'*The Girls* reimagines the Americ... ...ptures a defining friendship in its full humanity with a touch of rock-memoir, tell-it-like-it-really-was attitude'
Vogue

'Debut novels like this are rare, indeed… The most remarkable quality of this novel is Cline's ability to articulate the anxieties of adolescence in language that's gorgeously poetic without mangling the authenticity of a teenager's consciousness… With the maturity of a writer twice her age, Cline has written a wise novel that's never showy: a quiet, seething confession of yearning and terror'
Washington Post

'Breathtaking… So accomplished that it's hard to believe it's a debut. Cline's powerful characters linger long after the final page'
Entertainment Weekly

'Finely intelligent…with flashingly brilliant sentences… Cline's first novel, *The Girls*, is a song of innocence and experience… Much of this has to do with Cline's ability to look again, like a painter, and see (or sense) things better than most of us do'
New Yorker

'Outstanding… Cline's novel is an astonishing work of imagination… Cline painstakingly destroys the separation between art and faithful representation to create something new, wonderful, and disorienting'
Boston Globe

'Emma Cline's first novel positively hums with fresh, startling, luminous prose. *The Girls* announces the arrival of a thrilling new voice in American fiction'
Jennifer Egan

'Hypnotizing… Cline's eagle-eyed take on the churnings and pitfalls of adolescence – longing to be wanted, feeling seen, getting discarded – rarely misses its mark. In truth, it's this aspect of *The Girls*…that stays with us after Evie's whirlwind story concludes'
San Francisco Chronicle

'Gorgeous, disquieting, and really, really good… Cline's prose conveys a kind of atmospheric dread, punctuated by slyly distilled observation… What Cline does in *The Girls* is to examine, even dissect, these shifts between power and powerlessness that characterize a girl's coming of age… Cline, born years after the events she explores, brings a fresh and discerning eye to both the specific, horrific crime at her book's center, one firmly located in a time and place, and the timeless, slow-motion tragedy of a typical American girlhood'
Los Angeles Times

'A hypnotic, persuasively melancholy performance… The surprise of this novel is its almost studious avoidance of shock and sensationalism… What Ms. Cline delivers instead is an atmosphere of eerie desolation and balked desire thanks to her sensuous turns of phrase'
Wall Street Journal

EMMA CLINE

The Girls

VINTAGE

9 10 8

Vintage
20 Vauxhall Bridge Road,
London SW1V 2SA

Vintage is part of the Penguin Random House group of companies
whose addresses can be found at global.penguinrandomhouse.com.

Copyright © Emma Cline 2016

First published in Vintage in 2017
First published in hardback by Chatto & Windus in 2016

First published in the United States by Random House in 2016

penguin.co.uk/vintage

A CIP catalogue record for this book is available from the British Library

ISBN 9781784701741

Printed and bound by Clays Ltd, St Ives plc

Penguin Random House is committed to a sustainable future
for our business, our readers and our planet. This book is made
from Forest Stewardship Council® certified paper.

THE GIRLS

I LOOKED UP because of the laughter, and kept looking because of the girls.

I noticed their hair first, long and uncombed. Then their jewelry catching the sun. The three of them were far enough away that I saw only the periphery of their features, but it didn't matter—I knew they were different from everyone else in the park. Families milling in a vague line, waiting for sausages and burgers from the open grill. Women in checked blouses scooting into their boyfriends' sides, kids tossing eucalyptus buttons at the feral-looking chickens that overran the strip. These long-haired girls seemed to glide above all that was happening around them, tragic and separate. Like royalty in exile.

I studied the girls with a shameless, blatant gape: it

didn't seem possible that they might look over and notice me. My hamburger was forgotten in my lap, the breeze blowing in minnow stink from the river. It was an age when I'd immediately scan and rank other girls, keeping up a constant tally of how I fell short, and I saw right away that the black-haired one was the prettiest. I had expected this, even before I'd been able to make out their faces. There was a suggestion of otherworldliness hovering around her, a dirty smock dress barely covering her ass. She was flanked by a skinny redhead and an older girl, dressed with the same shabby afterthought. As if dredged from a lake. All their cheap rings like a second set of knuckles. They were messing with an uneasy threshold, prettiness and ugliness at the same time, and a ripple of awareness followed them through the park. Mothers glancing around for their children, moved by some feeling they couldn't name. Women reaching for their boyfriends' hands. The sun spiked through the trees, like always—the drowsy willows, the hot wind gusting over the picnic blankets—but the familiarity of the day was disturbed by the path the girls cut across the regular world. Sleek and thoughtless as sharks breaching the water.

PART ONE

IT BEGINS WITH THE FORD idling up the narrow drive, the sweet drone of honeysuckle thickening the August air. The girls in the backseat holding hands, the car windows down to let in the seep of night. The radio playing until the driver, suddenly jittery, snaps it off.

They scale the gate, still strung with Christmas lights. Encountering, first, the dumb quiet of the caretaker's cottage; the caretaker taking an evening nap on the couch, his bare feet tucked side by side like loaves. His girlfriend in the bathroom, wiping away the hazy crescents of eye makeup.

Then the main house, where they startle the woman reading in the guest bedroom. The glass of water quivering on the nightstand, the damp cotton of her underpants. Her five-year-old son by her side, murmuring cryptic nonsense to fight sleep.

They herd everyone into the living room. The moment the frightened people understand the sweet dailiness of their lives—the swallow of morning orange juice, the tilting curve taken on a bicycle—is already gone. Their faces change like a shutter opening; the unlocking behind the eyes.

I had imagined that night so often. The dark mountain road, the sunless sea. A woman felled on the night lawn. And though the details had receded over the years, grown their second and third skins, when I heard the lock jamming open near midnight, it was my first thought.

The stranger at the door.

I waited for the sound to reveal its source. A neighbor's kid bumping a trash can onto the sidewalk. A deer thrashing through the brush. That's all it could be, I told myself, this far-off rattle in the other part of the house, and I tried to picture how harmless the space would seem again in daylight, how cool and beyond danger.

But the noise went on, passing starkly into real life. There was now laughter in the other room. Voices. The pressurized *swish* of the refrigerator. I trawled for explanations but kept catching on the worst thought. After everything, this was how it would end. Trapped in someone else's house, among the facts and habits of someone else's life. My bare legs, jotted with varicose veins—how weak I'd appear when they came for me, a middle-aged woman scrabbling for the corners.

I lay in bed, my breath shallow as I stared at the closed door. Waiting for the intruders, the horrors I imagined taking human shape and populating the room—there would be no heroics, I understood. Just the dull terror, the physical pain that would have to be suffered through. I wouldn't try to run.

I only got out of bed after I heard the girl. Her voice was high and innocuous. Though it shouldn't have been comforting—Suzanne and the others had been girls, and that hadn't helped anybody.

I was staying in a borrowed house. The dark maritime cypress packed tight outside the window, the twitch of salt air. I ate in the blunt way I had as a child—a glut of spaghetti, mossed with cheese. The nothing jump of soda in my throat. I watered Dan's plants once a week, ferrying each one to the bathtub, running the pot under the faucet until the soil burbled with wet. More than once I'd showered with a litter of dead leaves in the tub.

The inheritance that had been the leftovers of my grandmother's movies—hours of her smiling her hawkish smile on film, her tidy cap of curls—I'd spent ten years ago. I tended to the in-between spaces of other people's existences, working as a live-in aide. Cultivating a genteel invisibility in sexless clothes, my face blurred with the pleasant, ambiguous expression of a lawn ornament. The pleasant part was important, the magic trick of invisibility only possible when it seemed to fulfill the correct order of things. As if it were something I wanted, too. My charges were varied. A kid with special needs, frightened of electrical outlets and traffic lights. An elderly woman who watched talk shows while I counted out a saucerful of pills, the pale pink capsules like subtle candy.

When my last job ended and another didn't appear, Dan offered his vacation house—the concerned gesture of an old friend—like I was doing him a favor. The skylight filled the rooms with the hazy murk of an aquarium, the woodwork bloating and swelling in the damp. As if the house were breathing.

The beach wasn't popular. Too cold, no oysters. The single road through town was lined with trailers, built up into sprawling lots—pinwheels snapping in the wind, porches cluttered with bleached buoys and life preservers, the ornaments of humble people. Sometimes I smoked a little of the furry and pungent marijuana from my old landlord, then walked to the store in town. A task I could complete, as defined as washing a dish. It was either dirty or clean, and I welcomed those binaries, the way they shored up a day.

I rarely saw anyone outside. The only teenagers in town seemed to kill themselves in gruesomely rural ways—I heard about their pickups crashing at two in the morning, the sleepover in the garage camper ending with carbon monoxide poisoning, a dead quarterback. I didn't know if this was a problem born of country living, the excess of time and boredom and recreational vehicles, or whether it was a California thing, a grain in the light urging risk and stupid cinematic stunts.

I hadn't been in the ocean at all. A waitress at the café told me this was a breeding ground for great whites.

They looked up from the bright wash of the kitchen lights like raccoons caught in the trash. The girl shrieked. The boy stood to his full, lanky height. There were only two of them. My heart was scudding hard, but they were so young—locals, I figured, breaking into vacation houses. I wasn't going to die.

"What the fuck?" The boy put down his beer bottle, the girl clinging to his side. The boy looked twenty or so, in cargo shorts. High white socks, rosy acne beneath a scrim of beard. But the girl was just a little thing. Fifteen, sixteen, her pale legs tinged with blue.

I tried to gather whatever authority I could, clutching the hem of my T-shirt to my thighs. When I said I'd call the cops, the boy snorted.

"Go ahead." He huddled the girl closer. "Call the cops. You know what?" He pulled out his cellphone. "Fuck it, I'll call them."

The pane of fear I'd been holding in my chest suddenly dissolved.

"Julian?"

I wanted to laugh—I'd last seen him when he was thirteen, skinny and unformed. Dan and Allison's only son. Fussed over, driven to cello competitions all over the western United States. A Mandarin tutor on Thursdays, the brown bread and gummy vitamins, parental hedges against failure. That had all fizzled and he'd ended up at the CSU in Long Beach or Irvine. There'd been some trouble there, I remembered. Expulsion or maybe a milder version of that, a suggestion of a year at junior college. Julian had been a shy, irritable kid, cowering at car radios, unfamiliar foods. Now he had hard edges, the creep of tattoos under his shirt. He didn't remember me, and why should he? I was a woman outside his range of erotic attentions.

"I'm staying here for a few weeks," I said, aware of my exposed legs and embarrassed for the melodrama, the mention of police. "I'm a friend of your dad's."

I could see the effort he made to place me, to assign meaning.

"Evie," I said.

Still nothing.

"I used to live in that apartment in Berkeley? By your cello teacher's house?" Dan and Julian would come over sometimes after his lessons. Julian lustily drinking milk and scuffing my table legs with robotic kicks.

"Oh, shit," Julian said. "Yeah." I couldn't tell whether he actually remembered me or if I had just invoked enough calming details.

The girl turned toward Julian, her face as blank as a spoon.

"It's fine, babe," he said, kissing her forehead—his gentleness unexpected.

Julian smiled at me and I realized he was drunk, or maybe just stoned. His features were smeary, an unhealthy dampness on his skin, though his upper-class upbringing kicked in like a first language.

"This is Sasha," he said, nudging the girl.

"Hi," she peeped, uncomfortable. I'd forgotten that dopey part of teenage girls: the desire for love flashing in her face so directly that it embarrassed me.

"And Sasha," Julian said, "this is—"

Julian's eyes struggled to focus on me.

"Evie," I reminded him.

"Right," he said, "Evie. Man."

He drank from his beer, the amber bottle catching the blare of the lights. He was staring past me. Glancing around at the furniture, the contents of the bookshelves, like this was my house and he was the outsider. "God, you must've thought we were like, breaking in or something."

"I thought you were locals."

"There was a break-in here once," Julian said. "When I was a kid. We weren't here. They just stole our wet suits and a bunch of abalone from the freezer." He took another drink.

Sasha kept her eyes on Julian. She was in cutoffs, all wrong for the cold coast, and an oversize sweatshirt that must have been his. The cuffs gnawed and wet looking.

Her makeup looked terrible, but it was more of a symbol, I suppose. I could see she was nervous with my eyes on her. I understood the worry. When I was that age, I was uncertain of how to move, whether I was walking too fast, whether others could see the discomfort and stiffness in me. As if everyone were constantly gauging my performance and finding it lacking. It occurred to me that Sasha was very young. Too young to be here with Julian. She seemed to know what I was thinking, staring at me with surprising defiance.

"I'm sorry your dad didn't tell you I'd be here," I said. "I can sleep in the other room if you want the bigger bed. Or if you want to be here alone, I'll figure something—"

"Nah," Julian said. "Sasha and I can sleep anywhere, can't we, babe? And we're just passing through. On our way north. A weed run," he said. "I make the drive, L.A. to Humboldt, at least once a month."

It occurred to me that Julian thought I'd be impressed.

"I don't sell it or anything," Julian went on, backpedaling. "Just transport. All you really need is a couple Watershed bags and a police scanner."

Sasha looked worried. Would I get them in trouble?

"How'd you know my dad again?" Julian said. Draining his beer and opening another. They'd brought a few six-packs. The other supplies in sight: the nutty gravel of trail mix. An unopened package of sour worms, the stale crumple of a fast-food bag.

"We met in L.A.," I said. "We lived together for a while."

Dan and I had shared an apartment in Venice Beach in the late seventies, Venice with its third world alleyways, the palm trees that hit the windows in the warm night winds. I was living off my grandmother's movie money while I worked toward my nursing certification. Dan was trying to be an actor. It was never going to happen for him, acting. Instead he'd married a woman with some family money and started a vegetarian frozen-food company. Now he owned a pre-earthquake house in Pacific Heights.

"Oh wait, his friend from Venice?" Julian seemed suddenly more responsive. "What's your name again?"

"Evie Boyd," I said, and the sudden look that came over his face surprised me: recognition, partly, but real interest.

"Wait," he said. He took his arm away from the girl and she looked drained by his absence. "You're that lady?"

Maybe Dan had told him how bad things had gotten for me. The thought embarrassed me, and I touched my face reflexively. An old, shameful habit from adolescence, how I'd cover up a pimple. A casual hand at my chin, fiddling with my mouth. As if that weren't drawing attention, making it worse.

Julian was excited now. "She was in this cult," he told the girl. "Right?" he said, turning to me.

A socket of dread opened in my stomach. Julian kept looking at me, tart with expectation. His breath hoppy and fractured.

I'd been fourteen that summer. Suzanne had been

nineteen. There was an incense the group burned sometimes that made us drowsy and yielding. Suzanne reading
aloud from a back issue of *Playboy*. The obscene and luminous Polaroids we secreted away and traded like baseball
cards.

I knew how easily it could happen, the past at hand,
like the helpless cognitive slip of an optical illusion. The
tone of a day linked to some particular item: my mother's
chiffon scarf, the humidity of a cut pumpkin. Certain patterns of shade. Even the flash of sunlight on the hood of
a white car could cause a momentary ripple in me, allowing a slim space of return. I'd seen old Yardley slickers—
the makeup now just a waxy crumble—sell for almost
one hundred dollars on the Internet. So grown women
could smell it again, that chemical, flowery fug. That's
how badly people wanted it—to know that their lives *had*
happened, that the person they once had been still existed inside of them.

There were so many things that returned me. The
tang of soy, smoke in someone's hair, the grassy hills
turning blond in June. An arrangement of oaks and boulders could, seen out of the corner of my eye, crack open
something in my chest, palms going suddenly slick with
adrenaline.

I anticipated disgust from Julian, maybe even fear.
That was the logical response. But I was confused by the
way he was looking at me. With something like awe.

His father must have told him. The summer of the
crumbling house, the sunburned toddlers. When I'd first

tried to tell Dan, on the night of a brownout in Venice that summoned a candlelit, apocalyptic intimacy, he had burst out laughing. Mistaking the hush in my voice for the drop of hilarity. Even after I convinced Dan I was telling the truth, he talked about the ranch with that same parodic goof. Like a horror movie with bad special effects, the boom microphone dipping into the frame and tinting the butchery into comedy. And it was a relief to exaggerate my distance, neatening my involvement into the orderly package of anecdote.

It helped that I wasn't mentioned in most of the books. Not the paperbacks with the title bloody and oozing, the glossed pages of crime scene photographs. Not the less popular but more accurate tome written by the lead prosecutor, gross with specifics, down to the undigested spaghetti they found in the little boy's stomach. The couple of lines that did mention me were buried in an out-of-print book by a former poet, and he'd gotten my name wrong and hadn't made any connection to my grandmother. The same poet also claimed that the CIA was producing porn films starring a drugged Marilyn Monroe, films sold to politicians and foreign heads of state.

"It was a long time ago," I said to Sasha, but her expression was empty.

"Still," Julian said, brightening. "I always thought it was beautiful. Sick yet beautiful," he said. "A fucked-up expression, but an expression, you know. An artistic impulse. You've got to destroy to create, all that Hindu shit."

I could tell he was reading my bewildered shock as approval.

"God, I can't even imagine," Julian said. "Actually being in the middle of something like that."

He waited for me to respond. I was woozy from the ambush of kitchen lights: didn't they notice the room was too bright? I wondered if the girl was even beautiful. Her teeth had a cast of yellow.

Julian nudged her with his elbow. "Sasha doesn't even know what we're talking about."

Most everyone knew at least one of the grisly details. College kids sometimes dressed as Russell for Halloween, hands splashed with ketchup cadged from the dining hall. A black metal band had used the heart on an album cover, the same craggy heart Suzanne had left on Mitch's wall. In the woman's blood. But Sasha seemed so young— why would she have ever heard of it? Why would she care? She was lost in that deep and certain sense that there was nothing beyond her own experience. As if there were only one way things could go, the years leading you down a corridor to the room where your inevitable self waited—embryonic, ready to be revealed. How sad it was to realize that sometimes you never got there. That sometimes you lived a whole life skittering across the surface as the years passed, unblessed.

Julian petted Sasha's hair. "It was like a big fucking deal. Hippies killing these people out in Marin."

The heat in his face was familiar. The same fervor as those people who populated the online forums that never seemed to slow down or die. They jostled for ownership, adopting the same knowing tone, a veneer of scholarship masking the essential ghoulishness of the endeavor. What were they looking for among all the banalities? As though the weather on that day mattered. All of the scraps seemed important, when considered long enough: the station the radio was tuned to in Mitch's kitchen, the number and depth of the stab wounds. How the shadows might have flickered on that particular car driving up that particular road.

"I was only hanging around them for a few months," I said. "It wasn't a big thing."

Julian seemed disappointed. I imagined the woman he saw when he looked at me: her unkempt hair, the commas of worry around her eyes.

"But yeah," I said, "I stayed there a lot."

That answer returned me firmly to his realm of interest.

And so I let the moment pass.

I didn't tell him that I wished I'd never met Suzanne. That I wished I'd stayed safely in my bedroom in the dry hills near Petaluma, the bookshelves packed tight with the gold-foil spines of my childhood favorites. And I did wish that. But some nights, unable to sleep, I peeled an apple slowly at the sink, letting the curl lengthen under the glint of the knife. The house dark around me. Sometimes it didn't feel like regret. It felt like a missing.

. . .

Julian shooed Sasha into the other bedroom like a peaceable teenage goatherd. Asking if I needed anything before he said good night. I was taken aback—he reminded me of the boys in school who'd become more polite and high functioning on drugs. Dutifully washing the family dinner dishes while they were tripping, mesmerized by the psychedelic magic of soap.

"Sleep well," Julian said, giving a little geisha bow before closing the door.

The sheets on my bed were mussed, the pang of fear still lingering in the room. How ridiculous I'd been. Being so frightened. But even the surprise of harmless others in the house disturbed me. I didn't want my inner rot on display, even accidentally. Living alone was frightening in that way. No one to police the spill of yourself, the ways you betrayed your primitive desires. Like a cocoon built around you, made of your own naked proclivities and never tidied into the patterns of actual human life.

I was still alert, and it took effort to relax, to regulate my breath. The house was safe, I told myself, I was fine. Suddenly it seemed ridiculous, the bumbling encounter. Through the thin wall, I could hear the sounds of Sasha and Julian settling into the other room. The floor creaking, the closet doors being opened. They were probably putting sheets on the bare mattress. Shaking away years of accumulated dust. I imagined Sasha looking at the family photographs on the shelf, Julian as a toddler holding a giant red telephone. Julian at eleven or twelve, on a whale-watching boat, his face salt lashed and wondrous. She was probably projecting all that innocence and sweetness on the almost-adult man who eased off his shorts and patted the bed for her to join him. The blurry leavings of amateur tattoos rippling along his arms.

I heard the groan of mattress.

I wasn't surprised that they would fuck. But then there was Sasha's voice, whining like a porno. High and curdled. Didn't they know I was right next door? I turned my back to the wall, shutting my eyes.

Julian growling.

"Are you a cunt?" he said. The headboard jacking against the wall.

"Are you?"

I'd think, later, that Julian must have known I could hear everything.

1969

1

It was the end of the sixties, or the summer before the
end, and that's what it seemed like, an endless, formless
summer. The Haight populated with white-garbed Process members handing out their oat-colored pamphlets,
the jasmine along the roads that year blooming particularly heady and full. Everyone was healthy, tan, and heavy
with decoration, and if you weren't, that was a thing,
too—you could be some moon creature, chiffon over the
lamp shades, on a kitchari cleanse that stained all your
dishes with turmeric.

But that was all happening somewhere else, not in
Petaluma with its low-hipped ranch houses, the covered
wagon perpetually parked in front of the Hi-Ho Restaurant. The sun-scorched crosswalks. I was fourteen but

looked much younger. People liked to say this to me. Connie swore I could pass for sixteen, but we told each other a lot of lies. We'd been friends all through junior high, Connie waiting for me outside classrooms as patient as a cow, all our energy subsumed into the theatrics of friendship. She was plump but didn't dress like it, in cropped cotton shirts with Mexican embroidery, too-tight skirts that left an angry rim on her upper thighs. I'd always liked her in a way I never had to think about, like the fact of my own hands.

Come September, I'd be sent off to the same boarding school my mother had gone to. They'd built a well-tended campus around an old convent in Monterey, the lawns smooth and sloped. Shreds of fog in the mornings, brief hits of the nearness of salt water. It was an all-girls school, and I'd have to wear a uniform—low-heeled shoes and no makeup, middy blouses threaded with navy ties. It was a holding place, really, enclosed by a stone wall and populated with bland, moon-faced daughters. Camp Fire Girls and Future Teachers shipped off to learn 160 words a minute, shorthand. To make dreamy, overheated promises to be one another's bridesmaids at Royal Hawaiian weddings.

My impending departure forced a newly critical distance on my friendship with Connie. I'd started to notice certain things, almost against my will. How Connie said, "The best way to get over someone is to get under someone else," as if we were shopgirls in London instead of inexperienced adolescents in the farm belt of Sonoma

County. We licked batteries to feel a metallic jolt on the tongue, rumored to be one-eighteenth of an orgasm. It pained me to imagine how our twosome appeared to others, marked as the kind of girls who belonged to each other. Those sexless fixtures of high schools.

Every day after school, we'd click seamlessly into the familiar track of the afternoons. Waste the hours at some industrious task: following Vidal Sassoon's suggestions for raw egg smoothies to strengthen hair or picking at blackheads with the tip of a sterilized sewing needle. The constant project of our girl selves seeming to require odd and precise attentions.

As an adult, I wonder at the pure volume of time I wasted. The feast and famine we were taught to expect from the world, the countdowns in magazines that urged us to prepare thirty days in advance for the first day of school.

Day 28: Apply a face mask of avocado and honey.

Day 14: Test your makeup look in different lights (natural, office, dusk).

Back then, I was so attuned to attention. I dressed to provoke love, tugging my neckline lower, settling a wistful stare on my face whenever I went out in public that implied many deep and promising thoughts, should anyone happen to glance over. As a child, I had once been part of a charity dog show and paraded around a pretty collie on a leash, a silk bandanna around its neck. How thrilled I'd been at the sanctioned performance: the way I went up to strangers and let them admire the dog, my smile as indulgent and constant as a salesgirl's, and how vacant I'd felt when it was over, when no one needed to look at me anymore.

I waited to be told what was good about me. I wondered later if this was why there were so many more women than men at the ranch. All that time I had spent readying myself, the articles that taught me life was really just a waiting room until someone noticed you—the boys had spent that time becoming themselves.

That day in the park was the first time I saw Suzanne and the others. I'd ridden my bike there, aimed at the smoke streaming from the grill. No one spoke to me except the man pressing burgers into the grates with a bored, wet sizzle. The shadows of the oaks moved over my bare arms, my bike tipped in the grass. When an older boy in a cowboy hat ran into me, I purposefully slowed so he would bump into me again. The kind of flirting Connie might do, practiced as an army maneuver.

"What's wrong with you?" he muttered. I opened my mouth to apologize, but the boy was already walking off. Like he'd known he didn't need to hear whatever I was going to say.

The summer gaped before me—the scatter of days, the march of hours, my mother swanning around the house like a stranger. I had spoken to my father a few times on the phone. It had seemed painful for him, too.

He'd asked me oddly formal questions, like a distant uncle who knew me only as a series of secondhand facts: Evie is fourteen, Evie is short. The silences between us would've been better if they were colored with sadness or regret, but it was worse—I could hear how happy he was to be gone.

I sat on a bench alone, napkins spread across my knees, and ate my hamburger.

It was the first meat I'd had in a long time. My mother, Jean, had stopped eating meat in the four months since the divorce. She'd stopped doing a lot of things. Gone was the mother who'd made sure I bought new underwear every season, the mother who'd rolled my white bobby socks as sweetly as eggs. Who'd sewn my dolls pajamas that matched mine, down to the exact pearly buttons. She was ready to attend to her own life with the eagerness of a schoolgirl at a difficult math problem. Any spare moment, she stretched. Going up on her toes to work her calves. She lit incense that came wrapped in aluminum foil and made my eyes water. She started drinking a new tea, made from some aromatic bark, and shuffled around the house sipping it, touching her throat absently as if recovering from a long illness.

The ailment was vague, but the cure was specific. Her new friends suggested massage. They suggested the briny waters of sensory deprivation tanks. They suggested E-meters, Gestalt, eating only high-mineral foods that had been planted during a full moon. I couldn't believe my mother took their advice, but she listened to everyone. Eager for an aim, a plan, believing the answer could come from any direction at any time, if only she tried hard enough.

She searched until there was only searching left. The astrologer in Alameda who made her cry, talking about the inauspicious shadow cast by her rising sign. The therapies that involved throwing herself around a padded room filled with strangers and whirling until she hit something. She came home with foggy tinges under the skin, bruises that deepened to a vivid meat. I saw her touch the bruises with something like fondness. When she looked up and saw me watching, she blushed. Her hair was newly bleached, stinking of chemicals and artificial roses.

"Do you like it?" she said, grazing the sheared ends with her fingers.

I nodded, though the color made her skin look washed by jaundice.

She kept changing, day by day. Little things. She bought handcrafted earrings from women in her encounter group, came back swinging primitive bits of wood from her ears, enameled bracelets the color of after-dinner mints jittery on her wrists. She started lining her eyes with an eyeliner pencil she held over a lighter flame. Turning the point until it softened and she could draw slashes at each eye, making her look sleepy and Egyptian.

She paused in my doorway on her way out for the

night, dressed in a tomato-red blouse that exposed her shoulders. She kept pulling the sleeves down. Her shoulders were dusted with glitter.

"You want me to do your eyes too, sweetheart?"

But I had nowhere to be. Who would care if my eyes looked bigger or bluer?

"I might get back late. So sleep well." My mother leaned over to kiss the top of my head. "We're good, aren't we? The two of us?"

She patted me, smiling so her face seemed to crack and reveal the full rush of her need. Part of me did feel all right, or I was confusing familiarity with happiness. Because that was there even when love wasn't—the net of family, the purity of habit and home. It was such an unfathomable amount of time that you spent at home, and maybe that's the best you could get—that sense of endless enclosure, like picking for the lip of tape but never finding it. There were no seams, no interruptions—just the landmarks of your life that had become so absorbed in you that you couldn't even acknowledge them. The chipped willow-print dinner plate I favored for forgotten reasons. The wallpaper in the hallway so known to me as to be entirely incommunicable to another person—every fading copse of pastel palm trees, the particular personalities I ascribed to each blooming hibiscus.

My mother stopped enforcing regular mealtimes, leaving grapes in a colander in the sink or bringing home glass jars of dilled miso soup from her macrobiotic cooking class. Seaweed salads dripping with a nauseating amber oil. "Eat this for breakfast every day," she said, "and you'll never have another zit."

I cringed, pulling my fingers away from the pimple on my forehead.

There had been many late-night planning sessions between my mother and Sal, the older woman she had met in group. Sal was endlessly available to my mother, coming over at odd hours, impatient for drama. Wearing tunics with mandarin collars, her gray hair cut short so her ears showed, making her look like an elderly boy. My mother spoke to Sal about acupuncture, of the movement of energies around meridian points. The charts.

"I just want some space," my mother said, "for me. This world takes it out of you, doesn't it?"

Sal shifted on her wide rear, nodded. Dutiful as a bridled pony.

My mother and Sal were drinking her woody tea from bowls, a new affectation my mother had picked up. "It's European," she'd said defensively, though I had said nothing. When I walked through the kitchen, both women stopped talking, but my mother cocked her head. "Baby," she said, gesturing me closer. She squinted. "Part your bangs from the left. More flattering."

I'd parted my hair that way to cover the pimple, gone scabby from picking. I'd coated it with vitamin E oil but couldn't stop myself from messing with it, flaking on toilet paper to soak up the blood.

Sal agreed. "Round face shape," she said with authority. "Bangs might not be a good idea at all, for her."

I imagined how it would feel to topple Sal over in her chair, how her bulk would bring her down fast. The bark tea spilling on the linoleum.

They quickly lost interest in me. My mother rekindling her familiar story, like the stunned survivor of a car accident. Dropping her shoulders as if to settle even further into the misery.

"And the most hilarious part," my mother went on, "the part that really gets me going?" She smiled at her own hands. "Carl's making money," she said. "That currency stuff." She laughed again. "Finally. It actually worked. But it was my money that paid her salary," she said. "My mother's movie money. Spent on that girl."

My mother was talking about Tamar, the assistant my father had hired for his most recent business. It had something to do with currency exchange. Buying foreign money and trading it back and forth, shifting it enough times so you were left, my father insisted, with pure profit, sleight of hand on a grand scale. That's what the French language tapes in his car had been for: he'd been trying to push along a deal involving francs and lire.

Now he and Tamar were living together in Palo Alto. I'd only met her a few times: she'd picked me up from school once, before the divorce. Waving lazily from her

Plymouth Fury. In her twenties, slim and cheerful, Tamar constantly alluded to weekend plans, an apartment she wished were bigger, her life textured in a way I couldn't imagine. Her hair was so blond it was almost gray, and she wore it loose, unlike my mother's smooth curls. At that age I looked at women with brutal and emotionless judgment. Assessing the slope of their breasts, imagining how they would look in various crude positions. Tamar was very pretty. She gathered her hair up in a plastic comb and cracked her neck, smiling over at me as she drove.

"Want some gum?"

I unwrapped two cloudy sticks from their silver jackets. Feeling something adjacent to love, next to Tamar, thighs scudding on the vinyl seat. Girls are the only ones who can really give each other close attention, the kind we equate with being loved. They noticed what we want noticed. And that's what I did for Tamar—I responded to her symbols, to the style of her hair and clothes and the smell of her L'Air du Temps perfume, like this was data that mattered, signs that reflected something of her inner self. I took her beauty personally.

When we arrived home, the gravel crackling under the car wheels, she asked to use the bathroom.

"Of course," I said, vaguely thrilled to have her in my house, like a visiting dignitary. I showed her the nice bathroom, by my parents' room. Tamar peeked at the bed and wrinkled her nose. "Ugly comforter," she said under her breath.

Until then, it had just been my parents' comforter, but abruptly I felt secondhand shame for my mother, for the tacky comforter she had picked out, had even been foolish enough to be pleased by.

I sat at the dining table listening to the muffled sound of Tamar peeing, of the faucet running. She was in there a long time. When Tamar finally emerged, something was different. It took me a moment to realize she was wearing my mother's lipstick, and when she noticed me noticing her, it was as if I'd interrupted a movie she was watching. Her face rapt with the presentiment of some other life.

My favorite fantasy was the sleep cure I had read about in *Valley of the Dolls*. The doctor inducing long-term sleep in a hospital room, the only answer for poor, strident Neely, gone muddy from the Demerol. It sounded perfect—my body kept alive by peaceful, reliable machines, my brain resting in watery space, as untroubled as a goldfish in a glass bowl. I'd wake up weeks later. And even though life would slot back into its disappointing place, there would still be that starched stretch of nothing.

Boarding school was meant to be a corrective, the push I needed. My parents, even in their separate, absorbing worlds, were disappointed in me, distressed by my mediocre grades. I was an average girl, and that was the biggest disappointment of all—there was no shine of greatness on me. I wasn't pretty enough to get the grades

I did, the scale not tipping heartily enough in the direction of looks or smarts. Sometimes I would be overtaken with pious impulses to do better, to try harder, but of course nothing changed. Other mysterious forces seemed to be in play. The window near my desk left open so I wasted math class watching the shudder of leaves. My pen leaking so I couldn't take notes. The things I was good at had no real application: addressing envelopes in bubble letters with smiling creatures on the flap. Making sludgy coffee I drank with grave affect. Finding a certain desired song playing on the radio, like a medium scanning for news of the dead.

My mother said I looked like my grandmother, but this seemed suspicious, a wishful lie meant to give false hope. I knew my grandmother's story, repeated like a reflexive prayer. Harriet the date farmer's daughter, plucked from the sunburned obscurity of Indio and brought to Los Angeles. Her soft jaw and damp eyes. Small teeth, straight and slightly pointed, like a strange and beautiful cat. Coddled by the studio system, fed whipped milk and eggs, or broiled liver and five carrots, the same dinner my grandmother ate every night of my childhood. The family holing up in the sprawling ranch in Petaluma after she retired, my grandmother growing show roses from Luther Burbank cuttings and keeping horses.

When my grandmother died, we were like our own country in those hills, living off her money, though I could bicycle into town. It was more of a psychological distance—as an adult, I would wonder at our isolation.

My mother tiptoed around my father, and so did I—his sideways glances at us, his encouragements to eat more protein, to read Dickens or breathe more deeply. He ate raw eggs and salted steaks and kept a plate of beef tartare in the refrigerator, spooning out bites five or six times a day. "Your outer body reflects your inner self," he said, and did his gymnastics on a Japanese mat by the pool, fifty push-ups while I sat on his back. It was a form of magic, being lifted into the air, cross-legged. The oat grass, the smell of the cooling earth.

When a coyote would come down from the hills and fight with the dog—the nasty, quick hiss that thrilled me—my father would shoot the coyote dead. Everything seemed that simple. The horses I copied from a pencil drawing book, shading in their graphite manes. Tracing a picture of a bobcat carrying away a vole in its jaws, the sharp tooth of nature. Later I'd see how the fear had been there all along. The flurry I felt when our mother left me alone with the nanny, Carson, who smelled damp and sat in the wrong chair. How they told me I was having fun all the time, and there was no way to explain that I wasn't. And even moments of happiness were followed by some letdown—my father's laugh, then the scramble to keep up with him as he strode far ahead of me. My mother's hands on my feverish forehead, then the desperate alone-ness of my sickroom, my mother disappeared into the rest of the house, talking on the phone to someone in a voice I didn't recognize. A tray of Ritz crackers and chicken noodle soup gone cold, sallow meat breaching the scrim of fat. A starry emptiness that felt, even as a child, something like death.

I didn't wonder how my mother spent her days. How she must have sat in the empty kitchen, the table smelling of the domestic rot of the sponge, and waited for me to clatter in from school, for my father to come home.

My father, who kissed her with a formality that embarrassed us all, who left beer bottles on the steps that trapped wasps and beat his bare chest in the morning to keep his lungs strong. He clung tight to the brute reality of his body, his thick ribbed socks showing above his shoes, flecked from the cedar sachets he kept in his drawers. The way he made a joke of checking his reflection in the hood of the car. I tried to save up things to tell him, combing through my days for something to provoke a glint of interest. It didn't occur to me, until I was an adult, that it was strange to know so much about him when he seemed to know nothing about me. To know that he loved Leonardo da Vinci because he invented solar power and was born poor. That he could identify the make of any car just by the sound of the engine and thought everyone should know the names of trees. He liked when I agreed that business school was a scam or nodded when he said that the teenager in town who'd painted his car with peace signs was a traitor. He'd mentioned once that I should learn classical guitar, though I had never heard him listen to any music except for those theatrical cowboy bands, tapping their emerald cowboy boots and singing about yellow roses. He felt that his height was the only thing that had prevented him from achieving success.

"Robert Mitchum is short too," he'd said to me once. "They make him stand on orange crates."

As soon as I'd caught sight of the girls cutting their way through the park, my attention stayed pinned on them. The black-haired girl with her attendants, their laughter a rebuke to my aloneness. I was waiting for something without knowing what. And then it happened. Quick, but still I saw it: the girl with black hair pulled down the neckline of her dress for a brief second, exposing the red nipple of her bare breast. Right in the middle of a park swarming with people. Before I could fully believe it, the girl yanked her dress back up. They were all laughing, raunchy and careless; none of them even glanced up to see who might be watching.

The girls moved into the alley alongside the restaurant, farther past the grill. Practiced and smooth. I didn't look away. The older one lifted the lid of a dumpster. The redhead bent down and the black-haired girl used her knee as a step, hoisting herself over the edge. She was looking for something inside, but I couldn't imagine what. I stood to throw away my napkins and stopped at the garbage can, watching. The black-haired girl was handing things from the dumpster to the others: a bag of bread, still in its packaging, an anemic-looking cabbage that they sniffed, then tossed back in. A seemingly well-established procedure—would they actually eat the food? When the black-haired girl emerged for the last time, climbing over the rim and slinging her weight onto the ground, she was holding something in her hands. It was a strange shape, the color of my own skin, and I edged closer.

When I realized it was an uncooked chicken, sheened in plastic, I must have stared harder, since the black-haired girl turned and caught my glance. She smiled and my stomach dropped. Something seemed to pass between us, a subtle rearranging of air. The frank, unapologetic way she held my gaze. But she jarred back to attention when the screen door of the restaurant banged open. Out came a hefty man, already shouting. Shooing them like dogs. The girls grabbed the bag of bread and the chicken and took off running. The man stopped and watched them for a minute. Wiping his large hands on his apron, his chest moving with effort.

By then the girls were a block away, their hair streaming behind them like flags, and a black school bus heaved past and slowed, and the three of them disappeared inside.

The sight of them; the gruesomely fetal quality of the chicken, the cherry of the girl's single nipple. All of it was so garish, and maybe that's why I kept thinking of them. I couldn't put it together. Why these girls needed food from the dumpster. Who had been driving the bus, what kind of people would paint it that color. I'd seen that they were dear to one another, the girls, that they'd passed into a familial contract—they were sure of what they were together. The long night that stretched ahead, my mother out with Sal, suddenly seemed unbearable.

That was the first time I ever saw Suzanne—her black hair marking her, even at a distance, as different, her smile at me direct and assessing. I couldn't explain it to myself, the wrench I got from looking at her. She seemed as strange and raw as those flowers that bloom in lurid explosion once every five years, the gaudy, prickling tease that was almost the same thing as beauty. And what had the girl seen when she looked at me?

I used the bathroom inside the restaurant. *Keep truckin'*, scrawled with a marker. *Tess Pyle eats dick!* The accompanying illustrations had been crossed out. All the silly, cryptic marks of humans who were resigned to being held in a place, shunted through the perfunctory order of things. Who wanted to make some small protest. The saddest: *Fuck*, written in pencil.

While I washed my hands, drying them with a stiff towel, I studied myself in the mirror over the sink. For a moment, I tried to see myself through the eyes of the girl with the black hair, or even the boy in the cowboy hat, studying my features for a vibration under the skin. The effort was visible in my face, and I felt ashamed. No wonder the boy had seemed disgusted: he must have seen the longing in me. Seen how my face was blatant with need, like an orphan's empty dish. And that was the difference between me and the black-haired girl—her face answered all its own questions.

I didn't want to know these things about myself. I splashed water on my face, cold water, like Connie had once told me to do. "Cold water makes your pores close up," and maybe it was true: I felt my skin tighten, water dripping down my face and neck. How desperately Connie and I thought that if we performed these rituals—washed our faces with cold water, brushed our hair into a static frenzy with a boar-bristle brush before bed—some proof would solve itself and a new life would spread out before us.

2

Cha ching, the slot machine in Connie's garage went, like a cartoon, Peter's features soaked in its rosy glow. He was eighteen, Connie's older brother, and his forearms were the color of toast. His friend Henry hovered at his side. Connie decided she had a crush on Henry, so our Friday night would be devoted to perching on the weight-lifting bench, Henry's orange motorcycle parked beside us like a prize pony. We'd watch the boys play the slot machine, drinking the off-brand beer Connie's father kept in the garage fridge. Later they'd shoot the empty bottles with a BB gun, crowing at each glassy burst.

I knew I'd see Peter that night, so I'd worn an embroidered shirt, my hair foul with hairspray. I'd dotted a pimple on my jaw with a beige putty of Merle Norman, but it collected along the rim and made it glow. As long as my hair stayed in place, I looked nice, or at least I thought so, and I tucked in my shirt to show the tops of my small breasts, the artificial press of cleavage from my bra. The feeling of exposure gave me an anxious pleasure that made me stand straighter, holding my head on my neck like an egg in a cup. Trying to be more like the black-haired girl in the park, that easy cast of her face. Connie narrowed her eyes when she saw me, a muscle by her mouth twitching, but she didn't say anything.

Peter had really only spoken to me for the first time two weeks before. I'd been waiting for Connie downstairs. Her bedroom was much smaller than mine, her house meaner, but we spent most of our time there. The house done up in a maritime theme, her father's misguided attempt to approximate female decoration. I felt bad for Connie's father: his night job at a dairy plant, the arthritic hands he clenched and unclenched nervously. Connie's mother lived somewhere in New Mexico, near a hot spring, had twin boys and another life no one ever spoke of. For Christmas, she had once sent Connie a compact of cracked blush and a Fair Isle sweater that was so small neither of us could squeeze our head through the hole.

"The colors are nice," I said hopefully.

Connie just shrugged. "She's a bitch."

Peter crashed through the front door, dumping a book

on the kitchen table. He nodded at me in his mild way and started making a sandwich—pulling out slices of white bread, an acid-bright jar of mustard.

"Where's the princess?" he said. His mouth was chapped a violent pink. Slightly coated, I imagined, with pot resin.

"Getting a jacket."

"Ah." He slapped the bread together and took a bite. He watched me while he chewed.

"Looking good these days, Boyd," he said, then swallowed hard. His assessment knocked me so off balance that I felt I had almost imagined it. Was I even supposed to say anything back? I'd already memorized the sentence.

He turned then at a noise from the front door, a girl in a denim jacket, her shape muffled by the screen. Pamela, his girlfriend. They were a constant couple, porous with each other; wearing similar clothes, silently passing the newspaper back and forth on the couch or watching *The Man from U.N.C.L.E.* Picking lint off each other as if from their own selves. I had seen Pamela at the high school, those times I'd ridden my bike past the dun-colored building. The rectangles of half-dry grass, the low, wide steps where older girls were always sitting in poor-boy shirts, pinkies linked, palming packs of Kents. The whiff of death among them, the boyfriends in humid jungles. They were like adults, even in the way they flicked the ashes of their cigarettes with weary snaps of the wrist.

"Hey, Evie," Pamela said.

It was easy for some girls to be nice. To remember your name. Pamela was beautiful, it was true, and I felt that submerged attraction to her that everyone felt for the beautiful. The sleeves of her jean jacket were bulked at her elbows, her eyes doped looking from liner. Her legs were tan and bare. My own legs were dotted with the pricks of mosquito bites I worried into open wounds, my calves hatched with pale hairs.

"Babe," Peter said with his mouth full, and loped over to give her a hug, burying his face in her neck. Pamela squealed and pushed him away. When she laughed, her snaggletooth flashed.

"Beyond foul," Connie whispered, entering the room. But I was quiet, trying to imagine how that would feel: to be so known to someone that you had become almost the same person.

We were upstairs, later, smoking weed Connie had stolen from Peter. Stuffing the space below the door with the fat twist of a towel. She kept having to pinch the rolling paper shut again with her fingers, the two of us smoking in our solemn, hothouse silence. I could see Peter's car out the window, parked awry like he'd had to abandon it under great duress. I'd always been aware of Peter, in the way I liked any older boy at that age, their mere existence demanding attention. But my feelings were suddenly amplified and pressing, as exaggerated and inevitable as events seem in dreams. I stuffed myself on banalities of him, the T-shirts he wore in rotation, the tender skin where the back of his neck disappeared into his collar. The looping horns of Paul Revere and the Raiders sounding from his bedroom, how he'd sometimes stumble around with a proud, overt secrecy, so I would know he had taken acid. Filling and refilling a glass of water in the kitchen with extravagant care.

I'd gone into Peter's bedroom while Connie was showering. It reeked of what I'd later identify as masturbation, a damp rupture in the air. All his possessions suffused with a mysterious import: his low futon, a plastic bag full of ashy-looking nugs by his pillow. Manuals to become a trainee mechanic. The glass on the floor, greased with fingerprints, was half-full of stale-looking water, and there was a line of smooth river stones on the top of his dresser. A cheap copper bracelet I had seen him wear sometimes. I took in everything as if I could decode the private meaning of each object, puzzle together the interior architecture of his life.

So much of desire, at that age, was a willful act. Trying so hard to slur the rough, disappointing edges of boys into the shape of someone we could love. We spoke of our desperate need for them with rote and familiar words, like we were reading lines from a play. Later I would see this: how impersonal and grasping our love was, pinging around the universe, hoping for a host to give form to our wishes.

. . .

When I was young, I'd seen magazines in a drawer of the bathroom, my father's magazines, the pages bloated with humidity. The insides crowded with women. The tautness of mesh pulled across crotches, the gauzy light that made their skin illuminate and pale. My favorite girl had a gingham ribbon tied around her throat in a bow. It was so odd and stirring that someone could be naked but also wear a ribbon around her neck. It made her nakedness formal.

I visited the magazine with the regularity of a penitent, replacing it carefully each time. Locking the bathroom door with breathless, ill pleasure that quickly morphed into rubbing my crotch along the seams of carpets, the seam of my mattress. The back of a couch. How did it work, even? That by holding the hovering image of the girl in my mind, I could build the sensation, a sheet of pleasure that grew until it was compulsive, the desire to feel that way again and again. It seemed strange that it was a girl I was imagining, not a boy. And that the feeling could be reignited by other oddities: a color-plate illustration in my fairy-tale book of a girl trapped in a spider's web. The faceted eyes of evil creatures, watching her. The memory of my father cupping a neighbor's ass through her wet swimsuit.

I'd done things before—not quite sex, but close. The dry fumbles in the hallways of school dances. The overheated suffocation of a parent's couch, the backs of my knees sweaty. Alex Posner worming his hand down my shorts in his exploratory, detached fashion, jerking away roughly when we heard footsteps. None of it—the kissing, the clawing hand in my underwear, the raw jumpiness of a penis in my fist—seemed in any way kin to what I did alone, the spread of pressure, like stairs going up. I imagined Peter almost as a corrective to my own desires, whose compulsion sometimes frightened me.

I lay back on the thin tapestry covering Connie's bed. She had a bad sunburn; I watched her rub cloudy skin loose from her shoulder and roll it into tiny gray balls. My faint revulsion was tempered by the thought of Peter, who lived in the same house as Connie, who breathed the same air. Who ate from the same utensils. They were conflated in an essential way, like two different species raised in the same laboratory.

From downstairs, I heard Pamela's tripping laugh.

"When I get a boyfriend, I'm going to make him take me out to dinner," Connie said with authority. "She doesn't even mind Peter just brings her here to screw."

Peter never wore underwear, Connie had complained, and the fact grew in my mind, making me nauseous in a not unpleasant way. The sleepy crease of his eyes from his permanent high. Connie paled in comparison: I didn't really believe that friendship could be an end in itself, not just the background fuzz to the dramatics of boys loving you or not loving you.

Connie stood at the mirror and tried to harmonize with one of the sweet, sorrowful forty-fives we listened to with fanatic repetition. Songs that overheated my own righteous sadness, my imagined alignment with the tragic nature of the world. How I loved to wring myself out that way, stoking my feelings until they were unbearable. I wanted all of life to feel that frantic and pressurized with portent, so even colors and weather and tastes would be more saturated. That's what the songs promised, what they trawled out of me.

One song seemed to vibrate with a private echo, as if marked. The simple lines about a woman, about the shape of her back when she turns it on the man for the last time. The ashes she leaves in bed from her cigarettes. The song played once through, and Connie hopped up to flip the record.

"Play it again," I said. I tried to imagine myself in the same way the singer saw the woman: the dangle of her silver bracelet, tinged with green, the fall of her hair. But I only felt foolish, opening my eyes to the sight of Connie at the mirror, separating her eyelashes with a safety pin, her shorts wedged into her ass. It wasn't the same to notice things about yourself. Only certain girls ever called forth that kind of attention. Like the girl I'd seen in the park. Or Pamela and the girls on the high school steps, waiting for the lazy agitation of their boyfriends' idling cars, the signal to leap to their feet. To brush off their seat and trip out into the full sun, waving goodbye to the ones left behind.

...

Soon after that day, I'd gone to Peter's room while Connie was sleeping. His comment to me in the kitchen felt like a time-stamped invitation I had to redeem before it slipped away. Connie and I had drunk beer before bed, lounging against the wicker legs of her furniture and scooping cottage cheese from a tub with our fingers. I drank much more than she had. I wanted some other momentum to take over, forcing action. I didn't want to be like Connie, never changing, waiting around for something to happen, eating an entire sleeve of sesame crackers, then doing ten jumping jacks in her room. I stayed awake after Connie passed into her deep, twitchy sleep. Listening for Peter's footsteps on the stairs.

He crashed to his room, finally, and I waited for what seemed like a long time before I followed. Creeping along the hallway like a specter in shortie pajamas, their polyester slickness stuck in the broody stretch between princess costumes and lingerie. The silence of the house was a living thing, oppressive and present but also coloring everything with a foreign freedom, filling the rooms like a denser air.

Peter's form under the blankets was still, his knobby man's feet exposed. I heard his breathing, brambled from the aftereffects of whatever drugs he'd taken. His room seemed to cradle him. This might have been enough—to watch him sleep as a parent would, indulging the privilege of imagining happy dreams. His breaths like the beads of a rosary, each in and out a comfort. But I didn't want it to be enough.

When I got closer, his face clarified, his features completing as I adjusted to the dark. I let myself watch him without shame. Peter opened his eyes, suddenly, and somehow didn't seem startled by my presence at his bedside. Giving me a look as mild as a glass of milk.

"Boyd," he said, his voice still drifty from sleep, but he blinked and there was a resignation in the way he said my name that made me feel he'd been waiting for me. That he'd known I would come.

I was embarrassed to be standing like I was.

"You can sit," he said. I crouched by the futon, hovering foolishly. My legs already starting to burn with effort. Peter reached a hand to pull me fully onto the mattress and I smiled, though I wasn't sure he could even see my face. He was quiet and so was I. His room looked strange, as seen from the floor; the bulk of the dresser, the slivered doorway. I couldn't imagine Connie in the rooms beyond. Connie mumbling in her sleep, as she often did, sometimes announcing a number like an addled bingo player.

"You can get under the blankets if you're cold," he said, caping open the covers so I saw his bare chest, his nakedness. I got in beside him with ritual silence. It was as easy as this—I'd entered a possibility that had always been there.

He didn't speak, after that, and neither did I. He hitched me close so my back was pressed against his chest and I could feel his dick rear against my thighs. I didn't want to breathe, feeling that it would be an imposition on him, even the fact of my ribs rising and falling too much of a bother. I was taking tiny breaths through my nose, a light-headedness overtaking me. The strident rank of him in the dark, his blankets, his sheets—it was what Pamela got all the time, this easy occupation of his presence. His arm was around me, a weight I kept identifying as the weight of a boy's arm. Peter acted like he was going to sleep, the casual sigh and shuffle, but that kept the whole thing together. You had to act as if nothing strange were happening. When he brushed my nipple with his finger, I kept very still. I could feel his steady breath on my neck. His hand taking an impersonal measurement. Twisting the nipple so I inhaled audibly, and he hesitated for a moment but kept going. His dick smearing at my bare thighs. I would be shunted along whatever would happen, I understood. However he piloted the night. And there wasn't fear, just a feeling adjacent to excitement, a viewing from the wings. What would happen to Evie?

When the floorboards creaked from the hall, the spell cracked. Peter withdrew his hand, rolling abruptly onto his back. Staring at the ceiling so I could see his eyes.

"I've gotta get some sleep," he said in a voice carefully drained. A voice like an eraser, its insistent dullness meant to make me wonder if anything had happened. And I was slow to get to my feet, a little stunned, but also in a happy swoon, like even that little bit had fed me.

. . .

The boys played the slot machine for what seemed like hours. Connie and I sat on the bench, vibrating with forced inattention. I kept waiting for some acknowledgment from Peter of what had happened. A catch in the eye, a glance serrated with our history. But he didn't look at me. The humid garage smelled of chilly concrete and the funk of camping tents, folded while still wet. The gas station calendar on the wall: a woman in a hot tub with the stilled eyes and bared teeth of taxidermy. I was grateful for Pamela's absence that night. There'd been some fight between her and Peter, Connie had told me. I wanted to ask for more details, but there was a warning in her face—I couldn't be too interested.

"Don't you kids have somewhere better to be?" Henry asked. "Some ice-cream social somewhere?"

Connie tossed her hair, then walked over to get more beer. Henry watched her approach with amusement.

"Give those to me," she whined when Henry held two bottles out of reach. I remember noticing for the first time how loud she was, her voice hard with silly aggressiveness. Connie with her whines and feints, the grating laugh that sounded, and was, practiced. A space opened up between us as soon as I started to notice these things, to catalog her shortcomings the way a boy would. I regret how ungenerous I was. As if by putting distance between us, I could cure myself of the same disease.

"What are you gonna give me for them?" Henry said. "Nothing's free in this world, Connie."

She shrugged, then lunged for the beers. Henry pressed the solid mass of his body against her, grinning as she struggled. Peter rolled his eyes. He didn't like this kind of thing either, the bleating vaudeville. He had older friends who'd disappeared in sluggish jungles, rivers thick with sediment. Who'd returned home babbling and addicted to tiny black cigarettes, their hometown girl-friends cowering behind them like nervous little shadows. I tried to sit up straighter, to compose my face with adult boredom. Willing Peter to look over. I wanted the parts of him I was sure Pamela couldn't see, the pricks of sorrow I sometimes caught in his gaze or the secret kindness he showed to Connie, taking us to Arrowhead Lake the year their mother had forgotten Connie's birthday entirely. Pamela didn't know those things, and I held on to that certainty, whatever leverage might belong to me alone.

Henry pinched the soft skin above the waist of Connie's shorts. "Hungry lately, huh?"

"Don't touch me, perv," she said, hitting his hand away. She giggled a little. "Fuck you."

"Fine," he said, grabbing Connie's hands by the wrist. "Fuck me." She tried halfheartedly to pull away, whining until Henry finally let her go. She rubbed her wrists.

"Asshole," she muttered, but she wasn't really mad. That was part of being a girl—you were resigned to whatever feedback you'd get. If you got mad, you were crazy, and if you didn't react, you were a bitch. The only thing you could do was smile from the corner they'd backed you into. Implicate yourself in the joke even if the joke was always on you.

I didn't like the taste of beer, the granular bitterness nothing like the pleasing hygienic chill of my father's martinis, but I drank one and then another. The boys fed the slot machine from a shopping bag full of nickels until they were almost out of coins.

"We need the machine keys," Peter said, lighting a thin joint he pulled from his pocket. "So we can open it up."

"I'll get them," Connie said. "Don't miss me too much," she crooned to Henry, fluttering a little wave before she left. To me, she just raised her eyebrows. I understood this was part of some plan she had hatched to get Henry's attention. To leave, then return. She had probably read about it in a magazine.

That was our mistake, I think. One of many mistakes. To believe that boys were acting with a logic that we could someday understand. To believe that their actions had any meaning beyond thoughtless impulse. We were like conspiracy theorists, seeing portent and intention in every detail, wishing desperately that we mattered enough to be the object of planning and speculation. But they were just boys. Silly and young and straightforward; they weren't hiding anything.

Peter let the lever ratchet to a starting position and

stepped back to give Henry a turn, the two of them passing the joint back and forth. They both wore white T-shirts that were thin from washings. Peter smiled at the carnival racket when the slot machine clattered out a pile of coins, but he seemed distracted, finishing another beer, smoking the joint until it was crushed and oily. They were speaking low. I heard bits and pieces.

They were talking about Willie Poteracke: we all knew him, the first boy in Petaluma to enlist. His father had driven him to register. I'd seen him later at the Hamburger Hamlet with a petite brunette whose nostrils streamed snot. She called him stubbornly by his full name, Will-*iam*, like the extra syllable was the secret password that would transform him into a grown, responsible man. She clung to him like a burr.

"He's always out in the driveway," Peter said. "Washing his car like nothing's different. He can't even drive anymore, I don't think."

This was news from the other world. I felt ashamed, seeing Peter's face, for how I only playacted at real feelings, reaching for the world through songs. Peter could actually be sent away, he could actually die. He didn't have to force himself to feel that way, the emotional exercises Connie and I occupied ourselves with: What would you do if your father died? What would you do if you got pregnant? What would you do if a teacher wanted to fuck you, like Mr. Garrison and Patricia Bell?

"It was all puckered, his stump," Peter said. "Pink."

"Disgusting," Henry said from the machine. He didn't

turn away from the looping images of cherries that scrolled in front of him. "You wanna kill people, you better be okay with those people blowing your legs off."

"He's proud of it, too," Peter said, his voice rising as he flicked the end of the joint onto the garage floor. He watched it snuff out. "Wanting people to see it. That's what's crazy."

The dramatics of their conversation made me feel dramatic, too. I was stirred by the alcohol, the burn in my chest I exaggerated until I became moved by an authority not my own. I stood up. The boys didn't notice. They were talking about a movie they had seen in San Francisco. I recognized the title—they hadn't shown it in town because it was supposed to be perverted, though I couldn't remember why.

When I finally watched the movie, as an adult, the palpable innocence of the sex scenes surprised me. The humble pudge of fat above the actress's pubic hair. How she laughed when she pulled the yacht captain's face to her saggy, lovely breasts. There was a good-natured quality to the raunch, like fun was still an erotic idea. Unlike the movies that came later, girls wincing while their legs dangled like a dead thing's.

Henry was fluttering his eyelids, tongue in an obscene rictus. Aping some scene from the movie.

Peter laughed. "Sick."

They wondered aloud whether the actress had actually been getting fucked. They didn't seem to care that I was standing right there.

"You can tell she liked it," Henry said. "Ooh," he crowed in a high feminine voice. "Ooh, yeah, mmm." He banged the slot machine with his hips.

"I saw it, too." I spoke before thinking. I wanted an entry point in the conversation, even if it was a lie. They both looked at me.

"Well," Henry said, "the ghost finally speaks."

I flushed.

"You saw it?" Peter seemed doubtful. I told myself he was being protective.

"Yeah," I said. "Pretty wild."

They exchanged a glance. Did I really think they'd believe I had somehow gotten a ride to the city? That I'd gone to see what was, essentially, a porno?

"So." Henry's eyes glinted. "What was your favorite part?"

"That part you were talking about," I said. "With the girl."

"But what part of that did you like best?" Henry said.

"Leave her alone," Peter said mildly. Already bored.

"Did you like the Christmas scene?" Henry continued. His smile lulled me into thinking we were having a real conversation, that I was making progress. "The big tree? All the snow?"

I nodded. Almost believing my own lie.

Henry laughed. "The movie was in Fiji. The whole thing's on an island." Henry was snorting, helpless with laughter, and cut a look at Peter, who seemed embarrassed for me, like you would be embarrassed for a stranger who tripped on the street, like nothing had ever happened between us at all.

I pushed Henry's motorcycle. I hadn't expected it to tip over, not really: maybe just wobble, just enough to interrupt Henry so he'd be scared for a second, so he'd make some jokey exclamations of dismay and forget my lie. But I had pushed with real force. The motorcycle fell over and crunched hard on the cement floor.

Henry stared at me. "You little bitch." He hurried to the downed motorcycle like it was a shot pet. Practically cradling it in his arms.

"It's not broken," I said inanely.

"You're a fucking nutcase," he muttered. He ran his hands along the body of the bike and held a shard of orange metal up to Peter. "You believe this shit?"

When Peter looked at me, his face solidified with pity, which was somehow worse than anger. I was like a child, warranting only abbreviated emotions.

Connie appeared in the doorway.

"Knock knock," she called, the keys hanging from a crooked finger. She took in the scene: Henry squatting by the motorcycle; Peter's arms crossed.

Henry let out a harsh laugh. "Your friend's a real bitch," he said, shooting me a look.

"Evie knocked it over," Peter said.

"You fucking kids," Henry said. "Get a babysitter next time, don't hang around with us. Fuck."

"I'm sorry," I said, my voice small, but nobody was listening.

Even after Peter helped Henry right the motorcycle, peering closely at the break—"It's just cosmetic," he announced, "we can fix it pretty easy"—I understood that other things had broken. Connie studied me with cold wonder, like I'd betrayed her, and maybe I had. I'd done what we were not supposed to do. Illuminated a slice of private weakness, exposed the twitchy rabbit heart.

3

The owner of the Flying A was a fat man, the counter cutting into his belly, and he leaned on his elbows to track my movements around the aisles, my purse banging against my thighs. There was a newspaper open in front of him, though he never seemed to turn the page. He had a weary air of responsibility about him, both bureaucratic and mythological, like someone doomed to guard a cave for all eternity.

I was alone that afternoon. Connie probably fuming in her small bedroom, playing "Positively 4th Street" with wounded, righteous indulgence. The thought of Peter was gutting—I wanted to skim over that night, calcifying my shame into something blurry and manageable, like a rumor about a stranger. I'd tried to apologize to

Connie, the boys still worrying over the motorcycle like
field medics. I even offered to pay for repairs, giving
Henry everything I had in my purse. Eight dollars, which
he'd accepted with a stiff jaw. After a while, Connie said it
was best if I just went home.

I'd gone back a few days later—Connie's father answered
the door almost instantly, like he'd been waiting for me.
He usually worked at the dairy plant past midnight, so it
was odd to see him at home.

"Connie's upstairs," he said. On the counter behind
him, I saw a glass of whiskey, watery and catching the
sunlight. I was so focused on my own plans that I didn't
pick up the air of crisis in the house, the unusual information of his presence.

Connie was lying on her bed, her skirt hitched so I
could see the crotch of her white underwear, the entirety
of her stippled thighs. She sat up when I entered, blinking.

"Nice makeup," she said. "Did you do that just for me?"
She threw herself back on the pillow. "You'll like this
news. Peter's gone. Like, gone gone. With Pamela, *quelle*
surprise." She rolled her eyes but articulated Pamela's
name with a perverse happiness. Cutting me a look.

"What do you mean, left?" Panic was already dislocating my voice.

"He's so *selfish*," she said. "Dad told us we might have
to move to San Diego. The next day, Peter takes off. He
took a bunch of his clothes and stuff. I think they went to

her sister's house in Portland. I mean, I'm pretty sure they went there." She blew at her bangs. "He's a coward. And Pamela is the kind of girl who's gonna get fat after she has a baby."

"Pamela's pregnant?"

She gave me a look. "Surprise—you don't even care I might have to move to San Diego?"

I knew I was supposed to start enumerating the ways I loved her, how sad I would be if she left, but I was hypnotized by an image of Pamela next to Peter in his car, falling asleep against his shoulder. Avis maps at their feet gone translucent with hamburger grease, the backseat filled with clothes and his mechanic manuals. How Peter would look down and see the white line of Pamela's scalp through her part. He might kiss her, moved by a domestic tenderness, even though she was sleeping and would never know.

"Maybe he's just messing around," I said. "I mean, couldn't he still show up?"

"Screw you," Connie said. She seemed surprised by these words, too.

"What'd I even do to you?" I said.

Of course we both knew.

"I think I'd rather be alone right now," Connie announced primly, and stared hard out the window.

Peter, fleeing north with the girlfriend who might even have his baby—there was no imagining the biology away, the fact of the multiplying proteins in Pamela's stomach. But here was Connie, her chubby shape on the bed so familiar that I could map her freckles, point out the blip on her shoulder from chicken pox. There was always Connie, suddenly beloved.

"Let's go to a movie or something," I said.

She sniffed and studied the pale rim of her nails. "Peter's not even around anymore," she said. "So you really have no reason to be here. You're gonna be at boarding school, anyway."

The hum of my desperation was obvious. "Maybe we can go to the Flying A?"

She bit her lip. "May says you're not very nice to me."

May was the dentist's daughter. She wore plaid pants with matching vests, like a junior accountant.

"You said May was boring."

Connie was quiet. We used to feel sorry for May, who was rich but ridiculous, but I understood that now Connie was feeling sorry for me, watching me pant after Peter, who'd probably been planning to go to Portland for weeks. Months.

"May's nice," Connie said. "Real nice."

"We could all see a movie together." I was pedaling now, for any kind of traction, a bulwark against the empty summer. May wasn't so bad, I told myself, even though she wasn't allowed to eat candy or popcorn because of her braces, and yes, I could imagine it, the three of us.

"She thinks you're trashy," Connie said. She turned back to the window. I stared at the lace curtains I had helped Connie hem with glue when we were twelve. I had waited too long, my presence in the room an obvious error, and it was clear that there was nothing to do but leave, to say a tight-throated goodbye to Connie's father downstairs—he gave me a distracted nod—and clatter my bike out into the street.

Had I ever felt alone like this before, the whole day to spend and no one to care? I could almost imagine the ache in my gut as pleasure. It was about keeping busy, I told myself, a frictionless burning of hours. I made a martini the way my father had taught me, sloshing the vermouth over my hand and ignoring the spill on the bar table. I'd always hated martini glasses—the stem and the funny shape seemed embarrassing, like the adults were trying too hard to be adults. I poured it in a juice cup instead, rimmed with gold, and forced myself to drink. Then I made another and drank that, too. It was fun to feel loose and amused with my own house, realizing, in a spill of hilarity, that the furniture had always been ugly, chairs as heavy and mannered as gargoyles. To notice the air was candied with silence, that the curtains were always drawn. I opened them and struggled to lift a window. It was hot outside—I imagined my father, snapping that I was letting the warm air in—but I left the window open anyway.

My mother would be gone all day, the liquor aiding the shorthand of my loneliness. It was strange that I could feel differently so easily, that there was a sure way to soften the crud of my own sadness. I could drink until my problems seemed compact and pretty, something I could admire. I forced myself to like the taste, to breathe slowly when I felt nauseous. I burbled acrid vomit onto my blankets, then cleaned so there was just a tart, curdled spice in the air that I almost liked. I knocked over a lamp and put on dark eye makeup with inexpert but avid attention. Sat in front of my mother's lighted mirror with its different settings: Office. Daylight. Dusk. Washes of colored light, my features spooking and bleaching as I clicked through the artificial day.

I tried reading parts of books I'd liked when I was young. A spoiled girl gets banished underground, to a city ruled by goblins. The girl's bared knees in her childish dress, the woodcuts of the dark forests. The illustrations of the bound girl stirred me so I had to parcel how long I could look at them. I wished I could draw something like that, like the terrifying inside of someone's own mind. Or draw the face of the black-haired girl I'd seen in town—studying her long enough so I could see how the features worked together. The hours I lost to masturbation, face pressed into my pillow, passing some point of caring. I'd get a headache after a while, muscles jumpy, my legs quivering and tender. My underpants wet, the tops of my thighs.

Another book: a silversmith accidentally spills molten silver on his hand. His arm and hand probably looked skinned after the burn had scabbed over and peeled. The skin tight and pink and fresh, without hair or freckles. I thought of Willie and his stump, the warm hose water he sloshed over his car. How the puddles would slowly evaporate from the asphalt. I practiced peeling an orange as if my arm were burned to the elbow and I had no fingernails.

Death seemed to me like a lobby in a hotel. Some civilized, well-lit room you could easily enter or leave. A boy in town had shot himself in his finished basement after getting caught selling counterfeit raffle tickets: I didn't think of the gore, the wet insides, but only the ease of the moment before he pulled the trigger, how clean and winnowed the world must have seemed. All the disappointments, all of regular life with its punishments and indignities, made surplus in one orderly motion.

The aisles of the store seemed new to me, my thoughts formless from drinking. The constant flickering of the lights, stale lemon drops in a bin, the makeup arranged in pleasing, fetishistic groupings. I uncapped a lipstick, to test it on my wrist like I'd read I should. The door rang its chime of commerce. I looked up. It was the black-haired girl from the park, in denim sneakers, a dress whose sleeves had been cut at the shoulder. Excitement moved through me. Already I was trying to imagine what I would say to her. Her sudden appearance made the day seem tightly wound with synchronicity, the angle of sunlight newly weighted.

The girl wasn't beautiful, I realized, seeing her again. It was something else. Like pictures I had seen of the actor John Huston's daughter. Her face could have been an error, but some other process was at work. It was better than beauty.

The man behind the counter scowled.

"I told you," he said. "I won't let any of you in here, not anymore. Get on."

The girl gave him a lazy smile, holding up her hands. I saw a prick of hair in her armpits. "Hey," she said, "I'm just trying to buy toilet paper."

"You stole from me," the man said, shading red. "You and your friends. Not wearing shoes, running around with your filthy feet. Trying to confuse me."

I would have been terrified in the focus of his anger, but the girl was calm. Even jokey. "I don't think that's true." She cocked her head. "Maybe it was someone else."

He crossed his arms. "I remember you."

The girl's face shifted, something hardening in her eyes, but she remained smiling. "Fine," she said. "Whatever your thing is." She looked over at me, her glance cool and distant. Like she hardly saw me. Desire moved through me: I surprised myself with how much I didn't want her to disappear.

"Get on outside," the man said. "Go."

Before she left, she stuck out her tongue at the man. Just a peep, like a droll little cat.

I'd only hesitated for a moment before following the girl outside, but she was already cutting across the parking lot, keeping up a brisk pace. I hurried behind.

"Hey," I called. She kept walking.

I said it again, louder, and she stopped. Letting me catch up to her.

"What a jerk," I said. I must have looked shiny as an apple. Cheeks flushed with half-drunk effort.

She glared in the direction of the store. "Fat fuck," she muttered. "I can't even buy toilet paper."

She finally seemed to acknowledge me, studying my face for a long moment. I could tell she saw me as young. That my bib shirt, a gift from my mother, was considered fancy. I wanted to do something bigger than those facts. I made the offer before I'd really thought about it.

"I'll lift it," I said, my voice unnaturally bright. "The toilet paper. Easy. I steal stuff from there all the time."

I wondered if she believed me. It must have been obvious how lightly I was wearing the lie. But maybe she respected that. The desperation of my desire. Or maybe she wanted to see how it would play out. The rich girl, trying out kid-glove criminality.

"You sure?" she said.

I shrugged, my heart hammering. If she felt sorry for me, I didn't see that part.

My unexplained return agitated the man behind the counter.

"Back again?"

Even if I'd really planned to try to steal something, it would have been impossible. I dawdled down the aisles, making an effort to wipe my face of any delinquent glimmer, but the man didn't look away. He glared until I grabbed the toilet paper and brought it to the register, shamed at how easily I snapped into the habit. Of course I wasn't going to steal anything. That was never going to happen.

He got on a tear as he rang up the toilet paper. "A nice girl like you shouldn't hang out with girls like that," he said. "So filthy, that group. Some guy with a black dog." He looked pained. "Not in my store."

Through the pocked glass, I could see the girl ambling in the parking lot outside. Hand shading her eyes. This sudden and unexpected fortune: she was waiting for me.

After I paid, the man looked at me for a long moment. "You're just a kid," he said. "Why don't you go on home?"

I had felt bad for him until then. "I don't need a bag," I said, and stuffed the toilet paper in my purse. I was silent while the man gave me change, licking his lips as if to chase away a bad taste.

The girl perked up as I came over.

"You get it?"

I nodded, and she huddled me around the corner, her arm hurrying me along. I could almost believe I had actually stolen something, adrenaline brightening my veins as I held out my bag.

"Ha," she said, peeking inside. "Serves him right, the asshole. Was it easy?"

"Pretty easy," I said. "He's so out of it, anyway." I was thrilling at our collusion, the way we'd become a team. A triangle of stomach showed where the girl's dress wasn't fully buttoned. How easily she invoked a kind of sloppy sexual feeling, like her clothes had been hurried on a body still cooling from sweat.

"I'm Suzanne," she said. "By the way."

"Evie." I stuck out my hand. Suzanne laughed in a way that made me understand shaking hands was the wrong thing to do, a hollow symbol from the straight world. I flushed. It was hard to know how to act without all the usual polite gestures and forms. I wasn't sure what took their place. There was a silence: I scrambled to fill it.

"I think I saw you the other day," I said. "By the Hi-Ho?"

She didn't respond, giving me nothing to grab on to.

"You were with some girls?" I said. "And a bus came?"

"Oh," she said, her face reanimating. "Yeah, that idiot was real mad." She relaxed into the memory. "I have to keep the other girls in line, you know, or they'd just fall all over themselves. Get us caught." I was watching Suzanne with an interest that must have been obvious: she let me look at her without any self-consciousness.

"I remembered your hair," I said.

Suzanne seemed pleased. Touching the ends, absently. "I never cut it."

I would find out, later, that this was something Russell told them not to do.

Suzanne nestled the toilet paper to her chest, suddenly proud. "You want me to give you some money for this?"

She had no pockets, no purse.

"Nah," I said. "It's not like it cost me anything."

"Well, thanks," she said, with obvious relief. "You live around here?"

"Pretty close," I said. "With my mom."

Suzanne nodded. "What street?"

"Morning Star Lane."

She made a hum of surprise. "Fancy."

I could see it meant something to her, me living in the nice part of town, but I couldn't imagine what, beyond the vague dislike for the rich that all young people had. Mashing up the wealthy and the media and the government into an indistinct vessel of evil, perpetrators of the grand hoax. I was only just starting to learn how to rig certain information with apology. How to mock myself before other people could.

"What about you?"

She made a fluttery motion with her fingers. "Oh," she said, "you know. We've got some things going on. But a lot of people in one place"—she held up the bag—"means a lot of asses that need wiping. We're low on money, at this exact moment, but that'll turn, soon, I'm sure."

We. The girl was part of a *we*, and I envied her ease, her surety of where she was aimed after the parking lot. Those two other girls I'd seen with her in the park, whoever else she lived with. People who'd notice her absence and exclaim at her return.

"You're quiet," Suzanne said after a moment.

"Sorry." I willed myself not to scratch my mosquito bites, though my skin was twisting with itchiness. I reeled for conversation, but all the possibilities that appeared were the things I couldn't say. I should not tell her how often and idly I had thought of her since that day. I should not tell her I had no friends, that I was being shunted to boarding school, that perpetual municipality of unwanted children. That I was not even a blip to Peter.

"It's cool." She waved her hand. "People are the way they are, you know? I could tell when I saw you," she continued. "You're a thoughtful person. On your own trip, all caught up in your mind."

I was not used to this kind of unmediated attention. Especially from a girl. Usually it was only a way of apologizing for being zeroed in on whatever boy was around. I let myself imagine I was a girl people saw as thoughtful. Suzanne shifted: I could tell this was a prelude to departure, but I couldn't think of how to extend our exchange.

"Well," she said. "That's me over there." She nodded to a car parked in the shade. It was a Rolls-Royce, shrouded in dirt. When she saw my confusion, she smiled.

"We're borrowing it," she said. As if that explained everything.

I watched her walk away without trying to stop her. I didn't want to be greedy: I should be happy I had gotten anything at all.

4

My mother was dating again. First, a man who introduced himself as Vismaya and kept massaging my mother's scalp with his clawed fingers. Who told me that my birthday, on the cusp of Aquarius and Pisces, meant my two phrases were "I believe" and "I know."

"Which is it?" Vismaya asked me. "Do you believe you know, or do you know you believe?"

Next, a man who flew small silver planes and told me that my nipples were showing through my shirt. He said it plainly, as if this were helpful information. He made pastel portraits of Native Americans and wanted my mother to help open a museum of his work in Arizona. Next, a real estate developer from Tiburon who took us out for Chinese food. He kept encouraging me to meet his daughter. Repeating again and again how sure he was that we'd get along like a house on fire. His daughter was eleven, I came to realize. Connie would have laughed, dissecting the way the man's teeth gummed up with rice, but I hadn't spoken to her since the day at her house.

"I'm fourteen," I said. The man looked to my mother, who nodded.

"Of course," he said, a tang of soy sauce on his breath. "I see now you're practically a grown-up."

"I'm sorry," my mother mouthed across the table, but when the man turned to feed her a slimy-looking snow pea from his fork, she opened her mouth obediently, like a bird.

The pity I felt for my mother in these situations was new and uncomfortable, but also I sensed that I deserved to carry it around—a grim and private responsibility, like a medical condition.

There had been a cocktail party my parents had thrown, the year before the divorce. It was my father's idea—until he left, my mother wasn't social, and I could sense a deep agitation in her during parties or events, a heave of discomfort she willed into a stiff smile. It had been a party to celebrate the investor my father had found. It was the first time, I think, that he'd gotten money from someone other than my mother, and he got even bigger in the heat of that, drinking before the guests arrived. His hair saturated with the dense fatherly scent of Vitalis, his breath notched with liquor.

My mother had made Chinese ribs with ketchup and they had a glandular sheen, like a lacquer. Olives from a can, buttered nuts. Cheese straws. Some sludgy dessert made from mandarin oranges, a recipe she'd seen in *McCall's*. She asked me before the guests arrived if she looked all right. Smoothing her damask skirt. I remember being taken aback by the question.

"Very nice," I said, feeling strangely unsettled. I'd been allowed some sherry in a cut pink glass: I liked the rotted pucker and snuck another glass.

The guests were my father's friends, mostly, and I was surprised at the breadth of his other life, a life I saw only from the perimeter. Because here were people who seemed to know him, to hold a vision of him informed by lunches and visits to Golden Gate Fields and discussions of Sandy Koufax. My mother hovered nervously around the buffet: she'd put out chopsticks, but no one was using them, and I could tell this disappointed her. She tried to urge them on a heavyset man and his wife, and they shook their heads, the man making some joke I couldn't hear. I saw something desperate pass over my mother's face. She was drinking, too. It was the kind of party where everyone was drunk early, a communal haze slurring over conversation. Earlier, one of my father's friends had lit a joint, and I saw my mother's expression downshift from disapproval to patient indulgence. Certain lines were getting dim. Wives staring up at the pass of an airplane, arcing toward SFO. Someone dropped a glass in the pool. I saw it drift slowly to the bottom. Maybe it was an ashtray.

I floated around the party, feeling like a much younger child, that desire for invisibility coupled with a wish to participate in an adjacent way. I was happy enough to point out the bathroom when asked, to parcel into a napkin buttered nuts that I ate by the pool, one by one, their salty grit fleecing my fingers. The freedom of being so young that no one expected anything from me.

I hadn't seen Tamar since the day she'd dropped me off after school, and I remember feeling disappointed when she arrived—I'd have to act like a grown-up now that she was there as witness. She had a man with her, slightly older. She introduced him around, kissing someone on the cheek, shaking hands. Everyone seemed to know her. I was jealous of how Tamar's boyfriend rested his hand on her back while she spoke, on the sliver of skin between her skirt and top. I wanted her to see that I was drinking: I made my way to the bar table when she did, pouring myself another glass of sherry.

"I like your outfit," I said, pushed to speak by the burn in my chest. She had her back to me and didn't hear. I repeated myself and she startled.

"Evie," she said, pleasantly enough. "You scared me."

"Sorry." I felt foolish, blunt in my shift dress. Her outfit was bright and new looking, wavy diamonds in violet and green and red.

"Fun party," she said, her eyes scanning the crowd.

Before I could think of a rejoinder, some crack to show

that I knew the tiki torches were stupid, my mother joined us. I quickly put my glass back on the table. Hating the way I felt: all my comfort before Tamar's arrival had transformed into painful awareness of every object in my house, every detail of my parents, as if I were responsible for all of it. I was embarrassed for my mother's full skirt, which seemed outdated next to Tamar's clothes, for the eager way my mother greeted her. Her neck getting blotchy with nerves. I slunk away while they were distracted with their polite chatter.

Queasy and sunbaked with discomfort, I wanted to sit in one place without having to talk to anyone, without having to track Tamar's gaze or see my mother using her chopsticks, announcing gaily that it wasn't so hard, even as a mandarin orange slithered back onto her plate. I wished Connie were there—we were still friends then. My spot by the pool had been occupied by a gossipy scrum of wives: from across the yard, I heard my father's booming laugh, the group surrounding him laughing as well. I pulled my dress down, awkwardly, missing the weight of a glass in my hands. Tamar's boyfriend was standing nearby, eating ribs.

"You're Carl's daughter," he said, "right?"

I remember thinking it was strange that he and Tamar had floated apart, that he was just standing by himself, powering through his plate. It was strange that he would even want to talk to me. I nodded.

"Nice house," he said, his mouth full. Lips bright and wet from the ribs. He was handsome, I saw, but there was something cartoonish about him, the upturn of his nose. The extra ruff of skin under his chin. "So much land," he added.

"It was my grandparents' house."

His eyes shifted. "I heard about her," he said. "Your grandmother. I used to watch her when I was little." I didn't realize how drunk he was until that moment. His tongue lingering in the corner of his mouth. "That episode where she finds the alligator in the fountain. Classic."

I was used to people speaking of my grandmother fondly. How they liked to perform their admiration, tell me that they'd grown up with her on their television screens, beamed into their living rooms like another, better, family member.

"Makes sense," the boyfriend said, looking around. "That this was her place. 'Cause your old man couldn't afford it, no way."

I understood that he was insulting my father.

"It's just strange," he said, wiping his lips with his hand. "What your mother puts up with."

My face must have been blank: he waggled his fingers in the direction of Tamar, still at the bar. My father had joined her. My mother was nowhere in sight. Tamar's bracelets were making noise as she waved her glass. She and my father were just talking. Nothing was happening. I didn't get why her boyfriend was smiling so rabidly, waiting for me to say something.

"Your father fucks anything he can," he said.

"Can I take your plate?" I asked, too stunned to flinch. That was something I'd learned from my mother: revert to politeness. Cut pain with a gesture of civility. Like Jackie Kennedy. It was a virtue to that generation, an ability to divert discomfort, tamp it down with ceremony. But it was out of fashion now, and I saw something like disdain in his eyes when he handed me his plate. Though maybe that is something I imagined.

The party ended after dark. A few of the tiki torches stayed lit, sending their bleary flames streaking into the navy night. The vivid oversize cars lumbering down the driveway, my father calling out goodbyes while my mother stacked napkins and brushed olive pits, washed in other people's saliva, into her open palm. My father re-started the record; I looked out my bedroom window and saw him trying to get my mother to dance. "I'll be look-ing at the moon," he sang, the moon's far-off face the focus of so much longing back then.

I knew I should hate my father. But I only felt foolish. Embarrassed—not for him, but for my mother. Smooth-ing her full skirt, asking me how she looked. The way she sometimes had flecks of food in her teeth and blushed when I told her so. The times she stood at the window when my father was late coming home, trying to decode new meaning out of the empty driveway.

She must know what was going on—she had to have known—but she wanted him anyway. Like Connie, jumping for the beer knowing she would look stupid. Even Tamar's boyfriend, eating with his frantic, bottomless need. Chewing faster than he could swallow. He knew how your hunger could expose you.

The drunk was wearing off. I was sleepy and hollow, cast uncomfortably back to myself. I had scorn for everything: my room with my childhood leftovers, the trim of lace around my desk. The plastic record player with a chunky Bakelite handle, a wet-looking beanbag chair that stuck to the backs of my legs. The party with its eager hors d'oeuvres, the men wearing aloha shirts in a sartorial clamor for festivity. It all seemed to add up to an explanation for why my father would want something else. I imagined Tamar with her throat circled by a ribbon, lying on some carpet in some too-small Palo Alto apartment. My father there—watching her? sitting in a chair? The perverse voltage of Tamar's pink lipstick. I tried to hate her but couldn't. I couldn't even hate my father. The only person left was my mother, who'd let it happen, who'd been as soft and malleable as dough. Handing money over, cooking dinner every night, and no wonder my father had wanted something else—Tamar's outsize opinions, her life like a TV show about summer.

It was a time when I imagined getting married in a simple, wishful way. The time when someone promised to take care of you, promised they would notice if you were sad, or tired, or hated food that tasted like the chill of the refrigerator. Who promised their lives would run parallel to yours. My mother must have known and stayed anyway, and what did that mean about love? It was never going to be safe—all the mournful refrains of songs that despaired *you didn't love me the way I loved you.*

The most frightening thing: It was impossible to detect the source, the instant when things changed. The sight of a woman's back in her low dress mingled with the knowledge of the wife in another room.

When the music stopped, I knew my mother would come say good night. It was a moment I'd been dreading—having to notice how her curls had wilted, the haze of lipstick around her mouth. When she knocked, I thought about pretending to be asleep. But my light was on: the door edged open.

She grimaced a little. "You're still all dressed."

I would've ignored her or made some joke, but I didn't want to cause her any pain. Not then. I sat up.

"That was nice, wasn't it?" she said. She leaned against the door frame. "The ribs came out good, I thought."

Maybe I genuinely thought my mother would want to know. Or maybe I wanted to be soothed by her, for her to offer a calming adult summary.

I cleared my throat. "Something happened."

I felt her tense in the doorway.

"Oh?"

Later I cringed, thinking of it. She must have already known what was coming. Must have willed me to be quiet.

"Dad was talking." I turned back to my shoes, working intently at the buckle. "With Tamar."

She let out a breath. "And?" She was smiling a little. An untroubled smile.

I was confused: she must know what I meant. "That's all," I said.

My mother looked at the wall. "That dessert was the one thing," she said. "Next time I would do macaroons instead, coconut macaroons. Those mandarins were too hard to eat."

I was silent, shock making me wary. I slipped off my shoes and put them under my bed, side by side. I murmured good night, tilted my head to receive her kiss.

"You want me to turn off the light?" my mother asked, pausing in the doorway.

I shook my head. She shut the door gently. How conscientious she was, turning the handle so it clicked shut. I stared at my red feet, marked by the outline of my shoes. Thought about how strangled and strange they looked, all out of proportion, and who would ever love someone whose feet could look like this?

My mother spoke of the men she dated, after my father, with the desperate optimism of the born-again. And I saw the devout labor it took: she did exercises on a bath towel in the living room, her leotard striped with sweat. Licked her palm and sniffed to test her own breath. She went out with men whose necks raised boils where they cut themselves shaving, men who fumbled for the check but looked grateful when my mother removed her Air Travel Card. She found men like this and seemed happy about it.

I'd imagine Peter, during our dinners with these men. Asleep with Pamela in a basement apartment in an unfamiliar Oregon town. Jealousy mingled strangely with a protectiveness for the two of them, for the child growing inside Pamela. There were only so many girls, I understood, that could be marked for love. Like that girl Suzanne, who commanded that response just by existing.

The man my mother liked best was a gold miner. Or that's how Frank introduced himself, laughing, a scud of spit in the corner of his mouth.

"Pleased to meet you, darlin'," he said the first night, his big arm reining me toward him in a clumsy hug. My mother was giddy and a little drunk, as if life were a world where nuggets of gold were hidden in streambeds or clustered at cliff bases, picked off as easily as peaches.

I had heard my mother tell Sal that Frank was still married but wouldn't be for long. I didn't know if that was true. Frank didn't seem the type to leave his family. He wore a shirt with creamy buttons, peonies embroidered in raised red thread on the shoulders. My mother was acting nervous, touching her hair, slipping her fingernail between her front teeth. She looked from me to Frank. "Evie's a very smart girl," she said. She was talking too loud. Still, it was nice to hear her say it. "She'll really blossom at Catalina." This was the boarding school I'd attend, though September seemed years away.

"Big brains," Frank boomed. "Can't go wrong there, can you?"

I didn't know if he was joking or not, and my mother didn't seem to know either.

We ate a casserole in silence in the dining room, and I picked out the blats of tofu and built a pile on my plate. I watched my mother decide not to say anything.

Frank was good-looking, even if his shirt was strange, too fussy and feminine, and he made my mother laugh. He was not as handsome as my father, but still. She kept reaching out to touch his arm with her fingertips.

"Fourteen years old, huh?" Frank said. "Bet you have a ton of boyfriends."

Adults always teased me about having boyfriends, but there was an age where it was no longer a joke, the idea that boys might actually want you.

"Oh, heaps," I said, and my mother perked to attention, hearing the coldness in my voice. Frank didn't seem to notice, smiling widely at my mother, patting her hand. She was smiling, too, in a masklike way, her eyes bouncing from me to him across the table.

Frank had gold mines in Mexico. "No regulations

down there," he said. "Cheap labor. It's pretty much a sure thing."

"How much gold have you found?" I asked. "So far, I mean."

"Well, once all the equipment is in place, I'll be finding a ton." He drank from a wineglass, his fingers leaving ghosts of grease. My mother went soft, in his glance; her shoulders relaxing, her lips parting. She was young looking that night. I had a queer twinge of motherly feeling for her, and the discomfort of it made me wince.

"Maybe I'll take you down there," Frank said. "Both of you. Little trip to Mexico. Flowers in your hair." He burped under his breath, swallowing it, and my mother blushed, wine moving in her glass.

My mother liked this man. Did her stupid exercises so she would look beautiful to him without any clothes on. She was groomed and oiled, her face eager for love. It was a painful thought, my mother needing anything, and I looked over at her, wanting to smile, to show her how we were fine, the two of us. But she wasn't watching me. She was alert to Frank instead, waiting to receive whatever he wanted to give her. I balled my hands tight under the table.

"What about your wife?" I asked.

"Evie," my mother hissed.

"That's all right," Frank said, holding up his hands. "That's a fair question." He rubbed his eyes hard, then put down his fork. "It's complicated stuff."

"It's not that complicated," I said.

"You're a rude girl," my mother said. Frank put his hand on her shoulder, but she'd already stood up to clear the plates, a grim busyness fixed on her face, and Frank handed over his plate with a concerned smile. Wiping his dry hands on his jeans. I didn't look at her or him. I was picking at the skin around my fingernail, tugging until there was a satisfying tear.

When my mother left the room, Frank cleared his throat.

"You shouldn't make your mom so mad," he said. "She's a nice lady."

"None of your business." My cuticle was bleeding a little: I pressed to feel the sting.

"Hey," he said, his voice easy, like he was trying to be my friend. "I get it. You wanna be out of the house. Tired of living with ol' mom, huh?"

"Pathetic," I mouthed.

He didn't understand what I had said, only that I hadn't responded how he wanted. "Biting your nails is an ugly habit," he said hotly. "An ugly, dirty habit for dirty people. Are you an ugly person?"

My mother reappeared in the doorway. I was sure she had overheard, and now she knew that Frank wasn't a nice man. She would be disappointed, but I resolved to be kinder, to help more around the house.

But my mother just wrinkled her face. "What's happening?"

"I was just telling Evie she shouldn't bite her nails."

"I tell her that, too," my mother said. Her voice rattled, her lips twitching. "She could get sick, ingesting germs."

I cycled through the possibilities. My mother was simply stalling. She was taking a moment to figure out how best to drive Frank from our lives, to tell him I was no one else's business. But when she sat down and allowed Frank to rub her arm, even leaning toward him, I understood how it would go.

When Frank went to the bathroom, I figured there would be some kind of an apology from her.

"That shirt is too tight," she whispered harshly. "It's inappropriate, at your age."

I opened my mouth to speak.

"We'll talk tomorrow," she said. "You better believe we'll talk." When she heard Frank's footsteps returning, she gave me one last look, then rose to meet him. They left me alone at the table. The overhead light on my arms and hands was severe and unlovely.

They went on the porch to sit, my mother keeping her cigarette butts in a mermaid tin. From my bedroom I heard their staggered talk late into the night, my mother's laugh, simple and thoughtless. The smoke from their cigarettes drifting through the screen. The night boiled inside me. My mother thought life was as easy as picking gold from the ground, as if things could be that way for her. There was no Connie to temper my upset, just the suffocating constancy of my own self, that numb and desperate company.

. . .

There are ways I made sense of my mother later. How fifteen years with my father had left great blanks in her life that she was learning to fill, like those stroke victims relearning the words for car and table and pencil. The shy way she looked at herself in the oracle of the mirror, as critical and hopeful as an adolescent. Sucking in her stomach to zip her new jeans.

In the morning, I came into the kitchen and found my mother at the table, her bowl of tea already drained, sediment flecking the bottom. Her lips were tight, her eyes wounded. I walked past her without speaking, opening a bag of ground coffee, purple and heady, my mother's replacement for the Sanka that my father liked.

"What was that about?" She was trying to be calm, I could tell, but the words were rushed.

I shook the grounds into the maker, turned on the burner. Keeping a Buddhist calm on my face as I went about my tasks, untroubled. This was my best weapon, and I could feel her getting agitated.

"Well, now you're quiet," she said. "You were very rude to Frank last night."

I didn't respond.

"You want me to be unhappy?" She got to her feet. "I'm talking to you," she said, reaching to snap the stove off.

"Hey," I said, but her face made me shut up.

"Why can't you let me have anything?" she said. "Just one little thing."

"He's not going to leave her." The intensity of my feeling startled me. "He's never going to be with you."

"You don't know anything about his life," she said. "Not anything. You think you know so much."

"Oh yeah," I said. "Gold. Right. Big success there. Just like Dad. I bet he asked you for money."

My mother flinched.

"I try with you," she said. "I've always tried, but you aren't trying at all. Look at yourself. Doing nothing." She shook her head, tightening her robe. "You'll see. Life will come up on you so fast, and guess what, you'll be stuck with the person you are. No ambition, no drive. You have a real chance at Catalina, but you have to try. You know what my mother was doing at your age?"

"You never did anything!" Something tipped over inside me. "All you did was take care of Dad. And he left." My face was burning. "I'm sorry I disappoint you. I'm sorry I'm so awful. I should pay people to tell me I'm great, like you do. Why did Dad leave if you're so fucking great?"

She reached forward and slapped me, not hard, but hard enough so there was an audible sound. I smiled, like a crazed person, showing too many teeth.

"Get out." Her neck was mottled with hives, her wrists thin. "Get out," she hissed again, weakly, and I darted away.

. . .

I took the bicycle down the dirt road. My heart thudding, the tightness of pressure behind my eyes. I liked feeling the sting of my mother's slap, the aura of goodness she had so carefully cultivated for the last month—the tea, the bare feet—curdled in an instant. Good. Let her be ashamed. All her classes and cleanses and readings had done nothing. She was the same weak person as always. I pedaled faster, a flurry in my throat. I could go to the Flying A and buy a bag of chocolate stars. I could see what was playing at the movie theater or walk along the brothy soup of the river. My hair lifted a little in the dry heat. I felt hatred hardening in me, and it was almost nice, how big it was, how pure and intense.

My furious pedaling went abruptly slack: the chain slipped its bearings. The bike was slowing. I lurched to a stop in the dirt by the fire road. My armpits were sweating, the backs of my knees. The sun hot through the cut-work lattice of a live oak. I was trying not to cry. I crouched on the ground to realign the chain, tears skimming off my eyes in the sting of the breeze, my fingers slippery with grease. It was too hard to grip, the chain falling away.

"Fuck," I said, then said it louder. I wanted to kick the bicycle, silence something, but that would be too pitiful, the theater of upset performed for no one. I tried one more time to hook the chain onto the spoke, but it wouldn't catch, snapping loose. I let the bike drop into

the dirt and sank down beside it. The front wheel spun a
little, then slowed to a stop. I stared at the bike, splayed
and useless: the frame was "Campus Green," a color that
had conjured, in the store, a hale college boy walking you
home from an evening class. A prissy fantasy, a stupid
bike, and I let the string of disappointments grow until
they looped into a dirge of mediocrity. Connie was probably with May Lopes. Peter and Pamela buying houseplants for an Oregon apartment and soaking lentils for
supper. What did I have? The tears dripped off my chin
into the dirt, pleasing proof of my suffering. This absence
in me that I could curl around like an animal.

I heard it before I saw it: the black bus lumbering
heavily up the road, dust rising behind the wheels. The
windows were pocked and gray, the blurred shapes of
people within. Painted on the hood was a crude heart,
crowned with drippy lashes, like an eye.

A girl wearing a man's shirt and knitted vest stepped
down from the bus, shaking back her flat orange hair. I
could hear other voices, a flurry at the windows. A moony
face appeared: watching me.

The girl's voice was singsongy. "What's wrong?" she
said.

"The bike," I said, "the chain's messed up." The girl
toed the wheel with her sandaled foot. Before I could ask
who she was, Suzanne came down the steps, and my heart
surged. I got to my feet, trying to brush the dirt from my

knees. Suzanne smiled but seemed distracted. I realized I had to remind her of my name.

"From the store on East Washington," I said. "The other day?"

"Oh yeah."

I expected her to say something about the bizarre luck of encountering each other again, but she looked a little bored. I kept glancing at her. I wanted to remind her of our conversation, how she'd said I was thoughtful. But she wouldn't exactly meet my eye.

"We saw you sitting there and thought, Oh shit, poor thing," the redhead said. This was Donna, I was to learn. She had a touched look, her eyebrows invisible so her face took on an alien blankness. She squatted to study my bike. "Suzanne said she knew you."

The three of us worked together to get the chain back on. The smell of their sweat as we propped the bike on its stand. I'd bent the gears somehow when the bike fell, and the teeth wouldn't line up with the spokes.

"Fuck." Suzanne sighed. "This is all messed up."

"You need pliers or something," Donna said. "You aren't gonna fix it now. Stick it in the bus, come hang with us for a while."

"Let's just give her a ride into town," Suzanne said.

She spoke briskly, like I was a mess that needed to be cleaned up. Even so, I was glad. I was used to thinking about people who never thought about me.

"We're having a solstice party," Donna said.

I didn't want to go back to my mother, to the forlorn guardianship of my own self. I had the sense that if I let Suzanne go, I would not see her again.

"Evie wants to come," Donna said. "I can tell she's up for it. You like to have fun, don't you?"

"Come on," Suzanne said. "She's a kid."

I surged with shame. "I'm sixteen," I lied.

"She's *sixteen*," Donna repeated. "Don't you think Russell would want us to be hospitable? I think he'd be upset if I told him we weren't being hospitable."

I didn't read any threat in Donna's voice, only teasing. Suzanne's mouth was tight; she finally smiled.

"Okay," she said. "Put the bike in the back."

I saw that the bus had been emptied and rebuilt, the interior cruddy and overworked in the way things were back then—the floor gridded with Oriental carpets, grayed with dust, the drained tufts of thrift store cushions. The stink of a joss stick in the air, prisms ticking against the windows. Cardboard scrawled with dopey phrases.

There were three other girls in the bus, and they turned to me with eagerness, a feral attention I read as flattering. Cigarettes going in their hands while they looked me up and down, an air of festivity and timelessness. A sack of green potatoes, pasty hot dog buns. A crate of wet, overripe tomatoes. "We were on a food run," Donna said, though I didn't really understand what that meant. My mind was preoccupied with this sudden shift of luck, with monitoring the slow trickle of sweat under my arms. I kept waiting to be spotted, to be identified as an intruder who didn't belong. My hair too clean. Little nods toward presentation and decorum that seemed to concern no one else. My hair cut crazily across my vision from the open windows, intensifying the dislocation, the abruptness of being in this strange bus. A feather hanging from the rearview with a cluster of beads. Some dried lavender on the dashboard, colorless from the sun.

"She's coming to the solstice," Donna chimed, "the summer solstice."

It was early June and I knew the solstice was at the end of the month: I didn't say anything. The first of many silences.

"She's gonna be our offering," Donna told the others. Giggling. "We're gonna sacrifice her."

I looked to Suzanne—even our brief history seemed to ratify my presence among them—but she was sitting off to the side, absorbed by the box of tomatoes. Applying pressure to the skins, sifting out the rot. Waving away the bees. It would occur to me later that Suzanne was the only one who didn't seem overjoyed to come upon me, there on the road. Something formal and distant in her affect. I can only think it was protective. That Suzanne saw the weakness in me, lit up and obvious: she knew what happened to weak girls.

. . .

Donna introduced me around, and I tried to remember their names. Helen, a girl who seemed close to my age, though maybe it was just her pigtails. She was pretty in the youthful way of hometown beauties, snub-nosed, her features accessible, though with an obvious expiration date. Roos. "Short for Roosevelt," she told me. "As in, Franklin D." She was older than the other girls, with a face as round and rosy as a storybook character.

I couldn't remember the name of the tall girl who was driving: I never saw her again after that day.

Donna made a space, patting the nub of an embroidered cushion.

"Come here," she said, and I sat down on the itchy pile. Donna seemed odd, slightly oafish, but I liked her. All of her greed and pettiness was right on the surface.

The bus lurched forward: my gut went jostled and tight, but I took the jug of cheap red wine when they passed it, splashing out over my hands. They looked happy, smiling, their voices sometimes breaking into snippets of song like campers around a fire. I was picking up the particularities—how they held hands without any self-consciousness and dropped words like "harmony" and "love" and "eternity." How Helen acted like a baby, pulling on her pigtails and talking in her baby voice, abruptly sinking into Roos's lap like she could trick Roos into taking care of her. Roos didn't complain: she seemed stolid, nice. Those pink cheeks, her lank blond hair falling in her eyes. Though later I'd think maybe it was less niceness than a muted void where niceness should be. Donna asked me about myself, and so did the others, a constant stream of questions. I couldn't help my pleasure at being the focus of their attention. Inexplicably, they seemed to like me, and the thought was foreign and cheering, a mysterious gift I didn't want to probe too much. I could even cast Suzanne's silence in a welcoming light, imagining she was shy, like me.

"Nice," Donna said, touching my shirt. Helen pinched a sleeve, too.

"You're just like a little doll," Donna said. "Russell's gonna love you."

She tossed out his name just like that, as if it were unimaginable that I might not know who Russell was. Helen giggled at the sound of his name, rolling her shoulders with pleasure, like she was sucking on a sweet. Donna saw my blink of uncertainty and laughed.

"You'll love him," she said. "He's not like anyone else. No bullshit. It's like a natural high, being around him. Like the sun or something. That big and right."

She looked over to be sure I was listening, seemed pleased that I was.

She said that the place we were headed was about a way of living. Russell was teaching them how to discover a path to truth, how to free their real selves from where it was coiled inside them. She talked about someone named Guy, who'd once trained falcons but had joined their group and now wanted to be a poet.

"When we met him, he was on some weird trip, just eating meat. He thought he was the devil or something.

But Russell helped him. Taught him how to love," Donna said. "Everyone can love, can transcend the bullshit, but so many things get us all stopped up."

I didn't know how to imagine Russell. I had only the limited reference point of men like my father or boys I'd had crushes on. The way these girls spoke of Russell was different, their worship more practical, with none of the playful, girlish longing I knew. Their certainty was unwavering, invoking Russell's power and magic as though it were as widely acknowledged as the moon's tidal pull or the earth's orbit.

Donna said Russell was unlike any other human. That he could receive messages from animals. That he could heal a man with his hands, pull the rot out of you as cleanly as a tumor.

"He sees every part of you," Roos added. As if that were a good thing.

The possibility of judgment being passed on me supplanted any worries or questions I might have about Russell. At that age, I was, first and foremost, a thing to be judged, and that shifted the power in every interaction onto the other person.

The hint of sex that crossed their faces when they spoke of Russell, a prom-night giddiness. I understood, without anyone exactly saying so, that they all slept with him. The arrangement made me blush, inwardly shocked. No one seemed jealous of anyone else. "The heart doesn't own anything," Donna chimed. "That's not what love is about," she said, squeezing Helen's hand, a look passing between them. Even though Suzanne was mostly silent, sitting apart from us, I saw her face change at the mention of Russell. A wifely tenderness in her eyes that I wanted to feel, too.

I may have smiled to myself as I watched the familiar pattern of the town pass, the bus cruising through shade to sunshine. I'd grown up in this place, had the knowledge of it so deep in me that I didn't even know most street names, navigating instead by landmarks, visual or memorial. The corner where my mother had twisted her ankle in a mauve pantsuit. The copse of trees that had always looked vaguely attended by evil. The drugstore with its torn awning. Through the window of that unfamiliar bus, the burr of old carpet under my legs, my hometown seemed scrubbed clean of my presence. It was easy to leave it behind.

They discussed plans for the solstice party. Helen up on her knees, tightening her pigtails with happy, brisk habit. Thrilling while they described the dresses they'd change into, some goofy solstice song Russell had made up. Someone named Mitch had given them enough money to buy alcohol: Donna said his name with a confusing emphasis.

"You know," she repeated. "Mitch. Like Mitch Lewis?"

I hadn't recognized Mitch's name, but I'd heard of his

band—I'd seen them on TV, playing in the hot lights of a studio set, sweat needling their foreheads. The background was a shag of tinsel, the stage revolving so the band members turned like jewelry-box ballerinas.

I affected nonchalance, but here it was: the world I had always suspected existed, the world where you called famous musicians by their first names.

"Mitch did a recording session with Russell," Donna told me. "Russell blew his mind."

There it was again, their wonder at Russell, their certainty. I was jealous of that trust, that someone else could stitch the empty parts of your life together so you felt there was a net under you, linking each day to the next.

"Russell's gonna be famous, like *that*," Helen added. "He has a record deal, already." It was like she was recounting a fairy tale, but this was even better, because she knew it would happen.

"You know what Mitch calls Russell?" Donna spooked her hands dreamily. "The Wizard. Isn't that a trip?"

After I'd been at the ranch a while, I saw how everyone spoke of Mitch. Of Russell's imminent record deal. Mitch was their patron saint, sending Clover Dairy shipments to the ranch so the kids could get calcium, supporting the place financially. I wouldn't hear the whole story until much later. Mitch had met Russell at Baker Beach, at a love-in of sorts. Russell attending in his buckskins, a Mexican guitar strapped to his back. Flanked by his women, begging for change with their air of biblical poverty. The cold, dark sand, a bonfire, Mitch on a break between records. Someone in a porkpie hat tending a pot of steamed clams.

Mitch, I'd learn, had been having a crisis—money disputes with a manager who'd been a childhood friend, a marijuana arrest that had been expunged, but still—and Russell must have seemed like a citizen of a realer world, stoking Mitch's guilt over the gold records, the parties where he covered the pool in Perspex. Russell offered up a mystic salvation, buttressed by the young girls who cast their eyes down in adoration when Russell spoke. Mitch invited the whole group back to his house in Tiburon, letting them gorge on the contents of his refrigerator, crash in his guest room. They drained bottles of apple juice and pink champagne and tracked mud onto the bed, thoughtless as an occupying army. In the morning, Mitch gave them a lift back to the ranch: by then Russell had seduced Mitch, speaking softly of truth and love, those invocations especially potent to wealthy searchers.

I believed everything the girls told me that day, their buzzy, swarming pride as they spoke of Russell's brilliance. How pretty soon he wouldn't be able to walk down the street without getting mobbed. How he'd be able to tell the whole world how to be free. And it was true that Mitch had set up a recording session for Russell. Thinking maybe Mitch's label would find Russell's vibe interesting and of the moment. I didn't know it until much later, but the session had gone badly, the failure legendary. This was before everything else happened.

There are those survivors of disasters whose accounts never begin with the tornado warning or the captain announcing engine failure, but always much earlier in the timeline: an insistence that they noticed a strange quality to the sunlight that morning or excessive static in their sheets. A meaningless fight with a boyfriend. As if the presentiment of catastrophe wove itself into everything that came before.

Did I miss some sign? Some internal twinge? The bees glittering and crawling in the crate of tomatoes? An unusual lack of cars on the road? The question I remember Donna asking me in the bus—casually, almost as an afterthought.

"You ever hear anything about Russell?"

The question didn't make sense to me. I didn't understand that she was trying to gauge how many of the rumors I'd heard: about orgies, about frenzied acid trips and teen runaways forced to service older men. Dogs sacrificed on moonlit beaches, goat heads rotting in the sand. If I'd had friends besides Connie, I might've heard chatter of Russell at parties, some hushed gossip in the kitchen. Might've known to be wary.

But I just shook my head. I hadn't heard anything.

5

Even later, even knowing the things I knew, it was impossible, that first night, to see beyond the immediate. Russell's buckskin shirt, smelling of flesh and rot and as soft as velvet. Suzanne's smile blooming in me like a firework, losing its colored smoke, its pretty, drifting cinders.

"Home on the range," Donna said as we climbed down from the bus that afternoon.

It took me a moment to see where I was. The bus had gone far from the highway, bumping down a dirt road that ended deep in the blond summer hills, cupped with oaks. An old wooden house: the knobby rosettes and plaster columns giving it the air of a minor castle. It was part of a grid of ad hoc existence that included, as far as I could see, a barn and a swampy-looking pool. Six fleecy llamas drowsing in a pen. Far-off figures were hacking at brush along the fence. They raised their hands in greeting, then bent again to their work.

"The creek is low, but you can still swim," Donna said.

It seemed magical to me that they actually lived there together. The Day-Glo symbols crawling up the side of the barn, clothes on a line ghosting in a breeze. An orphanage for raunchy children.

They had once filmed a car commercial at the ranch, Helen said in her baby voice. "A while ago, but still."

Donna nudged me. "Pretty wild out here, huh?"

I said, "How'd you even find this place?"

"This old guy used to live here, but he had to move out 'cause the roof was bad." Donna shrugged. "We fixed it, kind of. His grandson rents it to us."

To make money, she explained, they took care of the llamas and worked for the farmer next door, harvesting lettuce with their pocketknives and selling his haul at the farmer's market. Sunflowers and jars of marmalade gluey with pectin.

"Three bucks an hour. Not bad," Donna said. "But money gets tight."

I nodded, like I understood such concerns. I watched a young boy, four or five, hurtle himself at Roos, crash-landing into her leg. He was badly sunburned, his hair bleached white, and he seemed too old to still be wearing a diaper. I assumed the boy was Roos's child. Was Russell the father? The quick thought of sex raised a queasy rush in my chest. The boy lifted his head, like a dog roused from sleep, and looked at me with a bored, suspicious squint.

Donna leaned into me. "Come meet Russell," she said. "You'll love him, I swear."

"She'll meet him at the party," Suzanne said, cutting into our conversation. I hadn't noticed her approach: her closeness startled me. She handed a sack of potatoes to me and took up a cardboard box in her arms. "We're gonna dump this stuff in the kitchen, first. For the feast."

Donna pouted, but I followed Suzanne.

"Bye, dolly," she called, frittering her thin fingers and laughing, not unkindly.

I followed Suzanne's dark hair through a jumble of strangers. The ground was uneven, a disorienting slope. It was the smell, too, a heavy smokiness. I was flattered Suzanne had enlisted my help, like it confirmed I was one of them. There were young people milling around in bare feet or boots, their hair drifty and sun lightened. I overheard feverish invocations of the solstice party. I didn't know it yet, but it was rare for the ranch, all this efficient work. Girls wore their best thrift store rags and carried instruments in their arms as gently as babies, the sun catching the steel of a guitar and fractaling into hot dia-

monds of light. The tambourines rattling tuneless in
their arms.

"Those fuckers bite me all night," Suzanne said, swatting at one of the vicious horseflies that droned around
us. "I wake up all bloody from scratching."

Beyond the house, the land was scarred with boulders
and the filtery oaks, a few hollow cars in a state of disrepair. I liked Suzanne but couldn't shake the feeling that I
was struggling to keep pace with her: it was an age when
I often conflated liking people with feeling nervous
around them. A boy with no shirt and a chunky silver
belt buckle catcalled when we passed. "What you got
there? A solstice present?"

"Shut up," Suzanne said.

The boy smiled, raffish, and I tried to smile back. He
was young, his hair long and dark, a medieval droop to
his face I took as romantic. Handsome with the feminine
duskiness of a cinematic villain, though I'd find out he
was just from Kansas.

This was Guy. A farm boy who'd defected from Travis
AFB when he'd discovered it was the same bullshit scene
as his father's house. He'd worked in Big Sur for a while,
then drifted north. Gotten caught up in a group ferment-
ing around the borders of the Haight, the hobby Satanists
who wore more jewelry than a teenage girl. Scarab lock-
ets and platinum daggers, red candles and organ music.
Then Guy had come across Russell playing guitar in the
park one day. Russell in the frontier buckskins that maybe
reminded Guy of the adventure books of his youth, seri-

als starring men who scraped caribou hides and forded frigid Alaskan rivers. Guy had been with Russell ever since.

Guy was the one who would drive the girls later that summer. Tighten his own belt around the caretaker's wrists, that big silver buckle notching into the tender skin and leaving behind an oddly shaped stamp, like a brand.

But that first day he was just a boy, giving off a dirty fritz like a warlock, and I glanced back at him with a thrilled shiver.

Suzanne stopped a girl walking by: "Tell Roos to get Nico back to the nursery. He shouldn't be out here."

The girl nodded.

Suzanne glanced at me as we kept going, reading my confusion. "Russell doesn't want us to get too attached to the kids. Especially if they're ours." She let out a grim laugh. "They aren't our property, you know? We don't get to fuck them up just because we want something to cuddle."

It took me a moment to process this idea that parents didn't have the right. It suddenly seemed blaringly true. My mother didn't own me just because she had given birth to me. Sending me to boarding school because the spirit moved her. Maybe this was a better way, even though it seemed alien. To be part of this amorphous group, believing love could come from any direction. So you wouldn't be disappointed if not enough came from the direction you'd hoped.

. . .

The kitchen was much darker than outside, and I blinked in the sudden wash. All the rooms smelled pungent and earthy, some mix of high-volume cooking and bodies. The walls were mostly bare, except for streaks of a daisy-patterned wallpaper and another funny heart painted there, too, like on the bus. The window sashes were crumbling, T-shirts tacked up instead of curtains. Somewhere nearby, a radio was on.

There were ten or so girls in the kitchen, focused on their cooking tasks, and everyone was healthy looking, their arms slim and tan, their hair thick. Bare feet gripping the rough boards of the floor. They cackled and snipped at one another, pinching exposed flesh and swatting with spoons. Everything seemed sticky and a little rotten. As soon as I put the bag of potatoes on the counter, a girl started picking through them.

"Green potatoes are poisonous," she said. Sucking her teeth, sifting through the sack.

"Not if you cook them," Suzanne shot back. "So cook them."

Suzanne slept in a small outbuilding with a dirt floor, a bare twin mattress against each of the four walls. "Mostly girls crash here," she said, "it depends. And Nico, sometimes, even though I don't want him to. I want him to grow up free. But he likes me."

A square of stained silk was tacked above a mattress, a Mickey Mouse pillowcase on the bed. Suzanne passed me a rolled cigarette, the end wet with her saliva. Ash fell on her bare thigh, but she didn't seem to notice. It was weed, but it was stronger than what Connie and I smoked, the dry refuse from Peter's sock drawer. This was oily and dank, and the cloying smoke it produced didn't dissipate quickly. I waited to start feeling differently. Connie would hate all this. Think this place was dirty and strange, that Guy was frightening—this knowledge made me proud. My thoughts were softening, the weed starting to surface.

"Are you really sixteen?" Suzanne asked.

I wanted to keep up the lie, but her gaze was too bright.

"I'm fourteen," I said.

Suzanne didn't seem surprised. "I'll give you a ride home, if you want. You don't have to stay."

I licked my lips—did she think I couldn't handle this? Or maybe she thought I would embarrass her. "I don't have to be anywhere," I said.

Suzanne opened her mouth to say something, then hesitated.

"Really," I said, starting to feel desperate. "It's fine."

There was a moment, when Suzanne looked at me, when I was sure she'd send me home. Pack me back to my mother's house like a truant. But then the look drained into something else, and she got to her feet.

"You can borrow a dress," she said.

...

There was a rack of clothes hanging and more spilling out of a garbage bag—torn denim. Paisley shirts, long skirts. The hems stuttering with loose stitching. The clothes weren't nice, but the quantity and unfamiliarity stirred me. I'd always been jealous of girls who wore their sister's hand-me-downs, like the uniform of a well-loved team.

"This stuff is all yours?"

"I share with the girls." Suzanne seemed resigned to my presence: Maybe she'd seen that my desperation was bigger than any desire or ability she had to shoo me off. Or maybe the admiration was flattering, my wide eyes, greedy for the details of her. "Only Helen makes a fuss. We have to go get things back; she hides them under her pillow."

"Don't you want some for yourself?"

"Why?" She took a draw from the joint and held her breath. When she spoke, her voice was crackled. "I'm not on that kind of trip right now. Me me me. I love the other girls, you know. I like that we share. And they love me."

She watched me through the smoke. I felt shamed. For doubting Suzanne or thinking it was strange to share. For the limits of my carpeted bedroom at home. I shoved my hands in my shorts. This wasn't bullshit dabbling, like my mother's afternoon workshops.

"I get it," I said. And I did, and tried to isolate the flutter of solidarity in myself.

The dress Suzanne chose for me stank like mouse shit, my nose twitching as I pulled it over my head, but I was happy wearing it—the dress belonged to someone else, and that endorsement released me from the pressure of my own judgments.

"Good," Suzanne said, surveying me. I ascribed more meaning to her pronouncement than I ever had to Connie's. There was something grudging about Suzanne's attention, and that made it doubly valued. "Let me braid your hair," she said. "Come here. It'll tangle if you dance with it loose."

I sat on the floor in front of Suzanne, her legs on either side of me, and tried to feel comfortable with the closeness, the sudden, guileless intimacy. My parents were not affectionate, and it surprised me that someone could just touch me at any moment, the gift of their hand given as thoughtlessly as a piece of gum. It was an unexplained blessing. Her tangy breath on my neck as she swept my hair to one side. Walking her fingers along my scalp, drawing a straight part. Even the pimples I'd seen on her jaw seemed obliquely beautiful, the rosy flame an inner excess made visible.

Both of us were silent as she braided my hair. I picked up one of the reddish rocks from the floor, lined up beneath the mirror like the eggs of a foreign species.

"We lived in the desert for a while," Suzanne said. "That's where I got that."

She told me about the Victorian they had rented in San Francisco. How they'd had to leave after Donna had accidentally started a fire in the bedroom. The time spent in Death Valley where they were all so sunburned they couldn't sleep for days. The remains of a gutted, roofless salt factory in the Yucatán where they'd stayed for six months, the cloudy lagoon where Nico had learned to swim. It was painful to imagine what I had been doing at the same time: drinking the tepid, metallic water from my school's drinking fountain. Biking to Connie's house. Reclining in the dentist's chair, hands politely in my lap, while Dr. Lopes worked in my mouth, his gloves slick with my idiot drool.

The night was warm and the celebration started early. There were maybe forty of us, swarming and massing in the stretch of dirt, hot air gusting over the run of tables, the wavy light from a kerosene lamp. The party seemed much bigger than it actually was. There was an antic quality that distorted my memory, the house looming behind us so everything gained a cinematic flicker. The music was loud, the sweet thrum occupying me in an exciting way, and people were dancing and grabbing for one another, hand over wrist: they skipped in circles, threading in and out. A drunken, yelping chain that broke when Roos sat down hard in the dirt, laughing. Some little kids skulked around the table like dogs, full and lonesome for the adult excitement, their lips scabby from picking.

"Where's Russell?" I asked Suzanne. She was stoned, like me, her black hair loose. Someone had given her a shrub rose, half-wilted, and she was trying to knot it in her hair.

"He'll be here," she said. "It doesn't really start till he's here."

She brushed some ash off my dress and the gesture stirred me.

"There's our little doll," Donna cooed when she saw me. She had a tinfoil crown on her head that kept falling off. She'd drawn an Egyptian pattern on her hands and freckled arms with kohl before clearly losing interest—it was all over her fingers, smeared on her dress, along her jaw. Guy swerved, avoiding her hands.

"She's our sacrifice," Donna told him, her words already careening around. "Our solstice offering."

Guy smiled at me, his teeth stained from wine.

They burned a car that night in celebration, and the flames were hot and jumpy and I laughed out loud, for no reason—the hills were so dark against the sky and no one from my real life knew where I was and it was the *solstice*, and who cared if it wasn't actually the solstice? I had distant thoughts of my mother, houndish nips of worry, but she'd assume I was at Connie's. Where else would I be? She couldn't conceive of this kind of place even existing, and even if she could, even if by some miracle she showed up, she wouldn't be able to recognize me. Suzanne's dress was too big, and it often slipped off my shoulders, but pretty soon I wasn't as quick to pull the sleeves back up. I liked the exposure, the way I could pretend I didn't care, and how I actually started not to care, even when I accidentally flashed most of a breast as I hitched up the sleeves. Some stunned, blissed-out boy—a painted crescent moon on his face—grinned at me like I'd always been there among them.

The feast was not a feast at all. Bloated cream puffs sweating in a bowl until someone fed them to the dogs. A plastic container of Cool Whip, green beans boiled to structureless gray, augmented by the winnings of some dumpster. Twelve forks clattered in a giant pot— everyone took turns scooping out a watery vegetal pabulum, the mash of potatoes and ketchup and onion soup packets. There was a single watermelon, rind patterned like a snake, but no one could find a knife. Finally Guy cracked it open violently on the corner of a table. The kids descended on the pulpy mess like rats.

It was nothing like the feast I'd been imagining. The distance made me feel a little sad. But it was only sad in the old world, I reminded myself, where people stayed cowed by the bitter medicine of their lives. Where money kept everyone slaves, where they buttoned their shirts up to the neck, strangling any love they had inside themselves.

How often I replayed this moment again and again, until it gained a meaningful pitch: when Suzanne nudged me so I knew the man walking toward the fire was Russell. My first thought was shock—he'd looked young as he approached, but then I saw he was at least a decade older than Suzanne. Maybe even as old as my mother. Dressed in dirty Wranglers and a buckskin shirt, though his feet were bare—how strange that was, how they all walked barefoot through the weeds and the dog shit as if nothing were there. A girl got to her knees beside him, touching his leg. It took me a moment to remember the girl's name—my brain was sludgy from the drugs—but then I had it, Helen, the girl from the bus with her pigtails, her baby voice. Helen smiled up at him, enacting some ritual I didn't understand.

I knew Helen had sex with this man. Suzanne did, too. I experimented with that thought, imagining the man hunched over Suzanne's milky body. Closing his hand on her breast. I knew only how to dream about boys like Peter, the unformed muscles under their skin, the patchy hair they tended along their jaws. Maybe I would sleep with Russell. I tried on the thought. Sex was still colored by the girls in my father's magazines, everything glossy and dry. About beholding. The people at the ranch seemed beyond that, loving one another indiscriminately, with the purity and optimism of children.

The man held up his hands and boomed out a greeting: the group surged and twitched like a Greek chorus. At moments like that, I could believe Russell was already famous. He seemed to swim through a denser atmosphere than the rest of us. He walked among the group, giving benedictions: a hand on a shoulder, a word whispered in an ear. The party was still going, but everyone was now aimed at him, their faces turned expectantly, as if following the arc of the sun. When Russell reached Suzanne and me, he stopped and looked in my eyes.

"You're here," he said. Like he'd been waiting for me. Like I was late.

I'd never heard another voice like his—full and slow, never hesitating. His fingers pressed into my back in a not unpleasant way. He wasn't much taller than me, but he was strong and compact, pressurized. The hair haloed around his head was coarsened by oil and dirt into a boggy mass. His eyes didn't seem to water, or waver, or flick away. The way the girls had spoken of him finally made sense. How he took me in, like he wanted to see all the way through.

"Eve," Russell said when Suzanne introduced me. "The first woman."

I was nervous I'd say the wrong thing, expose the error of my presence. "It's Evelyn, really."

"Names are important, aren't they?" Russell said. "And I don't see any snake in you."

Even this mild approval relieved me.

"What do you think of our solstice celebration, Evie?" he said. "Our spot?"

All the while his hand was pulsing a message on my back I couldn't decode. I slivered a glance at Suzanne, aware that the sky had darkened without me noticing, the night gliding deeper. I felt drowsy from the fire and the dope. I hadn't eaten and there was an empty throb in my stomach. Was he saying my name a lot? I couldn't tell. Suzanne's whole body was directed at Russell, her hand moving uneasy in her hair.

I told Russell I liked it here. Other meaningless, nervous remarks, but even so, he was getting other information from me. And I never did lose that feeling. Even after. That Russell could read my thoughts as easily as taking a book from a shelf.

When I smiled, he tilted my chin up with his hand. "You're an actress," he said. His eyes were like hot oil, and I let myself feel like Suzanne, the kind of girl a man would startle at, would want to touch. "Yeah, that's it. I see it. You gotta be standing on a cliff and looking out to sea."

I told him I wasn't an actress, but my grandmother was.

"Right on," he said. As soon as I said her name, he was even more attentive. "I picked that up right off. You look like her."

Later I'd read about how Russell sought the famous and semifamous and hangers-on, people he could court and wring for resources, whose cars he could borrow and houses he could live in. How pleased he must have been at my arrival, not even needing to be coaxed. Russell reached out to draw Suzanne closer. When I caught her eye, she seemed to retreat. I hadn't thought, until that moment, that she might be nervous about me and Russell. A new feeling of power flexed within me, a quick tightening of ribbon so unfamiliar I didn't recognize it.

"And you'll be in charge of our Evie," Russell said to Suzanne. "Won't you?"

Neither looked at me. The air between them crisscrossed with symbols. Russell held my hand for a moment, his eyes avalanching over me.

"Later, Evie," he said.

Then a few whispered words to Suzanne. She rejoined me with a new air of briskness.

"Russell says you can stick around, if you want," she said.

I felt how energized she was by seeing Russell. Alert with renewed authority, studying me as she spoke. I didn't know if the jump I felt was fear or interest. My grandmother had told me about getting movie roles—how quickly she was plucked from a group. "That's the difference," she'd told me. "All the other girls thought the director was making the choice. But it was really me telling the director, in my secret way, that the part was mine."

I wanted that—a sourceless, toneless wave carried from me to Russell. To Suzanne, to all of them. I wanted this world without end.

The night began to show ragged edges. Roos was naked from the waist up, her heavy breasts flushed from the heat. Falling into long silences. A black dog trotted into the darkness. Suzanne had disappeared to find more grass. I kept searching for her, but I'd get distracted by the flash and shuffle, the strangers who danced by and smiled at me with blunt kindness.

Little things should have upset me. Some girl burned herself, raising a ripple of skin along her arm, and stared down at the scorch with idle curiosity. The outhouse with its shit stench and cryptic drawings, walls papered in pages torn from porno mags. Guy describing the warm entrails of the pigs he'd gutted on his parents' farm in Kansas.

"They knew what was coming," he said to a rapt audience. "They'd smile when I brought food and flip out when I had the knife."

He adjusted his big belt buckle, cackling something I couldn't hear. But it was the solstice, I explained to myself, pagan mutterings, and whatever disturbance I felt was just a failure to understand the place. And there was so much else to notice and favor—the silly music from the jukebox. The silver guitar that caught the light, the melted Cool Whip dripping from someone's finger. The numinous and fanatic faces of the others.

Time was confusing on the ranch: there were no clocks, no watches, and hours or minutes seemed arbitrary, whole days pouring into nothing. I don't know how much time passed. How long I was waiting for Suzanne to return before I heard his voice. Right next to my ear, whispering my name.

"Evie."

I turned, and there he was. I twisted with happiness: Russell had remembered me, he'd found me in the crowd. Had maybe even been looking for me. He took my hand in his, working the palm, my fingers. I was beaming, indeterminate; I wanted to love everything.

The trailer he brought me to was larger than any of the other rooms, the bed covered with a shaggy blanket that I'd realize later was actually a fur coat. It was the only nice thing in the room—the floor matted with clothes, empty cans of soda and beer glinting among the detritus. A peculiar smell in the air, a cut of fermentation. I was being willfully naïve, I suppose, pretending like I didn't know what was happening. But part of me really didn't. Or didn't fully dwell on the facts: it was suddenly difficult to remember how I'd gotten there. That lurching bus ride, the cheap sugar of the wine. Where had I left my bike?

Russell was watching me intently. Tilting his head when I looked away, forcing me to catch his eyes. He brushed my hair behind my ear, letting his fingers fall to my neck. His fingernails uncut so I felt the ridge of them.

I laughed, but it was uneasy. "Is Suzanne gonna be here soon?" I said.

He'd told me, back at the fire, that Suzanne was coming, too, though maybe that was only something I wished.

"Suzanne's just fine," Russell said. "I wanna talk about you right now, Evie."

My thoughts slowed to the pace of drifting snow. Russell spoke slowly and with seriousness, but he made me feel as though he had been waiting all night for the chance to hear what I had to say. How different this was from Connie's bedroom, listening to records from some other world we'd never be a part of, songs that just reinforced our own static misery. Peter seemed drained to me, too. Peter, who was just a boy, who ate oleo on white bread for dinner. This was real, Russell's gaze, and the flattered sickness in me was so pleasurable, I could barely keep hold of it.

"Shy Evie," he said. Smiling. "You're a smart girl. You see a lot with those eyes, don't you?"

He thought I was smart. I grabbed on to it like proof. I wasn't lost. I could hear the party outside. A fly buzzed in the corner, hitting the walls of the trailer.

"I'm like you," Russell went on. "I was so smart when I was young, so smart that of course they told me I was dumb." He let out a fractured laugh. "They taught me the word *dumb*. They taught me those words, then they told me that's what I was." When Russell smiled, his face soaked with a joy that seemed foreign to me. I knew I'd never felt that good. Even as a child I'd been unhappy— I saw, suddenly, how obvious that was.

As he talked, I hugged myself with my arms. It all started making sense to me, what Russell was saying, in the drippy way things could make sense. How drugs patchworked simple, banal thoughts into phrases that seemed filled with importance. My glitchy adolescent brain was desperate for causalities, for conspiracies that drenched every word, every gesture, with meaning. I wanted Russell to be a genius.

"There's something in you," he said. "Some part that's real sad. And you know what? That really makes me sad. They've tried to ruin this beautiful, special girl. They've made her sad. Just because they are."

I felt the press of tears.

"But they didn't ruin you, Evie. 'Cause here you are. Our special Evie. And you can let all that old shit float away."

He sat back on the mattress with the dirty soles of his bare feet on the fur coat, a strange calm in his face. He would wait as long as it took.

I don't remember what I said at that point, just that I chattered nervously. School, Connie, the hollow nonsense of a young girl. My gaze slid around the trailer, fingers nipping at the fabric of Suzanne's dress. Eyes coursing the fleur-de-lis pattern of the filthy bedspread. I remember that Russell smiled, patiently, waiting for me to lose energy. And I did. The trailer silent except for my own breathing and Russell shifting on the mattress.

"I can help you," he said. "But you have to want it."

His eyes fixed on mine.

"Do you want it, Evie?"

The words slit with scientific desire.

"You'll like this," Russell murmured. Opening his arms to me. "Come here."

I edged toward him, sitting on the mattress. Struggling to complete the full circuit of comprehension. I knew it was coming, but it still surprised me. How he took down his pants, exposing his short, hairy legs, his penis in his fist. The hesitant catch in my gaze—he watched me watching him.

"Look at me," he said. His voice was smooth, even while his hand worked furiously. "Evie," he said, "Evie."

The undercooked look of his dick, clutched in his hand: I wondered where Suzanne was. My throat tightened. It confused me at first, that it was all Russell wanted. To stroke himself. I sat there, trying to impose sense on the situation. I transmuted Russell's behavior into proof of his good intentions. Russell was just trying to be close, to break down my hang-ups from the old world.

"We can make each other feel good," he said. "You don't have to be sad."

I flinched when he pushed my head toward his lap. A singe of clumsy fear filled me. He was good at not seeming angry when I reared away. The indulgent look he gave me, like I was a skittish horse.

"I'm not trying to hurt you, Evie." Holding out his hand again. The strobe of my heart going fast. "I just want to be close to you. And don't you want me to feel good? I want you to feel good."

When he came, he gasped, wetly. The salt damp of semen in my mouth, the alarming swell. He held me there, bucking. How had I gotten here, in the trailer, found myself in the dark woods without any crumbs to follow home, but then Russell's hands were in my hair, and his arms were around me, pulling me up, and he said my name with intention and surety so it sounded strange to me, but smooth, too, valuable, like some other, better, Evie. Was I supposed to cry? I didn't know. I was crowded with idiot trivia. A red sweater I had lent Connie and never gotten back. Whether Suzanne was looking for me or not. A curious thrill behind my eyes.

Russell handed me a bottle of Coke. The soda was tepid and flat, but I drank the whole thing. As intoxicating as champagne.

I experienced the whole night as fated, me as the center of a singular drama. But Russell had put me through a series of ritual tests. Perfected over the years that he had worked for a religious organization near Ukiah, a center that gave away food, found shelter and jobs. Attracting the thin, harried girls with partial college degrees and neglectful parents, girls with hellish bosses and dreams of nose jobs. His bread and butter. The time he spent at the center's outpost in San Francisco in the old fire station. Collecting his followers. Already he'd become an expert in female sadness—a particular slump in the shoulders, a nervous rash. A subservient lilt at the end of sentences, eyelashes gone soggy from crying. Russell did the same thing to me that he did to those girls. Little tests, first. A touch on my back, a pulse of my hand. Little ways of breaking down boundaries. And how quickly he'd ramped it up, easing his pants to his knees. An act, I thought, calibrated to comfort young girls who were glad, at least, that it wasn't sex. Who could stay fully dressed the whole time, as if nothing out of the ordinary were happening.

But maybe the strangest part—I liked it, too.

I floated through the party in a stunned hush. The air on my skin insistent, my armpits sliding with sweat. It had happened—I had to keep telling myself so. I assumed everyone would see it on me. An obvious aura of sex. I wasn't anxious anymore, wasn't roaming the party squeezed by nervous need, the certainty that there was a hidden room I wasn't allowed access to—that worry had been satisfied, and I took dreamy steps, looked back into passing faces with a smile that asked nothing.

When I saw Guy, tapping a pack of cigarettes, I stopped without hesitation.

"Can I have one?"

He grinned at me. "The girl wants a cigarette, she shall have her cigarette." He held it to my mouth and I hoped people were watching.

I finally found Suzanne in a group near the fire. When she caught my eye, she gave me an odd, airless smile. I'm sure she recognized the inward shift you sometimes see in young girls, newly sexed. It's that pride, I think, a solemnity. I wanted her to know. Suzanne was giddy from something, I could tell. Not alcohol. Something else, her pupils seeming to eat the iris, a flush lacing up her neck like a trippy Victorian collar.

Maybe Suzanne felt some hidden disappointment when the game fulfilled itself, when she saw that I'd gone with Russell, after all. But maybe she'd expected it. The car was still smoldering, the noise of the party cutting up the darkness. I felt the night churn in me like a wheel.

"When's the car gonna stop burning?" I said.

I couldn't see her face, but I could feel her, the air soft between us.

"Jesus, I don't know," she said. "Morning?"

In the flicker, my arms and hands in front of me looked scaly and reptilian, and I welcomed the distorted vision of my body. I heard the brood of a motorcycle ignition, someone's wicked hoot—they'd thrown a box spring in the fire, and the flames soared and deepened.

"You can crash in my room if you want," Suzanne said. Her voice gave away nothing. "I don't care. But you have to actually be here, if you're going to be here. Get it?"

Suzanne was asking me something else. Like those fairy tales where goblins can enter a house only if invited by its inhabitants. The moment of crossing the threshold, the careful way Suzanne constructed her statements— she wanted me to say it. And I nodded, and said I understood. Though I couldn't understand, not really. I was wearing a dress that didn't belong to me in a place I had never been, and I couldn't see much farther than that. The possibility that my life was hovering on the brink of a new and permanent happiness. I thought of Connie with a beatific indulgence—she was a sweet girl, wasn't she—and even my father and mother fell under my generous purview, sufferers of a tragic foreign malady. The beam of motorcycle headlights blanched the tree branches and illuminated the exposed foundation of the house, the black dog crouching over an unseen prize. Someone kept playing the same song over and over. *Hey, baby*, the first lines went. The song repeated enough times that I started to get the phrase in my head, *Hey, baby*. I worked the words around with unspecific effort, like the idle rattle of a lemon drop against the teeth.

PART TWO

PART TWO

I WOKE TO A WASH OF FOG pressed against the windows, the bedroom filled with snowy light. It took a moment to reoccupy the disappointing and familiar facts—I was staying in Dan's house. It was his bureau in the corner, his glass-topped nightstand. His blanket, bordered in sateen ribbon, that I pulled over my own body. I remembered Julian and Sasha, the thin wall between us. I didn't want to think of the previous night. Sasha's mewlings. The slurred, obsessive muttering, "Fuck me fuck mefuckmefuckme," repeated so many times it failed to mean anything.

I stared at the monotony of ceiling. They'd been thoughtless, as all teenagers are, and the night didn't mean anything beyond that. Still. The polite thing to do was to wait in my room until they had left for Humboldt. Let them clear off without having to perform any dutiful morning niceties.

As soon as I heard the car back out of the garage, I got out of bed. The house was mine again, and though I expected relief, there was some sadness, too. Sasha and Julian were aimed at another adventure. Clicking back into the momentum of the larger world. I'd recede in their minds—the middle-aged woman in a forgotten house—just a mental footnote getting smaller and smaller as their real life took over. I hadn't realized until then how lonely I was. Or something less urgent than loneliness: an absence of eyes on me, maybe. Who would care if I ceased to exist? Those silly phrases I remembered Russell saying—cease to exist, he urged us, disappear the self. And all of us nodding like golden retrievers, the reality of our existence making us cavalier, eager to dismantle what seemed permanent.

I started the kettle. Opened the window to let a slash of cold air circulate. I gathered what seemed to be a lot of empty beer bottles—had they drunk more while I slept?

After taking out the trash, the tight heave of plastic and my own garbage, I caught myself staring at the poky blankets of ice plants along the driveway. The beach beyond. The fog had started to burn off, and I could see the crawl of waves, the cliffs above looking rusted and dry. A few people were out walking, obvious in performance wear. Most of them had dogs—this was the only beach around where you could take dogs off-leash. I'd seen the same rottweiler a few times, his coat a color deeper than black, his heavy churning run. A pit bull had recently killed a woman in San Francisco. Was it strange that people loved these creatures that could harm them? Or was it understandable—that they maybe even loved animals more for their restraint, for the way they blessed humans with temporary safety.

I hustled back inside. I couldn't stay in Dan's house forever. Another aide job would turn up soon. But how familiar that was—lifting someone into the warm, persistent waters of a therapy tub. Sitting in the waiting rooms of doctor's offices, reading articles on the effects of soy on tumors. The importance of filling your plate with a rainbow. The usual wishful lies, tragic in their insufficiency. Did anyone really believe in them? As if the bright flash of your efforts could distract death from coming for you, keep the bull snorting harmlessly after the scarlet flag.

The kettle was whistling, so at first I didn't hear Sasha come into the kitchen. Her abrupt presence startled me.

"Morning," she said. A streak of spit had dried along her cheek. She was wearing high-cut shorts made of sweatpant material, her socks dotted with tiny hot-pink symbols I realized were skulls. She swallowed, her mouth furry with sleep. "Where's Julian?" she asked.

I tried to hide my surprise. "I heard the car leave awhile ago."

She squinted. "What?" she asked.

"Didn't he tell you he was going?"

Sasha saw my pity. Her face tightened.

"Of course he told me," she said after a moment. "Yeah, of course. He'll be back tomorrow."

So he had left her. My first thought was irritation. I wasn't a babysitter. Then relief. Sasha was a kid—she shouldn't go with him to Humboldt. Ride an ATV through barbed-wire checkpoints to some shithole tarp ranch in Garberville just to pick up a duffel bag of weed. I was even a little glad for her company.

"I don't like the drive, anyway," Sasha said, gamely adapting to the situation. "I get sick on those small roads. He drives so crazy, too. Super fast." She leaned up against the counter, yawning.

"Tired?" I said.

She told me that she had been trying polyphasic sleep but had to quit. "It was too weird," she said. Her nipples were apparent through her shirt.

"Polyphasic sleep?" I said, pulling my own robe tight in a prudish surge.

"Thomas Jefferson did it. You sleep in hour bursts, like, six times a day."

"And you're awake the rest of the time?"

Sasha nodded. "It's kind of great, the first couple of days. But I crashed hard. It seemed like I'd never sleep normal again."

I couldn't link the girl I'd overheard the night before to the girl in front of me, talking about sleep experiments.

"There's enough hot water in the kettle if you want some," I said, but Sasha shook her head.

"I don't eat in the mornings, like a ballerina." She glanced at the window, the sea a pewter sheet. "Do you ever swim?"

"It's really cold." I had only seen the occasional surfer venture into the waves, their bodies sheathed in neoprene, hoods over their heads.

"So you've gone in?" she asked.

"No."

Sasha's face moved with sympathy. Like I was missing out on some obvious pleasure. But no one swam, I thought, feeling protective of my life in this borrowed house, the local orbits of my days. "There are sharks out there, too," I added.

"They don't really attack humans," Sasha said, shrugging. She was pretty, like a consumptive, eaten by an internal heat. I tried to spot some pornographic residue of the night before, but there was nothing. Her face as pale and blameless as a lesser moon.

Sasha's proximity, even for the day, forced some normalcy. The built-in preventative of another person meant I couldn't indulge the animal feelings, couldn't leave orange peels in the kitchen sink. I dressed right after breakfast instead of haunting my robe all day. Swiped on mascara from a mostly dried-up tube. These were the cogent human labors, the daily tasks that staved larger panics, but living alone had gotten me out of the habit—I didn't feel substantial enough to warrant this kind of effort.

I'd last lived with someone years ago, a man who taught ESL classes at one of the sham colleges that advertised on bus-stop benches. The students were mostly wealthy foreigners who wanted to design videogames. It was surprising to think of him, of David, to remember a time when I imagined a life with another person. Not love, but the pleasant inertia that could substitute. The agreeable quiet that passed over us both in car rides. The way I'd once seen him look at me as we crossed a parking lot.

But then it started—a woman who knocked on the apartment door at strange hours. An ivory hairbrush that had belonged to my grandmother went missing from the bathroom. I'd never told David certain things, so that whatever closeness we had was automatically corrupted, the grub twisting in the apple. My secret was sunk deep, but it was there. Maybe that was the reason it had happened, the other women. I had left open a space for such secrets. And how much could you ever know another person, anyway?

I'd imagined that Sasha and I would spend the day in courteous silence. That Sasha would be as hidden as a mouse. She was polite enough, but soon her presence was obvious. I found the refrigerator door left open, filling the kitchen with an alien buzz. Her sweatshirt thrown on the table, a book about the Enneagram splayed on a chair. Music came loud from her room through tinny laptop speakers. It surprised me—she was listening to the singer whose plaintive voice had been the perpetual aural back-drop for a certain kind of girl I remembered from college. Girls already swampy with nostalgia, girls who lit can-dles and stayed up late kneading bread dough in Danskin leotards and bare feet.

I was used to encountering remnants—the afterburn of the sixties was everywhere in that part of California. Ragged blips of prayer flags in the oak trees, vans eter-nally parked in fields, missing their tires. Older men in decorative shirts with common-law wives. But those were the expected sixties ghosts. Why would Sasha have any interest?

I was glad when Sasha changed the music. A woman singing over gothy electronic piano, nothing I recognized at all.

That afternoon, I tried to take a nap. But I couldn't sleep. I lay there, staring at the framed photo that hung over the bureau: a sand dune, rippling with mint grass. The ghoulish whorls of cobwebs in the corners. I shifted in the sheets, impatient. I was too aware of Sasha in the room next door. The music from her laptop hadn't stopped all afternoon, and sometimes I could make out scraps of digital noise over the songs, beeps and chimes. What was she doing—playing games on her phone? Texting with Julian? I had a sudden ache for the obliging ways she must be tending to her loneliness.

I knocked on her door, but the music was too loud. I tried again. Nothing. I was embarrassed by the exposure of effort, about to scurry back to my room, but Sasha appeared in the doorway. Her face still muted with sleep, her hair scraggled by the pillow—maybe she'd been trying to nap, too.

"Do you want some tea?" I asked.

It took her a moment to nod, like she'd forgotten who I was.

Sasha was quiet at the table. Studying her fingernails, sighing with cosmic boredom. I remembered this pose from my own adolescence—thrusting my jaw forward, staring out the car window like a wrongfully accused prisoner, all along desperately wishing that my mother would say something. Sasha was waiting for me to breach her reserve, to ask her questions, and I could feel her eyes on me while I poured the tea. It was nice to be watched, even suspiciously. I used the good cups and the buckwheat crackers I fanned along the saucers were only a little stale. I wanted to please her, I realized, setting the plate gently in front of her.

The tea was too hot; there was a lull while we huddled

over the cups, my face dampening in the thin vegetal steam. When I asked Sasha where she was from, she grimaced.

"Concord," she said. "It sucks."

"And you go to college with Julian?"

"Julian's not in college."

I wasn't sure if this was information Dan knew. I tried to remember what I'd last heard. When Dan did mention his son, it was with performative resignation, playing the clueless dad. Any trouble reported with sitcom sighs: boys will be boys. Julian had been diagnosed with some behavioral disorder in high school, though Dan made it sound mild.

"Have you guys been together long?" I asked.

Sasha sipped at the tea. "A few months," she said. Her face grew animate, like just talking about Julian was a source of sustenance. She must have already forgiven him for leaving her behind. Girls were good at coloring in those disappointing blank spots. I thought of the night before, her exaggerated moans. Poor Sasha.

She probably believed that any sadness, any flicker of worry over Julian, was just a problem of logistics. Sadness at that age had the pleasing texture of imprisonment: you reared and sulked against the bonds of parents and school and age, the things that kept you from the certain happiness that awaited. When I was a sophomore in college, I had a boyfriend who spoke breathlessly of running away to Mexico—it didn't occur to me that we could no longer run away from home. Nor did I imagine what we would be running to, beyond the vagueness of warm air and more frequent sex. And now I was older, and the wishful props of future selves had lost their comforts. I might always feel some form of this, a depression that did not lift but grew compact and familiar, a space occupied like the sad limbo of hotel rooms.

"Listen," I said, slotting into a parental role that was laughably unearned. "I hope Julian is being nice to you."

"Why wouldn't he be nice?" she said. "He's my boyfriend. We live together."

I could imagine so easily what would pass for living. A month-to-month apartment that smelled of freezer meals and Clorox, Julian's childhood comforter on the mattress. The girlish effort of a scented candle by the bed. Not that I was doing much better.

"We might get a place with a washing machine," Sasha said, a new defiance in her tone as she invoked their meager domesticity. "Probably in a few months."

"And your parents are okay with you living with Julian?"

"I can do what I want." She shuffled her hands into the sleeves of Julian's sweatshirt. "I'm eighteen."

That couldn't be true.

"Besides," she said, "weren't you my age when you were in that cult?"

Her tone was blank, but I imagined a slant of accusation.

Before I could say anything, Sasha got up from the table, listing toward the refrigerator. I watched her affected swagger, the easy way she removed one of the beers they'd brought. The cutout silvered mountains gleaming from the label. She met my gaze.

"Want one?" she asked.

This was a test, I understood. Either I could be the kind of adult to be ignored or pitied or I could be someone she could maybe talk to. I nodded and Sasha relaxed.

"Think fast," she said, tossing the bottle to me.

Night came on quick, as it did on the coast, with no mediation of buildings to temper the change. The sun was so low that we could look directly at it, watching it drift from sight. We each had had a few beers. The kitchen grew dark, but neither of us got up to turn on the lights. Everything had a blue shadow, soft and royal, the furniture simplifying into shapes. Sasha asked if we could make a fire in the fireplace.

"It's gas," I said. "And it's broken."

A lot of things in the house were broken or forgotten: the kitchen clock stopped, a closet doorknob coming off in my hand. The sparkly mess of flies I'd swept from the corners. It took sustained, constant living to ward off decay. Even my presence for the last few weeks hadn't made much of a dent.

"But we can try making one out in the yard," I said.

. . .

The sandy lot behind the garage was sheltered from the wind, wet leaves matted on the seats of plastic chairs. There had once been a fire pit of sorts, the stones scattered among the senseless archaeological relics of family life: add-ons to forgotten toys, a chewed-looking shard of Frisbee. We were both distracted by the hustle of preparation, tasks that allowed for companionable silence. I found a stack of three-year-old newspapers in the garage and a bundle of wood from the general store in town. Sasha toed the stones back into a circle.

"I was always bad at this," I said. "There's something you're supposed to do, right? Some special shape with the logs?"

"Like a house," Sasha said. "You're supposed to make it look like a cabin." She used her foot to neaten the ring. "We used to camp a lot in Yosemite when I was little."

Sasha was the one who actually got the fire going: squatting in the sand, keeping up a steady stream of breath. Gentling the flames until there was a satisfying burn.

We sat down in the plastic chairs, their surfaces stippled from sand and wind. I pulled mine close to the fire—I wanted to feel hot, to sweat. Sasha was quiet, looking at the jump of flames, but I could sense the whir of her mind, the faraway place she had disappeared to. Maybe she was imagining what Julian was doing up in Garberville. The musky futon he'd sleep on, using a towel for a blanket. All part of the adventure. How nice it must be to be a twenty-year-old boy.

"That stuff Julian was talking about," Sasha said, clearing her throat like she was embarrassed, though her interest was obvious. "Were you, like, in love with that guy or something?"

"Russell?" I said, poking at the fire with a stick. "I didn't think about him like that."

It was true: the other girls had circled around Russell, tracking his movements and moods like weather patterns, but he stayed mostly distant in my mind. Like a beloved teacher whose home life his students never imagined.

"Why'd you hang out with them, then?" she asked.

My first impulse was to avoid the subject. I'd have to pin down all the edges. Act out the whole morality play: the regret, the warnings. I tried to sound businesslike.

"People were falling into that kind of thing all the time, back then," I said. "Scientology, the Process people. Empty-chair work. Is that still a thing?" I glanced at her—she was waiting for me to go on. "It was partly bad luck, I guess. That it was the group I found."

"But you stayed."

I could feel the full force of Sasha's curiosity for the first time.

"There was a girl. It was more her than Russell." I hesitated. "Suzanne." It was odd to say her name, to let it live in the world. "She was older," I said. "Not by much, really, but it felt like a lot."

"Suzanne Parker?"

I stared across the fire at Sasha.

"I looked some things up today," she said. "Online."

I'd once lost hours to that kind of stuff. The fan sites or whatever you called them. The stranger corners. The website devoted to Suzanne's artwork from prison. Watercolors of mountain ranges, puffball clouds, the captions filled with misspellings. I'd felt a pang, imagining Suzanne working with great concentration, but closed the website when I saw the photo: Suzanne, in blue jeans and a white T-shirt—her jeans stuffed with middle-aged fat, her face a vacant scrim.

The thought of Sasha gorging on that macabre glut made me uneasy. Packing herself with particulars: the autopsy reports, the testimony the girls gave of that night, like the transcript of a bad dream.

"It's nothing to be proud of," I said. Recounting the usual things—it was awful. Not glamorous, not enviable.

"There wasn't anything about you," Sasha said. "Not that I could find."

I felt a lurch. I wanted to tell her something valuable, my existence traced with enough care that I would become visible.

"It's better that way," I said. "So the lunatics don't search me out."

"But you were there?"

"I lived there. Basically. For a while. I didn't kill anyone or anything." My laugh came out flat. "Obviously."

She was huddling into her sweatshirt. "You just left your parents?" Her voice was admiring.

"It was a different time," I said. "Everyone ran around. My parents were divorced."

"So are mine," Sasha said, forgetting to be shy. "And you were my age?"

"A little younger."

"I bet you were really pretty. I mean, duh, you're pretty now, too," she said.

I could see her puff up with her own generosity.

"How'd you even meet them?" Sasha asked.

It took me a moment to gather myself, to remember the sequence of things. "Revisit" is the word they always used in anniversary articles about the murder. "Revisiting the horror of Edgewater Road," as if the event existed singularly, a box you could close a lid on. As if I hadn't been stopped by hundreds of ghosted Suzannes on the streets or in the background of movies.

I fielded Sasha's questions about what they had been like in real life, those people who had become totems of themselves. Guy had been less interesting to the media, just a man doing what men had always done, but the girls were made mythic. Donna was the unattractive one, slow and rough, often cast as a pity case. The hungry harshness in her face. Helen, the former Camp Fire Girl, tan and pigtailed and pretty—she was the fetish object, the pinup murderess. But Suzanne got the worst of it. Depraved. Evil. Her sneaky beauty didn't photograph well. She looked feral and meager, like she might have existed only to kill.

Talking about Suzanne raised a rev in my chest that I was sure Sasha could see. It seemed shameful. To feel that helpless excitement, considering what had happened.

The caretaker on the couch, the coiled casing of his guts exposed to the air. The mother's hair soaked with gore. The boy so disfigured the police weren't sure of his gender. Surely Sasha had read about those things, too.

"Did you ever think you could have done what they did?" she asked.

"Of course not," I said reflexively.

In all the times I had ever told anyone about the ranch, few had ever asked me that question. Whether I could have done it, too. Whether I almost had. Most assumed a base level of morality separated me, as if the girls had been a different species.

Sasha was quiet. Her silence seemed like a kind of love.

"I guess I do wonder, sometimes," I said. "It seems like an accident that I didn't."

"An accident?"

The fire was getting weak and jumpy. "There wasn't that much difference. Between me and the other girls."

It was strange to say this aloud. To edge, even vaguely, around the worry I had worked over all this time. Sasha didn't seem disapproving or even wary. She simply looked at me, her watchful face on mine, as if she could take in my words and make a home for them.

We went to the one bar in town that had food. This seemed like a good idea, a goal we could aim toward. Sustenance. Movement. We'd talked until the fire had burned itself into a glowy mottle of newspaper. Sasha kicked sand over the mess, her scout's diligence making me laugh. I was happy to be with someone, despite the provisional reprieve—Julian would come back, Sasha would be gone, and I'd be alone again. Even so, it was nice to be the subject of someone's admiration. Because that's what it was, mostly: Sasha seemed to respect the fourteen-year-old girl I had been, to think I was interesting, had been somehow brave. I tried to correct her, but an expansive comfort had spread in my chest, a reoccupation of my body, like I'd woken from the twilight of pharmaceutical sleep.

We walked side by side on the shoulder of the road, along the aqueduct. The pointed trees were dense and dark, but I didn't feel afraid. The night had taken on a strange, festive air, and Sasha had started calling me Vee for some reason.

"Mama Vee," she said.

She seemed like a kitten, affable and mild, her warm shoulder bumping against mine. When I looked over, I saw that she was gnawing at her bottom lip, her face turned to the sky. But there was nothing to see—the stars were hidden by fog.

There were a few stools in the bar and not much else. The usual patchwork of rusted signs, a pair of humming neon eyes over the door. Someone in the kitchen was smoking cigarettes—the sandwich bread was humid with smoke. We stayed awhile after we'd finished eating. Sasha looked fifteen, but they didn't care. The bartender, a woman in her fifties, seemed grateful for any business. She looked worked over, her hair crispy from drugstore dye. We were almost the same age, but I wouldn't glance into the mirror to confirm the similarities, not with Sasha beside me. Sasha, whose features had the clean, purified cast of a saint on a religious medal.

Sasha swiveled around on her stool like a young child.

"Look at us." She laughed. "Partying hard." She took a drink of beer, then a drink of water, a conscientious habit I'd noticed, though it didn't prevent a visible slump from taking over. "I'm kind of glad Julian's not here," she said.

The words seemed to thrill her. I knew by then not to spook her, but instead to give her space to dawdle toward her actual point. Sasha kicked the bar rail absently, her breath beery and close.

"He didn't tell me he was leaving," she said. "For Humboldt." I pretended surprise. She laughed flatly. "I couldn't find him this morning and I just thought he was like, outside. That's kind of weird, right? That he just took off?"

"Yeah, weird." Too cautious, maybe, but I was wary of inciting a righteous defense of Julian.

"He texted me all sorry. He thought we'd talked about it, I guess."

She sipped her beer. Drawing a smiley face in the wood of the bar with a wet finger. "You know why he got kicked out of Irvine?" She was half-giddy, half-wary. "Wait," she said, "you're not gonna tell his dad, are you?"

I shook my head, an adult willing to keep a teenager's secrets.

"Okay." Sasha took a breath. "He had some comp teacher he hated. He was kind of a jerk, I guess. The teacher. He didn't let Julian turn in this paper late, even though he knew Julian would fail without a grade for it.

"So Julian went to the guy's house and did something to his dog. Fed him something that made him sick. Like bleach or rat poison, I don't really know what." Sasha caught my eye. "The dog died. This old dog."

I struggled to keep my face even. The plainness of her retelling, devoid of any inflection, made the story worse.

"The school knew he did it, but they couldn't prove it," Sasha said. "So they suspended him for other stuff, but he couldn't go back or anything. It's messed up." She looked at me. "I mean, don't you think?"

I didn't know what to say.

"He said he didn't mean to kill it or anything, just make it sick." Sasha's tone was tentative, testing out the thought. "That's not so bad, right?"

"I don't know," I said. "It sounds bad to me."

"But I live with him, you know," Sasha said. "Like he pays all the rent and stuff."

"There are always places to go," I said.

Poor Sasha. Poor girls. The world fattens them on the promise of love. How badly they need it, and how little most of them will ever get. The treacled pop songs, the dresses described in the catalogs with words like "sunset" and "Paris." Then the dreams are taken away with such violent force; the hand wrenching the buttons of the jeans, nobody looking at the man shouting at his girlfriend on the bus. Sorrow for Sasha locked up my throat.

She must have sensed my hesitation.

"Whatever," she said. "It was a while ago."

This is what it might be like to be a mother, I thought, watching Sasha drain her beer, wipe her mouth like a boy. To feel this unexpected, boundless tenderness for someone, seemingly out of nowhere. When a pool player sauntered over, I was prepared to scare him away. But Sasha smiled big, showing her pointed teeth.

"Hi," she said, and then he was buying us each another beer.

Sasha drank steadily. Alternating between distracted boredom and manic interest, feigned or not, in what the man was saying.

"You two from out of town?" he asked. His hair graying and long, a turquoise ring on his thumb—another sixties ghost. Maybe we'd even crossed paths back then, haunting the same well-worn trail. He hitched up his pants. "Sisters?"

His voice barely tried to include me in the purview of his effort, and I almost laughed. Still, even sitting next to Sasha, I was aware of some of the attention washing onto me. It was shocking to remember the voltage, even secondhand. How it felt to be a desired thing. Maybe Sasha was so used to it that she didn't even notice. Caught up in the rush of her own life, in her certainty of the meliorative trajectory.

"She's my mother," Sasha said. Her eyes were taut, wanting me to keep the joke going.

And I did. I huddled my arm around her. "We're on a

mother-daughter trip," I said. "Driving the 1. All the way up to Eureka."

"Adventurers!" the man exclaimed, pounding the table. His name was Victor, we learned, and the background wallpaper on Victor's cellphone was an Aztec image, he told us, so imbued with powers that just the contemplation of said image made you smarter. He was convinced that world events were orchestrated by complicated and persistent conspiracies. He took out a dollar bill to show us how the Illuminati communicated with one another.

"Why would a secret society lay out their plans on common currency?" I asked.

He nodded like he'd anticipated the question. "To display the reach of their power."

I envied Victor's certainty, the idiot syntax of the righteous. This belief—that the world had a visible order, and all we had to do was look for the symbols—as if evil were a code that could be cracked. He kept talking. His teeth wet from drink, the gray blush of a dead molar. He had plenty of conspiracies to explain to us in detail, plenty of inside information he could clue us into. He spoke of "getting on the level." Of "hidden frequencies" and "shadow governments."

"Wow," Sasha said, deadpan. "Did you know that, Mom?"

She kept calling me Mom, her voice exaggerated and comical, though it took me a while to see how drunk she was. To realize how drunk I was, too. The night had sailed into foreign waters. The fritzing of the neon signs, the bartender smoking in the doorway. I watched the bartender stamp the butt out, her flip-flops sliding around her feet. Victor said it was nice to see how well Sasha and I got along.

"You don't always see that, these days." He nodded, thoughtful. "Mothers and daughters who'd take a trip together. Who are sweet with each other like you two."

"Oh, she's great," Sasha said. "I love my mom."

She cut me a tricky smile before she leaned her face close to mine. The dry press of her lips, the stingy brine of pickles on her mouth. The most chaste of kisses. Still. Victor was shocked. As she'd hoped he would be.

"Goddamn," Victor said, both disgusted and titillated. Straightening his bulky shoulders, retucking his blousy shirt. He suddenly seemed wary of us, glancing around for support, for confirmation, and I wanted to explain that Sasha wasn't my daughter, but I was past the point of caring, the night stoking a foolish, confused sense that I had somehow returned to the world after a period of absence, had taken up residence again in the realm of the living.

1969

6

My father had always been in charge of pool maintenance—skimming the surface with a net, heaping wet leaves into a pile. The colored vials he used to test chlorine levels. He'd never been that assiduous with upkeep, but the pool had gotten bad since he'd left. Salamanders idling around the filter. When I propelled myself along the rim, there was some sloggy resistance, crud dispersing in my wake. My mother was at group. She'd forgotten a promise to buy me a new swimsuit, so I was wearing my old orange one: pale as cantaloupe, the stitching puckered and gaping around the leg holes. The top was too small, but the adult mass of cleavage pleased me.

It had only been a week since the solstice party, and already I'd been back to the ranch, and already I was stealing money for Suzanne, bill by bill. I like to imagine that it took more time than that. That I had to be convinced over a period of months, slowly broken down. Wooed as carefully as a valentine. But I was an eager mark, anxious to offer myself.

I kept bobbing in the water, algae speckling the hair on my legs like filings to a magnet. A forgotten paperback ruffled on the seat of the lawn chair. The leaves in the trees were silvery and spangled, like scales, everything full with June's lazy heat. Had the trees around my house always looked like that, so strange and aquatic? Or were things already shifting for me, the dumb litter of the normal world transforming into the lush stage sets of a different life?

Suzanne had driven me home the morning after the solstice, my bike shoved in the backseat. My mouth was leached and unfamiliar from smoking so much, and my clothes were stale from my body and smelled of ash. I kept picking bits of straw from my hair—proof of the night before that thrilled me, like a stamped passport. It had happened, after all, and I kept up a vivid catalog of happy data: the fact that I was sitting beside Suzanne, our friendly silence. My perverse pride that I'd been with Russell. I took pleasure in replaying the facts of the act, even the messy and boring parts. The odd lulls while Russell made himself hard. There was some power in the bluntness of human functions. Like Russell had explained to me: your body could hurtle you past your hang-ups, if you let it.

Suzanne smoked steadily as she drove, occasionally offering her cigarette to me with serene ritual. The quiet between us wasn't slack or uncomfortable. Outside the car, olive trees flashed by, the scorched summer earth. Far-off waterways, sloughing to the sea. Suzanne kept changing the radio station until she abruptly snapped it off.

"We need gas," she announced.

We, I echoed silently, *we* need gas.

Suzanne pulled into the Texaco, empty except for a teal-and-white pickup towing a boat trailer.

"Hand me a card," Suzanne said. Nodding at the glove box.

I scrambled to open it, loosing a jumble of credit cards. All with different names.

"The blue one," she said. She seemed impatient. When I handed her the card, she saw my confusion.

"People give them to us," she said. "Or we take them." She fingered the blue card. "Like this one is Donna's. She lifted it from her mom."

"Her mom's gas card?"

"Saved our ass—we would've starved," Suzanne said. She gave me a look. "Like you hustling that toilet paper, right?"

I flushed at the mention. Maybe she'd known I had lied, but I couldn't tell from her shuttered face—maybe not.

"Besides," she continued, "it's better than what they'd

do with it—more crap, more stuff, more me, me, me. Russell's trying to help people. He's not judgmental, that's not his trip. He doesn't care if you're rich or poor."

It made a kind of sense, what Suzanne was saying. They were just trying to equalize the forces in the world.

"It's ego," she went on, leaning against the car but keeping a sharp eye on the gas gauge: none of them ever filled up a tank more than a quarter full. "Money is ego, and people won't give it up. Just want to protect themselves, hold on to it like a blanket. They don't realize it keeps them slaves. It's sick."

She laughed.

"What's funny is that as soon as you give everything away, as soon as you say, Here, take it—that's when you really have everything."

One of the group had been detained for dumpster diving on a garbage run, and Suzanne was incensed, recounting the story as she pulled the car back onto the road.

"More and more stores get wise to it. Bullshit," she said. "They throw something away and they still want it. That's America."

"That is bullshit." The tone of the word was strange in my mouth.

"We'll figure something out. Soon." She glanced in the rearview. "Money's tight. But you just can't escape it. You probably don't know what that's like."

She wasn't sneering, not really—she spoke like she was just stating the truth. Acknowledging reality with an affable shrug. That's when the idea came to me, fully formed, as if I had thought of it myself. And that's how it seemed, like the exact solution, a baubled ornament shining within reach.

"I can get some money," I said, later cringing at my eagerness. "My mom leaves her purse out all the time."

It was true. I was always coming across money: in drawers, on tables, forgotten by the bathroom sink. I had an allowance, but my mother often gave me more, by accident, or just gestured vaguely in the direction of her purse. "Take what you need," she'd always said. And I'd never taken more than I should have and was always conscious of returning the change.

"Oh no," Suzanne said, flicking the last of her cigarette out the window. "You don't have to do that. You're a sweet kid, though," she said. "Nice of you to offer."

"I want to."

She pursed her lips, affecting uncertainty, igniting a tilt in my gut.

"I don't want you to do something you don't want to." She laughed a little. "That's not what I'm about."

"But I do want to," I said. "I want to help."

Suzanne didn't speak for a minute, then smiled without looking over. "Okay," she said. I didn't miss the test in her voice. "You want to help. You can help."

My task made me a spy in my mother's house, my mother the clueless quarry. I could even apologize for our fight when I ran into her that night across the stillness of the hallway. My mother gave a little shrug but accepted my apology, smiling in a brave way. It would bother me, normally, that wavery brave smile, but the new me bowed my head in abject regret. I was imitating a daughter, acting like a daughter would. Part of me thrilled at the knowledge I held out of her reach, how every time I looked at her or spoke to her, I was lying. The night with Russell, the ranch, the secret space I tended to the side. She could have the husk of my old life, all the dried-up leftovers.

"You're home so early," she said. "I thought you might sleep at Connie's again."

"I didn't feel like it."

It was strange to be reminded of Connie, to jar back to the regular world. I'd been surprised, even, that I could feel the ordinary desire for food. I wanted the world to reorder itself visibly around the change, like a mend marking a tear.

My mother softened. "I'm just glad because I wanted to spend some time with you. Just us. It's been a while, huh? Maybe I'll make Stroganoff," she said. "Or meatballs. What do you think?"

I was suspicious of her offer: she didn't buy food for the house unless I wrote notes for her to find when she got back from group. And we hadn't eaten meat in forever. Sal told my mother that to eat meat was to eat fear and that ingesting fear would make you gain weight.

"Meatballs would be good," I allowed. I didn't want to notice how happy it made her.

. . .

My mother turned on the radio in the kitchen, playing the kind of slight, balmy songs that I'd loved as a child. Diamond rings, cool streams, apple trees. If Suzanne or even Connie caught me listening to that sort of music, I'd be embarrassed—it was bland and cheerful and old-fashioned—but I had a grudging, private love of those songs, my mother singing along to the parts she knew. Rosy with theatrical enthusiasm, so it was easy to get caught up in her giddiness. Her posture was shaped by years of horse shows in adolescence, smiling from the backs of sleek Arabians, arena lights catching the crust of rhinestones on her collar. She had been so mysterious to me when I was younger. The shyness I had felt watching her move around the house, shuffling in her night slippers. The drawer of jewelry whose provenance I made her describe, piece by piece, like a poem.

The house was clean, the windows segmenting the dark night, the carpets plush beneath my bare feet. This was the opposite of the ranch, and I sensed I should be guilty—that it was wrong to be comfortable like this, to want to eat this food with my mother in the primness of our tidy kitchen. What were Suzanne and the others doing at that same moment? It was suddenly hard to imagine.

"How's Connie these days?" she asked, flicking through her handwritten recipe cards.

"Fine." She probably was. Watching May Lopes's braces scum up.

"You know," she said, "she can always come over here. You guys have been spending an awful lot of time at her house lately."

"Her dad doesn't care."

"I miss her," she said, though my mother had always seemed mystified by Connie, like a barely tolerated maiden aunt. "We should go on a trip to Palm Springs or something." It was clear she'd been waiting to offer this. "You could invite Connie, if you wanted."

"I don't know." It could be nice. Connie and I shoving each other in the sun-stifled backseat, drinking shakes from the date farm outside Indio.

"Mm," she murmured. "We could go in the next few weeks. But you know, sweetheart"—a pause. "Frank might come, too."

"I'm not going on a trip with you and your boyfriend."

She tried to smile, but I saw that she wasn't saying everything. The radio was too loud. "Sweetheart," she started. "How are we ever going to live together—"

"What?" I hated how automatically my voice tilted bratty, cutting any authority.

"Not right away, definitely not." Her mouth puckered. "But if Frank moves in—"

"I live here, too," I said. "You were just gonna let him move in one day, without even telling me?"

"You're fourteen."

"This is bullshit."

"Hey! Watch it," she said, tucking her hands into her armpits. "I don't know why you're being so rude, but you need to quit it, and fast." The nearness of my mother's pleading face, her naked upset—it stoked a biological disgust for her, like when I smelled the bellow of iron in the bathroom and knew she had her period. "This is a nice thing I'm trying to do," she said, "inviting your friend along. Can I get a break here?"

I laughed, but it was dripping with the sickness of betrayal. That's why she'd wanted to make dinner. It was worse now, because I'd been so easily pleased. "Frank's an asshole."

Her face flared, but she pushed herself to get calm. "Watch your attitude. This is my life, understand? I'm trying to get just a little bit happy," she said, "and you need to give me that. Can you give me that?"

She deserved her anemic life, its meager, girlish uncertainties. "Fine," I said. "Fine. Good luck with Frank."

Her eyes narrowed. "What does that mean?"

"Forget it." I could smell the raw meat coming to room temperature, a biting tinge of cold metal. My stomach tightened. "I'm not hungry anymore," I said, and left her standing in the kitchen. The radio still playing songs about first loves, about dancing by the river, the meat thawed enough so my mother would be forced to cook it, though no one would eat it.

It was easy after that to tell myself that I deserved the money. Russell said that most people were selfish, unable to love, and that seemed true of my mother, and my father, too, tucked away with Tamar in the Portofino Apartments in Palo Alto. So it was a tidy trade, when I thought about it like that. Like the money I was filching, bill by bill, added up to something that could replace what had gone missing. It was too depressing to think it had maybe never been there in the first place. That none of it had—Connie's friendship. Peter ever feeling anything for me besides annoyance at the obviousness of my kiddish worship.

My mother left her purse lying around, like always, and that made the money inside seem less valuable, something she didn't care enough about to take seriously. Still, it was uncomfortable, poking around in her purse, like the rattly inside of my mother's brain. The litter was too personal—the wrapper from a butterscotch candy, a mantra card, a pocket mirror. A tube of cream, the color of a Band-Aid, that she patted under her eyes. I pinched a ten, folding it into my shorts. Even if she saw me, I'd just say I was getting groceries—why would she suspect me? Her daughter, who had always been good, even if that was more disappointing than being great.

I'm surprised that I felt so little guilt. On the contrary— there was something righteous in the way I hoarded my mother's money. I was picking up some of the ranch bravado, the certainty that I could take what I wanted. The knowledge of the hidden bills allowed me to smile at my mother the next morning, to act like we hadn't said the things we'd said the night before. To stand patiently when she brushed at my bangs without warning.

"Don't hide your eyes," my mother said, her breath close and hot, her fingers raking at my hair.

I wanted to shake her off, to step back, but I didn't.

"There," she said, pleased. "There's my sweet daughter."

I was thinking of the money while I kicked in the pool, my shoulders above the waterline. There was a purity to the task, amassing the bills in my little zip purse. When I was alone, I liked to count the money, each new five or ten a particular boon. I folded the crisper bills on top, so the bundle looked nicer. Imagining Suzanne's and Russell's pleasure when I brought the money to them, lulled into the sweet wayward fog of daydreams.

My eyes were closed as I floated, and I only opened them when I heard thrashing beyond the tree line. A deer, maybe. I tensed, stirring uneasily in the water. I didn't think that it could be a person: we didn't worry about those kinds of things. Not until later. And it was a dalmatian anyway, the creature that came trotting out of the trees and right up to the pool's edge. He regarded me soberly, then started to bark.

The dog was strange looking, speckled and spotted, and it barked with high, human alarm. I knew it belonged to the neighbors on our left, the Dutton family. The father had written some movie theme song, and at parties I had heard the mother hum it, mockingly, to a gathered group. Their son was younger than me—he often shot his BB gun in the yard, the dog yelping in agitated chorus. I couldn't remember the dog's name.

"Get," I said, splashing halfheartedly. I didn't want to have to haul myself out of the water. "Go on."

The dog kept barking.

"Go," I tried again, but the dog just barked louder.

My cutoffs were damp from my swimsuit by the time I made it to the Dutton house. I'd put on my cork sandals, grimed with the ghost of my feet, and taken the dog by the collar, the ends of my hair dripping. Teddy Dutton answered the door. He was eleven or twelve, his legs studded with scabs and scrapes. He'd broken his arm last year falling from a tree, and my mother had been the one to drive him to the hospital: she'd muttered darkly that his parents left him alone too much. I had never spent much time with Teddy, beyond the familiarity of being young at neighborhood parties, anyone under age eighteen herded together in a forced march to friendship. Sometimes I'd see him riding his bike along the fire road with a boy in glasses: he'd once let me pet a barn kitten they'd found, holding the tiny thing under his shirt. The kitten's eyes were leaky with pus, but Teddy had been gentle with it, like a little mother. That was the last time I'd spoken to him.

"Hey," I said when Teddy opened the door. "Your dog."

Teddy was gaping at me like we hadn't been neighbors our whole lives. I rolled my eyes a little at his silence.

"He was in our yard," I went on. The dog moved against my hold.

It took Teddy a second to speak, but before he did, I saw him cut a helpless look at my swimsuit top, the exaggerated swell of cleavage. Teddy saw that I had noticed and got more flustered. He scowled at the dog, taking his collar. "Bad Tiki," he said, hustling the animal into the house. "Bad dog."

The thought that Teddy Dutton might be somehow nervous around me was a surprise. Though I hadn't even owned a bikini the last time I'd seen him, and my breasts were bigger now, pleasing even to me. I found his attention almost hilarious. A stranger had once shown Connie and me his dick by the movie theater bathrooms—it had taken a moment to understand why the man was gasping like a fish for air, but then I saw his penis, out of his zipper like an arm out of a sleeve. He'd looked at us like we were butterflies he was pinning to a board. Connie had grabbed my arm, and we'd turned and run, laughing, the Raisinets clutched in my hand starting to melt. We recounted our disgust to each other in strident tones, but there was pride, too. Like the satisfied way Patricia Bell had once asked me after class whether I'd seen how Mr. Garrison had been staring at her, and didn't I think it was *weird*?

"His paws are all wet," I said. "He's gonna mess up the floors."

"My parents aren't home. It doesn't matter." Teddy stayed in the doorway, awkward with an air of expectancy; did he think we were going to hang out?

He stood there, like the unhappy boys who sometimes got erections at the chalkboard for no reason at all—he was obviously under the command of some other force. Maybe the proof of sex was visible on me in a new way.

"Well," I said. I worried I would start laughing— Teddy looked so uncomfortable. "See you."

Teddy cleared his throat, trying to throttle his voice deeper. "Sorry," he said. "If Tiki was bothering you."

How did I know I could mess with Teddy? Why did my mind range immediately to that option? I'd only been to the ranch twice since the solstice party, but I'd already started to absorb certain ways of seeing the world, certain habits of logic. Society was crowded with straight people, Russell told us, people in paralyzed thrall to corporate interests and docile as dosed lab chimps. Those of us at the ranch functioned on a whole other level, fighting against the miserable squall, and so what if you had to mess with the straight people to achieve larger goals, larger worlds? If you checked yourself out of that old contract, Russell told us, refused all the bullshit scare tactics of civics class and prayer books and the principal's office, you'd see there was no such thing as right and wrong. His permissive equations reduced these concepts to hollow relics, like medals from a regime no longer in power.

I asked Teddy for a drink. Lemonade, I figured, soda, anything but what he brought me, his hand shaking nervously when he passed me the glass.

"Do you want a napkin?" he said.

"Nah." The intensity of his attention seemed exposing, and I laughed a little. I was just starting to learn how to be looked at. I took a deep drink. The glass was full of vodka, cloudy with the barest slip of orange juice. I coughed.

"Your parents let you drink?" I asked, wiping at my mouth.

"I do what I want," he said, proud and uncertain at the same time. His eyes gleamed; I watched him decide what to say next. It was strange to watch someone else calibrate and worry over their actions instead of being the one who was worrying. Was this what Peter had felt around me? A limited patience, a sense of power that felt heady and slightly distressing. Teddy's freckled face, ruddy and eager—he was only two years younger than me, but the distance seemed definitive. I took a large swallow from the glass, and Teddy cleared his throat.

"I have some dope if you want it," he said.

. . .

Teddy led me to his room, expectant as I glanced around at his boyish novelties. They seemed arranged for viewing, though it was all junk: a captain's clock whose hands were dead, a long-forgotten ant farm, warped and molding. The glassy stipple of a partial arrowhead, a jar of pennies, green and scuzzy as sunken treasure. Usually I'd make some crack to Teddy. Ask him where he got the arrowhead or tell him about the whole one I'd found, the obsidian point sharp enough to draw blood. But I sensed a pressure to preserve a haughty coolness, like Suzanne that day in the park. I was already starting to understand that other people's admiration asked something of you. That you had to shape yourself around it. The weed Teddy produced from under his mattress was brown and crumbled, barely smokable, though he held out the plastic bag with gruff dignity.

I laughed. "It's like dirt or something. No, thanks."

He seemed stung and stuffed the bag deep in his pocket. It had been his trump card, I understood, and he hadn't expected its failure. How long had the bag been there, crushed by the mattress, waiting for deployment? I suddenly felt sorry for Teddy, the neckline of his striped shirt gone limp with grime. I told myself there was still time to leave. To put down the now empty glass, to say a breezy thank-you and go back to my own house. There were other ways to get money. But I stayed. He eyed me, sitting on his bed, with a bewildered and attentive air, as if looking away would break the rare spell of my presence.

"I can get you some real stuff, if you want," I said. "Good stuff. I know a guy."

His gratitude was embarrassing. "Really?"

"Sure." I saw him notice as I adjusted my swimsuit strap. "You have any money on you?" I asked.

He had three dollars in his pocket, wadded and limp, and didn't hesitate to hand them over. I tucked the bills away, all business. Even possessing that small amount of money tindered an obsessive need in me, a desire to see how much I was worth. The equation excited me. You could be pretty, you could be wanted, and that could make you valuable. I appreciated the tidy commerce. And maybe it was something I already perceived in relationships with men—that creep of discomfort, of being tricked. At least this way the arrangement was put toward some use.

"What about your parents?" I said. "Don't they have money somewhere?"

He cut a quick glance at me.

"They're gone, aren't they?" I sighed, impatient. "So who cares?"

Teddy coughed. Rearranged his face. "Yeah," he said. "Let me check."

The dog banged at our heels while I followed Teddy up the stairs. The dimness of his parents' room, a room that seemed both familiar—the stale glass of water on the nightstand, the lacquered tray of perfume bottles—

and foreign, his father's slacks collapsed in the corner, an upholstered bench at the foot of the bed. I was nervous, and I could tell Teddy was, too. It seemed perverse to be in his parents' bedroom in the middle of the day. The sun was hot outside the shades, outlining them brightly.

Teddy went into the closet in the far corner, and I followed. If I stayed close, I was less like an intruder. He reached up on his toes to feel blindly through a cardboard box. While he searched, I shuffled through the clothes hanging from fussy silken hangers. His mother's. Paisley pussy-bow blouses, the grim, tight tweeds. They all seemed like costumes, impersonal and not quite real, until I pinched the sleeve of an ivory blouse. My mother had the same one, and it made me uneasy, the familiar gold of the I. Magnin label like a rebuke. I dropped the shirt back on its hanger. "Can't you hurry up?" I hissed at Teddy, and he made a muffled reply, rummaging farther, until he finally pulled out some new-looking bills.

He shoved the box back onto the high shelf, breathing hard, while I counted.

"Sixty-five," I said. Neatening the stack, folding it to a more substantial thickness.

"Isn't that enough?"

I could tell by his face, the effort of his breathing, that if I demanded more, he would find a way to get it. Part of me almost wanted to. To gorge myself on this new power, see how long I could keep it going. But then Tiki trotted in the doorway, startling us both. The dog panting as he nudged at Teddy's legs. Even the dog's tongue was spotted, I saw, the crimped pink freckled with black.

"This'll be fine," I said, putting the money in my pocket. My damp shorts gave off an itch of chlorine.

"So when will I get the stuff?" Teddy said.

It took a second to understand the significant look he gave me: the dope I'd promised. I'd almost forgotten that I hadn't just demanded money. When he saw my expression, he corrected himself. "I mean, no rush. If it takes time or whatever."

"Hard to say." Tiki was sniffing at my crotch; I pushed his nose away more roughly than I'd meant to, his snout wetting my palm. My desire to get out of the room was suddenly overwhelming. "Pretty soon, probably," I said, starting to back toward the door. "I'll bring it over when I get it."

"Oh, yeah," Teddy said. "Yeah, okay."

I had the uncomfortable sense, at the front door, that Teddy was the guest and I was the host. The wind chime over the porch rippling a thin song. The sun and trees and blond hills beyond seemed to promise great freedoms, and I could already start to forget what I'd done, washed over by other concerns. The pleasing meaty rectangle of the folded bills in my pocket. When I looked at Teddy's freckled face, a surge of impulsive, virtuous af-

fection passed through me—he was like a little brother.
The gentle way he'd mothered the barn kitten.

"I'll see you," I said, leaning to kiss him on the cheek.

I was congratulating myself for the sweetness of my
gesture, the kindness, but then Teddy adjusted his hips,
hunching them protectively; when I pulled away, I saw
his erection pushing stubbornly against his jeans.

7

I could ride my bike most of the way there. Adobe Road empty of cars, except for the occasional motorcycle or horse trailer. If a car passed, it was usually heading to the ranch, and they'd give me a lift, my bicycle half hanging out a window. Girls in shorts and wood sandals and plastic rings from the dispensers outside the Rexall. Boys who kept losing their train of thought, then coming to with a stunned smile, as if returned from cosmic tourism. The barest of nods we'd give one another, tuned to the same unseen frequencies.

It wasn't that I couldn't remember my life before Suzanne and the others, but it had been limited and expected, objects and people occupying their temperate orbits. The yellow cake my mother made for birthdays, dense and chilly from the freezer. The girls at school eating lunch on the asphalt, sitting on their overturned backpacks. Since I'd met Suzanne, my life had come into sharp, mysterious relief, revealing a world beyond the known world, the hidden passage behind the bookcase. I'd catch myself eating an apple, and even the wet swallow of apple could incite gratitude in me. The arrangement of oak leaves overhead condensing with a hothouse clarity, clues to a riddle I hadn't known you could try to solve.

I followed Suzanne past the motorcycles parked at the front of the main house, as big and heavy looking as cows. Men in denim vests sat on the nearby boulders, smoking cigarettes. The air was prickly from the llamas in their pen, the funny smell of hay and sweat and sunbaked shit.

"Hey, bunnies," one of the men called. Stretching so his belly strained pregnant against his shirt.

Suzanne smiled back but pulled me along. "If you stand around too much, they'll jump on you," she said, though she was pushing her shoulders back to emphasize her breasts. When I cut a glance over my shoulder, the man flicked his tongue at me, quick as a snake.

"Russell can help all kinds of people, though," Suzanne said. "And you know, the pigs don't mess with the motorcycle guys. That's important."

"Why?"

"Because," she said, like it was obvious. "The cops hate Russell. They hate anyone who tries to free people from the system. But they stay away if those guys are here." She shook her head. "The pigs are trapped, too, that's the bullshit. Their fucking shiny black shoes."

I stoked my own righteous agreement: I was in league with truth. I followed her to the clearing beyond the house, toward the campfire hum of voices in chorus. The money was banded tightly in my pocket, and I kept starting to tell Suzanne I'd brought it, then losing my nerve, concerned it was too meager an offering. Finally I stopped her, touching her shoulder before we joined the others.

"I can get more," I said, flustered. I just wanted her to know the money existed, imagining I would be the one to give it to Russell. But Suzanne quickly corrected that idea. I tried not to mind how swiftly she took the bills from my hand, counting them with her eyes. I saw that she was surprised by the amount.

"Good girl."

The sun hit the tin outbuildings and broke up the smoke in the air. Someone had lit a joss stick that kept going out. Russell's eyes moved around each of our faces, the group sitting at his feet, and I flushed when he caught my gaze—he seemed unsurprised by my return. Suzanne's hand touched my back lightly, possessively, and a hush came over me like in a movie theater or church. My awareness of her hand was almost paralyzing. Donna was playing with her orange hair. Weaving sections into tight, lacy braids, using her pinched fingernails to flay split ends.

Russell looked younger when he sang, his mess of hair tied back, and he played the guitar in a funny, mocking way, like a TV cowboy. His voice wasn't the nicest I'd ever heard, but that day—my legs in the sun, the stubble of oat grass—that day, his voice seemed to slide all over me, to saturate the air, so that I felt pinned in place. I couldn't move even if I wanted to, even if I could imagine there was any place I could go.

In the lull that followed Russell's singing, Suzanne got to her feet, her dress already thick with dust, and picked her way to his side. His face changed as she whispered to him, and he nodded. Squeezing her shoulder. I saw her slip him my wad of money, which Russell put in his pocket. Resting his fingers there for a moment as if giving a blessing.

Russell's eyes crinkled. "We've got good news. We've got some resources, sweethearts. Because someone has opened themselves up to us, they've opened their hearts."

A shimmer passed through me. And all at once, it seemed worth it—trawling my mother's purse. The stillness of Teddy's parents' bedroom. How cleanly that worry had been transmuted into belonging. Suzanne seemed gratified as she hurried to settle back beside me.

"Little Evie's shown us her big heart," Russell said. "She's shown us her love, hasn't she?" And the others turned to look at me, a current of goodwill pulsed in my direction.

...

The rest of the afternoon passed in a drowsy span of sunlight. The skinny dogs retreating under the house, tongues heaving. We sat alone on the porch steps—Suzanne rested her head on my knees and recounted scraps of a dream she'd had. Pausing to take ripping bites from a length of French bread.

"I was convinced I knew sign language, but it was obvious to me I didn't, that I was just flailing my hands around. But the man understood everything I was saying, like I actually did know sign language. But later it just turned out he was only pretending to be deaf," she said, "in the end. So it was all fake—him, me, the whole train."

Her laugh was an afterthought, a sharp addendum—how happy I was for any news of her interior, a secret meant for me alone. I couldn't say how long we sat there, the two of us cut adrift from the rhythms of normal life. But that's what I wanted—for even time to feel different and new, washed with special import. Like she and I were occupying the same song.

We were, Russell told us, starting a new kind of society. Free from racism, free from exclusion, free from hierarchy. We were in service of a deeper love. That's how he said it, a deeper love, his voice booming from the ramshackle house in the California grasslands, and we played together like dogs, tumbling and biting and breathless with sun shock. We were barely adults, most of us, and our teeth were still milky and new. We ate whatever was put in front of us. Oatmeal that gummed up in the throat. Ketchup on bread, chipped beef from a can. Potatoes soggy with PAM.

"Miss 1969," Suzanne called me. "Our very own."

And they treated me like that, like their new toy, taking turns hooking their arms through mine, clamoring to braid my long hair. Teasing me about the boarding school I'd mentioned, my famous grandmother, whose name some of them recognized. My clean white socks. The others had been with Russell for months, or years, even. And that was the first worry that the days slowly melted in me. Where were their families, girls like Suzanne? Or baby-voiced Helen—she spoke sometimes of a house in Eugene. A father who gave her enemas every month and rubbed her calves after tennis practice with mentholated balm, among other dubious hygienic practices. But where was he? If any of their homes had given them what they needed, why would they be here, day after day, their time at the ranch stretching on endlessly?

Suzanne slept late, barely up by noon. Groggy and lingering, her movements at half-speed. Like there would always be more time. By then, I was already sleeping in Suzanne's bed every few nights. Her mattress wasn't comfortable, gritty with sand, but I didn't mind. Sometimes she reached over blindly from sleep to sling her arm around me, a warmth coming off her body like baked bread. I would lie awake, painfully alert to Suzanne's nearness. She turned in the night so she kicked off the sheet, exposing her bare breasts.

Her room was dark and jungly in the mornings, the tar roof of the outbuilding getting bubbly in the heat. I was already dressed but knew we wouldn't join the others for another hour. Suzanne always took a long time to get ready, though preparation was mostly a matter of time and not action—a slow shrug into herself. I liked to watch her from the mattress, the sweet, blank way she studied her reflection with the directionless gaze of a portrait. Her naked body was humble at these moments, even childish, bent at an unflattering angle as she rummaged through the trash bag of clothes. It was comforting to me, her humanness. Noticing how her ankles were gruff with stubble, or the pin dots of blackheads.

Suzanne had been a dancer in San Francisco. The flashing neon snake outside the club, the red apple that cast an alien glow on the passersby. One of the other girls burned off Suzanne's moles backstage with a caustic pencil.

"Some girls hated being up there," she said, tugging a dress over her nakedness. "Dancing, the whole thing. But I didn't think it was so bad."

She assessed the dress in the mirror, cupping her breasts through the fabric. "People can be so prudish," she said. She made a lewd face, laughing a little at herself, and let her breasts drop. She told me, then, how Russell fucked her gently and how sometimes he didn't, and how you could like it either way. "There's nothing sick about that," she said. "The people who act so uptight, who act like it's so evil? They're the real perverts. It's like some of the guys who'd come to see us dance. All mad at us that they were there. Like we'd tricked them."

Suzanne didn't often talk about her hometown or family, and I didn't ask. There was a glossy pucker of scar tissue along one of her wrists that I'd seen her tracing with a tragic pride, and once she slipped and mentioned a humid street outside Red Bluff. But then she caught herself. "That cunt," she called her mother, peaceably. My dizzy solidarity overwhelmed me, the weary justice in her tone—I thought we both knew what it was to be alone, though it seems silly to me now. To think we were so alike, when I had grown up with housekeepers and parents and she told me she had sometimes lived in a car, sleeping in the reclined passenger seat with her mother in the driver's side. If I was hungry, I ate. But we had other things in common, Suzanne and I, a different hunger. Sometimes I wanted to be touched so badly I was scraped by longing. I saw the same thing in Suzanne, too, perking up like an animal smelling food whenever Russell approached.

Suzanne went into San Rafael with Russell to look at a truck. I stayed behind—there were chores, and I threw myself into them with an eagerness born of fear. I didn't want to give them any excuse to make me leave. Feeding the llamas, weeding the garden, scrubbing and bleaching the kitchen floors. Work was just another way to show your love, to offer up the self.

Filling the llamas' trough took a long time, the water pressure sluggish at best, but it was nice to be out in the sun. Mosquitoes hovered around my bare skin and I kept having to shiver them off. They didn't bother the llamas, who just stood there, as sultry and heavy-lidded as screen sirens.

I could see Guy beyond the main house, messing with the bus engine with the low-stakes curiosity of a science fair project. Taking breaks to smoke cigarettes and do downward dog. He went to the main house every once in a while to get another beer from Russell's stash, checking to make sure everyone did their chores. He and Suzanne were like the head counselors, keeping Donna and the others in line with a stray word or glance. Operating as satellite versions of Russell, though Guy's deference was different from Suzanne's. I think he stayed around because Russell was a way to get things he wanted—girls, drugs, a place to crash. He wasn't in love with Russell, didn't cower or pant in his presence—Guy was more like a sidekick, and all his blustery tales of adventure and hardship continued to star himself.

He approached the fence, his beer and cigarette in the same hand, his jeans low on his hips. I knew he was watching me, and I concentrated on the hose, the warm fill of water in the trough.

"The smoke keeps 'em away," Guy said, and I turned as if I'd just noticed his presence. "The mosquitoes," he said, holding out his cigarette.

"Yeah," I said, "sure. Thanks." I took the cigarette over the fence, careful to keep the hose trained on the trough.

"You seen Suzanne?"

Already Guy assumed I'd know her movements. I was flattered to be the keeper of her whereabouts.

"Some guy in San Rafael was selling his truck," I said. "She went with Russell to look at it."

"Hm," Guy said. Reaching to take his cigarette back. He seemed amused by my professionalism, though I'm sure he saw, too, the worship that hijacked my face whenever I spoke of Suzanne. My half-hitch step those times I hurried to her side. Maybe it confused him not to be the focus of all that desire—he was a handsome boy, used to the attention of girls. Girls who sucked in their stomachs when he put his hand down their jeans, girls who believed the jewelry he wore was the pretty evidence of his untapped emotional depths.

"They're probably at the free clinic," Guy said. He mimed scratching his crotch, his cigarette waving around. He was trying to get me to snicker at Suzanne, collude in some way—I didn't respond, beyond a grim smile. He tilted back on the heels of his cowboy boots. Studying me.

"You can go on and help Roos," he said in between the final slugs of his beer. "She's in the kitchen."

I'd already finished my chores for the day, and working with Roos in the hot kitchen would be tedious, but I nodded with a martyr's air.

Roos had been married to a policeman in Corpus Christi, Suzanne had told me, which seemed about right. She floated around the border with the dreamy solicitude of beaten wives, and even my offer of help with the dishes was met with a mild cower. I scrubbed gelatinous fug from their biggest stew pot, the colorless scraps of food gumming up the sponge. Guy was punishing me in his petty fashion, but I didn't care. Any irritation was softened by Suzanne's return. She gusted into the kitchen, breathless.

"The guy gave Russell the truck," Suzanne said, her face bright, casting around for an audience. She opened a cabinet, rooting inside. "It was so perfect," she said, "'cause he wanted, like, two hundred bucks. And Russell said, all calm, You should just give it to us."

She laughed, still residually thrilled, and sat up on the counter. Starting to crack her way through a bag of dusty-looking peanuts. "The guy was real angry, at first, that Russell was just asking for it. For free."

Roos was only half listening, picking through the makings of that night's dinner, but I turned off the faucet, watching Suzanne with my whole body.

"And Russell said, Let's just talk for a minute. Just let me tell you what I'm about." Suzanne spit a shell back into the bag. "We had some tea with the guy, in his weird log cabin house. For an hour or something. Russell gave him the whole vision, laid it all out. And the guy was real interested in what we were doing out here. Showed Russell his old army pictures. Then he said we could just have the truck."

I wiped my hands on my shorts, her giddiness making me so shy I had to turn away. I finished the dishes to the sound of her snapping open peanut after peanut from her perch on the counter, amassing an unruly pile of damp shells until the bag was gone and she went looking for someone else to tell her story to.

The girls would hang out near the creek because it was cooler, the breeze carrying a chill, though the flies were bad. The rocks capped with algae, the sleepy shade. Russell had come back from town in the new truck, bearing candy bars, comic books whose pages grew limp from our hands. Helen ate her candy immediately and looked around at the rest of us with a seethe of jealousy. Though she'd also come from a wealthy family, we weren't close. I found her dull except around Russell, when her brattiness took on a directed aim. Preening under his touch like a cat, she acted younger, even than me, stunted in a way that would later seem pathological.

"Jesus. Stop staring at me," Suzanne said, hunching her candy away from Helen. "You already ate yours." Her shape on the bank next to me, her toes curling into the dirt. Jerking when a mosquito swarmed by her ear.

"Just a bite," Helen whined. "Just the corner."

Roos glanced up from the chambray mess of cloth in her lap. She was mending a work shirt for Guy, her tiny stitches made with absent precision.

"You can have some of mine," Donna said, "if you be quiet." She picked her way to Helen, her chocolate bar craggy with peanuts.

Helen took a bite. When she giggled, her teeth washed with chocolate.

"Candy yoga," she pronounced. Anything could be yoga: doing the dishes, grooming the llamas. Making food for Russell. You were supposed to bliss out on it, to settle into whatever the rhythms were going to teach you.

Break down the self, offer yourself up like dust to the universe.

All the books made it sound like the men forced the girls into it. That wasn't true, not all the time. Suzanne wielded her Swinger camera like a weapon. Goading men to drop their jeans. To expose their penises, tender and naked in dark nests of hair. The men smiled shyly in the pictures, paled from the guilty flash, all hair and wet animal eyes. "There isn't any film in the camera," Suzanne would say, though she had stolen a case of film from the store. The boys pretended to believe her. It was like that with lots of things.

I trailed after Suzanne, after all of them. Suzanne letting me draw suns and moons on her naked back with tanning oil while Russell played an idle riff on his guitar, a coy up-and-down fragment. Helen sighing like the lovesick kid she was, Roos joining us with a drifty smile, some teenage boy I didn't know looking at us all with grateful awe, and no one even had to speak—the silence was knit with so much.

I prepared inwardly for Russell's advances, but it only happened after a while. Russell giving me a cryptic nod so I knew to follow him.

I'd been washing windows with Suzanne in the main house—the floor littered with the crumple of newspaper and vinegar, the transistor radio going; even chores took on the delight of truancy. Suzanne singing along, talking to me with happy, fitful distraction. She looked different, those times we worked together, like she forgot herself and relaxed into the girl she was. It's strange to remember she was just nineteen. When Russell nodded at me, I looked at her reflexively. For permission or forgiveness, either one. The ease in her face had drained into a brittle mask. Scrubbing the warped window with new concentration. She shrugged goodbye when I left, like she didn't mind, though I could sense her watchful gaze on my back.

Every time Russell nodded at me like that, my heart

contracted, despite the strangeness. I was eager for our encounters, eager to cement my place among them, as if doing what Suzanne did was a way of being with her. Russell never fucked me—it was always other stuff, his fingers moving in me with a technical remove I ascribed to his purity. His aims were elevated, I told myself, unsullied by primitive concerns.

"Look at yourself," he said whenever he sensed shame or hesitance. Pointing me toward the fogged mirror in the trailer. "Look at your body. It's not some stranger's body," he said evenly. When I shied away, goofing some excuse, he took me by the shoulders and pointed me back at the mirror. "It's you," he said. "It's Evie. Nothing in you but beauty."

The words worked on me, even if only temporarily. A trance overtaking me when I saw my reflection—the scooped breasts, even the soft stomach, the legs rough with mosquito bites. There was nothing to figure out, no complicated puzzles—just the obvious fact of the moment, the only place where love really existed.

Afterward he'd hand me a towel to clean myself, and this seemed like a great kindness.

When I returned to her purview, there was always a brief period when Suzanne was cool to me. Even her movements were stiff, as if braced, a lull behind her eyes, like someone asleep at the wheel. I learned quickly how to compliment her, how to ride by her side until she forgot to be aloof and deigned to pass her cigarette to me. It would occur to me later that Suzanne missed me when I left, her formality a clumsy disguise. Though it's hard to tell—maybe that is only a wishful explanation.

The other parts of the ranch flash in and out. Guy's black dog that they called by a rotating series of names. The wanderers who passed through the ranch that summer, crashing for a day or two before leaving. Denizens of the brainless dream, appearing at all hours of the day with woven backpacks and their parents' cars. I didn't see anything familiar in how quickly Russell talked them out of their possessions, put them on the spot so their generosity became a forced theater. They handed over pink slips to cars, bankbooks, once even a gold wedding ring, with the stunned and exhausted relief of a drowning person finally giving in to the tidal suck. I was distracted by their tales of sorrow, both harrowing and banal. Complaints of evil fathers and cruel mothers, a similarity to the stories that made us all feel like victims of the same conspiracy.

It was one of the few days it rained that summer, and most of us were indoors, the old parlor smelling damp and gray like the air outside. Blankets gridded the floor. I could hear a baseball game on the radio in the kitchen, rain dropping into the plastic bucket under a leak. Roos was giving Suzanne a hand massage, their fingers slick with lotion, while I read a years-old magazine. My horoscope from March 1967. An irritated sulk hung between us; we were not used to limitations, to being stuck anywhere.

The kids did better at being indoors. They passed only briefly through our watch, trundling by on their private missions. There was the bang of a fallen chair in the other room, but no one got up to investigate. Besides Nico, I didn't know who most of the other kids belonged to—all of them were thin wristed, like they'd gone to seed, powdered milk glazed around their mouths. I'd watched Nico for Roos a few times, had held him in my arms and felt his sweaty, pleasing weight. I combed his hair with my fingers, untangled his shark-tooth necklace. All those self-consciously maternal tasks, tasks that pleased me more than him and allowed me to imagine I alone had the power to make him calm. Nico was uncooperative with these moments of softness, breaking the spell bluntly, like he'd sensed my good feelings and resented them. Tugging his little penis at me. Demanding juice in a shrieking falsetto. Once hitting me so hard that I bruised. I watched him squat and take a shit out on the concrete by the pool, shits we'd sometimes hose away and sometimes not.

Helen wandered downstairs in a Snoopy T-shirt and too-big socks, the red heels bunched around her ankles.

"Anyone wanna play Liar's Dice?"

"Nah," Suzanne announced. For all of us, it was assumed.

Helen slumped onto a balding armchair stripped of cushions. She glanced at the ceiling. "Still leaking," she said. Everyone ignored her. "Can someone roll a joint?" she said. "Please?"

When no one answered, she joined Roos and Suzanne on the floor. "Please, please, please?" she said, nuzzling her head into Roos's shoulder, draping herself in her lap like a dog.

"Oh, just do it," Suzanne said. Helen jumped up to get the fake ivory box they kept the supplies in, while Suzanne rolled her eyes at me. I smiled back. It wasn't so bad, I thought, being inside. All of us huddled in the same room like Red Cross survivors, water boiling on the stove for tea. Roos working by the window, where the light was alabaster through the scrappy lace curtain.

The calm was cut by Nico's sudden whine, stampeding into the room as he chased a little girl with a bowl cut—she had Nico's shark-tooth necklace, and a yelping scrabble broke out between them. Tears, clawing.

"Hey," Suzanne said without looking up, and the kids got quiet, though they kept staring hotly at each other. Breathing hard, like drunks. Everything seemed fine, quickly handled, until Nico scratched the girl's face, raking her with his overgrown nails, and the screaming doubled. The girl clapped both hands over her cheek, wailing so her baby teeth showed. Sustaining a high note of misery.

Roos got to her feet with effort.

"Baby," she said, holding her arms out, "baby, you gotta be nice." She took a few steps toward Nico, who started screaming, too, sitting down heavy on his diaper. "Get up," Roos said, "come on, baby," trying to hold on to his shoulders, but he'd gone limp and wouldn't be moved. The other girl sobered in the face of Nico's antics, how he wrenched away from his mother and started banging his head against the floor. "Baby," Roos said, droning louder, "no, no, no," but he kept going, his eyes getting dark and buttony with pleasure.

"God." Helen laughed, a strange laugh that persisted. I didn't know what to do. I remembered the helpless panic I'd sometimes felt when babysitting, a realization that this child did not belong to me and was beyond my reach; but even Roos seemed paralyzed with the same worry. Like she was waiting for Nico's real mother to come home and fix everything. Nico was getting pink with effort, his skull knocking on the floor. Yelling until he heard the footsteps on the porch—it was Russell, and I saw everyone's faces condense with new life.

"What's this?" Russell said. He was wearing one of Mitch's cast-off shirts, big bloody roses embroidered along the yoke. He was barefoot, wet all over from the rain.

"Ask Roos," Helen chirped. "It's her kid."

Roos muttered something, her words going wild at the end, but Russell didn't respond on her level. His voice was calm, seeming to draw a circle around the crying child, the flustered mother.

"Relax," Russell intoned. He wouldn't let anyone's upset in, the jitter in the room deflected by his gaze. Even Nico looked wary in Russell's presence, his tantrum taking on a hollow cast, like he was an understudy for himself.

"Little man," Russell said, "come on up here and talk to me."

Nico glared at his mother, but his eyes were drawn, helpless, to Russell. Nico pushed out his fat bottom lip, calculating.

Russell stayed standing in the doorway, not bending down eager and wet toothed like some grown-ups did with kids, and Nico was mostly quiet, settling into a whimper. Darting another look between his mother and Russell before finally scurrying over to Russell and letting himself be picked up.

"There's the little man," Russell said, Nico's arms clinging tight around his neck, and I remember how strange it was to see Russell's face change as he talked to the boy. His features mutable, turning antic and foolish, like a jester's, though his voice stayed calm. He could do that. Change himself to fit the person, like water taking on the shape of whatever vessel it was poured into. He could be all these things at once: The man who crooked his fingers in me. The man who got everything free. The man who sometimes fucked Suzanne hard and sometimes fucked her gently. The man who whispered to the little boy, his voice grazing his ear.

I couldn't hear what Russell said, but Nico swallowed his crying. His face was thrilled and wet: he seemed happy just to be in someone's arms.

Helen's eleven-year-old cousin Caroline ran away from home and stayed for a while. She'd been living in the Haight, but there had been a police crackdown: she'd hitched to the ranch with a cowhide wallet and a ratty fox fur coat she petted with skittish affection, like she didn't want anyone to see how much she loved it.

The ranch wasn't that far from San Francisco, but we didn't go there very often. I'd gone only once with Suzanne, to pick up a pound of grass from a house she called, jokingly, the Russian Embassy. Some friends of Guy's, I think, the old Satanist hangout. The front door was painted a tarry black—she saw my hesitation and hooked her arm through mine.

"Doomy, huh?" she said. "I thought so too, at first."

When she hitched me closer, I felt the knock of her hipbones. These moments of kindness were never anything but dazzling to me.

Afterward, she and I walked over to Hippie Hill. It was grayed-out, and drizzling, empty, except for the undead stumbling of junkies. I tried hard to squeeze out a vibe from the air, but there was nothing—I was relieved when Suzanne laughed, too, halting any labor for meaning. "Jesus," she said, "this place is a dump." We ended up

back in the park, the fog dripping audibly from the eucalyptus leaves.

I spent almost every day at the ranch, except for brief
stopovers at my house to change clothes or leave notes on
the kitchen table for my mother. Notes that I'd sign,
"Your Loving Daughter." Indulging the overblown affection my absence made room for.

I knew I was starting to look different, the weeks at
the ranch working me over with a grubby wash. My hair
getting light from the sun and sharp at the edges, a tint
of smoke lingering even after I shampooed. Much of my
clothes had passed into the ranch possession, morphing
into garments I often failed to recognize as my own:
Helen clowning around in my once precious bib shirt,
now torn and spotted with peach juice. I dressed like Suzanne, a raunchy patchwork culled from the communal
piles, clothes whose scrappiness announced a hostility to
the larger world. I had gone with Suzanne to the Home
Market once, Suzanne wearing a bikini top and cutoffs,
and we'd watched the other shoppers glare and grow hot
with indignation, their sideways glances becoming out-
right stares. We'd laughed with insane, helpless snorts,
like we'd had some wild secret, and we had. The woman
who'd seemed about to cry with baffled disgust, clutching
for her daughter's arm: she hadn't known her hatred only
made us more powerful.

I prepared for possible sightings of my mother with
pious ablutions: I showered, standing in the hot water until

my skin splotched red, my hair slippery with conditioner. I put on a plain T-shirt and white cotton shorts, what I might have worn when I was younger, trying to appear scrubbed and sexless enough to comfort my mother. Though maybe I didn't need to try so hard—she wasn't looking closely enough to warrant the effort. The times we did have dinner together, a mostly silent affair, she would fuss at her food like a picky child. Inventing reasons to talk about Frank, inane weather reports from her own life. I could have been anyone. One night I didn't bother to change, showing up at the table in a voile halter top that showed my stomach. She didn't say anything, plowing her spoon through her rice with a distracted air until she seemed suddenly to remember my presence. Darting a slanted look at me. "You're getting so skinny," she announced, gripping my wrist and letting it drop in jealous measurement. I shrugged and she didn't bring it up again.

When I finally met him in person, Mitch Lewis was fatter than I expected someone famous to be. Swollen, like there was butter under his skin. His face was furred with sideburns, his feathered golden hair. He brought a case of root beer for the girls and six netted bags of oranges. Stale brownies with German-chocolate frosting, in individual frilled cups like Pilgrims' bonnets. Nougat candy in bright pink tins. The dregs of gift baskets, I assumed. A carton of cigarettes.

"He knows I like this kind," Suzanne said, hugging the cigarettes to her chest. "He remembered."

They all spoke of Mitch with that possessiveness, like he was an idea more than an actual person. They'd preened and prepared for Mitch's visit with girlish eagerness.

"You can see the ocean from his hot tub," Suzanne told me. "Mitch put lights up so the water is all glowy."

"His dick is really big," Donna added. "And like, purple."

Donna was washing her armpits in the sink, and Suzanne rolled her eyes. "Whore's bath," she murmured, but she'd changed into a dress. Even Russell slicked back his hair with water, giving him a polished, urbane air.

Russell introduced me to Mitch, saying, "Our little actress," his hand at my back.

Mitch studied me with a questioning, smug smile. Men did it so easily, that immediate parceling of value. And how they seemed to want you to collude on your own judgment.

"I'm Mitch," he said. As if I hadn't already known. His skin was fresh looking and poreless in the way of wealthy overeaters.

"Give Mitch a hug," Russell said. Nudging me. "Mitch wants a hug, just like the rest of us. He could use a little love."

Mitch looked expectant, opening a present he'd already shaken and identified. Usually, I would have been eaten by shyness. Conscious of my body, some error I could make. But already I felt different. I was one of them, and that meant I could smile back at Mitch, stepping forward to let him mash himself against me.

The long afternoon that followed: Mitch and Russell took turns playing guitar. Helen sitting on Mitch's lap in a bikini top. She kept giggling and ducking her pigtailed head into his neck. Mitch was a much better musician than Russell, but I tried not to notice. I got stoned with a new and furious concentration, passing beyond the point of nervousness and into a blunted state. Smiling almost involuntarily, so my cheeks started to ache. Suzanne sat cross-legged in the dirt beside me, her fingers grazing mine. Our faces cupped and attentive as tulips.

It was one of those slurry days we offered up to the shared dream, a violence in our aversion to real life; though it was all about connecting, tuning in, we told ourselves. Mitch had dropped off some acid, sourced from a lab tech at Stanford. Donna mixed it with orange juice in paper cups and we drank it for breakfast, so the trees seemed to thrum with energy, the shadows purpling and wet. It was curious, later, to think of how easily I fell into things. If there were drugs around, I did them. You were in the moment—when everything back then happened. We could talk about *the moment* for hours. Turn it over in conversation: the way the light moved, why someone was silent, dismantling all the layers of what a look had really meant. It seemed like something important, our desire to describe the shape of each second as it passed, to bring out everything hidden and beat it to death.

Suzanne and I were working on the childish bracelets the girls had been trading among ourselves, collecting them up our arms like middle-schoolers. Practicing the V stitch. The candy stripe. I was making one for Suzanne, fat and wide, a poppy-red chevron on a field of peach thread. I liked the calm collection of the knots, how the colors vibrated happily under my fingers. I got up once to get Suzanne a glass of water, and there was a domestic gentleness in that act. I wanted to meet a need, put water in her mouth. Suzanne smiled up at me as she drank, gulping so fast I could see her throat ripple.

Helen's cousin Caroline was hanging around that day. She seemed more knowing than I had ever been at eleven. Her bracelets shook with the kiss of cheap metal. Her terry-cloth shirt was the pale yellow of a lemon slushie and showed her small stomach, though her knees were scraped and ashy like a boy's.

"Far-out," she said when Guy tipped a paper cup of juice to her lips, and like a windup toy, she kept repeating this phrase when the acid began to hit. I'd started to detect the first signs in myself, too, my mouth filling with saliva. I thought of the flooded creeks I'd seen in childhood, the death cold of the rainwater as it came swift over the rocks.

I could hear Guy spinning nonsense on the porch. One of his meaningless stories, the drug making his bluster echo. His long hair pulled into a dark knot at the base of his skull.

"This fella was banging on the door," he was saying, "shouting that he'd come to take what was his, and I was like aw, hell, big fuckin' deal," he droned, "I'm Elvis Presley," and Roos was nodding along. Squinting up at the sun while Country Joe sounded from the house. Clouds drifting across the blue, outlined in neon.

"Check out Orphan Annie," Suzanne said, rolling her eyes at Caroline.

Caroline was overdoing it at first, her stumbling, dopey affect, but soon the drug actually caught up to her and she got wild-eyed and a little scared. She was thin enough that I could see the glandular throb at her throat. Suzanne was watching her, too, and I waited for her to say something, but she didn't. Helen, Caroline's supposed cousin, didn't say anything, either. She was sunstruck, catatonic, stretched out on a piece of old carpet and listing a hand over her eyes. Giggling to no one. I went over to Caroline finally, touching her tiny shoulder.

"How's it going?" I said.

She didn't look up until I said her name. I asked her where she was from; she screwed her eyes tight. It was the wrong thing to say—of course it was, bringing up all that bad shit from the outside, whatever rotten memories were probably doubling right then. I didn't know how to pull her back from the bog.

"You want this?" I said, holding up the bracelet. She peeked at it. "Just have to finish it," I said, "but it's for you."

Caroline smiled.

"It's gonna look real nice on you," I went on. "It'll go good with your shirt."

The electricity in her eyes calmed. She held her own shirt away from her body to study it, softening.

"I made it," she said, fingering the embroidered outline of a peace sign on the shirt, and I saw the hours she'd spent on it, maybe borrowing her mother's sewing box. It seemed easy: to be kind to her, to put the finished bracelet around her wrist, burning the knot with a match so she'd have to cut it off. I didn't notice Suzanne eyeing us, her own bracelet ignored in her lap.

"Beautiful," I said, lifting Caroline's wrist. "Nothing but beauty."

As if I were an occupant of that world, someone who could show the way to others. Such grandiosity mixed up in my feelings of kindness; I was starting to fill in all the blank spaces in myself with the certainties of the ranch. The cool glut of Russell's words—no more ego, turn off the mind. Pick up the cosmic wind instead. Our beliefs as mild and digestible as the sweet rolls and cakes we hustled from a bakery in Sausalito, stuffing our faces with the easy starch.

In the days after, Caroline followed me like a stray dog. Hovering, in the doorway of Suzanne's room, asking if I wanted one of the cigarettes she'd cadged from the bikers. Suzanne stood up and clasped her elbows behind her back, stretching.

"They just gave you them?" Suzanne said archly. "For free?"

Caroline glanced at me. "The cigarettes?"

Suzanne laughed without saying anything else. I was confused, in these moments, but translated them into further proof: Suzanne was prickly with other people because they didn't understand her like I did.

I didn't say it out loud to myself or even think about it too much. Where things were heading with Suzanne. The dredge of discomfort I got when she disappeared with Russell. How I didn't know what to do without her, seeking out Donna or Roos like a lost kid. The time she came back smelling of dried sweat and roughly wiped herself between the legs with a washcloth, like she didn't care I was watching.

I got up when I saw how nervously Caroline fingered the bracelet I'd given her.

"I'll take a cigarette," I said, smiling at Caroline.

Suzanne hooked her arm in mine.

"But we're gonna feed the llamas," Suzanne said. "Don't want them to starve, do you? Waste away?"

I hesitated, and Suzanne reached out to play with a part of my hair. She was always doing that: picking burrs off my shirt, once wedging a fingernail between my front teeth to dislodge a bit of food. Breaching the boundaries to let me know they didn't exist.

Caroline's desire to be invited was so blatant that I felt almost ashamed. But it didn't stop me from following Suzanne outside, shrugging an apology at Caroline. I could feel her watching us go. The hooded attentions of a child, that wordless understanding. I saw that disappointment was already something familiar to Caroline.

I was scanning the contents of my mother's refrigerator, the glass jars mortared with dried spills. The fumes of cruciferous vegetables, roiling in plastic bags. Nothing to eat, as usual. Little things like this reminded me why I'd rather be somewhere else. When I heard my mother shuffling in the front door, the razzle of her heavy jewelry, I tried to slink off without crossing paths.

"Evie," she called, coming into the kitchen. "Wait up a minute."

I was out of breath from the bike ride from the ranch and at the tail end of being stoned. I tried to blink an ordinary number of times, to present a blank face that would give her nothing.

"You're getting so tan," she said, lifting my arm, and I shrugged. She idly brushed the hair on my arm back and forth, then paused. There was an uncomfortable moment between us. It occurred to me: she'd finally caught on to the trickle of money that had been disappearing. The thought of her anger didn't scare me. The act had been so preposterous that it took on the safety of the unreal. I'd almost started to believe that I had never really lived here, so strong was the feeling of disassociation as I crept through the house on my errands for Suzanne. My excavation of my mother's underwear drawer, sifting through the tea-colored silks and pilly lace until I closed in on a roll of bills banded with a hair tie.

My mother furrowed her brows. "Listen," she said. "Sal saw you out on Adobe Road this morning. Alone."

I tried to keep my face blank, but I was relieved—it was just one of Sal's bovine observations. I'd been telling my mother I'd been at Connie's house. And I was still home some nights, trying to keep the balance in check.

"Sal said there's some very strange people out there," my mother said. "Some kind of mystic or something, but he sounds"—her face screwed up.

Of course—she would love Russell if he lived in a mansion in Marin, had gardenias floating in his pool, and charged rich women fifty dollars for an astrology reading. How transparent she seemed to me then, always on constant guard against anything lesser than, even as she opened the house up to anyone who smiled at her. To Frank and his shiny-buttoned shirts.

"I've never met him," I said, my voice impassive. So my mother would know I was lying. The fact of the lie hovered there, and I watched her till for a response.

"I just wanted to warn you," she said. "So you know that this guy is out there. I expect you and Connie to take care of each other, understand?"

I could see how badly she wanted to avoid a fight, how she strained for this middle ground. She'd warned me, so she had done what she was supposed to do. It meant she was still my mother. Let her feel this was true—I nodded and she relaxed. My mother's hair was growing out. She was wearing a new tank top with knit straps, and the skin of her shoulders was loose, showing a tan line from a swimsuit—I had no idea when or where my mother had been swimming. How quickly we'd become strangers to each other, like nervous roommates encountering each other in the halls.

"Well," she said.

I saw, for a moment, my old mother, the cast of weary love in her face, but it disappeared when her bracelets made a tinny sound, falling down her arms.

"There's rice and miso in the fridge," she said, and I made a noise in my throat like I might eat it, but we both knew I wouldn't.

8

The police photos of Mitch's house make it look cramped and spooky, as if destined for its fate. The fat splintered beams along the ceiling, the stone fireplace, its many levels and hallways, like something in the Escher lithographs Mitch collected from a gallery in Sausalito. The first time I encountered the house, I remember thinking it was as spare and empty as a coastal church. There was very little furniture, the big windows in the shape of chevrons. Herringbone floors, wide and shallow steps. From the front door, you could already see the black plane of bay spreading past the house, the dark, rocky bank. The houseboats knocking peaceably against each other, like cubes of ice.

Mitch poured us drinks while Suzanne opened his refrigerator. Humming a little song as she peered at the shelves. Making noises of approval or disapproval, lifting tinfoil off a bowl to sniff at something. I was in awe of her at moments like that. How boldly she acted in the world, in someone else's house, and I watched our reflections wavering in the black windows, our hair loose on our shoulders. Here I was, in this famous man's kitchen. The man whose music I'd heard on the radio. The bay out the door, shining like patent leather. And how glad I was to be there with Suzanne, who seemed to call these things into being.

Mitch had a meeting with Russell earlier that afternoon— I remember noticing it was strange that Mitch had been late for it. Two o'clock had passed, and we were still waiting for Mitch. I was silent, like they all were, the quiet between us expanding. A horsefly bit at my ankle. I didn't want to shoo it away, conscious of Russell a few feet away, perched on his chair with his eyes closed. I could hear him humming under his breath. Russell had decided it would be best for Mitch to come upon him sitting there, his girls surrounding him, Guy at his side, the troubadour with his audience. He was ready to perform, guitar laid across his knees. His bare foot jiggling.

There was something in the way Russell was fingering the guitar, pressing silently on the strings—he was nervous in a way I didn't know how to decipher yet. Russell didn't look up when Helen started whispering to

Donna, just a low whisper. Something about Mitch, prob-ably, or some stupid thing Guy had said, but when Helen kept talking, Russell got to his feet. He took a moment to lay the guitar against his chair, pausing to make certain it was stable, then walked over swiftly and slapped Helen in the face.

She gave an involuntary yip, a strange burble of sound. Her wide-eyed hurt draining quickly into apology, blink-ing fast so the tears wouldn't fall.

It was the first time I had ever seen Russell react that way, the cut of anger aimed at one of us. He couldn't have hit her—the stupid blare of sun made that impossible, the hour of afternoon. The idea was too ludicrous. I looked around for confirmation of the frightening breach, but everyone was staring pointedly away or had arranged their faces into disapproving masks, like Helen had brought this on herself. Guy scratched behind an ear, sighing. Even Suzanne seemed bored by what had hap-pened, like it was no different from a handshake. The vin-egar in my throat, my sudden, despairing shock, seemed like a failing.

And soon enough, Russell was petting Helen's hair, tightening her lopsided pigtails. Whispering something in her ear that made her smile and nod, like a goopy-eyed baby doll.

When Mitch finally showed up at the ranch, an hour late, he was bearing much-needed supplies: a cardboard flat of canned beans, some dried figs, and chocolate spread. Rock-hard Packham pears, individually wrapped in pink tissue paper. He let the kids clamber up his legs, though normally he shook them off.

"Hi, Russell," Mitch said. A lace of sweat on his face.

"Long time no see, brother," Russell said. He kept his grin steady, though he didn't get up from his chair. "How goes the Great American Dream?"

"Things are good, man," he said. "Sorry I'm late."

"Haven't heard from you in a while," Russell said. "Breaking my heart, Mitch."

"Been busy," Mitch said. "A lot going on."

"There's always a lot going on," Russell said. Looking around at us, making long eye contact with Guy. "Don't you think? Seems like there's a lot going on and that's what life is. Think it only stops when you die."

Mitch laughed, like everything was fine. Passing out the cigarettes he'd brought, the food, like a sweating Santa. The books would identify this as the day things turned between Russell and Mitch, though I didn't know any of this at the time. Didn't pick up on any meaning in the tension between them, Russell's fury muffled by a calm, indulgent exterior. Mitch had come to give Russell the bad news that there would be no record deal for Russell, after all: the cigarettes, the food, all of it meant as a consolation. Russell had been hounding Mitch for weeks about the supposed record deal. Pushing and pushing, wearing Mitch down. Sending Guy to deliver cryptic messages to Mitch that could oscillate between threatening and benign. Russell was trying to get what he believed he deserved.

We smoked some grass. Donna made peanut-butter sandwiches. I sat in the circle of shade cast by an oak. Nico was running around with one of the other kids, chins crusted with remnants of breakfast. He snapped a stick at a bag of trash, the garbage spilling everywhere—nobody noticed but me. Guy's dog was out in the meadow, the llamas high-stepping in agitation. I was stealing looks at Helen, who seemed, if anything, insistently happy, like the exchange with Russell fulfilled a comforting pattern.

The slap should have been more alarming. I wanted Russell to be kind, so he was. I wanted to be near Suzanne, so I believed the things that allowed me to stay there. I told myself there were things I didn't understand. I recycled the words I'd heard Russell speak before, fashioned them into an explanation. Sometimes he had to punish us in order to show his love. He hadn't wanted to do it, but he had to keep us moving forward, for the good of the group. It had hurt him, too.

Nico and the other kid had abandoned the trash pile, squatting in the grass with their heavy diapers sagging. They spoke rapidly to each other in serious Asiatic voices, with sober, rational inflection, like the conversation of two little sages. Breaking into sudden hysterical laughter.

. . .

It was late in the day. We drank the dirty wine they sold by the gallon in town, sediment staining our tongues, a nauseous heat. Mitch had gotten to his feet, ready to head home.

"Why don't you go with Mitch?" Russell suggested. Squeezing my hand in submerged code.

Had a look passed between him and Mitch? Or maybe I am imagining that I witnessed that exchange. The logistics of the day were shrouded in confusion, so that somehow it was dusk and Suzanne and I were driving Mitch back to his house, hurtling along the back roads of Marin in his car.

Mitch was sitting in the backseat, Suzanne driving. I was up front. I kept catching sight of Mitch in the mirror, lost in an aimless fog. Then he'd jolt back into himself, staring at us with wonderment. I didn't fully understand why we'd been chosen to take Mitch home. Information passed through selectively, so all I knew was that I got to be with Suzanne. All the windows open to the smell of summer earth and the secret flash of other driveways, other lives, along that narrow road in the shadow of Mount Tam. The loops of garden hoses, the pretty magnolia. Suzanne drove in the wrong lane sometimes, and we shrieked with happy and confused terror, though there was a flatness to my yelling: I did not believe anything bad could ever happen, not really.

. . .

Mitch changed into a white pajama-like suit, a souvenir from a three-week sojourn in Varanasi. He handed us each a glass—I caught the medical whiff of gin and something else, too, a tinge of bitterness. I drank it easily. I was almost pathologically stoned, and I kept swallowing, my nose getting stuffy. I laughed a little to myself. It seemed so odd to be in Mitch Lewis's house. Among his cluttered shrines and new-looking furniture.

"The Airplane lived here for a few months," he said. He blinked heavily. "With one of those dogs," he continued, staring around at his house. "The big white ones. What are they called? Newfoundlands? It tore up the lawn."

He didn't seem to care that we were ignoring him. He was out of it, glazing over with silence. Abruptly he got to his feet, putting a record on. Turning the volume up so loud I startled, but Suzanne laughed, urging him to make it louder. It was his own music, which embarrassed me. His heavy belly pressed against his long shirt, as flowing as a dress.

"You're fun girls," he said dimly. Watching Suzanne start to dance. Her dirty feet on the white carpet. She'd found chicken in the refrigerator and had torn off a piece with her fingers, chewing while she moved her hips.

"Kona chicken," Mitch remarked. "From Trader Vic's." The banality of this remark—Suzanne and I caught each other's eyes.

"What?" Mitch said. When we kept laughing, he did, too. "This is fun," he repeated over the music. He kept saying how much some actor he knew liked the song. "He really got it," he said. "Wouldn't stop playing it. Tuned-in guy."

It was new to me, that you could treat someone famous like they weren't that special, that you could see all the ways they were disappointing and regular or notice the way his kitchen smelled of trash that hadn't been taken out. The phantom squares on the wall where photographs had once hung, the gold records leaned against the baseboard, still wrapped in plastic. Suzanne acted like it was really only she and I that mattered, and this was all a little game we were playing with Mitch. He was the background to the larger story, which was our story, and we pitied him and felt grateful to him, at the same time, for how he sacrificed himself for our enjoyment.

Mitch had a little coke, and it was almost painful to watch him shake it out carefully onto a book about TM, staring at his own hands with a queer distance, like they didn't belong to him. He cut three lines, then peered at them. He fussed around until one was markedly bigger and snorted it quickly, breathing hard.

"Ahh," he said, leaning back, his throat raw and pricked with golden stubble. He held out the book to Suzanne, who danced over, sniffing up a line, and I did the last one.

The coke made me want to dance, so I did. Suzanne grabbing my hands, smiling at me. It was a strange moment: we were dancing for Mitch, but I was eaten up by her eyes, how she urged me on. She watched me move with pleasure.

Mitch was trying to talk, telling us some story about his girlfriend. How lonesome he'd been since she'd left for Marrakesh, on some tear about needing more space.

"Baloney," he kept saying. "Ah, baloney."

We were indulging him: I took my lead from Suzanne, who nodded when he spoke but rolled her eyes at me or loudly urged him to tell us more. He was talking about Linda that night, though her name meant nothing to me. I was barely listening: I'd picked up a small wooden box rattling with tiny silver balls and tipped it, trying to get the balls to drop into holes painted to look like the mouths of dragons.

Linda would be his ex-girlfriend by the time of the murders, only twenty-six, though that age seemed vague to me then, like a knock on a faraway door. Her son, Christopher, was five years old but had already been to ten countries, bundled along on his mother's travels like the pouch of her scarab jewelry. The ostrich-skin cowboy boots she stuffed with rolled-up magazines so they'd keep their shape. Linda was beautiful, though I'm sure her face would've grown bawdy or cheap. She slept in bed with her golden-haired little boy, like a teddy bear.

I was so lulled into feeling that the world had winnowed itself around Suzanne and me, that Mitch was just the comic fill—I didn't even consider other possibilities. I'd gone to the bathroom, used Mitch's strange black soap and peeked in his cabinet, loaded with bottles of Dilaudid.

The enamel shine of the bathtub, the cut of bleach in the air so I could tell he had a cleaning lady.

I had just finished peeing when someone opened the bathroom door without knocking. I was startled, reflexively trying to cover myself. I saw the man sliver a glance toward my exposed legs before he ducked back into the hallway.

"Apologies," I heard him say from the other side of the door. A chain of stuffed marigold birds swung gently from where they hung by the sink.

"My deepest apologies," the man said. "I was looking for Mitch. Sorry to bother you."

I sensed him hesitate on the other side of the door, then tap the wood lightly before he walked away. I pulled up my shorts. The adrenaline that spread through me lessened but didn't disappear. It was probably just a friend of Mitch's. I was jumpy from the coke, but I wasn't frightened. Which made sense: nobody thought until later that strangers might be anything but friends. Our love for one another boundless, the whole universe an extended crash pad.

I'd realize a few months after that this must have been Scotty Weschler. The caretaker who lived in the back house, a tiny white-paneled cabin with a hot plate and a space heater. The man who cleaned the hot tub filters and watered the lawn and checked that Mitch hadn't overdosed in the night. Prematurely balding, with wire glasses: Scotty had been a cadet at a military academy in Pennsylvania before dropping out, moving west. He never shook his cadet idealism: he wrote letters to his mother about the redwoods, the Pacific Ocean, using words like "majestic" and "grandeur."

He'd be the first. The one who tried to fight back, to run.

I wish I could squeeze more out of our brief encounter. To believe, when he opened the door, that I had felt a shiver of what was coming. But I'd made out nothing but the flash of a stranger, and I thought of it very little. I didn't even ask Suzanne who the man was.

The living room was empty when I came back. The music blaring, a cigarette leaching smoke in the ashtray. The glass door that led out to the bay was open. I was surprised by the suddenness of the water when I went out on the porch, the wall of woolly lights: San Francisco in the fog.

No one was out on the bank. Then I heard, over the water, a distorted echo. And there they were, both of them, splashing in the waves, the water foaming around their legs. Mitch flapping around in his white outfit, now like soggy bedsheets, Suzanne in the dress she called her Br'er Rabbit dress. My heart lurched—I wanted to join them. But something held me in place. I kept standing on the stairs that led to the sand, smelling the sea-softened wood. Did I know what was coming? I watched Suzanne shed her dress, shrugging it off with drunken difficulty, and then he was on her. His head lowering to lick at her bare breast. Both of them unsteady in the water. I watched for longer than seemed right. I was buzzy and adrift by the time I turned my back and wandered into the house.

I turned the music down. Shut the refrigerator door, which Suzanne had left open. The picked-over carcass of the chicken. Kona chicken, as Mitch had insisted: the sight made me a little nauseous. The too-pink flesh emanating a chill. I would always be like this, I thought, the person who closed the refrigerator. The person who watched from the steps like a spook while Suzanne let Mitch do whatever he wanted. Jealousy started to oscillate in my gut. The strange gnaw when I imagined his fingers inside her, how she'd taste of salt water. Confusion, too—how quickly things had changed and I was the one on the outside again.

The chemical pleasure in my head had already faded, so all I recognized anymore was the lack of it. I wasn't tired, but I didn't want to sit on the couch, waiting for them to come inside. I found an unlocked bedroom that looked like a guest room: no clothes in the closet, a bed with slightly mussed sheets. They smelled like someone else, and there was a single gold earring on the nightstand. I thought of my own home, the weight and feel of my own blankets—then a sudden desire to sleep at Connie's house. Curled up against her back in our familiar,

ritual arrangement, her sheets printed with chubby cartoon rainbows.

I lay in the bed, listening for the sound of Suzanne and
Mitch in the other room. Like I was Suzanne's thick-
necked boyfriend, the same ratchet of righteous anger. It
wasn't aimed at her, not exactly—I hated Mitch with a
fierceness that kept me wide-awake. I wanted him to
know how she'd been laughing at him earlier, to know the
exact degree of pity I had for him. How impotent my
anger was, a surge with no place to land, and how familiar that was: my feelings strangled inside me, like little
half-formed children, bitter and bristling.

I was almost certain, later, that this was the same bedroom that Linda and her little boy were sleeping in.
Though I know there were other bedrooms, other possibilities. Linda and Mitch were broken up by the night
of the murder, but they were still friends, Mitch deliver-
ing an oversize stuffed giraffe on Christopher's birthday
the week before. Linda was only staying at Mitch's because her apartment in the Sunset was crawling with
mold—she'd planned on being at his house for two
nights. Then she and Christopher would stay in Woodside with her boyfriend, a man who owned a series of
seafood restaurants.

After the murders, I had seen the man on a talk show:
face red, pressing a handkerchief to his eyes. I wondered
if his fingernails were manicured. He told the host he'd

been planning to propose to Linda. Though who knows if that was true.

Around three in the morning, there was a knock on my door. It was Suzanne, stumbling inside without waiting for an answer. She was naked, bringing a gusty smell of brine and cigarette smoke.

"Hi," she said, pulling at my blankets.

I'd been half-asleep, lulled by the sameness of the dark ceiling, and she was like a creature from a dream, storming into the room, smelling as she did. The sheets getting damp when she crawled in beside me. I believed she had come for me. To be with me, a gesture of apology. But how quickly that thought disappeared when I took in her urgency, her stoned, glassy focus—I knew this was for him.

"Come on," Suzanne said, and laughed. Her face new in the strange blue light. "It's beautiful," she said, "you'll see. He's gentle."

Like that was the most you could hope for. I sat back, grabbing the covers.

"Mitch is a creep," I said. It was clear to me that we were in a stranger's house. The oversize, empty guest room, with its unsavory off-gassing of other bodies.

"Evie," she said. "Don't be like that."

Her nearness, the dart of her eyes in the dark. How easily she pressed her mouth to mine, then, edging her tongue past my lips. Running the tip along the ridges of my teeth, smiling into my mouth, and saying something I couldn't hear.

I could taste the cocaine drip in her mouth, the brackish sea. I went to kiss her again, but she had already drifted away, smiling like this was a game, like we'd done something funny and unreal. Playing lightly with my hair.

I was happy to twist the meanings, willfully misread the symbols. Doing what Suzanne asked seemed like the best gift I could give her, a way to unlock her own reciprocal feelings. And she was trapped, in her way, just like I was, but I never saw that, shifting easily in the directions she prompted for me. Like the wooden toy, clattering with the silver ball I'd tilted and urged into the painted holes, trying for the winning drop.

Mitch's room was big, and the tile floor was cold. The bed was on a raised platform, carved with Balinese figures. He grinned when he saw me behind Suzanne, showing a quick flash of teeth, and opened his arms to us, his bare chest foaming with hair. Suzanne went right to him, but I sat on the edge of the bed, hands folded in my lap. Mitch raised up on his elbows.

"No," he said, patting the mattress. "Here. Come here."

I scooted over to lie beside him. I could feel Suzanne's impatience, how she sidled to him like a dog.

"I don't want you yet," Mitch said to her. I couldn't see Suzanne's face, but I could imagine the swift hurt.

"Can you take these off?" Mitch tapped at my underwear with his hand.

I was ashamed: they were full-seated and childish, the elastic limp. I lowered them down my hips until they were around my knees.

"Oh God," Mitch said, sitting up. "Can you open your legs a little?"

I did. He crouched over me. I could feel his face close to my childish mound. His snout had the wet heat of an animal.

"I'm not going to touch you," Mitch said, and I knew he was lying. "Jesus," he breathed. He gestured Suzanne over. Murmuring low, placing us like dolls. Announcing fussy asides to no one in particular. Suzanne looked to me like a stranger in that strange room, like the part of her I recognized had retreated.

He sucked my tongue into his mouth. I could stay still, mostly, while Mitch kissed me, and accept his probing tongue with a hollow distance, even his fingers inside me like something curious and without meaning. Mitch lifted himself and pushed inside me, groaning a little when it was difficult. He spit on his hand and rubbed me, then tried again, and how sudden it was, his jacking between my legs, and how I kept thinking to myself with some surprise and disbelief that it was actually happening, and then I felt Suzanne's hand snake over and grab mine.

Maybe Mitch nudged Suzanne in my direction, but I didn't see. When Suzanne kissed me again, I was lulled into thinking she was doing it for me, that this was our way to be together. That Mitch was just the background noise, the necessary excuse that allowed for her eager mouth, the curl of her fingers. I could smell myself and smell her, too. A sound deep in her throat that I believed was meant for me, as if her pleasure were at some pitch Mitch couldn't hear. She moved my hand to her breast, shivering when I touched the nipple. Closing her eyes like I had done something good.

Mitch rolled off me in order to watch. Kneading the wet head of his dick, the mattress slanting toward his weight.

I kept kissing Suzanne, so different from kissing a man. Their forceful mash getting across the idea of a kiss, but not this articulation. I pretended Mitch wasn't there, though I could feel his gaze, his mouth as slack as the open trunk of a car. I was skittish when Suzanne tried to push apart my legs, but she smiled up at me, so I let her. Her tongue was tentative, first, then she used her fingers, too, and I was embarrassed at how wet I was, the noises I made. My mind fritzing from a pleasure so foreign I didn't know how to name it.

Mitch fucked us both after that, like he could correct our obvious preference for each other. Sweating hard, his eyes crimping with effort. The bed moving away from the wall.

When I woke up in the morning and saw the soiled twist of my underwear on Mitch's tile floor, such helpless embarrassment bubbled up in me that I almost cried.

...

Mitch drove us back to the ranch. I was silent, looking out the windows. The passing houses seemed long dormant, the fancy cars shrouded in their putty-colored covers. Suzanne was sitting in the front. She turned around to smile at me from time to time. An apology, I could tell, but I was stone-faced, my heart a tight fist. A grief that I didn't fully indulge.

I was shoring up the bad feelings, I suppose, like I could preempt sorrow with my bravado, with the careless way I thought about Suzanne to myself. And I'd had sex: so what? It was no big deal, another working of the human body. Like eating, something rote and accessible to everyone. All the pious and pastel urgings to wait, to make yourself into a present for your future husband: there was relief in the plainness of the actual act. I watched Suzanne from the backseat, watched her laugh at something Mitch said and roll down the window. Her hair lifting in the rush.

Mitch pulled up at the ranch.

"Later, girls," he said, raising a pink palm. Like he'd taken us for ice cream, some innocent outing, and was returning us to the cradle of our parents' house.

Suzanne had gone immediately in search of Russell, cleaving from me without a word. I realized later that she must have been giving Russell a report. Letting him know how Mitch had seemed, whether we'd made him happy enough to change his mind. At the time, I only noticed the abandonment.

I tried to busy myself, peeling garlic in the kitchen with Donna. Smashing cloves between the flat blade of a knife and the counter like she showed me. Donna slid the radio knob from one end of the dial to the other and back, getting varying degrees of static and alarming strains of Herb Alpert. She gave up finally and returned to jabbing at a mess of black dough.

"Roos put Vaseline in my hair," Donna said. She gave a shake and her hair barely moved. "It's gonna be real soft when I wash it."

I didn't answer. Donna could tell I was distracted and catted her eyes over at me.

"Did he show you the fountain in the backyard?" she said. "He got it from Rome. Mitch's place has high vibes," she went on, "all the ions, 'cause of the ocean."

I reddened, trying to concentrate on separating the garlic from its woody husks. The buzz of the radio suddenly seemed nasty, polluting, the announcer talking too fast. They'd all been there, I understood, to Mitch's strange house by the sea. I'd enacted some pattern, been defined, neatly, as a girl, providing a known value. There was something almost comforting about it, the clarity of purpose, even as it shamed me. I didn't understand that you could hope for more.

I hadn't seen the fountain. I did not say so.

Donna's eyes were bright.

"You know," she said, "Suzanne's parents are actually real rich. Propane or something. She never was homeless or anything, either." She was working the dough on the counter as she spoke. "Didn't end up in any hospital. Any of that shit she says. Just scratched herself up with a paper clip, on some freaky jag."

I was queasy from the stench of food scraps softening in the sink. I shrugged like I didn't much care either way.

Donna went on. "You don't believe me," she said. "But it's true. We were up in Mendocino. Crashing with an apple farmer. She'd done too much acid, just started working away at herself with that clip until we made her quit. She didn't even bleed, though."

When I didn't respond, Donna slammed the dough into a bowl. Punching it down. "Think whatever you want," she said.

Suzanne came into her bedroom later, while I was changing. I hunched myself protectively over my naked chest: Suzanne noticed and seemed ready to mock me but stopped herself. I saw the scars on her wrist but didn't indulge the uneasy questions—Donna was just jealous. Never mind Donna and her stiff Vaseline hair, shanky and foul as a muskrat's.

"Last night was a trip," Suzanne said.

I pulled away when she tried to sling her arm around me.

"Oh, come on, you were into it," she said. "I saw."

I made a sick face—she laughed. I occupied myself with tidying the sheets, as if the bed could ever be anything but a dank nest.

"Aw, it's fine," Suzanne said. "I got something to cheer you up."

I thought she was going to apologize. But then it occurred to me—she was going to kiss me again. The dim room got airless. I almost felt it happen, an imperceptible lean—but Suzanne just hefted her bag onto the bed, the fringe pooling on the mattress. The bag was full of a strange weight. She gave me a triumphant look.

"Go on," she said. "Look inside."

Suzanne huffed at my stubbornness and opened it herself. I didn't understand what was inside, the odd metallic flash. The sharp corners.

"Take it out," Suzanne said, impatient.

It was a gold record framed in glass, much heavier than expected.

She nudged me. "We got him, huh?"

Her expectant look—was this meant to explain something? I stared at the name, engraved on a small plaque: Mitch Lewis. The *Sun King* album.

Suzanne started laughing.

"Man, you should see your face right now," she said. "Don't you know I'm on your side?"

The record glinted dully in the dark room, but even its pretty Egyptian gleam failed to stir me—it was just an artifact of that strange house, nothing so valuable. Already the weight was making my arms tired.

9

The clatter on the porch startled me, followed by the sound of my mother's dissolving laughter, Frank's heavy steps. I was in the living room, stretched out in my grandfather's chair and reading one of my mother's *McCall's*. Its pictures of genitally slick hams, wreathed with pineapple. Lauren Hutton lounging on a rocky cliff in her Bali brassieres. My mother and Frank were loud, coming into the living room, but stopped talking when they caught sight of me. Frank in his cowboy boots, my mother swallowing whatever she'd been saying.

"Sweetheart." Her eyes were filmy, her body swaying just enough so I knew she was drunk and trying to hide it, though her pink neck—exposed in a chiffon shirt—would have given it away.

"Hi," I said.

"Whatcha doing home, sweetheart?" My mother came over to wrap her arms around me, and I let her, despite the metallic smell of alcohol on her, the wilt of her perfume. "Is Connie sick?"

"Nah." I shrugged. Turning back to my magazine. The next page: a girl in a butter-yellow tunic, kneeling on a white box. An advertisement for Moon Drops.

"You're usually in and out so quick," she said.

"I just felt like being home," I said. "Isn't it my house, too?"

My mother smiled, smoothing my hair. "Such a pretty girl, aren't you? Of course it's your house. Isn't she a pretty girl?" she said, turning to Frank. "Such a pretty girl," she repeated to no one.

Frank smiled back but seemed restless. I hated that unwilling knowledge, how I'd started to notice each tiny shift of power and control, the feints and jabs. Why couldn't relationships be reciprocal, both people steadily accruing interest at the same rate? I snapped the magazine shut.

"Good night," I said. I didn't want to imagine what would happen later, Frank's hands in the chiffon. My mother aware enough to turn out the lights, eager for the forgiving dark.

These were the fantasies I goaded: that by leaving the ranch for a while, I could provoke Suzanne's sudden appearance, her demand that I return to her. The loneliness I could gorge myself on, like the saltines I ate by the sleeve, relishing the cut of sodium in my mouth. When I watched *Bewitched*, I had new irritation for Samantha. Her priggish nose, how she made a fool of her husband. The desperation of his doltish love turning him into the punch line. I paused one night to study the studio photo of my grandmother that hung in the hall, her shellacked cap of curls. She was pretty, awash in health. Only her eyes were sleepy, as if just woken from flowery dreams. The realization was bracing—we looked nothing alike.

I smoked a little bit of grass out the window, then fingered myself to tiredness, reading a comic book or a magazine, it didn't matter which. It was just the form of bodies, my brain let loose on them. I could look at an advertisement for a Dodge Charger, a smiling girl in a snow-white cowboy hat, and furiously project her into obscene positions. Her face slack and swollen, sucking and licking, her chin wet with saliva. I was supposed to understand the night with Mitch, be easy with things, but I had only my stiff and formal anger. That stupid gold record. I tried hard to mash up new meaning, like I'd missed some important sign, a weighted look Suzanne had given me behind Mitch's back. His goatish face, dripping sweat onto me so I had to turn my head.

The next morning I'd been pleased to find the kitchen empty, my mother taking a shower. I tipped sugar in my coffee, then settled at the table with a sleeve of saltines. I liked to crumble a saltine in my mouth, then flood the starchy mess with coffee. I was so absorbed in this ritual that Frank's sudden presence startled me. He scraped out the other chair, hitching it close as he sat down. I saw him take in the debris of saltines, inciting my vague shame. I was about to slither away, but he spoke before I could.

"Big plans for today?" he asked me.

Trying to pal around. I twisted the sleeve of crackers closed and wiped my hands of crumbs, suddenly fastidious. "Dunno," I said.

How quickly the veneer of patience drained away. "You just going to mope around the house?" he asked.

I shrugged; that's exactly what I'd do.

A muscle in his cheek jumped. "At least go outside," he said. "You stay in that room like you're locked in there."

Frank wasn't wearing his boots, just his blaring white socks. I swallowed a helpless snort; it was ridiculous to see a grown man's socked feet. He noticed my mouth twitch and got flustered.

"Everything's funny to you, huh?" he said. "Doing whatever you want. You think your mom doesn't notice what's going on?"

I stiffened but didn't look up. There were so many things he could be talking about: the ranch, what I'd done with Russell. Mitch. The ways I thought about Suzanne.

"She got real confused the other day," Frank went on. "She's missing some money. Gone right from her purse."

I knew my cheeks had flushed, but I stayed quiet. Narrowing my eyes at the table.

"Give her a break," Frank said. "Hm? She's a nice lady."

"I'm not stealing." My voice was high and false.

"Borrowing, let's say. I'm not gonna tell. I get it. But you should stop. She loves you a lot, you know?"

No more noise from the shower, which meant my mother would appear soon. I tried to gauge whether Frank really wouldn't say anything—he was trying to be nice, I understood, not getting me in trouble. But I didn't want to be grateful. Imagine him trying to be fatherly with me.

"The town party is still happening," Frank said. "Today and tomorrow, too. Maybe you could go on down there, have some fun. I'm sure that would make your mother happy. You staying busy."

When my mother entered, toweling the ends of her hair, I immediately brightened, arranging my face like I was listening to Frank.

"Don't you think so, Jeanie?" Frank said, gazing at my mother.

"Think what?" she said.

"Shouldn't Evie go check out that carnival?" Frank said. "That centennial thing? Keep busy?"

My mother took up this pet notion like it was a flash of brilliance. "I don't know if it's the centennial, exactly—" she said.

"Well, town party," Frank broke in, "centennial, whatever it is."

"But it's a good idea," she said. "You'll have a great time."

I could feel Frank watching me.

"Yeah," I said, "sure."

"Nice to see you two having a good talk," my mother added shyly.

I made a face, collecting my mug and crackers, but my mother didn't notice: she had already bent to kiss Frank. Her robe falling open so I saw a triangle of shadowy, sun-spotted chest and had to look away.

The town was celebrating 110 years, after all, not 100, the awkward number setting the tone for the meager affair. To even call it a carnival seemed overly generous, though most of the town was there. There had been a box social in the park and a play about the town's founding in the high school amphitheater, the student council members sweating in theater department costumes. They'd closed the road to street traffic, so I found myself in a bobbing press of people, pushing and grabbing at the promise of leisure and fun. Husbands whose faces were tight with aggrieved duty, flanked by kids and wives who needed stuffed animals. Who needed pale, sour lemonade and hot dogs and grilled corn. All the proof of a good time. The river was already clotted with litter, the slow drift of popcorn bags and beer cans and paper fans.

My mother had been impressed by Frank's miraculous ability to get me to leave the house. Just as Frank wanted her to be. So she could imagine the neat way he'd slot into a father shape. I was having exactly as much fun as I'd expected to have. I ate a snow cone, the paper cup weakening until the syrup leaked out over my hands. I threw the rest away, but my hands scudded with the residue, even after I wiped them on my shorts.

I moved among the crowd, in and out of shade. I saw kids I knew, but they were the background fill from school, no one I had ever spent concentrated time with. Still, I incanted their first and last names helplessly in my head. Norm Morovich. Jim Schumacher. Farm kids, mostly, whose boots smelled of rot. Their soft-spoken answers in class, speaking only when specifically called upon, the humble ring of dirt I saw in the upturned cowboy hats on their desks. They were polite and virtuous, the trace of milk cows and clover fields and little sisters on them. Nothing at all like the ranch population, who would pity boys who still respected their father's authority or wiped their boots before entering their mother's kitchen. I wondered what Suzanne was doing—swimming in the creek, maybe, or lying around with Donna or Helen or maybe even Mitch, a thought that made me bite my lip, working a ruff of dry skin with my teeth.

I'd have to stay at the carnival only a little while longer and then I could go back home, Frank and my mother satisfied with my healthy dose of sociable activity. I tried to make my way toward the park, but it was packed—the parade had started, the pickup beds heavy with crepe-paper models of town hall. Bank employees and girls in Indian costumes waving from floats, the noise of the marching band violent and oppressive. I weaved out of the crowd, scuttling along the periphery. Sticking to the quieter side streets. The sound of the marching band grew louder, the parade winding down East Washington. The laughter I heard, pointed and performative, cut through my focus: I knew, before I looked up, that it was aimed at me.

It was Connie, Connie and May, a netted bag stretching from Connie's wrist. I could make out a can of orange soda and other groceries straining inside, the line of a swimsuit under Connie's shirt. Encoded within was their whole simple day—the boredom of the heat, the orange soda going flat. The bathing suits drying on the porch.

My first feeling was relief, like the familiarity of turning into my own driveway. Then came an uneasiness, the clicking together of the facts. Connie was mad at me. We were not friends anymore. I watched Connie move past her initial surprise. May's bloodhound eyes squinted, eager for drama. Her braces thickening her mouth. Connie and May exchanged a few whispered words, then Connie edged forward.

"Hey," she said cautiously. "What's going on?"

I had expected anger, derision, but Connie was acting normal, even a little glad to see me. We hadn't spoken in almost a month. I looked at May's face for a clue, but it was insistently blank.

"Nothing much," I said. I should have been fortified by the last few weeks, the existence of the ranch lessening the stakes of our familiar dramas, and yet how quickly the old loyalties return, the pack animal push. I wanted them to like me.

"Us either," Connie said.

My sudden gratitude for Frank—it was good that I had come, good to be around people like Connie who were not complicated or confusing like Suzanne, but just a friend, someone I'd known beyond daily changes. How she and I had watched television until we got blinky headaches and popped pimples on each other's backs in the harsh light of the bathroom.

"Lame, huh?" I said, gesturing in the direction of the parade. "A hundred and ten years."

"There's a bunch of freaky people around." May sniffed, and I wondered if she was somehow implicating me. "By the river. They stunk."

"Yeah," Connie said, kinder. "The play was really stupid, too. Susan Thayer's dress was pretty much see-through. Everyone saw her underwear."

They shot each other a look. I was jealous of their shared memory, how they must have sat together in the audience, bored and restless in the sun.

"We might go swimming," Connie said. This statement seemed vaguely hilarious to both of them, and I joined in, tentative. Like I understood the joke.

"Um." Connie seemed to silently confirm something with May. "Do you want to come with us?"

I should have known that it wouldn't end well. That it was happening too easily, that my defection wouldn't be tolerated. "To swim?"

May stepped up, nodding. "Yeah, at the Meadow Club. My mom can drive us. You wanna come?"

The thought that I might go with them was such a ludicrous anachronism, as if an alternate universe were unfolding where Connie and I were still friends and May Lopes was inviting us to the Meadow Club to swim. You could get milkshakes there and grilled cheese sandwiches with lacy frills of burnt cheese. Simple tastes, food for children, everything paid for by signing your parent's name. I allowed myself to feel flattered, remembering an easy familiarity with Connie. Her house so known to me that I didn't even think about where each bowl went in the cabinet, each plastic cup, their rims eaten by the dishwasher. How nice that seemed, how uncomplicated, the cogent march of our friendship.

That was the moment May stepped toward me, pitching the can of orange soda forward: the soda inside hit my face at an angle, so it didn't douse me so much as dribble. Oh, I thought, my stomach dropping. Oh, of course. The parking lot tilted. The soda was tepid and I could smell the chemicals, the unsavory drip on the asphalt. May dropped the mostly empty can. It rolled a ways and then stopped. Her face was as shiny as a quarter, and she looked spooked by her own audacity. Connie was more uncertain, her face a flickering bulb, coming to full-watt attention when May rattled her bag like a warning bell.

The liquid had barely grazed me. It could have been worse, a real soaking instead of this meager attempt, but somehow I longed for the soaking. I wanted the event to be as big and ruthless as the way my humiliation felt.

"Have a fun summer," May trilled, linking arms with Connie.

And then they were walking away, their bags jostling and their sandals loud on the sidewalk. Connie turned to glance back at me, but I saw May tug her, hard. The bleed of surf music carried across the road from an open car window—I thought I saw Peter's friend Henry at the wheel, but maybe that was my imagination. Projecting a larger net of conspiracy onto my childish humiliation, as if that were an improvement.

I kept a lunatic calm on my face, afraid someone might be watching me, alert for signs of weakness. Though I'm sure it was obvious—a tightness in my features, a wounded insistence that I was fine, everything was fine, that it was just a misunderstanding, girlish high jinks between friends. *Ha ha ha*, like the laugh track on *Bewitched* that drained the look of horror on Darrin's marzipan face of any meaning.

It had only been two days without Suzanne, but already I had slipped back so easily into the dull stream of

adolescent life—Connie and May's idiot dramas. My
mother's cold hands, sudden on my neck, like she was
trying to startle me into loving her. This awful carnival
and my awful town. My anger at Suzanne was hard to
access, an old sweater packed away and barely remembered. I could think of Russell slapping Helen and it sur-
faced as a little glitch at the back of certain thoughts, a
memory of wariness. But there were always ways I made
sense of things.

I was back at the ranch the next day.

I found Suzanne on her mattress, bent intently over a
book. She never read, and it was odd to see her stilled in
concentration. The cover was half-torn and had a futuris-
tic pentagram on it, some blocky white type.

"What's that about?" I asked from the doorway.

Suzanne looked up, startled.

"Time," she said. "Space."

The sight of her brought flashes of the night with
Mitch, but they were unfocused, like a secondhand reflection. Suzanne didn't say anything about my absence.
About Mitch. All she did was sigh and toss the book
down. She lay back on the bed, studying her nails. Pinching the skin of her upper arm.

"Flabby," she declared, waiting for me to protest. As
she knew I would.

...

I had a hard time sleeping that night, shifting on the mattress. I was returned to her. So alert to every cue in her face that I made myself sick, watching her, but happy, too.

"I'm glad I'm back," I whispered, the darkness allowing me to say the words.

Suzanne laughed a little, half-asleep. "But you can always go home."

"Maybe I never will."

"Free Evie."

"I'm serious. I don't ever want to leave."

"That's what all the kids say when summer camp is over."

I could see the whites of her eyes. Before I could say anything, she let out a sudden heavy breath.

"I'm too hot," she announced. Kicking off the sheet and turning from me.

10

The clock was loud in the Dutton house. The apples in the netted basket looked waxy and old. I could see photos on the mantel: the familiar faces of Teddy and his parents. His sister who'd married an IBM salesman. I kept waiting for the front door to open, for someone to identify our intrusion. The sun lit a folded paper star in the window so it went bright. Mrs. Dutton must have taken the time to tape that up, make her home nice.

Donna disappeared into another room, then reappeared. I heard the shudder of drawers, of things being moved.

I saw the Dutton house that day as if for the first time. Noticing that the living room was carpeted. That the rocking chair had a cross-stitched pillow on the seat that looked handmade. The wonky antennae of the television, a smell like stale potpourri in the air. Everything was waterlogged by the knowledge of the family's absence: the arrangement of papers on the low table, an uncapped aspirin bottle in the kitchen. None of it made any sense without the animation of the Duttons' presence, like the blurry glyphs of 3-D pictures before the glasses knocked them into clarity.

Donna kept reaching to bump something out of its place: little things. A blue glass of flowers moved four inches to the left. A penny loafer kicked away from its mate. Suzanne didn't touch anything, not at first. She was picking things up with her eyes, ingesting it all—the framed photos, the ceramic cowboy. The cowboy made Donna and Suzanne weaken into giggles, me smiling, too, but I did not get the joke; only a queer feeling in my stomach, the starkness of the hollow sunlight.

The three of us had gone on a garbage run earlier that afternoon, in a borrowed car, a Trans Am, possibly Mitch's. Suzanne turned up the radio, KFRC, K. O. Bayley on the big 610. Both Suzanne and Donna seemed energized, and so was I. Happy to be back among them. Suzanne pulled into a glass-fronted Safeway that was familiar to me, the cant of its green roof. Where my mother shopped occasionally.

"Grubby grub time," Donna announced, making herself laugh.

Donna hoisted herself over the lip of the dumpster, avid as an animal, knotting her skirt around her hips so she could dig deep. She got off on it, happy to muck around in the trash, the wet squelch.

On the way back to the ranch, Suzanne made an announcement.

"Time for a little trip," she said, loudly recruiting Donna into the plan.

I liked knowing she was thinking of me, trying to placate me. I noticed a new desperation around her after Mitch. I was more conscious of her attentions, of how to keep her eyes on me.

"Where?" I asked.

"You'll see," Suzanne said, catching Donna's gaze. "It's like our medicine, like a little cure for what ails you."

"Ooh," Donna said, leaning forward. She seemed to have understood immediately what Suzanne was talking about. "Yes, yes, yes."

"We need a house," Suzanne said. "That's the first thing. An empty house." She flashed a look at me. "Your mom's gone, right?"

I didn't know what they were going to do. But I recognized a tinge of alarm, even then, and had the sense to spare my own home. I shifted in the seat. "She's there all day."

Suzanne made a disappointed hum. But I was already

thinking of another house that might be empty. And I offered it up to them, easily.

I gave Suzanne directions, watching the roads grow
more and more familiar. When Suzanne stopped the car
and Donna got out and smeared mud on the first two
numbers of the license plate, I only worried a little. I
gathered an unfamiliar braveness, a sense of pushing past
limitations, and tried to give myself up to the uncertainty.
I was locked into my body in a way that was unfamiliar. It
was the knowledge, perhaps, that I would do whatever
Suzanne wanted me to do. That was a strange thought—
that there was just this banal sense of being moved along
the bright river of whatever was going to happen. That it
could be as easy as this.

Suzanne was driving erratically, rolling through a
stop sign and gazing away from the road for long stretches
of time, caught in a private daydream. She turned onto
my own road. The gates like a familiar string of beads,
one following the other.

"There," I said, and Suzanne slowed the car.

The windows of the Dutton house were plain with
curtains, the flagstone path cutting a line to the front
door. No car in the carport, just a glisten of oil on the
asphalt. Teddy's bike wasn't in the yard—he was gone,
too. The house looked empty.

Suzanne parked the car down the road a little bit, mostly
out of sight, while Donna went briskly to the side yard. I

trailed Suzanne, but I was hanging back slightly, shuffling my sandals through the dirt.

Suzanne turned to me. "Are you coming or what?"

I laughed, but I'm sure she saw the effort it took. "I just don't understand what we're doing."

She cocked her head and smiled. "Do you really care?"

I was scared and couldn't say why. I mocked myself for letting my mind range furiously to the very worst thing. Whatever they were going to do—steal, probably. I didn't know.

"Hurry up," Suzanne said. She was getting annoyed, I could tell, though she was still smiling. "We can't just stand here."

Afternoon shadows were starting to slant through the trees. Donna reemerged from the wooden side gate. "The back door's open," she said. My stomach sank—there was no way to stop whatever was about to happen. And then there was Tiki, scrambling in our direction, barking in wretched alarm. Yips shook his whole body, his skinny shoulders twitching.

"Fuck," Suzanne muttered. Donna backed off, too.

The dog could have been enough of an excuse, I suppose, and we could've piled back into the car and gone back to the ranch. A part of me wanted that. But another part wanted to fulfill the sick momentum in my chest. The Dutton family seemed like perpetrators, too, just like Connie and May and my parents. All quarantined by their selfishness, their stupidity.

"Wait," I said. "He knows me."

I squatted, holding out my hand. Keeping my eyes on the dog. Tiki approached, sniffing my palm.

"Good Tiki," I said, petting him, scratching under his jaw, and then the barking stopped and we went inside.

I couldn't believe nothing happened. That no cop cars were whining after us. Even after shifting so easily into the Dutton domain, crossing the invisible boundaries. And why had we done that? Jarred the inviolate grid of a home for no reason? Just to prove we could? The calm mask of Suzanne's face as she touched the Duttons' things confused me, her odd remove, even as I fluoresced with a strange, unreadable thrill. Donna was looking over some treasure from the house, a bauble of milky ceramic. I peered closer and saw it was a little figure of a Dutch girl. How bizarre, the detritus of people's lives removed from their context. It made even things that were precious seem like junk.

The lurch in me made me think of an afternoon when I was younger, my father and I hunched over the shoreline at Clear Lake. My father squinting in the harshness of midday, the fish white of his thighs in his swimming shorts. How he pointed out a leech in the water, quivering and tight with blood. He was pleased, poking at the leech with a stick to make it move, but I was frightened. The inky leech caused some drag on my insides that I sensed again, there, in the Dutton house, Suzanne's eyes meeting mine across the living room.

"You like?" Suzanne said. Smiling a little. "Wild, right?"

Donna came out into the entryway. Her forearms shone with sticky juice, and she held a triangle of watermelon in her hand, the spongy pink of an organ.

"Greetings and salutations," she said, chewing wetly. There was an almost feral percolation emanating from Donna like a bad smell, her dress whose hem was ratty from being stepped on: how out of place she looked next to the polished coffee table, the tidy curtains. Drops of watermelon juice fell on the floor.

"There's more in the sink," she said. "It's real good."

Donna picked a black seed from her mouth with a delicate little pinch, then flicked it off into the corner of the room.

We were there only a half hour or so, though it seemed much longer. Snapping the TV on and off. Paging through the mail on the side table. I followed Suzanne up the stairs, wondering where Teddy was now, where his parents were. Was Teddy still waiting for me to bring him his drugs? Tiki banged around in the hallway. I realized with a start that I'd known the Dutton family my whole life. Under the hanging photographs, I could make out the line of wallpaper, just starting to peel, the tiny pink flowers. The smear of fingerprints.

I would often think of the house. How innocent I told myself it was: harmless fun. I was reckless, wanting to win back Suzanne's attention, to feel like we were arranged again against the world. We were ripping a tiny seam in the life of the Dutton family, just so they'd see themselves differently, even if for a moment. So they'd notice a slight disturbance, try to remember when they'd moved their shoes or put their clock in the drawer. That could only be good, I told myself, the forced perspective. We were doing them a favor.

Donna was in the parents' bedroom, a long silk slip pulled over her dress.

"I'll need the Rolls at seven," she said, swishing the watery fabric, the color of champagne.

Suzanne snorted. I could see a cut-glass bottle of perfume tipped on the nightstand and the golden tubes of lipstick like shell casings in the carpet. Suzanne was already sifting through the bureau, stuffing her hand inside the flesh-tone nylons, creating obscene bulges. The brassieres were heavy and medical looking, stiff with wire. I lifted one of the lipsticks and uncapped it, smelling the talcum scent of the orangy red.

"Oh, yeah," Donna said, seeing me. She grabbed a lipstick, too, and made a cartoonish pucker, pretending to apply it. "We should leave a little message," she said. Looking around.

"On the walls," Suzanne said. The idea excited her, I could tell.

I wanted to protest: leaving a mark seemed almost

violent. Mrs. Dutton would have to scrub the wall clean, though it would probably always have a phantom nap, the receipt of all the scrubbing. But I stayed quiet.

"A picture?" Donna said.

"Do the heart," Suzanne added, coming over. "I'll do it."

I had a startling vision of Suzanne then. The desperation that showed through, the sudden sense of a dark space yawning in her. I didn't think of what that dark space might be capable of, only a doubling of my desire to be near it.

Suzanne took the lipstick from Donna but hadn't yet pressed the tip to the ivory wall when we heard a noise in the driveway.

"Shit," Suzanne said.

Donna's eyebrows were raised in mild curiosity: What would happen next?

The front door opened. I tasted my own stale mouth, the rancid announcement of fear. Suzanne seemed scared, too, but her fear was distant and amused, like this was a game of sardines and we were just hiding until the others found us. I knew it was Mrs. Dutton when I heard high heels.

"Teddy?" she called. "You home?"

They'd parked the ranch car down the road, but still: I'm sure Mrs. Dutton took note of the unfamiliar car. Maybe she thought it was a friend of Teddy's, some older neighborhood pal. Donna was giggling, her hand pressed over her mouth. Eyes bulged in mirth. Suzanne made an exaggerated shushing face. My pulse was loud in my ears. Tiki clattered through the rooms downstairs and I heard Mrs. Dutton cooing to him, the heaving sighs he made in response.

"Hello?" she called.

The wake of silence that followed seemed obviously uneasy. She'd come upstairs soon enough, and then what?

"Come on," Suzanne whispered. "Let's sneak out the back."

Donna was laughing silently. "Shit," she said, "shit."

Suzanne dropped the lipstick on the bureau, but Donna kept the slip on, hitching the straps.

"You go first," she said to Suzanne.

There was no way out but to pass Mrs. Dutton in the kitchen.

She was probably wondering at the pink mess of watermelon in the sink, the sticky patches on the floor. Maybe just starting to pick up the disturbance in the air, the itch of strangers in the house. A nervous hand fluttering at her throat, a sudden wish for her husband at her side.

Suzanne took off down the stairs, Donna and I hustling behind. The racket of our footsteps as we plowed past Mrs. Dutton, barreling at full speed through the kitchen. Donna and Suzanne were laughing their heads off, Mrs. Dutton shrieking in fright. Tiki came barking after us, quick and hectic, his nails skittering on the floor. Mrs. Dutton backed up, nakedly afraid.

"Hey," she said, "stop," but her voice wavered.

She bumped against a stool and lost her balance, sitting down hard on the tile. I looked back as we banged past—there was Mrs. Dutton splayed on the floor. Recognition tightened her face.

"I see you," she called from the floor, struggling to right herself, her breath going wild. "I see you, Evie Boyd."

PART THREE

JULIAN RETURNED FROM HUMBOLDT with a friend who wanted a ride to L.A. The friend's name was Zav. It seemed vaguely Rastafarian, how he pronounced it, though Zav was fishy white with a bog of orange hair held back by a woman's elastic. He was much older than Julian, maybe thirty-five, but dressed like an adolescent: the same too-long cargo shorts, the T-shirt worn to a pulp. He walked around Dan's house with an appraising squint, picking up a figurine of an ox, carved from bone or ivory, then putting it down. He peered at a photo of Julian in his mother's arms on the beach, then replaced the frame on the shelf, chuckling to himself.

"It's cool if he stays here tonight, right?" Julian asked. As if I were the den mother.

"It's your house."

Zav came over to shake my hand. "Thanks," he said, pumping away, "that's real decent of you."

Sasha and Zav seemed to know each other, and soon all three were talking about a gloomy bar near Humboldt owned by a gray-haired grower. Julian had his arm around Sasha with the adult air of a man returning from the mines. It was hard to imagine him harming a dog, or harming anyone, Sasha so obviously pleased to be near him. She'd been girlish and veiled with me all day, no hint of our conversation the night before. Zav said something that made her laugh, a pretty, subdued laugh. Half covering her mouth, like she didn't want to expose her teeth.

I'd planned to walk to town for dinner, leave them alone, but Julian noticed me heading for the door.

"Hey, hey, hey," he said.

They all turned to look at me.

"I'm gonna go into town for a bit," I said.

"You should eat with us," Julian said. Sasha nodded, scooting into his side. Giving me the sloppy half attention of someone in the orbit of her beloved.

"We got a bunch of food," she said.

I made the usual smiling excuses, but finally I took off my jacket. Already getting used to attention.

. . .

They'd stopped for groceries on the way back from Humboldt: a giant frozen pizza, some discount ground beef in a Styrofoam tray.

"A feast," Zav said. "You've got your protein, your calcium." He pulled a pill bottle from his pocket. "Your vegetables."

He started rolling a joint on the table, a process that involved multiple papers and much fussing over the construction. Zav eyed his work from a distance, then pinched a little more from the pill bottle, the room marinating in the stench of damp weed.

Julian was cooking the beef on the stove, the meat losing its sheen. He poked at the crude patties with a butter knife, prodding and sniffing. Dorm-room cookery. Sasha slid the pizza in the oven, balling up the plastic wrap. Setting out paper towels at each chair, a suburban memory of chores, of setting the table for dinner. Zav drank a beer and watched Sasha with amused contempt. He hadn't lit the joint yet, though he twirled it in his fingers with obvious pleasure.

I listened while he and Julian talked about drugs with the intensity of professionals, exchanging stats like bond traders. Greenhouse yield vs. sun-grown. Comparing THC levels in varying strains. This was nothing like the hobby drugs of my youth, pot grown alongside tomato plants, passed around in mason jars. You could pick out seeds from a bud and plant them yourself, if you felt like it. Trade a lid for enough gas to get to the city. It was strange to hear drugs flattened to a matter of numbers, a knowable commodity instead of a mystic portal. Maybe Zav and Julian's way was better, cutting out all the woozy idealism.

"Fuck," Julian said. The kitchen smelled of ashes and burning starch. "Damn, damn, damn." He opened the oven and pulled the pizza out with his bare hands, swearing as he tossed it on the counter. It was black and smoky.

"Man," Zav said, "that was the good kind, too. Expensive."

Sasha was frantic. Hurrying over to consult the back of the pizza box. "Preheat to four fifty," she droned. "I did that. I don't understand."

"What time did you put it in?" Zav asked.

Sasha's eyes moved to the clock.

"The clock's frozen, idiot," Julian said. He grabbed the box and stuffed it in the garbage. Sasha looked like she might cry. "Whatever," he said with disgust. Picking at the burnt shell of cheese, then rubbing his fingers clean. I thought of the professor's dog. The poor animal, limping in circles. Vascular system slushy with poison. All the other things Sasha had probably not told me.

"I can make something else," I said. "There's some pasta in the cabinet."

I tried to catch Sasha's eye. Willing some combination of warning and sympathy to pass from me to her. But Sasha was unreachable, stung by her failure. The room got quiet. Zav fussing the joint between his fingers, waiting to see what would happen.

"There's a lot of beef, I guess," Julian said finally, his anger slipping from sight. "No big thing."

He rubbed Sasha's back, roughly, I thought, though the movement seemed to comfort her, returning her to the world. When he kissed her, she closed her eyes.

We drank a bottle of Dan's wine at dinner, the sediment settling in the cracks of Julian's teeth. Beer after that. Alcohol cut the fat on our breath. I didn't know what time it was. The windows black, the squeeze of wind through the eaves. Sasha was corralling wet pieces of the wine label into a meticulous pile. I could feel her glance at me from time to time, Julian's hand working the back of her neck. He and Zav maintained a constant patter all through dinner, Sasha and I fading into a silence familiar from adolescence: the effort to break through Zav and Julian's alliance wasn't worth the return. It was simpler to watch them, to watch Sasha, who acted like just sitting there was enough.

"'Cause you're a good guy," Zav kept saying. "You're a good guy, Julian, and that's why I don't make you pay up front with me. You know I have to do that with McGinley, Sam, all those retards."

They were drunk, the three of them, and maybe I was, too, the ceiling drab with expired smoke. We'd shared a burly joint, a sexual droop descending on Zav. A pleased, overcome squint. Sasha had drawn further into herself, though she'd unzipped her sweatshirt, her chest sunless and crossed with faint blue veins. Her eye makeup was heavier than it had been: I didn't know when she'd put more on.

I got to my feet when we finished eating. "I've got to do a few things," I said.

They made halfhearted efforts to get me to stay, but I waved them off. I closed the door to the bedroom, though bits of their conversation slipped through.

"I respect you," Julian was saying to Zav, "I always have, man, ever since Scarlet was like, You have to meet this guy." Performing an extravagant admiration, the stoned person's tendency toward optimistic summary.

Zav responded, resuming their practiced volley. I could hear Sasha's silence.

When I passed through later, nothing had really changed. Sasha was still listening to their conversation like she'd be tested someday. Julian's and Zav's intoxication had passed into a strenuous state, their hairlines wet with sweat.

"Are we being too loud?" Julian asked. That weird politeness again, how easily it clicked in.

"Not at all," I said. "Just getting some water."

"Sit with us," Zav said, studying me. "Talk."

"That's okay."

"Come on, Evie," Julian said. The odd intimacy of my name in his mouth surprised me.

The table was stamped with rings from the bottles, the litter of dinner. I started to clear the dishes.

"You don't have to do that," Julian said, scooting back so I could reach his plate.

"You cooked," I said.

Sasha made a peep of thanks when I added her plate to the stack. Zav's phone lit up, shivering across the surface of the table. Someone was calling: a blurry photograph of a woman in underwear flashed on the screen.

"Is that Lexi?" Julian asked.

Zav nodded, ignoring the call.

A look passed between Julian and Zav: I didn't want to notice it. Zav belched. They both laughed. I could smell the memory of chewed meat.

"Benny is doing computer shit now," Zav said, "you know that?"

Julian hit the table. "No fucking way."

I walked the dishes to the sink, gathering the balled paper towels from the counter. Sweeping crumbs into my hand.

"He's fat as fuck," Zav said, "it's hilarious."

"Is Benny the guy from your high school?" Sasha asked.

Julian nodded. I let the sink fill with water. Watching Julian swivel his body to mirror Sasha's, knocking his knees into hers. He kissed her on the temple.

"You guys are too fucking much," Zav said.

His tone had a tricky bite. I sank the dishes in the water. A scummy network of grease formed on the surface.

"I just don't get it," Zav went on, addressing Sasha, "why you stay with Julian. You're too hot for him."

Sasha giggled, though I glanced back and saw her labor to calculate a response.

"I mean, she's a babe," Zav said to Julian, "am I right?"

Julian smiled what I thought of as the smile of an only son, someone who believed he would always get what he wanted. He probably always had. The three of them were lit like a scene from a movie I was too old to watch.

"But Sasha and I know each other, don't we?" Zav smiled at her. "I like Sasha."

Sasha held a basic smile on her face, her fingers tidying the pile of torn label.

"She doesn't like her tits," Julian said, pulsing the back of her neck, "but I tell her they're nice."

"Sasha!" Zav affected upset. "You have great tits."

I flushed, hurrying to finish the dishes.

"Yeah," Julian said, his hand still on her neck. "Zav would tell you if you didn't."

"I always tell the truth," Zav said.

"He does," Julian said. "That's true."

"Show me," Zav said.

"They're too small," Sasha said. Her mouth was tight like she was making fun of herself, and she shifted in her seat.

"They'll never sag, so that's good," Julian said. Tickling her shoulder. "Let Zav see."

Sasha's face reddened.

"Do it, babe," Julian said, a harshness in his voice making me glance over. I caught Sasha's eye—I told myself the look in her face was pleading.

"Come on, you guys," I said.

The boys turned with amused surprise. Though I think they were tracking where I was all along. That my presence was a part of the game.

"What?" Julian said, his face snapping into innocence.

"Just cool it," I told him.

"Oh, it's fine," Sasha said. Laughing a little, her eyes on Julian.

"What exactly are we doing?" Julian said. "What exactly should we 'cool'?"

He and Zav snorted—how quickly all the old feelings came back, the humiliating interior fumble. I crossed my arms, looking to Sasha. "You're bothering her."

"Sasha's fine," Julian said. He tucked a strand of her hair behind her ear—she smiled faintly and with effort. "Besides," he went on, "are you really someone who should be lecturing us?"

My heart tightened.

"Didn't you, like, kill someone?" Julian said.

Zav sucked his teeth, then let loose a nervous laugh.

My voice sounded strangled. "Of course not."

"But you knew what they were going to do," Julian said. Grinning with the thrill of capture. "You were there with Russell Hadrick and shit."

"Hadrick?" Zav said. "Are you shitting me?"

I tried to rein in the hysterical lean coming into my voice. "I was barely around."

Julian shrugged. "That's not what it sounded like."

"You don't really believe that." But there was no entry point in any of their faces.

"Sasha said you told her so," Julian went on. "Like you could have done it, too."

I inhaled sharply. The pathetic betrayal: Sasha had told Julian everything I'd said.

"So show us," Zav said, turning back to Sasha. I was already invisible again. "Show us the famous tits."

"You don't have to," I said to her.

Sasha flicked her eyes in my direction. "It isn't a big deal or anything," she said, her tone dripping with cool, obvious disdain. She plucked her neckline away from her chest and looked pensively down her shirt.

"See?" Julian said, smiling hard at me. "Listen to Sasha."

I had gone to one of Julian's recitals when Dan and I were still close. Julian must have been nine years old or so. He was good at the cello, I remembered, his tiny arms going about their mournful adult work. His nostrils rimed with snot, the instrument in careful balance. It didn't seem possible that the boy who had called forth those sounds of longing and beauty was the same almost-man who watched Sasha now, a cold varnish on his eyes.

She pulled her shirt down, her face flushed but mostly dreamy. The impatient, professional tug she gave when the neckline caught on her bra. Then both pale breasts were exposed, her skin marked by the line of her bra. Zav exclaimed approvingly. Reaching to thumb a rosy nipple while Julian looked on.

I had long outlived whatever usefulness I had here.

1969

11

I got caught; of course I did.

Mrs. Dutton on her kitchen floor, calling my name like a right answer. And I hesitated for just a moment—a stunned, bovine reaction to my own name, the knowledge that I should help the fallen Mrs. Dutton—but Suzanne and Donna were far ahead, and by the time I jarred back into that realization, they had almost disappeared. Suzanne turned back just long enough to see Mrs. Dutton clamp a trembling hand on my arm.

My mother's pained and baffled declarations: I was a failure. I was pathological. She wore the air of crisis like a flattering new coat, the stream of her anger performed for an invisible jury. She wanted to know who had broken into the Dutton house with me.

"Judy saw two girls with you," she said. "Maybe three. Who were they?"

"Nobody." I tended my rigid silence like a suitor, full of honorable feelings. Before she and Donna disappeared, I tried to flash Suzanne a message: I would take responsibility. She didn't have to worry. I understood why they'd left me behind. "It was just me," I said.

Anger made her words garbled. "You can't stay in this house and spout lies."

I could see how rattled she was by this confusing new situation. Her daughter had never been a problem before, had always zipped along without resistance, as tidy and self-contained as those fish that clean their own tanks. And why would she bother to expect otherwise or even prepare herself for the possibility?

"You told me you were going to Connie's all summer," my mother said. Almost shouting. "You said it so many times. Right to my face. And guess what? I called Arthur. He says you haven't been there in months. Almost two months."

My mother looked like an animal then, her face made strange with rage, a gaspy run of tears.

"You're a liar. You lied about that. You're lying about this, too." Her hands were clenched hard. She kept lifting them, then dropping them at her sides.

"I was seeing friends," I snapped. "I have other friends besides Connie."

"Other friends. Sure. You were out screwing some boyfriend, God knows what. Nasty little liar." She was barely looking at me, her words as compulsive and fevered as the muttered obscenities of a pervert. "Maybe I should take you down to the juvenile detention center. Is that what you want? It's clear to me I just can't control you anymore. I'll let them have you. See if they can straighten you out."

I wrenched away, but even in the hallway, even with my door closed, I could still hear my mother at her bitter chant.

Frank was called in as reinforcement: I watched from the bed as he took my bedroom door off its hinges. He was careful and quiet, though it took him a while, and he eased the door out of the frame as if it were made of glass instead of cheapo hollow-core. He placed it against the wall gently. Then hovered for a moment in the now empty doorway. Rattling the screws in his hands like dice.

"Sorry about this," he said, like he was just the hired help, the maintenance man carrying out my mother's wishes.

I didn't want to have to notice the actual kindness in his eyes, how immediately it drained my hateful narration of Frank of any real heat. I could picture him in Mexico for the first time, slightly sunburned so the hair on his arm turned platinum. Sipping a lemon soda while overseeing his gold mine—I pictured a cave whose interior was cobblestoned in stony growths of gold.

I kept expecting Frank to tell my mother about the stolen money. Pile on more problems to the list. But he didn't. Maybe he'd seen that she was already angry enough. Frank kept up a silent vigil at the table during her many phone calls with my father while I listened from the hallway. Her high-pitched complaints, all her questions squeezed to a panicked register. What kind of person breaks into a neighbor's house? A family I'd known my whole life?

"For no reason," she added shrilly. A pause. "You think I haven't asked her? You think I haven't tried?"

Silence.

"Oh, sure, right, I bet. You want to try?"

And so I was sent to Palo Alto.

I spent two weeks at my father's apartment. Across from a Denny's, the Portofino Apartments as blocky and empty as my mother's house was sprawling and dense. Tamar and my father had moved into the biggest unit, and everywhere were the still lifes of adulthood she had so obviously arranged: a bowl of waxed fruit on the counter, the bar cart with its unopened bottles of liquor. The carpet that held the bland tracks of the vacuum.

Suzanne would forget me, I thought, the ranch would

hurtle on without me and I'd have nothing. My sense of persecution gobbled up and grew fat off these worries. Suzanne was like a soldier's hometown sweetheart, made gauzy and perfect by distance. But maybe part of me was relieved. To take some time away. The Dutton house had spooked me, the blank cast I'd seen in Suzanne's face. These were little bites, little inward shifts and discomforts, but even so, they were there.

What had I expected, living with my father and Tamar? That my father would try to sleuth out the source of my behavior? That he would punish me, act like a father? He seemed to feel punishment was a right he'd relinquished and treated me with the courtly politeness you'd extend to an aging parent.

He startled when he first saw me—it had been over two months. He seemed to remember that he should hug me and made a lurching step in my direction. I noticed a new bunching at his ears, and his cowboy shirt was one I had never seen before. I knew I looked different, too. My hair was longer and wild at the edges, like Suzanne's. My ranch dress was so worn I could hook my thumb through the sleeve. My father made a move to help me with my bag, but I'd already hefted it into the backseat before he reached me.

"Thanks, though," I said, trying to smile.

His hands spread at his sides, and when he smiled back, it was with the helpless apology of a foreigner who needed directions repeated. My brain, to him, was a mysterious magic trick that he could only wonder at. Never bothering to puzzle out the hidden compartment. As we took our seats, I could sense that he was gathering himself to invoke the parental script.

"I don't have to lock you in your room, do I?" he said. His halting laugh. "No breaking in to anyone's house?"

When I nodded, he visibly relaxed. Like he'd gotten something out of the way.

"It's a good time for you to visit," he went on, as if this were all voluntary. "Now that we're settled. Tamar's real particular about the furniture and stuff." He started the ignition, already beyond any mention of trouble. "She went all the way to the flea market in Half Moon Bay to get this bar cart."

There was a brief moment I wanted to reach for him across the seat, to draw a line from myself to the man who was my father, but the moment passed.

"You can pick the station," he offered, seeming as shy to me as a boy at a dance.

The first few days, all three of us had been nervous. I got up early to make the bed in the guest room, trying to heft the decorative pillows back into completion. My life was limited to my drawstring purse and my duffel of clothes, an existence I tried to keep as neat and invisible as possible. Like camping, I thought, like a little adventure in self-reliance. The first night, my father brought home a cardboard tub of ice cream, striated with chocolate, and scooped free heroic amounts. Tamar and I just picked at ours, but my father made a point of eating another bowl. He kept glancing up, as if we could confirm his own pleasure. His women and his ice cream.

Tamar was the surprise. Tamar in her terry shorts and shirt from a college I had never heard of. Who waxed her legs in the bathroom with a complicated device that filled the apartment with the humidity of camphor. Her attendant unguents and hair oils, the fingernails whose lunar surfaces she studied for signs of nutritional deficiencies.

At first, she seemed unhappy with my presence. The awkward hug she offered, like she was grimly accepting the task of being my new mother. And I was disappointed, too. She was just a girl, not the exotic woman I'd once imagined—everything I'd thought was special about her was actually just proof of what Russell would call a straight world trip. Tamar did what she was supposed to. Worked for my father, wore her little suit. Aching to be someone's wife.

But then her formality quickly melted away, the veil of adulthood she wore as temporarily as a costume. She let me rummage through the quilted pouch that held her makeup, her blowsy perfume bottles, watching with the pride of a true collector. She pushed a blouse of hers, with bell sleeves and pearl buttons, onto me.

"It's just not my style anymore." She shrugged, picking at a loose thread. "But it'll look good on you, I know. Elizabethan."

And it did look good. Tamar knew those things. She

knew the calorie count of most foods, which she recited in sarcastic tones, like she was making fun of her own knowledge. She cooked vegetable vindaloo. Pots of lentils coated with a yellow sauce that gave off an unfamiliar brightness. The roll of powdery antacids my father swallowed like candy. Tamar held out her cheek for my father to kiss but swatted him away when he tried to hold her hand.

"You're all sweaty," she said. When my father saw that I had noticed, he laughed a little but seemed embarrassed.

My father was amused at our collusion. But it sometimes shook out so we were laughing at him. Once Tamar and I were talking about Spanky and Our Gang, and he chimed in. Like the Little Rascals, he figured. Tamar and I looked at each other.

"It's a band," she said. "You know, that rock-and-roll music the kids like." And my father's confused, orphaned face set us off again.

They had a fancy turntable that Tamar often spoke of moving to another corner or room for varying acoustic or aesthetic reasons. She constantly mentioned future plans for oak flooring and crown moldings and even different dish towels, though the planning itself seemed to satisfy. The music she played was more slick than the ranch racket. Jane Birkin and her froggy old-man husband, Serge.

"She's pretty," I said, studying the record cover. And she was, tan as a nut with a delicate face, those rabbit teeth. Serge was disgusting. His songs about Sleeping Beauty, a girl who seemed most desirable because her eyes were always closed. Why would Jane love Serge? Tamar loved my father, the girls loved Russell. These men who were nothing like the boys I'd been told I would like. Boys with hairless chests and mushy features, the flocking of blemishes along their shoulders. I didn't want to think of Mitch because it made me think of Suzanne— that night had happened somewhere else, in a little doll-house in Tiburon with a tiny pool and a tiny green lawn. A dollhouse I could look onto from above, lifting the roof to see the rooms segmented like chambers of the heart. The bed the size of a matchbox.

Tamar was different from Suzanne in a way that was easier. She was not complicated. She didn't track my attention so closely, didn't prompt me to shore up her declarations. When she wanted me to move over, she said so. I relaxed, which was unfamiliar. Even so, I missed Suzanne—Suzanne, who I remembered like dreams of opening a door on a forgotten room. Tamar was sweet and kind, but the world she moved around in seemed like a television set: limited and straightforward and mundane, with the notations and structures of normality. Breakfast, lunch, and dinner. There wasn't a frightening gap between the life she was living and the way she thought about that life, a dark ravine I often sensed in Suzanne, and maybe in my own self as well. Neither of us could fully participate in our days, though later Suzanne would participate in a way she could never take back. I mean that we didn't quite believe it was enough, what we were offered, and Tamar seemed to accept the world happily, as an end point. Her planning wasn't actually about making anything different—she was just rearranging the same known quantities, puzzling out a new order like life was an extended seating chart.

Tamar made dinner while we waited for my father. She looked younger than usual—her face washed with the cleanser she'd explained had actual milk proteins in it, to prevent wrinkles. Her hair wet and darkening the shoulders of the big T-shirt she wore, her lace-edged cotton shorts. She belonged in a dorm room somewhere, eating popcorn and drinking beer.

"Hand me a bowl?"

I did, and Tamar set aside a portion of lentils. "Without spices." She rolled her eyes. "For the tender heart's stomach."

I had a bitter flash of my mother doing that for my father: little consolations, little adjustments, making the world mirror my father's wants. Buying him ten pairs of the same socks so he never mismatched.

"It's almost like he's a kid sometimes, you know?" Tamar said, pinching out a measure of turmeric. "I left him for a weekend, and there was nothing to eat when I came back but beef jerky and an onion. He'd die if he had to take care of himself." She looked at me. "But I probably shouldn't tell you this, huh?"

Tamar wasn't being mean, but it surprised me—her ease in dismantling my father. It hadn't occurred to me before, not really, that he could be a figure of fun, someone who could make mistakes or act like a child or stumble helplessly around the world, needing direction.

Nothing terrible happened between me and my father. There was not a singular moment I could look back on, no shouting fight or slammed door. It was just the sense I got, a sense that seeped over everything until it seemed obvious, that he was just a normal man. Like any other. That he worried what other people thought of him, his eyes scatting to the mirror by the door. How he was still trying to teach himself French from a tape and I heard him repeating words to himself under his breath. The way his belly, which was bigger than I remembered, sometimes showed through the gap in his shirts. Exposing segments of skin, pink as a newborn's.

"And I love your father," Tamar said. Her words were careful, like she was being archived. "I do. He asked me to dinner six times before I said yes, but he was so nice about it. Like he knew I would say yes even before I did."

She seemed to catch herself—both of us were thinking it. My father had been living at home. Sleeping in bed with my mother. Tamar flinched, obviously waiting for me to say as much, but I couldn't muster any anger. That was the strange thing—I didn't hate my father. He had wanted something. Like I wanted Suzanne. Or my mother wanted Frank. You wanted things and you couldn't help it, because there was only your life, only yourself to wake up with, and how could you ever tell yourself what you wanted was wrong?

Tamar and I lay on the carpet, knees bent, heads angled toward the turntable. My mouth was still buzzing from the tartness of the orange juice we'd walked four blocks to buy from a stand. The wood heels of my sandals slapping the sidewalk, Tamar chatting happily in the warm summer dark.

My father came in and smiled, but I could tell he was annoyed by the music, the way it skittered on purpose. "Can you turn that down?" he asked.

"Come on," Tamar said. "It's not that loud."

"Yeah," I echoed, thrilled by the unfamiliarity of an ally.

"See?" Tamar said. "Listen to your daughter." She reached blindly to pat at my shoulder. My father left without saying anything, then returned a minute later and lifted the needle, the room abruptly silent.

"Hey!" Tamar said, sitting up, but he was already stalking away and I heard the shower start in the bathroom. "Fuck you," Tamar muttered. She got to her feet, the backs of her legs printed with the nub of the carpet. Glancing at me. "Sorry," she said absently.

I heard her talking in low tones in the kitchen. She was on the phone, and I watched her fingers piercing the loops of the cord, over and over. Tamar laughed, covering her mouth as she did, cupping the receiver close. I had the uncomfortable certainty that she was laughing at my father.

I don't know when I understood that Tamar would leave him. Not right away, but soon. Her mind was already somewhere else, writing a more interesting life for herself, one where my father and I would be the scenery to an anecdote. A detour from a larger, more correct journey. The redecoration of her own story. And who would my father have then, to make money for, to bring dessert home to? I imagined him opening the door on the empty apartment after a long day at work. How the rooms would be as he'd left them, undisturbed by another person's living. And how there would be a moment, before he flicked on the light, when he might imagine a different life revealed within the darkness, something besides the lonely borders of the couch, the cushions still holding the shape of his own sleepy body.

A lot of young people ran away: you could do it back then just because you were bored. You didn't even need a tragedy. Deciding to go back to the ranch wasn't difficult. My other house wasn't an option anymore, the ludicrous possibility of my mother dragging me to the police station. And what was there at my father's? Tamar, the way she insisted on my youthful alliance. The chocolate pudding after dinner, cold from the refrigerator, like our daily allotment of pleasure.

Maybe before the ranch, that life would have been enough.

But the ranch proved that you could live at a rarer pitch. That you could push past these petty human frailties and into a greater love. I believed, in the way of adolescents, in the absolute correctness and superiority of my love. My own feelings forming the definition. Love of that kind was something my father and even Tamar could never understand, and of course I had to leave.

While I had been watching television all day in the stuffy, overheated dark of my father's apartment, the ranch was going sour. Though I wasn't aware to what degree until later. The problem was the record deal—it wasn't going to happen, and that was not something Russell could accept. His hands were tied, Mitch told Russell; he could not force the record company to change their minds. Mitch was a successful musician, a talented guitar player, but he did not have that kind of power.

This was true—my night with Mitch seems piteous for that reason, a groundless whir of wheels. But Russell didn't believe Mitch, or it didn't matter anymore. Mitch became the convenient host for a universal sickness. The pacing rants that increased in frequency and length, Russell pinning it all on Mitch, that overfed Judas. The .22s traded for Buntlines, the frenzy of betrayal Russell worked in the others. Russell wasn't even bothering to hide his anger anymore. Guy was bringing speed around, he and Suzanne running to the pump house, coming back with eyes black as berries. The target practice in the trees. The ranch had never been of the larger world, but it grew more isolated. No newspapers, no televisions, no radio. Russell began to turn away visitors and send Guy out with the girls on every garbage run. A shell hardening around the place.

I can imagine Suzanne waking up, those mornings, with no sense of the days passing. The food situation getting dire, everything tinted with mild decay. They didn't eat much protein, their brains motoring on simple carbohydrates and the occasional peanut-butter sandwich. The speed that scraped Suzanne of feeling—she must have moved through the filtery electricity of her own numbness like moving through deep ocean.

Everyone, later, would find it unbelievable that anyone involved in the ranch would stay in that situation. A situation so obviously bad. But Suzanne had nothing else: she had given her life completely over to Russell, and by then it was like a thing he could hold in his hands, turning it over and over, testing its weight. Suzanne and the other girls had stopped being able to make certain judgments, the unused muscle of their ego growing slack and useless. It had been so long since any of them had occupied a world where right and wrong existed in any real way. Whatever instincts they'd ever had—the weak twinge in the gut, a gnaw of concern—had become inaudible. If those instincts had ever been detectable at all.

They didn't have very far to fall—I knew just being a

girl in the world handicapped your ability to believe yourself. Feelings seemed completely unreliable, like faulty gibberish scraped from a Ouija board. My childhood visits to the family doctor were stressful events for that reason. He'd ask me gentle questions: How was I feeling? How would I describe the pain? Was it more sharp or more spread out? I'd just look at him with desperation. I needed to be *told*, that was the whole point of going to the doctor. To take a test, be put through a machine that could comb my insides with radiated precision and tell me what the truth was.

Of course the girls didn't leave the ranch: there is a lot that can be borne. When I was nine, I'd broken my wrist falling from a swing. The shocking crack, the blackout pain. But even then, even with my wrist swelling with a cuff of trapped blood, I insisted I was fine, that it was nothing, and my parents believed me right up until the doctor showed them the X-ray, the bones snapped clean.

12

As soon as I'd packed my duffel, the guest room already looked like no one had ever stayed there—my absence quickly absorbed, which was maybe the point of rooms like that. I'd figured Tamar and my father had already left for work, but when I came into the living room, my father grunted from the couch.

"Tamar's buying orange juice or some stupid thing," he said.

We sat together and watched television. Tamar was gone a long time. My father kept rubbing his freshly shaven jaw, his face seeming undercooked. The commercials embarrassed me with their strident feeling, how they seemed to mock our awkward quiet. My father's nervous measurement of the silence. How I would have been, a month ago, tense with expectation. Dredging my life for some gem of experience to present to him. But I couldn't summon that effort anymore. My father was both more knowable to me than he had ever been, and at the same time, more of a stranger—he was just a man, sensitive to spicy foods, guessing at his foreign markets. Plugging away at his French.

He stood up the moment he heard Tamar's keys fussing in the door.

"We should have left thirty minutes ago," he said.

Tamar glanced at me, reshouldered her purse. "Sorry." She cut him a tight smile.

"You knew when we had to go," he said.

"I said I was sorry." She seemed, for a moment, genuinely sorry. But then her eyes drifted helplessly to the television, still on, and though she tried to click back to attention, I knew my father had noticed.

"You don't even have any orange juice," he said, his voice flickering with hurt.

A young couple was the first to pick me up. The girl's hair was the color of butter, a blouse knotted at her waist, and she kept turning to smile and offer me pistachios from a bag. Kissing the boy so I could see her darting tongue.

I hadn't hitchhiked before, not really. It made me nervous to have to be whatever strangers expected from a girl with long hair—I didn't know what degree of outrage to show about the war, how to talk about the students who threw bricks at police or took over passenger planes, demanding to be flown to Cuba. I'd always been outside all that, like I was watching a movie about what should have been my own life. But it was different, now that I was heading to the ranch.

I kept imagining the moment when Tamar and my father, home from the office, would realize I was actually gone. They would understand slowly, Tamar probably coming to the conclusion faster than my father. The apartment empty, no trace of my things. And maybe my father would call my mother, but what could either of them do? What punishment could they possibly pass down? They didn't know where I'd gone. I had moved beyond their purview. Even their concern was exciting, in its way: there would be a moment when they'd have to wonder why I'd left, some murky guilt rising to the surface, and they would have to feel the full force of it, even if it was only for a second.

The couple took me as far as Woodside. I waited in the parking lot of the Cal-Mart until I got a ride from a man in a rattly Chevrolet, on his way to Berkeley to drop off a motorcycle part. Every time he went over a pothole, his duct-taped glove compartment clattered. The shaggy trees flashed past the window, thick with sun, the purple stretch of the bay beyond. I held my purse on my lap. His name was Claude, and he seemed ashamed of how it jarred with his appearance. "My mother liked that French actor," he mumbled.

Claude made a point of flipping through his wallet,

showing me pictures of his own daughter. She was a chubby girl, the bridge of her nose pink. Her unfashionable sausage curls. Claude seemed to sense my pity, suddenly grabbing the wallet back.

"None of you girls should be doing this," he said.

He shook his head and I saw how his face moved a little with concern for me, an acknowledgment, I thought, of how brave I was. Though I should have known that when men warn you to be careful, often they are warning you of the dark movie playing across their own brains. Some violent daydream prompting their guilty exhortations to "make it home safe."

"See, I wish I'd been like you," Claude said. "Free and easy. Just traveling around. I always had a job."

He slid his eyes to me before turning them back to the road. The first twinge of discomfort—I'd gotten good at deciphering certain male expressions of desire. Clearing the throat, an assessing nip in the gaze.

"None of you people ever work, huh?" he said.

He was teasing, probably, but I couldn't tell for sure. There was sourness in his tone, a sting of real resentment. Maybe I should have been frightened of him. This older man who saw that I was alone, who felt like I owed him something, which was the worst thing a man like that could feel. But I wasn't afraid. I was protected, a hilarious and untouchable giddiness overtaking me. I was going back to the ranch. I would see Suzanne. Claude seemed barely real to me: a paper clown, innocuous and laughable.

. . .

"This good?" Claude said.

He'd pulled over near the campus in Berkeley, the clock tower and stair-step houses thickening the hills behind. He turned off the ignition. I felt the heat outside, the close wend of traffic.

"Thanks," I said, gathering my purse and duffel.

"Slow down," he said as I started to open the door. "Just sit with me a second, hm?"

I sighed but sat back in the seat. I could see the dry hills above Berkeley and remembered, with a start, that brief time in winter when the hills were green and plump and wet. I hadn't even known Suzanne then. I could feel Claude looking at me sideways.

"Listen." Claude scratched at his neck. "If you need some money—"

"I don't need money." I was unafraid, shrugging a quick goodbye and opening the door. "Thanks again," I said. "For the ride."

"Wait," he said, grabbing my wrist.

"Fuck off," I said, wrenching my arm away from the bracelet of his grasp, an unfamiliar heat in my voice. Before I slammed the door, I saw Claude's weak and sputtering face. I was walking away, breathless. Almost laughing. The sidewalk radiating even heat, the pulse of the abrupt sunshine. I was buoyed by the exchange, as if suddenly allowed more space in the world.

"Bitch," Claude called, but I didn't turn back to look.

. . .

Telegraph was packed: people selling tables of incense or concho jewelry, leather purses hung from an alley fence. The city of Berkeley was redoing all the roads that summer, so piles of rubble collected on the sidewalks, trenches cracking through the asphalt like a disaster movie. A group in floor-length robes fluttered pamphlets at me. Boys with no shirts, their arms pressed with faint bruising, looked me up and down. Girls my age lugged carpetbags that banged against their knees, wearing velvet frock coats in the August heat.

Even after what had happened with Claude, I wasn't afraid of hitchhiking. Claude was just a harmless floater in the corner of my vision, drifting peacefully into the void. Tom was the sixth person I approached, tapping his shoulder as he ducked into his car. He seemed flattered by my request for a ride, like it was an excuse I'd made up to be near him. He hurriedly brushed off the passenger seat, raining silent crumbs onto the carpet.

"It could be cleaner," he said. Apologetic, as if I might possibly be picky.

Tom drove his small Japanese car at exactly the speed limit, looking over his shoulder before changing lanes. His plaid shirt was thinning at the elbows but clean and tucked, a boyishness to his slim wrists that moved me. He took me all the way to the ranch, though it was an hour from Berkeley. He'd claimed to be visiting friends at the junior college in Santa Rosa, but he was a bad liar: I could see his neck get pink. He was polite, a student at Berkeley. Premed, though he liked sociology, too, and history.

"LBJ," he said. "Now there was a president."

He had a large family, I learned, and a dog named Sister, and too much homework: he was in summer school, trying to get through prereqs. He'd asked me what my major was. His mistake excited me—he must have thought I was eighteen, at least.

"I don't go to college," I said. I was about to explain I was only in high school, but Tom immediately got defensive.

"I was thinking of doing that, too," he said, "dropping out, but I'm gonna finish the summer classes. I already paid fees. I mean, I wish I hadn't, but—" He trailed off. Gazing at me until I realized he wanted my forgiveness.

"That's a bummer," I said, and this seemed like enough.

He cleared his throat. "So do you have a job or something? If you're not in school?" he said. "Gee, unless that's a rude question. You don't have to answer."

I shrugged, affecting ease. Though maybe I was feeling easy on that car ride, like my occupation of the world could be seamless. These simple ways I could meet needs. Talking to strangers, dealing with situations.

"The place I'm going now—I've been staying there," I said. "It's a big group. We take care of each other."

His eyes were on the road, but he was listening closely as I explained the ranch. The funny old house, the kids.

The plumbing system Guy had rigged in the yard, a knotty mess of pipes.

"Sounds like the International House," he said. "Where I live. There are fifteen of us. There's a chore board in the hall, we all take turns with the bad ones."

"Yeah, maybe," I said, though I knew the ranch was nothing like the International House, the squinty philosophy majors arguing over who'd left the dinner dishes unwashed, a girl from Poland nibbling black bread and crying for a faraway boyfriend.

"Who owns the house?" he said. "Is it like a center or something?"

It was odd to explain Russell to someone, to remember that there were whole realms in which Russell or Suzanne did not figure.

"His album's gonna come out around Christmas, probably," I remember saying.

I kept talking about the ranch, about Russell. The way I tossed free Mitch's name, like Donna had that day on the bus, with studied, careful deployment. The closer we got, the more worked up I became. Like horses that bolt with barn sickness, forgetting their rider.

"It sounds nice," Tom said. I could tell my stories had charged him, a dreamy excitement in his features. Mesmerized by bedtime tales of other worlds.

"You could hang out for a while," I said. "If you wanted."

Tom brightened at the offer, gratitude making him

shy. "Only if I'm not intruding," he said, a blush clotting his cheeks.

I imagined Suzanne and the others would be happy with me for bringing this new person. Expanding the ranks, all the old tricks. A pie-faced admirer to raise his voice with ours and contribute to the food pool. But it was something else, too, that I wanted to extend: the taut and pleasant silence in the car, the stale heat raising vapors of leather. The warped image of myself in the side mirrors, so I caught only the quantity of hair, the freckled skin of my shoulder. I took on the shape of a girl. The car crossed the bridge, passing through the shit-stench veil of the landfill. I could see the span of another distant highway, sided by water, and the marshy flats before the sudden drop into the valley, the ranch hidden in its hills.

By that time, the ranch I'd known was a place that no longer existed. The end had already arrived: each inter-action its own elegy. But there was too much hopeful mo-mentum in me to notice. The leap in me when Tom's car had first turned down the ranch drive: it had been two weeks, not long at all, but the return was overwhelming. And only when I saw everything still there, still alive and strange and half-dreamy as ever, did I understand I'd worried it might be gone. The things I loved, the miraculous house—like the one in *Gone with the Wind*, I'd realized, coming upon it again. The silty rectangle of pool, half-full, with its teem of algae and exposed concrete: it could all pass back into my possession.

As Tom and I walked from the car, I had a flash of hesitation, noticing how Tom's jeans were too clean. Maybe the girls would tease him, maybe it had been a bad idea to invite him along. I told myself it would be fine. I watched him absorbing the scene—I read his expression as impressed, though he must have been noticing the disrepair, the junked-out skeletons of cars. The crispy package of a dead frog, drifting on the surface of the pool. But these were details that no longer seemed notable to me, like the sores on Nico's legs that stuck with bits of gravel. My eyes were already habituated to the texture of decay, so I thought that I had passed back into the circle of light.

13

Donna stopped when she caught sight of us. A nest of laundry in her arms, smelling like the dusty air.

"Trou-ble," she hooted. "Trouble," a word from a long-forgotten world. "That lady just nabbed you, huh?" she said. "Man. Heavy."

Dark circles made crescents under her eyes, a hollow sink to her features, though these details were overshadowed by the swell of familiarity. She seemed happy enough to see me, but when I introduced Tom, she zipped a look at me.

"He gave me a ride," I supplied helpfully.

Donna's smile teetered, and she hitched the laundry higher in her arms.

"Is it cool that I'm here?" Tom whispered to me, as if

I had any power at all. The ranch had always welcomed visitors, putting them through their jokey gauntlet of attention, and I couldn't imagine why that would have changed.

"Yeah," I said, turning to Donna. "Right?"

"Well," Donna said. "I don't know. You should talk to Suzanne. Or Guy. Yeah."

She giggled absently. She was being odd, though to me it was just the usual Donna rap—I could even feel affection for it. Some movement in the grass caught her attention: a lizard, scuttling in search of shade.

"Russell saw a mountain lion a few days ago," she remarked to no one in particular. Widening her eyes. "Wild, huh?"

"Look who's back," Suzanne said, a flounce of anger in her greeting. Like I had disappeared on a little vacation. "Figured you'd forgotten how to get here."

Even though she'd seen Mrs. Dutton stop me, she kept glancing at Tom like he was the reason I'd left. Poor Tom, who wandered the grassy yard with the hesitant shuffle of museumgoers. His nose pricking from the animal smells, the backed-up outhouse. Suzanne's face was shuttered with the same distant confusion as Donna's: they could no longer conceive of a world where you could be punished. I was suddenly guilty for the nights with Tamar, the whole afternoons when I didn't even think of Suzanne. I tried to make my father's apartment sound worse than it had been, as if I'd been watched at every moment, suffered through endless punishments.

"Jesus," Suzanne snorted. "Dragsville."

The shadow of the ranch house stretched along the grass like a strange outdoor room, and we occupied this blessing of shade, a line of mosquitoes hovering in the thin afternoon light. The air crackled with a carnival sheen—the familiar bodies of the girls jostling against mine, knocking me back into myself. The quick metal flash through the trees—Guy was bumping a car through the back ranch, calls echoing and disappearing. The drowsy shape of the children, mucking around a network of shallow puddles: someone had forgotten to turn off the hose. Helen had a blanket around herself, pulled up to her chin like a woolly ruff, and Donna kept trying to snap it away and expose the homecoming queen body underneath, the hematoma on Helen's thigh. I was aware of Tom, sitting awkwardly in the dirt, but mostly I thrilled to Suzanne's familiar shape beside me. She was talking quickly, a glaze of sweat on her face. Her dress was filthy, but her eyes were shining.

Tamar and my father weren't even home yet, I realized, and how funny it was to already be at the ranch when they didn't even know I was gone. Nico was riding a tricycle that was too small for him, the bike rusted and clanging as he pedaled hard.

"Cute kid," Tom said. Donna and Helen laughed.

Tom wasn't sure what he'd said that was funny, but he blinked like he was willing to learn. Suzanne plucked at a stalk of oat grass, sitting in an old winged chair pulled from the house. I was keeping an eye out for Russell but didn't see him anywhere.

"He went to the city for a bit," Suzanne said.

We both turned at the sound of screeching: it was just Donna, trying to do a handstand on the porch, the flail of her kicking feet. She'd knocked over Tom's beer, though he was the one apologizing, looking around as if he'd find a mop.

"Jesus," Suzanne said. "Relax."

She wiped her sweating hands on her dress, her eyes pinging a little—speed made her stiff as a china cat. The high school girls used it to stay skinny, but I'd never done it: it seemed at odds with the droopy high I associated with the ranch. It made Suzanne harder to reach than usual, a change I didn't want to acknowledge to myself. I assumed she was just angry. Her gaze never exactly focusing, stopping at the brink.

We were talking like we always did, passing a joint that made Tom cough, but I was noticing other things at the same time with a slight drift of unease—the ranch was less populated than before, no strangers milling around with empty plates, asking what time dinner would be ready. Shaking back their hair and invoking the long car ride to L.A. I didn't see Caroline anywhere, either.

"She was weird," Suzanne said when I asked about

Caroline. "Like you could see her insides through her skin. She went home. Some people came and picked her up."

"Her parents?" The thought seemed ludicrous, that anyone at the ranch even had parents.

"It's cool," Suzanne said. "A van was heading north, I think Mendocino or something. She knew them from somewhere."

I tried to picture Caroline back at her parents' house, wherever that was. I didn't push much further than those thoughts, Caroline safe and elsewhere.

Tom was clearly uncomfortable. I was sure he was used to college girls with part-time jobs and library cards and split ends. Helen and Donna and Suzanne were raw, a sour note coming off them that struck me, too, returned from two weeks with miraculous plumbing and proximity to Tamar's obsessive grooming, the special nylon brush she used only on her fingernails. I didn't want to notice the hesitation in Tom, the shade of a cower whenever Donna addressed him directly.

"So what's new with the record?" I asked loudly. Expecting the reassuring invocation of success to shore up Tom's faith. Because it was still the ranch, and everything I'd said was true—he just had to open himself to it. But Suzanne gave me a strange look. The others watching for her to set a tone. Because it hadn't gone well, that was the point of her stare.

"Mitch is a fucking traitor," she said.

I was too shocked to fully take in the ugly cast of Suzanne's hatred: how could Russell really not have gotten his deal? How could Mitch not have seen it on him, the aura of strange electricity, the air around him murmuring? Was it specific to this place, whatever power Russell had? But Suzanne's gaudy anger recruited me back in, too.

"Mitch freaked, who knows why. He lied. These people," Suzanne said. "These fucking dopes."

"You can't fuck with Russell," Donna said, nodding along. "Saying one thing, then going back on it. Mitch doesn't know how Russell is. Russell wouldn't even have to lift a finger."

Russell had slapped Helen, that time, like it was nothing. The uncomfortable rearranging I had to do, the mental squint in order to see things differently.

"But Mitch could change his mind, right?" I asked. When I finally looked toward Tom, he wasn't paying attention, his gaze trained beyond the porch.

Suzanne shrugged. "I don't know. He told Russell not to call him anymore." She let out a snort. "Fuck him. Just disappearing like he didn't make promises."

I was thinking about Mitch. His desire, that night, making him brutish so he didn't care when I winced, my hair caught under his arm. His fogged-over gaze that kept us indistinct, our bodies just the symbol of bodies.

"But it's cool," Suzanne said, forcing a smile. "It's not—"

She was cut off by the sudden surprise of Tom, surging to his feet. He clattered down from the porch and sprinted in the direction of the pool. Shouting something I couldn't make out. His shirt coming untucked, the naked, vulnerable holler.

"What's his problem?" Suzanne said, and I didn't know, flushing with desperate embarrassment that morphed into fear: Tom was still shouting, scrambling down the steps into the pool.

"The kid," he said, "the boy."

Nico: I flashed on the silent shape of his body in the water, his little lungs sloshing and full. The porch tilted. By the time we hurried over to the pool, Tom already slogging the kid out of the slimy water, it was immediately clear that he was okay. Everything was fine. Nico sat down on the grass, dripping, an aggrieved look on his face. Fisting at his eyes, pushing Tom away. He was crying more because of Tom than anything else, the strange man who'd yelled at him, who'd dragged him from the pool when he was just having fun.

"What's the big idea?" Donna said to Tom. Patting Nico on the head roughly, like a good dog.

"He jumped in." Tom's panic was reverberating through his whole body, his pants and shirt sopping. The wet suck of his shoes.

"So?"

Tom was wide-eyed, not understanding that trying to explain would make it worse.

"I thought he'd fallen into the pool."

"But there's water in there," Helen said.

"That wet stuff," Donna said, sniggering.

"The kid's fine," Suzanne said. "You scared him."

"Glug glug glug." A fit of giggling overtook Helen. "You thought he was dead or something?"

"He still could have drowned," Tom said, his voice going high. "No one was watching him. He's too young to really swim."

"Your face," Donna said. "God, you're all freaked, aren't you?"

The sight of Tom wringing the biological stink of pool water from his shirt. The junk in the yard catching the light. Nico got to his feet, shaking out his hair. Sniffing a little with his weird childish dignity. The girls were laughing, all of them, so Nico trundled off easily, no one noticing his departure. And I pretended I hadn't worried, either, that I'd known everything was fine, because Tom seemed pathetic, his panic right on the surface with no place to retreat, and even the kid was mad at him. I was ashamed for bringing him around, for how he'd caused such a fuss, and Suzanne was staring at me, so I knew exactly what a stupid idea it had been. Tom looked at me for help, but he saw the distance in my face, the way I slid my eyes back to the ground.

"I just think you should be careful," Tom said.

Suzanne snorted. "We should be careful?"

"I was a lifeguard," he said, his voice cracking. "People can drown even in shallow water." But Suzanne wasn't listening, making a face at Donna. Their shared disgust including me, I thought. I couldn't bear it.

"Relax," I said to Tom.

Tom looked wounded. "This is an awful place."

"You should leave, then," Suzanne said. "Doesn't that sound like a good idea?" The rattle of speed in her, the vacant, vicious smile—she was being meaner than she needed to be.

"Can I talk to you for a second?" Tom said to me.

Suzanne laughed. "Oh, man. Here we go."

"Just for a second," he said.

When I hesitated, Suzanne sighed. "Go talk to him," she said. "Christ."

Tom walked away from the others and I followed him with halting steps, as if distance could prevent contagion. I kept glancing back to the group, the girls heading to the porch. I wanted to be among them. I was furious with Tom, his silly pants, his thatchy hair.

"What?" I said. Impatient, my lips tight.

"I don't know," Tom said, "I just think—" He hesitated, darting a look at the house, pulling at his shirt. "You can come back with me right now, if you want. There's a party tonight," he said. "At the International House."

I could picture it. The Ritz crackers, earnest groups crammed around bowls of watery ice. Talking SDS and comparing reading lists. I half shrugged, the barest shift of a shoulder. He seemed to understand this gesture for the falsehood it was.

"Maybe I should write down my number for you," Tom said. "It's the hall phone, but you can just ask for me."

I could hear the stark billow of Suzanne's laughter carrying in the air.

"That's okay," I said. "There's no phone here, anyway."

"They aren't nice," Tom said, catching my eyes. He looked like a rural preacher after a baptism, the wet pants clinging to his legs, his earnest stare.

"What do you know?" I said, an alarming heat rising in my cheeks. "You don't even know them."

Tom made an abortive gesture with his hands. "It's a trash heap," he said, sputtering, "can't you see that?"

He indicated the crumbling house, the tangle of overgrown vegetation. All the junked-out cars and oil drums and picnic blankets abandoned to the mold and the termites. I saw it all, but I didn't absorb anything: I'd already hardened myself to him and there was nothing else to say.

Tom's departure allowed the girls to deepen into their natures without the fracture of an outsider's gaze. No more peaceful, sleepy chatter, no balmy stretches of easy silence.

"Where's your special friend?" Suzanne said. "Your old pal?" Her hollow affect, her leg jiggling even though her expression was blank.

I tried to laugh like they did, but I didn't know why I

got unnerved at the thought of Tom returning to Berkeley. He was right about the junk in the yard, there was
more of it, and maybe Nico really could have been hurt,
and what then? I noticed all of them had gotten skin-
nier, not just Donna, a brittle quality to their hair, a dull
drain behind the eyes. When they smiled, I glimpsed
the coated tongues seen on the starving. Without con-
sciously doing so, I pinned a lot of hope on Russell's return. Wanting him to weigh down the flapping corners
of my thoughts.

"Heartbreaker," Russell catcalled when he caught
sight of me. "You run off all the time," he said, "and it
breaks our hearts when you leave us behind."

I tried to convince myself, seeing the familiarity of
Russell's face, that the ranch was the same, though when
he hugged me, I saw something smeared at his jawline. It
was his sideburns. They were not stippled, like hair, but
flat. I looked closer. They were drawn on, I saw, with
some kind of charcoal or eyeliner. The thought disturbed
me; the perverseness, the fragility of the deception. Like
a boy I'd known in Petaluma who shoplifted makeup to
cover his pimples. Russell's hand worked my neck, passing along a fritter of energy. I couldn't tell if he was
angry or not. And how immediately the group jolted to
attention at his arrival, trooping in his wake like ragged
ducklings. I tried to pull Suzanne aside, hook my arm
through hers like the old days, but she just smiled, low
burning and unfocused, and shook herself loose, intent
on following Russell.

. . .

I learned that Russell had been harassing Mitch for the last few weeks. Showing up unannounced at his house. Sending Guy to knock over his trash cans, so Mitch came home to a lawn junked with flattened cereal boxes and shredded wax paper and tinfoil slick with food scraps. Mitch's caretaker had seen Russell there, too, just once— Scotty told Mitch he'd seen some guy parked at the gate, just staring, and when Scotty had asked him to leave, Russell had smiled and told him he was the house's previous owner. Russell had also shown up at the recording engineer's house, trying to cadge the tapes from his session with Mitch. The man's wife was home. Later she'd recall being irritated at the sound of the doorbell: their newborn was asleep in the back bedroom. When she opened the door, there was Russell in his grubby Wranglers, his squinty smile.

She'd heard stories of the session from her husband, so she knew who Russell was, but she wasn't afraid. Not really. He was not a frightening man when first encountered, and when she told him her husband wasn't home, Russell shrugged.

"I could just grab the tapes real quick," he said, straining to look past her. "In and out, just like that." That's when she got a little uneasy. Plowing her feet deeper into her old slippers, the fussing of the baby drifting down the hall.

"He keeps all that at work," she said, and Russell believed her.

The woman remembered she heard a noise in the yard later that night, a thrash in the roses, but when she looked out the window, she didn't see anything except the pebbled driveway, the stubble of the moonlit lawn.

My first night back was nothing like the old nights. The old nights had been alive with a juvenile sweetness in our faces—I'd pet the dog, who'd nose around for love, give him a hearty scratch behind his ears, my coursing hand urging me into a happy rhythm. And there had been strange nights, too, when we'd all taken acid or Russell would have to get in some drunk motorcycle guy's face, using all his flip-flop logic on him. But I had never felt scared. That night was different, by the ring of stones with the barest of fires going. No one paid any attention when the flames dissolved to nothing, everyone's roiling energy directed at Russell, who moved like a rubber band about to snap.

"This right here," Russell said. He was pacing, dinking out a quick song. "I just made it up and it's already a hit."

The guitar was out of tune, twanging flat notes—Russell didn't seem to notice. His voice rushed and frantic.

"And here's another one," he said. He fussed with the

tuning pegs before letting loose a jangle of strums. I tried to catch Suzanne's eye, but she was trained on Russell. "This is the future of music," he said over the din. "They think they know what's good 'cause they got songs on the radio, but that's not shit. They don't have true love in their hearts."

No one seemed to notice his words unraveling around the borders: they all echoed what he said, their mouths twisting in shared feeling. Russell was a genius, that's what I'd told Tom—and I could picture how Tom's face would have moved with pity if he were there to see Russell, and it made me hate Tom, because I could hear it, too, all the space in the songs for you to realize they were rough, not even rough, just bad: sentimental treacle, the words about love as blunt as a grade-schooler's, a heart drawn by a chubby hand. Sunshine and flowers and smiles. But I could not fully admit it, even then. The way Suzanne's face looked as she watched him—I wanted to be with her. I thought that loving someone acted as a kind of protective measure, like they'd understand the scale and intensity of your feelings and act accordingly. That seemed fair to me, as if fairness were a measure the universe cared anything about.

There were dreams I had sometimes, and I'd wake from the tail end assuming some image or fact to be true, carrying forward this assumption from the dreamworld into my waking life. And how jarring it would be to realize that I was not married, that I had not cracked the code to flight, and there would be a real sorrow.

The actual moment Russell told Suzanne to go to Mitch Lewis's house and teach him a lesson—I kept thinking I had witnessed it: the black night, the cool flicking chirps of crickets, and all those spooky oaks. But of course I hadn't. I'd read about it so much that I believed I could see it clearly, a scene in the exaggerated colors of a childhood memory.

I'd been waiting in Suzanne's room at the time. Irritable, desperate for her return. I'd tried to talk to her at multiple points that night, tugging at her arm, tracking her gaze, but she kept brushing me off. "Later," she said, and that was all it took for me to imagine her promise fulfilling itself in the darkness of her room. My chest tightened when I heard footsteps enter the room, mind swelling with the thought—Suzanne was here—but then I felt the soft glancing hit and my eyes flew open—it was just Donna. She'd thrown a pillow at me.

"Sleeping Beauty," she said, sniggering.

I tried to settle back into pretty repose; the sheet overheated from the nervous shuffle of my body, ears suggestible for any sound of Suzanne's return. But she didn't come to the room that night. I waited as long as I could, alert to every creak and jar, before passing into the drowsy patchwork of unwilling sleep.

In fact, Suzanne had been with Russell. The air of his trailer probably going stuffy from their fucking, Russell unraveling his plan for Mitch, he and Suzanne staring up at the ceiling. I can imagine how he got right up to the edge before swerving around the details, so maybe Suzanne would start to think she'd had the same idea, that it was hers, too.

"My little hellhound," he had cooed to her, his eyes pinwheeling from a mania that could be mistaken for love. It was strange to think Suzanne would be flattered in this moment, but certainly she was. His hand scratching her scalp, that same agitated pleasure men like to incite in dogs, and I can imagine how the pressure started to build, a desire to move along the larger rush.

"It should be big," Russell had said. "Something they can't ignore." I see him twisting a lock of Suzanne's hair around a finger and pulling, the barest tug so she wouldn't know if the throb she felt was pain or pleasure.

The door he opened, urging Suzanne through.

Suzanne was distracted the whole next day. Going off by herself, face announcing her hurry, or having urgent, whispered conferences with Guy. I was jealous, desperate that I couldn't compete with the fraction of her that was deeded to Russell. She'd folded herself up and I was a distant concern.

I nursed my own confusion, tending hopeful explanations, but when I smiled at her, she blinked with delayed recognition, like I was a stranger returning her forgotten pocketbook. I kept noticing a soldered look in her eyes, a grim inward turning. Later I'd understand this was preparation.

Dinner was some reheated beans that tasted of aluminum, the burned scrapings of the pot. Stale chocolate cake from the bakery with a hoary pack of frost. They wanted to eat indoors, so we sat on the splintered floor, plates crooked on our laps. Forcing a primitive caveman hunch—no one seemed to eat very much. Suzanne pressed a finger to the cake and watched it crumb. Their looks at one another across the room were bursting with suppressed hilarity, a surprise-party conspiracy. Donna handing Suzanne a rag with a significant air. I didn't understand anything, a pitiful dislocation keeping me blind and eager.

I'd steeled myself to force a talk on Suzanne. But I looked up from the nasty slop of my plate and saw she was already getting to her feet, her movements informed by information invisible to me.

They were going somewhere, I realized when I caught up to her, following the play of her flashlight beam. The lurch, the gag of desperation: Suzanne was going to leave me behind.

"Let me come too," I said. Trying to keep up, following the swift rupture she cut through the grass.

I couldn't see Suzanne's face. "Come where?" she said, her voice even.

"Wherever you're going," I said. "I know you're going somewhere."

The teasing lilt. "Russell didn't ask you to go."

"But I want to," I said. "Please."

Suzanne didn't say yes, exactly. But she slowed enough so I could match her stride, a pace new to me, purposeful.

"You should change," Suzanne said.

I looked down, trying to discern what had offended her: my cotton shirt, my long skirt.

"Into dark clothes," she said.

14

The car ride was as slurred over and unbelievable as a long illness. Guy at the wheel, Helen and Donna beside him. Suzanne sat in the backseat, staring out the window, and I was right next to her. The night had dropped deep and dark, the car passing under the streetlights. Their sulfur glow gliding across Suzanne's face, a stupor occupying the others. Sometimes it seemed like I never really left the car. That a version of me is always there.

Russell stayed at the ranch that night. Which didn't even register with me as strange. Suzanne and the others were his familiars, loosed out into the world—it had always been that way. Guy like his second in a duel, Suzanne and Helen and Donna not hesitating. Roos was supposed to have gone, too, but she didn't—she claimed, later, that she'd gotten a bad feeling and stayed behind, but I don't know if that is true. Did Russell hold her back, sensing a stubborn virtue in her that might yoke her to the real world? Roos with Nico, a child of her own. Roos, who did become the main witness against the others, taking the stand in a white dress with her hair parted straight down the middle.

I don't know if Suzanne told Russell I was coming— no one ever answered that question.

The car radio was on, playing the laughably foreign soundtrack to other people's lives. Other people who were getting ready to sleep, mothers who were scraping the last shreds of chicken dinner into the garbage. Helen was jawing away about a whale beaching down in Pismo and did we think it was true that it was a sign a big earthquake was gonna happen? Getting up on her knees then, like the idea thrilled her.

"We'd have to go to the desert," she said. No one was taking her bait: a hush had fallen over the car. Donna muttered something, and Helen set her jaw.

"Can you open the window?" Suzanne said.

"I'm cold," Helen whined in her baby voice.

"Come on," Suzanne said, pounding the back of the seat. "I'm fucking melting."

Helen rolled the window down and the car filled with air, flavored with exhaust. The salt of the nearby ocean.

And there I was among them. Russell had changed, things had soured, but I was with Suzanne. Her presence corralled any stray worries. Like the child who believes that her mother's bedtime vigil will ward off monsters. The child who cannot decipher that her mother might be frightened, too. The mother who understands she can do nothing for protection except offer up her own weak body in exchange.

Maybe some part of me had known where things were headed, a sunken glimmer in the murk: maybe I had a sense of the possible trajectory and went along anyway. Later that summer, and at various points throughout my life, I would sift through the grain of that night, feeling blindly.

All Suzanne said was that we were paying Mitch a visit. Her words were spiked with a cruelty I hadn't heard before, but even so, this was the furthest my mind ranged: we were going to do what we'd done at the Dutton house. We'd perform an unsettling psychic interruption so Mitch would have to be afraid, just for a minute, would have to reorder the world anew. Good—Suzanne's hatred for him allowed and inflamed my own. Mitch, with his fat, probing fingers, the halting, meaningless chatter he kept up while looking us over. As if his mundane words would fool us, keep us from noticing how his glance dripped with filth. I wanted him to feel weak. We would occupy Mitch's house like tricky spirits from another realm.

Because I did feel that, it's true. A sense that something united all of us in the car, the cool whiff of other worlds on our skin and hair. But I never thought, even once, that the other world might be death. I wouldn't really believe it until the news gathered its stark momentum. After which, of course, the presence of death seemed to color everything, like an odorless mist that filled the car and pressed against the windows, a mist we inhaled and exhaled and that shaped every word we spoke.

We had not gone very far, maybe twenty minutes from the ranch, Guy easing the car along the tight dark curves of the hills, emerging into the long empty stretches of the flat land and picking up speed. The stands of eucalyptus we passed, the chill of fog beyond the window.

My alertness held everything in precise amber. The radio, the shuffle of bodies, Suzanne's face in profile. This is what they had all the time, I imagined, this net of mutual presence like something too near to identify. Just a sense of being buoyed along the fraternal rush, the belonging.

Suzanne rested her hand on the seat between us. The familiar sight stirred me, remembering how she'd grabbed for me in Mitch's bed. The spotty surface of her nails, brittle from poor diet.

I was sick with foolish hope, believing I would ever stay in the blessed space of her attention. I tried to reach for her hand. A tap of her palm, like I had a note to pass. Suzanne startled a little and jarred from a haze I had not noticed until it broke.

"What?" she snapped.

My face dropped all ability to costume itself. Suzanne must have seen the needy swarm of love. Must have taken the measure, like a stone dropped in a well—but there was no sound marking the end. Her eyes went dull.

"Stop the car," Suzanne said.

Guy kept driving.

"Pull over," Suzanne said. Guy glanced back at us, then pulled into the shoulder of the right lane.

"What's the matter—," I said, but Suzanne cut me off.

"Get out," she said, opening the door. Moving too fast for me to stop her, the reel snapping ahead, the sound lagging behind.

"Come on," I said, trying to sound bright with the joke. Suzanne was already out of the car, waiting for me to leave. She wasn't joking.

"But there's nothing here," I said, circling a desperate look at the highway. Suzanne was shifting, impatient. I glanced to the others for help. Their faces were lit by the dome light, leaching their features so they seemed as cold and inhuman as bronze figures. Donna looked away, but Helen watched me with a medical curiosity. Guy shifted in the driver's seat, adjusting the mirror. Helen said something under her breath—Donna shushed her.

"Suzanne," I said, "please," the powerless tilt in my voice.

She said nothing. When I finally shuffled along the seat and got out, Suzanne didn't even hesitate. Ducking back inside the car and closing the door, the dome light snapping off and returning them to darkness.

And then they drove away.

I was alone, I understood, and even as I tended some naïve wish—they would return, it was only a joke, Suzanne would never leave me like that, not really—I knew that I had been tossed aside. I could only zoom away, to hover up somewhere by the tree line, looking down on a girl standing alone in the dark. Nobody I knew.

15

There were all kinds of rumors those first days. Howard Smith reported, erroneously, that Mitch Lewis had been killed, though this would be corrected more swiftly than the other rumors. David Brinkley reported six victims had been cut up and shot and left on the lawn. Then the number was amended to four people. Brinkley was the first to claim the presence of hoods and nooses and Satanic symbols, a confusion that started because of the heart on the wall of the living room. Drawn with the corner of a towel, soaked in the mother's blood.

The mix-up made sense—of course they'd read a ghoulish meaning in the shape, assume some cryptic, doomy scrawl. It was easier to imagine it was the left-over of a black mass than believe the actual truth: it was

just a heart, like any lovesick girl might doodle in a note-
book.

A mile up the road, I came upon an exit and nearby Texaco station. I went in and out of the sulfur lights, the
sound they made like bacon frying. I rocked on my toes,
watching the road. When I finally gave up on anyone
coming for me, I called my father's number from the pay
phone. Tamar answered. "It's me," I said.

"Evie," she said. "Thank God. Where are you?" I could
picture her twining the cord in the kitchen, gathering the
loops. "I knew you'd call soon. I told your dad you would."

I explained where I was. She must have heard the
crack in my voice.

"I'll leave now," she said. "You stay right there."

I sat on the curb to wait, leaning on my knees. The air
was cool with the first news of autumn, and the constel-
lation of brake lights was going along 101, the big trucks
rearing as they picked up speed. I was reeling with excuses for Suzanne, some explanation for her behavior
that would shake out. But there wasn't anything but the
awful, immediate knowledge—we had never been close. I
had not meant anything.

I could sense curious eyes on me, the truckers who
bought bags of sunflower seeds from the gas station and
spit neat streams of tobacco on the ground. Their fatherly
gaits and cowboy hats. I knew they were assessing the
facts of my aloneness. My bare legs and long hair. My

furious shock must have sent out some protective scrum, warning them off—they left me alone.

Finally I caught sight of a white Plymouth approaching. Tamar didn't turn off the ignition. I got into the passenger side, gratitude for Tamar's familiar face making me fumble. Her hair was wet. "I didn't have time to dry it," she said. The look she gave me was kind but mystified. I could tell she wanted to ask questions, but she must have known that I wouldn't explain. The hidden world that adolescents inhabit, surfacing from time to time only when forced, training their parents to expect their absence. I was already disappeared.

"Don't worry," she said. "He didn't tell your mom you took off. I told him that you'd show up and then she'd just be worried for no reason."

Already my grief was doubling, absence my only context. Suzanne had left me, for good. A frictionless fall, the shock of missing a step. Tamar searched her purse with one hand until she found a small gold box, overlaid with pink stamped leather. Like a card case. There was a single joint inside, and she nodded to the glove compartment— I found a lighter.

"Don't tell your dad?" She inhaled, eyes on the road. "He might ground me, too."

Tamar was telling the truth: my father hadn't called my mother, and though he was shaky with rage, he was sheepish, too, his daughter a pet he'd forgotten to feed.

"You could've been hurt," he said, like an actor guessing at his lines.

Tamar calmly patted his back on her way to the kitchen, then poured herself a Coke. Leaving me with his hot, nervous breath, his blinky, frightened face. He regarded me across the living room, his upset trailing off. Everything that had happened—I was unafraid of this, my father's neutered anger. What could he do to me? What could he take away?

And then I was back in my bland room in Palo Alto, the light from the lamp the featureless light of the business traveler.

The apartment was empty by the time I emerged the next morning, my father and Tamar already at work. One of them—probably Tamar—had left a fan going, and a fake-looking plant shivered in the wake of air. There was only a week before I had to leave for boarding school, and seven days seemed too long to be in my father's apartment, seven dinners to soldier through, but, at the same time, unfairly brief—I wouldn't have time for habits, for context. I just had to wait.

I turned on the television, the chatter a comforting soundtrack as I foraged in the kitchen. The box of Rice Krispies in the cabinet had a barest coating of cereal left: I ate it by the handful, then flattened the empty box. I poured a glass of iced tea, balanced a stack of crackers with the pleasing quantity and thickness of poker chips. I ferried the food to the couch. Before I could settle back, the screen stopped me.

The crowd of images, doubling and spreading.

The search for the perpetrator or perpetrators still unsuccessful. The newscaster said Mitch Lewis was not available for comment. The crackers crimped into shards by my wet hands.

Only after the trial did things come into focus, that night taking on the now familiar arc. Every detail and blip made public. There are times I try to guess what part I might have played. What amount would belong to me. It's easiest to think I wouldn't have done anything, like I would have stopped them, my presence the mooring that kept Suzanne in the human realm. That was the wish, the cogent parable. But there was another possibility that slouched along, insistent and unseen. The bogeyman under the bed, the snake at the bottom of the stairs: maybe I would have done something, too.

Maybe it would have been easy.

They'd gone straight to Mitch's after leaving me by the side of the road. Another thirty minutes in the car, thirty minutes that were maybe energized by my dramatic dismissal, the consolidation of the group into the true pilgrims. Suzanne leaning on folded arms over the front seat, giving off an amphetamine fritz, that lucid surety.

Guy turning off the highway and onto the two-lane road, crossing the lagoon. The low stucco motels by the off-ramp, the eucalyptus loomy and peppering the air. Helen claimed, in her court testimony, that this was the first moment she expressed reservations to the others. But I don't believe it. If anyone was questioning themselves, it was all under the surface, a filmy bubble drifting and popping in their brains. Their doubt growing weak as the particulars of a dream grow weak. Helen realized she'd left her knife at home. Suzanne shouted at her, according to trial documents, but the group dismissed plans to go back for it. They were already coasting, in thrall to a bigger momentum.

They parked the Ford along the road, not even bothering to hide it. As they made their way to Mitch's gate, their minds seemed to hover and settle on the same movements, like a single organism.

I can imagine that view. Mitch's house, as seen from the gravel drive. The calm fill of the bay, the prow of the living room. It was familiar to them. The month they'd spent living with Mitch before I'd known them, running up delivery bills and catching molluscum from dank towels. But still. I think that night they might have been newly struck by the house, faceted and bright as rock candy. Its inhabitants already doomed, so doomed the group could feel an almost preemptive sorrow for them.

For how completely helpless they were to larger movements, their lives already redundant, like a tape recorded over with static.

They'd expected to find Mitch. Everyone knows this part: how Mitch had been called to Los Angeles to work on a track he'd made for *Stone Gods*, the movie that was never released. He'd taken the last TWA flight of the night out of SFO, landing in Burbank, leaving his house in the hands of Scotty, who had cut the grass that morning but not yet cleaned the pool. Mitch's old girlfriend calling in a favor, asking if she and Christopher could crash for two nights, just two nights.

Suzanne and the others had been surprised to find strangers in the house. No one they had ever met. And that could have been the abortive moment, a glance of agreement passing between them. The return to the car, their deflated silence. But they didn't turn back. They did what Russell had told them to do.

Make a scene. Do something everyone would hear about.

The people in the main house were preparing to go to bed, Linda and her little boy. She'd made him spaghetti for dinner and had snuck a forkful from his bowl but not bothered to make anything for herself. They were sleeping in the guest bedroom—her quilted weekend bag leaking clothes on the floor. Christopher's grimy stuffed lizard with its jet button eyes.

Scotty had invited his girlfriend, Gwen Sutherland, to listen to records and use Mitch's hot tub while Mitch was away. She was twenty-three, a recent graduate of the College of Marin, and she'd met Scotty at a barbecue in Ross. Not particularly attractive, but Gwen was kind and friendly, the kind of girl that boys are forever asking to sew on buttons or trim their hair.

They had both had a few beers. Scotty smoked some weed, though Gwen had not. They passed the evening in the tiny caretaker's cottage Scotty kept to military standards of cleanliness—the sheets on his futon tight with hospital corners.

Suzanne and the others came across Scotty first. Nodding off on the couch. Suzanne cleaved away to investigate the sound of Gwen in the bathroom, while Guy nodded at Helen and Donna to go search the main house. Guy nudged Scotty awake. He snorted, jolting back from a dream. Scotty didn't have his glasses on—he'd rested them on his chest as he fell asleep—and he must have thought Guy was Mitch, returning early.

"Sorry," Scotty said, thinking about the pool, "sorry." Blindly tapping for his glasses.

Then Scotty fumbled them on and saw the knife smiling up from Guy's hand.

• • •

Suzanne had gotten the girl from the bathroom. Gwen was bent over the sink, splashing water on her face. When Gwen straightened, she saw a shape in the corner of her eye.

"Hi," Gwen said, her face dripping. She was a girl who had been well raised. Friendly, even when surprised.

Maybe Gwen thought it was a friend of Mitch's or Scotty's, though within seconds it must have been obvious that something was wrong. That the girl who smiled back (because Suzanne did, famously, smile back) had eyes like a brick wall.

Helen and Donna collected the woman and the boy in the main house. Linda was upset, her hand fluttering at her throat, but she went with them. Linda in her underpants, her big T-shirt—she must have thought that as long as she was quiet and polite, she'd be fine. Trying to reassure Christopher with her eyes. The chub of his hand in hers, his untrimmed fingernails. The boy didn't cry until later; Donna said he seemed interested at first, like it was a game. Hide and go seek, red rover, red rover.

I try to imagine what Russell was doing while all this was happening. Maybe they'd made a fire at the ranch and Russell was playing guitar in its darty light. Or maybe he'd taken Roos or some other girl to his trailer, and maybe they were sharing a joint and watching the smoke drift and hover against the ceiling. The girl would have preened under his hand, his singular attention, though of course his mind would have been far away, in a house on Edgewater Road with the sea out the door. I can see his tricky shrug, the inward coiling of his eyes that made them polished and cold as doorknobs. "They wanted to do it," he'd say later. Laughing in the judge's face. Laughing so hard he was choking. "You think I made them do anything? You think these hands did a single thing?" The bailiff had to remove him from the court-room, Russell was laughing so hard.

They brought everyone to the living room of the main house. Guy made them all sit on the big couch. The glances between the victims that did not know, yet, that they were victims.

"What are you gonna do to us?" Gwen kept asking.

Scotty rolled his eyes, miserable and sweating, and Gwen laughed—maybe she could see, suddenly, that Scotty could not protect her. That he was just a young man, his glasses fogged, his lips trembling, and that she was far from her own home.

She started to cry.

"Shut up," Guy said, "Christ."

Gwen tried to halt her sobs, shaking silently. Linda at-tempted to keep Christopher calm, even as the girls tied everyone up. Donna knotting a towel around Gwen's hands. Linda squeezing Christopher one last time before Guy nudged them apart. Gwen sat on the couch with her skirt hitched up her legs, keening with abandon. The exposed skin of her thighs, her still wet face. Linda murmuring to Suzanne that they could have all the money that was in her purse, all of it, that if they just took her to the bank, she could get some more. Linda's voice was a calm monotone, a shoring up of control, though of course she had none.

Scotty was the first. He'd struggled when Guy put a belt around his hands.

"Just a second," Scotty said, "hey." Bristling at the rough grasp.

And Guy lost it. Slamming the knife with such force that the handle had splintered in two. Scotty struggled but could only flop onto the floor, trying to roll over and protect his stomach. A bubble of blood appearing from his nose and mouth.

Gwen's hands had been tied loosely—as soon as the blade sank into Scotty, she jerked free and ran out the front door. Screaming with a cartoon recklessness that sounded fake. She was almost to the gate when she tripped and fell on the lawn. Before she could get to her feet, Donna was already on her. Crawling over her back, stabbing until Gwen asked, politely, if she could die already.

. . .

They killed the mother and son last.

"Please," Linda said. Plainly. Even then, I think, hoping for some reprieve. She was very beautiful and very young. She had a child.

"Please," she said, "I can get you money." But Suzanne didn't want money. The amphetamines tightening her temples, an incantatory throb. The beautiful girl's heart, motoring in her chest—the narcotic, desperate rev. How Linda must have believed, as beautiful people do, that there was a solution, that she would be saved. Helen held Linda down—her hands on Linda's shoulders were tentative at first, like a bad dance partner, but then Suzanne snapped at Helen, impatient, and she pressed harder. Linda's eyes closed because she knew what was coming.

Christopher had started to cry. Crouching behind the couch; no one had to hold him down. His underwear saturated with the bitter smell of urine. His cries were shaped by screams, an emptying out of all feeling. His mother on the carpet, no longer moving.

Suzanne squatted on the floor. Holding out her hands to him. "Come here," she said. "Come on."

This is the part that isn't written about anywhere, but the part I imagine most.

How Suzanne's hands must have already been sprayed with blood. The warm medical stink of the body on her clothes and hair. And I can picture it, because I knew every degree of her face. The calming mystic air on her, like she was moving through water.

"Come on," she said one last time, and the boy inched toward her. Then he was in her lap, and she held him there, the knife like a gift she was giving him.

By the time the news report was finished, I was sitting down. The couch seemed sheared off from the rest of the apartment, occupying airless space. Images blistered and branched like nightmare vines. The indifferent sea beyond the house. The footage of policemen in shirtsleeves, stepping from Mitch's front door. There was no reason for them to hurry, I saw—it was over. Nobody would be saved.

I understood this news was much bigger than me. That I was only taking in the first glancing flash. I careened toward an exit, a trick latch: maybe Suzanne had broken off from the group, maybe she wasn't involved. But all these frantic wishes carried their own echoed response. Of course she had done it.

The possibilities washed past. Why Mitch hadn't been home. How I could have intersected with what was coming. How I could have ignored all the warnings. My breath was squeezed from the effort of trying not to cry.

I could imagine how impatient Suzanne would be with my upset. Her cool voice.

Why are you crying? she'd ask.

You didn't even do anything.

It's strange to imagine the stretch of time when the murders were unsolved. That the act ever existed separately from Suzanne and the others. But for the larger world, it did. They wouldn't get caught for many months. The crime—so close to home, so vicious—sickened everyone with hysteria. Homes had been reshaped. Turned suddenly unsafe, familiarity flung back in their owners' faces, as if taunting them—see, this is your living room, your kitchen, and see how little it helps, all that familiarity. See how little it means, at the end.

The news blared through dinner. I kept turning at a jump of motion in the corner of my eye, but it was just the stream of television or a headlight glinting past the apartment window. My father scratched his neck as we watched, the expression on his face unfamiliar to me—he was afraid. Tamar wouldn't leave it alone.

"The kid," she said. "It wouldn't be so bad if they didn't kill the kid."

I had a numb certainty they would see it on me. A rupture in my face, the silence obvious. But they didn't. My father locked the apartment door, then checked again before he went to bed. I stayed awake, my hands limp and clammy in the lamplight. Was there the merest slip between the outcomes? If the bright faces of planets had orbited in another arrangement, or a different tide had eaten away at the shore that night—was that the membrane that separated the world where I had or had not done it? When I tried to sleep, the inward reel of violence made me open my eyes. And something else, too, chiding in the background—even then, I missed her.

The logic of the killings was too oblique to unravel, involving too many facets, too many false clues. All the police had were the bodies, the scattered scenes of death like note cards out of order. Was it random? Was Mitch the target? Or Linda, or Scotty, or even Gwen? Mitch knew so many people, had a celebrity's assortment of enemies and resentful friends. Russell's name was brought up, by Mitch and by others, but it was one of many. By the time the police finally checked out the ranch, the group had already abandoned the house, taking the bus to campgrounds up and down the coast, hiding out in the desert.

I didn't know how stalled the investigation was, how the police got caught up following trivia—a key fob on the lawn that ended up belonging to a housekeeper, Mitch's old manager under surveillance. Death imbued the insignificant with forced primacy, its scrambled light turning everything into evidence. I knew what had happened, so it seemed the police must know, too, and I waited for Suzanne's arrest, the day the police would come looking for me—because I'd left my duffel behind.

Because that Berkeley student Tom would put together the murders and Suzanne's hissing talk of Mitch and contact the police. My fear was real, but it was unfounded—Tom knew only my first name. Maybe he did speak to the police, good citizen that he was, but nothing came of it—they were inundated with calls and letters, all kinds of people claiming responsibility or some private knowledge. My duffel was just an ordinary duffel, and it had no identifying feature. The things inside: clothes, a book about the Green Knight. My tube of Merle Norman. The possessions of a child pretending at an adult's accrual. And of course the girls probably had gone through it, tossing the useless book, keeping the clothes.

I had told many lies, but this one colonized a bigger silence. I thought of telling Tamar. Telling my father. But then I'd picture Suzanne, imagine her picking at a fingernail, the sudden cut of her gaze turning to me. I didn't say anything to anyone.

The fear that followed the wake of the murders is not hard to call up. I was barely alone the week before boarding school, trailing Tamar and my father from room to room, glancing out windows for the black bus. Awake all night, as if my labored vigil would protect us, my hours of suffering a one-to-one offering. It seemed unbelievable that Tamar or my father didn't notice how pale I was, how suddenly desperate for their company. They expected life would march on. Things had to be done, and I got shunted along their logistics with the numbness that had taken the place of whatever had made me Evie. My love of cinnamon hard candies, what I dreamed—that had all been exchanged for this new self, the changeling who nodded when spoken to and rinsed and dried the dinner plates, hands reddening in the hot water.

I had to pack up my room at my mother's house before I went to boarding school. My mother had ordered me the Catalina uniform—I found two navy skirts and a middy blouse folded on my bed, the fabric stinking of industrial cleaner, like rental tablecloths. I didn't bother to try on the clothes, shoving them into a suitcase on top of tennis shoes. I didn't know what else to pack, and it didn't seem to matter. I stared at the room in a trance. All my once beloved things—a vinyl diary, a birthstone charm, a book of pencil drawings—seemed valueless and defunct, drained of an animating force. It was impossible to picture what type of girl would ever have liked those things. Ever worn a charm around her wrist or written accounts of her day.

"You need a bigger suitcase?" my mother said from my doorway, startling me. Her face looked rumpled, and I could smell how much she'd been smoking. "You can take my red one, if you want."

I thought that she'd notice the change in me even if Tamar or my father couldn't. The baby fat in my face disappeared, a hard scrape to my features. But she hadn't mentioned anything.

"This is fine," I said.

My mother paused, surveying my room. The mostly empty suitcase. "The uniform fits?" she asked.

I hadn't even tried it on, but I nodded, wrung into a new acquiescence.

"Good, good." When she smiled, her lips cracked and I was suddenly overcome.

I was shoving books into the closet when I found two milky Polaroids, hidden under a stack of old magazines. The sudden presence of Suzanne in my room: her hot feral smile, the pudge of her breasts. I could call up disgust for her, hopped up on Dexedrine and sweating from the effort of butchery, and at the same time be pulled in by a helpless drift—here was Suzanne. I should get rid of the photo, I knew, the image already charged with the guilty air of evidence. But I couldn't. I turned the picture over, burying it in a book I'd never read again. The second photo was of the smeary back of someone's head, turning away, and I stared at the image for a long moment before I realized the person was me.

PART FOUR

SASHA AND JULIAN AND ZAV left early, and then I was alone. The house looked as it had always looked. Only the bed in the other room, the sheets scrabbled and smelling of sex, indicated anyone else had ever been here. I would wash the sheets in the machine in the garage. Fold and slot them on the closet shelves, sweep the room back to its previous blankness.

I walked along the cold sand that afternoon, stippled with broken bits of shell, the shifting holes where sand crabs burrowed. I liked the rush of wind in my ears. The wind drove people off—students from the junior college yelping while their boyfriends chased down the ripple of a blanket. Families finally giving up and heading toward their cars, toting folding chairs, the poky splay of a cheap kite, already broken. I was wearing two sweatshirts and the bulk made me feel protected, my movements slower. Every couple of feet, I'd come across the giant, ropy seaweed, tangled and thick as a fireman's hose. The purging of an alien species, seemingly not of this world. It was kelp, someone had told me, bull kelp. Knowing its name didn't make it any less strange.

Sasha had barely said goodbye. Burrowing into Julian's side, her face set like a preventative against my pity. She had already absented herself, I knew, gone to that other place in her mind where Julian was sweet and kind and life was fun, or if it wasn't fun, it was *interesting*, and wasn't that valuable, didn't that mean something? I tried to smile at her, to speed her a message on an invisible thread. But it had never been me she wanted.

The fog had been denser in Carmel, descending over the campus of my boarding school like a blizzard. The spire of the chapel, the nearby sea. I had started school that September, just as I was supposed to. Carmel was an old-fashioned place, and my classmates seemed much younger than they were. My roommate with her collection of mohair sweaters arranged by color. The dormitory walls softened with tapestries, the after-curfew creeping. The Tuck Shop, run by seniors, which sold chips and soda and candy, and how all the girls acted like this was the height of sophistication and freedom, being allowed to eat in the Tuck Shop from nine to eleven thirty on weekends. For all their talk, their bluster and crates of records, my classmates seemed childish, even the ones from New York. Occasionally, when the fog obscured the spires of the chapel, some girls could no longer orient themselves and got lost.

For the first few weeks, I watched the girls, shouting to one another across the quad, their backpacks turtled on their backs or slung from their hands. They seemed to move through glass, like the well-fed and well-loved scamps of detective series, who tied ribbons around their ponytails and wore gingham shirts on weekends. They wrote letters home and spoke of beloved kittens and worshipful younger sisters. The common rooms were the domain of slippers and housecoats, girls who ate Charleston Chews cold from miniature refrigerators and huddled by the television until they seemed to have psychologically absorbed the cathode rays. Someone's boyfriend died in a rock-climbing accident in Switzerland: everyone gathered around her, on fire with tragedy. Their dramatic shows of support underpinned with jealousy—bad luck was rare enough to be glamorous.

I worried I was marked. A fearful undercurrent made visible. But the structure of the school—its particularities, its almost municipal quality—seemed to cut through the dim. To my surprise, I made friends. A girl in my poetry class. My roommate, Jessamine. My dread appeared to others as a rarefied air, my isolation the isolation of weary experience.

Jessamine was from a cattle town near Oregon. Her older brother sent her comic books where female superheroes burst out of their costumes and had sex with octopuses or cartoon dogs. He got them from a friend in Mexico, Jessamine said, and she liked the silly violence, reading them with her head hung over the side of the bed.

"This one's nuts," she'd snort, tossing a comic to me. I'd try to hide a vague queasiness incited by the starbursting blood and heaving breasts.

"I'm on a diet where I just share all my food," Jessamine had explained, giving me one of the Mallomars she kept in her desk drawer. "I used to throw half of everything away, but then the dorms got a mice infestation and I couldn't."

She reminded me of Connie, the same shy way she plucked her shirt away from her belly. Connie, who'd be at the high school in Petaluma. Crossing the low steps, eating lunch at the splintered picnic tables. I had no idea how to think of her anymore.

Jessamine was hungry for my stories of home, imagining I lived in the shadow of the Hollywood sign. In a house the sherbet pink of California money, a gardener sweeping the tennis court. It didn't matter that I was from a dairy town and told her so: other facts were bigger, like who my grandmother had been. The assumptions Jessamine made about the source of my silence at the beginning of the year, all of it—I let myself step into the outline. I talked about a boyfriend, just one in a series of many. "He was famous," I said. "I can't say who. But I lived with him for a while. His dick was purple," I said, snorting, and Jessamine laughed, too. Casting a look in my direction all wrapped up in jealousy and wonder. The way I had looked at Suzanne, maybe, and how easy it was to keep up a steady stream of stories, a wishful narrative that borrowed the best of the ranch and folded it into a new shape, like origami. A world where everything turned out as I'd wanted.

I took French class from a pretty, newly engaged teacher who let the popular girls try on her engagement ring. I took art class from Miss Cooke, earnest with first-job anxiety. The line of makeup I could sometimes see along her jaw made me pity her, though she tried to be kind to me. She didn't comment when she noticed me staring into space or resting my head on my folded arms. Once she took me off campus for malteds and a hot dog that tasted of warm water. She told me how she had moved from New York to take her job, how the city asphalt would reflect sheets of sun, how her neighbor's dog shit all over the apartment stairs, how she'd gone a little crazy.

"I would eat just the corners of my roommate's food. Then it would all be gone, and I would get sick." Miss Cooke's glasses pinched her eyes. "I've never felt so sad, and there was no real reason for it, you know?"

She waited, obviously for me to match the story with

one of my own. Expecting a sad, manageable tale of the defection of a hometown boyfriend or a mother in the hospital, the cruel whispers of a bitchy roommate. A situation she could make heroic sense of for me, cast in older and wiser perspective. The thought of actually telling Miss Cooke the truth made my mouth tighten with unreal hilarity. She knew about the still-unsolved murders—everyone did. People locked doors and installed dead bolts, bought guard dogs at a markup. The desperate police got nothing from Mitch, who had fled in fear to the South of France, though his house wouldn't be razed until the following year. Pilgrims had started driving past the gate, hoping to pick up horror like a vapor in the air. Idling in their cars until weary neighbors shooed them off. In his absence, detectives were following leads from drug dealers and schizophrenics, bored housewives. Even enlisting a psychic to walk the rooms of Mitch's house, straining to pick up vibes.

"The killer is a lonely, middle-aged man," I'd heard the psychic say on a call-in show. "He was punished as a youth for something he hadn't done. I'm getting the letter K. I'm getting the town Vallejo."

Even if Miss Cooke would believe me, what would I tell her? That I had not slept well since August because I'd been too afraid of the unmonitored territory of dreams? That I woke certain that Russell was in the room—taking soggy gasps for breath, the still air like a hand over my mouth? That the cringe of contagion was on me: there was some concurrent realm where that night had not happened, where I insisted Suzanne leave the ranch. Where the blond woman and her teddy-bear son were pushing a cart down a grocery store aisle, planning a Sunday dinner, snippy and tired. Where Gwen was wrapping her damp hair in a towel, smoothing lotion on her legs. Scotty clearing the hot tub filters of debris, the silent arc of the sprinkler, a song floating into the yard from a nearby radio.

The letters I wrote my mother were willful acts of theater, at first. Then true enough.

Class was interesting.

I had friends.

Next week we would go to the aquarium and watch the jellyfish gape and parry in their illuminated tanks, suspended in the water like delicate handkerchiefs.

By the time I'd walked the farthest spit of land, the wind had picked up. The beach empty, all the picnickers and dog walkers gone. I stepped my way over the boulders, heading back to the main stretch of sand. Following the line between cliff and wave. I'd done this walk many times. I wondered how far Sasha and Julian and Zav had gotten by then. Probably still an hour from L.A. Without having to think about it, I knew Julian and Zav were sitting in the front seats and Sasha was in the back. I could imagine her leaning forward from time to time, asking for a joke to be repeated or pointing out some funny road sign. Trying to campaign for her own existence, before finally giving up and lying back on the seat. Letting their conversation thicken into meaningless noise while she watched the road, the passing orchards. The branches flashing with the silver ties that kept away birds.

I was passing by the common room with Jessamine, on our way to the Tuck Shop, when a girl called, "Your sister's looking for you downstairs." I didn't look up; she couldn't be talking to me. But she was. It took me a moment to understand what might be happening.

Jessamine seemed hurt. "I didn't know you had a sister."

I suppose I had known Suzanne would come for me.

The cottony numbness I occupied at school wasn't unpleasant, in the same way a limb falling asleep isn't unpleasant. Until that arm or leg wakes up. Then the prickles come, the sting of return—seeing Suzanne leaning in the shade of the dorm entrance. Her hair uncombed, her lips bristling—her presence knocked the plates of time ajar.

Everything was returned to me. My heart strobed, helpless, with the tinny cut of fear. But what could Suzanne do? It was daytime, the school filled with witnesses. I watched her notice the fuss of landscaping, teachers on their way to tutoring appointments, girls crossing the quad with tennis bags and chocolate milk on their breath, walking proof of the efforts of unseen mothers. There was a curious, animal distance in Suzanne's face, a measurement of the uncanny place she'd found herself.

She straightened when I approached. "Look at you," she said. "All clean and scrubbed." I saw a new harshness in her face: a blood blister under a fingernail.

I didn't say anything. I couldn't. I kept touching the ends of my hair. It was shorter—Jessamine had cut it in the bathroom, squinting at a how-to article in a magazine.

"You look happy to see me," Suzanne said. Smiling. I smiled back, but it was hollow. That seemed, obliquely, to please Suzanne. My fear.

I knew I should do something—we kept standing under the awning, increasing the chance someone would stop to ask me a question or introduce herself to my sister. But I couldn't make myself move. Russell and the others couldn't be very far away—were they watching me? The windows of the buildings seemed alive, my mind flashing to snipers and Russell's long stare.

"Show me your room," Suzanne announced. "I want to see."

The room was empty, Jessamine still at the Tuck Shop, and Suzanne pushed past me and through the doorway before I could stop her.

"Just lovely," she trilled in a fake English accent. She sat down on Jessamine's bed. Bouncing up and down. Looking at the taped-up poster of a Hawaiian landscape, the unreal ocean and sky sandwiching a sugary rib of beach. A set of the *World Book* Jessamine had never opened, a gift from her father. Jessamine kept a stack of letters in a carved wooden box and Suzanne immediately lifted the lid, sifting through. "Jessamine Singer," she read off an envelope. "Jessamine," she repeated. She let the lid bang shut and got to her feet. "So this one's your bed." She stirred my blanket with a mocking hand. My stomach tilted, a picture of us in Mitch's sheets. Hair sticking to her forehead and neck.

"You like it here?"

"It's okay." I was still in the doorway.

"Okay," Suzanne said, smiling. "Evie says the school is just okay."

I kept watching her hands. Wondering what they'd done exactly, as if the percentage mattered. She tracked my glance: she must have known what I was thinking. She got abruptly to her feet.

"Now I get to show you something," Suzanne said.

The bus was parked on a side street, just outside the school's gate. I could see the jostle of figures inside the bus. Russell and whoever was still around—I assumed everyone. They'd painted over the hood. But everything else was the same. The bus beastly and indestructible. My sudden certainty: they would surround me. Back me into a corner.

If anyone had seen us standing there on the slope, we

would have looked like friends. Chatting in the Saturday air, my hands in my pockets, Suzanne shading her eyes.

"We're going to the desert for a while," Suzanne announced, watching the flurry that must have been visible on my face. I felt the meager borders of my own life: a meeting that night for the French Club—Madame Guevel had promised butter tarts. The musty weed Jessamine wanted to smoke after curfew. Even knowing what I knew, did a part of me want to leave? Suzanne's dank breath and her cool hands. Sleeping on the ground, chewing nettle leaves to moisten our throats.

"He's not mad at you," she said. Keeping a steady simmer of eye contact. "He knows you wouldn't say anything."

And it was true: I hadn't said anything. My silence keeping me in the realm of the invisible. I had been frightened, yes. Maybe you could pin some of the silence on that fear, a fear I could call up even later, after Russell and Suzanne and the others were in jail. But it was something else, too. The helpless thoughts of Suzanne. Who had sometimes colored her nipples with cheap lipstick. Suzanne, who walked around so brutish, like she knew you were trying to take something from her. I didn't tell anyone because I wanted to keep her safe. Because who else had loved her? Who had ever held Suzanne in their arms and told her that her heart, beating away in her chest, was there on purpose?

My hands were sweating, but I couldn't wipe them on my jeans. I tried to make sense of this moment, to hold an image of Suzanne in my mind. Suzanne Parker. The atoms reorganizing themselves the first time I'd seen her in the park. How her mouth had smiled into mine.

No one had ever looked at me before Suzanne, not really, so she had become my definition. Her gaze softening my center so easily that even photographs of her seemed aimed at me, ignited with private meaning. It was different from Russell, the way she looked at me, because it contained him, too: it made him and everyone else smaller. We had been with the men, we had let them do what they wanted. But they would never know the parts of ourselves that we hid from them—they would never sense the lack or even know there was something more they should be looking for.

Suzanne was not a good person. I understood this. But I held the actual knowledge away from myself. How the coroner said the ring and pinky fingers of Linda's left hand had been severed because she had tried to protect her face.

Suzanne seemed to look at me as if there could be some explanation, but then a slight movement behind the shrouded windshield of the bus caught her attention—even then, she was alert to Russell's every shift—and a businesslike air came over her.

"Okay," she said, urged by the tick of an unseen clock. "I'm taking off." I had almost wanted a threat. Some indication that she might return, that I should fear her or could draw her back with the right combination of words.

I only ever saw her again in photographs and news reports. Still. I could never imagine her absence as permanent. Suzanne and the others would always exist for me; I believed that they would never die. That they would hover forever in the background of ordinary life, circling the highways and edging the parks. Moved by a force that would never cease or slow.

Suzanne had shrugged a little, that day, before walking down the grassy slope and disappearing into the bus. The queer reminder in her smile. Like we had a meeting, she and I, at some appointed time and place, and she knew I would forget.

I wanted to believe Suzanne kicked me out of the car because she'd seen a difference between us. That it was obvious to her that I could not kill anyone, Suzanne still lucid enough to understand that she was the reason I was in the car. She wanted to protect me from what was going to happen. That was the easy explanation.

But there was a complicating fact.

The hatred she must have felt to do what she'd done, to slam the knife over and over again like she was trying to rid herself of a frenzied sickness: hatred like that was not unfamiliar to me.

Hatred was easy. The permutations constant over the years: a stranger at a fair who palmed my crotch through my shorts. A man on the sidewalk who lunged at me, then laughed when I flinched. The night an older man took me to a fancy restaurant when I wasn't even old enough to like oysters. Not yet twenty. The owner joined our table, and so did a famous filmmaker. The men fell into a heated discussion with no entry point for me: I fidgeted with my heavy cloth napkin, drank water. Staring at the wall.

"Eat your vegetables," the filmmaker suddenly snapped at me. "You're a growing girl."

The filmmaker wanted me to know what I already knew: I had no power. He saw my need and used it against me.

My hatred for him was immediate. Like the first swallow of milk that's already gone off—rot strafing the nostrils, flooding the entire skull. The filmmaker laughed at me, and so did the others, the older man who would later place my hand on his dick while he drove me home.

None of this was rare. Things like this happened hundreds of times. Maybe more. The hatred that vibrated beneath the surface of my girl's face—I think Suzanne recognized it. Of course my hand would anticipate the weight of a knife. The particular give of a human body. There was so much to destroy.

Suzanne stopped me from doing what I might be capable of. And so she set me loose into the world like an avatar for the girl she would not be. She would never go to boarding school, but I still could, and she sent me spinning from her like a messenger for her alternate self. Suzanne gave me that: the poster of Hawaii on the wall, the beach and blue sky like the lowest common denominator of fantasy. The chance to attend poetry class, to leave bags of laundry outside my door and eat steaks on parents' visiting days, sopping with salt and blood.

It was a gift. What did I do with it? Life didn't accumulate as I'd once imagined. I graduated from boarding school, two years of college. Persisted through the blank decade in Los Angeles. I buried first my mother, then my father. His hair gone wispy as a child's. I paid bills and bought groceries and got my eyes checked while the days crumbled away like debris from a cliff face. Life a continuous backing away from the edge.

There were moments of forgetting. The summer I had visited Jessamine in Seattle after she had her first child—when I saw her waiting at the curb with her hair tucked into her coat, the years unknit themselves and I felt, for a moment, the sweet and blameless girl I had once been. The year with the man from Oregon, our shared kitchen hung with houseplants and Indian blankets on the seats of our car, covering the rips. We ate cold pita with peanut butter and walked in the wet green. Camping in the hills around Hot Springs Canyon, far down the coast, near a group who knew all the words to *The People's Song Book*. A sun-hot rock where we lay, drying from the lake, our bodies leaving behind a conjoined blur.

But the absence opened up again. I was almost a wife but lost the man. I was almost recognizable as a friend. And then I wasn't. The nights when I flicked off the bedside lamp and found myself in the heedless, lonely dark.

The times I thought, with a horrified twist, that none of this was a gift. Suzanne got the redemption that followed a conviction, the prison Bible groups and prime-time interviews and a mail-in college degree. I got the snuffed-out story of the bystander, a fugitive without a crime, half hoping and half terrified that no one was ever coming for me.

It was Helen, in the end, who ended up talking. She was only eighteen, still desirous of attention—I'm surprised they stayed out of jail as long as they did. Helen had been picked up in Bakersfield for using a stolen credit card. Just a week in a county jail and they would have let her go, but she couldn't help bragging to her cellmate. The coin-operated television in the common room showing a bulletin of the ongoing murder investigation.

"The house is way bigger than it looks in those pictures," Helen said, according to her cellmate. I can see Helen: nonchalant, thrusting her chin forward. Her cellmate must have ignored her at first. Rolling her eyes at the girlish bluster. But then Helen kept going, and suddenly the woman was listening closely, calculating reward money, a reduced sentence. Urging the girl to tell her more, to keep talking. Helen was probably flattered by the attention, unspooling the whole mess. Maybe even exaggerating, drawing out the haunted spaces between words, as in the incantation of a ghost story at a sleepover. We all want to be seen.

. . .

All of them would be arrested by the end of December. Russell, Suzanne, Donna, Guy, the others. The police descending on their tent encampment in Panamint Springs: torn flannel sleeping bags and blue nylon tarps, the dead ash of the campfire. Russell bolted when they came, as if he could outrun a whole squad of officers. The headlights of the police cruisers glowing in the bleached pink of morning. How pitiful, the immediacy of Russell's capture, forced to kneel in the scrub grass with his hands on his head. Guy handcuffed, stunned to discover there were limitations to the bravado that had carried him that far. The little kids were herded onto the Social Services van, wrapped in blankets, and handed cold cheese sandwiches. Their bellies distended and scalps boiling with lice. The authorities didn't know who had done what, not yet, so Suzanne was just one of the skinny jumble of girls. Girls who spit in the dirt like rabid dogs and went limp when the police tried to handcuff them. There was a demented dignity to their resistance—none of them had run. Even at the end, the girls had been stronger than Russell.

It would snow in Carmel that same week, the barest slip of white. Class was canceled, frost crunching thinly under our shoes as we tromped across the quad in our jean jackets. It seemed like the last morning on earth, and we peered into the gray sky as if more of the miracle were coming, though it all melted into a mess in less than an hour.

...

I was halfway back to the beach parking lot when I saw the man. Walking toward me. Maybe a hundred yards away. His head was shaved, revealing the aggressive outline of his skull. He was wearing a T-shirt, which was strange—his skin flushed in the wind. I didn't want to feel as uneasy as I did. A helpless accounting of the facts: I was alone on the sand. Still far from the parking lot. There was no one else around but me and this man. The cliff, starkly outlined, each striation and pulse of lichen. The wind lashing my hair across my face, dislocating and vulnerable. Rearranging the sand into furrows. I kept walking toward him. Forcing myself to keep my gait.

The distance between us fifty yards, now. His arms were honeycombed with muscle. The brute fact of his naked skull. I slowed my pace, but it didn't matter—the man was still heading briskly in my direction. His head was bouncing as he walked, an insane rhythmic twitch.

A rock, I thought crazily. He'll pick up a rock. He'll break open my skull, my brain leaking onto the sand. He'll tighten his hands around my throat until my windpipe collapses.

The stupid things I thought of:

Sasha and her briny, childish mouth. How the sun had looked in the tops of the trees lining my childhood driveway. Whether Suzanne knew I thought of her. How the mother must have begged, at the end.

The man was bearing down on me. My hands were

limp and wet. Please, I thought. Please. Who was I addressing? The man? God? Whoever handled these things.

And then he was in front of me.

Oh, I thought. Oh. Because he was just a normal man, harmless, nodding along to the white headphones nested in his ears. Just a man walking on the beach, enjoying the music, the weak sun through the fog. He smiled at me as he passed, and I smiled back, like you would smile at any stranger, any person you didn't know.

ACKNOWLEDGMENTS

I would like to thank Kate Medina and Bill Clegg for invaluable guidance. Thank you also to Anna Pitoniak, Derrill Hagood, Peter Mendelsund, Fred and Nancy Cline, and my brothers and sisters: Ramsey, Hilary, Megan, Elsie, Mayme, and Henry.

penguin.co.uk/vintage

the
jesus
man

CHRISTOS
TSIOLKAS

ATLANTIC BOOKS

London

First published in Australia in 1999 by Random House Australia, a division of
Random House, Inc., New York.

First published in paperback and e-book in Great Britain in 2016 by Atlantic Books,
an imprint of Atlantic Books Ltd.

10 9 8 7 6 5 4 3 2

A CIP catalogue record for this book is available from the British Library.

Paperback ISBN: 978 178 2397250
E-book ISBN: 978 178 2397267

Printed and bound CPI Group (UK) Ltd, Croydon, CR0 4YY

Atlantic Books
An Imprint of Atlantic Books Ltd
Ormond House
26–27 Boswell Street
London
WC1N 3JZ

www.atlantic-books.co.uk

for Shane Laing, in faith
for Jessica Migotto, in trust

and for Wayne van der Stelt, in gratitude and in love

Contents

Acknowledgements

A book is not just an object. It doesn't just belong to the writer. What is written is all my responsibility but it being written depends on the labour and support of others. So thanks to the friends around me—to George Papaellinas, Sasha Soldatow, Megan Nicholson, Spiro Economopolous, Jeana Vithoulkas, Miriam Iuricich, Helen Tamme, Cathy Woodfield, John Harrison and Dawn Jackson. And always, thanks to Alan 'Sol' Sultan. This all has only been made possible by the faith of my family. Thank you George and Georgia Tsiolkas, John, Catherine, Vicky, Pete, Bill and Eva. Thanks to Thea Diamanta, and in memory of Theo Illias Triantafyllou. As well, gratitude for the assistance and enthusiasm of Julia Stiles, Fiona Inglis and Linda Funnell. And especially, Jane Palfreyman. Gracias amigo! Thanks also to Paul Dougdale and Heather Brooks for helping with the printing—and for making Canberra inviting.

This book is also a hope for the future. For Geordie Moran Dalzell, for Caitlin, Illias and Zoe, for Kate and Michael. For Carl Reed, for Jack Harrison and Zachariah Stathis.

I want to extend a big thanks to the Maritime Union of Australia for giving me optimism. In a time when everything and everyone is announcing that greed has won, the MUA showed that no, it's winning, but it ain't over yet.

I am an atheist but I once did experience the shock of a vision. I was with my brother Dominic, his wife Eva, and their children; we were walking the gloomy and empty beaches at the southern most tip of the Australian coast. Even though it was summer, a sharp wind had foamed the sea. As we emerged from scrub and onto the beach, we saw a line of crows, a horizontal dotting along the shoreline; they were pecking into the sand. The first bird we approached was tearing into a dark object, and it refused to move as our shadows fell across it. Then my niece Lisa spotted what it was pecking.

—Get away, you dirty bird.

She let go of my hand and ran towards the creatures. She stopped abruptly.

A heart, large; too big to be human. All along the shore the crows were feeding on blood and innards, liver and stomach and lung. Each crow kept a respectful solitaire. They ate alone, a few metres away from each other. The terror I experienced is indescribable. All I can say of it is that I had stumbled across the mad order of nature: it was screaming out the riddle of God. When we looked out to the chopping sea, a dark mirror of oil caught our attention. The oil slick rode with the waves, rippling and shaking, but it retained its ovular form. Caught in the middle were large grey birds, those still alive were squealing weakly. I've never again—thankfully, never since that day—experienced such sound: the hopeless feeble lamentations, the will betrayed by exhaustion.

Why did we feel fear? It was the insane symmetry, the *mathematical* symmetry of what I saw—the neat column of birds feeding on blood and flesh. I can understand why the crow appears again and again in folk superstition as the herald of death. I saw them hungry for meat, *famished*, their zeal murderous.

This book is about a family, my family, which has been followed by the crow for generations. This is a myth and, like all myths, atheists and skeptics will scorn it. I'm not sure that I myself can claim a faith in what I am about to tell you.

•

On the beach Dominic rushed towards his child, scooped her in his large strong arms, held her, Shush Litsa, Shush. And he kicked at the crows. They circled above. Let's turn back, he said, his only thought his children. But part of me wanted to stay, I wanted to face this terror, examine it, wanted to comprehend it. Dominic has a particular strength that I wish were mine, this ability to turn away. He hates the crow, whatever that might mean, and he turns away from it. He has a faith that I don't have. We walked in a single file back away from the ocean, Dom holding Lisa, Eva with the baby, and me the last in line. I turned back and saw that the crows had returned to their feast. I heard the whimpering of the dying birds caught in their greasy prison.

Later, around the fire, the children asleep in the tents, I started questioning Dominic about the crow. What did it mean? Why had it followed us all our lives? He was exasperated by my questions. Eva was smoking a joint, in and out of the conversation.

—It's a myth, Louie, he told me. Understand? It's part of our family, who we are. Hasn't it always been with us?

—But myths aren't true, I insisted.

He laughed and stoked the fire.

—That's university talking, he goaded me, you just want to question everything.

—So myths are true?

—Some are. He. was stroking Eva's knee. She was smiling at me.

—What do you think, Eva?

We both looked at her.

—I don't know, she answered, offering me the joint. This is about your family, what I think doesn't matter.

—But you're family, insisted Dominic, what are we if not a family?

—I'm your wife, Dom, she answered softly. She got up and wiped her pants clean of dirt and twigs. I'm going to bed, she said, and kissed us both goodnight. I watched my brother kiss his wife, he closed his eyes as their lips touched, and I was jealous. Such a strong man, my brother, the way he had rushed towards Lisa on the beach. I know, I know that he must have shared my terror, shared my loathing of those birds. But he acted, for his daughter. I reached out and touched him, softly, on his knee.

—What?

—Nothing.

He ruffled my hair.

—Louie, Louie, he sang, and began rolling another joint. Don't worry about what doesn't make sense, what you can't understand. Just worry about what is real, what you can touch, what you can feel.

—Our family are a bit obsessed with myths, aren't they? I was doodling, with a stick, in the dirt. He didn't answer, I had made him sad.

—The crow is nothing, Lou, all right? You don't need the crow to understand our family. He sat up, handed me the joint, and when he spoke again his voice was firm, the older brother's voice. I'm going to the tent. Make sure the fire's out when you pack it in, right?

I nodded. I was alone. I looked into the slowly dwindling fire and could hear the light snores of the children, the shifting of the adult bodies. A family at sleep. I looked into the fire and thought about family.

•

It was Dominic who taught me how to clean underneath my foreskin. I don't know who taught him, he never said. Dad just never thought of it. He was cut and so he probably had no idea of the hygiene required for uncircumcised cocks. That the three of us boys kept our foreskins was Mum's idea, a decision she made straight after Dominic's birth, against the protestations of the doctor and the mild questioning of my father. I wonder whether she thought that somehow this would connect us boys to her land and to her history: our cocks were matriarchal and Greek, not patriarchal and Australian.

I was twelve and Dominic was about to get married. We had visited a store in Prahran that hired out suits and tuxedoes. I was to be the youngest groomsman. I was growing impatient—I hate clothes shopping! Mum kept fiddling with the tuxedo trouser leg, slipping in pins and recalculating measurements. Our brother Tommy had stepped outside, in his tux, middle of the day in High Street, smoking a cigarette.

—It'll be all right, I groaned.

—It looks fine, agreed Dom.

—Too short.

We couldn't sway her. Dominic knelt down beside her and checked. It's fine, he repeated. Reluctantly she stood up.

Later, back home, Dominic entered the bedroom I shared with Tommy. Tom was on his bed, reading *Mad* magazine. Dom ordered him out.

—Get fucked.

My oldest brother never once took an order from Tommy.

—Out, he warned.

Tommy, bitching, left the room.

—What, is it? Everything for the last month had been the wedding. Dom was tense. He sat on my bed and refused to look at me.

—Louie, you know about cleaning yourself?

There's no way to hide from a question like that. Looking back now I realise that, at twelve years of age, I was a shy and nervous kid. Easily humiliated. Dom was gentle, but loud waves of blood smashed against my ears. What he said to me sounded muffled, came from a long way away.

—Listen, you know how to pull back the skin on your dick? It was the first time he looked at me. I nodded. It was a lie.

—Good, well when you shower just pull back the skin and give yourself a wash. He took a deep breath, relieved it was over, and came over and hugged me. I was burning. He left me alone. He didn't say why he had decided to bring the subject up now— he didn't need to. I knew. It was when he was kneeling before me, it was then he must have sniffed my crotch. The accumulated scum. And I realised, an aching humiliation, that Mum had smelt it as well.

That night two things happened. I showered and slowly pulled back my foreskin. It was tight and it hurt, hurt badly; it stung. But I pulled it back and started to lather up, spent five fucking minutes rubbing my cock raw till there wasn't a fleck of dried old scum on it. And the second thing? Later, in bed, Tommy still watching TV in the lounge, I tried masturbating by tugging for the first time. Before, what I did was to roll my cock between my palms. It felt different, it didn't feel as good, but it felt the right thing to do. This was how Dom did it, how boys were meant to do it.

Tommy and I never really talked about such things. It was a code set up between us from when we were very young. I don't think Dom and Tommy spoke about that kind of stuff either. They weren't close. It was like there was me, the baby, there was

Dom, the oldest and a man, and somewhere in between was Tommy. He was happiest watching TV, sitting close to the screen, the rest of the family behind Him, not in view.

Of course, I remember the television as well, that it was always on. But some of my earliest memories—very early memories, those memories that reach back beyond when time became concrete, before time became clocked—are of being a small child and listening to the adults tell stories, their words competing with the TV. And I still remember one evening vividly, sitting on my father's lap. Mum and Yiota were telling stories about life back in Greece. They were talking about the priests. Mum always said that you could trust the Church, never the priest. Her Aunt Yianoula had had an affair for years with Father Vassili. This night Yiota was telling us about the priest in her village. He was more into boys than girls and was having it off with a boy who minded the goats up in the mountain. One day the priest's wife was returning from collecting firewood and she saw her husband, bent over, his robe discarded, being fucked by the shepherd boy. She screamed and started giving chase to both of them. Yiota says the men tore down the hill and ran into the valley where Yiota, still a girl, was helping her mother collect wild greens. She recalled that Father Yianni flew past, disrobed, only a white undershirt covering his torso. And you know what, chuckled Yiota, the big crucifix around his neck was swinging in time with his dick as he was running.

I remember the whole family collapsed into hysteria as Yiota told her tale. My father was laughing so much I can still remember his tears falling on my face as I looked up at him. Mama, Dom, Tommy, Spiro and Yiota, me and Dad, all of us were laughing.

•

I want to offer a history of my family. I can do that by fixing the dates—births and marriages, divorces and deaths. I can tell you the shared stories, the facts that have been sanctioned and passed down. But remember, please, this is also my story, in my own words. I'll try and be honest, tell you what I know. But it is an interpretation; and I have to go back to beginnings and in the beginning I wasn't there. So it may be that some of what I say is bullshit, is speculation, lies and fabrications passed on. Myth. But in wishing to describe a family it would be ludicrous to deny it its myths. Memory and myth, like fiction, tend towards the cataclysm, the catharsis, the tragic and the painful. Before I begin there is one thing I must insist on, that you must understand: we also shared laughter.

SECTION ONE

Dominic Stefano

Ghosts are not the resurrection but the insurrection of the dead.

FYODOR DOSTOYEVSKY

Dominic watched the clock, the slow creep towards the end of the lesson. He looked at the dark black sheen of Lynette's hair in front of him. With one hand he scratched letters into the desk, with the other he softly rubbed his crotch, thinking of Lynette, listening to the murmuring of the teacher, words descending without meaning or sense, aware only of the rhythm. Lynette's arse was big, squeezed into tight jeans. Dominic scratched the word *fuck* into the desk.

I should have wagged. He was bored by the regime and the monotony of school, the numbing repetition of knowledge. A map of Australia behind him, a picture of Queen Elizabeth, her face made ghostly by dust. A snakeskin, from an excursion in the country, was wrapped around the frame. Dominic took his hand off his crotch, yawned and again glanced at the clock. The hands tortured him with their exquisite laggard pace.

There was a sudden commotion in the corridor. A sobbing, then a knocking at the door. Mr Clifford entered, ignoring the students and walking straight up to the surprised Miss Ahrn. He whispered in her ear. The door was open and some students giggled, noticing that in the corridor thin Miss Lunerman was crying.

—Someone's died, whispered Lynette to the stolid Olga sitting beside her. Wonder who it is.

Dominic watched Miss Ahrn. She had gripped the desk, her eyes stared wide. Mr Clifford put his arm around her. She shook it off. Clearing heir throat, then with an unsteady voice, she asked for attention. Her adolescent audience sat up, obedient. Even Dominic, feigning his usual boredom, was eager to hear what she had to say.

—Class, we're dismissing early. It has just been announced on the radio. Miss Ahrn paused, she gripped the desk tighter. The bastards have sacked the Prime Minister.

The class broke into furore. Shouting, yelling. What happened? How? When? The pandemonium rang through the portable, shaking the air, joining the erupting thunder from throughout the school. Miss Ahrn and Mr Clifford watched silently.

—The cunts, the cunts, the cunts. Spiro Matheopolous was singing his disgust.

Only Dominic sat quietly. He was thinking, Mum will be furious.

He jumped up, took his thick history book and threw it against the back wall, towards the map. It crashed into the solemn face of the Queen. The snakeskin withered to dust and the glass fell as confetti to the floor. The room was immediately silent. He turned around, triumphant. Miss Ahrn smiled and Mr Clifford coughed nervously.

—Stefano, clean that mess up. The rest of you, go outside. There will be an early break.

Dominic did not move. His fellow classmates filed out into the yard. Mr Clifford glanced at him, then at the quiet Miss Ahrn, and he too left. The teacher and the student stood watching each other. She was the first to move.

—I'll help you clean up.

The woman bent over and with an exercise book began scraping up the glass. Dominic crouched, watching the slow

movement of her hands. Her long hair fell around her face, still
wet from tears, and her tight sweater stretched across her thin
breasts. The boy, clumsily, began to scoop up glass with his hand.

—No, Dom, get a broom and a pan.

The boy scrambled. He returned, handed them to the teacher
and sat down next to her. He watched her collect the glass, sweep
the dust. Her hands were long, thin, no polish on her nails. She
finished her task and smiled at him, handing him back the pan.

—Empty it.

He touched her skin.

—And this? He held up the portrait which had come loose
from the frame. Without a word, Miss Ahrn took it then tore it
into pieces. Dominic listened to the tearing then laughed. They
laughed together.

•

In the yard the school was dividing into factions. Dominic
walked over to where three boys were sitting on a fence, their
backs to the road. He sat with them.

—What you reckon, Dom?

—About what?

—Jesus, what do you reckon, dickhead? Whitlam's sacking.

—I reckon it stinks.

—Bound to happen. This from Zalate. He's an idiot.

—Why?

Zalate didn't answer that.

—Funny it should happen today.

—Why?

—You know, Gallipoli.

—What the fuck? Harry glanced around quickly, took a pack
of Winfield from his shirt pocket. He handed them around.
Dominic saw that Mr Zeidars was looking at them. The teacher
turned his back and Dominic took the smoke.

—Not fucking Gallipoli, you ignorant Croat cunt, it's
Armistice Day.

Zalate shrugged.

—You know what I mean, the minute silence for all the Aussies slaughtered by the Turks.

Harry giggled.

—Good on the Turks.

The boys stopped talking. A thin pale girl slid up to them.

—Can I speak to you, Dom?

Dominic nodded. The other boys moved on, a few metres away, pretending ignorance. Cheryl climbed up next to him.

—Have you been thinking about what I said?

—Whitlam's been sacked.

Cheryl wasn't looking at him.

—I don't know anything about that. She looked at him. I don't give a shit about that. She grabbed his smoke, puffed and handed it back.

—Well?

—Well what?

—What are we going to do?

Cheryl was the first girl Dominic had fucked. Standing up, a bedroom at a party, 'The Song Remains the Same'. Jeans still on, her fingers on his arse, a matter of minutes. The first thrust had hurt, a little, as if his foreskin was tearing, then once in, she was grimacing, breathing hard, not enjoying it, but for him it had felt terrific, it had felt warm. He came and cried at the same time. They had done it again and again. Stupidly, without thinking of the consequences, but it wasn't consequences he had wanted to think about. He kept wanting to return to her warm cunt. His mother talked of heaven, said that God existed but heaven did not. But God and heaven were there, together, in Cheryl's cunt.

—What do you want to do?

—Keep it?

She didn't know. She was asking him. She was frail, small tits, freckles and dirty blonde hair. Her stomach still flat. He no longer wanted the rush of her sex, not since the baby. The baby inside her made him stop wanting to fuck her. Made him stop wanting to be with her.

—We can't.

We, which we? Me, you, the baby? God?

—I told my mum.

—Jesus Fucking Christ! He threw the cigarette at her, she ducked; the boys looked up, then quickly looked away.

—Did you tell her it was me?

Cheryl got furious.

—She didn't have to ask. You're the only one I've been with.

Dominic took her hand, she let him. The teachers were calling the students, an assembly was forming. Mr Zeidars came up.

—Fall to assembly. He reached into Harry's pocket and took the cigarettes. If I catch you again . . . The threat was left open. They moved on, Mr Zeidars behind them, and Dominic let go of Cheryl's hand.

She whispered in his ear, Mum says you have to pay for it, and then she rushed off.

They were let off early. Dominic avoided Cheryl, searched for his brother. He found Tommy in the library, playing chess with Glenn, a cretin. Dominic knocked away the pieces with a wave of his hand.

—Let's go.

Sulking, Tommy stood up. Glenn whimpered but did not attempt to argue with the older boy. A quick goodbye, then Tommy followed after his brother.

The sacking was everywhere, in the air, on radios, in the milk bar where Dominic stopped for fags. The street that headed home was full of factories. Outside, workers in their blue overalls and aqua uniforms were arguing. Curses, obscenities everywhere. Dominic walked ahead, thinking of Cheryl. Tommy kicked stones up the street.

—Why did they sack him?

Dominic turned round, his brother had stopped, was looking up to him.

—'Cause he was a good man. That's what they do to good people.

When they arrived home, their mother was already there, still in her pale blue factory dress.

—Go pick up the baby from Yiota's, she ordered Tommy. The boy complained but headed off. Dominic sat down. His mother could not stand still, she was pacing the kitchen, her lungs devouring the cigarette. Dominic reached for one, and this time she did not stop him.

—Where's your fucking father?

—At work? This was offered quietly.

—He should be on fucking strike.

—Maybe he's at the pub.

Maria stopped, looked sharply at her son.

—That's the problem with the Australians. They are probably all at the pub, drinking, talking. Her voice rose. Instead of doing. She broke into Greek curses and Dominic looked out of the window.

In his bedroom his mother had placed a holy icon, the Virgin and the Child. An old broken piece of wood, the picture faded. Sometimes a small candle was lit, floating in oil, and placed next to the icon. A portrait of Whitlam stood beside it. His mother rarely talked of God, gave Him no definition. But she spoke of the Panagia, the Virgin, and she spoke of the Prime Minister. He could hear her, she was wild, swiping the air with her fists and cursing her fate. Listening to her brute fury, Dominic was scared.

Tommy arrived with the baby and Yiota. She was frightened. The two women rushed to each other with long cries. All Greek, fast, furious, and Dominic could not understand them. He was holding the baby, Lou was struggling in his arms, and Tommy, scared, ran to the television.

The emerging sound from the lounge room halted the

women's tears. They too rushed to the television. Dominic stayed
in the kitchen, playing with Lou, lifting the baby up high on his
knee, dropping him onto his lap, repeating the game. Lou
gurgled, smiled. Dominic could hear the channels changing, the
click of the dial, Tommy complaining.

—Quick, quick, Dom, his mother called. Come here.

Whitlam was on the television, camera in his face, a crowd
before him.

—Look what a giant he is, his mother praised.

—What's he saying? Yiota asked.

His mother translated. That only God can save that slut's
crawling slave, that bastard John Kerr, because the people are
going to hang the animal.

His mother never referred to Elizabeth Windsor as Queen.
She was simply the Poutana.

Yiota shook her head.

—There will be war.

—There has to be war, thundered his mother. A revolution.
She was excited, beneath the tears there was an excitement. This
is a coup, this is another junta.

Yiota crossed herself.

Dominic watched Whitlam. All strength.

The phone rang. His mother rushed to it. She came back,
frowning.

—It's Cheryl. Be quick.

Cheryl was crying.

—Dom, what are we going to do?

He whispered, pulling tight on the phone cord, trying to
shelter in the safety of his bedroom. He could see his mother and
his brother intent on the television.

—We have to get rid of it.

His own words shocked him. He turned his back to the icon.
Cheryl said nothing, only sobbed.

—I'll go with you.

—Mum says we can't go to a hospital. More sobbing. She

doesn't want any questions asked. She knows a doctor who'll do it. A scream in the background. Jesus, Dom, she's threatening to call the cops on you.

Dominic cleared his throat. Stay calm. Whitlam had disappeared from the screen. A journalist's head, bobbing rapidly.

—How much will it cost?

—Three hundred dollars.

—Fucking hell. Dominic groaned.

—Mum says you have to pay for it.

Dominic did not reply. He understood the justice.

—When?

—Soon.

An awkward silence.

—I love you, Dom.

He said nothing. He heard her sniffing.

—What are you doing?

—I'm watching Whitlam, on the TV.

—Who fucking cares about Whitlam?

He slammed the phone on her.

—What did she want?

—Nothing.

—I don't like her.

Dominic stared hard at the television.

—Don't trust the Australian girls, Dom. His mother pointed to the black and white images on the television. See what they do to people who like dagos in this country, see what they do to Whitlam because he cared about us migrants. Don't trust the Australians.

—I am Australian. His shouting made the baby cry. His mother picked Lou up, stared down at the sullen Dominic.

—You're not, she said in Greek. Maybe when they stop calling you wog. Her voice was cruel, he was shocked that she was laughing at him. In English.

—You're a wog, aren't you, wog boy, that's what Cheryl calls you behind your back, no?

—Shut the fuck up!

His mother turned away from him.

—Maybe you are Australian. Shut the fuck up, shut the fuck up. That's what they've been telling me for years.

Dominic was slapped by her sadness.

•

The cat sprawled at his touch and he rubbed her fat belly. Across the street the factory was all banging and whirring of machines. The cat's purring was the only softness.

His mother did not allow the cat in the house, she had to shelter underneath. She trusted only Dominic, took food straight from his hands. He rubbed her belly, felt the sharp ridges of the scarring.

—Hey cat, Dominic whispered, you pregnant too?

Every few months Dominic was sent to drown the new litter in the river.

—Hey, Dom, is it World War Three in there?

The cat ran off, a sleek flash, at Artie's voice. He kicked after her.

—Mum's pretty angry.

—I thought she would be. Artie dropped his bag, sat down next to his son and offered him a cigarette. The man was sweating, his hands black from the grease of the machines.

—Bad news, bad news.

Dominic did not answer.

—That's the end of a Labor government for another twenty years. Artie nudged his son. Don't listen to your mum, she thinks like a Red. She doesn't know Australia, sometimes I think she never will. People like it slow here, like it easy. They don't like change.

—Where were you?

Maria was behind the screen door, arms folded. Artie did not turn around.

—At work, where else?

—I thought maybe the pub.

—Oh Jesus, Maria, give us a break.

She opened up the door and stood above them.

—I'm on strike.

Artie swiftly turned around.

—Have they called a general strike?

—They will.

Dominic watched a dog across the street squat and piss in the factory's driveway.

—Well, I've heard nothing about it.

—This is a coup, Arto.

Dominic stood up.

—I'm going to the park.

Maria shook her head.

—You're staying home tonight.

—Let the boy go, what's he going to do, stay home listening to your raving?

—Aren't you upset? the son quizzed the father.

—Yes. Artie stood up, messed the boy's hair. But it's the end of Whitlam. He faced his wife. No amount of complaining is going to change that.

By that night the house was crowded with visitors. His Uncle Peter and his Aunt Elisabet; the Kyriakous from down the road; the drunk, Colin McCabe, his father's work friend. Yiota helped Maria with the food and the drink and the kitchen clouded with smoke. Tommy sat with the baby in the lounge room and Dominic sat with the adults. Tonight they let him smoke in front of the relatives. The conversation was all politics, all anger. A young woman from the biscuit factory, a Yugoslav, arrived and he was entranced by the beauty of her broad features. She said little, and when she did she spoke softly. Dominic watched the fine threads of hair on her arms.

The phone rang and it was his Uncle Joe from Western Australia. His mother answered the call and she returned, stern.

—It's for you, she said to her husband. All contempt. He's celebrating.

The room went quiet. Unlike the others, Dom did not strain to hear the conversation from the hall. The Slav woman was wearing an orange dress patterned with white leaves. He imagined fucking her and the desire was too sweet; his crotch, his face, they felt as if they were burning.

The next morning there was no school. Though initially protesting, Artie gave in and followed his wife and children to the demonstration. Dominic walked ahead of his family, not looking behind, keeping his distance. Outside Town Hall an immense crowd had gathered, through which Maria proudly weaved her pram. Tommy held tight to his brother's shirt, fearful of the noise, overwhelmed by the mass of people. Men with megaphones walked through, calling for action. All placards and ribbons. The police were everywhere, a long line of blue, watching, waiting. The protesters chanted and screamed and, carried away, Dominic began chanting with them. They marched through the streets, and his blood released a venom that became a passion that became a hate. A very thin blond policeman passed by his side. Dominic spat. On the footpaths strangers stood and watched. He could not understand their reticence, for in the middle of this crowd Dominic had found a voice that made him strong. He screamed poison and his voice rose above Cheryl, rose above the child in her womb, the temptation of her cunt. Safe within the crowd, Dominic urged murder.

He did not listen to the speeches. The men with the megaphones were too far away, their talk senseless. He looked up at the sweep of the Parliament steps, then down the stretch of boulevard. The vast crowd was behind him, around him. Beside him his mother was crying; his father, sullen, bored, smoked a cigarette.

Strike. The word began slowly, then moved serpentine throughout the crowd. His mother was fire, alive with the word. Strike, strike, strike. Banging, thumping, clapping. The crowd pushed forward, mocking the block of frightened police protecting the steps. Dominic slapped his hands together, took the word and threw it back; the world spoke in one voice. Strike.

Then there was a silence, another man on the podium, urging patience and restraint; the crowd descended back to peace. The tight fence of policemen stood firm across the steps. A final applause, a retreat, and then it was over.

And back at home, as his brother turned the television on, and his mother stirred the coffee, Dominic found that all the strength from the morning had left him. Cheryl came back and the thought of her was obscene. He yelled, I'm going out, and ran from the house.

Tiger snakes lived in the park. Last summer a young girl had been bitten, had died. This is what was said. Dominic lumped hard on the grass, announcing his presence.

The park, the great grounds of the river, was empty. He slashed through the grass, keeping to the water's edge. The foliage was all dark greens and shades of yellow. He walked towards the prison. The construction sites were quiet, huge piles of stone and dirt ready for the freeway. That's the future, his father had said, pointing towards morning, a house out east.

The prison's grey walls were impenetrable. He touched the granite. Behind the prison lay an empty stretch of grass; on one side a hospital protected by wire fencing, on the other a stretch of the city. A small city. Dominic sat on the grass, lit a cigarette, looked at the thin spires on the horizon.

An old man was walking a black labrador. Both animal and human walked slowly, both elderly. Dominic recognised the man, one of the faces he had grown up with, saw in the milk bar or coming out of the pub, a familiar stranger. The man was wearing a long-sleeved white shirt and faded blue jeans, baggy, folds of denim fluttering around his spindly legs. The dog barked, once, and Dominic gestured.

It was a licky dog; his face got wet. He pushed the animal away.

—Rex, come here!

The old man's voice was harsh.

—It's right, mate, he ain't bothering me.

Dominic got up and they stood together, looking out to the city.

—No school today?

—Nah. Nervously. Went to a demo.

The old man nodded, slowly. His eyes were tender, they searched Dominic's face. Sad eyes. Dominic, shy, not wishing to talk, smoked silently. He felt the man's gaze on him.

—You a Greek?

—Italian. Dominic was going to continue, to explain further, then decided against it. The question rattled him, it had no answer.

—Whitlam supporter?

There was longing, an appetite, in the old man's eyes. The man held his hand out as if to touch Dominic's arm, then the hand fluttered down to rest on the labrador's back.

—I should get going. Dominic turned around and began running.

—Nice to meet you, the old man called after him.

The boy sped off, rushing across the oval, jumping the creek, running all the way home.

•

He did not attend school for a week, threatening Tommy with violence if he dobbed to the parents, avoiding Cheryl. She rang, he told his mother to say he wasn't home if she called. Maria was glad to assist in this lie.

—You gonna flunk, mate.

—Who cares?

Dominic and Victor were drinking beer, cans, in the old sheds by Victoria Park Station. Saturday night.

—What you gonna do?

—Apprenticeship. Carpentry, maybe. Dad's trying to find something for me.

—You want to do that?

The sun was setting as the boys drank.

—Yeah, should be all right.

Victor was smart, going to go to university. Maybe. His mother liked Victor, he was passionate about similar things. Whitlam. Free universities, his mother raged, the man made the universities free and still this bloody country complains. Yeah, his father would answer, but everything fucking costs a bloody lot more. Think of your children, Maria would scream, and the argument would be on.

—Tina says Cheryl's pregnant.

Dominic didn't answer.

—Well, is she?

—Yeah, she is.

—What you gonna do?

—Kill it. Kill her. Kill my fucking self.

Victor laughed and sucked on the can.

—She'll have the abortion. Her mum's a Christian psycho. She's not going to put up with a pregnant fifteen year old. What would the neighbours say?

The platform was empty except for a young Greek man, drunk, in a shirt and tie, waiting for the city train.

—Hey, Vic, you know that old Aussie guy with the black labrador on Ramsden Street?

Victor sniffed.

—Yeah, the guy just down the road from us?

—Yeah. Whereabouts is the house?

—Two doors down from the station. Must cause a racket. Victor threw an empty can against a graffitied wall. Why do you ask?

—He said hello the other day.

—Zoron reckons he's a pervert.

The sun had set and the breeze was now cold. Dominic folded his arms.

—Zoron is full of it.

—Yeah, I know, king of the bullshitters. Victor looked over at Dominic. But he reckons he got ten bucks once for showing the queer his dick.

No answer.

Guess it's an easy ten bucks, Victor shrugged.

Dominic jumped up.

—What do you want to do?

—Where's there to go?

—See you then?

—See you.

The boys scaled the wall, headed home.

•

He knocked twice on the door then almost ran off. There was no answer but for the barking of the dog. He tried again. Slow shuffled steps, the barking of the dog. A latch undone, the door slowly opened.

—What do you want?

Three hundred dollars.

—Hello, sir, we met the other day. At the park. I'm Dominic Stefano, from down the road.

—Yeah? And what do you want?

Three hundred dollars.

—Can I come in?

The dog sniffed through the crack of the door, Dominic let it lick at his fingers. The old man hesitated, then opened the door wide.

—Come in then.

Dominic at fifteen was never to be more handsome. His hair was tight brown curls and his olive eyes were outlined with long lashes. He was lean, tough. Hair had begun to sprout all over his body, and though it confused the boy himself, so much so that he refused to be seen without a singlet or T-shirt, shocked by the pace of becoming an adult, it was the sight of the rich curls beneath the boy's collar that drew the old man. He wanted to reach for the boy's neck, to touch the curls, to kiss goodbye to the boy.

The house was full of the clutter of history. Photographs and books, an old ship's compass. The man shuffled slowly to the kitchen.

—Would you like a tea?

—No, answered the boy.

—A soft drink? A beer?

—I'll have a beer.

A man in military uniform, standing up, handsome. Beside him, sitting, a pretty woman in white. The sallow old man's face just discernible in the proud eyes of the young soldier.

—Is this you? asked Dominic when the man returned with a glass of beer.

—Yes. And me wife.

Dominic quickly looked around.

—Sorry, she asleep?

—She's dead.

The dog was wagging its tail, pawing the boy. Dominic stroked its head.

The man continued.

—That was taken when I returned from Malaysia. I was in the war.

—She's beautiful. And she was. The woman was lean and pretty, elegant.

The man cleared his throat and extended his hand across the couch.

—I'm Bill.

—I'm Dominic.

—So you said. What can I do for you, Dominic?

Give me three hundred dollars, you fucking poofter cunt. He

was ashamed at the thought. The man was old, frail. He could kill him, injure him, it would be easy.

—Take your time.

Dominic laughed.

—I don't have too much of that.

—Bullshit! The reply was almost fury. Bill gazed on the youth, blinked his eyes shut tight. The arrogance of his handsome body.

—You live in Roseneath Street?

The boy nodded. The man poured more beer.

—My girlfriend's pregnant. He noticed the crucifix, hanging on the wall. I need money.

—Don't we all.

—Three hundred bucks. Then breathlessly, I don't want her to have the baby, we couldn't afford it, we're too young, now he was beginning to cry, ashamed but doing it, breathing heavily, and I can't tell Mum and Dad, they'd kill me for being so fucking stupid. Abrupt stop.

—Sorry, I didn't mean to swear.

The old man laughed.

—S'all right, mate.

The boy wiped his eyes, sniffed, the tears, stopped.

—What do you want from me?

Dominic stared ahead, hard; Bill was again defeated by the arrogance in the dark eyes.

—I want some money. And I've heard you'll pay.

—Why should I give you money for nothing? The man signalled for the dog, did not take his eyes off Dominic.

And Dominic was thinking, while looking down at the rug, red floral swirls, that murder would be easier.

—I've heard that you will . . . How was he to say this? You can fuck me if you want to, sir. I need the money and I won't tell anyone. Dominic had lifted his head, returned the man's defiant stare. The old man said nothing, got up and left the room. The dog followed. Dominic took a large swig of beer.

The man returned with two glasses, an amber liquid. He handed one to the boy and Dominic sniffed it warily; he had no taste for whisky, but he drank, a large gulp down, and screwed up his face.

—Thanks, sir.

The man sat down.

—First, I don't know what you heard and what little lying cunt it came from, but know this, I don't fuck men. I'm not a poof, not that way. I don't want to fuck you. Fucking, and it sounds like you already know this, fucking is what you do with a woman. That's how it's meant to be and that's how it is best.

The man hesitated. He's like a teacher, thought Dominic, wonder if he is a teacher?

—I'm sorry, sir.

—You've got to be careful of poofters, son, they'll corrupt you. The man downed the whisky. Three hundred dollars?

Dominic hung his head.

—Can't you work?

Dominic nodded.

—But I have to give any money to Dad.

—Can't you tell him?

—He'd fucking kill me.

—I haven't got three hundred dollars to give you.

Dominic got up. He left his whisky unfinished.

—Sorry to disturb you, sir.

—Wait. The man pointed to the glass. Drink up. He patted the dog, no longer looking at the boy, lost in the room and its memories.

—I can give you some of it.

Dominic excited, almost gleeful. Yeah?

—Yes. But not for nothing.

A train screeched, the house began to slowly rumble, then to shake, the noise drowned the heavy panting of the dog. Then, abruptly, a last whistle and the train had passed.

—What do I have to do?

The man coughed, then blushed. He did not look at the boy.

—You just have to comfort me. I'll give you twenty dollars for every time you comfort me.

How? Dominic was humiliated to find that his cock was now erect under the soft cotton of his pants. The man poured another whisky. Softly he mumbled an order.

—What?

—Come here.

The boy rose, walked over to the sitting man. The man put down his glass and looked up to the shaking boy.

—Don't be scared, I won't hurt you. That's the last thing I want to do. Dominic was quiet. The man smiled nervously. With one hand he began to massage the boy's crotch.

Throughout, Dominic watched the dog. The man, embarrassed, removed his dentures, lay them next to the empty glass. Sorry, sorry.

—That's all right, replied the boy.

The man's mouth was dry, not wet at all, and he licked at cock and balls, none of Cheryl's mechanical sucks. The boy closed his eyes, the man's bristles stung. He opened them once, looked down, the man was tugging a loose and long thin cock. He closed his eyes, dreamt nothing but space, black and lonely space, nothing but the wheezing of the dog, the stink of whisky, and when he came, he came inside the hole.

The man drank his fill of the boy. His hands clutched the boy's buttocks, he pushed the boy towards him, ate from him. When he had finished, had cleaned the cock of semen, the man sat back, closed his eyes and mourned his age. He picked up his dentures, mumbled an apology and left the room, hanging onto his belt, his pants falling. The dog looked up expectantly, then fell again to rest.

Dominic looked down at his naked crotch, pulled back the foreskin. His cock was wet, pink. He rubbed it with a handkerchief, then quickly pulled up his pants, zipped his fly. The man had not yet returned. Dominic looked at the photo of the beautiful thin woman, her white lace. A watch, gold, lay beside a thick leather book. The man had still not returned. The boy pocketed the watch. The dog did not stir. There was flush of a toilet, then the man was back.

To corrupt the silence, the man poured another whisky. Dominic drank again, this time there was no scouring. He wondered if he was drunk.

—Thank you.

—That's all right. Dominic wanted to laugh. The man's face was white, wrinkled. The thin pink veins were ugly. The boy fixed his eyes, tried not to look away.

—Please don't tell anyone.

—I won't.

Of course I fucking won't.

The man stared into his glass.

—You shouldn't do this too often.

—I won't. The boy cleared his throat, drank from the whisky, the spirit was making him loud. I'm not like you, I like women.

—So do I. The voice was a quiet rumble, like distant thunder.

Have you always been like this, the boy wished to ask.

—I was married for thirty-five years, the man answered his thought, and I was not unfaithful once. Not once.

Dominic was getting impatient. He wanted the night, to feel a breeze. He finished the whisky.

—I never betrayed Cynthia.

—You must have been in love.

Did she know you were a fucking queer?

—We were. Then she died and I was alone. The man was no longer looking at Dominic. He's pissed, out of it, thought the boy, pay up, pay up, where's the bloody money?

—Don't do this too often.

—I won't.

—I have two sons, I'd hate to think they were doing this.

The gold watch was sinking in Dominic's pocket.

The man sighed. He took some notes from his pocket, threw them at the boy.

—Here it is. Dominic clutched at the cash, scooping it up. It was a hundred dollars. He pocketed the money, a large smile lit his face.

—Can I trust you?

The boy nodded.

—I'll give you two hundred all up. That's ten times you come here, right, ten nights you comfort me.

Dominic hesitated. Who you going to tell, arsehole, if I just pocket this? The old man was staring hard at the youth. Dominic extended his hand.

—I'll shake on it.

So they did.

—Sorry, sir, got to go. The room was disappearing, the man was disappearing. The boy was eager, smiling, impatient to leave. Without a word the man rose and walked Dominic to the door. The black sky danced with stars. Dominic breathed in the infinite space, jumped into the night.

—Can you come this Sunday? Sunday afternoon.

—Yeah, said the boy. Thanks.

And he meant it, the cash in his hand, the watch in his pocket. And it had not hurt, and he had not had to do anything but stand there, and he had not had to be fucked, so he was still clean.

—Thanks, he repeated, and jumped into the street.

•

His mother was in the lounge room, talking with Yiota. In the kitchen his father was with the men, playing cards. The house was full of smoke.

—Where have you been?

—Out. He kissed his mother, kissed Yiota.

—Cheryl rang.

In the kitchen the men were drunk, a line of beer bottles on the bench. Dominic ate cold moussaka, watched the men play.

—Had a good night?

Dominic nodded to his father.

He brushed his teeth slowly, filling his mouth with the paste, washing away the evening. Tommy was still awake, reading. Dominic stripped to his underpants and jumped into bed.

—Were you with Victor?

—Yeah.

Dominic looked at the icon above Tommy's bed. The Virgin's face was clouded, black, soiled from age. The boy Jesus with the old man's face. Once, Tommy had run screaming from the room, had dissolved in hysterical tears. The baby Jesus had turned his face, had beckoned him. Tommy was sometimes crazy.

—Turn off the light.

—I want to read some more.

—Turn off the fucking light!

The younger boy obeyed.

Dominic could hear his brother praying. Tommy prayed all the time, sometimes for hours into the night. A murmur, indecipherable, a steady stream.

—Mum and Dad had a fight.

—What about?

—Mum wants to go back to Greece, reckons we all should go.

Dominic laughed.

—Yeah, right. It's okay for her, she can speak the language. What are we meant to do?

—That's what Dad said.

—It's not going to happen. She's just upset about Whitlam.

Dominic looked up again, at the icon. Next to it the Prime Minister's face was smiling.

Tommy followed his gaze.

—He shouldn't be there. That's blasphemy.

—Shut up with that Christian shit. That photo stays there.

Tommy fell silent.

Dominic lay awake, listening to the occasional shouts from

the kitchen, the muffled music from the radio. At one point his mother played a Greek song. Tommy was still praying.

Dominic waited for his brother's snores. They finally came, the whimper of sleep. Then Dominic pulled down his shorts, closed his eyes and filled his thoughts with dreams of women. He sunk into Yiota's firm large breasts, licked from Cheryl's cunt. He conjured up movie stars and pop stars. He pulled at his dick and Tommy disappeared, the house disappeared, the money and the old man disappeared. And when he came he was dreaming of Lynette's large behind, kissing her neck, eating at the thick strands of her hair.

Next morning he rushed to Cheryl's house. Her mum and dad were at church. She answered the door in a white bath robe, her eyes still full of sleep.

—I've got the money. Or I will have, I've got half of it.

The girl let him in, they sat on the couch and watched sports on television.

—Maybe I'll keep it.

Dominic wanted to smash her pretty little face in. He took her hand.

—We can't.

—Why not?

—We're too young.

I don't love you, I don't want you. Dominic was tasting freedom, his youth was back.

Cheryl started to cry. They made love on the sofa, his cock inside her, once inside her he wanted to stay there forever. And then, spluttering to orgasm, the feeling went. He couldn't wait to leave.

—Tell your mum to organise it, as soon as.

Monday he went back to school. Order had returned. The Queen was back in her place, a new frame. The snakeskin gone. After school he sold the watch. It was not gold at all, and he only received ten dollars for it. Dominic visited the old man twice every week for a month, cleared the debt. His visits to the old man occurred outside his world. In the old man's world they would talk, a little; the man would get his comfort, they would share a drink and the old man would tell him some stories. As soon as the sex was finished, Dominic forgot it, a chore wiped from his memory.

Only once did the two worlds merge. In the bedroom, when he ordered Tommy to stop reading, to turn off the light.

—Dom.

—Go to sleep.

—Dom, Bruno says he saw you visiting that old guy in Ramsden Street.

Dominic held his breath. Tommy waited in the silence.

—Dom?

—Your mate Bruno is a fucking poofter cunt.

—Did you?

—What?

—Visit the old man?

—Yeah.

—What for?

For money.

—Victor kicked a footy in his place. I was going to collect it.

Tommy lay back, closed his eyes. He wanted to ask more but he was scared. There was a danger in his brother's voice.

Dominic continued to visit, to honour his debt, after this conversation. But only at night, when the street was empty. And he left by the old man's back gate, disappeared along the railway line.

•

On the day of Cheryl's abortion, the Australian people voted against Gough Whitlam and his social-democratic government. Dominic saw her the morning after. She was pale and sick, could hardly look at him, all tears.

—This is all your bloody fault, you fucking wog bastard, her mother hissed at him.

Cheryl's father, oblivious to the truth of his daughter's illness, greeted him with a wide smile. In silence, Dominic held Cheryl's hand.

—Whitlam didn't get in.

—Who fucking cares?

And that was all that was said.

At home his mother was crying, angry, inconsolable. His father had escaped to the garden and Tommy was reading in their bedroom. Dominic grabbed two of his mother's cigarettes and ran down to the river. He sat and smoked on a small hill that overlooked the grey thin buildings of the city. The sun was high, not hot but pleasant. A crow danced in the air above him. That's my baby, thought Dominic, and for one brief moment he was sad. Then the crow was no more and the day was warm and the air was still and the year was closing and the world had changed and Dominic had escaped. He smoked his cigarette, prayed a small thanks, watched the lazy city.

SECTION TWO

Thomas Stefano

When you stand in front of me and look at me, what do you know of the griefs that are in me and what do I know of yours? And if I were to cast myself down before you and weep and tell you, what more would you know about me than you know about Hell when someone tells you it is hot and dreadful? For that reason alone we human beings ought to stand before one another as reverently, as reflectively, as lovingly as we would before the entrance to Hell.

FRANZ KAFKA

1

Blonde Mary

The television was on. The women were preparing the table, the men were round the barbecue. Tommy was alone in the lounge room, watching the TV. The birth of Christ. Mary was blonde, an LA nymph. Joseph was soap-opera handsome, young and smooth.

Tommy was thinking, sipping at his beer, how cheap Mary looked, what a cheap American slag. There was dancing in Jerusalem, the young Mary had just spotted the pretty Joseph. The camera cut back and forth, back and forth, to the blonde Mary with the silicon breasts, to the bearded Joseph with the sculptured chest. Their eyes met. Commercial break.

—What are you watching?

—The Christmas story.

Lou was going to be handsome, no doubt about that. His eyes were dark, his skin, even at the height of adolescence, smooth. His body was trim from swimming. And he was tall. Tommy patted his paunch, put down the beer.

—How's things?

—Good. The boy had become fixated on the television.

Their conversation was always stilted, always short. Between Dom and Lou it was different. Dom spoilt him, that was that. Dominic had never indulged Tommy. Sometimes, Tommy thought, watching the Virgin's face, lewd at Joseph's advances, he wanted a world in which there were no brothers.

Punch hard, punch fast. Dominic had a great right fist.

Lou got up.

—Looks pretty boring.

—Go and help Dad.

—No, you go and help Dad.

In the kitchen his mother and his aunts were baking. Greek pies. His Aunt Sophia was across from the west, with Duke, her fat dull husband. Sophia was trying to help.

He was going to bring Soo-Ling, introduce her around, but at the last moment he couldn't. He couldn't bear the tension, the looks, the judgements.

A Chinese girl's slash is horizontal not vertical. Dom once told him that. And nigger cunt smells like mango.

I've got an Asian girlfriend.

—Get up, Tom, go help your father.

His mother still carried a trace of the Mediterranean in her voice. The thick vowels and the soft consonants. He didn't take his eyes off the screen. Joseph was stripped to the waist, drawing water from the well. Mary's tits were plastic. They didn't move with her body.

He went to the toilet. Splashed piss on the floor and had to clean it up. Sometimes he pissed a split stream, as if his cock had two holes. He wiped the floor with tissue paper. In the bathroom he pulled up his shirt, looked at his belly. The fine black hair, the stretch of fat. He clutched at the flab, shook it, wished he could tear it off. He dropped his shirt and washed his hands.

Outside, Artie handed Tommy the fork. Look after them. The meat was still red, seeping blood. Tommy turned the pieces over. His brother was kicking a soccer ball across the yard, back to boyhood. He kicked the ball over to Tommy and it shook the barbecue.

—Watch it!

Dominic too was getting fat. His legs were thick, the T-shirt he wore stretched tight across chest and stomach. But he still looked good, still played footy, still worked hard. His arms were long and strong, the arms of a carpenter. His hair, never black, had been dulled by successive summers to a dull bronze with flashes of red.

When he was young, Dominic's pubic hair had been bright red. The flamed bush, when he first spied it, had shocked Tommy.

The air sizzled with the smell of charcoal and meat. His Uncle Duke was already drunk, slurring and smoking cigarettes. Maria, inside the house, had her lips closed, her mouth thin, she hated her husband's family. Tommy watched her through the window, at the sink, her long dyed hair. His mother always had long hair, refused to cut it with age the way other wog women did. She still looked beautiful. Tommy turned away.

—How's work?

Dominic opened a beer, sat on a plastic chair and wiped away sweat.

—Okay, replied Tommy.

—They still talking of getting rid of people?

—They always do.

Work, thought Tommy, I don't want to talk about fucking work.

—And how are you going?

—Good, good. Business is fine, Dominic replied, and they fell into uncomfortable silence.

Few people guessed, on first meeting, that Dominic and Tommy were brothers. They shared dark skin, their mother's delicate mouth, but that was all.

Dominic took off his T-shirt. His skin was olive, tanned by the sun. His chest and belly an explosion of fine blond hair. He's not fat, he's bulky, thought Tommy, and again he wished he could rip through his skin, get to the meat, to the flab, to the excess. Rip it up and start again.

—Put your shirt on.

Dominic laughed at Eva's taut command. He slapped his belly.

—Aren't you proud of your old man?

Eva was tall and thin, and Tommy thought her sophisticated. He envied his brother his wife.

She did not reply. Instead she took a seat offered to her by Duke and ruffled Tommy's hair.

—You all right?

—Sure, he smiled, it's Christmas.

The Stefano men all loved Eva.

—Where's Soo-Ling?

—With friends.

—When do we meet her? Dominic sat up.

—Soon.

—How soon? Artie was looking up, squinting from the smoke. He was balding, he was all grey.

Tommy didn't answer.

Eva quickly changed the subject.

—Dom, go check on the baby.

—You do it, answered her husband.

—Please, you go, Eva turned away from Dom, I want to talk to Tommy.

Dom went in and checked on his child.

The lunch was on the verandah, under the grapevines, with lots of beer and wine. Yiota arrived with the gangly Spiro and she brought octopus, salad and fresh bread. Their daughter, the dark gorgeous little Ourania, ran into the yard and jumped into Artie's arm. Hello Uncle Thanassi, she whispered in his ear. Yiota joined Maria in the kitchen.

The food was good, very good, and the group ate rapidly and ferociously. Maria kept refilling the wine, Artie the beer. Yiota kept serving the food.

—Sit down, ordered Maria to Yiota, in Greek.

—She never sits down, not till we finish. Spiro.

Which is true, thought Tommy, Yiota rarely sat still. He smiled at Yiota, she came around to the back of his chair, hugged him. My little Thomas, she whispered, Thomaki.

The day Spiro and Yiota had left the old house, stopped being boarders, Tommy had cried all night. Inconsolable.

The conversation kept to family and work. That was safe. Lou took no part, just kept eating, until politics came up. It started with Dominic, who winked slyly to both his brothers and mentioned the word. Maria responded immediately.

The argument was simple. The responsibility that government had to working people and to people unable to find work. Maria was defending socialism, Duke and Sophia arguing that Australians expected too much from welfare. Artie did not speak, he quietly ate. Lou, too, was quiet. Dominic didn't give a shit.

—I'd like to take some of those bludgers out to the farm and show them work. They don't know what work is.

—Farming isn't work. Not in this country.

Duke nearly choked on the barbecued meat. He glared at Maria.

—I get up at four-thirty in the morning, he warned her.

—And you're drunk by midday. Only labouring people, factory people, know work.

Dominic and his mother smiled at one another.

Tommy felt the weight of his white collar.

—Farmers work too, Mum.

Maria turned to him, angry at his betrayal.

—And what would you know?

Tommy could not look at her. It was his father who interrupted.

—As much as you do, Maria. Now shut up.

His mother snorted, rose and went to the kitchen. She clicked on the stereo. A Greek song; they heard her softly singing. When she came back with a platter of fruit, she was smiling.

Tommy was still hurting. He was scared by how much he did not understand of his parents. He had spent his childhood listening to arguments, shouting and bickering, but also to the breathless fucking from across the thin walls of the Clifton Hill house. He had been happy that when they moved out into the suburbs he was given the back bedroom. He was spared the sounds of his parents loving each other.

His mother thought him soft because he did not believe enough, his father thought him soft because his body and his work was, and Dominic thought him soft because that's what everyone thought of Tommy. Except Lou maybe. Lou never insulted him. The boy was sitting down next to the Christmas tree, dividing up the presents. Lou was now firmly a teenager and not a child; he looked awkward performing this traditional activity. Soon, in a year or two, baby Lisa, now asleep, would be doing the honours. Tommy wondered what kind of man his youngest brother would be.

Lou handed Tommy the first parcel.

—That's yours, mate.

He got a towel from his Aunt Sophia and his Uncle Duke. Body Shop cosmetics from Dominic and Eva. Fifty dollars in an envelope and a tie from his parents. And a CD from Lou.

—What's this?

—It's a rap thing.

—Oh. He never listened to rap.

—It's good, urged Lou, You should listen to it.

Strictly Business. EPMD. Which was the band, which was the title?

—Rap sucks, complained Dominic. Lou had given him and Eva a CD as well, the soundtrack to *Bagdad Cafe*.

Eva was excited by the present. She gave Lou a huge kiss.

—I really want to see this movie.

—It's good, said Lou, embarrassed by the kiss but grinning widely. Mum and I saw it the other week.

—That one with the fat woman?

The boy nodded.

—Yes, Maria said to Yiota, it was good. In Greek. She made me laugh a lot, the fat one. And she was beautiful.

Maria had received a book, a biography of Frida Kahlo, from her youngest son. A Greek translation Lou had hunted out in the city. She hugged the book close. She had exclaimed, been grateful, over Dominic and Tommy's presents, the scarf, the perfume, but she had quickly discarded them on the floor.

Tommy noticed that. He had run around and around the department store, from counter to counter. He had rushed in after work, assuming he would find presents quickly; but caught up in the movement and frenzy of the Christmas rush, he could not decide on anything for his mother. He had smelt and smelt perfumes till his body was dizzy, his head sore. His mother had liked, but no more than liked, the present.

Tommy counted down the remainder of the day, counted down the drinks. Wine, with fruit. Wine, with dessert. A short whisky with the coffee. Now he could go home.

—Stay, pleaded Maria, your uncles are coming, later. Stay the night.

—No, Mum.

Stop it, stop it, let me go.

It was Artie who stepped in, putting a hand on his wife's shoulder.

—Let him go.

—Do what you want, replied Maria, and she stormed into the kitchen.

Tommy kissed the women, hugged his brothers and his father. Lou was playing video games, slouched on the floor. Maria walked Tommy out, with a tray of food—the meat and pita—with a plastic bag of vegetables and fruits. He kissed her, held her tight.

—Sorry, he said.

—What are you going to do?

—Stuff. Go out with friends.

—Be careful, she said. She stood, waiting, till he disappeared from view. In the rear-view mirror he saw her make the sign of the Cross.

When he turned the corner, when he knew he was left to himself, alone, in the car, it was a supreme joy. He put on the radio loud, travelled the roads, took the long way. The breeze. He had been holding in his body for hours.

He got home, turned on the television, phoned Soo-Ling. He heard her answering machine clicking over. He hesitated. Hello, it's Tommy. Happy Christmas. He hung up and was about to ring Nadia's house, Soo-Ling was probably there, join another party; he put down the phone instead. He was enjoying the quiet.

He took a walk down the road to the Food Plus. It was changing hands, becoming a Shell. There was a new guy at the counter, a young guy.

Tommy wandered the store, searching for something to eat. Not the chocolate, you fat cunt. He searched the store and found the crisps. Low salt.

The guy at the counter had a tag on his orange uniform jacket. The tag read *Stephen*.

—Hi, Stephen.

—My name's not Stephen. The new uniforms haven't arrived. The man looked down at his jacket.

—This is shitty, isn't it? The colour.

Tommy said nothing. The man didn't give his name. Tommy didn't ask.

Two dollars for a two hundred gram bag of shit.

The neighbourhood was quiet. Only barks and wind in the air. He got home and turned on the television, watched the end of a movie. He went to his room, shuffled under the mattress, pulled out a magazine. A young blonde girl with ponytail, semen running down her cheek. Big red hooded dick.

Tommy wanked, quickly.

He finished, his yawned and he put the magazine back under the bed. He turned off the television and he brushed his teeth.

The bed was hot. He tossed off the doona. In the dark,

nothing was visible except for the shining eyes of the Virgin above his bed. Her eyes were moonlight.

Tommy closed his eyes, fell asleep.

2
The Stepford Husband

In the movie *The Stepford Wives*, Katherine Ross plays a young woman who moves with her husband and children from Manhattan into a lush and wealthy suburban life. But she doesn't like it, she wants to be a photographer—she misses New York. And she notices that all the ladies in Stepford, and indeed they are ladies, are all zombies. It turns out that the men of Stepford are replacing their wives with machines. The last shot of the film is Ross wheeling her trolley down a supermarket aisle, a soft-porn goddess in white. Her eyes are dead. They are the only part of the flesh that remains of the real woman and they are lifeless.

Tommy Stefano saw the movie on a Saturday night in 1977, when he was fourteen and the family had just moved into their new house. In the suburbs, where no-one walked at nights and where every home had a garden. The television was a connection with a previous life and he immersed himself in it. His old friendships were now a bus and a train ride away. So they stopped. The kids in the new school were strange. Only a very few had mothers who spoke with an accent. A sea of blondes, and he had became a foreigner in his own country. When Tommy saw *The Stepford Wives*, he was mesmerised. Because, scared of the sudden smashing of his world, he had only one desire. To not be hurt, picked on, accused. Tommy had decided to become a zombie.

•

The train was not on time and the crowd on the platform were beginning to shuffle impatiently. Tommy knew he would be late, he'd just scraped in, the 8.53 train. Nine-thirty, just about stretching it thin, people would disapprove. If time could stop, now, he thought, I'd like it to stop now. So I could walk around the statues.

This had been Tommy's fantasy ever since he'd been very young. He would fantasise about stopping time, but only for humans. And never for himself. He could then wander the world and do whatever he liked. Then finally, tired or bored, he would snap his fingers and everything would return to normal. When they moved to the new suburb, he began to close himself in his room, wank, watch a small black and white television. He began to stop time and within that eternity he could be anyone he wanted.

—Why don't you do something, mate, his father would say, waste some energy, get some of that fat off you.

But Tommy preferred to masturbate.

Dominic had escaped the new suburb. There had been the disco, the beach, and he had the car. The car was freedom. Dominic had moved out to Blackburn only reluctantly, the fucking arse-end of the world he called it. His mother's crying and entreaties finally swayed him. But he spent the weekends with the boys in the city, picking up chicks at night. On week-days he had an early rise and, returning from work, he would blot himself out with smoke, crash early. Or he'd stay in town. I'm staying over at Harry's place, yeah, his mum says hello. For Dominic home became the place you ate in and slept in. And the rest of the world was his to take—home just kept him safe. His mother wanted more of him, but Dominic was firm.

—Too much dancing to do, too many good-looking gomines to kiss. That harsh and pretty Greek word, around which Tommy could rarely get his tongue, what did it translate to? His ladies? It always made his mother smile, it was a phrase she remembered her brother Thimio using.

—He looks like you too. One day you'll see him, in Greece, she would tell him.

And so no matter what Dominic did, his mother would eventually forgive him. You're so very handsome, you devil, she would say, and then she would clean up after him.

But we never did get to bloody Greece and that fucking gutless Dom didn't ever bring home the girls he picked up from the disco.

The train was running five minutes late, smokers were lighting up cigarettes, and a particularly well-dressed gentleman was frowning and growling. European suit, thought Tommy. That girl, the one with the long legs, that trendy short skirt, I could fuck her. She was reading a magazine, flicking her eyes constantly to the end of the platform. Tommy could sense she was late for work too. Pull up that skirt, push apart the legs, bush and arse. Fuck her.

Tommy blinked and concentrated on the railway tracks.

Work had gone bad since the change, the selling of the mail room to a contractor. Previously Tommy had reported to one manager, an old guy who rarely interfered with anything. Since the takeover, he had to report to two managers. Somers and Pathis. They were both sharper and less aloof than old Mr Crankshaw.

—This is a new regime, lean, it has to be to make up for the mess of the past. But rewarding.

Tommy had listened to the words and thought how the new guy, Pathis, seemed pretty young for a manager. A manager. Tommy was running scared and he couldn't think what he could do about it. The job had changed and his competence alone was no longer enough. Now he was required to show initiative.

What the fuck for, thought Tommy, I'm still printing fine.

Tommy had no vanity when it came to work, he knew he wasn't special. But he assumed a trust: if he was getting his job done, nothing more should be expected of him.

The train arrived into Flagstaff Station at 9:27. He was late.

Even running across the park, he was late. So slow down, might as well enjoy it.

Somers was brown. Tommy couldn't work out how. Somers had taken only the days between Christmas and New Year off. Tommy was dark only on his face and hands. He knew that beneath his lab coat, beneath his shirt and pants, his skin was a distinct pale. The beach seemed an effort and his own holidays had not gone on long enough. What had he done? Reclined, not thought, just dreamt.

—How are you, Tom?

—Fine, Kev.

—The printing on the bromides has been a bit dark recently.

—Only on the brochures for the electronics sale. And they always complain but they'll only use the lowest grade paper.

—Do your best, Tom, all right?

These would most probably be the only words exchanged between them all day.

The print shop was small, in a red-brick warehouse. From the roof the view was overwhelming. On one side the industrial geometry of the western suburbs, the flat stretch; and on the other side, the towering prisms of the city.

At eleven o'clock he took a coffee break on the roof, took a smoke off John. Sue was fixing the line of her stockings.

—Tommy, what's a systems analyst?

John was frowning as he smoked, looking down, embarrassed. Nadia too looked up.

—That's like Pathis, right, someone who comes in and works out how your job, you know, where you work, how that could be better. Tommy paused, not convinced of his authority.

—Efficient, that's it. Make things more efficient.

Sue lit her cigarette.

—That Pathis is an arsehole.

—I thought you girls upstairs think he's cute.

Nadia ignored John.

—He's checking the three of us out at the moment, working

out which one he's going to keep on. She glared at John. He's not that cute. His eyes are wrong. With that insult, she turned her face away from the men, looked up to the building floating above her.

—I'm looking for work, anywhere, but I'll miss the city.

—You looking for work? Tommy liked Sue, she had always welcomed him.

—Gotta. Mayal should stay on, she's got the kids. Anyway, I don't want to work for that Pathis prick. He wouldn't want me, I don't suck up to him. She pointed sharply at John. Not like him.

—I don't suck up to anyone.

Tommy only half finished the cigarette, regretted the sourness. Pathis had spoken to him on the first day.

—You Greek?

—Half. Half Italian.

Pathis, in Greek, asked if Tommy spoke the language.

—Sorry, no, I don't speak any Greek.

From then on they mostly only nodded to each other.

John did suck up to Pathis. Their fathers came from neighbouring villages.

—Time's up, said Tommy, looking at his watch. It said 11:14.

The day was to be taken up with a catalogue for the store's fashion show. The print shop and the adjacent mail room in which the girls worked were satellites. They served the needs of a department store in the middle of the city, a grand store born of the gold boom. Tommy looked at the artwork sent in for the current job. It was pathetic: sloppy typesetting and bad illustration.

—The computer, mate, argued John, that's the future. They don't need to waste time with all this running back and forth from the typesetter to us. And fuck, they don't even need high quality printing for the shit they give us. He threw the pages on the desk. This place is fucking obsolete.

Tommy had never used a computer.

He had to think about study. Soo-Ling said that all the time. Go back to school, do a computer course.

Inside, all the time, Tommy groaned. I just want to not think, I just want to stop.

At lunchtime he bought a roll—salad and beef—got the paper and read in the park. The day was fine. A guy had murdered five children, blasted about thirty more, a place called Stockton in California. They seemed to be getting crazier over there. Another article on the Madonna and Sean Penn divorce. And a good picture of Gabriela Sabatini. Tommy loved the tennis. The legs, the photo had caught her legs.

Tommy lay in the sun, closed his eyes. He had a hard-on, thinking of her legs. He turned on his stomach. On the hill two office girls were chatting. He watched them. No-one could tell, he was discreet. He rubbed his crotch on the ground.

All too soon it was one-thirty and he was back to work.

That afternoon two things happened. The globe went on the bromide machine and John had forgotten to replenish the stock. This resulted in a humiliating request to the annoyed Somers who signed over some petty cash.

—Sorry, sir, apologised John.

Stop sucking on that cunt's cock, you fucking piece of weak shit.

Tommy said nothing.

The second incident threw the entire warehouse into panic. The young kid who delivered the internal mail for the whole department store and its offices had a faint of some sort. He came to, but he was shaky, and it was clear that he could not continue.

Somers and Pathis walked over, saw that the kid was all right, and then began to walk away.

—Who'll deliver the mail? Sue stepped in front of them.

Pathis frowned and turned around. His eyes fell on old Stan Rodgers. Rodgers had been in the mail room since forever, or so it seemed to everyone else.

—Can he go? Pathis asked Somers.

—Yes. The sorting has all been done.

Pathis continued back to his office. Without turning his head, he said, simply, loudly, Rodgers, deliver the mail today. Thanks.

Sue stopped him again.

—What is it? He was annoyed now.

She whispered something to him. He ignored her.

—He's too frail. Not a whisper.

The old man blushed. He blushed deeply, a scarlet that flooded his face.

Tommy cleared his throat.

—I'll do it, he said loudly.

Pathis turned around and for a moment looked as if he was going to yell. Then he fell back, smiled and, turning, dismissed everyone again.

—Sure. Somers, that all right?

The two men went back to their offices. The kid was on his way home, Old Rodgers sat in his corner. Tommy grabbed the trolley and headed out the door. The sun was glowing, the light was brilliant and the pavement hot. Tommy took off his tie, wrapped it around the trolley's handle. He forgot about Pathis, about that smile.

Pathis thought he was weak.

Tommy wanted to hurt Pathis very very much.

The afternoon was spent circumnavigating the guts of the organisation. He walked through distracted shoppers, busy office staff, through rooms and corridors he had not known existed. He followed a map. The buyers, boys in designer suits, girls in fashion, no-one looked at him. He handed over the mail to young secretaries. He memorised faces. Faces to blow on, faces to kiss, faces to hit. He was a mail boy.

At 3.55 he took the trolley into a toilet. He pissed. He spat.

At 4.20 he was ordered by a fat man in an ill-chosen shirt to deliver a parcel to the east wing of the store.

—I've already been there.

—You fucking do what you're told.

The Stockton guy, coming in, gun, shooting up and down the corridor. Shooting this prick, this sweaty ugly cunt. Shooting that snotty bitch in the buyers section, that up-herself blonde, fucking her, gun in her mouth, shooting.

At 5.15 the shop assistants were getting ready for the end of the day. Tommy could see it in the restless faces, the glancing at watches, looking at the clocks. The customers were now frantic, hunting, rushing. Tommy wheeled the trolley back to the mail room. He had been invisible for the last few hours. He liked it.

—All done?

Tommy nodded at Pathis.

—You enjoyed that?

—It was all right.

Tommy was waiting for a thanks.

—Bloody waste of time.

Shit-kicking. Pathis smiled again.

—And you enjoyed it?

Tommy glanced at the clock, white face, black numerals. He couldn't wait till six, he'd leave at five-thirty, fuck who noticed, fuck whoever said anything. Tommy looked at the clock so he wouldn't look at Pathis. If he looked at Pathis, he felt the poison flood his guts, soar into his blood.

Tommy did not look at Pathis.

•

The train was express. Flagstaff. Richmond. Camberwell. Box Hill. Then stopping all stations.

At Richmond a young woman in a blue dress got on. Tommy spent the journey looking down at her large brown breasts.

When Tommy hopped off at Laburnum, he was exhausted. Needing to pee.

—How was your day?

—Fine. Tommy cradled the phone under his chin, switched on the television. The news. And yours?

Soo-Ling was singing gossip.

—Should we get together tonight?

—I'm a bit tired.

—So am I.

—Tomorrow?

—Yeah, tomorrow.

They said their goodbyes. He left the phone off the hook.

At seven-forty Tommy was hungry. He switched off all the lights, left the television on. He jumped into the car, headed for McDonald's.

—Two quarter-pounders, large fries, a Coke.

Tommy sat in the car, feeling his girth. Tomorrow, I'll change tomorrow.

The girl at the service window was barely fifteen. He smiled at her. She did not smile back.

Bitch.

He ate the food in the car, parked across the road at a servo. Four teenage boys were mucking about on bikes. They looked over at him for just one moment and then quickly looked away. He tasted the salt and the oil on his lips. The car smelt of grease.

One of the boys said something. In Italian. Fuck.

Tommy drove the suburb, listening to the radio, catching the breeze. A love song. A sad song. He drove down Middleborough Road, turned towards Box Hill. The Asian restaurants were the only lights. Except for the video shop. He parked the car in a side street. Two girls were coming out of a local college, hugging their books, laughing. He waited till they had passed, turned the corner. He put the lock on the wheel, got out. A young Vietnamese boy was smoking, taking a break from the kitchen. They did not look at each other. Tommy turned up the alley, through the car park, went through the back of the video store.

Club X. Was the boy looking at him? He was embarrassed but not shamed. He did not know any Vietnamese. The boy couldn't tell on him.

The store was empty. A thin man was reading a magazine at the counter. The two men nodded.

Tommy scanned the videos. He moved slowly across the shelves. A black girl was being fucked by a black cock, sucking on a white cock. The white guy was old, grey and with a gut. The black guy was young and thick. The black girl had a shaved cunt. Thirty-nine dollars and ninety-five cents.

Piss, on the back of one slick, a white girl was getting pissed on. Another frame. She was squatting. Pissing.

A young bloke, dark-haired, entered the shop. He moved over to the back wall, the faggot wall. Tommy looked over. The faggot wall had a large poster of a man with a tremendous cock, a cock that fell to his knees. Tommy wondered what that cock would feel like to hold. To wank with, to use two hands to come.

He picked up another video, *Thai Sex Excursions*. He massaged his crotch. The young man had also picked up a video.

Tommy and the homo reached the counter at the same time. The man wanted to book a booth.

—It's busy, can you wait twenty minutes?

The young man nodded, embarrassed. He put the video case on the counter. I'll come back. He almost squeaked.

—Thirty bucks, mate.

Tommy handed over the money. You fucking idiot, you fucking idiot. Save. His father said. Save. Soo-Ling said. Save. Save. He kept promising himself, one day, he would save.

Three hundred and fifty-seven dollars in the bank. Rent due next week. Thank God for fucking work.

As he left the shop, Tommy became aware that the taste of the food had lingered on his breath, on his clothes. The young man was smoking in the street, pacing, waiting for the booth. They looked at each other for one moment. Tommy didn't smile. They looked away.

When he got home Tommy turned on the lights. The room was buzzing. The television. Below its call, a loud silence. Tommy wandered the flat, checking every room, the video in its brown bag under his arm. It was a superstition, he never could shake the feeling: someone was watching him.

Then he put on the video.

He was clothed.

A Thai girl, naked, in a motel room. She opens her cunt wide to the camera.

Tommy pulls out his cock, not quite hard, pulls.

The Thai girl gets on her knees, sticks a finger up her arse-hole, turns around, licks her breasts.

Tommy is pulling at his cock.

The Thai girl masturbates. She is loud. Tommy lowers the volume, conscious of the neighbours.

Tommy slows, drops his hand from his cock. Don't blow. The head of his cock is wet. Tommy sits on his hands.

The Thai girl comes.

There is a knock on the door. Two white American men enter the motel room. One is blond, in his thirties, one is younger, darker.

Tommy fast-forwards.

Tommy fingers his balls, plays the video.

The Thai girl is sucking one, sucking both.

Tommy gets up, pauses the video.

He hunts for the cigarettes, hidden at the back of the kitchen cupboards in an old saucepan. There's just one. Just one fucking fag.

On the screen, eternity, the Thai girl's mouth is extended, wide, her eyes screwed up, she's dribbling. Two fat white cocks in her mouth. Tommy lights the cigarette. His cock is limp again.

The video plays.

She's fucked and she sucks, and the blond guy is up her cunt and the dark guy is in her mouth. Tommy smokes and he wanks. The Thai girl is turned around. The blond guy is in her arse.

Tommy wanks, comes close, slows down, watches, fast-forwards, she's getting fucked, the dark guy holds her head, forces her on his cock. He groans. Tommy turns up the volume.

—I'm coming, I'm coming.

Obviously dubbed. No connection between mouths and sounds.

The dark guys comes on her face, she has her eyes shut tight, He smears his cock on her cheeks, white spoof runs down her throat.

Tommy comes, the white streak falls on his shirt, on his arm.

He looks at the screen.

He is disgusted.

He is aware of sound. Can the neighbours downstairs hear? He turns off the video. 'LA Law'. The volume is deafening. He switches it off.

He takes off his shirt, cleans himself up. He hates the look, the smell of semen, it makes him sick.

He takes out the video. He forces it into its case, he grabs a key, goes to the bedroom, opens the lid to the trunk, throws the video in there. He doesn't look into the trunk. He closes it up.

He goes to the bathroom. He washes his hands, wipes his chest and stomach with a towel. His fat gut, his rolling gut, the obscene flesh.

The hair on his chest is wet.

He washes his hands, scrubs, rinses, scrubs, rinses.

He goes back into the lounge room. The news is on the television. A story about the missing schoolgirl. Three weeks and still no sign of her. Fears that she may have been murdered.

Tommy gets into bed, fully clothed, looks up at the Madonna and Child on the wall. His hands move to prayer. His prayer is an apology.

•

Tommy tries to sleep.

Tommy takes a Valium.

Tommy thinks about the missing schoolgirl. She's eleven.

Tommy thinks about what it would be like stealing a girl, how would he do it.

He would pretend to be a tradesman, hire a station wagon.

He would drive around the streets and maybe a schoolgirl would be walking home alone. And he'd pull up next to her and ask her if she knew the way to somewhere. And he'd pull out a road map and maybe she would come over and look at it with him. He would drug her, with ether. That's what they did on TV. And take her home. Then he would blindfold her and just keep her in a room, just for a few days. He would just get her to suck him off, slap her if she refused, he'd just fuck her, a few times. Just to see what it was like. A girl's cunt, hairless, smooth, tight.

Tommy blew a jerk of thin semen. It fell on his groin, ran down his legs.

Tommy closed his eyes tight, so tight it began to hurt. Tommy saw red dots and a million lights flooded his head.

Tommy didn't open his eyes again, lay there, wet, not daring to look into the dark. The Virgin Mary and the Baby Jesus were there, on the wall, looking down at him.

Tommy wiped his crotch. He could smell the stench of come.

Tommy prayed and kept his eyes tight shut.

It took a long time for the world to vanish.

3

Chinese girls are not sluts

Sloo-Ling Kwok was born in Ballarat, a town built on gold mining and violence. She was not the only Chinese girl at her school, there were a few, descendants of prospectors, but Soo-Ling grew up aware of the demarcations provoked by the slant of her eyes. Her father ran a grocery, her mother worked the till. Kevin Kwok was a tame man, that's what all of Ballarat thought of him. He too had been born in the bush, but his father's country had infected his tongue: there was a chopped rhythm to his accent, a miniscule variation that confirmed his foreignness.

—Malaysia is a beautiful place, her father would tell Soo-Ling, but it's very harsh. When you go to Malaysia, he would always add, you must never forget you are Chinese. Not Malay, you are Chinese.

I'm never going to fucking Malaysia.

Malaysia was her mother, the quiet shy An. An never yelled, rarely spoke above a whisper. The marriage had been arranged in a room in Kuala Lumpur. Grandfather Kwok and Grandfather Lee had dealt their children's future.

—And you didn't mind?

An was reading from a Chinese novel, Soo-Ling was thirteen, back from school.

—I didn't know to mind.

—What does that mean?

—Soo-Ling, he was your grandfather, my father, I had to listen to him.

Soo-Ling chucked her schoolbag over her shoulder, marched out of the shop.

Kevin was gentle, kind to his daughter. But he was strict with her time. If she arrived from school after four o'clock, he would fret.

—Where have you been?

—Just out. With Sharon.

—Sharon is no good.

—Why?

—Her family is no good. They drink.

Soo-Ling kept quiet.

Soo-Ling was not allowed to go to parties.

—Australian parties are bad. Too much drug, too much alcohol.

An lived in terror of drugs.

—Mum, it's all right. I won't drink.

—No, would interrupt Kevin, and that was that. His face would collapse into disappointment if Soo-Ling attempted to argue with him.

—I said no!

An would touch her daughter's sleeve.

—Be quiet, she'd whisper.

Kevin Kwok is all right, not bad for a Chinaman. That's what the locals said.

Soo-Ling had God in common with the other girls. Milk-shakes with Sharon, Karen and Sally after Mass. The Catholic God mesmerised her with His passionate martyrdom, His death on the Cross. His feminine and savaged body. Soo-Ling prayed to Jesus every night to get her out of Ballarat.

Kevin Kwok never hit Soo-Ling until 20 November, 1979.

She had rung her mother.

—Mum, I'm out with Sharon, I'll be back soon. Mrs Corrs invited me for dinner.

An put down the phone.

At nine-thirty Soo-Ling had still not come home.

—Ring her, ordered Kevin.

An dialled the number.

—Good evening, Mrs Corr, this An Kwok. Is Soo-Ling there?

—How you doing, An? How's Kev?

—Please, Mrs Corr, can I speak to my daughter?

—Sorry, love, the kids are out. I haven't seen them all night.

—Thank you.

An put down the phone and shuddered.

Kevin found Soo-Ling in the back of a panel van belonging to red-haired, red-faced, red-arsed Steven Jacobs. This was a sight he was to carry forever. The boy's pale arse, the shock of red halo around the swinging balls. The quick ugly flash of his daughter's thickly black snatch. Kevin Kwok roared.

—You slut, you've shamed me, you slut! He cried into the night, frightening the empty bush into a cacophony of bird shrieks and marsupial wails. Chinese girls are not sluts.

Kevin swung open the van doors, tore the boy off his daughter and threw him into the shrubs. He pummelled his daughter, breaking her face. The young Steven, naked, tried to stop the violence. The man, disgusted and ashamed, cried tears over his cowering daughter. The boy pulled the man away. Soo-Ling jumped back, covering her breasts, her cunt. She huddled, heaving, inside her boyfriend's denim jacket.

Kevin looked at the frightened Steven. The boy's penis, long, the head thick. Kevin covered his eyes, again ashamed. A man had fucked his daughter.

—Get dressed, he gasped, and turned away from the couple.

Soo-Ling and Steven did not exchange one word. They quickly got dressed, not looking at each other, and Soo-Ling came and stood next to her father.

—You leave for Melbourne tomorrow.

Blood was pouring down the girl's cheek, drenching her shirt.

An began screaming when she saw her daughter's face, but

her husband ordered her to stop. Tj-Shin, Jack, also cried and ran up to his sister.

—Don't touch her. Kevin stopped his son. Soo-Ling flinched. Go to your room.

The boy hesitated.

—Now!

The boy obeyed.

Her father did not speak to her again that night. Her mother packed her bags, cleaned her face. In Soo-Ling's shaking hands she placed five crisp fifty dollar bills and a mess of soiled twenties, tens and fives. She gave her child an address.

—She will help you find a room, a job. An softly touched her daughter's cheek. The girl was sobbing.

—You cannot stay here, daughter, it isn't possible. You have to disappear. An started praying, in her first language.

Soo-Ling watched her mother pray, heard the words to God in a foreign tongue. Mum is very beautiful, Mum is so fragile. Soo-Ling sniffed. I'm not that.

She arrived in Melbourne, sleepless and cold. A job, cleaning, was found for her immediately. She had a room with the Chin family; at night she drifted into dreams fed by smell, tracing the stories of the oils and the spices, the food and the grease that dominated the Chins' shop. Soo-Ling missed her mother's patience and she missed the space offered by the bush. But apart from that, she missed nothing of Ballarat. Her nose healed, but it was always crooked, imperceptible to others, but not to Soo-Ling. Jack, she was ashamed to discover, she did not miss at all; in fact she was relieved to no longer have to take care of him. Her father she thought of not at all; if she did, the passionate hatred humiliated her. Of Steve, she missed the kisses, the hard tenderness of his mouth.

•

Maria was watching her. Tommy scowled and pushed away his plate.

—What is it?

—Nothing, Ma. I'm not hungry.

—Eat, you idiot.

Dominic patted his thick stomach and then quickly cut up another chop.

—You should watch it, fatty, said Eva, and smiled at Soo-Ling. The boys in this family have it too good, she continued, and quickly glanced at Maria. They need a daughter. Or two.

Maria got up from the table.

—Any more wine?

—Sit down, growled Artie. You haven't eaten anything.

She was very attractive, Tommy's mother, thought Soo-Ling. Not in the same way as An, not thin. But not quite plump. Maria Stefano's style was defined by the icons of the fifties and the sixties. But a Mediterranean definition. Sophia Loren, Gina Lollobrigida, and the dark Hollywood beauties, someone like Ava Gardner. Maria's hair was dyed black, swept over her neck. The dress she wore was cut fine across her breasts, and though not expensive, it fitted well and looked good.

—I like your dress, Mrs Stefano.

The woman smiled.

—Are you still hungry, darling?

Soo-Ling shook her head.

Maria said something in Greek. Tommy jerked angrily, Dominic laughed and Artie looked up, quizzical, and then glanced over at Soo-Ling.

—Fuck off, Mum. Soo-Ling was shocked at Tommy's profanity. She touched his arm, a warning. He was fuming.

His mother continued in Greek, defensive. Soo-Ling kept her eyes low, aware and thankful that Eva was with her. Tommy answered his mother in angry broken Greek.

—Soo-Ling, I said nothing bad, I promise. Maria was smiling at her.

—What did you say?

Soo-Ling liked the father. He was staring at his wife, patient, waiting.

—I said that Chinese girls are so beautiful, have very good figures, because they don't eat much.

—That's not all you said, Mum. Lou looked over to Soo-Ling, he stared right at her. Soo-Ling, Mum said that, well, it's one good thing about the Chinese girls, they're cheap to keep.

Soo-Ling immediately burst out laughing, and so did Lou. Maria exploded. Shut up, Louie. She was blushing.

Tommy had one thought. He wanted to grab his brother's young face and push it hard against the wall. He wanted to hear the crack.

After lunch enormous amounts of food were still left on the table. A pile of charred meat, dripping fat. Two bowls of salad: tomato and fetta, coleslaw. Maria allowed Soo-Ling to help clear the table, but she was not allowed to help wash up. Eva did the drying.

Outside, Artie and Dominic were scraping the barbecue. Tommy sat on the verandah, watching his niece play, watching the men.

—Is work good, Soo-Ling?

—Yes. I like it. Soo-Ling neither liked nor disliked work. She had to do it and so did it.

—How's Tommy's job. He is happy?

—Yes. A flicker of hesitation and Maria pounced on it.

—Very tough, very tough now for people. Especially when there is no jobs. Maria touched wood. That's all I want for my children, that they find secure jobs. And good wives.

—Excuse me, said Soo-Ling, where's the bathroom?

It was a house solid with objects. It was small, smaller than the house she had grown up in. From walls hung photographs and tapestries. The toilet smelt of air freshener—pine—and disinfectant sat quietly next to the toilet brush. On the wall hung a painting done on glass, an ocean view from a villa. The marble steps, the dark blue of the sea. A garden from a Hollywood musical.

Just outside the bathroom, on the wall opposite, was a portrait taken when the family had just arrived in the new house. Lou was still a toddler, a cherub. Tommy was smiling widely, almost beginning a laugh. Artie was handsome, Maria beautiful. Their clothes were ludicrous. Soo-Ling giggled at the flares and pinstripes, the wide unflattering collars. From the hall there was a faint stir of unfamiliar music.

She knocked on the door where the sound was coming from.

Lou was sitting in the middle of the room, against his bed. The television was on. Silent, a football game. The radio was playing electronic dance music Soo-Ling did not recognise. A cluttered desk with a computer.

Lou smiled at her.

—Welcome. This is my room.

Soo-Ling sat on the bed. The boy's window opened onto the garden. Artie and the sons were opaque beneath the heavy lace and folds of the curtain. Above Lou's desk were naked images of Madonna, the *Playboy* spread.

Soo-Ling pointed.

—What's your mother think of that?

—She don't mind that. That's what freaked her out. Lou pointed above her head.

Soo-Ling swung around. Posters, images. Who the fuck are the Sonic Youth? she wondered. She finally caught the offending poster. Torn from a magazine, an AIDS notice. Two boys kissing.

—Mum hates that.

—What's that song, on the radio?

Lou shrugged.

—Some acid house thing, I think.

He squizzed at the radio, screwed up his face. No. He hesitated, then nodded. Yeah, I think it's acid house.

—What's the station?

—Triple R. Noncommercial. You don't ever listen?

—No. I'm a bit of a dag, I guess.

—Doesn't Tommy listen to it?

—I don't think so.

Lou turned back to the television.

—Tommy used to listen to it all the time. That's how I got into it.

Mentioning his brother had reminded Lou of the intimacy of the situation he was in right how. This woman's long and slim legs. He blushed and fixed on the television screen. The football had dissolved to advertising.

—You barrack for anyone?

Soo-Ling shook her head.

—I guess you Asians aren't that into football, eh? My mate Vinnie is the same, he can't stand footy. He's Vietnamese, not Chinese, the boy added.

—Maybe it's a girl thing with me.

The boy grinned.

—Nah, can't get away with that. Heaps of girls like footy. His embarrassment had disappeared.

Protesting students. Lou followed the woman's gaze. Flash back to the newsreader.

—Tiananmen? I guess you're following all that, eh?

Soo-Ling smiled at the boy and got up.

—I know nothing about that shit. See you.

A shape ran from under the bed, it jumped onto Lou's lap. A small black and white cat, adult, stretched its neck towards the boy. Lou lowered his head and they touched, nose to nose. Soo-Ling laughed.

Lou turned to her, a finger to his lips.

—Don't tell anyone, she's not meant to be inside. The boy stroked the cat, which began purring and clawing his thigh. Lou turned to Soo-Ling.

—Mum goes all woggy about animals inside the house. Don't tell her.

—I won't, promised Soo-Ling.

As she was leaving she had a strong urge to play with the boy's hair. But she didn't.

In the kitchen Maria was making coffee.

—You want one? Greek?

—I guess. I've never had one. I'll try it.

Soo-Ling was to serve the coffee. The tray had gilt edges, an Acropolis scene on a black shiny surface. Four Greek coffees, two Australian.

—Is Lou having one?

Maria yelled loudly through the house. In Greek.

The boy yelled back.

—No!

The men were sitting on the verandah. Soo-Ling felt the chill. She served the coffee and went inside for her jacket.

Tommy sipped at the coffee, there was not enough milk. Eva was breastfeeding the baby and Tommy did not look at her.

Dominic whispered loudly in Greek.

—Eva, do you have to do it here?

Eva gave him a fuck-you sign.

—I don't speak Greek, remember.

Artie laughed.

—There's nothing wrong, Dom. And I don't mind catching a perv of Eva's tits.

Tommy thought his father was a stupid ignorant cunt.

Eva ignored the men and ministered to the baby. Soo-Ling joined her, sat next to her on the verandah.

—She's beautiful.

—Yeah, she's good. Eva looked proud. She hardly cries, we're lucky.

Artie sipped at his coffee.

—You like yours? he asked Soo-Ling.

The coffee tasted harsh, the thick sediment stained her lips.

—It's fine.

Artie laughed.

—I've never been able to drink that shit.

—Stop. Said in Greek. Maria was shaking her head. You Australians don't know anything about coffee, she spat.

—I'm part Greek, protested Artie, winking to his sons.

—Bullshit you're part Greek, laughed his wife. You're one hundred per cent *kangarootha*.

Tommy looked over at Soo-Ling. She was pretty. He hoped everyone could see how pretty she was.

—How's work, Tommy?

—Fine, Dad.

—They still talking of selling up?

—Yep. Tommy didn't look at Soo-Ling.

—Well, you should keep your eye out for other jobs.

—It ain't that easy, Dad.

—It was easy for me. Maximum two days and I'd find me a new job. I'd knock at every factory door. And you've been to fucking college. You gotta get off your bum.

It isn't that fucking easy any more. Soo-Ling wanted to scream the words. She did not realise it but her fingers uncoiled, they were reaching out for Tommy. Maria was looking at her.

—Arto, you're a malaka, an idiot. There's a recession on, it's not like when you and I started.

Tommy was thankful for his mother's intervention. Now shut up. But she turned to him.

—Tommy, you need a house. It's stupid living at the flat, wasting your money on rent.

—I'm saving. Tommy was frowning.

—How much have you saved? his father asked.

—About three thousand. Again, Tommy did not look at Soo-Ling. His savings account now held nine hundred and fifty-seven dollars and twenty-five cents. It was pay week.

—That's fucking nothing, mate. Dominic shut the paper he was reading. Mum's right, move back here. Everything's done for you, you'll save heaps.

Don't listen to him, Tommy, prayed Soo-Ling.

—I like the flat.

—Why? demanded his mother.

—I like the independence.

His mother exploded into Greek. Independence! Contempt ate at the word.

Fuck you, you bitch. Tommy said nothing. He stood up.

—I've got to go to the toilet.

He deliberately pissed over the seat, splashed on the floor. Then he feverishly sprayed, disinfectant, tore paper from the roll, vigorously cleaned up. He felt sick, his stomach was bloated. He had eaten too much.

Outside, the talk was of politics. Maria berating the collapse of the socialist government in Greece. For her, Papandreou was a hero. The recent coalition formed between the communists and the conservatives made her furious.

—Traitors.

—Why do you care, Mama, what's it to you? The Greeks are fucked, always have been, you say that yourself.

Maria turned swiftly to Dominic.

—I'm still Greek.

—Well, we're not.

Tommy wanted to take back the words as soon as his mother turned her eyes on him. They were fire.

—You're nothing, right. Nothing! The last word Greek.

—Okay, okay, we're nothing.

Maria stared hard at her middle son; she was waiting. Tommy was silent.

You!

She was disgusted. And turned away from him.

Soo-Ling had been quiet throughout, angry for Tommy, She waved to him and pointed across the garden.

—Look, Tom, there's a crow.

Everyone followed her finger.

Dominic laughed.

—She's looking at you, Tommy Boy.

—Bullshit!

Soo-Ling was at a loss to understand the hilarity her innocent observation had caused.

Eva leant close to her and whispered.

—It's a family lunacy.

Maria was laughing hardest.

•

In the car Soo-Ling fiddled with the radio.

—Is this Triple R?

Tommy nodded. He was driving at eighty, he wanted to floor it. He was stung. By his father's casual dismissal. Three years at a fucking college. Just three lousy years of study and his father and his brother were not going to let him forget it. Jealous pricks. Dumb as fucking dogshit, that's what they were.

—I like Lou. I like him a lot.

—He's all right.

He's fucking spoilt. Because he's the baby.

At the lights, waiting for the green, Tommy turned to Soo-Ling.

—You want to stay the night?'

She nodded.

He had cleaned the flat, washed the dishes, wiped down the small kitchen table. He had stuffed his dirty clothes into a plastic bag, kicked it under the bed. His pornography was in the trunk, under an old blanket, under sheets and linen.

Tommy walked into the house, and turned the television on. Soo-Ling went to the toilet. The room was bare. Toothbrushes, soap, deodorant and shaving kit, that was all. The room was cold.

The television was on. She glanced at it, a documentary, some animal in Africa.

—What are you watching?

—I'm waiting for *Sixty Minutes*.

Soo-Ling made herself a tea, sat next to her lover, and they watched the television. An ad break.

—Lou said that you were into music, when you were younger.

—Still am. His eyes on the screen, Tommy waved to his CDs. Two long racks next to the stereo.

—You don't play them much. Do you still have your records?

Tommy turned to Soo-Ling. Why, he wondered, is this happening? This past does not include you.

—No. I don't have my records any more.

Tommy sat back, drank some beer, put his arm around Soo-Ling. This was her comfort, this was where her love began. The solid weight of his arm around her.

On the television a journalist was interviewing the protesting Chinese students. She watched, listened and did not understand anything. China, its size, its history, overwhelmed her. Soo-Ling did not deliberately eschew politics but she did not believe in the possibility of her own engagement. China was too big, she had been raised in this simple but important awareness. The individual was at a loss to assist in anything. She voted, but on a whim.

—What you reckon? Tommy pointed to the screen. Maybe they'll change things.

The China bogey. Everyone had the China bogey.

Tommy relaxed into the couch, tightened the squeeze. Soo-Ling's disinterest in politics delighted him.

—Don't you care, his mother would sometimes scream at him. Look, look. Look what's happening!

No, I don't care. Just leave me alone.

Ad break.

Tommy wanted food. His stomach was still large from the lunch. But he craved sensation. His flab was constrained by the tightness of the belt. He punched his stomach softly.

—You all right? Soo-Ling nestled into him.

—You hungry?

—No, she smiled, I ate so much today.

You fucking bitch. Tommy withdrew his arm, went into the kitchen. He munched a biscuit, poured a Coke.

A woman gang raped in Central Park. Six teenage black

youths bashed her, raped her, tore her apart. Left her barely breathing. Tommy stood in the doorway, watching the report. Better they had finished the job.

—This is terrible. Soo-Ling was crying for the woman.

—I can see how it happened.

—What do you mean?

—She was an idiot. Jogging in fucking Central Park at night. A bloody white woman. What did she expect?

Not that.

—So women are to blame for getting raped, eh? Soo-Ling had crossed her arms, petulant.

You look so pretty. Tommy smiled. Niggers on juice, he was thinking, that's all I meant. Pissed-off kids, didn't she know how angry kids could get?

—Suzie, I'm tired. This isn't worth an argument. He sat down next to her, grabbed the remote and changed the channel. Comedy. American. He turned to her.

—It's all fucked, you know that.

—I don't. You don't want to argue about anything.

Soo-Ling left the room, went to the toilet, brushed her hair, wondered what she would wear for work tomorrow. Did not return until the next ad break.

Selling insurance.

—How is work, Tommy?

Tommy crashed, Tommy closed his eyes. Tommy was close to screaming.

—It's fine.

Soo-Ling did not believe him.

They watched the movie, mostly in silence, she lay against him. They smoked a joint. He went to the convenience store, chips and chocolate. Soo-Ling fell asleep before the movie ended.

She wandered groggy to bed, slipped into the man's sheets, smelt Tommy everywhere, in the wrinkles of the folds. He undressed in the light, she was naked. He lay next to her and hugged her, she shivered, she clutched him, spreading him across her body, needing his warmth. She touched his chest, her finger played with the curls. He kissed her.

Nearly every time sex began, Tommy was conscious of his weight. He sucked in his stomach. His cock was thick, pressing into Soo-Ling's thigh. He looked at her, kissed her face, her eyes. He gently pushed apart her legs and entered her.

Soo-Ling twitched, arched her back, took him in. She kissed his mouth and closed her eyes.

Tommy was fucking her slowly, looking at her, smelling her.

Soo-Ling was dreaming the three brothers. The tender Lou, the brawn of Dominic. She shut them out.

Tommy was dreaming six black giant cocks raping a white cunt. He slammed into his lover, pushing far inside her.

Soo-Ling tried to move to his rhythm, he was speeding to climax.

Tommy came in a shout, screamed in her ear. Nigger cock coming on bleeding whitey's face. He came, shuddered, and detested his dreaming.

Soo-Ling breathed slowly as he lay on top of her. She rubbed her hands across his back, the hair that coated his hips, she rubbed his fat, enjoyed the solidity. His cock was still erect inside her. She moved and he winced. Tommy pulled out.

—I got to go to the toilet.

Quickly she thrashed inside her cunt, speeding to orgasm. The icon was staring down at her. A sound. Tommy was at the door.

He switched on the light. His penis, softening, but still thick from the fucking.

—Don't stop, he asked.

She closed her eyes and relented to her hand, she sniffed the pungency of her own sweat.

—Open your legs, wide.

She kept her eyes shut, moved to his voice.

He had come close, his finger, wet, stroked her, rubbed the boundaries of her cunt, went inside her.

—Harder, she whispered.

—Your cunt, he whispered above her, two, then three fingers, your cunt is so beautiful.

And it was, he was inside her and all the room was the smell of her.

She came, she saw diamonds, his eyes were huge. He was smiling. He moved next to her, held her. She closed her eyes. A black flash, as a flying bird.

—So you fear crows, Tom?

He held her close. He did not answer.

They fell asleep.

At seven o'clock the alarm was the radio. On the news a man with a gruff voice announced the news of the day. The young girl, the eleven year old, the girl gone missing. Her body was found, raped and slaughtered.

Soo-Ling put on her lipstick, sipped her coffee. Tommy shaved, ate the remainder of last night's chocolate. Taking the train into the city, Soo-Ling pointed out the suburbs in which she would like to live. Surrey Hills, Camberwell, Hawthorn.

Tommy looked out the window; at the passing roofs, the swimming pools, the neat gardens.

We can't fucking afford them.

4

Chocolate City

After his first visit to a whore Tommy was convinced that the encounter had soiled him forever. He tasted syphilis on her mouth, licked gonorrhoea off her skin. Her cunt was venereal. Tommy washed and washed when he got home, washed the whore off his skin. He scrubbed and washed, to get rid of the sickness.

Tommy had adored the whore, her size, her age, her beauty. She must have been in her mid-forties, weighed about seventy-five kilos, and her face was a crazy jigsaw maze of lines and wrinkles. But pale, a face painted white. Tommy had closed his eyes and dived into her, the ferocious splendour of her breasts, an unquenchable thirst for her cunt. Seventeen and still a virgin, though he had managed to force two hand-jobs from a disapproving girlfriend, it had been Dominic who had shouted him the extravagance of a prostitute. Drunk, on a bottle of bourbon and the thick oily smoke of hashish, Tommy was initiated into the pleasures of women. He came thrusting above the whore, his elbow hard on the back of her head, pinning her down on the massage table, fucking her from behind and inserting two of his fingers far up her arse. When he first stripped, unzipped, as she took out the flaccid cock, and asked, Have you washed? he had a moment of panic, a fear of his inadequacy. But she breathed on his cock and he scrambled across her body, snatching flesh. He had dreamt her, called out to her, had been waiting, an excruciating waiting, for years. For this fat old slut's breath. On his cock. When he exploded inside her, Tommy opened his eyes and looked down at the weary blubbery shoulders of the woman. He shuddered, his desire had evaporated to loathing, and he quickly lifted his trousers. Embarrassed, he left the room, rushing, gathering shirt and socks, and stumbled into the foyer of the brothel where his brother and two mates were waiting and laughing, laughing and waiting for the boy.

That was 1979 and a prostitute cost fifty dollars. He had quickly forgotten her face, the contours of her skin. He could not recall her at all. What he did remember was the smell. Her perfume, her cunt, and that the massage table smelt of disinfectant. And her voice, he could still remember her voice. Soft, not the harshness he had expected. A little girl's breathy glee, but the hard consonants of a difficult life.

Tommy was preparing the artwork for printing, the mail room was nearly empty and that same voice was now on the radio. The newsreader's well-enunciated expression lacked the whore's vigour, but the accent was familiar.

They'd found, the girl's body in a stretch of bush in Pakenham. The body was poorly concealed under scattered branches and torn shrubs. Her face had appeared on newsprint, on television screens, had made the glossy pages of the magazines. Eleven, dark, pretty; and her distraught weeping parents. The mother, Filipino and extravagant, had broken into howls, a reminder of wolves, when she had been interviewed on *A Current Affair*.

—My daughter, please. Please God, bring my daughter back safe.

The father, stoic, the ruddy coarse skin of the Irishman, had wept quietly, holding tight to his wife.

She had been missing for four months; her tortures were referred to obliquely and therefore seemed even more tantalising. Was her corpse sodomised? The torture is unimaginable, thought Tommy. His eyes were moist, her suffering was tragic.

But it was also perverse. His eyes were moist, he was conscious of his cock.

The story ended. Christopher Skase to buy United Artists. Oliver North on trial. Eleven million gallons of oil in Prince William Sound, somewhere off the Alaskan coast. Football and the prediction of rain, rain throughout the weekend. It's six o'clock and seventeen degrees in the city. A truck has overturned on the South Eastern Freeway near the Toorak Road exit and cars are advised to avoid Punt Road.

A commercial for a tyre specialist, a commercial for Pepsi, a station promo. A blistering thrash of guitar, a burst of heavily bassed rap, then a cut. Proudly announcing, No weird new sounds, no rap, no heavy rock, just Golden Oldies. 3TT FM. And into the first song. 'When You See A Chance', Steve Winwood. Tommy lay down his scalpel, looked at the clock. 6.05.

That fucking prick, he's doing it to spite me.

Pathis was in his office, clear behind the glass, working on his computer. His tie was still tight around his shirt collar. Tommy had loosened his own once the rest of the shop had begun to leave. It was Friday night and he wanted to head off, to make work disappear. But he also wanted to be the last to leave, to leave after Pathis. But the wog wasn't moving.

Tommy was working on a brochure for the electronics unit, a sale on stereo equipment. The brochure was cheap, black and white, to be printed on a lazy cream paper stock. The task was finished and Tommy was not in the mood for starting new work. He rolled the artwork, placed it in a plastic envelope and walked towards the offices.

Pathis did not look up at the knock.

—Come in.

Tommy handed him the envelope.

—The job's finished.

Pathis nodded. Thanks. His eyes on the computer.

—See you.

Pathis farewelled him in Greek. Gia sou. Tommy grimaced, he hated that.

He made no answer.

The daylight had begun its surrender to night. In the park, secretaries and clerks were scrambling towards the station. The wind was slight but it brought drizzle and chill. Tommy stuffed his hands deep into the pockets of his bomber jacket. The rough cotton lining tickled his fingers. At the entrance to Flagstaff Station the kiosk that sold papers and magazines was shutting up. Three posters. The dead girl's pretty face. The oil on the icy waters. The tall lean body of a footballer. Her face, she was grinning, in her school uniform, a self-conscious joy for the camera. Sexually assualted and murdered. Tommy spat on the ground, stepped onto the escalator and descended into the bowels of the station.

When they find him, he thought to himself, hanging his bag over his shoulder, I hope they crucify the arsehole, I hope they make him suffer. I hope he pays.

Tommy would have him fucked, arse, mouth and cock, with a broken bottle. An eye for an eye.

The carriage was not full. Tommy avoided the drunk youth up the back and plonked himself down next to a couple, Indian, the man with his arm around the woman's shoulder. Across the aisle a drunk old man with a red and veined nose dribbling. A man in blue overalls stood in the doorway, a large bushy blond moustache, a tattoo of a snake creeping up his exposed right arm. Tommy glanced behind him. The drunk youths, making noise, he avoided their eyes. A beautiful woman. Dark. Thick red lipstick. He turned back around. The Indian couple. She too was sweet.

At Richmond the door opened and a woman, fell into the carriage. Windcheater and faded blue jeans. She was not young, she was not old. Drugs had lacerated her face. She was shrivelled and ugly. Thin. She staggered through the carriage. The train started to move and she fell onto Tommy. Sorry, love. Her breath stunk, cheap nasty wine. He assisted her to her feet and she sat hard next to the old drunk man, who groaned, shifted his weight and rested his head on the window.

—What are you looking at?

The Indian woman had been staring. She bowed her head, embarrassed, and indicated she was sorry. The woman in the windcheater wouldn't leave it alone.

—What the fuck were you looking at?

Around the carriage heads turned. The Indian woman ignored her.

—Well? An insistent highly unpleasant noise. A cheap Australian accent.

—Fucking niggers.

The carriage went quiet. The Indian man's face hardened. And on the Indian woman's face there was an acceleration of contempt. They both said nothing.

—Fucking niggers, I can't stand them.

Around the carriage there were faint murmurs of dissent. Tommy kept praying, Shut up you stupid cunt, just shut up.

But she wouldn't shut up. She began a slow drugged rave, a mixture of fantasy and bile. Fucking niggers, this place is full of them now, fucking niggers and slopes. Anyone want sex with me? she screamed out. The old man opened his eyes, took a look, shook his head and went back to sleep.

—Who'd want to fuck you? yelled one of the boys from the back and his mates started to laugh and jeer.

—Fuck you, scum, she screamed back. There was laughter in her cruel stark voice.

She's young, thought Tommy. He was praying, Shut it, shut up. He could not look at the couple in front of him, and instead he looked out into the night, the suburbs whizzing past.

She would not shut up.

—You black bastards stink.

Inside Tommy exploded. He heard his mother. All Australian girls are sluts, dirty, stupid sluts. He wanted to take her, grab her hair, smash her fucking face against the glass, again and again, bleeding, shards of glass in her mouth. Hurt her, bruise her, bash her. He wanted her dead.

—Fucking too many slopes.

He wanted her dead.

—It's all niggers and wogs and slopes these days.

She deserves to die. He looked up, the Indian man was staring straight ahead, beyond him, beyond the train, beyond the world. The Indian man looked at him. Tommy smiled.

•

Do I too believe this, that a woman like that deserves to die?

•

At Box Hill she got off, swaying drunk to the doors, shooting off final insults. The young men followed her into the dark of the underground station. The train pulled away and Tommy peered out into the grey and black. She was riding the escalator, still mouthing curses, the boys behind her.

Rape her. I hope they rape her.

He relaxed back in the seat. He could not look at the couple. He felt that his silence had been a betrayal, though what could he have done?

You could have said something. Again, his mother's voice.

The Indian woman sighed deeply and she looked up at him. He smiled arid she, tentatively, she smiled back.

He walked home quickly, in the dark, bashing against the cold. The flat was freezing. He tore off his tie, threw his shirt and trousers in a corner and jumped into track pants and a windcheater. As his arms shot into the sleeves he glimpsed his body in the bedroom mirror. Fat. In the lonely room Tommy rang out a cry. I've got to go to the gym, I haven't been all week. He thought of the sausage roll and chips he had eaten for lunch. He traced the path of the fat, of the grease, of the salt. He banged his fist into the hideous softness of his body. He checked the time on the alarm clock. 6.53. The red numbers blinked. He grabbed his keys.

The gym change room was quiet. An old white-haired man was dressing slowly. A young swimmer showering. Tommy changed into a T-shirt and shorts and walked upstairs to the gym. In the fluorescent cavern he began his routine.

He stretched. And thought of the bogan bitch on the train. How he should have punched her, shut her up.

He began the weights, twenty lifts of twenty-five kilos, and thought, No, I couldn't, she's a woman, someone would have stopped me. I'd have been arrested.

He cycled and listened to the thundering music from the room next-door, the thumping of aerobics. He pushed his feet hard against the pedals, felt the muscles in his thighs stretch. No, the boyfriend should have done something, fucking gutless Indian prick.

The rhythm of movement stilled his mind. He withdrew into counting and action. There were six men in the gym, and three women. A blonde in lycra shorts and a black bikini top. An older woman, overweight, grunting on a bike. And the woman in the wheelchair.

There was the man, the man with the beard, the tall man. His legs, shocking in their barbaric strength.

The minutes began to lag into a shuddering boredom. He looked around the cavern. The woman in the wheelchair, her black hair in a ponytail, was pulling down on a bar, her face closed, she never smiled at him, working the machine. The time code on the bike read 3.58. Twelve minutes to go and the world began to come in again. Pathis, the obscenity of his sneer. That was who Tommy should punch. He pedalled furiously on the machine.

4.43. He had never fucked a woman in a wheelchair. Did their cunts have any feelings?

5.13. The song on the radio was Roberta Flack, 'First Time Ever I Saw Your Face': His cycling slowed, he was unaware of it, the song soothed him, made the time go faster. Pathis was going to get rid of him. Tommy closed his eyes. Rent due. He closed his eyes tight. He had to make more money.

7.02. Soo-Ling. He was so fucking lucky to have Soo-Ling. Jesus, he had forgotten to ring Soo-Ling.

8.02. He wasn't going to go for fifteen minutes. Ten, he'd make it, ten minutes.

9.13. Again, the 13. Was he willing it?

9.28. His fat was shaking as he pedalled. He was being lazy. He should do fifteen.

10.00. He stopped. The sweat was pouring down his back, his T-shirt sticking to his skin. The smell of man. Tommy breathed heavily, picked up his towel and walked out of the gymnasium. He stood on the balcony overlooking the pool. Two boys diving. They laughed and shivered on the board, pushing each other, daring each other. Tommy walked downstairs to the showers.

He did not often shower at the gym, waited till he was home and safe in the isolation of his own bathroom instead. But tonight the change room was empty. He stripped and relaxed into the hot swoosh of the water. The rush fell on his head, on the back of his neck, and he had an urge to piss. Tommy opened his mouth to the water and closed his eyes. The water was a sea in which he floated. He opened his eyes and looked down to the swirl of soap at his feet, the hair on his chest and belly splattered long and thin on his skin. Abruptly Tommy leant across, jerked the hot water tap off and the cold blast of ice tore him out of dreaming and into a savage present. His body jumped back, startled by the shivering cold.

In front of the mirror Tommy looked at his body. Shouts from the swimming pool. He dried, first his hair, then his chest and shoulders. Between his thighs. In the mirror his body was warm, red and warm.

Tommy was the darkest of the brothers. His hair, his lips, the olive of his skin, they were Maria's, and though he did not know it, they were also his grandmother's. The dark swirls on his chest and his legs. Tommy was not ugly but this too was not known to him. The mirror reflected back the asymmetry of his weight. His tits hung, just a slight podge, but he could only see a hideous limp bulk. The heavy lead of his stomach. The long thin piece of foreskin that made his cock a spike. Tommy turned from the mirror. And thought of nothing more but the ecstasy of excising his body from the world.

A man entered the change room. Abruptly Tommy turned his back to the stranger and quickly put pants over his nakedness. Tommy dressed and ran a red comb through his hair. The man was in the shower, his back to Tommy, soap and water. Tommy looked into the mirror, then quickly, a flash, glanced over his shoulder to the showers. The man's cock was short, the balls shrunken and cold. Tommy sighed, relieved, and left.

Still hot from the workout, he did not feel the cool of the night. He walked to the car and the hunger gnawed. No, fuckwit. Don't eat tonight. You've got to lose some weight. Tommy pushed a cassette savagely into the stereo. A blast of U2. The *War* album. He revved, he revved hard, and journeyed home.

He loved U2. Had been there from the beginning. 'Gloria'. He had loved U2. Three years ago, three young people, students, on the train. He had not long been a worker. They were discussing U2. They were laughing at U2.

Daggy.

Boring.

Pompous.

People who liked U2 were into cock-rock, that's what they said.

Tommy was not to know that these were adjectives they had learnt from the *Rolling Stone*. He was not to know that the three students were simply playing at snobbery, innocuous snobbery but, like all snobbery, meant to ruthlessly extinguish all opposition.

It was Tommy's failure that instead of embracing the opposition—I think you're wrong, I like U2—he acquiesced to their opinion. It did not make him stop listening to the band, to his music, but something changed for him; the belief in the integrity of his own opinions. If he had resisted the shame—because it was shameful, his belief that he was proven *wrong*—he could have laughed instead. He could have leant over and explained to the three young people that taste should never be the basis for an ethics or a politics.

Daggy, maybe. Depends on your class and social circle.

Boring. Yes, some of it is.

Pompous. Yes, often.

All people who like U2 were into cock-rock. An absurdity. A statistical impossibility. A *prejudice*.

•

I'm blushing. I'm intervening here. It was me, I told Tommy U2 were pompous.

•

He played U2, drove home.

The first thing he did on entering the flat was ring Soo-Ling.

—Hi, it's me.

He could hear her smoking, the stilted puff. She sounded tired.

—Where have you been?

—I worked late. Then I went to the gym.

—What are you doing tonight?

A high pitch on the last syllable. He was tired, the thought of collapsing at his own place, within his own space, was very attractive. But on the other end of the phone Soo-Ling was breathing, waiting, and he also desired her softness.

—I thought I might come over.

—Good. I'd like that. He could sense her smile. Have you eaten yet? she asked.

—No. I'm not that hungry.

—I'll cook you something, something small.

—You don't have to.

—I know. She sniffed on the other end. Waiting.

—Okay, thanks. Is Sonja home tonight?

—No, she's out at Ronnie's.

Good. Tommy found it difficult to communicate with the diffident, suspicious Sonja.

—I'll be over soon.

He put down the phone.

He stuffed underwear and a T-shirt into a bag, grabbed the old mustard jar where he kept the dope, and locked up the flat. He debated leaving on a light but thought about the money.

Rent, he recalled, frustrated, angry, rent was due. He switched off the lights.

•

They kept flashing her picture throughout the night, in between every program break. Soo-Ling pointed the remote at the screen and the little girl's face jerked, flashed and disappeared into darkness. Soo-Ling jumped up and walked into the kitchen, grabbing food and saucepans, but she could not forget the face. It was not that she was particularly shocked by the rape and murder. Nothing new there. It was the vulnerable youth of the victim that hurt. Soo-Ling sliced the chicken fillets methodically, neatly. The violence of the murderer struck her as absurd, a madness in men which she had no wish to understand.

God says forgive, she thought to herself, her fingers wet from the carcass, but He surely can't ask me to forgive this? Soo-Ling prayed, silently, only a tremor of the lips.

Pray, she had taught Tommy. Just pray, because even if it is not answered, the praying helps.

She prayed that the child's parents could live with the annihilation the rapist had wreaked.

I wish I hadn't watched the fucking television.

Music. She put on a tape of Sonja's, a compilation. And the music did its work. She concentrated on the cooking, coordinating sauce and pasta, a quick washing up. The tape segued across time and genre, and she sang along to the words. Cat Stevens, 'Father and Son'. And it made her think of Tommy.

The little girl's face. *From the moment I could talk I was ordered to listen.* She swept hair away from her eyes with the back of her hand and attempted again to forget the image. Thank God Tommy will be here tonight.

The kitchen, bathed in electric light, seemed large tonight and very cold. The backyard was dark. She turned away from the darkness and glanced up at the clock. It had been twenty minutes since Tommy had called.

She was praying. Please come, Tommy, please get here soon.

Soo-Ling had first seen Tommy when he'd delivered a set of pamphlets to her work. She was on the phone, doing reception, and he had waited patiently for her to finish. He had tried to pretend that he was not looking at her but he was not successful. Soo-Ling made no such pretence. She had initially thought him sweet rather than handsome, a little boy still hiding somewhere in the shy young man. The unruliness of his dark hair, the large eyes, a dog's sad eyes. Injured. It had been the eyes.

They had talked, a perfunctory exchange. Where do I deliver this? Here will do. She had signed, he smiled and left. At the glass door, he had turned, looked at her again.

She smiled back.

They had met again over a lunch. Nadia, whom Tommy worked with, was friendly with Soo-Ling; they had been at TAFE together. They were having lunch and Tommy was in the same cafeteria. Nadia invited him over. He had sat in silence for most of the conversation, nervous. He left quickly and blushed on saying goodbye.

—He's strange, real quiet.

—That's okay, replied Soo-Ling.

And they did not talk of him again. On leaving the cafeteria they discovered that he had paid for both their bills.

Their third encounter was again over the reception desk at

work. This time he was more effusive, away from the alert Nadia, and he made her laugh, quietly, by impersonating the staid English prickliness of her boss. And she asked him out to lunch.

This was not characteristic of Soo-Ling, for in her aloofness from men she resembled her mother. But her assertiveness, its very accident, in this instance was to cement the future.

—Would you have asked me for a date? she demanded from Tommy a year after their first outing.

—No, replied Tommy, honestly, I wouldn't have had the guts.

She had thought at first that Nadia was right, he was strange. His shyness, though attractive, had initially disturbed her. Conversation proved difficult but she found herself touched by his generosity. He followed her, let her decide which films they watched, paid for most things. She was impressed by his attentiveness and was considerate of his hesitancies.

But it was after fucking that Soo-Ling discovered she was in love. In bed, freed from the contract of conversation, Tommy allowed himself to express the depth of his devotion. His kissing first hurt, he bit into her and drew blood. He pummelled her body and his sweat covered her. She had been with men more experienced, possibly even more considerate, but Tommy was the first to show her the immensity of passion. His body, which when clothed had appeared clumsy, assumed a potent grandeur when naked. Tommy's body, in its softness and its solidity, was the first body in which Soo-Ling allowed herself to disappear. His smells, his touch, the roughness of his hands, the swell of his cock inside her, the taste of his mouth. His lips praised every part of her body. She emerged from their lovemaking convinced of the virtue of their union. His silences continued to disturb her but she began to learn to listen to his kisses instead. On occasion, on making love, he would cry, tears would fall on her. This, in a man, this amazed her.

For Tommy, it was far more simple. He could not believe that Soo-Ling had chosen him for a partner. He thought her the most beautiful woman he had ever seen. In sex he worshipped her.

And only in sex with her was he not ugly. And, for him, his silences proved that he could protect her.

Tommy arrived with stubbies of beer. Soo-Ling laid out the food on the coffee table. Tommy turned on the television—David Letterman beamed in from America—opened a beer and began rolling a joint.

—Can't that wait till later?

Fuck you.

—Sure.

They ate in silence, watching the television. It's nice, Tommy nodded to Soo-Ling and continued eating. When he had finished, had wiped the plate clean with bread, he sat back and lit the joint.

Soo-Ling took three quick puffs, coughed and passed it over. The effect was immediate. She sunk back, she sunk into torpor.

—I must clean up. She got up, steadied herself on the armrest and cleared away the plates. Tommy took hold of her hand.

—It can wait.

—I know. But you know me.

He let go.

In smoke they found an equilibrium. For Tommy he could relax into silence, close to her, smelling her. In smoke Soo-Ling found a slowness that numbed her lips and tongue.

She washed up, the warm water falling smooth on her hands. She dried the dishes, rubbed oil into her palms, sniffed the fruity aroma. She could hear Tommy laughing.

The television did annoy her. It created a space between them, a white noise, a stranger separating them. She hated Letterman.

—Anything else on?

She sat down beside him, took his arm and stretched it around her shoulders. She leant in to him, smelt the soap and the sweat. She put her hand under the sweatshirt and rubbed her palm across his wiry hair.

Tommy shifted, a slight move away. Her hand was feeling his fat, the horror of his weight. He looked at his beer. The tan thick liquid. He drank from it, returned to the television, straightened, and Soo-Ling fell back. He began rolling another joint.

—How was work?

—All right. Pretty busy.

—Same.

Soo-Ling was a secretary in an accounting firm. Twenty-four thousand six hundred and twenty-eight dollars per annum.

The comedian on the Letterman show was not funny.

—I don't see why we have to watch crap from America.

Tommy offered her the joint, laughing.

—Haven't we been doing that all our lives?

The comedian was making New York jokes.

—Do you want to go to America?

Soo-Ling shook her head.

—I think I'd hate it.

Tommy wanted to visit Graceland, maybe Disneyland, hire a hooker for the night. A sexy black hooker who looked like the girl from Salt N Peppa. Was she Salt or was she Peppa?

—I don't know, some of it would be all right.

Soo-Ling handed him the joint, rubbed his palm.

—We'll travel.

I want to see the world on my own, thought Tommy, no-one there with me. Then I could be a stranger, do anything I wanted and no-one would know, no-one would see me, no-one could tell on me.

Except God.

And God knows already.

Tommy stretched his arms, yawned, kissed Soo-Ling. She smelt of the moisturiser on her hands. His cock shifted, suddenly he was aware of her. The smoke had dulled his movements and accentuated his senses. He rubbed her thigh slowly.

Soo-Ling rested back on the couch, shifted her legs.

Tommy moved his hand under her skirt, traced his finger along the mound of her crotch.

Soo-Ling took the joint.

Tommy pushed his thumb tight into her cunt.

Soo-Ling expelled the smoke.

Tommy took her hand, placed it on his thigh. He slowly guided it along the crescent of his erection.

Soo-Ling squeezed the cotton, squeezed the cock head.

On the television a phone sex ad. Blonde girls with big tits.

Tommy pushed Soo-Ling's hand vigorously across his crotch. He pushed her panties down, sunk his fingers into her still dry hole. He pushed far into the coarseness.

It hurt. Soo-Ling pushed his arm away.

Tommy butted out the joint. Her hand slid off his body.

—I'm sorry. Later. I'm a little tired.

—That's all right. The end credits of the Letterman show.

Suck my cock. He could grab her hair, shove her face on his dick. Push down hard, blow deep into her mouth.

The news. A five minute grab. The little girl's face. The hunt for the killer.

Soo-Ling crossed her arms. Tommy got up.

—Where are you going?

—To the toilet.

Pissing, hard, a stream of beer, his cock was still half tight. He could smell the decay beneath the foreskin, the sharp ugly bitterness of dry sperm. When he came back the news was football.

The happiness that is relief.

They did not talk of the girl.

The night descended into a marijuana lull. Soo-Ling slept on the couch and Tommy watched videos on *Rage*. He too fell asleep and only woke, startled, when he recognised a bass riff.

On screen: black men, loud funk, garish costumes, spacemen.

He knew this song.

The bass riff, he knew this riff.

Chocolate City. Dominic had this album, from the days of disco. Dominic had been a disco king, a dancer. Tommy rarely danced and never to disco. That was for the wogs in Clifton Hill.

Dominic, the oldest, had chosen disco, dance. Tommy had to turn to rock, to punk. He switched off 'Chocolate City'.

Tommy yawned. He shook Soo-Ling.

—Honey, let's go to bed.

She yawned, smiled. They cleaned their teeth in silence, a quick furious scrubbing. In bed the sheets were cold and Tommy hugged Soo-Ling tight, grabbing at the warmth of her body. She in turn wrapped his arms tight around her and fell immediately asleep, protected by his solidity.

For Tommy it took a long time. His cock went stiff. The little girl. He thought of masturbating, listened to the deep rhythms of Soo-Ling's sleep, but embarrassment stopped him. He thought of work, of Pathis, thought of rent. The little girl. He thought of work. He thought of work and Pathis and thought of rent. He felt the pleasant roughness of Soo-Ling's nipple. She squirmed in her sleep. He heard bass in his head. *Chocolate City*. He hummed, he breathed, he let the smoke and the drink do its work. He heard music in his head, forgot the girl, and he eventually fell asleep.

5

Fitzroy vs Collingwood
at Victoria Park

The Stefano family all supported the Collingwood Football Club, all except Tommy. He barracked for Fitzroy. This difference caused an isolation Tommy felt keenly even from the very borders of his memory. The choice was now impossible to decipher. He had always barracked for Fitzroy; whether from defiance or simply because he had liked the colours on the guernseys, he did not know. It had happened and it marked his difference.

—C'arn the Pies.

And he hated Collingwood with a murderous passion. He had been born not far from Victoria Park, Collingwood's home ground. It seemed that his childhood years had always been punctured with the raucous ferocious screams of supporters. Collingwood, Collingwood forever. And it followed that between himself and Dominic a rivalry had grown, a violence over football that erupted in savage moments of bickering and hate.

—The fucking Fitzroy Lions are all poofters. They're a fucking disgrace.

Tommy would leap at his brother, screaming, and batter him with his fists. Dominic would laugh, push back, and Tommy would fall crying to the floor.

—See. Told ya. You're all a pack of poofters.

His father, laughing, would pick up the shaking hysterical child. It's only footy, mate, it's only footy. He would turn, to his older son. Leave him alone, all right. Don't upset him.

His mother would get angry at their obsession with the sport. Bloody football. But she too, when pressed, would admit her preference for the black and white of the Collingwood Football Club.

—We live here, she would argue, it's a working class team, it's our team.

—It's not, it's not my fucking team, yelled Tommy.

•

—This is Susan McIntyre, she'll be with us for a few weeks. She's a consultant.

Pathis had introduced her and from that moment Tommy became aware that the world was spinning in directions far from his control. She was young, possibly younger even than himself. She was blonde, smart and spoke good English and she spoke it tough. She was thin, no meat on her at all.

The anorexic bitch. That's what everyone called her. Nadia was the most contemptuous.

—She'll be the one, you'll see, she's come in to do the hatchet job.

The company was to shut down the print shop. That decision had already been made though it had not yet been communicated to staff. But the threat of closure had been a strong rumour for months and the unease and fear had begun to accentuate the petty differences among the staff. For a long time the print shop and the mail room had been divided. Among the printers, the five men reaching retirement age, there was one hundred per cent union membership. They were old school, tradespeople who had assumed the rightness and inevitability of unions. They had also seen the results. For the administrative staff and among the mail clerks—young, some straight out of school—the union did not exist.

Tommy had paid union dues from the day he started work. It had been a familial obligation.

Nadia, too, was union.

—Those fucking stupid bitches, she spat through her cigarette, referring to the women she typed with. They don't know a thing.

Tommy looked at her long legs, shivering behind the nylon. She doesn't shave them enough, he thought, and looked across the roof down to the city. He was falling; he knew it. He was going to lose this job and he had no idea and no inclination for future work.

—What are you going to do?

Tommy didn't answer. He was watching skyscrapers.

—Hey, I'm talking to you.

He turned around, beckoned for a cigarette. He'd give up again tomorrow.

—Fuck, I hate botters. She handed him a fag. What you thinking about?

—Wondering if Fitzroy will beat Collingwood on Saturday.

Nadia laughed and stamped out her cigarette.

—Bullshit. They're a pack of losers.

This was the first time in the five years Tommy had worked in the print shop that no-one had organised a footy tipping competition. Whatever factions and animosities, the weekly tipping had been a cement for the workplace. The rushed marking off of teams on a Friday night. Largely it had been organised by the brash Richmond-supporting Sue. She collected the money at the beginning of the year, organised the pre-finals evening bash. Chips and dips, salami and kabana. The wine and the beer. They'd all get drunk. Secretaries and printers, designers and clerks. Even the manager came along. But the football season had been hushed this year. Tommy and John would exchange opinions, team colours worn on a Monday after a successful weekend. But no-one else really bothered.

McIntyre was conducting interviews with staff. John had already gone up.

—What's she asking?

—Stuff. John said little more. It was likely he would keep his job. He had done his best to impress the stiff Somers and the arrogant Pathis. With McIntyre he was attentive and a little flirtatious. He was also studying the new computer graphics in his own time and with his own money. That put him ahead.

—Yeah, but we don't all live at home and have Mummy to wipe our arses for us, snarled Nadia.

—What she asking?

—Nothing, Tom, nothing. She's just asking about our work.

—She say anything about me?

—Nothing, Tom, I told you. They're just simple questions.

Tommy watched McIntyre talking to Pathis through the glass partition. He had no attention for the flyer he was working on. She was laughing at something Pathis had said. Her tits were quivering. Pathis was laughing, mild, standing above her, black suit.

Fuck her.

McIntyre had asked John Karthidis simple questions. She wanted to know his plans, his ambitions, the nature of his studies. And John gave quick and humorous answers but impressed on her the strength of his aspirations, the tenacity of his will and the loyalty of his greed. She noticed that his pants were fine linen and fitted neatly around his arse.

She likes a good fast root, thought John. And he smiled at her again.

John Karthidis was going to keep his job. He was making sure of it. Studying computers, Pagemaker and Photoshop, Quark Express. He was getting into it, paving the future. This is what John Karthidis wanted.

Money.

John Karthidis was sniffing the change, it was all in the air. His mother would iron his shirts, press the trousers. Mama, Mama, there's still a crease on this sleeve. I told you, Jesus, they notice everything. You don't want me to lose my job, do you?

—Jesus, Mama, you want to ruin it for me?

So he flirted with McIntyre, he was a pal to Somers, he was

respectful with the arrogant Pathis. He knew what he was doing. John sat across the desk from McIntyre.

You've hardly got tits at all, you ugly bitch.

He nodded his head in agreement.

—I agree, Susan. Can I call you Susan?

I'll lick your clit, I'll suck his cock, I'll lick all your arses. I'll keep my job, I'll keep a future.

John stepped out into the mail room. Nadia was at her desk, her arms folded, her computer quiet. She was glaring at him.

—Weak bastard, she mouthed.

John ignored her. I'm going to keep my job, bitch. He walked over to his desk and sat down. Tommy walked over.

—What she asking?

—Nothing, Tom, nothing. She's just asking about our work.

—She say anything about me?

—Nothing, Tom, I told you. They're just simple questions.

Tommy nodded and walked back to the layout table, picked up the scalpel and began work again. John punched some buttons on the keyboard and looked over at his workmate.

John could not understand Tommy. The lack of ambition, the Asian girlfriend. And that old fashioned loyalty to the union! John's parents too had been union, but they had to be, he would argue to himself. But his was a different kind of work. His was a *career*.

Tommy slid the scalpel down the length of the steel ruler. He cut the bromide and pasted it on the shining sheet.

See, thought John, pushing a button on the brand new keyboard, Control X. *Cut*. Then Control V. *Paste*. Tommy, my man Tommy, you're behind the times.

•

—I want to see *Field of Dreams*.

—We'll do it after the football.

—I don't want to go to the football. Soo-Ling was sulking, the silence was heavy.

—Okay then, don't come.

—I won't.

The line went dead. Tommy put down the receiver.

—Who was that?

Tommy spun around. McIntyre, smiling.

—One of the buyers. Asking after the leaflet.

McIntyre continued her rounds.

Soo-Ling hated the football, not the game itself, but the way the rites excluded her. Tommy had managed to take her to a few matches but she sat still, bored, patiently waiting for the game to finish, and as soon as it did she would begin to walk away, in a hurry, determined. Her face stone.

At the football everyone looked at her face. There was white and there was black, there was Latin and there was European. There was everyone at the football. Except Asian.

She hated the football. Everyone looked at her. As if she was handicapped. As if she was crippled.

Tommy did not see any of this. He thought she was disinterested and it exasperated him. Football became one of those topics they refused to speak about, a language they did not share.

But though she had never liked the game, she had begun to barrack for Fitzroy.

Tommy quickly rang the number.

—Simpsons and Jakovitch. Please hold the line.

Tommy glanced around. Pathis was in deep conversation with Somers in the mail room front office. McIntyre was nowhere to be seen.

—Sorry to keep you waiting.

Tommy interrupted. Karen, it's Tom Stefano. Is Soo-Ling there?

—Hi, Tommy. I'll connect you.

McIntyre was walking along the ramp, up from the printing presses, walking towards the main offices.

—Sorry. I won't go to the footy this weekend. I'll call you later.

Tommy put down the phone. McIntyre walked past the desk. She said nothing.

That weekend Fitzroy lost to Collingwood by ten goals. Tommy and Soo-Ling went to see *Field of Dreams* and he hated it and she did not mind it. They smoked a joint walking back to the car in the Shoppingtown car park. Tommy turned on the radio in the car, searched for the footy results, listened, and banged his fist on the dashboard.

—See, isn't it better we didn't go?

—No! he screamed at her and she cowered in the passenger seat. They drove along home in silence, the rain falling on the car beating a cruel and erratic tattoo.

6

Hiroshima Day, 1989

This is a conversation that took place between Eva and Soo-Ling on 8 August 1989. It occurred after work in a coffee shop in the city, at the top end of Bourke Street. Eva, who finished work in the factory at three-thirty, had spent two hours walking the shops.

It had been Eva who had rung Soo-Ling. Though friendly, both were still uncertain of the rules that bound their relationship. Eva, a wedding ring on her finger, was embedded now in the Stefano family. Soo-Ling, de facto and an outsider, being Asian, did not fit neatly into the family structure. An assumption had been made that Soo-Ling and Tommy would marry. He's nearly thirty, he has to marry soon, that was Maria's verdict. Artie never said a thing about the relationship. It was Dominic who was most concerned. He doesn't think about the fucking future. Tommy had begun not turning up to the Sunday lunches, making excuses, sleeping in, not answering the phone. Maria was ringing Eva, complaining, worrying.

And Eva, frustrated, having begun work again, still adjusting to motherhood, had rung Soo-Ling.

She is beautiful. That was Eva's first thought as Soo-Ling walked through the door and into the bar. Eva had arrived first and had been nervous as she took a seat. The bar was full of office workers, men in suits and well-coiffured women. Young. She was conscious that something in her own style marked her out as alien from the rest of the room. Not that Eva was not attractive and not that she did not know how to look after herself. But her dress, her hair, the way she applied her make-up was not in kilter with the crowd. There is no restraint with Eva. Her lipstick was blood scarlet and her light blue dress was tight around her tits and arse. This is a crude description and she does have a crudity that could be described as vulgar. Possibly the men that glanced at her as she sat down had this very thought. Probably the women too. But vulgar is always too easy a dismissal. Eva, I'm sure, would have been by far the prettiest woman in the place.

Soo-Ling came in and took a look at Tommy's sister-in-law. Her first thought, the first word, was correct. Alive, Eva was alive.

Soo-Ling ordered a glass of wine. Eva, a bourbon and Coke. Soo-Ling had had a hard day of answering phones, sending last-minute faxes waved in her face by harassed managers, Eva had done her three days at the factory, working the machines that worked the dough. She had stripped herself clean from the assembly line and looked fresh, except for her hands. The lines on her hands told a different story to the glow of her face.

—How's work?

—It stinks. Eva lit a cigarette and took a drink. I can't wait for Dom to start building up the business. Then I'm through with this factory shit.

—And how's Lisa?

—She's fine. Can't complain at all. I can take her wherever and she sleeps through or just sits happily in the corner. Eva dragged hard on the cigarette. But she tires me out. The thought of going out makes me sick.

Soo-Ling laughed. Hard.

—Me too, me too. It's been ages since I've been dancing. She calculated. Two years. Christ, I think it's two years.

—Dom misses it. I can tell.

—Tommy doesn't talk about it at all.

—Dom says Tommy was never one for dancing.

Eva looked at Soo-Ling's hands. Smooth hands.

—How is Tommy?

—He's good. Soo-Ling sipped the wine. Can I have a cigarette?

—Sure. I didn't think you smoked.

—I don't.

Soo-Ling struck a match, waited and lit the cigarette.

—How's his work?

Soo-Ling noticed a man at the far end of the bar, tall, silver haired, in a leather jacket. He was a client with the firm. She turned back to Eva.

—His work is not good.

Soo-Ling's hand, a murmur, began to shake.

—Well, it's tough. I think they're going to close down the shithole I'm working in. Eva finished her drink, waved at the man behind the counter, beckoned him. It's all right, I'm not interested in staying on there, but for some of the others . . . Eva stopped. Well, for some of the others it's going to be hard.

—Tommy should have left ages ago.

The silver haired man had looked up, begun a smile, then dropped it and returned to his newspaper, pretending he did not recognise her.

—They're a fucked company, always have been. They've given him no training. He's got to go back to school.

—And do what?

—Computers.

Eva had never used a computer in her life. And she doubted she ever would. She was already bored by them, by their familiarity.

—He'll get a job. And you never know, they might keep him on.

—He's not so sure. He reckons this new woman they've got, some kind of consultant, she's out to roll heads.

—What kind of consultant?

—Don't know. A consultant.

—I can imagine the fucking bitch. Eva snorted and handed a ten dollar bill to the barman. She lightly slapped Soo-Ling's hand away. My shout. They clinked glasses. And laughed, suddenly girlish. I hate those power bitches. I can imagine what she's like exactly. Cold, rude. And she hates women.

—Why do you say that?

—'Cause, that's what they're like. I know them, mate, I get on the train with them. They don't look at me, I'm not good enough. Eva laughed again. She probably needs a good root.

—Yeah? You reckon?

—I reckon. She probably goes home at night, clutching her big salary and her expensive purse and then sobs into her pillow. Those career women are too uptight for sex.

—Jeez, Eva. That sounds really sexist.

—Does it? It sounds like the truth to me.

Neither Eva nor Soo-Ling considered themselves feminists, but they were virulently opposed to misogyny, to visible expressions of hatred towards women by men, to violence in particular. This combination, a feminist nonfeminism, though apparently paradoxical, was not an anomaly at all. They were both intelligent women and intolerant of intolerance.

But they had prejudices. Including an envy of other women which could be expressed with harsh cruelty.

—You don't want a career?

—I want another baby.

—Yeah. Are you and Dom planning?

Eva giggled into her glass. He's not so sure, says wait and see how the business goes, but I'm ready for it. She drops her voice to a whisper. I've been putting holes in the condoms.

Soo-Ling broke out in laughter, a rich peal that made the people around them look up.

—What are you doing? Puncturing the packets?

—Nah, Dom gets me to put them on for him, reckons it keeps him hard. So, you know, I'm doing things down there. Eva stopped, blushed. Laughed and turned away. Don't look at me, you know what I mean; anyway I make sure to put holes in the tip.

—How often do you have sex?

Soo-Ling looked away as she asked the question. The bar was filling up. The noise, conversation and music, the second drink, was flooding her head. The song was dance, a floating bass. The singer's voice, feminine and cruising. *It's a natural thing.* Soo-Ling could no longer see the silver haired man; he was obscured by bulky Italian men in European suits.

—With the baby? Hardly fucking ever. We're both too tired. But, you know, an occasional quickie on Sunday night.

Soo-Ling realised that she was the only Asian face in the bar. She disliked this thought immensely. She hated it.

—Tommy's not wanted it for a month now.

A flash, a memory. When Eva first met Tommy it was summer and he was wearing black shorts. He sat across from her, smiling, legs apart, and his crotch was heavy. On occasion, when Dom was fucking her, Eva closed her eyes and thought of Tommy. This, of course, was a thought she shared with no-one.

—Well, you know, if he's worried and stuff, about work . . . He's probably just tired.

—I guess. But he's usually so horny, much more than me. Soo-Ling's voice was soft. The consciousness of the crowd.

—I reckon all the Stefano men are horny little buggers. Artie still looks pretty sexy for an old guy. And don't forget they're Greek.

—I don't know much about Greeks. There weren't many around in Ballarat.

—Well, there were fucking heaps of them in Lalor, mate, and all of them randy little buggers. They'd fuck anything.

Soo-Ling had at first been shocked by Tommy's body, his hair; on his chest, his arms, his buttocks and the faint curls on his lower back, the thick bush of his crotch. And then the stark contrast to her smooth father had enraptured her.

—What do you think I should do?

—Be patient. Eva sniffed, hard. The next question was delicate. Are you talking about marriage?

The Italians had parted, the silver haired man was folding his newspaper. He walked the length of the bar, looking ahead, avoiding her eyes. He exited.

—He doesn't like me talking about it.

—Bloody men.

Soo-Ling laughed. Yeah, they hate that subject, don't they?

—Dom took ages to ask me.

—Did you say yes immediately?

—You betcha. Eva downed the bourbon, tried to catch the barman's eye. I knew from the start I wanted him.

Soo-Ling wanted to marry Tommy.

—It's just time, Suze. You understand? Men, you know, they get so wound up about work and they forget everything else. Tommy loves you, you know.

Then why the fuck has he not said it to me?

Soo-Ling shrugged.

—I know, or I guess he does.

—I'm sure of it.

I don't know, does he love you? Eva could not imagine fucking an Asian man; somewhere, inside, guiltily, the thought repelled her. No, not the fucking, the kissing. She searched Soo-Ling's face. But maybe it was different with the women. Again she was very aware, in the crowded bar, of how beautiful the woman sitting opposite her was.

Soo-Ling searched her bag. Eva tried to stop her but Soo-Ling was victorious.

—No, said firmly. This one's, my shout.

They drank, falling into silence. The wine had begun its magic. Soo-Ling drifted with the music, the repetition of the beat. Men were looking their way. She felt attractive.

—There was a demo in the City Square. Hiroshima Day, I think.

—Yeah? Soo-Ling fingered the stem of her glass.

—Yeah.

—They should just forget it. No-one listens to them.

—A pity, isn't it?

Soo-Ling scrutinised Eva's face. Her tone had been sad, almost despairing. Soo-Ling was suddenly ashamed of her indifference.

—Well, good on them. You're right. At least they're not shutting up.

The beat was getting more rapid, the sounds harsher, a stern rap waved through the bar.

Eva took Soo-Ling's hand. You'll be all right, mate, and so will Tommy.

—Yeah, I know.

Stop it, stop it. Soo-Ling was yelling inside her head, forcing back the crying. She finished her drink, fast.

—Another one?

Eva looked at her watch. Just one, otherwise my mum will go ballistic when I go to pick up Lisa.

—What's she like, your mum?

—Fine. I love her. She can give me the shits. Uptight Polish bitch.

—I don't know many Poles.

—There are a few around. Lots of them Jews. Mum can't stand the Jews.

—Really?

—Yeah, hates them.

An uncomfortable silence.

Eva continued.

—I don't mind them. Jesus, they suffered enough. But they are in control, don't you reckon? She handed another ten dollar bill to the barman. And they stick together.

—Doesn't everyone?

—What do you mean?

—The Chinese are the same.

—True. You're good at making money too.

Inside, Soo-Ling flinched.

—And the Poles?

—Too fucking lazy. Except the Jewish ones. Eva accepted the drinks. The barman winked at her. Eva smiled back.

—What are you up to tonight?

—I'd like to see a movie. But I don't think Tommy's into it. So I don't know, a quiet night at home.

—Getting shitfaced.

Soo-Ling laughed. Yeah, getting shitfaced.

—Been ages since Dom and I saw a movie. Too long. But with the baby and all, it's a bit hard. What are you thinking of seeing?

—*Do The Right Thing.*

—Yeah, who's in that?

—Don't know, but it had some good reviews. People say it's interesting.

—What's it about?

—I think some racial trouble in New York. Something like that.

Eva was getting pissed, she could feel it, the world had sped up, her skin was flushed.

—Sounds heavy, Sure. I'm in no mood for that. I'll get Dom to go down and get some vids tonight, something funny. You and Tom want to come along? You're welcome.

No. I'm not. Not yet. Status undecided.

—No. You know what Friday is like, you're too knackered to do anything.

—Yeah, fucking working life, eh? It stinks. I'm just going to make babies, Suze. I know some women get pissed off with that attitude, you know, I should care about career and all that, but seriously, mate, what the fuck for? Eva sculled her drink. A factory is not much of a career, is it?

—It's work.

—Well, someone else can have it. I'll do my bit for the unemployment problem.

—Eva, I'm scared what'll happen if Tommy loses his job.

Soo-Ling clasped the glass tight, aware that for the first time in the conversation she had been honest.

And the honesty had scared her.

Eva took her hand.

—Suze, love, don't worry. If he does, it's no shame. Christ, love, there's heaps of people on the dole. It's not like it's his fault. And he'll find a job, Tommy's smart.

Dominic's voice: My brother's a fucking idiot, he's always been a fucking idiot.

The crucifix, petite, gold, on Soo-Ling's neck. Eva touched it, gently.

—It's nice.

—It was my mother's.

—Are you Christian? Eva stumbled over the words.

—Yes.

Under the counter a pile of newspapers. A tabloid photo of a large black man. Eva pointed to the picture.

—That's that Abo guy, the one who's been done for murder in the States.

Soo-Ling looked down at the image. The man's eyes, there was nothing in those eyes. She shuddered at the ugliness.

—He's horrible.

—Do you reckon? Eva took up the newspaper, scanned the print. I feel a bit sorry for him, you know. He's had a tragic life, taken away from his family, all that. Put in institutions. Eva shook her head. It's all sad. She put the paper back, the other side up. An advertisement for Mazda.

How about her? How about the woman he killed? Blonde woman, raped, cut. Like the little girl. The little schoolgirl. And Soo-Ling thought of six young black youths, the battered body of a woman jogging in Central Park.

Tommy: What did she expect?

Big Aboriginal man with nothing behind his eyes.

The loud music. Bass.

Fuck *Do The Right Thing*. Eva was right. Enough depression, she and Tommy should see a comedy tonight.

—Eva, what's the crow?

Eva pulled her hand away.

—A story and a joke. Some bullshit. She touched, softly, Soo-Ling's hair. The crow is a Stefano obsession. Dom reckons that when there's something bad about to happen, he'll always see a crow. It can terrify him. Stupid, isn't it?

—Do you believe it?

Eva looked hard into Soo-Ling's eyes, too hard, and Soo-Ling turned away.

—What's Tommy say?

Tommy doesn't talk about it. Tommy doesn't talk about fucking anything.

—He says it's bullshit.

—Then he's probably right. Eva raised her glass. Let's drink to the smartest Stefano brother.

The smartest Stefano brother is Lou. Soo-Ling, suddenly, a humiliation, could not stop the tears falling. Eva, herself embarrassed, looked away. Italian men in European suits.

Soo-Ling wiped at her eyes, finished the drink.

—Eva, thank you, I've got to go. It's getting late and I don't like the trains at night.

—I know, I know, all those boozy louts.

—How you getting home?

—Tram to Mum's. Dom will pick us up from there. Eva finished her drink, grabbed her bag and hugged Soo-Ling.

—Honey, seriously, it will be all right.

Soo-Ling was stiff, the hug choked.

They stood in the cold, arms tight around their bodies, adjusting to night. The street was full of young people, milling around the disco next-door, chomping on fast food.

—How about a barbecue next week?

Soo-Ling nodded. They kissed, and they parted.

The descent into Parliament Station unbalanced Soo-Ling.

She clutched the escalator rail tight. Fortunately the train arrived quickly, and she sat in the middle of the carriage, away from the drunk young men who threw her dirty looks. As the train pummelled down the tracks she counted down the stations, eager for the trip to be over. Richmond, Burnley, Hawthorn, Glenferrie. The ride seemed long, the window looked out into a lonely black. Beside her a couple, a man in his thirties and a woman much younger, were holding hands. They did not look at her. The stations passed slowly. East Camberwell, Canterbury, Cotham, Surrey Hills. Too slowly, and the sound of boom gates clashed in her head. As the train slid into Box Hill Station and she waited to get off, Soo-Ling realised there was a tension in her stomach that the alcohol had not quite alleviated. She stepped off the train and glanced around her. A boy in a thick black jacket pushed hard against her. Above her a billboard proclaimed the fifty year anniversary of the beginning of World War Two. Celebrations were being prepared. Soo-Ling walked slowly up the ramp— there was no-one checking the tickets—and headed for the bus. She was heading for Tommy, eager, anxious, wanting him. She was, heading for Tommy, and she realised as she waited, feeling the cold, looking down at the suburbs stretched across a night horizon, that she was scared. The fear had no meaning. It was fear, pure, concrete. It touched her, engulfed her. She thought of Tommy, his arms, holding her. Inside his arms the fear couldn't get to her.

7
Grand Final

Laika was the first living creature in space. She was a dog. Her picture, wavering frames on a black and white television screen, had never been forgotten by Tommy. Her long thin face and the pert ears. The accomplishments of humanity were listed in a monotonous tone by the scowling Mr Morris; the classroom repeated them by rote. Ancient Greece. The birth of Christ. The printing press. The discovery of the Americas. The Renaissance. The Industrial Revolution. The World Wars. Man on the moon. Tommy mouthed the words but he couldn't forget the dog.

Starving to death, in perpetual orbit.

At home, his father drinking beer, his mother preparing dinner, Dominic reading *Mad* magazine in bed. Tommy started crying.

—Laika, Laika, they just left her, Laika. It's horrible, it's horrible.

He was screaming.

And his father was laughing.

And his mother said, shaking her head, Why are you worrying about a stupid dog?

And Dominic, who had risen to find out what the tears were all about, joined his father in laughter.

—What do you care about some stupid mutt?

And Tommy called his brother a cunt, and shouted to Maria that she was a stupid wog, and before he could say anything to his father, the man delivered the thundering slap.

And then Tommy stopped crying and fell silent.

When Somers, coughing, not looking at him, told Tommy that he was to be retrenched, that the corporation was downsizing to reflect the realities of the current economic situation, Tommy's first thought was of Laika, a fuzzy black and white image of a sad dog in space.

His next thought was that he wanted to find a church and to pray. And then—fuck prayer—his thoughts turned to sex. To find some woman, some stranger and fuck her so hard, so hard that she bled. Or he bled. There had to be blood.

Somers coughed a lot. He was clearly uncomfortable and Tommy was only one of many who were to be fired. He's so pale. Somers's skin was flushed, a corpulent red.

—I'm sorry, Tom.

—That's all right.

Immediately: Why the fuck did I say that?

The two men, made tense by the silence, looked out across the partition to the print room. John was staring at them and quickly looked down to his work. Pathis knocked on the door.

—Kevin, are you finished?

Tommy stood up.

—If it's all right, I may take the rest of the day off.

Pathis shook his head.

—Have you finished the sale catalogue?

Tommy ignored him. He looked at Somers.

—Is that all right?

Somers mouthed, One moment. He dialled a number.

—Hello, Susan, can you see Stefano now? Somers waited, then interrupted. Can you make some time now? His voice was insistent. He put down the phone.

—Go see Susan McIntyre and then you can have the day off. There's some things she'll want to talk to you about.

Tommy stood up, shook Somers's limp hand and brushed past Pathis. Wog. He whispered it.

Pathis laughed. The door shut.

The noise from in the print room was disorienting. Tommy

walked slowly to his desk, ignored John's eager, nervous glances.

—What did he say?

Tommy picked up his work, put it in a neat pile, loosened his tie and took off his white coat. He turned to his workmate.

—I'm fired.

Of course, after that, there was nothing to add.

McIntyre was nervous. She thought Tommy Stefano was lazy, lacking ambition and lacking drive, and it had been easy to argue for keeping on John Karthidis and getting rid of Stefano. John was expanding his skills, studying new computer graphics, he showed a commitment to the organisation. Stefano was surly; competent but not an innovator.

Still, Susan McIntyre was anxious when the man knocked on the door.

—Hello, Tom, please take a seat.

His face was unreadable. There was a sternness there.

—I'm sorry, this isn't pleasant.

He nodded, once. Simply.

Susan opened a manila folder.

—Tom, you've been working with the company for just over four years. Restructuring is never easy, but as I'm sure you well understand, the current recession combined with the new technologies in your profession mean that this whole section of the company will have to change. She stopped, searched his face. A cold impassivity. She continued.

—I doubt that in a year the print shop will be running. Unfortunately we have to let you go.

The decision, seven o'clock, Susan sipping a wine, Pathis and Somers, drinking beer.

Somers. We could retrain him.

Pathis. He's not worth the, investment.

Susan, tired, rubbing her neck. Wishing to be home.

Pathis, handsome, turning to her.

—Susan, what's your opinion?

McIntyre: I have to agree. Neither his performance nor his attitude justify the investment.

The manila folder is shut.

—What am I entitled to?

Susan coughed.

—The company has offered you quite a generous package. Two weeks for every year of work, that's eight weeks' pay, plus all your entitlements. Susan sang a list: annual leave loading and one week extra as a show of gratitude for his years of service.

The company is a cunt.

She closed the folder. His face was still cold. She hated it when they cried, the men. If she could see the tears approaching, their shocked faces, the shivering of their cheeks, she would make an excuse and leave them alone for five minutes. Their recomposure was never completely convincing but she realised that for her to be witness to their vulnerability would be the greater humiliation.

There was no cruelty in Susan. Though efficiency was her profession, her commitment, she did not enjoy seeing the pain of the superfluous.

Expendable. That was what Tommy Stefano was. Sometimes, when she was drunk or very stoned, she thought her world was a whorehouse.

She would prefer the vulnerability to this though. His frozen anger mocked her.

—I'll also make you an appointment, Tom, with an agency that specialises in placing retrenched people back into the workforce. Would you like that?

Nothing.

—How about next Monday?

Nothing. Then, a slow shift of his chin. An affirmative.

Relieved, she made a notation in her diary.

—Any other questions, Tom?

—Yes. How about sick leave?

—What about it?

—Do I get that paid out?

McIntyre shook her head.

—Tom, sick leave is rarely paid out at the end of employment. This company definitely doesn't.

—My mum worked for years at Repco, the car parts factory, they paid her out her sick leave when she got retrenched.

—That's very rare, Tom.

—She had a good union.

He bit hard on the word. Union. She understood it as the slap it was intended to be. Her voice, which throughout the interview had been soft, feminine, became brittle and harsh.

—Anything else, Tom?

Yes, can you get on the desk, can you spread your thighs? Do you want a big fat fuck, you frigid bitch?

—No.

Tommy closed the door and entered the discordant moans of machines and the wicked clacking of computer keys.

Nadia hugged him hard. She, like many others in the mail room, had been notified of her retrenchment the week before. The mail room, full of paper and repetitive motion, the filing of mail in slots, was to be rapidly shut down. Pathis had circulated a sheet praising the future, the technology that would make the organisation efficient. Nadia, angry and defiant, had torn up the memo in front of the smiling cold manager.

—I'm sorry, Tom. Will you be okay?

Tommy wanted to disappear into her skin, to breathe from her. He pulled apart.

—Sure.

Failure has the smell of sweat, but not the euphoric stench of physical exertion. Nothing of the erotic. Failure smells of decay, of stagnation. Tommy leant into the mirror, staring hard at his face. He pulled back. The fleshy cheeks, the beginning spread of a double chin. He swept a hand through his hair; the thickness waning. He pulled back and surveyed his body.

—You're ugly, he said to the mirror. He could smell the ugliness with the failure.

He packed his briefcase, put on his jacket and left. Swift goodbyes. Outside, the traffic screaming, he paused for breath. He was fighting an urge to giggle, to laugh, to skip. Beyond the moment lay a vast uncertainty. But within the moment he experienced a freedom. Tommy had never longed for liberation —freedom was terrifying not exciting. This moment, however, was an exception. He suddenly craved for music.

Tommy did not want anyone around, not even Soo-Ling. He walked across the park, down William Street into the city. Lawyers and clients smoking outside the courts, the passage of traffic. He entered a small coffee shop that smelt of pastry and grease.

The woman behind the counter, heavily made-up to hide deep, long wrinkles, was packing away food trays.

—Are you still serving coffee?

She nodded slowly.

—A coffee, please.

He watched the street. A woman in a long black dress was swinging her handbag. A man in overalls was scratching at his crotch, smoking a cigarette. Labourers always reminded him of his older brother, their straightforward masculinity. He blinked and wrapped his palms around the coffee mug. It tasted pallid and it was far too hot. He set down the mug and went inside his head.

Pathis. Somers. That bitch McIntyre. The urge for fucking was immense, overwhelming. He could feel the tightness of the fabric constraining his hard-on. He stared at the woman and she, uncomfortable, turned her back to him and began scrubbing the sink.

To her, Tommy's sadness was appalling; it repulsed compassion.

For Tommy her retreat, her rejection of him, made his cock stiffen, his anger palpable. He drank the coffee noisily and picked up a newspaper to close his mind and refuse his erection.

It was the week leading to the football Grand Final and the paper was celebrating. Colour pages, a lift-out and a poster. Hawthorn and Geelong. The writers were all in praise of Geelong's Gary Ablett, the pug ugly man with the sure kick and the tough squat body. Tommy, who had no strong affection for either team, was hoping for a Geelong victory. They, at least, were a working-class team.

Inside, he groaned. He and Soo-Ling were supposed to go to a Grand Final barbecue at Dominic's. The cold pumped through his stomach.

I'm fired. How could he begin to express those words? Again, he could smell the failure leaking through his skin.

An article, venomous in its anger, was directed towards the bleeding hearts asking for clemency for the Aboriginal man on America's death row. A tiny black and white photo, badly reproduced, smudged. A man alone. Tommy thought his crime pitiful but he did not want to see the man dead for it. He closed the newspaper.

Fists smashing into the angular blonde Susan McIntyre. A black cock raping her arse. Tommy brought the scalding coffee to his lip, sipped from it, but could not ingest the hot bitter liquid. He spat it back in the cup, put a two dollar coin on the table and left. The day demanded alcohol.

No, the man didn't deserve to be hanged. Get the white bitch instead!

He drank. First pots of beer, then whisky. Straight, no ice nothing to soften the harsh warm taste. He drank in a quiet, almost empty pub, downstairs, under the city, the city which was hard at work. He sank the alcohol and listened to the barman discussing football with the other lone customer, an old man, a damaged red nose. They were comparing the teams, Geelong had Ablett but Hawthorn had the tall good-looking Dunstall. That poofter Brereton, chuckled the old man.

—Michael Tuck, offered Tommy.

They paused, glanced at him, and quietly resumed their conversation.

Michael Tuck, he's good, whispered Tommy to himself.

Tommy tried out for his high school football team once. He had dreams of playing in the ruck. The first time the football soared towards him, his stomach jumped, his skin flushed cold and he closed his eyes, just for a second, even less, but that was enough time for him to lose the ball. Another boy jumped on his shoulders and the mark was fumbled.

—Fucking idiot, Stefano! screamed the boys.

He had failed.

The whisky was a dream and the print shop, Pathis and Somers, the consultancy bitch, that cock-sucking John, all of them, they receded. Soo-Ling too. She was far away and he did not want to reach towards her. He drank the whisky, finished it and headed up the stairs into the city. The barman asked, You all right, mate? You want a coffee?

—No, slurred Tommy, ashamed because suddenly he wanted to hug this stranger, I'll be fine, mate.

The city screamed his exile. Couriers on bikes rushed past him, men in suits were catching cabs, and everywhere there were tall prim women rushing for lights. The day was cold but Tommy felt exhausted from the city's electricity. His belly was a hole. He struggled, walking clumsily, to a McDonald's.

The city was not in McDonald's. There, slouched on the red and yellow plastic furniture, young kids wagged school and old ladies chewed on their hamburgers and dribbled over their chips. A woman in a black jumper was drowsing on a table. Tommy headed straight to the counter and impatiently shot out his order to a sullen young woman.

—Three quarter-pounders, a large fries, an apple pie, a shake. And a large Coke.

He tapped the counter, his hunger ferocious.

He ate the meal in lightning minutes, forcing the sugar and the grease straight down his throat. He clumped handfuls of chips, munched and wished he had ordered more. He ate two of the burgers, finished the chips and then attacked the third. The apple pie crumbled around his teeth, a liquid pastry, and he dunked the end of the pie in his shake. He slurped hard from the shake and drowned the whole meal with Coca-Cola. When he had finished, he looked up. Two young mothers were feeding chips to toddlers. Tommy burped quietly, pushed the tray away, and lay back on the seat. He patted his stomach, felt the bulge of his inflated stomach, and he groaned.

You fat stupid fuck. Fuck fuck fuck.

He pinched the flesh hard.

The two women across from him were very young, still teenagers. One, the prettiest, was skeletal. Her thinness almost shocking. The other one, plump, dark, she looked Turkish, was talking football. Geelong's going to cream them.

—Richmond, Richmond, sang one of the toddlers.

The thin woman laughed and touched the toddler's hair.

—Honey, Richmond ain't playing.

—Richmond, Richmond, insisted the child.

Tommy laughed and the thin woman smiled at him.

—You barrack for Richmond, do ya? she asked him.

Tommy shook his head.

—Fitzroy.

The woman grinned.

You are so beautiful, do you want to fuck me?

—Poor you, they're worse than us at the moment.

Tommy stood up, rushed past, ran down the stairs and hit the street. The cool air brushed away the nausea but his head pumped poison. He held out his hand, a cab stopped, and he crashed into the back seat.

Money. The word frightened him. But immediately a defiance shattered the fear.

He wanted to spend lots of money. He wanted to empty his wallet, his account, his pockets, his credit. He wanted to splurge, to drink. He was dying for smoke, for speed which he had not touched for years.

—Where do you want to go?

Tommy clutched his wallet and pointed straight ahead.

—Footscray.

He sank back into the seat, smelling the McDonald's, smelling the whisky. The sweat had not gone away. He was wet, perspiration lining his face, his shirt glued to his back, his armpits seeping. Money and stink, money and stink.

The brothel was on Barkly Street, no shop-front, an ordinary house except for the small white sign with the neat black lettering. *Rosie's. All Cards Welcome.*

Tommy did not move in the back seat. The driver turned around.

—Is this where you want, mate?

Tommy eyes closed, mouth moving. Praying.

—Mate, insisted the driver, are we here?

Tommy looked out of the window. He slowly nodded, opened his wallet and paid the fare. The driver went to return his change and Tommy stopped him.

—Keep it.

He jumped out of the cab and, drunk, wavering up the path, he knocked at the door.

Prostitution had soon lost its dread. The anxiety, of Tommy's first time, having to decipher the economic and moral codes which bound the brothel, was never to be repeated. But even once the costs and procedures were explained and made sense of, there still remained the shame. Entering the brothel was a humiliation: the terror that his mother, Soo-Ling, that *someone* was watching; even if it was only God, that was still someone bearing witness. But the hesitation, the fear was short-lived and the relief on crossing the threshold was magnificent—it heightened the intensity of the sexual anticipation. Tommy was not a frequent visitor. He had to be led by alcohol, he had to be smashed to go.

What alcohol did was to carve away the voices. Alcohol dismissed them all. What remained was only the appetite for lust. He hungrily handed over his money to the receptionist. Soo-Ling crossed his mind and he quickly set her aside, set her far back into consciousness. He was now aware of only one thing: he wanted sex with a stranger. The thought of disappearing in sex was so delicious he shivered as he handed over the money.

I want to fuck.

To not fuck today, this hour, this moment, to not fuck was inconceivable.

The woman he chose was nineteen, but she was really twenty-two. Everyone at Rosie's was nineteen. There were only four available and Tommy blushed as he looked at them. They were all pretty, all dressed in tight short skirts. One was Asian. He immediately discounted her. He searched their faces, their legs, their bodies, their smiles. His decision needed to be quick and he felt foolish in front of them. A blonde woman, on a couch, smoking a cigarette, had large thick thighs and her sharp mouth was thin. He chose her, paid his money, and she took his hand.

He washed. The room they had entered was red, lit with soft lights. The woman, aware that he was drunk, simply stripped him and pushed him gently into the shower. There, under the water, Tommy stood in delight, enjoying the motion of the water sliding on his skin. The woman leant across, turned off the tap, and offered him a towel.

—Feel better, sunshine?

She was expert. Nude, his cock erect, she fell on her knees and began sucking him. He looked down at her blonde hair bobbing at his waist. Her hand slid up his body and played with his nipple. He pushed it roughly away and laid a hand on her head, forcing her onto him. She stopped her work.

—Careful, she whispered softly. But firmly.

Tommy saw that her mouth had wrapped his cock in a

condom. Her neat trick, her professional accomplishment, it nearly sickened him. He sat on the ridiculously lavish bed.

—What do you want, honey?

He didn't know. Taking his silence for approval, she began working his cock again. The sensation was delightful, he was aroused, but the technique and its effect were mechanical. He lay back on the bed, playing with her hair, his other hand rolled across his stomach. The day came in. Work, Pathis. The Aboriginal man rapes and kills a blonde woman.

He closed his eyes and drifted far into the fantasy, imagining himself black and violent, the woman on her knees before him someone he could kill. It would be so easy, she was so young, so soft. Slowly his torso jerked forward, forward to his fantasy, rapid thrusts into the prostitute's mouth. He imagined the Aboriginal man above the bleeding body of the blonde, her face bruised, her lips fat, her cunt raw, shitting herself. Fucking her from behind. Fucking her so hard she was bleeding.

—Quickly, I want to fuck you.

Tommy got up from the bed. The woman lay down and looked up at him. She was smiling.

—Turn around!

The woman stopped smiling at the order.

—Be careful, right?

She turned around and Tommy looked down at her arse. It was surprisingly large, the cheeks fat. He pushed her legs apart and groaned when he saw the meat of her cunt. He pushed inside her, closed his eyes and felt her hand checking that his condom was still on. He fell into her, pushing hard, trying to fit all of himself into her cunt. He was murdering her, cutting her, fucking her, hurting her. He farted and the room smelt of his acrid, shit. He jumped into her, a machine, and he came in a spasm: groans, the kicking back of his body, a tremor through-out. The woman quickly moved away from him, turned and carefully took the condom from his now embarrassed dick. The smoking liquid inside the plastic. He stood there, sweating. He blushed and dressed fast, refusing to look at her. The smells of his body were everywhere, nauseating the room. McDonald's and come. Whisky and farts. The room smelling of shit.

He noticed, on leaving Rosie's, that above the reception desk both the Hawthorn and Geelong colours were proudly displayed.

He roamed the streets, his tie loose, his shirt not tucked in. The briefcase in his hand ridiculous. Footscray was unfamiliar but in the daylight, everything grey in the drizzle, it was also pragmatically suburban. Women with prams, men in overalls taking a smoko. He walked into a street mall, kids laughing, and passed a porn shop. The neon yellow X stopped him. Only minutes had passed but already the disgust had again been replaced by a hunger. He walked on.

He was not looking for a church but on coming across one he was violently happy. Protestant; simple, that did not matter. That it had the cross was enough. He tried the door. It would not budge and he stepped back, first shocked and then accepting. He hadn't the courage to knock. He prayed on the steps, a simple chanting. The repetition of apology.

The rain had stopped. He touched his skin, the wetness. The whore's wet meat, that enormous arse on her. He should have fucked her up the arse. He remembered the cross and he moved off the stairs.

I should have fucked her up the arse.

Money? Scared, he checked for his wallet and feeling it in his jacket pocket was relieved. He could go back, pay her the extra if she'd let him. He hadn't used that fat arse, its pulpy invitation. He'd get out some money, get another one. The dark one this time. No. He wanted that arse, to sink his body into her sweet hole.

He groaned. God, can you help me?

—Hello? Can I help you?

He jerked around. A man, nearly bald, was walking around the church. He wore garden boots and a baggy old jumper that sagged around a thin frame. He looks like, a cartoon, thought Tommy.

—I just wanted to, I guess, come inside. Tommy pointed to the door. It's locked.

The man approached the steps and took out some keys.

—It's fine. I'm the pastor here. He turned around and pointed to a sad brick veneer house on the adjacent grounds. That's where I live.

Tommy shook his head.

—It's fine, thanks, but I'm not . . . He stopped.

The pastor understood.

—You're Catholic, he asked?

Neither Catholic nor Orthodox but both. He knew God in Greek, Italian and English.

—Yes, he answered the man.

—You can still pray here, mate. Laughing.

Tommy disliked him, his normalcy. The cheap grey jumper struck him as an absurdity, ill befitting his role. He waved, limply, turned and walked away.

Coincidence, a rationalist and a secularist would say, is the root of all superstition. A door locked is not at all improbable, let alone a miracle. But for Tommy, drunk, desiring to sedate all his hungers, it was a sign. God did not want him either. The thought was not brutal and Tommy was calm.

Before making his way home, he chased the neon X and used his credit card to buy himself a video and two magazines. He circled the pornography in the shop, oblivious to the wary attendant, flicking through magazines, picking up and putting down video slicks. He knew exactly where to search. The shop was not familiar but he was accustomed to the layout. A young poofter, maybe just eighteen, was throwing him glances, his naked desperation repulsive, and Tommy refused to look at him. He searched through packets of magazines, *Kink* and *Teenager* his favourite. Tape bound the magazines so his decision was based on the front and back covers. He searched, could not

decide. An older woman, smiling, come pouring down her
cheek, a large cock resting on her face. A young girl, hair in
plaits, two cocks in her mouth. The back cover. Cock in her arse.
Cock in her enormous cunt, the pubes red and sparse. A woman
pissing to the camera. An Asian girl, legs apart, laughing, her
fingers playing with her clit. In the end he chose the cover with
the come; the thick liquid enticing. And he chose the Asian girl.

The video was harder to choose. He walked up and down, up
and down the racks. Professional models from the United States.
Amateur, badly lit shorts, from Europe. He settled for *Arse
Bangers*, a slick group of five men—one fat, one old and grey,
one young and hung, one chubby and hairy, one a boy—over a
large breasted brunette with enormous tits. On the back, three
small screens. Cocks up her arse. And again, the come.

—That'll be seventy-five bucks, mate.

Tommy handed over the card.

—This is good. The young man looked at the video approvingly.

Tommy said nothing, placed the package in his briefcase and
left the store. Outside, a trio of school-kids were smoking. One
of the girls looked at him, bored, and turned away. He shook,
looked at no-one, saw nothing, walked to the curb, looking for a
taxi.

No taxis. He felt for his wallet. He was sobering up. He felt
for his wallet and scanned the buildings. A sad pub on a corner.
He lunged towards it and ordered more drink until he was once
more sated by the heat of the alcohol and the world had again
become pleasurable. He wondered if he should take the train
home, save the money, but realising the distance of the journey,
knowing the train would be filling with workers rushing home
from work, he decided against that humiliation. He finished his
drink and went out to the street.

Up in the sky he could see a crow flying. Speak to me, he
wished. He would court madness for that experience. The crow

dived, disappeared behind a Victorian facade. Tommy raised his hand and stopped a cab.

He was anxious to be home, safe in his flat, playing the video, skimming the magazines. He was eager for dope, for more alcohol. He was eager to splash his semen across pages, across his belly, to disappear in the stench. The driver was a foreigner; soft music on the stereo.

Handclapping.

—Is that Laurie Anderson, mate?

—Sorry? A heavy accent.

—The music. The clapping, slow, beneath it a solid rhythm. It was familiar. The music you're playing, is it Laurie Anderson?

The driver shook his head.

—Sorry. This from Pakistan. He turned and looked at Tommy. Me. I am from Pakistan.

—It sounds like Laurie Anderson. Tommy strapped the seat belt across his middle. I used to be into Laurie Anderson, mate, all the time. I saw her in concert a few years ago. Tommy was smiling. I used to see a lot of bands, when I was younger. I used to know them all. He started humming. I like Laurie Anderson, she was weird, wasn't she?

The driver was simply pleased that this drunk had got into his cab. His only worry was that the man might not have the money to pay the long fare to Blackburn.

—You got the money, mate? The last word, clipped.

Tommy took out his wallet, opened it. Two fifties.

The driver smiled.

—You want me to play music loud?

—Yeah, yeah, said Tommy, play Laurie Anderson. They passed under a bridge. A newspaper ad and the large head of Gary Ablett.

—Who do you think will win the final?

—Geelong.

—Me too. Tommy closed his eyes, began to doze off.

The driver turned up the volume, headed east. He hated

football and he had never heard of Laurie Anderson. He did not like much western music, except for Michael Jackson.

It was getting dark when they reached the suburbs. The houses zipped past, a collage of brick and green. They turned into Tommy's street. He was still holding tight to his briefcase.

—Twenty nine dollars, demanded the driver.

Tommy paid.

He rushed up the stairs, anticipating the freedom of his home. On the doorstep, huddled in her thick black coat, was Soo-Ling. Tommy stopped. The anticipation vanished. His body slouched. He could smell his filth.

Soo-Ling jumped up.

—Tommy, are you all right?

He simply stared at her, aware of the damage in his briefcase, the need to keep her from it.

Soo-Ling approached and touched his cheek. The touch, its tenderness, hurt. Tommy nestled his face into her hand; she stroked him, wanting to say simply, I love you, but fearing his distress. The future, which her whole life and experience had taught her to respect, was ignored by those words.

—I should give you keys. His words were a penance, but she was not aware of this and was suddenly frightfully happy.

—I love you.

He rushed into her, his head on her chest, immersed in her softness and her hardness. The crying that began was shocking, he was howling. It was a relief so exquisite that he refused to stop, even as he knew, from her stiffening body, from her own tears, that he was frightening her. He spent himself.

Inside the flat she made him coffee, prepared him food, asked no questions. He, drunk, went into his room and kicked the briefcase under the bed. He stood before the icon of the Virgin and Child and said sorry, softly. He promised tomorrow he would burn the contents of the case, burn the trunk. Tomorrow he would begin again.

In the middle of drinking coffee, he suddenly sprang up,

went scrounging in a box, seeking a cassette. Laurie Anderson.
He pulled out a tape from its dusty cover and spent minutes in
front of the stereo, rewinding, fast-forwarding, trying to find a
song. Soo-Ling, worried about the mania of his search, watched
silently. He found the song and sat back, relieved. He closed his
eyes.

She said.

Soo-Ling wanted to take him, clean him, he smelt of exhaustion.

She said it.

Soo-Ling knelt by him, taking his hand. He clenched it hard.

She said it to.

Soo-Ling listened to the unfamiliar song, all electronics. She
let go of his hand, she wanted to stop the music. It sang a past
that did not belong to her.

She said it to no-one.

Tommy opened his eyes, saw her, shuddered, and closed
them again.

Isn't it just like a woman?

Underneath the song, infecting it, destroying it, he caught
the whiff of his come, stale on his skin. He pushed Soo-Ling's
hand away and spoke one word.

—Laika.

—What Tommy, what, what's that?

He repeated the word.

She did not know what he meant. He opened his eyes.

She was sitting on the couch, not crying, not speaking,
looking at him. He turned away; the tiny red light on the stereo.
The song ended. He could hear the retreat of the needle from the
vinyl, caught on tape.

•

Tommy and Soo-Ling watched the Grand Final at Dominic and
Eva's house. Tommy was quiet and his mother tried to talk to
him but he brushed her concerns aside. I'm all right, Mum.

Yeah, work's fine. I can't tell them, not yet, he said to Soo-Ling. And she, though she disliked this weakness, agreed to the deception.

Hawthorn beat Geelong by six points, an exciting game, the result anyone's up to the final siren. Tommy stayed close to the twenty-eight centimetres of the television frame, away from his family, away from Soo-Ling. There, close to the electric rays, there he felt safe.

8

What do you do?

When we were children our mother taught us the Ancient Greek myths, told us about the twelve gods of Olympus. My favorite was Hephaestos. He, the child of Zeus and Hera, was the celestial artist. He created his father's shield; his smith's hands created thunder and light, the dawn and destruction. It is said that his mother threw him from heaven because he was born lame and Hera was mortified that she, the queen of the gods, could have given birth to such a monster. Hephaestos's fall, his descent to earth, placed him at the bidding of both the mortals and the immortals. His blemishment, the club foot, meant he understood all too well, was compassionate to, human weakness. He was the only god who worked, who made things. That too made him human, like my father, like my mother.

In my mother's ancestral Anatolian village, in her own mother's time, there too lived an Hephaestos. At first the arrival of the child was greeted with great joy by the exhausted mother and the proud father. He was the youngest of four children, the rest daughters, and the woman's inability to bear a son had made her almost insensible with fear and shame. Her husband had become cold, brutal and disapproving. However, their happiness at the birth of the firstborn son was not to last. It soon became apparent that the child was an idiot. He was slow, unable to learn much speech. Terrorised by the humiliation—the village men mocked the father at the coffee shop; the women chuckled into their scarves at church—the father refused to have the idiot in the house and banished him to the dung and cold of the cellar.

The child was not allowed to see the light of the world and soon believed there existed only night. His mother and his older sister would feed him, cloak him, but if they made one move that startled him or shocked him, he would run at them, howling, trying to bite them. His father would rush into the cellar, hurling abuse at his demon son, kicks and lashings of wood. The boy would run into the cloak of darkness whenever he heard the man approaching.

Hephaestos died the day his younger brother was born.

—How did he die? asked a curious young Dominic.

Tommy, holding his breath, waited for the answer.

—They say his father killed him.

Maria crossed herself and was quiet. The children tugged at her clothes, wanting more. She snapped at them, pulling away. No matter how much she detested the harsh taste of exile, she was remembering the reasons she left Greece.

Maria told her children that when she was a young girl and the war with the Germans raged around her, she was walking home from school down the twisted urban streets of Nea Smyrni.

—You can't understand, you little half and halves, you little Australezoi, what European streets are like. They are, and she put her palms close together, they are tiny, narrow, and at night, during the Occupation, we had no light.

She was walking home from school, it was winter and already dark, and there appeared in front of her a divine vision of the Virgin. The apparition took her hand, and though frightened, the little girl placed her trust in the holy vision. The Virgin took her home the long way, through the desolate empty shells of buildings abandoned during the famine, and along the way Maria heard the quick studding of gun fire. She wanted to stop, turn back and look, but the Virgin gripped her hand tighter. When she arrived home her mother fell on her with screams and hugs. Resistance snipers on top of the hill had chosen that afternoon to retaliate against a convoy of Germans who were stationed at the bottom, of Sygrou.

Sygrou, explained Maria to her sons, is one of the main streets of Athens.

The young girl, realising her fortunate escape, turned to thank the Virgin. But the Holy Mother had disappeared.

—Bullshit, Dom always laughed when Maria told the story.

Tommy, dubious, questioning, asked: Are you sure? You weren't dreaming?

Maria would shake her head, cross herself and promise her son it was all true.

—What did she look like? Artie once asked.

Maria pointed to a cheap Catholic print on the kitchen wall.

—Like that. Long blonde beautiful hair. Shining blue eyes.

Artie smiled and kissed his wife.

—Bullshit. And he hugged her.

I, the baby, heard the stories much later of course. Recently I asked my mother why she never spoke of the thirteenth god, Dionysus, the god of wine and ecstacy.

—I never got taught about him. Are you sure he was one of the Greek gods?

—Yeah, I'm reading about him now.

—We had a skata education, Louie, much was censored. Maybe they thought Dionysus should be censored. Did you learn about him at school?

No, I didn't. Even in my time, even in my school, in another hemisphere, we only heard about the twelve Gods. Dionysus— wine, lust, celebration—he was excised.

•

Maria rang Tommy at nine o'clock in the morning. He was up, making a coffee, reading the paper.

—Anything in the newspaper? Any jobs?

—No. Through clenched teeth. The conversation was short, his replies monosyllabic.

—I'm looking, Mum.

I know, son. Greek. It's not your fault, there are no jobs. Maria began a harangue, of politicians, of economics. The Americans.

—Please, Mama. I've got to go.

He went through the employment section, marking in yellow highlighter every available position. He had initially concentrated only on jobs in print shops and to do with finished art and graphic design, but he quickly realised that the work was limited.

—Finished artist? John had laughed at him. They don't exist any more, Tommy, and if they do, they get paid shit. Get into computers.

He began to hate that word.

He marked five jobs. Four were sales positions. One was for a temporary clerk in a municipal office. Four positions supplied a phone number. One gave an address and asked for a resume.

He rang.

882 3456. Engaged.

543 2323. Engaged.

428 4076. Engaged.

652 6765. A woman's voice.

—Laser Write. Can I help you?

—I'm inquiring about the position advertised in today's paper. The sales position. Can I have a job description?

The woman took down his name and address and quickly put down the phone.

428 4076. Engaged.

882 3456. Engaged.

543 2323. A woman's voice.

—Quickprint. Can I help you?

—I'm inquiring about the position advertised in—

The woman cut him off.

—Sorry, sir, position filled.

428 4076. Engaged.

882 3456. A man's voice.

—Hello. Klein Group.

—Hello, sir, I'm inquiring about the position advertised for a sales person.

—Yeah. Okay. Hold a minute. I'll grab a pen.

Tommy waited, sipping the cooling coffee.

—What's your experience?

Tommy told him.

—Can you use Macintosh?

—Yes. Tommy lied.

—Quark?

What the fuck was Quark?

—Yes.

The man hesitated.

—What else?

—Pagemaker. Tommy tried to think of some other program John had spoken of. Corel Draw.

—That's IBM.

—Oh, sorry.

The man gave Tommy an address. Send in a resume.

Tommy went to the toilet and pissed. A tender relief. He looked at the pad. Two more numbers.

428 4076. Engaged.

Tommy put down the phone and picked up the newspaper. Another schoolgirl had gone missing; she had disappeared after school, walking home. The suburb of Bentleigh was being combed by police and investigating detectives. A massive door-knock was being undertaken and a large reward was posted for any information on the kidnapping. The girl's distraught mother was crying on the front page. A small shot. The main picture, the top half of the tabloid page, was of a smiling freckled pigtailed young girl in blue and white checked school uniform.

Tommy tickled at his arse, scratched, and his balls shook. He turned the page.

Fourteen women shot at a Canadian University. Another

thirteen wounded. A male student had taken a rifle to a seminar and proceeded to murder. Pictures of crying students. An editorial. Violence, against girls, against women. Stiffer penalties for sex offenders.

Tommy shut the paper and turned on the television. Noni Hazlehurst on *Play School*. He thought of fucking her in the mouth. He twisted in anger, furious, as he came on his pyjamas, his eyes closed, Noni Hazlehurst replaced by the little schoolgirl.

He tore off his pyjamas, stuffed them at the bottom of a basket, ignored the Virgin on the bedroom wall and turned on the taps to the shower. He scrubbed his thighs and stomach. He pulled back his foreskin and the fresh smegma had formed a milky foam. He scrubbed hard at that. A fleck of dry come, stuck on his cock head; that fleck could not be washed away.

After the initial shock of being fired, Tommy had regained his composure. He told his family, he returned to work, and though conscious of the silences that began whenever he was near, he pretended relief at the opportunity for another future. Pathis he could not speak to, his hate was full of violence. He wanted to murder the man. His farewell—a round of drinks and chicken lunch at the pub—was not attended by Pathis or, Somers. He did not want them there but he was stung by their absence.

Even when he had finished work he continued the routine. He woke early, at seven-thirty, and walked to the shop for the morning paper. He would dress in neat clothes and visit the Commonwealth Employment Service; he would inquire for work. In the afternoons he was at the gym. Losing his fat, becoming trim, this became his obsession. Conscious of his lack of funds, he stopped going to the cinema, going out to dinners, and Soo-Ling, not wishing to embarrass him, also stopped going out. She too felt herself scrutinised by Tommy's lack of work.

The gym offered routine, daily. He would rise, check the papers, ring for work, post his resume, and then he would walk into Box Hill, past the shops, through the park and into the gymnasium. His workout would last an hour and a half and he would sweat furiously, working off the fat. He began to look in mirrors again. But his weight refused to descend at a rate that made him happy. His lust for food did not diminish, if anything it increased, and he would gulp down chips and bread, sausage and meat.

—You smoke too much. Soo-Ling said this to him nervously. He was rolling a joint, they were on her couch, watching Cosby on television. He felt annihilated.

—Please, Soo-Ling.

She refused the smoke.

He wished he could leave her. Then there were nights when he would wake sweating, terrified of all things that lay beyond the bed, and he would reach out for her. Those nights she was not beside him he could not return to sleep. He'd numb himself with marijuana. He had been given a script for Serapax, to relieve his anxiety. But only Soo-Ling lying next to him could bring real peace.

The simplest comfort remained the gym. There he realised that his weight was not obscene. He found that even with his sagging belly, his fat thighs, there were faggots who would stare at him in the shower. He was both repulsed and attracted to their greed for his sex. He would wash his cock carefully, pull at his balls to extend their length. This narcissism was another pleasure of the gym. But outside that closed world, his doubts returned. Among women he compared his girth to other men around him. They wore their shirts loose, their leanness was mesmerising. He would glance in mirrors and find that he still seemed bloated and unshapely.

There was one more sanctuary. His visits to the porn shop. After the gym he would wander in and take his time walking along the shelves, picking up videos, putting them back, glancing at the covers and the backs of magazines. During the day a blond curly haired young man would sit at the counter, reading, listening to the radio and smoking his cigarettes. The young man would nod to Tommy then return to his reading. No fuss was made if Tommy remained in the shop for hours. Feeling the absence of a fortnightly salary, dependent on the dole, Tommy rationed his pornography. One magazine per week. No more than fifteen dollars. One video per fortnight, exchanged with another from his collection. Another fifteen dollars. Once, sometimes twice a week, always on the Thursday when the benefits got paid, Tommy would enter one of the booths and masturbate. Eight dollars for half an hour.

The dole office, the gymnasium, the porn shop. The routine.

He had taken the icon off his bedroom wall, had wrapped it in cloth and stored it carefully in his trunk, separated from the videos and magazines by sheets and blankets.

•

—Maybe we should move in together. Soo-Ling took the remote control and switched channels. They settled into an old Benny Hill.

Why? He said nothing.

—You're always here, which I like, she added quickly, but it seems a waste for you to pay rent on the flat.

He nodded. Six hundred and forty-three dollars, sixty-seven cents remained in his account. What she said made lots of sense. He would ask her to marry him when he found another job.

—You're right. We'll talk about it when the lease ends.

She nodded, happy, and turned to the screen. The images flashed past, nonsensical, hypnotic. She was planning the future.

Tommy laughed. An old man, rubbery face, toothless, was smothered in the bosom of a blonde tart with gigantic tits.

Tommy clenched his stomach tight. The thought of not being alone, of living with Soo-Ling, every day, every moment, filled him with a vertiginous nausea that was close to disgust. But so did the thought of losing her.

•

December 15. Lou's birthday.

Tommy drove slowly. Soo-Ling was putting on lipstick, rubbing her lips and looking in the mirror.

It had been a month since he had visited his parents. Maria's calls had become increasingly hysterical. One night she had rung up crying, cursing him for his indifference.

—I'll be there, he screamed into the phone, I'll be there for Lou's birthday.

—You're my son, I need to see you, she sobbed.

I don't need to see you.

He fantasised, always, about her death. Her absence would be a relief. And then his guilt would confirm what he already knew: that he was hardly human, something obscene.

Maria kissed Soo-Ling warmly, hugged her. The initial distance between them had vanished, replaced with a guarded intimacy: they rarely talked of Tommy, only of everything around him. Soo-Ling's being Chinese no longer mattered once Maria saw she would stand firm alongside her son. An, Australian girl would have left him as soon as he became unemployed, she said to Artie.

—So would a Greek one, he replied.

Politics had also cemented the affection between the two women. Soo-Ling, who had previously avoided politics, thought herself bored by it, had discovered an overwhelming interest in it once Tommy had become unemployed. The world of economics and politics no longer seemed a distant soap opera played out daily on the news at six but had begun to impact and force changes in her own life. The dole bludger was Tommy.

—Imagine if the Liberals get in next year. Maria shook her head in horror.

—It won't make a fucking difference, said Artie.

—Yes it will. Soo-Ling, quiet, amazed them with the force of her exclamation.

—They're the same, argued Dominic. Hawke's mates with all the fucking capos.

They're racist. Soo-Ling remembered the previous leader of the conservatives, his call for a restriction of Asian immigration.

But she said nothing.

—Bloody Vietnamese everywhere. Dominic had once sung this complaint. He looked up, Soo-Ling carrying a tray of coffee.

—Sorry, Sue, I didn't mean you.

I know, arsehole, I'm Chinese.

Only Maria seemed a true ally. Once, tipsy on wine at a barbecue, just before Tommy got the sack, she had made a comment, crude, that Soo-Ling always remembered. She was referring to the short balding leader of the opposition in Parliament.

—That bastard, what a wanker. And so ugly. There are Australian men, so pale, so lacking passion, they are like fish. Being with them would be like fucking a bloody fish. He reminds me of my bosses at the factories. I'd rather stitch up my mouni five times over than fuck a man like that.

Artie had got up from the table, taken her drink and said, furious, That's enough.

Soo-Ling had smiled, grinned, and fallen in love with the woman.

Tommy kissed his mother, shook hands with his father and excused himself to go to the toilet. He opened the bathroom door. Lou was naked except for a towel around his slender waist, combing his wet hair in front of the mirror.

—Sorry, Tommy blushed and shut the door. On his brother's flat stomach a thick web of hair had formed.

—It's all right, Lou yelled from inside, you can come in.

Tommy opened the door. The boy smiled, leant over and kissed his brother. Tommy went stiff.

—How are you? Is Soo-Ling here?

Tommy nodded.

—Great.

There was a silence.

—I'll leave. Lou grabbed deodorant from the sink and walked out of the bathroom.

—Put something on!

The boy simply laughed.

They were both embarrassed, though for Lou it was a response to his brother's mistrust rather than a response to the situation. But Lou was aware that Tommy was distant from him, almost suspicious of him, and that their intimacy inside the bathroom was uncomfortable; it was almost ugly. In his bedroom the boy winked at the cat, stroked its fine short hair and stripped the towel from his waist. He looked at his body in the mirror.

Jesus, you need to be bigger. He started to dress and forgot Tommy.

You forgot to say happy birthday, you dickhead. Tommy pissed, holding his cock, resting the thickness in his palm. The boy's lean body, no fat, no sagging or decay. A spurt of semen in a young child's mouth. He thought of the kidnapped girl. He flushed, looked in the mirror.

Had he always been a sicko? From birth?

His face had begun to lose the podge, the outline of cheekbone was now visible. But the double chin was still there. He stretched his jaw and then clenched his teeth hard, angry at his own foolishness. He knocked on Lou's door.

—Come in.

The boy was fastening his belt, a black T-shirt and faded jeans.

—Happy birthday, mate.

Lou smiled.

—Soo-Ling's got your present.

—Thanks. The boy bolted past, heading for the kitchen. Tommy felt as if he had been slapped.

Maria had organised a sumptuous feast. In the kitchen. Soo-Ling and Eva were preparing salads. There was roasting gemista, tomatoes, peppers and zucchini flowers filled with meat and rice, a large pan of creamy pasticchio and a platter of oily dolmades, the vine leaves shiny and deep jade. There was a roast chicken and golden slices of potato. Taramasalata and tzatziki, fresh bread and wine. Outside, drinking beer, Dominic and Artie were cooking souvlakia. Soo-Ling was made dizzy by the smells, the kitchen was full of the succulent ether of oil and spice, oregano and basil. She stroked her chin, she felt encased in the oil. Lou was at her side, chopping tomatoes. The boy's fresh face was smiling.

—How's the cat?

—She's good. She's probably out in the garage.

—Not in your room?

Maria turned around sharply.

—She's not allowed in the house.

Soo-Ling made a face, an apology.

—That's all right. He whispered it softly.

Soo-Ling had chosen Lou's present, a shirt of red silk. He opened it and impulsively kissed her. He put the shirt on, over the T-shirt, and it hung loose across his frame.

—Tuck it in, urged his mother.

—It looks fine like that, smiled Soo-Ling.

Faggot.

Tommy retreated from the women, out to the garden, to his older brother and his father around the barbecue.

—How's the job hunting going, eh Tom?

Tommy opened a beer, looked around the garden. His father winked at him.

—You'll find one soon, won't you, Tommy.

And what if I don't want to?

—Sure Dad, after Christmas.

Dominic turned the meat over.

—Where's Eva?

—At her mum's. She'll be here soon. She had to pick up some stuff.

The conversation turned to cricket and the weather. Lou

came into the yard, calling for the cat. The three older men turned and looked at the boy.

—Bass! Where are you?

Tommy excused himself. He could not stay still.

Dominic turned over the skewers of meat and the oil sizzled.

—You think he's all right?

Artie nodded.

—It's been nearly six months now.

—Jobs are hard to get. Lou came over next to his brother.

—What the fuck would you know about it?

Lou smiled and started calling for the cat.

—How's school going anyway?

Lou shrugged. Okay.

The cat was hiding under a canopy of lettuce leaves. Lou spied it and walked over. The cat slithered cautiously up to his hand.

—Boo! Dominic screamed and the cat became liquid, dived over the fence.

Lou turned around, shaking his head.

—You're an arsehole. He sat down next to his father. Can I have a beer?

Artie handed over a stubby.

—Well, Dad, has he told you anything? Tom, I mean. Has he got any interviews?

Artie stood up and took the tongs off Dominic.

—He doesn't talk about it much. Shut it, all right Dom, around him. Don't give him a hard time.

—I don't fucking give him a hard time.

—Yes you do. Lou said this quietly. He sniffed the air and scowled, I hate the smell of meat.

—You're not turning vego on us?

—Maybe.

Dominic laughed. That'll piss Mum off.

Lou tapped the bottle. Soft thick short notes.

—Soo-Ling reckons he should do more study.

—Who?

—Tommy.

—Soo-Ling doesn't know what she's talking about.

Artie tasted a slice of steaming meat.

—Dom's right. He's already been to college. He needs a job. He needs to settle down.

—Soo-Ling's got him hooked. Dominic laughed and, in a whisper, A china doll for a bride, hey Dad?

Lou got up to go inside. She's smarter than both of you idiots. He walked up to the laundry door, brushed past Tommy.

—What are they laughing about?

Lou didn't turn around.

—Just bullshit.

The lunch dragged on for hours. In the background the television played the cricket and the radio played songs. The feast of pastries and meat was followed by fruit: grapes, and deep red plums from the garden, watermelon and peaches. Throughout the meal wine was drunk, and a bottle of champagne was opened to celebrate the boy's birthday. The three brothers slowly all got drunk. Eva and Soo-Ling began drinking water. Maria, safe in her home, drank with her sons.

The conversation nervously and studiously avoided the subject of work. But the alcohol loosened lips and concentration. Soo-Ling sat quietly, listening in. Maria, charged with drink, began to curse the fall of the Wall. Soo-Ling was shocked. She had watched the television over the last few months, a gratuitous happiness at seeing the division of Europe shattered by the exuberant celebrations of will. But Maria was damning.

Tommy filled his glass, shaking his head. He tried to interject.

—Mum, how can you believe that shit? You think it was better for people under communism. You're a fool.

Maria laughed cruelly.

—I'm the fool? No, you're the fools. A whining, mocking voice. Excuse me, Mr Bush, we're Australia. What can we do for you? Whatever you want, Mr Bush. In Greek. The Americans fuck everyone. Only Australia, however, only Australia rolls over and lets them do it willingly.

Tommy, furious, raised his glass.

—To capitalism.

Artie laughed and raised his glass as well.

Soo-Ling realised the danger. The mother's eyes were moist but angry.

—Is capitalism offering you a job, son?

Tommy sculled the glass, banged it on the table and poured himself another drink. His mother's contempt lacerated him and he wished he had the guts to overturn the table, to bash his fist hard in her sly face. To walk out. To walk away and not return.

Maria did not wish to hurt her son. But what Tommy did not realise, what none of them realised, even the husband who had lived with her for so long, was that when they dismissed her faith with jokes and light banter, they compounded a hurt which isolated her from them. Even within her own family, Maria had no-one with whom she could share her exile.

The approach of menopause made it worse. The headaches and the fevers, the inability to sense the fury and the impossibility of keeping it in control. She was lashing, lashing out, Arto had never been so far away from her. Sometimes, next to her in bed, the touch of his skin repulsed her. Her despair was becoming poisonous.

After lunch the men sat bloated in the lounge room, watching the television, reading the newspapers, while the women restored order to the kitchen. Lou walked the spaces in between, watching the cricket, drying the dishes. Maria had fallen into a silence, not angry but distant. Eva and Soo-Ling attempted conversation but Maria's answers were short. They washed in silence. The young boy and the mother stayed close to one another, and Soo-Ling marvelled at the affection between them. Maria stroked the boy's cheek, a soft line of suds. She blew it away and the boy giggled.

—I'm going to go out after this, okay, Mum?

—Where to?

—Kylie's. We're just going out, a group of us. Celebrate my birthday. Dinner and then there's this party.

—How late are you going to be?

—Not too late. All right?

The mother nodded.

But not too late. Greek.

In the lounge room, Tommy heard the exchange. Bitch, he thought, you wouldn't have let me out without a fight when I was his age. He's just fucking turned sixteen.

—Can Pete stay over?

—Why? Maria looked suspiciously at her youngest son.

—Can he?

—Why can't he sleep at home? He's just down the road.

Lou shifted uncomfortably, foot to foot. He looked over at Soo-Ling.

—Why? demanded Maria.

—He's not at home at the moment.

—Why?

—He's had a fight with his mum. She chucked him out again.

Maria turned off the tap. She faced her son.

—Where has he been sleeping?

—I don't know. Around. At the bus shelter in the plaza. Can he sleep over tonight?

Maria said nothing. She stormed out of the kitchen. Lou and Soo-Ling silently continued the washing up.

Tommy heard his mother in her bedroom. She slammed a drawer hard. He looked over at his father who was concentrating intently on the television.

Maria came into the kitchen and handed a roll of notes to her son.

—He can sleep here tonight. Give him this.

Lou unrolled the notes.

—Jesus, Mum, he exclaimed, this is one hundred dollars.

Artie roared from inside the lounge room, What the fuck are you thinking of, woman?

—It's my money, screamed back Maria. Mine, all right!

Tommy watched a ball claim a wicket. The television cut to an ad. He wanted his father to scream back. He didn't. Instead he shook his head. Dominic pointed a finger to his forehead, rolled his eyes, indicated towards the kitchen.

—She's always been crazy, agreed his father.

—Thanks, Mum.

Maria turned away from Lou and shoved Soo-Ling aside.

—I'll finish them, she said gruffly. There was a tear in her left eye.

Bloody Australians. In Greek. The slut, and she spat into the water. The fucking slut. In English. Who would leave her fifteen year old son to fend for himself? She asked this question to Soo-Ling. Australians, that's who.

Lou pocketed the money and kissed his mother.

—Thanks, Mum.

Eva went into the lounge room and asked the men if they wanted more coffee. Dominic, his eyes on the screen, shook his head. He lifted a beer glass towards her. She took it.

Tommy looked up.

—Do you want some help?

—No, thanks, Tom. She hesitated. You look good, you know. You've lost weight.

—I've been working out. He was pleased, exhilarated.

Dominic turned.

—Well, he's got all the time in the world, hasn't he?

Tommy wished he could kick at the table, at the vase, at the symmetry of the room, at the symmetry of family.

Dominic, realising his spite, cringed and avoided his wife's eyes.

Eva, walking back to the kitchen, found herself fearful of eternity.

Artie closed his eyes, pretended to fall asleep.

Before he left, Lou kissed all his family goodbye. Dominic hugged him, then lifted him high. The boy struggled and laughed. Soo-Ling was struck by the softness of the teenager's lips.

On the couch, Artie was snoring. Tommy leant over to his older brother.

—You got any dope, Dom?

Dominic nodded.

—Can I have some?

—It's two fifty an ounce.

I haven't got the money. You cunt, I haven't got the money.

—I'll get you a quarter; pick it up over the week. You can have it for free.

Nothing more was said.

Driving home, Tommy was annoyed by Soo-Ling's presence. He wanted nothing more than to shed the stain of family, to remove himself from the forced attentions of the world. Soo-Ling asked him to stop at a milk bar and he snarled at her, What do you want?

Soo-Ling answered quietly. Tampons.

He thought of her blood and was sickened. He wanted to drive straight to the porn shop, become immersed in the comfort of sterile vaginas, to be among women who didn't talk, who didn't bleed, who didn't answer back. He wanted Soo-Ling far away from him.

She came back to the car.

—You all right? She took Tommy's hand. He pushed her away.

—I've got to drive.

●

A week before Christmas Soo-Ling was invited to a dinner in the city, a Christmas break-up for work. She urged Tommy to come. They dressed up, he wore a tie and she looked stunning in a dark blue mini and a long vinyl black jacket. The night was full of drink and jokes, the expectation of holidays, the abdication of work and responsibility. High on smoke, drinking the free wine,

Tommy felt happy, content. All night his eyes were on a tall woman with golden hoop earings and a full oval mouth. From time to time the woman smiled at him, then returned to her conversation. Late in the evening, when the seating had been upset and the table was full of empty glasses and overflowing ashtrays, Tommy, inspired by drink, moved over to the woman. He introduced himself.

—You're Soo-Ling's boyfriend.

He nodded.

The woman shook his hand.

—I'm Alanah. I work with Soo-Ling. Upstairs.

She smelt of cigarettes and the hint, simple, of tea-tree.

—What do you do?

Tommy stared at her. Her breasts were not large but they were perfectly formed, sweet round curves. The low neckline of her tight red dress.

He could not put words together. He looked around the room. A man, fifties, grey beard, had his arm across the back of Soo-Ling's chair. Suddenly the noise was everywhere. The noise was a dizzy buzzing, a discord and a ferocious thrashing. He had to cough. His mouth was dry. Alanah was looking at him strangely.

What do you do?

Tommy, without apology, got up and walked slowly to the toilets. In there a young man was pissing loudly in the urinal. Tommy closed the cubicle door and sat heavily on the seat. The woman's question was not new. It was unavoidable. Previously he had answered it with the past or concocted a future. The answer always implied a continuum. I am. I will be. But tonight the present was the past and was the future and in this present there was no answer he could give.

A flush. The young man leaving the toilet.

There was one answer, the only possible answer.

Nothing.

What do you do?

Nothing.

The full force of the word hurt Tommy so much that he began to shake, a sweat, uncontrollable, gathered on his brow. From somewhere there was music. Possibly Kylie Minogue. Tommy waited for the shaking to stop and when it didn't, when he realised the palpitations were going to continue, he stood up, pissed, flushed, washed his hands, walked back to the table, held tight to Soo-Ling and, like a baby, whispered, was crying, Take me home, take me home.

9

Freedom '90

On 11 February 1990 Nelson Mandela walked free from prison and Tommy Stefano filled out his fifteenth dole form. Mandela's walk out of the prison, televised on a billion screens, only served to deepen Tommy's despair. The world was celebrating. The Wall had fallen, apartheid was ending, and the future was free of nuclear menace. But Tommy was still unemployed. He left social security, crossed the railway tracks and entered the back entrance of the porn shop. There was a new man working the counter, he was watching the television, the replay of Mandela's release the night before. A long shot, a dusty wide road, crowds waiting. Mandela was coming. A newsreader, excited, loud pink lipstick. The man at the counter flicked the remote control. A white woman, feline face, was staring hard at a bulbous cock head. A furious masturbation. The come fell, buckets, on her face. On the radio, Mike and the Mechanics.

—Free Nelson Mandela, the man behind the counter mocked.

Tommy laughed. He remembered the song.

—Do you think anything will change in South Africa? The man was looking at him. Tommy was scouting video slicks.

—Don't know.

—I don't reckon. The niggers at the bottom will still be the niggers at the bottom.

Tommy felt slapped by the harsh racist word.

The man was large, tall and burly. He had a thick moustache, and though his smoky hair was closely cropped, he was obviously balding. Tommy wandered the store and finally settled on a video. On the back a black woman was holding two black cocks in her hand. They were huge. He took the video over to the counter.

—Is the booth empty? He did not look at the man. Embarrassed.

—Sure, mate. It's quiet. He took the video cover. Need any change?

Tommy handed over a ten dollar bill and the man handed him back five coins.

—Enjoy, it's a good one. I'll fast forward it for you. There's a bit of talking at the beginning.

—Thanks.

He entered the booth. He locked the door.

•

There had been a long line at the DSS, even though he arrived just before ten o'clock. Lots of scared young girls with prams, holding the hands of snotty children. The regulars were there as well. A pock-marked young man, losing his hair, an ACDC T-shirt. The Punk Princess who never smiled. The fat slag and her stained shirt. The line progressed slowly. At the counter a man in a tie was having an argument.

—I can't hang around all day. Can't I see someone now?

The girl behind the counter shook her head.

—Take a number and take your seat. I've told you, you have to wait your turn.

The fat slag, who was before him, turned around.

—She's a cunt, ain't she that one?

Tommy nodded.

•

The booth was clean. It was still early. He turned on the fan, a slow whirring began. A box of tissues on a shelf, a small pink bin lined with white plastic. The black walls had been scrubbed but the faint marks of ancient semen were still visible. They re-minded Tommy of the slimy trails of slugs.

He put his coins in the slot, the screen flickered, a fuzzy line, and the video began. A woman sitting on the phone, talking sex, pulling down her panties. Her breasts were full and sagging, round pink nipples. Her eyes were dull. She was rubbing at her furry cunt. Tommy sat down on the plastic chair, undid his belt, pulled down his zip. His cock was soft.

•

The man in the tie had taken his seat, muttering, threatening to call his MP, to take decisive action. Everyone else ignored him. The Punk Princess shook her head, rolled her eyes. Tommy got to the counter. He handed over his form. The woman glanced at it, stamped it.

—I've got an appointment. Tommy had handed her the slip.

She looked at it, nodded and asked him to take a seat. He walked over to the man in the tie, sat next to him. The man shifted, did not look at Tommy. They sat in silence and waited. On the screen a woman was selling crockery. Only forty-nine dollars and ninety-five cents. A set of plates, an oven dish, cups and saucers. And if you rang within the next hour, a set of carving knives. Tommy got up and headed to the toilet. He took a packet of pills from his top pocket, threw two down the back of his throat and cupped water to his mouth. Outside, he could hear a baby crying.

•

Tommy waited to get hard. The sound on the monitor was loud and it closed off the world outside. Her moans were squeals. They punctuated the heavy breathing on the soundtrack. The loudness filled his ears and his cock twitched. He closed his eyes and simply listened to the ecstasy. He opened his eyes. The camera was right up the woman's cunt, her skin made yellow by the careless shooting on video. Tommy spat in his hand and greased his cock. The woman's face flooded the screen, her eyes closed, her breathing loud. The screen flickered, a break in the soundtrack. Outside, he could hear a woman's voice. He stopped, lifted the seat of his trousers. He flicked at the switch that controlled the volume, turned it down. He was enraged that the booth was no longer empty.

•

The interview had been monotonous. A red haired man, young, with a crucifix in his left earlobe, had methodically gone through a list of questions.

—How long have you been unemployed?

—Six months.

You fucking know that.

—What work are you looking for?

—Graphic design, sales. Anything really.

Nothing.

—You live on your own?

—Yes.

—Seeing anyone?

None of your fucking business.

—No.

—When was your last interview?

Tommy faltered. November?

—January.

—Where?

He tracked his mind, tried to remember some of the names he had put on the dole form.

—Club X, the porn shop.

The young man looked up.

—That's a far call from graphic design.

Tommy blushed. And hated himself for blushing.

—It's a job, ain't it?

—Yes. That's it?

Tommy nodded.

The young man sat back in his seat.

—In two months you are eligible for some training assistance. Are there any courses you feel would assist you in expanding your professional skills?

Tommy wanted to laugh in his face. The Serapax had kicked in.

—I did graphics before computers. It would be good to get some computer experience.

—Do you own a computer?

—No.

—It would probably be a good idea to get one, Mr Stefano. As you know, it's a tough job market out there. You'll need to get proficient on the computer.

A poster behind the man read: *Domestic Violence. Sharing the Responsibility.*

—Mr Stefano?

—Yes.

—A computer. I suggest you get a computer.

Two hundred and twenty-three dollars left in the bank.

—Sure.

The young man made notations on Tommy's sheet.

—We'll see if we can find you a TAFE course. If you're still unemployed in a few months.

—Thanks. Tommy got up.

—Good luck.

Suck my fat cock, you piece of poofter shit.

Outside, the man in the tie was still waiting, the anger long dissipated, his body slumped into the plastic orange chair, a dejected curve. At his feet a baby played with plastic blocks. Tommy, walking past, was seized with a strong desire to smash his foot into the child's wet face. He walked out, the air was warm. He had one thought. Pornography. His body was bursting to expel the red haired man's face from his memory.

•

The woman came, lifted her panties. The camera settled on her contented face. A pimple evaded the foundation. Tommy could no longer hear the woman outside. The radio in the shop was playing commercials. He turned up the volume and lowered his pants. He freed his limp cock from his underwear. The woman in the video rose to answer a knock on the door. A startlingly thin black man with a sliver of a moustache was at the door. He was in overalls. The woman let him in and he began to work on the kitchen sink. The woman sat on the bench, her legs apart, smiling and flirting with the man. Her black underwear was visible. The man stood up and moved towards her. She fumbled with the buttons to his overalls. He kneaded her breasts and began to suck, in close up, on one of her nipples. Tommy began a slow tug. The man stepped back and pulled his overalls off his shoulders. The woman ran her tongue down his chest, his belly. She pulled his cock out of his thin blue underwear. It was thick and arced a long curve. She began to suck on it.

—Fuck her, nigger. Said softly, to himself. The final word excited him. Tommy's semen splashed across his shirt, fell all over his fist. Immediately the ugliness of the jerking figures on the screen disgusted him. He pulled three tissues from the box, wiped himself. The actors on the screen had begun fucking. She was leaning across the kitchen table. He was fucking her. She was squealing. The fucking bored him and Tommy left the booth.

•

When Tommy reached home he phoned Soo-Ling. She was short with him.

—What's wrong?

—It's busy. She sighed. I hate this job, she whispered to him. On the television Phil Donahue was working the audience.

—I haven't even had time for lunch.

He suddenly realised he was happy.

—Are you coming over tonight?

He hesitated. No.

—Fine. See you later then.

She was angry.

—I'll call you tomorrow.

She didn't reply. She hung up the phone.

He scouted the cupboards for food. Five slices of stale bread, two mouldy apples. In the back of one drawer he found a tin of beans and spaghetti. He thought of his stomach. He kicked at a cupboard door. He poured the contents of the tin into a sauce-pan. On *Donahue* they were discussing date rape.

He had become lazy with the gym and lazy with his diet. Now, after a shower, the room steaming, he refused to look in the mirror. If he glanced at the folds of his belly, his day was shattered. His self-hatred would be so staggering that he'd be incapable of action.

When he judged the food hot enough, he poured it over two pieces of stale bread and sat in front of the television. He munched on the bread.

A woman, crying, was talking of having met a man at a dance, his invitation home, her shyness and her fear as she realised he wanted sex. She let him kiss her, she let him undo her bra, and then she wanted him to stop.

Tommy put down his plate. The woman's speech was halted by her increasing sobbing. He wouldn't stop, he wouldn't stop, she pleaded with the audience. Close-up of Donahue's sym-pathetic frown. Close-up to a cold-eyed white woman in the front row.

When Tommy first had sex with a girlfriend, she had resisted him. He kept pleading, please, please, please. She finally relented. Her obvious anger was disconcerting but he was grateful that she let him come inside her. He rolled off her without speaking. He was relieved at her assent for he had been tempted to cover her mouth, shut off her refusal.

The woman was being comforted by another woman. Donahue then spoke with the man, who told a different story.

He had not heard no, she was kissing him, she helped him take off her bra. Then he was fucking her and not aware of anything until he had finished and awoke to her screaming. The audience booed. Tommy fantasised the rape. He fell asleep on the couch, the television on. He didn't bother to clean himself up. When he woke up, startled, the night had begun. He smelt of urine.

•

Soo-Ling had typed up close to ten thousand words on the computer. It had been nonstop all morning. Up to the election her work itself had slowed down, a trickle. Immediately after the results, the phones had not stopped ringing, clients were demanding extra attention, and her manager, harassed, tired, depended on her for extra work and extra hours. Soo-Ling was methodical, organised, she knew herself to be an asset in the unit. But she hated the work.

Nadia had rung up out of the blue, unexpected, cheerful, and Soo-Ling had eyed the clock nervously throughout their conversation. Two other women were typing furiously at their keyboards.

—Nadia, good to hear from you. When did you come back?

—Last week. I can't believe it. I'm still not sure if I made the right decision. She talked of overseas and Soo-Ling realised that the conversation was painful for her. She had not travelled yet.

—How's Tommy?

—Good. She winced, anticipating the question.

—Is he working?

—No. Softly. She looked around her as she gave the answer.

—Yeah, must be hard. I haven't even started looking yet.

—Where are you living?

—At my sister's, in Brunswick. I'm houseminding. She's away up north for a few weeks. Then fuck knows.

Soo-Ling looked at the clock again.

—Sorry, Nadia, but I've got to go. It's hell here at the moment.

—Understand. Look, do you and Tommy want to come around for dinner next week?

—We'd love to.

Nadia gave her a number and an address. Soo-Ling put down the phone and turned back to the computer terminal. She clicked the mouse and the screen exploded into line and curve. She began typing.

•

—I don't want to go.

—Please, Tom, you like Nadia and we haven't been anywhere for ages.

On the news there were two photographs, two young men. In Holland. Killed by a bomb. They were Australian and one of them looked Greek. The photo grabbed Soo-Ling's attention.

—That's so sad.

No, it isn't. Tommy didn't feel sad at all. His indifference was complete.

—Please, Tommy? Soo-Ling was pleading. In the kitchen she could hear Sonja laughing on the phone.

—Tom. She nestled under his arm. He groaned and assented.

That night she wanted sex. She touched his arm softly with her fingers, tried to kiss his mouth.

—Hon, I'm tired.

She stopped, shamed. She waited till she heard the regular harshness of his snoring and then, cradled in his arms, softly rubbed at her clitoris. She masturbated without image, without memory. The orgasm that came was soft, a ripple, unsatisfying, but it allowed her to fall asleep.

The young man, the one who died in the bombing, was fresh faced, handsome. In the dream he called out to her across a busy road and she kept losing sight of him as she attempted to negotiate the buses and the cars, the trucks and motorbikes. There was an explosion and the world collapsed to rubble. She was not hurt. In the dream she moved slowly towards the fallen body of the man who had called out to her. She knew it was Tommy and the dread so disturbed her that she awoke, clutching air, before she could witness any more. What disturbed her most was that in the middle of the rubble a young girl sat foetal, her hand between her legs, rocking, masturbating. This, more than the bomb, more than the death, this distressed her most.

·

Nadia had changed. At first Soo-Ling could not pick it. The hair, of course, was shorter and instead of the neat pressed work skirts and blouses, Nadia now wore tight fitting black. They drank wine, Tommy hardly spoke, and Soo-Ling was shy. The rituals of dinner, she was shocked to discover, she had forgotten. Nadia put down her wine glass and excused herself.

—I've still got some stuff to do in the kitchen.

—Can I help you? Soo-Ling stood up suddenly, eagerly. Nadia nodded.

—Can I put on the telly?

Without waiting for a reply, Tommy flashed on the screen.

He had taken a pill to steady his anxiety. Nadia reminded him of the old life and it seemed so long ago that he could hardly remember any of it. The faces of work had begun to disappear and all he retained of the place was the smell of the printing press. Ink. The pill had begun its work and he settled into the couch. The world compacted into the distance between himself and the screen, the bobbing miniatures of actors. Outside his vision, Nadia and Soo-Ling disappeared. The emanation of the screen kept him warm.

—Things all right?

Soo-Ling was chopping up tomatoes. She pulled her hair back from her face and smiled at Nadia.

—They are, she dropped her voice, it's just hard with Tommy, his not having work.

—Are you engaged yet?

Soo-Ling shook her head.

—He won't do it until he gets a job. He reckons he doesn't want to have me supporting him.

Nadia squeezed drops of lemon into a jar.

—And would you put up with that?

The question shocked her. Soo-Ling had started to feel annoyed at the poverty of Tommy's existence, she wanted to lash out at him when he refused activities because of the cost. She knew that in her head she kept a mental tally of what she spent on him. She was unhappy at her own greed. But this was the first moment in which she understood it clearly. She wanted him to have a job, she wanted him to have money. She hated giving him money.

She thought him weak now. She blushed.

—He'll find a job soon.

—It's hard.

—What are you thinking of doing? Same sort of thing as before?

—No fucking way.

Nadia's vehemence was exhilarating.

—So, what?

—I'm going to study. I'm not sure what, but that's what I'm going to do.

—Can you afford it?

—Nah. Nadia laughed. I'll try and get some part-time work.

Nadia turned towards Soo-Ling, shaking a jar of salad dressing.

—No more offices, no more shit work. That's all I know.

Soo-Ling was jealous.

—Good on you.

—Mum thinks I'm mad, she told me I was wasting my time. Not married, unemployed. She hates the fact that I blew my retrenchment on overseas. Wog mothers, Nadia shrugged, you know what they're like.

Soo-Ling realised what was different about the woman. Except for the faint pink of lipstick and a casual application of eyeliner, Nadia's face was clean of make-up. She looked years younger and the harshness around her mouth had gone.

Dinner proceeded slowly. Tommy shovelled down the food, ravenous: the salad, the cream and mushroom tortellini, the cheesecake. Conversation stumbled between Soo-Ling and Nadia. They both, at separate moments in the evening, shared the same thought: I wish Tommy was not here. He desperately attempted conversation but beyond the television and the food there was nothing he could talk about. Nadia was shocked at his thinness, the loss of colour in his skin. He seemed desperately unhappy and she could find no way to bridge his isolation. She kept pouring wine.

After dessert she put on a CD and they retreated to the couches.

—What's this?

—George Michael. It was playing everywhere in Europe. Nadia took out a bottle of vodka from the fridge.

—Want some?

—Yes.

—Are you sure, Tommy, aren't you driving?

Fuck off.

—I'll be fine.

—I'll have one too. Soo-Ling wished to be drunk, to be intoxicated. Nadia brought in the glasses and Soo-Ling finished hers in two sharp swigs.

—I'll have another one.

Nadia giggled.

—That's what I like to see.

Tommy watched the women. The drink and the food, the pill inside his head. He wanted to fuck. Both of them. He tasted the sour softness of the vodka and for a moment, gratefully, he touched happiness. A swift bounce of rhythm jumped through the speakers. Nadia got up and began dancing. Come on, she roared, and clapped her hands at Soo-Ling. Come dance.

First nervously, then excited, Soo-Ling followed Nadia into a dance. Tommy reclined back on the couch, his eyes closed, feeling the music. Freedom, the song sung and he smiled at his own detachment. Dinner with Nadia had not revived the past and for that he was grateful. He opened his eyes. Soo-Ling, her eyes shut, her face to heaven, was laughing as she swayed. Nadia walked to the stereo, turned a dial, and the music flooded the room, the house.

—Come dance, she mouthed to Tommy.

He refused, closed his eyes again, and listened to the song. He wanted it to go on forever, for an eternity, to find death within it. But the song ended and the silence at its demise saddened all three of them.

—I haven't danced for ages, said Soo-Ling as she sat down next to Tommy, a trembling of sweat on her lips.

Six years, maybe longer, thought Tommy, and I used to go out to bands all the time.

Nadia turned down the volume.

—Maybe we should all go dancing soon.

—Where? asked Soo-Ling.

—Anywhere.

—We're too old. Tommy.

—Bullshit. Nadia poured another round of vodka. You're never too old.

—We are.

—Speak for yourself.

I am.

—That's so Australian. In Greece and Italy, you idiot, where you come from, they dance till they're dead.

I'm not from Italy or Greece.

—How old are you Tommy?

—He's thirty. Next February. Soo-Ling said this quietly.

—That's not old, said Nadia, and she drank from her glass.

They watched a video of Nadia's trip overseas. At first Soo-Ling watched politely. The tourist shots of London. The Houses of Parliament. Big Ben. The Tower. Then the images began to change. The camera no longer focused on buildings and icons but stayed to measure the everyday life of the city. A group of backpackers, over breakfast, laughed and talked into the camera.

—Hello Australia. A big faced woman with a thick accent.

An old woman, a bright orange sari, washing down a wall.

—That's Brick Lane, in London. The only decent place to get food.

The wall washed clean, the old woman turned to the camera and smiled. She had no teeth. The video paused, then there was a close-up of the old woman's brown face, speaking slowly into the microphone. She was wishing Nadia luck and prosperity.

—Where are you from? Nadia's voice.

—India.

—How long have you been in England?

—Forty years. The old woman laughed. Since I was a young girl.

Scotland. An old man searching through rubbish bins, a young girl playing hopscotch on the street. A line of bright washed clothing. A handsome young man, a mop of dirty blond hair covering his eyes, avoiding the camera. Suddenly smiling.

—That's Alan.

—Who's he? asked Soo-Ling.

—A man I met in Glasgow.

A line of apartment blocks, grey, ugly.

—That's where he lived.

Alan on a balcony of a council estate. Waving to the camera, diminishing, disappearing.

France. A woman in a field digging the earth. A man with an accordion, playing. The camera left him and encircled the watching crowd of villagers. In the very middle a teenage girl with a white T-shirt that fell to her knees. *Aciieeed!* it read. Yellow smiling face.

—Now that was huge everywhere. Acid house. I'd never fucking heard of it before.

—Lou likes that, doesn't he?

Tommy nodded, fixated on the images. And they came and came; the camera journeyed across Europe, picking on faces and moments. The faces were handsome and ugly, beautiful and damaged. The country on the screen was green and ablaze with geometry. Hills and towers, slopes and troughs. The camera wound around the faces and the land. In Romania lined old faces, sitting round a table, sung a plaintive song for Nadia. His mother had sung such songs. Nadia's grandmother, raising a glass to her grand-daughter, crying; all shawls and scarves. Then the children, their faces dirty and their hair not brushed, picking at food and smiling and hiding from the camera. In the lounge room, watching the video, Nadia was crying. Soo-Ling took her hand.

A river black; beyond it a factory poured a rain of dark smoke. Under a tree a woman was laughing. She too was dirty, her face marked by lines of grease. She was shaking and laughing. The camera stayed on her, the jerking of Nadia's hands, the woman jumping up and chasing her.

—Who's that?

—Eleni, remarked Nadia quietly. And Soo-Ling understood, shocked, that the two women had been lovers.

Nadia. Getting dressed, a bra and panties. On the floor Nadia hid her face and giggled. Tommy wanted to fix the image. He noticed that the hair around the lace white of Nadia's panties was thick and wiry.

Nadia. Walking through a monumental desolation. A square of grey monstrous power; steps that seemed to lead to heaven.

—Bucharest.

Eleni waving at the camera. In a tiny cubicle of a room, a single bed, a swirl of damp and dirt on the wall. Pan across a wooden table. A photo of a man and a woman, around the frame a crown of thorns. Fuzzy image, clumsy framing. Then a close up of the frame: an entwining wreath of skulls and bones.

—What's that?

—Eleni made it. That's a picture of Ceaucescu and his wife.

Requiem for a Dictator, she calls it. She carved the frame out of wood.

—That would have taken ages.

—She has plenty of time. Nothing but time.

Tommy had watched the dictator and his wife be executed. On television. The woman rather than the man had stayed with him. Faced with the savage glee welcoming her death, she had responded with a defiant hate. Tommy thought the cheering crowds were fools. Her defiance had betrayed their victory.

Greece. The waves of the Aegean rolled on the screen and then the camera focused on jutting rocky islets. A queue of people, T-shirts and shorts, disembarking. Men gathering nets onto boats. A frail young girl at a window, a lane of smoky white houses. The abrupt scream of the Athenian skyline, the jutting ugliness of dull concrete. A kiosk stand. A group of old men arguing and shouting.

Soo-Ling turned to Tommy.

—What are they saying?

—I don't know.

The whisper of a wind at the Parthenon, tourists standing on the ruined steps, their hair flying with the breeze. A close-up of scaffolding.

Tommy reached towards the screen.

The video spluttered, flashed white lines across an empty blackness, stopped and became static.

Nadia turned on the lights.

The brightness disoriented Soo-Ling. Nadia offered coffee and, not touching, apart, on the floor, Tommy and Soo-Ling nodded in agreement. They looked at the blank television. Tommy reached for the remote control. Soo-Ling stopped his hand.

—No television now, Tommy. I couldn't bear it.

In the kitchen Nadia was humming a song.

—We should go. Soon.

—Home?

—No! Overseas.

—I can't afford it, you know that. And I thought you wanted to save up for a house. Can't have both, you know, not with me out of a job.

Soo-Ling, staring at blankness, wondered if he hated her.

Over coffee Nadia began to tell the stories of the video images. She described the casual drug hedonism of Glasgow, Alan, and the wounded intensity of the beautiful Eleni. She talked of walking through Romanian fields made putrid by chemical emissions.

—When we came back home, the rubber of my runners had turned grey.

She described a war across the borders, the serenity of France and the confusion of Greece. She spoke of the loneliness of London and the nervous anxiety about a united Germany.

—I can't wait to go.

—You should, Soo-Ling, you should. Nadia was eager in her passion. Oh, how can I explain it. We are so far away, everything is happening so fast over there. It could all be fucking ugly, I know. There's a war in Europe, the Wall's collapsed. She moved back, sipped her coffee. We're so far away.

Shut up. Just shut up. A panic crept through Tommy, a fear of the black night outside.

Nadia turned to him.

—You too, mate, you too, Tom. Greece, you've got to go to Greece.

—Why?

—That's where you're from. She turned to Soo-Ling. And you, you must want to see China.

Soo-Ling and Tommy went quiet, watched the liquid turning slowly in their cups.

They drove home in silence, Soo-Ling gazed out onto the elongated emptiness of the freeway. Tommy turned to her.

—Do you mind if I don't come in?

The television was throwing sparse light onto the windows. Sonja was home.

—I'm tired.

—We can go straight to bed.

—I just want to be alone tonight, Soo. Is that okay?

It's ending, isn't it, Tommy? Soo-Ling scraped her shoes on the vinyl mat on the floor. Drunk. She wanted to say, simply, Please be with me tonight. But she didn't. She leant across, touched his cold cheek with her lips, and said goodnight.

Sonja was lounging on the floor, a man by her side, watching video. The roar of *The Terminator*. Sonja paused the video.

—Where's Tom?

—He had stuff to do.

—Dinner good?

Soo-Ling nodded.

—Soo-Ling, this is Andrew.

They shook hands. The video came back on. Soo-Ling waited fifteen minutes, rang Tommy's number. No-one answered. She watched more of the movie, another fifteen minutes. Rang again. No-one answered. She washed, brushed her teeth, fell into bed. It would be foolish to say that she was sad. Her exhaustion was not from sadness. She was dreaming of a flight, across oceans and territories. In her imaginings she was, flying. But alone. Tommy had disappeared.

•

The shop was quiet. An old man, migrant, was thumbing the gay videos when Tommy walked in. Immediately the man moved aside, embarrassed, and left the shop.

The man at the counter looked up as Tommy approached.

—Closing up soon, mate. In ten minutes.

Tommy stood there, engulfed by the mechanics of sex; the hunger to scout the room, to immerse himself in the siren call of mute genitalia. At Nadia's he had watched the video with increasing horror, the gulf between himself and the world was immense. He *needed* to walk the shelves of video and magazines, to find equilibrium. Even with the store closing, his anticipation refuted, he was glad to stand still and arouse himself in merchandise. At the counter the man was settling the till. Tommy pulled the first video he saw off a shelf and brought it over.

—Have I got time to buy this?

There was a click, the red engaged sign slipped to the green vacant, and a man came out of the video booth. On seeing Tommy he was immediately distraught. He turned away and rushed out of the store. The man behind the counter laughed.

—Scaring off the customers, you are.

Tommy said nothing. The man who had emerged from the cell had disgusted him. He was fat, grossly overweight, rolls of flab. He was sweating. His thinning hair, his double chin. He was fat and ugly and obscene. He was familiar too. The dole office? Yes, probably, that was his world too. The dole office. This filthy frightened man, caught out by Tommy, scurrying away, an animal in flight. The eyes that could not look ahead, could only look down, look away. His eyes.

—Have you got the right money?

Tommy did not hear. The man behind the counter repeated his question. Tommy blankly banded over the money, took the video wrapped in the brown paper bag. He left, wordlessly.

Tommy had just looked into a mirror. His reflection was repulsive.

10
The Great Schism

When he was fifteen, Tommy began attending the North Blackburn Baptist Church. This was something he did not tell his family. Maria had refused to allow her children to sit in on religious instruction at school. These classes at the local primary school in Clifton Hill were taken by volunteer officers from the Salvation Army and Maria would not allow her children to be indoctrinated by Protestants. Tommy and Dominic visited the library the one hour a week allotted to religion. There, with assorted Irish and Italian Catholics, Greek and Serbian Orthodox, with the Muslim Turks, they would tease and make jokes and avoid the lazy eye of the librarian. The Bible was Easter and Christmas, the biblical stories glimpses of fables in storybooks.

Tommy began attending the Baptist church because he badly wanted to fuck Helen Thompson. Nights were furious thrashings, a silent, self-conscious masturbation interrupted by sleep or the sudden intrusion of a human sound.

Helen. He did not know what fucking was but he knew he wanted to fuck Helen. This was the sound, always there in his head, always. Fuck Helen. Fuck her. Fuck her. The thought of cunt obsessed him, its complete unfamiliarity. He didn't even know what cunt looked like, not really. He once spied his mother undressing. He was held by the beauty of this foreign body. Breasts and hips, a glimpse of the snatch. He turned, ashamed of himself for looking, and that was when the repulsion came. For it was his mother. And the repulsion was not for her body but for himself.

Tommy fell in love with Helen Thompson.

She was attentive to him, thrilled at bringing a convert to the church. But he stuck out, was visibly a stranger. They were all fair and pale, these churchgoers. The women, unlike his mother, wore the most insipid of fashions. No bright colours and no black, nothing tight fitting. The men wore shirt and tie, and they too appeared unattractive. Not that some women there were not pretty, not that some men were not handsome. But they did everything to diminish any spark. Only the ministers, when they got fired up, were impressive. They spoke tough and looked strong.

Helen was upset when they, went to Sally Manton's party and he got drunk, shitfaced on cheap wine. He put his arm around her and tried to kiss her. She pushed him off.

Pull me then, he thought.

But he said nothing and stopped going to church. There was nothing there, the only thing the sermon. He couldn't believe without the evidence of God's face: the statues and the icons, the angels in the architecture.

But he did not stop believing in God. This faith had its basis in one feeling, a sensation he carried with him all of his life: that he was always watched. Even though he would have preferred not to believe, to be atheist, he experienced God through this fear. It might just as well be the Devil. It did not matter to Tommy whether this presence was good or evil. It being unknown was what terrified him.

•

Tommy was watching *Twin Peaks*, Tommy was watching Oprah Winfrey and Sally Jesse Raphael. Tommy was watching the World Cup Soccer beamed in from Italy. Tommy was watching television.

It had been two months since he'd paid his rent and an eviction notice had been sent. He threw it on the laminex bench; it fell among a scattering of paper and bills. He promptly forgot it.

He had split up with Soo-Ling on the phone.

She spat out her contempt. You could have told me face to face.

He could make no reply to that.

She cursed him. To hell and beyond.

He did not leave the house and was nursed by the confessions from the television. American confessions. Fast confessions that could wrap themselves easily around the commercial breaks. From eleven o'clock till two o'clock he heard of rape and murder, adultery and thievery, of betrayal and falsehood. Dull-eyed adolescents told him that they had sex with their priests, their teachers, their fathers, their mothers. Best friends destroyed best friends. Children were bashed and left in strange cities by parents who no longer wished for responsibility. The world was crumbling, he heard it every day, and he rejoiced in the end. He no longer felt separated from anyone.

A man can spend much time masturbating. It is a pleasure readily accessible and requiring little effort. Tommy recognised that he was spiralling out of control, that a big bang was approaching. He was running out of money and he had no will to work. The rent was long overdue and there were bills for gas and electricity, for phone and insurance. He had made one decision. He wasn't going to take out insurance on the contents of the flat again.

And he spent a lot of time wanking. Watching television.

The man who was a mirror had frightened him. He compared his own body to the apparition's. His own fat body, his weak ugly body.

Tommy was also spending a lot of time dwelling on the past, on everything he could remember of youth. And he was shocked at how little made sense, or rather, that he had so little memory of time. Everything was all jumbled up and he had no idea how life had happened.

His thinking was made easier by the Serapax. Tommy had three doctors whom he rotated, ensuring a constant supply. One, however, had grumbled while filling out the last prescription.

—If you want another script after this one, I'm going to recommend you see a psychologist.

Tommy nearly laughed in his face. Will a shrink give me a fucking job, cunt, will a shrink pay my rent?

Instead, he said nothing, took the script and told himself to find a fourth doctor.

And everywhere there was the crow. They had started descending, he had not noticed them before, in the bushy yard of number 127 across the street. They sat on thick elm branches and watched him. He looked out from his bedroom window into their eyes. Their ugly black eyes, their rings of white.

Failing. Had he always been a failure, he wondered. He didn't even want to think of that.

And he wondered why he had decided to pursue graphics at tech. He thought of his first fuck, with the prostitute, and he sometimes thought of how he missed Soo-Ling. He thought of finding a job and he thought of killing himself. He thought of his first friend at school, the quiet Glenn Anderson. He thought of childhood, he thought of adulthood. He thought himself unlucky and he thought himself a fool. He couldn't stop thinking. That's where the Serapax helped. It didn't stop him thinking, it just made him incapable of remembering. The pills cancelled everything out. Just one thought at a time.

Tommy was watching television.

There were pleasures, that must be said. He found that he enjoyed not washing regularly. He used to wash every day, a shower in the morning. Now it all depended on his mood. He sometimes sniffed at himself, particularly after a wank, and was disgusted at the sweat. He'd wash then. There were days when he just walked around the suburbs, five dollars budgeted for the day, and he'd sink two drinks around lunchtime at the Blackburn Pub. With the pills, that made him high. Sometimes he was so delighted by not having to deal with the confines of office life that he thought himself lucky, blessed. He enjoyed waking up at

whatever time he needed to, enjoyed zonking out to the television. He enjoyed his rediscovery of music. He played tapes
from 1982, the Go Betweens and David Bowie. This was not a
life without moments of joy.

But he also knew he was spiralling and he knew he was
incapable of decisions, let alone action. So he had started
praying again, for he needed a miracle. He had not seen his
parents' for weeks, not contacted them, not answered the phone.
It rang still, and he let it die to silence. Though Maria came in
and out of his thoughts, his father was hardly a presence. Artie
was a shadow in his life. Kind, considerate, not brutal. But there
seemed nothing there in the past that spoke of a connection.
Arthur Stefano was a man of action. And Tommy was inert,
possibly had always been inert. Tommy knew his mother's
favourite colour was red, that her favourite movie was *Letter
from an Unknown Woman*, that she was a socialist and that the
food she adored most was a fig fresh off the tree. Of his father he
knew nothing. Artie Stefano was a man who worked.

Tommy was watching television. He no longer moved far
from the perimeters of his flat. The bedroom, the kitchen, the
lounge room. He was safe inside, wasn't safe in the streets. He
refused to go outside in the morning or the early evening, when
people were going to or returning from offices, from factories,
from warehouses. He had no uniform. Even the short walk to the
milk bar, to buy the milk, to buy the bread and chocolate, even
that short work required effort and interaction with strangers. He
was anxious, barely moved his lips. He was happiest alone. He
neither watched the news nor read the papers. He was aware—
how could he not be for there were regular bites interrupting his
favourite programs—that something menacing was happening in
the Middle East. The American President—what was his name?—
was gunning for war. There was an Arab, real wog looking guy,
who had invaded another Arab country. He knew this. Kuwait
and Iraq, but he was a little confused as to which was the

aggressor. He switched channels with the remote control. He was bored of the world.

He was not paying his bills, he was facing eviction and he was hoping for a miracle. Till then he was content to watch television and to wank. He was disgusted at himself but his only joy was in the restful calm of his inertia.

Once, every fortnight, he took his dole form into the office.

•

It had been a harsh winter with much rain, and the Tuesday morning brought the first taste of summer. He awoke with a strong sun's light on his face. He jumped out of bed and pulled a blue shirt and Mickey Mouse boxer shorts over his naked body. He did not wash, he ran the toothbrush five strokes along his teeth. He turned on the television and made a coffee.

He watched *Play School*. He enjoyed the show, the remarkable consistency it had to his childhood memories. *Play School* and *Sesame Street*, they were familiar and loving. He watched till the end and when it finished he placed a video in the player. The machine, coughed and a woman being fucked was on the screen. He rewound, watched the mechanics of sex backwards, and stopped at the moment he liked best. The rest of the video now bored him. An image, the woman's face caked in come. He was not even erect, but he came. He switched off the video. On the television an Aboriginal man was discussing the early resistance to white settlement. Wiping his semen off with an old T-shirt, he felt a repugnance. He threw the T-shirt into a corner of the bedroom.

Dole day. He filled out the form. Name. No, he had not changed his address, no he was not enrolled in study. Yes, he was looking for work. He opened the Yellow Pages and searched. Medline Graphics, Moorabbin. Bluestone, Fitzroy. No, he had no dependants. No, he had received no monies over the last fortnight. He signed and dated. He was aware that he was liable for prosecution if any of the above information was false.

He folded the paper, stuck it in his shirt pocket, put his track pants on, his runners. He had four dollars in coins. He placed those in his pants' pocket. He switched off the television and walked into Box Hill.

The line was long. The Punk Princess and the slags with kids were sitting on the orange plastic seats, talking, out of it. He waited behind a big man who was shuffling impatiently, new to this. He waited, nodded to the man at the counter and handed in the form.

The walk had been pleasant, the enjoyable rush of sun on his skin. But he was sweating by the time he arrived at the dole office. He walked into the toilets and brushed his lips with water. He was hungry but refused to eat outside of home. Too expensive. Instead he walked into the cool auditorium of the mall. He went, in and out of shops, looking at merchandise. It was eleven o'clock and the stores were full of women. Women with prams, women with shopping bags. He walked through, his head buzzing. He had learnt to control his hunger, rarely eating now, but he was still ashamed of the flesh on his body. He was still pinching at his flab, wishing it to disappear. He refused his hunger and walked out of the mall into the sunshine. He stopped and watched a young kid busking with a saxophone. He closed his eyes and felt the sunshine. This was a certain happiness.

—When all is darkness, when everyone else has disappeared, Jesus will still be there.

He opened his eyes. Outside the barber shop a man was proclaiming God. He was handing out small leaflets to whoever would take them. Most people were shunning him, but he persisted, talking God and flashing paper. Tommy thought, Jesus freak. But the man was familiar. He walked over.

The man was enormous, all soft weight. He was wearing, even in the heat, an ill fitting suit, a white shirt. His brow was wet, his black hair flat and damp across his scalp. His fingers were fat bulbs. He turned and Tommy and the fat man looked at each other. They blushed at the same time.

The fat man turned quickly away and his voice rose in pitch. Jesus will save you as long as you open your heart to him.

Tommy walked over, enjoying the cruelty, stood beside the fat man,

—Can I have one of those?

The man stopped talking. Slowly he handed Tommy a leaflet. An image of the Cross, a prayer, the promise of heaven. Tommy glanced at it then pocketed it.

—Do I know you?

He wanted to be mean to this man, to express his disgust at this man. This obscenity.

—I don't think so.

—Yeah, I know you from somewhere.

The man hung his head, his body slumped. And in that moment Tommy felt a pain at his own ruthlessness.

—Sorry, mate, I was thinking of someone else. Tommy began to walk away.

—Wait. The fat man followed him. He extended his hand. They shook.

—Neil.

He smelt of sweat but something else besides, something bitter. Tommy sniffed. Neil continued to speak.

—You have seen me before. They were walking towards the porn shop, further down the square. Tommy could see the bright red X across the road. They stopped on the corner and Neil pointed.

—You have seen me there.

Tommy felt an acute shame.

—You visit there regularly, don't you?

Tommy shook his head.

—That was put there by the Devil, to tempt us. He tempts me, tempts me all the time. Then Neil laughed, a loud arid long laugh, and his body shook. But I've been saved and Jesus forgives me. Have you been saved?

Tommy shook his head again.

—Would you like to be saved?

—No, it's all right.

—Would you like a drink?

The two men stared at each other. It had been a long time since Tommy had been in the company of another person, so long he could barely remember being social. He hesitated.

—I'll shout you, urged Neil.

Tommy thought of the four dollars in his pocket.

—Okay.

They took the bus along Whitehorse Road and got off outside the Blackburn Pub. All through the journey Tommy was aware of Neil's bulk, the looks he received from the strangers on the bus. Did he hear a small child say, Look at those two fat guys? He turned around. The child was silent, next to its mother, drawing circles in the window dust.

They got drunk, very drunk, and Neil did not stop talking of his love for God. God was everywhere for Neil, in the beer and in the bar, in the silences between them. Can't you feel him, Tom, can't you feel him? Tommy was only aware of the sweet numbness of the alcohol.

—You're a Papist, Tom, you know that? Neil was not looking at him, looking morosely into his beer. Orthodox, Catholic, it's all the same. You don't worship God but men, those fucking arsehole priests. That is not God, Tom. You hear me?

Tommy nodded, drank more beer.

They ended up at Neil's house. It was a tiny place but with a large front yard overrun with weeds and naked rosebushes. Inside, the smell was of decay. Scattered clothes everywhere, soiled dishes on the sink. The toilet, when Tommy went in for a piss, had a black ring around the enamel basin. It stunk of shit and urine.

Neil had plonked a cask of red wine on the table. He grimaced as Tommy entered the room.

—Sorry, mate. This is all I have.

The television was on. Scenes from America, the President

standing strong against the Arab foe. Neil was excited by the images and the rhetoric, ignoring Tommy, focusing on the small screen. Tommy glanced around the room. Nil, nothing on the white walls.

—There will be war, Tom, you know it? War, but not just a war, The War. This is the Apocalypse, Tom. Understand? It's all in the Bible.

The man was excited, his eyes glistening. Tommy stared back at the screen. Pictures of aeroplanes, bombers. Neil was almost chuckling in delight. And Tommy realised that for Neil the Apocalypse was a wish, a desire. He was suddenly aware that he too wanted this cataclysmic shower, he too wanted a deluge. Both men were laughing.

The sound of a key in the door. A youth entered the room and Tommy recognised the charcoal grey pants of high school. He was no more than sixteen, dark and thin. He hardly glanced at the two men around the television.

—Darren, this is Tommy.

The boy looked up, looked down.

—Anything to eat? His voice was shy, surprisingly feminine.

—Toast.

Darren groaned. He made his way to the back of the house.

—My brother. Neil's eyes were still on the screen.

The boy came back out, changed into jeans and a red sweatshirt.

—I'm going out.

—Where?

—Out.

—Coming home tonight?

—Maybe.

—You've got school tomorrow.

The two brothers looked at each other.

—I know, conceded Darren.

—They'll kick you out if you wag too much.

—Give a fuck.

Neil sprung up. The boy jumped back, frightened.

—I want you back here tonight.

Silence.

—Hear me?

The boy nodded.

As the youth left, Tommy heard the muttered, Fuck you.

They continued drinking, watching television. Late in the evening Neil ordered pizzas, and Tommy, watching the big man eat, found it impossible to put any of the food in his own mouth. Neil grabbed at the pieces, munched on them quickly, pieces of vegetable and meat and grease lined his chin. The food fell and stained his shirt. Tommy looked away. He clenched his stomach, feeling the fat, feeling the excess. He could not look at the other man.

They finished the cask and Neil descended into a maudlin monologue about God and about his own weakness and failures. He was not even talking to Tommy, he was talking to the air. He was praying.

—Pray with me, Tom.

Tommy sat still.

—Pray with me. Neil had stood up and was walking down the small hall, he opened a door.

—Come, he ordered.

Standing up, Tommy realised how drunk he was. He followed the other man into the room. It was not very large, more a storeroom than a bedroom; a single mattress covered by a dirty sheet lay on the floor. There was nothing on the walls except for a small framed picture of Christ. Neil knelt before the picture. He indicated for Tommy to kneel with him.

Christ, his wrists and ankles tied up, his body scarred. An angel and a cherub contemplating him. The picture was dark except for the soft colours that illuminated the Saviour's body. Tommy hung his head and listened to the man's monotonous prayer. He noticed stains running down the wall, underneath the picture. Stains like the trails of slugs.

The room smelt. Of man.

Forgive me Jesus sweet Jesus forgive me for my weakness. Forgive me Lord for my drinking and my dirty thoughts. Forgive my friend here for his being led astray by the Devil. Lord show yourself to him. Save him Lord. He is a good man.

There was a groan. Tommy opened his eyes. Neil had slashed at his arm, a slight wound but it was bleeding. He did it one more time. The blood was falling in large drops on the floor. Tommy struggled for the knife.

—What the fuck are you doing?

But Neil's face was ablaze with a light and a happiness. He was joy.

—Jesus loves you, he whispered to Tommy, and he stood up. You can sleep here tonight. He walked out of the room, his arm red, the blood still falling on the floor.

There was also a trunk in the room, half covered by a blanket. Tommy lay on the mattress and closed his eyes. He instinctively reached for his cock to begin a quick wank, but he knew that the tortured Christ was above him. He drew his hand away and turned on his side, away from the Saviour's gaze. He was immediately asleep.

He awoke with shit in his mouth, his head throbbing, his throat sore. He rolled off the mattress. There was a tightness that hurt in his bladder. He walked out of the room.

It was all confusion in the darkness, and the unfamiliarity of the stranger's house stopped him. He could hear a tap dripping and he made his way towards the sound. From one of the rooms there was a light and Tommy, aware of the late hour, stepped quietly down the hall. He glanced into the lit room, the door half open, and he stopped still. A low wattage of light. Neil was kneeling, his back to Tommy, folds and folds of fat, a wide expanse of arse, a shocking white in the soft umber cavern of the room. Tommy walked towards the light. Darren, naked as well, was standing above his brother, his dark brown skin glistening. A prayer, spoken, chanted, sung. The youth's eyes were closed but he stood there, bored, no expression; below him the filthy white body was quivering. Tommy walked into the room. Darren, startled, opened his eyes—terror—jumped back. His cock, erect, a thin trace of spittle shone in the light. The prayer stopped.

He heard his father's voice, a scream: You animal, you don't do that to your brother, you don't do that to anyone!

The sound that came from Tommy's throat was animal. He rushed into the room, grabbed the man's shoulders and threw him away from the boy. Neil lay on the floor, his body shuddering; a smile, an illumination on his face. There was a whisper, Do it. Do it. Do it.

Tommy looked on the misshapen body, white paste. And he kicked, and he kicked again. His fury was savage. He smashed his foot hard onto the man's face. And he kicked again. The sound was a crack. A shot of blood jumped in the air. The blood was seeping down the face, covering the cheeks, the eyes, pouring from the broken nose. Tommy raised his fist and the youth jumped on him, took his arm. Sound came back.

—Stop it, stop it! the boy was screaming. Tommy's fury evaporated. Everything was still. The boy had gone to his brother, cradling him. Neil's body was all scars and lines, a tattoo of wounds. Tommy stepped back.

Darren raised a weary face.

—Go. Said softly.

On the floor Neil, bloodied, hands clasped, was praying, was smiling in an ecstatic bliss.

Tommy turned, left the room. He put on his socks, his shoes. About to walk out, he turned around and looked at the picture on the wall. Automatically he crossed himself. He almost ran out of the door, into the night air.

Disorientated, frightened, he wandered the unfamiliar streets until he hit the coned lights of Canterbury Road. Cars, even at this early hour, were zooming past. The night was chilly and he was shaking. His head was hurting from the alcoholic poison. He passed an all-night store and fingered the change: in his pocket. The four dollars were still there. He bought a sausage roll and a can of Coke and gulped them down. Outside in the night again he was aware that he was being watched, a thousand eyes were on him. The night sky was a blanket of crows.

He walked to the station and sat in the small cavern of the shelter. A woman in blue uniform was shivering, waiting for the first train. She refused to look at him. He, in turn, hardly registered her presence. He wanted to extinguish the brothers, the crow, the sickness inside him. He wanted to escape the dark. There was only one place he could think to go.

He hesitated in front of the house. There was a light. He knocked on the door and Soo-Ling answered. She saw him and instinctively reached for him. He tied himself in the embrace. He was unaware that he was heaving.

She was shocked by his smell. She remembered the stink of his sweat, had missed it, but tonight she also smelt the acrid alcohol. She dragged him into the house and into the bedroom. He fell on top of her and she allowed him to cry. His eyes were red, his skin pale. She was horrified at his thinness, his once solid body was now weak and limp. The flesh had gone from his face. He felt wrong in her arms.

He was trying to kiss her. She resisted and then happily devoured his mouth. He pulled her dressing gown off her shoulders and began a soft biting at her breasts. His hands were everywhere, his fingers in her cunt, on her thighs, pushing hard into her bowels. She tried to pull away.

—No.

—Please. His cock was free of his zip, it was rubbing against her leg.

—No.

—Please. He was on top of her, pushing into her. She closed her eyes. He was fucking her furiously, and though she could not feel the pleasure, she wrapped herself tight in the strangeness of his new body. She was providing warmth and he shook her with the force of his thrusts. When he shuddered, when he screamed his orgasm, she too was wet with tears.

They sat apart. He could not look at her. Nothing had disappeared. The crows were still outside the door, his head was full of what he had seen, the obscene man slobbering over the child. The bloody face. He had hoped for an escape and he had only brought the ugliness to Soo-Ling. He got up and she reached for him. He pushed her hand away.

—Stay. I won't go to work.

Her pleading shamed him. He pulled up his zip and walked out.

—Stay, she screamed. He shut the door and walked outside to greet the darkness.

He reached home, exhausted, craving sleep. He put on the orange tubes of the heater and turned on the television. The rays of light soothed him. He walked into the bedroom and opened the trunk. He searched, blindly. He pulled out the icon and prepared to pray. Then he noticed that the Virgin's face had gone black. She was burnt. He brought the icon out in the light, delirious from the terror, but her eyes were still not visible. The baby Jesus looked on him with adult sadness. He threw the icon across the room, then scampered after it, pleaded with it to change, pleaded, to see the light of Her grace once more. It remained black. He took it, placed it back in the trunk and went to the television. He wrapped himself in front of the flickering images, his face criss-crossed by blue light. He closed his eyes and prayed. He was not praying for sleep. He was saying to God that even if eternity was the Devil, then he wished for it. He closed his eyes and prayed for death.

Tommy was watching television.

11
Radiation

Maria knocked hard on the door. Silence greeted her. She knocked harder, bashing at the cheap wood. Artie steadied her hand.

—Enough, Maria.

She was crying now. She called through the door.

—Tom, Tommy, speak to us.

The silence again.

—He's not here, Maria.

She would not move.

—Tommy, she called, I'm calling the police.

—It's all right, Maria, he's all right. He spoke to Dominic the other week. He's all right.

Then where the fuck is he? Her Greek was a scream.

—He'll call when he's ready.

She banged on the door one more time. From down the corridor an old woman poked out her head then quickly shut her door again.

Artie led the crying Maria down the stairs and to the car. He glanced back at the block of flats. From his son's window he saw a curtain rise and fall.

Tommy had lain huddled in the middle of the floor, his head in his hands, listening to his mother's pleas. When he heard his parents begin to walk away he had crawled to the couch, lifted the curtain and blinds, watched the figures descend the stairs.

The telephone was off. Unpaid bill. He had begun to pay the electricity in instalments, terrified of a world without light, without television. He had begun sleeping in front of the screen now, unable to deal with the wide expanse of the bedroom, all that space. He allowed the TV to play all hours, fell asleep to the shuddering light.

The mirror taunted him. Even though he was hardly eating, even though he had lost the taste for food, he was angry at his body's refusal to change. The white pale flesh of his thighs, the large stretch of his belly. One night he took a knife and traced a path across his stomach. He would cut here and there, he would cut away at the flab. Then his legs, carve his calves and thighs, the round paste of his arms. He threw the knife in the sink.

He still watched his pornography but he had placed the blackened icon on top of the television, so every time he masturbated to the revolting images on the screen, he was watched by the Madonna and the Child. The porn had ceased to be even a sexual pleasure, instead it was now simply a need, as reflexive as breathing. He hated it, *hated it*. Hated the models who paraded their bodies on the screen. But he could not resist it. Every morning, every afternoon, every night, he drained himself, tugging away at his flaccid cock. Bile, everything was bile.

And he was hunting for Neil. He walked the mall of Box Hill, the car parks and shopping strips of Blackburn and Nunawading. He scouted Shoppingtown, walking aimlessly through stores, looking for the demon. But Neil eluded him.

He called Dominic, aware that his exile from family would not be tolerated for much longer. He got Eva,

—Jesus, Tommy. Where the fuck have you been? Are you all right?

—I'm fine, he answered.

—Jesus, Tommy. Eva went silent. Come around, now. We'll come and get you.

—No. He almost shouted. He lowered his voice. I just need to be alone for a while, understand?

—We're family, Tommy.

I know.

—Is Dom there?

—Yes, he wants to speak to you. She hesitated. We love you, Tommy.

Her words were devastating.

Dominic came to the phone. His voice was harsh.

—Where the fuck have you been?

—Here.

—You know Mum's worried sick about you.

Tommy wanted to smash the phone booth, wanted to kick and kick.

—I'm sorry, Dom. It's been a hard time.

—Are you working?

He was stunned by the question. He hadn't thought of work for months.

—Yes, he lied.

—Where?

—In the city.

—Doing what?

Fucking children, you cunt.

—What I was doing before.

At the same moment both brothers realised that every conversation between them, throughout their lives, every conversation had revealed nothing. Dominic waited for an apology. There was only silence.

—Go and see Mum and Dad.

—I will but not yet. I've got some thinking to do.

—About what?

—Jesus, Dom, give me a break.

—You don't deserve a break, you useless piece of shit.

Tommy hung up. The relief was immediate, an intensity, and he was laughing as he left the phone booth. His duty done, his brother cleaved from his life, he walked confidently, happily home.

•

Tommy was talking to the television. The Americans kept coming in, discussing sex and love, marriage and failure, deviance and truth. Daughters were raped and sons were bashed, women slept with their fathers and fathers slept with their sons. Tales punctured by commercials and flashes from the Persian Gulf.

War. Tommy so desperately wanted war.

He was made sick by the force of his need to communicate with the figures on the television. Watching a woman berate her daughter, live in front of a studio audience, the daughter sullen and overweight, watching the mother yell at the daughter for her laziness, her refusal to respect her parents, Tommy wanted to reach inside the television and place his hands around the older woman's throat, to destroy her. Destroy her. He was talking back to the television.

He wanted to kill them all, every last one of them, every person on the planet.

He was seeking Neil. Neil had become his twin, his real brother, more concrete, much closer than either Lou or Dominic. A vacillation between love and hate. He fantasised, and this was arousal, that he would find the man again and that he would kill him, slash at his meat, tear him apart, finish him, destroy the ugliness. And he fantasised that he would meet the man, fall on him, be immersed in his weight and solidity, that he would kiss him. Pray together. Two women were sixty-nining on the screen, tongues around clits, finger fucking. He came, moaned, shook his head violently, stopped the flow of images. The screen returned to daytime television. He looked up at the black face of the Madonna. He swiftly turned around.

There was no-one there, but he was sure that someone was watching him. God or the Devil or the Crow. It did not matter. He wasn't alone; even his home had become polluted, unsafe. He never ventured into the bedroom any more, he was even frightened by the confined space of the toilet. When he shat, he shat with the door open, the television loud. Close to sound.

When he pissed, he pissed in the kitchen sink, watching the television. He couldn't shower, he couldn't close the door to whatever was watching him.

And he prayed and he prayed.

•

He found Neil again. He was walking the streets, window living. A group of schoolkids were smoking by a bus shelter. One of the boys was smoking alone. He looked up as Tommy passed. The boy, Darren.

The boy did not recognise him. Tommy walked past then stopped, waited for the bus. The orange vehicle came and Tommy boarded with the schoolkids. They were loud. The boys were teasing the girls, the girls were giggling. Darren sat next to a tall youth, dirt blond hair, a white school shirt open to the navel. A hairless pale chest. Tommy sat two seats back. The tall youth called down the bus.

—Kirrie, when's the party?

—Who says you're invited? mocked a young girl.

—I reckon I am.

—Saturday, ain't that right? called a dark short youth.

The girl turned in her seat, faced the boys at the back of the bus.

—Pirizzi, you're not coming.

—Take that, you wog, called out the tall youth.

—Fuck you!

The bus driver, yelled sharply, No fucking swearing. Everyone laughed. Darren called out, the trace of child, high, still in his voice.

—Sorry, cunt!

More laughter. The tall youth punched the boy's shoulder affectionately.

—Shut up, you Abo cunt.

Darren giggled.

Of course, the dark skin; the boy's features were not white.

But Neil, Neil's pale coarse skin, he was all white? Neil was the ugliest white man Tommy had ever seen.

The bus stopped and Darren grabbed his school bag from the floor, lifted himself over the seat and rushed to the back door. Tommy rose and followed him.

He walked behind the boy. When Darren reached his house —Tommy recognised the feral lawn—the boy turned around and faced him.

—What do you want?

—Is Neil home?

The youth walked up to Tommy, quizzed his face. Then he smiled.

—Oh, you're the guy from the other week.

There was definitely the feminine in the boy. Neil must have done that to him. The girl in the boy's smile. He invited Tommy in.

The house was empty, warm, it stunk of tobacco. There was mould in the cups on the coffee table. Darren went into a room and Tommy sat on the couch. The youth emerged, changed, in an Adidas top and black shorts, a bong in his hands. He sat beside Tommy.

—Want a cone?

Tommy nodded slowly.

The boy took an envelope from his pocket, began a mix. The first rush of smoke was elation. Tommy lay back on the couch.

—Neil's probably at church. The boy smirked and drew his knees to his chest. You a Jesus freak?

Tommy shook his head.

—Me neither. The boy packed another bong. He handed it to Tommy. The man inhaled, the water bubbled. Darren placed a hand on Tommy's knee. Tommy slammed it away.

—Okay, okay. The boy straightened his body and rose. He was hurt. Tommy couldn't look at him. It felt good to hurt him, very good. He wanted to continue.

—Neil will be back. You want to stay?

Tommy nodded.

Darren hesitated, and then spoke rapidly.

—Neil, he don't have many friends. No-one. Church people but they never visit. You're the first visitor for a long time. He likes you. Darren bit his lower lip and a smile played around his mouth, almost a cruelty: he thinks he can save you, you don't have to tell anyone. He's just lonely. Then the smile disappeared, and his voice was earnest, pleading. What you saw the other night, he's lonely. He's really lonely. It doesn't hurt me, it isn't sex, it doesn't happen often. Understand? He's my brother, he looks after me, he loves me.

Tommy said nothing. Understand? pleaded the boy. He don't really hurt me, he wouldn't hurt me.

The man, the boy, they looked at each other and there was silence.

The boy left, banged the front door shut.

Alone, the room, the house, hummed. Tommy walked to the prayer room, opened the door. The picture on the wall. He fingered the face of Christ. A fresh stain ran down the wall. The blanket was no longer on the trunk. He walked over to it, tried to raise the lid, then noticed the small lock. He left the room and searched the house, opening drawers, looking on shelves. He found a hammer and walked back into the room. The lock was fragile. Four sharp blows, they pealed, they clanged through the house. The lock gave way and Tommy sat in the echoes. The humming continued. He listened but heard no-one human and he raised the lid.

A mountain of paper. Bills and receipts. Letters and cards, school reports. Tommy dived into the pile, fingered the bottom of the trunk and found an old photo album. Rectangular pictures of the past, gum trees and the shimmering of a lake. Photos of women with children, black women, wide flat faces. Naked children playing in the lake. Smiles, food being roasted around a bush fire. Two envelopes hid in the back of the album. He opened the first. Black and white photographs, two men in leather masks, a naked young body tied to a crucifix. The naked body being penetrated by a cock. The naked body with splashes of semen on the chest and cock. He put the photographs back. The second envelope was thicker, packed. He opened it.

And then he knew why he was here, why he had been brought here. He recognised the faces. The three schoolgirls, their young faces smiling, the blue and white checks of the school uniforms. And the pile of newsprint detailing the abductions, the rapes and the murders. He sat back. Carefully he piled the clippings back into the envelope, pushed it to the bottom of the trunk, closed the lid. In the stoned silence he waited. No voices, nothing called. He attempted to fit the lock back onto the hinge of the trunk. He had broken it. He had broken it, it would not fit.

The picture was watching him. Tommy pressed his lips to Jesus's face. He knelt and he prayed. He closed the door and left the house. The day was becoming night and the clouds in the sky were wisps of red and yellow streaks. He breathed in the air and his lungs expanded. He was alone, the trees, the sky, it was empty of birds. He was alone, invigorated. He began to run and by the time he reached home, sweating, his breath short, his thighs aching, he was smiling widely. He went into the bathroom and turned on the shower. He closed the bathroom door behind him, scrubbed at his skin, every inch of it, shampooed his hair, brushed his teeth, brushed savagely for minutes, washed and brushed his body clean. Naked, dry, he sat in the centre of the room, looking at the Madonna's face: still black but that was because she was waiting. It would be soon. The television was off, he sat in darkness. He sat in the silence of his home, no noise, no light, but he was not frightened.

He fell asleep and awoke to the light of early morning. He stretched and looked at the television. He wandered into the kitchen, put on the kettle. On the bench was a black video cassette. He tried not to look at it. But as the kettle boiled he turned on the television. He stirred the coffee and then, knowing this was an instinct not an act of will, he grabbed the video and slotted it into the player. The familiar grind of machinery. The naked bodies filled the screen. He came quickly.

Without looking at their faces, he prayed his apologies to the Mother and to the Child. The room was yet not his. He left the television on, dependent on—it was *crucial*—the noise. He prayed and promised that soon, very soon, all this would be gone.

12

Conversations about drugs, war and food

They'll win, I reckon.

Lou had the branches splayed in front of him. The pungent smell of marijuana was intoxicating. He was stripping the tightly clumped heads, tearing off the leaves.

—Keep the seeds, warned Dom.

—What do you reckon? Lou insisted.

Dom looked up from the scales.

—I'm sick of hoping they'll win. They never win.

He was to be proved wrong. Collingwood, one of the oldest and one of the most popular of the Australian Football teams, had not won a Grand Final for over thirty years. In 1990 they won the flag.

—How much can I have?

—A couple of Safeway bags full.

Lou whistled happily.

—Cool.

They were in the shed, huddled by an occasionally spasming electric heater. The light from the globe was strong and their faces were pale. The youth was sucking on a straw.

Eva hated the plants, worried about the police. Dom's greenhouse ran the narrow gutter of the side of the house, concealed from the street by a tall brick fence, and the plastic roof was opaque. But Eva feared the helicopters.

—We don't need to do this, she said.

But Dom wanted a boat, he wanted to pay off the mortgage

and, probably most acutely, he was sick of carpentry. His back hurt, his wrists were getting stiff and he had worked for fifteen years. That already seemed too long a time. And Eva was pregnant again. He needed the money.

—Has Tommy rung?

Lou shook his head.

—Fucking jerk, I want to slam him. He knows how worried Mum gets.

Lou paused from his task, played with the wet straw.

—I wrote him a letter.

—Did he answer it?

—No.

The brothers sat in silence. Dominic broke it.

—Got a girlfriend yet?

Lou blushed. He shook his head.

—Why not?

—Don't know.

—Dunno, mimicked Dom, He glanced over at his younger brother, then ruffled his hair.

—Don't!

There were ten plants in the greenhouse. An expert gardener, Dom had sired hefty booming plants. He was to make a profit of ten thousand on the dope and this did not include the generous share he was to leave aside for himself and Eva. Lou would sell most of the dope he received among his friends, keeping a little stash for himself. He found marijuana at times perplexing, the stone more anxious than pleasurable. But sometimes, if relaxed, if alone in the house, just dreaming, he found a smoke intensified every pleasure: the sensual pleasures of food and touch, of laughter and music. He was to get four hundred dollars from his dealing. He could have made maybe double that, but he preferred to give chunks of it away.

—Mum said Eva's spoken to Soo-Ling.

—Yeah, she has.

—How is she?

Lou asked the question with a forced bravado. But he spoke low, into his chest. Dom noticed.

—You liked her, didn't you?

—Yeah, I thought she was cool. Lou wiped his mouth, quickly, the back of his hand.

—Well, she's upset of course. That dickhead of a brother fucking dumped her. Dom shook his head in disbelief. Where the fuck is that arsehole going to find another girl like that?

Lou fingered the plants. He couldn't wait to wash. The pungent smell was all over him.

—What do you reckon's wrong?

As soon as he asked the question he realised that he did not want to hear Dom's answer. He adored his older brother, sometimes with a passion so intense he knew it to be sexual, which embarrassed him immensely. But he found Dominic complacent.

—He's always been like this. He can't look after himself.

The shed was tall and wide. Tools lay all over the shelves and a wall of packed boxes was covered by blankets. Lou stood up and walked over to the boxes, lifted the covers and searched.

—What are you looking for?

—Your old records.

Dominic pointed to the plants.

—Finish this first.

—Nah. I want a break.

Dom stood up and walked over.

—There they are.

There were twelve boxes of vinyl. Seven inches and twelve inches. Lou's face flushed with excitement. Dom watched his brother take down a box and begin flicking through them. I should sell them, he mused, but he as yet was unable to part with them.

Dancing, more than anything, Dom missed dancing with all his soul.

The records were all marked. D and T. Mostly D.

—You got lots of Tommy's as well.

—He left them behind at Mum and Dad's. He didn't want them.

Lou pulled out a record.

—Kraftwerk?

—Yeah, I didn't realise I had that.

—It's Tommy's.

—They did dance stuff, kind of, didn't they?

—Dunno. Yeah, I guess. Dominic began singing a song in his head. He clicked the beats with his tongue.

—Can I borrow it?

—Sure.

Dom returned to his seat and began putting the dope into small sandwich bags. He looked around. Lou was lifting down another box.

—No, you don't.

—Just a second.

Dom groaned.

—Mate, get over here. This is going to take all night otherwise. I've got to go to bed soon.

The boy returned to his seat, a group of records in his hand. He put them down and began stripping the plants.

—What else did you get?

—Led Zeppelin. The one with that photo of the old man on the cover.

—That's mine, said Dom proudly.

Lou checked his records.

—This. The Velvet Underground and Nico.

—Tommy's, said Dom.

—Do you like them?

—Some.

—I like that song 'Heroin'.

—What else you got there?

Lou showed Dom the record. A twelve inch single.

Dom smiled.

—Musical history, mate. That's the original.

—Yeah.

—Don't lose it, warned Dom.

—Promise, answered his brother. He even crossed himself.

The single was 'Rapper's Delight'. The Sugarhill Gang.

They finished stripping the plants and Dom packed the dope into shopping bags and placed them in an old trunk under a work table. He covered the trunk with thick cloth.

—Want a joint?

Lou hesitated then nodded. He watched his brother roll the cigarette. Dom's hands were raw, the skin puffed, lined and savage.

—Have you ever done heroin, Dom?

The older brother stopped his work.

—Why you asking that?

—Just wondering.

—Are you using? Dom's voice was suspicious.

—Dom, no, Jesus! I'm just asking.

—No, I haven't.

Dom lit the joint, puffed and handed it to Lou.

—Have you?

—Once. The boy said it quietly.

Dominic slammed the table hard. Lou jumped back.

—You fucking little idiot!

—It was just once, wailed the boy.

Lou was silent.

—Who?

—I'm not telling.

—You fucking will!

—Would you want me to tell anyone about this? Lou pointed to the trunk. Dom was silenced.

—Fair enough. He shook his head, threw his hand towards Lou. The boy jumped back again.

—Just once?

—Promise, just once.

Dominic looked sad.

—Man, it's fucked. What are you, grade eleven, and you've had smack? It's unbelievable.

He passed the joint.

—Things are really fucked.

They finished the smoke in silence. Dom butted out the end and stood up. He touched his younger brother on the shoulder.

—Lou, please, don't do it again. But if you do, tell me.

The boy was quiet.

—Tell me?

—Yeah, sure. Thanks, he added.

—And I'll fucking kill you, all right? And the cunt who gave it to you.

Dom wiped the table clean, brushed the scales and hid them in a tin box. He placed a cloth around the scissor and utensils and sprayed the air with deodorant. It did not totally eclipse the smell of the drugs but it bathed it in the more subtle hints of pine.

•

—And what is the cup of manna?

The preacher's strong blue eyes surveyed the circle. The chairs formed a circle and he was at the head. Ten sets of eyes rested on him, waiting.

—In the Arc of the Covenant, continued the preacher, there are the Ten Commandments; the code for life for every, *every* human being on this planet—black and white—there is Aaron's Rod and there is the cup of manna. Is manna the chequebook? Is that what God's covenant with us promises? Wealth? Money?

Again, his eyes surveyed the room. He smiled.

—Remember the children, of Israel. They were loaded, his thick American accent carried a giggle, they were loaded, rich with jewels and coins when they fled into the wilderness. Do you think that they could buy their provisions in the wilderness? With money?

The old woman, Mrs Carey, started shaking her head. The preacher smiled at her, encouraging.

—No! Of course not. The cup of manna is not money, is not gold, it is God's promise to us that if we wash ourselves in the water of his Word, He will provide. Understand? That is faith, this is faith. He banged the wood of his chair with his fist. God will provide.

A chorus of amens.

Darren, whispered, O thank you, Lord.

—And what sits above the Commandments and the cup of manna in the Covenant? Above the Commandments? he insisted. You must know, he pleaded with the circle. Come on, tell me. Tell me.

—Jesus? Mrs Carey answered shyly.

—Bless you! screamed the preacher and he laughed, a rich strong laugh that echoed through the sparse wooden building. The Mercy Seat, the seat with the blood of Jesus. We are washed in the blood of Jesus, God's supreme promise to us. In Jesus we are pure we are cleansed we are free. Understand? In Jesus.

Darren shook, an exhilaration. O Jesus, wash me pure. The eleven bodies clasped each other's hands, kissed, brows met brows in joy and contemplation. He experienced it, Mrs Carey's arms around his shoulders, her frail arms, loving him; Jesus was there, loving him, washing him clean.

The preacher broke the communion with a cough. Neil was conscious of the sweat on his palm, and he drew his hand away, apologetically, from Mr Chee's frail grip. He was blushing now as the final prayer was read. When it was finished, the group quickly dispersed. Neil took the broom and the pan and began sweeping the floor.

The Church of Christ was small, empty except for the ten rows of pews, the lectern on the raised stage. A simple white crucifix on the wall. He swept away at the dust. When he had finished he wet his face, scrubbed his hands. The gaunt preacher approached him as he came out of the toilet.

—Neil, here's your money.

The man handed him four twenty dollar bills.

—We sure appreciate you helping us out like this, Neil.

—That's fine, Mr Weston.

Even though the lay preacher preferred to be called Bill, Neil found it difficult to refer to a man of God by his first name. So he still called the American by his surname. Or simply, sir.

—Neil, we'll need you early on Sunday. Expecting a big congregation. There'll be a lot of setting up.

Neil nodded. This Sunday they were to pray for the soldiers going to serve in the Gulf. War seemed inevitable. He wondered if he would be paid any extra money. The American read his thoughts.

—You know it's hard for us to afford even the eighty we pay you a month, Neil. We do appreciate the work you do for us. You're one of the most committed of Christians.

—Thank you, sir. It was a mumble.

—God provides, doesn't he?

—Yes, sir.

The American grinned. He thought Neil was slow. And undisciplined. He prayed that Neil would find, through God's grace, the ability to overcome the laziness that compromised his covenant with God. That body, that obscene body, it spoke the Devil's work. Bill was thin, exercised religiously—of course—every morning, swam three times a week. His was a fit body for Jesus's army.

—This is it, Neil, this war. This is the war that was prophesied. It's all there, in the Book. Russia defeated, the ancient battle between Christian and Jew, Christian and Arab.

—Yes, sir. Neil spoke slowly. Is it the Apocalypse, Mr Weston?

—Sure is, Neil. The man was smiling broadly. Sure is.

—I'm ready for it.

—I know you are, Neil. But we'll be there, we'll be there with Jesus in the end. But we got to continue our work. We've got to fight the enemies of God, and that includes the Iraqis, because the Antichrist is rising. Can you feel it, Neil?

The two men nodded to each other.

—Should we pray, Neil?

The two men knelt on the floor, heads lowered, almost touching. The American led the prayer.

—Dear Lord, the time of your arrival is here and we pray that we have the strength to resist the temptations of your adversary, that we may live through the horror of the approaching war to preach your gospel. May our boys in the Gulf, all of them, American and British, and of course, the Australians, may they be victorious in their battle against the forces of evil. Above all, Lord, may our enemies hear your Word, may our enemies be washed in your Word to be reborn in your love. Amen, Lord.

There was a silence. Weston rose to his feet.

—Five-thirty, all right, Neil? On Sunday morning?

Neil slowly rose to his feet, with assistance from the American.

—You know, Neil, the American spoke warmly, gluttony is a sin.

The Australian blushed. He could not look up. Weston patted his shoulder.

—Now, now, didn't mean anything by that. I know you're a good Christian. None of us is perfect, boy, we're all prey to temptation.

He smiled. And waited.

—Thank you, sir.

—That's fine, Neil. That's what I'm here for.

Neil watched the man walk away.

The banks were closing and he argued with the young woman at the door to let him in. She gave him a filthy look and pointed to a clock on the wall. She slammed the door.

Filthy Indian bitch.

He went to the automatic teller and pressed four buttons. He placed three of the fresh notes into an envelope and slid them into the machine. He had two accounts. This was for his brother.

Neil was saving as much as he could for Darren. There was one thousand dollars already in the account.

Neil had no doubt about his relationship with his brother. It was evil. When Neil was drunk, the devil made the excuses for him. Look, he wants it, look at that little faggot. Look at how he walks past you, almost naked, swinging those hips. He's asking for it.

In the morning, knowing the enormity of his sin, he would grab the knives, the nails, the cut glass, draw blood from his skin. His body, his mind, his heart was filth.

He crossed the road, entered a phone booth and dialled a number. Five rings and it was answered. She was drunk.

—Yeah?

—Mum, it's Neil.

—Everything right?

—Yeah, Mum. How are you?

—Good, mate. Real good. Need some money. You got any money?

—Mum, I told you. I'm putting it away for Darren.

—I need it, I'll look after my son.

Then why don't you, why don't you take him, you fucking black cunt?

—Are you still living with Steve?

—Why?

—Are you?

—Of course. Me and Steve love each other.

—Then Darren's staying with me.

There was a cackle on the other end of the phone.

—You can keep the little poofter. Her voice lowered. Don't trust him, Neil, right? Don't believe him. Stevo did nothing to him, nothing. It was that little cunt that tried to do things to my Stevo. He's sick he is.

—Mum, he's your son.

—Yeah, well he's welcome here any time he wants. But he

can't order me around. If he lives here he lives with Stevo and me.

—Stephen's a cunt! Neil exploded.

—None of that language, and you pretending to be a bloody Christian and all.

—Sorry, Mum.

Her voice was soft.

—That's all right, love. You a good boy. She shifted tone again. I need some money, love.

For grog.

—What for?

—Life's hard, Neil. You know that.

—I'm on the dole, Mum. Like you.

—Darren told me you got a job, at the church.

—That's nothing, Mum, just a pittance. I do it for the church.

—I wouldn't worry about the fucking church, Neil boy, they got money, they always got money.

—That's not true, Mum. They're not like the Catholics.

She snapped at him.

—Don't you go insulting my faith.

—Sorry, Mum.

She softened again.

—Can you send up some money, Neil?

—Got none.

—How about Darren?

—No.

She was angry.

—By law I should be minding his money.

—It's my money, Mum, till he's eighteen.

—Well fuck you then, you look after the little shit.

—He needs you, Mum.

She began to cry.

—I'm bad, aren't I? It's been hard, Neil, been real hard. You kids are lucky. You don't know what it was like for me. The rambling began. He knew the litany. Your dad walked out on me.

I got no education. I wasn't a servant, I was a slave.

He watched the neon lights on the telephone screen. Thirty cents worth of time remaining.

—Got to go, Mum.

—I understand. She was almost incoherent, sadness and alcohol.

—Mum, it's near the end, you know.

—What is, love?

—The Apocalypse. This Gulf War, it's in the Bible.

—Love, it's their Apocalypse, not ours. She laughed. Son, there'll be plenty of Apocalypse. I promise you that, love.

The line went dead.

He went back to the church. The building was dark, cold. He switched on the radio. A commercial for mufflers. The radio announced the five o'clock news. He emptied the bin and lined it with new plastic. The selling of the State Bank, the Kuwait refugees, the war between the Serbians and the Croatians, the chance to win free tickets to *Goodfellas*. The lead-up to the Grand Final. He began a sweeping again, aimlessly, for no reason except he didn't want to go home. He was safe here, with God.

•

Soo-Ling knocked on the door. Once, softly. Three times hard. The blinds were drawn, there was no light, but she was sure she had heard the sound of television. There was no noise now.

—Tom, open up. It's me, I need to speak to you.

There was nothing.

Her mouth was dry. And her anger ferocious. She began banging at the door.

Inside, Tommy was curled, a ball, rocking back and forth.

—Open the fucking door!

Soo-Ling kept bashing away, determined.

The door finally opened.

She was shocked at how thin he was. The chubbiness in his cheeks which had first attracted her to his face was now all gone.

A soiled white T-shirt was hanging off his body. He was un-shaven, his hair long and greasy. She stared at him. He attempted a smile.

He did not want her inside. She was a past he could raver return to. But she waited there, shivering, and he invited her in.

The smell was a pollution. She closed her eyes. Sheets, a blanket on the floor, in front of the television. The refuse of junk food and its wrapping on the floor. She could smell urine everywhere. He sat on the floor, cross-legged, not looking at her.

She could not begin to speak. She had arrived determined and prepared. A speech. But nothing was possible now. She wanted only to get as far from him as she could. He was not even the body of a man she once knew, once loved. She cringed. The smell of piss and McDonald's. She sat on the sofa, felt a wetness under her thigh. Her feet kicked at an object. She looked down. A porno. A woman with a dick in her face.

—I'm sorry, I'm sorry. Tommy lunged for the magazine and hid it into his chest.

Soo-Ling put up a hand. It said, please, this is nothing.

He was dying. His eyes, enormous in the sunken face, were tearful.

—Tommy, Tommy, she whispered, what's wrong?

He recoiled from the sound of her voice. It terrified her. She stretched out a hand and he jolted back, pushing against the television. The hurt tempered her compassion. She sat back.

—So how's things, Tommy?

The question sounded like, a blasphemy.

—Fine, fine. He still refused to look at her.

—Are you eating? She could not avoid this question.

He nodded, quickly.

—Are you sure? You look so thin.

He defiantly shook his head.

—Nah, I'm still too fat. Always have been.

—Tommy, look at you, you're so skinny.

He scratched at his body. He pulled at skin. He tugged at his

T-shirt, wishing to go beyond to the fat, to escape the obscenity of his obesity. She returned to the subject of food. Everything else seemed dangerous.

—Should I get you something to eat? I can drive down the road to the Chinese take-away. How about I do that?

His refusal was violent. He stood up, walked agitated back and forth across the room. Her eyes followed him.

—I'm not hungry, I'm not hungry, I tell you, I'm eating.

—Have you seen your parents?

He stood still, faced her. His face was a howl, an immense sadness. She bit her lip. He reminded her of a Christ on the Cross.

She prayed.

—Lord help me.

Tommy heard her whisper. He could not touch her. That would spread the contamination. Instead he walked towards her, towered over her and implored her with his silence. Stop.

And she did.

Soo-Ling got to her feet. She touched him softly on his arm and this time he did not panic from the touch. He looked down to her hand.

She walked straight to the door and said the word without looking back.

—Goodbye.

They both waited a beat, paused as the door shut between them, before they both started crying.

•

Tommy crouched on the floor, turned on the television, flickered furiously through the channels. Every image disturbed him. He left it on static, requiring the radiation, but jumped to his feet and searched a shelf. He kicked the porno, looked down, grabbed it and flung it against the wall.

Go to hell.

He switched on the radio, hustling through stations. Words

made him sick. He found a song, an electronic shudder of noise. Only beats and snatched words. He poured the music through the flat, the decibels corrosive, and finally lay relaxed on the floor. The bass of the music massaged his body and a voice above him ordered: Beat dis, beat dis. His fingers searched the floor and curled around a pen. He pushed the ballpoint and started slaying at his arm. It wasn't until the pen scratched and punctured skin that he was at peace; he smelt the blood flowing. The light from the television. Even with the music screaming he could hear the crackle of the screen. Keeping on slashing at his arm, he relaxed into sedation. The dancing electronic light, the crashing beat; he could no longer hear the demons shrieking in the room next-door.

Soo-Ling had come to tell Tommy that she was pregnant and that the child, he must know, was his. But his decay had forced her to a different decision. She arrived home and called her mother.

—Mother, it's me.

There was a rush of words. Soo-Ling interrupted. Can I speak to Dad?

Her fist was tight around the telephone. A man was breathing, waiting.

—Father, I ask your forgiveness. And she collapsed into waves of crying.

She arrived a week later with a suitcase. He answered the door. She bowed her head and she was again welcome in his house. That night, alone in her old bedroom, she stopped crying. She ordered her heart to steel. In humbling herself before her father she had forsaken the one refusal that had given her pride. She now felt shame. She closed her eyes, she cursed Tommy, wished his death. She abandoned God.

13
War

Sisters, brothers, we'll make it to the Promised Land. A young woman was singing, kicking at her chair, a song in her head. A bomb in Jerusalem. The young woman's hair was straight and limp, her face a raw paleness. Tommy watched the television, blood and limbs, hysterics and prayer.

The dole queue was slow and crowded. The last few months he had noticed that they were beginning to penalise recipients who came in late in the morning or came in the afternoon. There were less staff waiting at the counter, they pored over the form. He never made it in by the morning. From time to time he forgot, had to argue his case the next day. They knew him by name now. And he knew the others in line with him.

She was Mattie. Matilda really, but she hated that name. She was pale from blood and pale from drugs. She always sung, to herself but audible, in a surprisingly deep and soulful voice.

Brothers, sisters, we'll make it to the Promised Land.

There was Stan. Stan Kandouris. He was permanently stoned. He hated work and he was hoping to move over to sickness benefits.

—You should get on the pension, mate. Stan pointed to the scars on Tommy's arms. They'll certify you, dead set, with bullshit like that. Stan spat on the floor. On the pension you don't have to go through this crap.

There was Clara. Forty-three and deeply embarrassed to be there. She shuffled in, eyes down, always neat, always her clothes ironed. I am a secretary, she told Tommy once, have been for twenty years. Her eyes were frightened. I'll get a job, soon, she had also said, just a matter of time. She was still shuffling in.

Barry. Kev. Theo. Sandra One and Sandra Two. Van. Vin. Tim. Ahmed. Candy with the big tits. Savirio with the big hands. Candy and Sav had begun fucking. There was Oprah and Phil and Sally Jesse Raphael on the television. There was a bomb in Jerusalem. In some Muslim church. Nineteen dead, a hundred and forty wounded.

—Fucking Muslims.

Mattie had dated a Muslim last year. He dumped her.

—I hope they blast the shit out of them.

—Fuck off, sulked Kev. He was sitting across from her. I hope that Hussein blasts the fuck out of those lousy Jew bastards. He pointed to the television. That's what Saddam wants to stop.

—Fuck all of them, said Stan.

Clara stood up, walked to the toilet.

—Don't swear around her, she don't like it.

Kev laughed.

—How about you, bitch, you fucking swear all the time.

Mattie held up her finger and turned back to the television. She half sang, half spoke.

—*Suckers to the side I know you hate my 98. You're gonna get yours.*

There was the Punk Princess, all chains and earrings and tattoos. Who'd give her a job? This week she was talking to the single mums, they'd made up. But they didn't trust her. Weirdo, they called her. Everyone called her that. No-one knew her name.

Tommy, had washed this morning. They were to arrive tomorrow. He did not know who they would bring. The police? A sheriff? Did Australia have sheriffs? This was the last night he could legally stay in the flat. He owed them one thousand two hundred and thirty-six dollars. He knew he could never afford to pay them back. He washed, showered, even cleaned his teeth. He drank his coffee.

He filled out the form.

Have you sought work for the period 8/11/90–22/11/90?

He was happy, this time, not to go through the humiliation of looking through the Yellow Pages. He marked the space. No.

If not, why not?

Jesus was a maker of crosses.

Have you changed your address since your last application? Yes.

Where and why have you changed address?

He left the spaces empty. He signed the form.

They called his name. When he slipped the form into the woman's hand she glanced at it, bored, was about to stamp it and then she stopped.

—Mr Stefano, the form is not complete.

He insisted that it was.

—Excuse me. She walked away. Tommy turned and stared at the people waiting. They all avoided his eyes.

The woman returned.

—Mr Stefano, you'll have to sit an interview.

And so he waited.

They called his name and the young man James, with the slicked back hair, the polite smile, waved him into a booth.

—How are you doing, Tommy?

—Fine.

James laid Tommy's dole form on the desk.

—Tommy, have you looked for work the last fortnight?

Tommy shook his head.

—Why is that?

—I have my work.

James looked up.

—What's that?

Tommy squirmed in his seat and said nothing.

—Tom, we can't make a payment to you. This is a contract. James pointed to the dole form. If you don't honour your side of the contract, which is to look for work, then we can't pay you.

—I don't need your money.

Your money is death.

—You've changed address.

Tommy nodded.

—Where are you living?

—You don't need to know.

The two men stared at each other. James was dying for a cigarette.

—Tom, I'm going to make an appointment for you to see one of our counsellors.

—I don't want to.

James sighed. Fuck this idiot, he thought to himself. He fingered his cigarette packet.

—Up to you, Tommy. But this means you're off the dole.

Tommy stood up. His task here was accomplished. He shook James's hand.

—Thank you.

As he was leaving he spun around in the doorway.

—I don't need you any more, I got Jesus, he said.

James nodded politely, watched the man walk out and flicked a cigarette to his mouth.

Tommy walked through the shopping mall. Young mothers pushing prams and old men sitting, smoking, reading the newspaper. He waited for the bus and recognised a stranger from the gym. The man was gargantuan, his body all ripples and muscles. His neck thick. All this flesh is evil, thought Tommy, it is all disease. He tried to smile at the stranger. The man turned away, uncomfortable, a glare on his face. The bus arrived and he made his last ride home.

He stood in front of the door, his knees weak. He had not been in the bedroom for weeks. He pushed open the door. It was all a coldness. The room was leaden with ice and the heavy weight of stink. He crossed to the trunk and lifted the lid. The video cassettes, the magazines. He doused the contents of the trunk with methylated spirits. He struck a match. In the living room he took the icon in his hands. The Virgin's face was still dark, her eyes invisible in the black. The Son stared back at him, aloof and reproving. Soon, thought Tommy, I'm going to make it up to you.

He left the house, the icon in his hand. And in his jacket pocket a knife.

He walked to the sinner's house, clutching the icon. Two young boys followed him, taunting him. Jesus freak, Jesus freak. He kept touching the knife in his pocket, and even though the air was warm, he kept his jacket on. He passed a school, young girls skipping rope. He was making it safe. In the treetops the crows were waiting.

He knocked once and he heard a bang, a short curse, a shadow in the glass. Neil opened the door. His cheeks were dark with stubble, there was no surprise in his eyes.

—I was expecting you. Darren said you'd been around. He let Tommy in.

Neil was drunk, he stunk of it, the pharmaceutical stench of red wine. Tommy placed the icon on the table.

—What's that?

Neil took the icon then grimaced.

—Papist shit.

The television was on. The preparations for war.

—Want a coffee?

Tommy shook his head.

—Want a drink?

Again a refusal. The two men looked at each other.

—What do you want?

—Let's pray, Neil, I've come to pray with you.

The room was as before: the filthy mattress, the trunk. The lock had gone. Neil knelt on the floor before the picture of Jesus. A fresh stain of slime trailed down the wall, bubbles had dried to form white flecks in the plaster. Neil's mouth moved to worship. Tommy listened to the murmurs from the foul mouth. He did not pray. Instead he drew up close to the picture on the wall, studied Jesus. Tiny black writing beneath the image: *Christ After the Flagellation Contemplated by the Christian Soul, Diego Velazquez, National Gallery of London*. The Christ figure, his arms and legs tied to a post, his anguished eyes, had been painted with a virile economy. This was a man's body, even in his humiliation. The strength of Jesus shocked Tommy who was more familiar with the softness of the Catholic God or the anorexic poverty of the Orthodox Christ. Tommy's eyes moved across the picture; the dark flesh, the thick folds of cloth wrapped around Christ's genitals. Tommy's own cock responded to the sensuality and to the suffering. He turned sharply from the wall and looked down at the gross man on his knees.

—Shut up, he screamed at him.

—I'm just praying, pleaded the abomination.

Did you let them pray, you bastard, did you let the little girls pray, you fucking cocksucking scum!

Tommy watched the man pray. Neil's eyes were closed, his head high, his hands outstretched. Tommy moved behind him.

I did it.

Tommy was looking at the Christ. Jesus was speaking.

I killed them, I cut them up. I was foul with them.

Why did you do it?

I wanted to feel what their bodies would be like, what their young bodies would feel like, to touch.

Neil turned round. He was staring up at Tommy.

To foul their pure white bodies. Do you understand that?

Yes.

—No! Tommy roared. You're sick. You're evil.

The man dropped his head, his lips moved silently.

—What? ordered Tommy.

Yes. Jesus had spoken. Evil.

Neil sighed, his massive frame shuddered, jerked, danced.

—Oh Lord, he whispered, I am exhausted.

Neil raised his head, eyes closed, to heaven, to Christ. He was waiting.

The first cut was swift but the fleshy bulk around the man's neck did not allow for a deep incision. There was a line of blood and Neil had begun a groaning. Tommy grabbed the man's head, tilted it back, and stuck the knife straight, deep into his neck. The blood, black not red, splashed across the wall, on the print. Jesus was bleeding. And then, quickly, in a rapid succession of jabs, Tommy sliced through the oesophagus. The head lopped clumsily to the left side, veins and meat exposed. Neil's body collapsed into his arms and Tommy held him, caressed the greasy hair. He looked down at his hands, everything scarlet. And there was the smell. Tommy staggered out of the room.

The Madonna's face was still turned away from him, her eyes shrouded in the darkness. He heaved, retched. His arm hurt, the arm that held the knife. The exertion had been violent. He felt a pressure between his legs. He looked down, he felt the wetness inside his underpants. He groaned.

He tightened his grip on the knife's sharp blade, the pain was a relief. Eyes were still watching and in the empty house he blushed. The stain on his pants.

He walked into the living room. On one wall there was a mirror and on the mantelpiece there were photos. Darren in school uniform, a large dark woman. He stood before the mirror and looked closely into his face. His eyes were animal, savage and thirsty. His skin rough and taut around his skeletal face. His body appalling, an ugly mass of flab and skin. He started, slowly, then with a rapid pleasure, to scratch at himself. The lines of blood were a comfort. He looked away from the mirror. The Virgin's black face, her vanished eyes, reproved him. He looked back in the mirror. Neil's face. He smashed his fist into the glass. The slivers, like rain, fell around him.

He knew now what to do. He took a long angular piece of glass, he ripped at his stomach. The pain stopped him, not the blood, not the visibility of his own meat. He stopped, gasped for air and tried again. He screamed and doubled over. He looked at the Virgin, at the sad eyes of the child-man Jesus. They were still unsatisfied. He touched the stain on his trousers, it stung as if it were poison.

A sound. He turned around.

No-one there.

They were all waiting.

He lowered his pants. His cock was thick, the head peeping from underneath the foreskin purple in its wetness and from its work. He wished it expunged. He said the Lord's name and took up again the sliver of glass. Blood was seeping all around him. The mat of hair on his groin had coloured crimson. He took the sliver, closed his eyes and slashed.

The pain, when it came, was all white light. From somewhere beyond the room there was a shuddering howling. He opened his eyes. The pain was gone and there were loops of fine veins falling across his thigh. A petit testicle, a pale jelly, lay seeping on the floor. His grip tight, his palm bleeding, he held his severed penis in his hand. Again, the Lord's name on his lips, praying for this one moment of strength, he raised the sliver and sliced. A thick injection of blood slammed against the mirror, spraying the room. There was pain, there was the penis in his hand, and then there was relief. He crashed onto the coffee table and the contents tipped around him. He looked across to God. The Virgin's face was white, her eyes a gleaming pride. The child-man too was smiling. Then there was the pain, a cruel annihilating pain. But, there was the face of the Virgin, her smiling eyes, forgiving him, loving him. The pain drank from her light and he was swimming towards it. Her love and, finally, her respect vanquished all.

There was the fluttering of wings, the angry flight of the demon.

Then there was nil.

•

Lou and Dominic cleaned out Tommy's life from the flat. The landlord, furious at the damage done to his property, at first refused to let the family in. But Artie, patient even in his grief, assured the man that all damages would be paid for. But Artie refused to clean up the remainder of his dead son's life. And it was inconceivable that Maria would do it.

Her grief was all hysteria and shame. The funeral had come close to destroying her. For her family their concern over her health helped stay the horror they experienced at recognising the suicide.

—Jesus Christ! Dominic stood in the middle of the room, looking at the charred walls. The room still smelt of fire.

Lou took a large green plastic bag from his brother.

—Let's get to it.

There was little remaining to pick up. A few prints off the wall, a family photograph, the baby Luigi in Maria's arms; the surly Tommy and the swaggering Dominic, arms folded, next to their tall father. The photograph miraculously unscarred. Lou popped it in a box.

—I'll do the bedroom, he yelled to his brother.

He noticed the cold first. He shivered and looked around. The bed, the walls, the mirror, all black. The wooden trunk was a sad pyre. Lou carefully lifted the lid. It fell to ash and charcoal. Inside, everything was black. He lifted fragments of cloth and stuffed them inside the plastic bag. He suddenly had to stop as he came across an album of photographs. He opened it and the photographs were all curled and bubbled. Nothing remained. He was crying as he slipped it into the bag.

Lou hesitated. The disjointed shapes of video cases, a mad sculpture; the corroded blackened magazines, the mad catalogues of the body and its uses; he touched a smoked crucifix. He hesitated, then threw it in the bag.

He took the pornography and pushed it deep in the bag, to the back, to be hidden under the dust and wood and fabric. He cleared the trunk and then kicked at it and kicked at it. It fell to rubble.

Dominic was at the door.

—Found anything?

Without looking at his brother, Lou shook his head.

—Let's go then. There's nothing left. Even the stereo's fucked. I just grabbed some kitchen stuff.

Dominic walked over to his younger brother and put a hand on the kneeling boy's shoulder.

—You all right?

Lou nodded and got to his feet. His grip was firm around the bag. Dominic reached for it but Lou refused.

They walked out of the flat, not bothering to lock it up behind them. Under the sun, in its warmth, Lou stood still and closed his eyes.

—You all right?

Lou smiled at his brother.

—It's good to get out of there.

On the way to their parents' house, Lou stopped and placed the rubbish bags in a large industrial bin. The bang of the shutting lid echoed through the quiet street.

The brothers drove home. Wordlessly, music on the radio.

The weekend after the funeral, in Edithvale, a bayside suburb at the edge of the city, a little girl, in her checked school uniform, walked to the corner milk bar to buy a bag of lollies and some milk for her mother. She went missing, abducted, and she was never to return.

INTERMISSIONS

Fremantle, 1947

A black crow had followed Artie Stephens for all his life.

It had been there at his birth, he had been told, as it had been at the birth of his brothers and his sisters. It was there on the day of his marriage, a shining liquid sky and the gentlest of breeze. Showered with confetti, holding Maria's hand, he noticed the birds keeping a vigil on the stone fence of the Orthodox Church. He stared straight into one bird's opium yellow eye and shivered, wished to raise his arm to Catholic prayer. Instead he tightened his grip on his wife's hand and wrist, silently mouthed a promise to her. I will protect you.

Artie fell in love with Maria at a barbecue, watching her slim dark body, watching her bring out trays of salad, meat and bread. She had smiled shyly as her brother Peter introduced them.

She spoke Greek and he blushed.

—He's an Aussie, laughed Peter.

—Sorry, replied Maria, her English crisp and broken.

—I'm half Greek, half Italian, he stammered, and his face was a wide grin.

—He's an Aussie, insisted Peter, and slapped him hard on the back. Maria had continued smiling. The few words she spoke to him that afternoon, in the company of men, they were all in English.

He had kissed her, a stolen kiss, unasked, he had kissed her lightly on the mouth while she was alone in the kitchen preparing peppers in oil. He tasted lemon juice on her lips. She had returned his kiss and then quickly stepped away, refused to look at him. He stammered an apology to her in his half forgotten Greek and he went back to the men circling the fire.

For Maria, the kiss had sealed a fate. No-one else would have dared, she told him much later. Are you kidding, in my brother's house, no-one would have dared touch me. It had excited her, the risk of that kiss. It promised the adventure she had not yet found in this strange land, this large and ugly land.

He wooed her. He sent flowers and took her dancing. He helped her learn the intricacies of Australian English. She taught him caresses in Greek and pleaded with him all the time to speak his love in Italian. It is, she said to him, pouring over magazines featuring black and white pictures of Rossellini and Bergman, Anita and Frederico, it is the language of love.

Her brother Peter had been appalled. He liked Artie, admired him as a man, they worked together affixing engines to the new hulls of automobiles, but Artie was not Greek. And his wife Aphrodite warned him against the crime of giving away his younger sister to a stranger.

—You'll regret it, ordered Peter. We'll find you a Greek husband.

—He is Greek, insisted Maria.

—He's a bastard, warned Aphrodite, half and half. Your children, think about them, they will not be Greek if you marry him. This warning silenced Maria.

But he was too handsome. She had found, to her shame, that she had fallen in love.

Maria had arrived in Australia convinced that love was a sham. She found the new country strange and isolated, no life in the streets and no passion in conversation. Unlike the other Greek women who worked with her, threading textiles through the clanking teeth of industrial machines, she was an Athenian, a girl of the city, and she had known the delights of cafes and bars, of dancing and movie houses. She felt as estranged from the village gossip of the migrants as she did from the harsh bigotry of the Australians. Melbourne had disappointed her, horrified her: the closing of the bars at six in the evening, the tame unsophistication of a colonial town. She fell asleep, every night, dreaming of Athens. Sipping coffee, eating cake, smoking cigarettes on the sidewalks of Kolonaki; being pestered by the kamaki, the seductions of boys walking along Sygrou. Every night she prayed to God to return her, one day, when she had made some money, to return her to Greece.

Greece, where she had been the youngest girl in a family of four daughters. Greece, where her lazy generous father had no money to pay for her dowry. Greece, where she was ordered to marry louts and idiots. Or take up whoring, her father had screamed at her in a drunken rage, we cannot afford to marry you to gentlemen. No, she had grown into a woman who did not believe in love. She had seen the cruel contract of marriage and knew herself to be poor. She was attractive, she was hard working, she was intelligent and a dancer. But she was poor. No man in Greece had bothered to ask her to be his wife.

Artie Stephens told her, quietly, in English and in Italian, I Love you. Ti Amo.

And I love you too, she had breathed it into herself.

—We must marry in the Orthodox Church, she ordered. I will not be a Catholic.

—Yes, he had promised.

—And our children, they will be raised Greek?

He had hesitated. I'm a mongrel, he had thought, I don't know what that means.

—Yes, he had answered. Above all, I promise to protect you, to protect our children. Maria, there will only be you. Understand. Only you.

She had said yes and that night, whistling 'Summertime', he had skipped home, back to the little room in Carlton he shared with three Italians. I will buy you a house, he had promised, I will give you everything. In the blackening sky, a crow had swooped. He stopped. Cursed. I will protect you, Maria, he whispered. Defying the bird.

He had always thought of the bird as female. His Nonna had always spoken of a young woman's ghost.

—How do you know, Nonna? he once asked, when still a child.

—I've seen her.

His grandmother had been a strange sullen woman who rarely left the house. She sat in the kitchen or on the back verandah, with her tobacco, chewing and spitting. The grandchildren spent their childhoods in the shadow of her glare. But she had a special affection for Artie, she called him Turro, and only to him was she indulgent with her love. She took to teaching him her own language, small words, affections. And dirty words.

—Poutsa! he'd repeat and she would clap her hands and laugh and laugh.

—Skata? She'd grab him and hold him in her black folds. She told him the stories of her faith, the Panagia, Christ's mother, a statue in the holy church of Agia Sophia who cried tears of blood and would, continue to cry tears of blood till Constantinopli was once again returned to the Greeks. She told him of the ancient gods, and it was Apollo who was his favourite, riding the chariot across the sky each dawn.

But mostly, especially if anyone else but Artie was in the room, she would just glare.

Only English and Italian were allowed in the house, his Papa's orders. And as the children began school, it was, finally, only English that was spoken. The Greek had been forbidden Nonna, a condition of entering her son-in-law's house. Even her title was foreign. Not Giagia, but Nonna, or Nana.

•

It is, 1947 and the war has been over for two years. At fourteen, Artie Stephens' body has already been hardened by work. There is nothing of the plumpness, the softness of childhood. He is handsome, and dark but his Mediterranean face has been scorched by an alien sun; a fairness is emerging, in the hair, even in the shade of the skin. Stephens is not his real name. As war became inevitable, Artie's father took the children to an office, and there, silently watched over by sullen men in suits, he changed their name from Stefano to Stephens. Though this did not completely save Papa Stefano—he was interned for three months, at the beginning of the war—it did mean his children could continue their schooling. They faced insults and exclusion from the sons and daughters of patriotic Australians but the school in Fremantle included enough dark faces to allow for the possibility of mateship. Artie's best friend, Victor, was Portuguese, his sister Sophia's best friend was the Greek girl. Marina. When Italy became an ally, the taunt *dago* lost some venom and became a word that simply marked a difference.

It is 1947 and a black crow is circling the sky.

Artie laid down the saw and winked at the man beside him on the wall.

—Too hot.

—Yeah, mate, too bloody hot.

Simultaneously the two men lit cigarettes and put them to their lips. Bill spat, and watched the thick white trace spin to the earth below. His brow, his neck, his shirt was wet, his hair plastered flat under his cap.

—Too fucking hot, he emphasised.

Artie was silent, he was looking down at the harbour. They were sealing a roof and the building faced the firm solidity of the Port Authority. Beyond that, there were the ships in the port. Beyond them there was only ocean.

—We should chuck it in, go for a swim. Artie searched the street below. Where's Pickett, you reckon?

—The old bastard. Down at the pub, of course.

Artie winked again. But Bill was apprehensive.

—We can't leave, mate. Sorry, he'll skin us.

The sea. Artie didn't speak the words, he had no need to. The gentle breeze off the water was invitation enough.

Bill was shaking his head.

—Sorry, mate, can't do it.

It was not the possibility of a beating from Pickett that halted Artie. Not only work had made him strong. He had painfully, almost from the beginning of boyhood, with a fierce determination, skilled himself at defiance. Pickett did not dare hit Artie with the ferocity he showed to his other apprentices. And Pickett's strength was nothing compared to Papa's. Artie's father had softened, weakened with age, but his fury could still make the boy flinch. Only the Nonna dared to challenge Papa: even after so many years the mother and the son-in-law still refused to show each other a respect. But Papa did not spare the children. Artie had been slapped when they had returned from the Town Hall, their name no longer dago but Australian—he had addressed his father with the English word, Dad. The slap had knocked him to the floor.

—Papa! the man roared at Artie, and he kicked at the boy.

He may be getting old, thought Artie, but he'll still knock me out if Pickett docks me a day's pay.

—Right you are, Bill, we'll wait till knock-off.

The other youth relaxed.

They bathed nude, behind the bluestone jetty, a small cove with rocks on its beach instead of sand, and one which families never entered. They were hidden from the town, visible only to the passing ships. The two young men became boys again, splashing in the shallows. The sky was still.

The water was cool, refreshing, but by the time Artie was climbing home along South Terrace, he was sweating again. He turned left into Little Howard Street and walked up to the house. In the afternoon sun, children were playing. His brother Joseph was sitting on the porch, his eyes closed, a soft snoring. Artie took a seat beside him.

—Good day?

Joseph's eyes remained shut. He grunted.

—Too hot, eh?

Another grunt; the smell of oil, of grease and fish.

—You smell, mate, you need a wash.

—Piss off. Joseph opened his eyes. He turned back to the house.

—Nonna's upset.

—What's happened?

—She got a telegram. Some dago in Greece just died.

Along the horizon a ship was lazily sailing into view. Artie got up and entered the house.

Joseph closed his eyes again.

His Nonna was silent in her chair. No tears, just the silence. He glimpsed the blue paper in her hand. He walked over and touched her face. She grabbed his hand.

—Can I read it, Nonna?

She offered him the telegram. *Kosta Papapouchitis died. Stop.*

—Who was he, Nonna?

—My brother.

He sat with her, searching for tears, but there was nothing but the soft sounds of her breathing. He got up, she released his hand, and he went outside to the water trough to wash. He removed sawdust and sweat from his neck and underneath his arms. He put a coffee on to boil and sat silently and patiently next to his Nonna.

The arrival of his Mama and sister Sophia, both in starch blue uniforms, returned order to the house. His Mama had frozen on seeing the telegram.

—What does it say, she whispered to her daughter. Sophia read out the three stark words. Mama started a moaning. The expected tears of mourning satisfied Artie. But his Nonna remained dry eyed. Artie went outside again, joined his brother on the front steps.

—Everything all right?

Artie nodded.

Joseph spat at a mangy dog that shuffled close to the boys. The dog whimpered arid walked away.

—I didn't even know she had a brother.

—Who cares? Joseph had no time for Nonna.

—How was work?

—Same.

—Where's Papa?

—The pub.

The boys fell to silence. On the horizon the ship was still sailing. Artie scooped his hand across the sea, willing the ship, the water, the world to rest in his palm. A crow danced in the air above him. He dropped his arm and went inside.

Papa arrived and noticed his wife's red eyes.

—What's happened?

—Nonna's brother Kosta has died. The man nodded slowly and glanced over to the old woman. Her glare was stern, there was only contempt. He shook his head, was about to speak, and instead walked out to the trough. Mama sighed a relief. They ate dinner in silence.

The next day, as he returned from work, his Nonna was waiting for him on the front steps.

—Turro!

—Yes, Nonna? He kissed.

—Tomorrow we go to Perth. It was an order.

Artie groaned. Saturday. He was hungry for a day in the ocean.

—Why tomorrow, Nonna?

—Tomorrow, she repeated. And he agreed.

He spent the night with Bill, at a pub near the port. They drank beer and smoked and listened to drunk Persian sailors. It was dark when they made their way home. Outside the National Hotel, lights out, all long shadows, three black bastards were sitting on the ground. Pissed. One of them, a woman, possibly young, possibly old, impossible to tell for her face was made bitter with drink, shouted after them.

—Spare a shilling.

They walked on without turning. They heard her stumbling footsteps behind them.

—Spare a shilling.

—Go to hell, spat Bill.

The woman was fat, horrible, no teeth and a broken nose. She clutched at Artie's arm and he shook her off. Underneath the thin cotton of her dress, her breasts were naked. Large. He pushed her away. She cursed and they walked free.

Joseph was asleep and Artie quietly stripped himself. He slid into bed next to his brother and Joseph snored, once, shook, then turned over. Artie watched his brother's naked form, his head spinning. His limbs ached, he wanted water. Softly, holding his breath still, he began a soft stroking of his cock. Joseph stirred and Artie stopped, scared, awaiting humiliation. Then again snores. Slowly Artie stroked himself to climax, thinking of the gin's massive tits, the strong sphere of her nipple. He splashed into his hand and he wiped it under the mattress, careful not to make a sound, embarrassed that he had aroused himself through dreaming of such ugliness.

The morning arrived with a demanding sunshine and Nonna's knock on the bedroom door. Joseph had already risen, for he had to work on Saturdays, and Artie threw the bed sheet on the floor.

—Coming.

A banging in his head.

They took the bus into the city. He was conscious of the stares the Nonna received from the other passengers. Two young women, one very pretty, turned around then giggled at the old woman wrapped in her black shrouds. The bus followed the sea, crossed the bridge, and the water spread for miles below. They passed the long sheds in which Joseph and Papa worked: men, stripped to their waists, were moving boxes and crates. Then the bus turned away from the ocean and the view changed to bush. Shrubs had turned from green to gold in the summer heat. Artie pushed his nose, his face, tight to the window. Watching the world outside. He turned around and noticed tears on his Nonna's cheeks.

—What's wrong, Nonna? he asked, concerned. She took hold of his hand and began to speak in Greek. The two young women turned around again and Artie felt his face flush. He pulled his hand away.

—Talk Australian.

The old woman turned away from him, wiped her eyes. Artie returned to the lopped kaleidoscope world outside the window.

The city was hot, pools of light on the concrete, and there were people everywhere. Again Artie was embarrassed by the foreignness of his Nonna, wished she did not wrap her body and head in thick black cloth. But he was excited to be in the city. He peered through windows, noted the hotels and the streets be-hind the markets that led into dark passages and corners in which women did not enter. He wanted to stay around the markets, to wander freely through the city, but his Nonna's steps were eager, impatient. They crossed a small park and stopped before a small building, yellow brick. It was a Church. He was disappointed. All this way and only for God.

The Nonna did her sign of the Cross, not like Papa, she crossed right then left. They entered the building.

He noticed the smell first, strong waves of spice that stroked his nose, entered through his mouth. He felt dizzy. An older man, older than the Nonna, sat on a chair and he guarded a box of yellow candles. The Nonna grabbed two, deposited two pennies and they walked into the church.

Long elongated figures, purple and gold. Candles, thin, and flickering with heat and light. The pews. The Nonna lit her candle, ordered him to do the same, and they placed them in a box of sand. Artie watched her face the altar, kneel and cross herself. This did not look, did not smell like real church. The figures painted on the wall were dark and sinister. Gaunt men with lined faces, their gaze admonishing and their poverty frightening. One saint bled from his feet. The Nonna took Artie's

arm and pushed him towards a stand on top of which sat a small
icon, a picture of Our Lady holding the baby Jesus; the picture
was haloed by flowers. But this was not a smiling benevolent
Madonna. Her face was stern, and she and the baby were not soft
but hard. His body was that of a child but it had the face of a
man.

—Kiss it.

Artie shook his head.

—Kiss it, she ordered. He brushed his lips against the glass.
The Nonna did the same and then walked towards the altar.

There, under the gaze of the saints and of Jesus, under the
severe eyes of the Lady that was not Our Lady, she threw herself
onto the floor and began a wailing.

Artie watched, shocked, scared, but made immobile by her
grief. The woman started banging the stone floor with her fists.
Artie finally rushed to her, attempted to raise her. She fought
him off but he held her until her heaving slowly descended to
quiet anguished spasms. She got up without looking at her
grandson. Her lips were praying and her eyes were raised. Artie
looked up.

God was looking down on him from the ceiling. His beard
was long, white, his hands were outstretched across the earth.
Gold flecks shone in his hair. The church itself was small, much
smaller than the church near home. Artie understood the pews
and altars, the symmetry of the building, but was lost in the
unfamiliar images. Beside him the Nonna was still praying. He
moved away from her, walked towards an open door that was
leading to sunshine. He stepped outside.

The building was fairly new, no more than ten years, if
that. His experienced eyes travelled across the window frames,
investigated the structure of the building. It was simple, in-
expensive. The frames already in need of more paint.

A moan, from inside the church, stopped him. He ran to his
Nonna.

She was standing next to a priest, a man in black with a short stubby beard. Artie stood under a painting of a disapproving old man, his halo cracked and fading, a snake under his foot. The snake was thin, twisted, a voluminous black. The priest had placed a hand on the Nonna.

She recoiled, angry.

No. She was defiant but Artie was also surprised to hear in her voice a rare and reluctant respect.

He could not make out the conversation, all of it in Greek. The priest looked towards him. He said something to the old woman and she turned around.

—Thanassi, come here. It was the priest who spoke.

He walked over.

—It's Arthur. He coughed. It's Arthur, Father.

—You don't speak Greek?

Artie shrugged.

—Take your grandmother away, Arthur. She is tired. His accent was musical, but there was a chilled retreat in his voice, in his manner.

The Nonna, eyes lowered, said one more thing in Greek. The priest turned to Artie.

—You are Catholic, boy?

Artie nodded.

The priest whispered.

—And so is your grandmother. He turned to the old woman.

—You should go to the Catholic Church, that's your Church now.

The Nonna shook her head in refusal. The priest sighed, his face unhappy, as miserable as the icons on the wall. He turned to the youth, and said tenderly, Your father wished his family to have one faith. Take your giagia to the church your family attends. The priest there, I am sure, he will help her.

The Nonna touched the man's sleeve.

—No, you have to leave.

And with this he briskly turned and walked away from them,

disappeared behind the altar. The Nonna stood quiet, her hand outstretched, stood still for what seemed an eternity.

Artie took her hand, lowered it into his.

This one moment would continue to surface, in waves of memory, be entrapped in his dreams, for the rest of Artie's life. The priest's sweet accent, his dark steel beard: he could not forget him. Not that memory is faithful. Sometimes the priest is an old man, sometimes young. Sometimes there are other figures praying behind them, sometimes he and the Nonna are alone. The story would change, his memory would fade; facts lost to time. The Nonna's grief and the priest's sadness, however, were never to disappear. This solemn tableau of his Nonna and himself banished from the church was to be his only witness to the ferocity of God. He was to grow old believing not in the promises of his Catholic faith but in the beauty and the despair of this exile. He walked his Nonna away from the altar, and as they passed the burning candles, he hesitated. And swiftly, his hands a wind, he snatched the icon from its frame.

•

Outside, in the daylight, with strangers passing, the Nonna spat savagely on the footpath. A thin woman recoiled, shuddered. An old man laughed. Bloody dagoes. They walked in silence in the heat.

—Are you hungry, Nonna? Artie asked finally.

She shook her head.

—Should we go home?

He didn't want to. Now that he was in the city, he wanted to play, he wanted to roam. They were walking through the park.

—Marta! The voice that screamed out to them was shrill. The old woman spun around. Artie, horrified, saw a large black gin, all belly and breasts, run towards them.

Then a further shock.

—Bess! The Nonna walked towards the gin, her hands outstretched. They met and they fell into hugging, into tears, into kisses. Artie stood still. Behind the two old women, now tight in a circle, he spotted a younger gin, much younger, sitting on the grass. The old gin pulled away from the Nonna but took her hand and pointed to the younger woman.

—There's daughter. Come meet daughter.

Like his Nonna, her English was broken.

The Nonna turned to Artie and signalled him to follow.

—This is my grandson. Arthur. Arthur, this is Bess.

The old gin held out her hand. Artie did not move. The woman smiled but dropped her arm to her side.

—Thanassi, shake her hand!

—It doesn't matter.

Artie's eyes went wide. The boong had just spoken *Greek*.

The daughter was called Jen and, despite her black skin, Artie thought her pretty. She was young but her belly was round, with child. Jen too was surprised at the familiarity between the two old women. They sat, holding hands, talking, a mixture of languages, their gestures also a voice. Jen winked at Artie.

—Who'd believe this?

He smiled weakly. Above him he was conscious of people walking through the park; the looks, the distaste in a man's eyes as he spotted the two old women. They were grotesque.

—We have to leave.

The Nonna refused to listen.

—You married?

Artie shook his head. Jen was offering him a bottle of wine, to suck from. Though thirsty, he wanted nothing that had touched her lips.

—You?

She laughed. No.

He was looking at her belly. She followed his gaze.

—This one's Tom's.

—You've got another?

—A little girl. But her daddy's a white man, the nuns took her away. Jen pointed to the sky. Up north. I'll see her one day.

A young couple were passing. Artie hid his face in embarrassment. When he looked up, Jen was smiling at him, drinking from the bottle.

—You sure you don't want some?

He scratched a twig into the dirt. Jen asked for tobacco. He rolled her a cigarette. The icon spilt from underneath his jacket. She grabbed it.

—What's this? She teased. But Bess looked up and scolded her in blackfella language. Jen handed back the icon sheepishly.

—What's she say? asked Artie, curious.

—That's the Greek gods and I got to respect them.

—God isn't Greek. Artie was sullen and wrapped his jacket around the icon. Jen smiled and offered him the bottle again.

Again he refused and turned to his Nonna.

—We've got to go. His voice was now almost a childish wail.

The old black woman was ugly, thick lips and her small eyes, radiant white, were crossed with red lines. The old women were touching each other's faces.

—Can I come see you, Marta?

The Nonna looked at her grandson, who was on his feet, scowling, his arms crossed.

—His Papa a bad man.

Artie flinched. How dare she insult Papa in front of that black bitch?

—Would not be right, eh? Not right.

The two old women hugged, kissed and there were tears when they parted. Artie walked ahead, not turning around, not saying goodbye, only wishing to escape the park.

—Goodbye, Thanassi, Bess called after him. Her voice stopped him. He turned around. Her tears were a stream. He softened.

—Goodbye, he replied. In Greek.

The Nonna walked behind him. When they reached the street, away from the park, heading back towards the station, he stopped and waited for her to catch up. She was far away.

—You shouldn't speak to the boongs, Nonna. Papa doesn't like it.

—She's a friend.

—Friend?

—Yes, replied the Nonna in harsh English. Only friend.

—Where did you meet?

The Nonna chuckled. She spat.

—Your Papou was married to her sister.

Artie did not believe her. He was outraged.

—You're lying.

The Nonna shook her head.

—Nonno was married to an Abo?

—Yes.

—Before you?

—Yes. Bess was sister.

—And what happened to her?

The Nonna was sad. She put an arm around her grandchild.

—It doesn't matter.

—Please, Nonna. What happened?

—She died.

—How?

Above there was a fluttering. Artie looked up to the sky. The sun burnt his eyes, there was a diving flash of black and the flash became the crow. It danced in the harsh light for a moment.

Your grandfather killed her.

The crow spoke in his Nonna's voice.

•

It was still light when they reached home and Artie ran from the house to the beach, jumped in the water and washed away the city and the church, washed away Jen and Bess. Washed away the crow. He danced in the water. When he arrived back home his father was washing in the trough. The Nonna was sitting, scowling, in the kitchen. Mama was cooking and Johnny was playing at her feet.

—Where were you today?

Artie sat down and looked first at his Nonna, then at his father. Her face told him nothing.

—Perth.

—What the hell for?

—I took Nonna to church.

—What church? The Papa was sponging underneath his arms. His gaze was firm on his son.

—Don't know.

—Bloody Greek, eh?

—Yes, Greek.

Papa turned on the old woman.

—Shut up, you cow.

—You shut up.

Everyone looked at Mama, even Johnny was startled by her raising her voice at Papa. And, immediately aware of her error, she softened her voice.

—She wanted to light a candle, for her brother. Leave her be.

Papa stared hard at his wife. She slowly walked over, touched his cheek. He smiled and began whistling.

—Not my problem. It's the boy who had his day wasted.

Papa put on a clean shirt, prepared for a night of drinking. He left and the whole house seemed to breathe more contently, to settle peacefully with the setting sun.

Sleep was shattered by the sound of a bashing door, the loud curses of the Papa. Joseph sprung out of bed and moved to the door.

—What's happening? whispered Artie.

—Dunno.

They listened.

The Papa was screaming for the Nonna to rise. Then he was screaming for Artie. The youth looked nervously at his older brother. Joseph opened the door and they walked into the hall.

The Papa, drunk, a belt in his hand was standing over the

tumbled body of the Nonna. Mama was crying at the old woman's side.

—Please Joseph, please. Stop.

—Papa?

Artie felt the blow, his face was fire; he fell across the wall.

—Where did you go today?

—To Perth.

—Where else?

—Nowhere.

—Who did you see?

Artie hesitated.

—Who did you fucking see?

—No-one, he screamed back. Another blow. He could hear Sophia and Therese sobbing. In the front room, Johnny was howling.

—That's not what O'Malley told me tonight. He told me my son, and Papa spat, he told me he saw my son drinking with the abos in a park in Perth.

—I didn't.

—Don't lie, you fucking cunt. Italian.

—Stop, screamed the Nonna. Papa kept his eyes on Artie.

—To your room, he ordered. Artie did as he was told. The Papa turned to the old woman.

—You did this to him, right, you hurt him. He spat on her. If you ever see any of those filthy black bastards again, I'm going to skin you alive. 'Cause that's what those abos deserve and you're no fucking better. He tugged, violently at her hair, snapping her head forward.

—You don't poison my son. I'm not going to let you.

He pushed her away. She fell moaning on her daughter.

—Understand? he ordered in Italian.

—Understand! he repeated when she did not reply.

—I understand.

He walked out and the old woman crumbled in her chair. The Mama dropped to her knees shuddering. There were three sounds: the lash that whistled then cracked as it tore at flesh; the exertions of Papa's breath; the sobbing of the frightened girls. The Nonna clenched her fists, fear had collapsed her face.

—Stop him! My God, stop him!

—Be quiet, her daughter shouted. This is all your fault!

Eventually the hatred stopped. The Papa walked into the kitchen, his hair wet, his hands shaking. Two drops of blood on his shirt. He was already doubting his virulence, shaken by his son's ferocious will not to collapse. Artie had not made a sound. Nonna climbed to her feet, pushed hard past him and ran into the boys' bedroom.

Joseph was under the covers, looking across to his younger brother who was staring hard into the dark through the window. The blood was a trickle from Artie's nose to his chin. The Nonna approached him, her hands in prayer, crying softly. She curled herself around him and began a wailing.

She fell on her knees and apologised. She screamed her apology and it was in Greek and it was in English, it was Italian and it was Turkish. There was just the word, an infinite repeating.

Sorry, my Thanassi, I'm sorry.

But Artie was not in the room. He was above it, watching the tiny brother and the distraught Nonna. Artie flew up into the ceiling, and through, through into the sky. And in the sky he was travelling across the ocean, he was flying, driving a chariot and he was no longer Artie and this was not his bed and this was not his room and this was not his people. This was not his home.

•

He left Western Australia that year, left his family and his apprenticeship. He took his Nonna with him. They travelled across the desert and he found work in Port Augusta. But there too, a port town, blackfellas on the street, he was reminded too much of Fremantle. They moved further east, to Horsham, to Ballarat. There he buried his Nonna and sent a telegram home. It was only himself and a priest at the funeral. He ordered a simple white cross, the words—her name—in Greek. As her body descended to earth, around him the wind and the birds, he found himself at last alone. You were wrong, Nonna, he prayed, there is no God. And Jesus was just a man who wept and pissed and shat and came. Just like me, Nonna. It was me, not God, not Jesus; not the Virgin, it was me who loved you, Nonna. He shamed himself with the force of his grief. He drank himself into a stupor, into unconsciousness that night.

Years later, in Melbourne, he was invited to a barbecue and Maria's soft beauty reminded him of loss and reminded him of the joy he had felt in escaping, in fleeing, in taking his Nonna away from the harshness of his Papa's house. He promised Maria his protection, the only gift he knew to offer. And he did not turn back on his word. He changed his name back to Stefano—at Maria's insistence. He filled his home with Greeks, offered a room to Spiro and to Yiota so that Maria would not be alone; he built her a new house in the suburbs, nursed her through the terror when the colonels took over Greece, her father thrown into prison. He did not wince, did not reject her when she began to scorn him and lash out at him, as she slowly realised, her children now Australian, she could never again return to Greece. And he never struck her once. Not once. Maria, Dominic, Thomas and Luigi. His grandchildren. They—not Greece, not Italy or Australia—they were the only home he wished to know.

He returned to Fremantle twice, each time to assist in burying one of his parents. His duty done, his respect shown, he returned to Melbourne, returned to a city where he had a wife and he had children, where there was laughter and where there was hope. Where there was no desert and no lazy ocean; no black bitches to disturb your dreams.

Greece, 1991

The first thing Maria did on arriving at the ancestral birthplace of her father's people, far up in the eastern mountains of Greek Macedonia, was to climb off the bus, get on her knees and crawl to the Church of the Prophet Elijah. The small church, tiny and carefully tended by the few remaining old women in the village, was perched high among the poplars, two kilometres above the village square. Maria made the journey supported by grieving, the wailing and the tears of her sisters and her cousins. Behind them all walked her frightened youngest son. Lou, on seeing his mother's knees shredded and weeping blood, himself began to cry and attempted to stop this insane work. But he was ordered away by his mother. She had made this journey, after decades, to repent of her sins. And to plead with her God that her son's suicide, his sins, would not deny him God's grace.

—Fuck God, is all that Artie said when both the Churches, the Catholic and the Orthodox, refused to bury his son. We don't need those fucking poofter priests.

But for Maria the knowledge of her son's eternal loneliness filled her with bitter agony and shame. A trail of blood led up to the church on the mountain. Through this sacrifice she hoped to make a bargain with heaven.

Lou, who cared nothing for eternity, who only understood that his brother no longer existed, thought his mother, the grim priest, the weeping women, he thought all of them mad. Athens had shocked him with its thundering noise and sweating heat. This medieval torture only accentuated his difference.

Alone, silent in the back of the church, he refused to pray. His mother was spread on the stone floor. A white-bearded old man stared down gloomy from the icons. Lou concentrated on the rhythm of the chant, not understanding a word. He was the one person, apart from the priest, not crying. Lou was beginning to understand that he might not be European.

Lou was happiest when he was alone with his giagia. Only from her did he sense respect. For his cousins he was nothing but an Amerikanaki, a faux American, without a point of view and too immersed in pop culture. As for his uncles and his aunts, they all sniggered at the atrocity of his Greek. He slipped into silence and into observation. Only his grandmother listened to him. They spoke a language that was half gesture and half sound. The ideas and emotions conveyed had, by necessity, to be simple, not abstract. The cousins offered complicated theories and philosophies as to the reason for the war on their northern border. His *giagia*, remembering the civil war she had lived through, only said, My child, my child, war is always bad.

And Lou, who had spent a lifetime witnessing the sterility of the slaughter on the television news, could only agree.

He had not been prepared for Greece. That he now understood. The Athenians described their city as chaos, and the word in Greek was pronounced *house*. This made perfect sense to Lou. He discovered an insistent beat emerging from the cacophony.

His mother warned him to cover the tattoo on his arm, but Lou refused to acquiesce to her ideas of shame and honour. She pointed to his flesh, the golden snake wrapped around his arm. What will people say?

—I don't give a fuck what people say.

His vehement opposition to propriety had become an ideal after the death of his brother.

He wore the tattoo, openly, proudly, throughout Greece.

They did not spend a night in the village. The family had long disbanded, moved across the country and across continents. Only a few old people remained, those abandoned by kin. They eyed Lou suspiciously. He had learnt quickly, in Athens, that a smile and the beauty of his young face would appease their distaste for his foreignness, but the madness of his mother's flagellation had left him ill-humoured, even hateful, towards the stoic archaic villagers. He was glad to pile back in the bus, with his mother and relatives, and leave the Church of the Prophet Elijah behind.

They stopped in Thessaloniki and in this city Lou first experienced the joy of travelling. He was entranced by the city's history and he wandered up to the castle overlooking the bay, thinking how beautiful it was. He drank ouzo and watched the people. He forgot the pain of witnessing his mother's sacrifice.

He detested her commitment to religion. He doubted it was faith. He had always suspected that her piety was only an attempt to order the extremities of exile, a repetition of ritual that in moments made her forget the dislocations wreaked on her soul by migration. Since Tommy's death, the rituals had become imperative.

—House, he whispered to the Thessalonikan night. Chaos music.

Somewhere, in a cafe below, a radio was playing REM's 'Losing My Religion'. In competition was the mellifluous sensuality of 'Fool's Gold'. If he closed his eyes, he could still be in Australia, on a couch, at a party. He wished he was stoned. When he returned to Athens he would find the courage to ask his cousins where to score.

Maria and Lou argued when he refused to go back to Athens with her.

—I want to travel a bit, on my own.

They argued but he won. He knew that because Maria could not expunge a sense of guilt over her son's suicide, a guilt Lou understood, she was no longer prepared to battle her children as viciously, with that fierce determination she had when they were younger. Tommy's death had finally eradicated her youth. Not only through the greying of her hair, the encroachment of wrinkles on her still vibrant face, but through an understanding of the immensity and scale of the past she had lived.

—Go, she said finally and turned away. Lou grabbed her and kissed her neck softly. He did not wish to hurt her. But he felt no compulsion to do her bidding any more. Maybe he never did. The Greek youths around him were certainly more sophisticated, more erudite, more confident than those he knew back home. But they were still shadowed, wherever they went, whoever they were with, by family. Lou loved his family without commitment. He loved and he knew he was loved. He could see no reason to obey.

He wanted to visit the island of Cos, where his great-grand-mother came from. Maria had returned to Greece to seek the solace and forgiveness of the saints. Lou, not a believer, was seeking an answer to Tommy's extinction in the stories of the past.

•

On the day of Tommy's funeral, a tall slowly weeping elm at the cemetery had been studded with the thick black shadows of the crow. The birds had observed the burial. All the Stefano men had noticed. Artie and Dominic were overwhelmed by a shattering fury. Not Lou. He stared at the birds, glad for their distraction. The descent of the coffin into the soil sickened him. Maggots and worms, decomposition. The knowledge of the castrated Tommy. Lou's eyes were wet. The tree, the birds, the sky, everything was ashimmer.

Maria too had noticed the crows and for the first time she too experienced a terror. She mentioned it, later, sitting crying in her chair, her face a darkness beneath the veil.

—The crows, did you see them?

The men shuffled uneasily. She looked straight at her husband.

—See them? she insisted.

Artie nodded.

Maria groaned and fell to more loud crying. Lou stood up, weaved past the mourners, walked to the shop. A black suit, black tie. The clothes, the grief, the sociality of burial, all this had made him weary. The short walk he had taken around the block, simply passing rows of brick veneer and hedge, was a respite. He had felt almost happy. There had been a moment when it *was* happiness, a drizzle on his face, the smell of lawn. But as soon as he'd experienced the joy, he'd remembered the day. And again all there was was Tommy.

Greece, never having known Tommy, felt safe. Lou watched a drunk girl take off her slippers, run up the steps to the top of the castle. She looked down and grinned at him. He grinned back. She ran after her boyfriend, then turned once more. Lou looked away.

After the funeral, when they were all back home, Eva had prepared a light meal. Maria had refused to eat. Her daughter-in-law slipped a pill into her coffee and the Valium soon took effect. Artie put her to bed, returned, and they put on the television; the children laughed at the animation and it was a relief.

Dominic hugged his brother tight, kissed the top of his head. Lou wished to sink into him. They pulled apart. Dom was crying. Lou hurt to see the tears, a rare vulnerability. Eva was shaking as she kissed him goodbye. The television was throwing harsh light through the room. Lou was alone with his father.

—Dad. A pause. Dad, are you all right?

Artie was staring at the motion of light on the TV screen. He was thinking of his dead son, the crisp almost metallic inviolability of the corpse. He heard Lou repeat his question.

—Just thinking about things, Lou.

—Mum okay?

—Yeah. She's sleeping.

Lou flicked the buttons on the remote. He settled on a documentary: wild carnivore birds attacking the maggoted hide of a zebra.

—Your mum's a strong woman, Lou. I've always known that. He leaned forwards in the armchair, towards his son. But we've got to look after her for a while. She doesn't have anything else, Louie, it is just *you* kids.

Lou realised that his father had been as shaken by Maria's despair at the funeral as he had. His father spoke, and it was true, they were sharing the same thought. It scares me that she was babbling on about the crow bullshit, today. She's always laughed at it before.

—What is the crow, Dad? Lou pushed another button. An American comedy—*The Cosby Show*.

—Turn it off! It was a harsh order, then Artie's voice mellowed. Please Lou. Artie walked over to a shelf and picked up a small framed photograph. Lou turned down the volume on the TV but the images still played. His father handed him the photograph.

—Your great-grandmother, Louie, she's the one to ask about the crows.

A scrap of black and white, a small woman, all in black. The hard sad face that had always alarmed Lou as a child. A stern face.

—She looks so tough, Dad.

—She had to be. Lou felt the love in his father's voice—and the defensiveness. She had to be, son. She was just fifteen when she sailed from Turkey. And ended up in Kalgoorlie. Louie, you can't imagine Kalgoorlie. A strip of two lousy streets in the middle of the desert, in the middle of fucking nowhere. Every kind of scum came to Kalgoorlie. My grandfather came to find gold.

Lou glanced at the advertisements, the cheerful colours of the television.

—They say that my grandfather had a previous wife, that he killed her.

Lou swung round.

—I don't know if that's true, Louie. My Mama says it isn't true and I could never ask my Papa. But Nonna knew. She told me that this dead woman was the crow. Her husband told her nothing, but she said that from her wedding night the crow would not leave her alone. She says the blackfellas told her. Told her that her husband had killed their sister.

—And she believed them?

—Nonna hated my grandfather. Artie took the photograph from his son. He was smiling.

—Nonna was always friendly with the blacks. My father hated that. His smile vanished. He stood up. I'm going to bed, Louie.

Father and son hugged, holding on tight to one another. Lou could hear tears in his father's voice and he did not dare glance up at him.

—They were cruel, Lou, people back then. Don't ever believe the bullshit about the good old days. They were savage days. It was a cruel life for Nonna. She could be cruel too. That's what makes me think she's the crow now, watching me, wanting me to be better. Always wanting me to be better, stronger. His faltering voice broke. Angry at me for my failures.

Tommy was around them, between them, over them.

—No! urged Lou. The youth tightened his grip around the man. You haven't failed, Papa, you haven't. You haven't.

Artie pulled away from his son.

—Thanks, Lou. Gruff, he did not bother to wipe away his tears. I'm going to bed.

Lou turned up the volume but the television was far away from him. He still felt Tommy next to him. But also another presence. Lou was not frightened. If there is a curse, he thought, I refuse it. He realised, his eyes shut tight, his hands fisted together, his body rocking, that he was in the throes of prayer. He had not prayed since childhood. Go away, go away, his breathing was a chant. He opened his eyes. The colours of the television and the American accents. He clumsily loosened his body from the submission of prayer. The room was empty.

When his father persuaded Maria to visit Greece, Lou had decided that he too would go and he too would make a pilgrimage. Certainly not to seek an answer from God. At sixteen, as the silent earth covered his brother's body, Lou had discovered the profound silence of God. But his father's story had promised something stranger. The overwhelming presence of the past.

•

Lou ordered another ouzo, surprised at the lackadaisical attitude the Greeks had to age and drinking. He was drunk and tomorrow he was to visit the place that maybe he had come from. Or some part of him. He sung as he staggered down the steps. It was the Violent Femmes, 'Add It Up'. *Why can't I get just one fuck?* A memory of being twelve and listening to Tommy's old records.

The ferry left early in the morning. His mother came with him to the wharf and slipped a small gold crucifix around his neck. Lou squirmed.

—Shh, answered Maria in Greek. This is protection.

All through the journey, as the boat slid east across the Aegean, Lou felt the weight of the cross around his neck. But he did not remove it. Instead, he received comfort from the gift, a superstition that calmed him. Swedish and American tourists tanned themselves and drank beer. On the radio REM were again singing 'Losing My Religion' and Madonna was answering with 'Like A Prayer'. And, then, as everywhere in Europe that year, Massive Attack brought calm with 'Unfinished Sympathy'.

In the Macedonian village up in the mountains Lou had become aware that an old Greece existed. It struck him as funny that it was the absence of cisterns that was most indicative of the distance between himself and Greece. He really was Amerikanaki. At the back of the Church of, the Prophet Elijah he went to have a shit. Flies circled around the small back hole that dived deep into the earth. He could not release. He was embarrassed at his softness but kept his shit inside till they reached the Europe of Thessaloniki, ancient walls and modern plumbing.

Cos had cisterns, where the tourists stayed. His great-grandmother's village, however, no longer really existed. Many of the houses now belonged to fourth generation American Greeks and to first generation Germans and Australians. There was rubble. And two old Greek women.

He approached them. They were sitting in the shade of an awning, a small village store. They started whispering to each other as he approached. Lou, who had learnt all he knew about Greek women from his mother and her factory mates, bowed, smiled widely and asked in halting Greek: Aunt, Aunt, can I please speak to you?

But they were content in their age and dismissive of charm. So he blushed and one of them laughed.

—Where are you from?

The other was still not smiling. She stared at the tattoo of the snake.

—Austra-lia. Lou scratched at his arm.

—Far, far, my son. She now smiled and patted the bench next to her. Lou sat down.

—I have children and grandchildren in Australia.

—Whereabouts?

—What do you mean?

—Which . . .? Lou stopped. He had forgotten the word for city. He looked around the square. It was late afternoon but the sun still caked the land. The village, high in a cleft on a cliff, was sheltered from the sea but also from its breeze. Lou mopped his forehead. The old women had fallen silent.

—My family from here. He pointed down at his feet, not confident in the words he was using.

—From here? From Cos? The old women turned straight back to him.

—What's your name? they demanded.

Lou hesitated.

—Luigi Stefano, he said proudly.

The women looked away, bored.

—He's Italian, he heard the second woman say.

—And Greek, he interrupted. My mother and my . . . Again he had to stop. He didn't know the words for kin beyond immediate family. The mother of my father's mother was Cos, he finally managed to say.

The first woman said, quietly, That's a long time ago. She looked Lou in the eyes and saw a question there. This time she took his hand.

—And her name?

—Marta, he whispered.

His father knew her as Nonna Marta and he remembered what she called her village, a thick dusty Turkish word. But he could not recollect her maiden name. His uncles, in Victoria, they were the Pippas. That, an abbreviation, said nothing; it was only a migrant shorthand, assigned to them as they got off the boats. He was unsure of the original Greek word. Pirratiris, Patitis? Pappipadis?

Pappappapalopolous, thought Lou, wishing to laugh but not wishing to offend the old women. He stood up.

—Thank you, he said, but all I know is her name was Marta.

The two women made the sign of the Cross, to protect him. He walked into the shop.

A half bottle of retsina later, he was alone on a beach, an unbuttoned white shirt and loose skater shorts. He was watching the setting sun, the vanishing waves. He sat on sand and hard round rocks. He threw them into the sea. On the horizon he could see land and the vaguest silhouettes of cliff and buildings. The only sounds the splashing water, his breathing. And the faint beginning of a hungry note.

—That is the Caliphs.

He swirled around. A woman, tall, blonde, a khaki singlet and the darkest of tans. He began to stand up but she stopped him and then sat beside him.

—I'm Anna.

A German accent.

—My name is Lou. He offered her the bottle. She accepted. The note, still faint, was very sweet.

—That's Turkey, said Anna. She pointed to the horizon. It's very close, no? They're calling for prayer.

He nodded. Her English was excellent. She had a joint in the pocket of her trousers which they smoked. There were lines around her eyes.

They talked into the night, about Berlin and about Melbourne. The fall of the Wall, the civil war in Yugoslavia, but those subjects were very soon abandoned and instead they talked of music and film, about Greece and the sea. The smoke was hash, intense. In between worlds, touching Europe, touching Asia, Lou came close to saying everything. To talking of Tommy. But before he found the way to put the words together, stumbling in the pleasant fog of intoxication, she placed her hand on his thigh.

He had not thought of sex.

She was flirting, she was strong and insistent. He spread his legs and she worked at his crotch. But feeling young and silly, he could not build to erection. She laughed it off.

—It's all right, she said, and lay back on the stubbled beach. And because she was beautiful and because he was stoned, and because it was the end of a long day in which he had discovered the impossibility of answers, he kissed her and placed his hands beneath her shorts and forced his hand slowly inside her. He kept kissing her and his hand led her to orgasm. Almost embarrassed, he brought himself off, sniffing the punch of her sweating arms and neck.

They washed in the water, splashed, and walked back together to the village. They did not touch again. He slept on the bench outside the store and she went back to the room she was sharing with her girlfriends.

The next day he visited the cemetery, a pitifully squeezed

block of land, and he walked beside the rusting iron and the eroded stone. He found a small square patch of earth, yellow weeds, and he began digging. He placed an icon, given to him by his father, an icon of a child with an old man's face held in the solid arms of the Madonna, into the earth. He finished, sweating, and he made a clumsy sign of the Cross, forgetting which side was first for the Orthodox and hoping that for his ancestors it might not matter.

His father had said to him, handing him the icon, just before he was leaving for the airport: If you are going to visit her island, take this with you and leave it there. That was a promise I made my grandmother which I could not manage to keep.

Marta Euginia Papapouchitis would have believed that by her grandson ensuring his son accomplished the task, the promise had finally been honoured.

Back in Athens Lou became restless. His cousins, out of duty, involved him in their activities, and two of them, Erini and Yianni, he genuinely liked and admired. But cursed with a stumbling illiterate Greek tongue, he was often mistaken for ignorant and boring. With Erini he shared a love for music. She was unapologetically into thrash and she had posters of the Hard Ons and Lou Reed on her bedroom wall. She loved his tattoo. Yianni was simply easy to talk to, free of the arrogance that Lou found in many of the Greeks. He preferred Athens in the day, when he could walk it alone and lose himself in the shrill. And he enjoyed watching European MTV. Not that nights did not also offer pleasure. He drank till nausea in a tavern in Pyreaus, and finally allowed himself to dance to the tranced seduction of Greek blues. At a nightclub call Stadium he mock-danced to Michael Jackson while he looked out across to the moon and to the Acropolis. He was high that night. But most of all he was lonely. He kept seeing it all through Tommy's eyes.

One night Maria went to bed early. She had made herself weary reliving the years of exile, the death of her son, the crawl for God's forgiveness. Lou followed her, concerned and a little scared. She held his hand and she kissed it. She told him that she loved him.

Returning to the kitchen he stopped on hearing the giggling of his aunts. Their rapid Greek confused him. He heard fragments and stayed in the shadows.

She was always spoilt. Did you see those shoes, bet they were expensive. The good life. Australia. She thinks she's had it hard. They're ignorant over there. He's a good boy but so slow. So slow. They don't know anything. It's true. They haven't changed at all. Imagine crawling to the church. Only old women do that.

Giggling and cruel laughter.

—The poor woman, she has suffered.

Silence. The murmuring of God's name.

—We've all suffered. So, she's had two. A word he did not understand. The word kept being repeated.

—What's done is done.

Lou coughed and walked into the kitchen.

—What's ektrosi?

The aunts looked at him, surprised, guilty.

—What's ektrosi? he repeated.

His older aunt, brash, large, beautiful, answered him.

—When you're pregnant and you don't want the kid. You go to the doctor to stop the pregnancy. Do you understand?

Her gaze was strong, she looked right at him. He looked right back.

—I understand.

His aunt lowered her eyes.

—You're nothing but a fucking lazy housewife. You haven't worked a day in your life. If you think my mum's had it easy, then you know shit. You wogs know shit. He said all this in English. It was not important to him that they understand.

He walked into the bedroom he was sharing with his mother and put on a new shirt.

—Where are you going? She was not yet asleep.

—Out. Just around the block, Mum. I'll be fine.

Maria raised her head. She continued to speak in English.

—I heard. You were very rude to your aunts.

They both giggled.

His mother signalled him over. She took his hand.

—I had two abortions, between Tommy and you. That was a sin.

Lou shook his head.

—No, it wasn't.

Maria rested again on the pillow. She smiled up at her son.

—There is a God, my little Louie, she said in Greek. There is for me. For you. She began a choked sobbing. There is for Thomas.

Lou went to comfort her but she pushed him away.

—Don't walk far, she ordered, I'll be all right. God help me, I don't deserve you.

Lou walked, the streets, ignoring people, beginning to realise that he might possibly detest the European.

•

After a tour of Santorini, which he loved, and a tour of Mykonos and Paros, which he hated, Lou spent his final week in Athens, being taken on a circuit of farewell dinners and parties. One night at his Aunt Olga's a group of all ages sat around drinking coffee, spirits and wine. The argument moved to politics. The platitudes of the conservatives, the bankruptcy of the left. The European Community, the New World Order and the consequences of the Gulf War. As the conversation zipped past fast around him, Lou retreated further away. His mother had become almost as fiery as the Greeks, forgetting her grief and enjoying the triumphs and castigations of argument. He himself was unable to contribute further than the most basic of observations. And beyond this he was beginning to accept their hushed derision of his unsophistication. He *was* ignorant, he *was* naive.

Lou got up, excused himself and dropped onto his cousin

Basili's bed. He picked up the remote, switched on the television. A metal atrocity on MTV. He switched stations.

In yellow print there was the word. Laros. He stared at the images, at first confusing them for old footage from the Second World War but then realising that the pixelated sepia of the video stock made this an impossibility. The drone of the CNN reporter came on. This was Laros, Greece, 1990.

He had heard the story but it had been just one of an infinite number of media bites and he had not pursued it. The images were savage. Naked men, their hands bound, shivering in the cold, were belted with a surge of water from a fire hose. They screamed and howled, fell over in the water. The camera moved across the soiled damp beds, the chains and the lashes. The EC demanded an investigation and the immediate overhaul of the Greek government's treatment of the mentally ill.

From inside, conversation, philosophising, the clink of glass. Laughter.

A young boy, mongoloid eyes, being dragged along the ground screaming.

Lou is alone in the dark room. The light from the television illuminates a pale face, the tattoo snake glistens almost silver.

The boy is a mess, a shaking, a doubled-up quiver; blood from biting his lips to stop himself howling. Every boy, every girl, the terrified haunted strangers on the screen, every one is Tommy.

Later, back home, Dominic asked him: So, did you like it?

Lou answered, No.

That was not the whole truth. He would remember, forever, dancing above the Parthenon. He would take pleasure in recalling smoking a joint with Erini and Yianni, pumping up the volume and listening to Died Pretty's *Winterland*. And every time he was to hear joy in prayer, he was to be reminded of how, in reaching towards the horizon from the island of Cos, one is close to touching Turkey. And that in the isolation of that touch is a remoteness and an expanse that he once thought uniquely Australian.

SECTION THREE

Luigi Stefano

Call yourself alive? I promise you you'll be defeated by dust falling on the furniture, you'll feel your eyebrows turning to two gashes, and every memory you have will begin at Genesis.

NINA CASSIAN

1

The last record shop

I'm in love with Soo-Ling. I've got to be up front about that. She laughs it off, says I'm being adolescent, but I know she's wrong. When she's around there's no-one else. No, that's not quite true. There's Betty. She's the best fucking kid in the world. When Betty's around she's the centre of everything.

And there's Tommy. He's dead but not dead. Maybe that's what happens with all deaths: the ghosts always remain, haunting us forever. But I've decided, just speculation, that it is different with suicides. The anger plus the guilt. Suicide ghosts are poltergeists, always capable of disturbing the peace.

Why did he do it? Soo-Ling never asks me this question, neither does Dad. Mum does, so does Dom. I think we all ask it of ourselves. I'm nervous about the day Betty asks it. It's going to come soon.

—Why did Daddy die?

Fuck knows. And that isn't an evasion. Fuck knows is the truth.

The world has gone mad with the vote. Booths everywhere. I haven't voted, I'm not even enrolled. Mum and Soo-Ling bitch to me about this. They are heaps more political than I am, much more radical. I think sometimes they despair of my generation.

—You're all so bloody lazy.

Mum will nod her head in agreement.

—You haven't lived under the Liberals, Mum yells at me. Just wait and see.

I just shut up. What can I say? My vote don't matter shit. I'm going to find out what it's like to live under the capital C conservatives. That's my fate. Too many deadheads around me, in the 'burbs, in the city, in the bush, are going to have their way. Anyway, I've lived through Labor. I'm paying fees again for study, I've spent four years getting shit pay for working sinks and staffing a counter. I shut up because I don't know as much as Mum and Soo-Ling but they're wrong to think my disinclination to vote is simply apathy. I wish it were. Apathy is easy. It's really confusion. I just don't know.

I'm in a record shop in Blackburn, a great place to pick up cheap vinyl and cheap CDs. I want to make a tape for Soo-Ling, I've been working on it for a week. She's got the best attitude to music, no pretension. She likes what she likes. We argue about rap and techno: she doesn't listen carefully enough sometimes. It's a mellow tape I'm making, music to sink into a bath with, but I want to find three songs for her. They're among her favourites but because she's no collector, she doesn't have them. The songs are, 'Save The Best Till Last', Vanessa Williams. 'Freedom', George Michael. And 'Ever Fallen in Love with Someone Who Loves You', The Buzzcocks. Now ain't that cool? You can't place her with those choices, can't pigeonhole her. They come from the heart.

Isn't she fucking amazing?

I have a theory, just a small one, probably worth shit, but I think Tommy lost some of his soul when he gave up music. That's how I best remember him, in his room, forbidding me to enter, listening to the radio and playing his records. He would do that for hours and he would spend all his available money on vinyl. He was sick of me, always having to look after me, having to babysit. But sometimes, if he was in a good mood, he'd let me sit in and he'd play stuff to me. He'd laugh at my taste. I was a child and all I wanted to hear was Culture Club and the Thompson Twins. But in the long run it was good for me, I learnt something. Most of the thrashy sounds from the speakers sounded like white noise to me but I remember Gun Club. They had a song with a nursery rhyme kind of chorus. Tommy used to laugh when I'd go around singing it.

—It's about a serial killer, you know that, don't you?

I just nodded. I don't think I quite knew what a serial killer was back then. Just another bogey man.

Soo-Ling says that Tommy had given up on music by the time she met him. That's so sad. There are so many questions I want to ask him and the fucker is dead. Did it happen suddenly? Did he decide one day that music was no longer valuable or precious to him? Did it remind him of home? Did someone he liked, because Tommy was easily shamed, did someone scoff at his tastes? Possibly. I realised early that was how to get Tommy to do something for me that he didn't particularly want to do. Just call him lazy, stupid, tell him his taste sucked. He never had faith in his own opinions. Maybe once the music escaped from his room, once it got tainted by other people, maybe it stopped being part of him.

I found The Buzzcocks, an old EP, in Dom and Eva's garage. But the vinyl is scratched to buggery. I can't use it for the tape so I'm going through the racks, trying to find it. 'Freedom' was easy. Picked up *Listen Without Prejudice*, on CD, for six bucks. I'm going to put 'Waiting For The Day' on the tape. I think Soo-Ling will like that. But Vanessa Williams is harder. I just want the single. It's on the *Priscilla* soundtrack but I don't want to get that out of principle. I hate 'I Love The Nightlife' and that's on it. Don't know why, just one of those songs that has no blood. Vampire songs I call them.

I love going through second-hand seven-inch records. This is a great store for it. Unlike the inner-city stores, everyone feels free here to unload their taste and make some money. Serious hip-hop next to coloured vinyl. The Smiths next to mid-seventies Status Quo. I've already got a handful of records. Fifty cents a pop. Madonna's 'Burning Up', Don Henley's 'The Boys of Summer', Mel and Kim's 'Showing Out' and The Saints 'I'm Stranded', a twelve inch. I've been in here for a couple of hours, smelling the dust, listening to Neil Young being played by the scruffy girl at the counter. Around me the whole country is probably voting in a new age. I don't want to go out. I'm protected in here.

Dominic was into music too. I still call him the disco king. But he has stopped as well, he's not listening to new music, not going forward. And not going back. What he has in his collection is incredible, from his old dj days when it was all bonging on, screwing the chicks and playing at being Travolta. But it all starts at the Pasadena sound and stops at Michael Jackson. I try him out on new things but he thinks it's all crap. I've mined his collection for all it's worth. He's got original Parliament and Funkadelic from back in the seventies, when you could only get funk through mail order. And when he dances, even I want to fuck him. Eva says, all the time, that's what made her love him. Turn up the bass, clear the floor and watch the man dance. Mum loves it when Dom dances, she claps her hand and sings along. Ah, freak out. She says he may be an Aussie, act like an Aussie, dress like an Aussie, but he's got Greek hips.

Tommy never danced.

Mum went apeshit at me one day soon after the funeral. She said I wasn't allowed to play music, not for three months, out of respect for Tommy. I thought that was bullshit but Dad asked me to go along with it, just for a while, just until she calmed down. I lasted a week then I was home alone and I put on the radio. And the radio made me think of music I'd like to listen to. It was such a shithouse time, such an awful collapse in our lives, that all I wanted to hear was something that spoke of light. I put on a dance compilation, I put it on loud and I roared in my bedroom. I danced up a mighty sweat. I was the hass and I was thunder. I didn't hear Mum come in.

She slapped me and I went ballistic.

—What the fuck you do that for?

—Your brother is dead, shame on you. She started crying and because I hated to see her cry and because I know how to lash out at her, I said the first thing that came to mind.

—Shame, always fucking shame with you. That's what killed Tommy.

There are moments of regret in everybody's life. That's one I live with. Her face just went white and she looked so vulnerable and so scared. I reached out to her and she wrapped her body in mine. She pulled away, kissed me, and left my room. I stopped the tape. From inside the kitchen, on the little cassette player she's had for years, I heard the sound of Greek music. A slow painful dirge.

The funeral was small. None of the Western Australian relos came down. Dad didn't want them there. Tommy's death changed everything, changed Dad. We all used to depend on him, he was the calm that made it safe for all of us to go crazy from time to time. The suicide made him, finally, sad. He held Mum's hand throughout the service and he cried. That shook us all up. He held her hand throughout the burial. On the walk back along the cemetery path, back to the cars, he turned to Mum and said, not angry, not bitter, he said just quietly: That's the last time I enter a church. He let go of her hand.

The Catholics and the Orthodox refused to bury Tommy. They make their rules. Dominic, Dad and I, we stopped going to church after that. I'll go to a wedding, I'll do that for someone, but my brother's exile is my exile as well. Mum, it's hard on Mum because God has been the only constant in her life, but I think she also understands. I think she might even respect us.

—God is a drug, she told me once.

They didn't bury Tommy because he offed himself. If it had just been the murder, it would have been okay.

Soo-Ling was at the funeral. I hadn't seen her for months and I leapt towards her. My mother pulled me back. Instead she walked up to her alone, hugged her and Soo-Ling began to cry. The two women held onto each other for a long time.

Eva had told us about the pregnancy the day before the funeral. Dom lost it, thought she should have kept her mouth shut, but she did the right thing. Dom didn't want Soo-Ling to keep the baby, he thought it was a mistake. He wanted an abortion, I guess a cleaning of the slate. For the rest of us, maybe even for Soo-Ling, from the start Betty was a way of going back to Tommy, rescuing him from the past. We all adore her, including Dom.

—Aren't you glad she was born? I asked, him recently.

—Of course, he grumbled. She's a fantastic kid, a great kid. But that's just fate. Imagine if she was sick, imagine if she was a real fucking brat. How would Soo-Ling have coped?

—Soo-Ling can cope with anything. I immediately sprung to Soo-Ling's defence.

—She couldn't save Tommy.

That silenced me. I know that, for all of us, Tommy's death is possibly hardest on my oldest brother. He never liked Tommy and while Tommy was alive the contempt between them was manageable, did not necessarily intrude on Dom's life, did not disturb him. But the suicide changed all that. Dom, among all the sorrow, is grieving for an absence of love.

For two years Soo-Ling lived in Ballarat in her parents' house, looking after Betty and doing a TAFE course. Community development. I'd hitchhike up every couple of months, not stay with her but spend a day walking the town, being with the baby. The house was dark, there were subtle borders between Soo-Ling and her parents. I didn't mind them. They just seemed scared. Her father was tough. A big Chinese man who smoked and swore a lot. He was handsome even though he was well into his sixties. Her mother was small, disappeared in the silences of the house.

—You can't stay here, I argued with Soo-Ling.

—Where should I go?

I didn't have an answer to that.

There's no Vanessa Williams, only the *Priscilla* soundtrack. And it's fifteen bucks, an expensive second hand. I count out my money. I can afford it, but then I can't afford a present for myself,

and I've still got to find The Buzzcocks. I give up my independence and ask the girl behind the counter for assistance.

She finds me a compilation of punk and new wave. It's eleven
bucks but it's worth it. 'Anarchy'. 'Eton Rifles'. And The Buzzcocks. I ask for Vanessa Williams on an off-chance and she
laughs. I buy the soundtrack. Twenty-six dollars and I've got
what I need. I hit the brisk cool air and I'm happy.

Soo-Ling told me that once, long months after the suicide,
she was changing the baby's nappy and *Video Hits* was on
morning television. She looked up and saw the most beautiful
woman she had ever seen. The song was sad and optimistic. The
tears would not stop. She so missed Tommy. Her mother came
in and, seeing her heaving daughter, rushed to her side. They
could not talk. Tommy was an impossible subject. Her family
had been hurt by the media frenzy, as had mine, as had all of us.
Tommy had been news. He was page one on a Thursday, page
three on a Friday and page twenty-six after the funeral. He was
copy for *Woman's Weekly* and for *Woman's Day*. He was even a
joke.

—Hey, Stefano, heard your brother's starring in a snuff
movie.

Giggles.

—Hey Stefano, here's a blade. Show us what you can do.

This was my final year at school. The good people told me
they were sorry, the strangers didn't talk about it. The fuck-ups
told me jokes. Soo-Ling could not talk about any of this with
anyone in her family. So when her mother found her crying,
shaking, all they could do was touch heads across the struggling
smelly baby. And in the background a beautiful woman was
singing 'Save The Best Till Last'.

I've got my tape. I jump on the train, head home, ready to
compile it. I've just moved back home after six months away. I
know, I know, pretty gutless. But Jesus, I can't bloody afford it.
Rent is really ridiculous. I'm not going to stay there long, I've
told Mum and Dad that, and I know that Dad definitely

understands. My father is, an Aussie, though he looks what he is: Southern Mediterranean. But when he opens his mouth, you know he's Aussie. He's comfortable in jeans and overalls and pyjamas. Dad's retiring; that means he's doing less and less work. A roof for a friend, a neighbour's loo. He'll freak, I know, for a while when he finishes working, and unlike my mother he doesn't have the garden. She'll be all right. She'll be forever sad, but.

Mum's cleaning at the moment, a factory in Abbotsford, an office building on Burwood Road, so she's not around in the early evenings. I do all my shit then because Dad will be at the pub. I wank, I watch porno, I smoke grass, I get ready to go out, not always at the same time but always in combination. It actually beats living in a shared household. I didn't dare watch a porno in the houses I was living in. I picked badly, virgins in many things. I don't mean sexual virgins, I mean life virgins, experience virgins. Everyone I lived with—mostly students, and some people on the run—they thought I was uptight about sex. And I thought they were uptight about everything else.

It cost seventy dollars a week for a shitty little box in Fitzroy and when I had to leave that, I paid fifty-five for an abomination in Kensington. I liked the areas. Christ, they were much more interesting, much more appealing than where I grew up. I don't live very far from where the *Neighbours* house is situated, that round the world TV show about the average Australian. I didn't get a chance to become addicted to *Neighbours*. Mum has always ruled over the six o'clock to seven-thirty timeslots. The television is now in the kitchen, that's where she spends her time. It is so bizarre the way my mother interacts with the split, dislocating segments of the news. She damns the television for its lies.

—That is bullshit! she roars. She knows her stuff. I'm out in the eastern suburbs and that's solidly middle class. And my mother is one of those people born working class who will die working class and let no cunt tell her otherwise. She reckons her years of factory service entitles her to that. I tell you, she knows her stuff. She's always gets the blue cheese in Trivial Pursuit. She did it all herself, on her minimum English and her will to know. And her English, though she still finds the written word difficult, is pretty good now.

—That's how; I survived all of you, you bloody Australian drongo men!

Off she went. We just ran. She lost the battle in giving us Greek; it began with Dom and then it was easy for me and Tommy to follow. So she cursed us when she was upset, and of course she was upset a lot in a household of men. In some strange way, and I am not justifying myself here, I think she gained a dignity from me, I respected her *precisely* because she was a woman. You've got to understand, my mother experienced, at the exact same time, the commencement of menopause and the suicide of her second child. Her otherness from me—I was a male and a native to this country—meant I knew there was a limit to how far I could understand anything of what she was going through. I was the baby of the family and she was the head of this world. Tommy died and I responded by wanting comfort and reassurance and she was only too happy to grant that to me.

I'm very self-conscious about living with my parents. It's kind of daggy, I guess.

When we cut ourselves from the Greek tongue, we also cut ourselves off from the Greeks. This was probably inevitable, nothing any of us did could have stopped it. My mother, the only one of us a migrant and therefore unapologetic for her right to be a Greek, thinks we're a failure as a migrant family, not a success story to write back home about. But I guess that's the rub: we weren't really a migrant family. I'm not even a wog. Or at least that's what the wogs tell me.

I'm very self-conscious about who I am.

But I always thought I was lucky, until I became the very public evidence of the tragedy of our situation. There's a picture of me, in *New Idea*, which I hate. Don't know what soulcatcher took that one. I can't stand to look at it. I'm obviously freaked out, just a scared kid, and I'm a little scrawny and I'm dressed in black. I look pathetic and tearful. So now everyone outside the family treats me as unlucky, but I can't afford to do that. I can't do it to Mum, I can't do it to Soo-Ling or Dad. I can't do it to Betty. Tommy has forced me to survive and to live, that's the curse he's given me. Maybe he did love me. I won't ever know.

Mum is not happy when I get home. She's got the *Age* in front of her, the *Australian* on the floor, the radio on the Greek channel. The TV's on Channel Seven with the sound off.

—Hi, Mum. I kiss her. She pats me on the arm but she's far away, listening to the radio. The announcers are way too fast for my Greek, I only catch names and exclamations. I go to the lounge, grab the remote and switch on the stereo. A flash of shrieking. I hastily turn it down.

—Lou-ie! yells Mum.

—What?

—No bloody music today, not with the elections. Elections is a word she always says in Greek. For her, that English pronunciation is difficult.

—Have you voted yet?

—No. She's in the lounge, looking down to me. I waited to go with you.

I whine, writhe to get out of it.

—Mum, you know I don't believe in elections.

She cracks it.

—That's so stupid. So so so stupid. You know how many countries in the world there are where people are dying for the freedom to vote? She holds up her hand, ready to begin counting.

—Okay, okay. In Greek, You win. I hold up a hand. But can I listen to some songs first?

—One, she says.

—Three, I counter.

—Two, she answers firmly, it's in Greek. And I concede.

She prepares to vote and dresses up for the occasion; there is a ritual to her participation in democracy. I, of course, am going to escort her exactly as I am. Dirty black jeans, runners and baggy T-shirt. She thinks I'm a boor.

I play the punk CD first, shuffling through the tracks, listening to a few seconds, skipping boring bits.

All my music is in my room, the records and the CDs. So's my turntable. Mum and Dad have one shelf of records and a handful of CD's. Mum used to collect music, her kind—the Greek or show tunes. Whatever records Dad has they've been presents. I've got to admit to thieving some of their records for my collection. From Dad, Ray Charles and Herb Alpert; from Mum, *Zorba, West Side Story, Cabaret* and *Folk Tunes of Arcadia*. The vinyl of the last one resides in a white label twelve inch sleeve, DJ USE—NOT FOR SALE marked in black. The cover was on the lounge wall of my place in Fitzroy, a hefty peasant woman digging the earth, another woman, mouth open in feverish song, brandishing a pitchfork in the air. The jacket, the glorious reds and yellows, were perfectly social-realist kitsch, but the music was quite incredible. I used it on my house-mates when we got really stoned. Very trance. And the singer was good, a banshee. But yes, there's certainly nothing recent in my parents' collection. Not since Tommy and all that . . . all that bullshit.

I'm trying hard not to blame Tommy.

I go into my room and play 'The Boys Of Summer' because it was the last song I can remember Tommy liking. I look at myself in the mirror, ruffle my hair, it looks stupid, needs a cut.

—Mum, I'm ready.

She's voting at my old primary school. The day is not cold, not quite warm. Mum looks pretty good, a white vest, a long skirt with a discreet split. The grounds are full of people handing out leaflets, how to vote cards. My mum dismisses all of them and goes straight up to the Labor Party representative. The smiling woman tries to hand me one as well.

—No, no thanks.

Her smile fades.

—Take one, Mum orders in Greek. I shake my head.

She walks into line exasperated.

—She'll think you're a Liberal, she whispers, then finishes loudly, and we know there is nothing more embarrassing than being a Liberal.

The people in line, most don't seem happy about her statement. Except for a grey haired older gentleman with sun roughened blond skin.

—I'm with you, love.

My mum votes straight down the ALP ticket for the House of Representatives and numbers her preferences in order for the Senate. We argue over her choices.

—Put the Greens first in the Senate, you don't have to vote ALP all the way.

She refuses. She reminds me that I have forfeited my right to counsel by refusing to vote myself. She puts in her ballots and says loudly to the room, Paul Keating is the best politician since Whitlam.

—He's a fucking dog.

There are cheers.

Then a silence. There are neighbours here, real ones, not like on television; we don't really talk to each other. But they know something about us. The cheer ended abruptly, as if at the same time they all remembered the child that killed an innocent man and then cut his own dick off with a knife.

My mum swirls, marches out. I know she is cursing every single person who voted right wing to eternal hell. She will not countenance conciliation. She hates too much.

The right wing wins. Dad is back from the pub, early, but even by then the results seem clear. By seven o'clock both my parents are drunk. Dad knew it was coming, but he too seems surprised. My mother simply becomes melodramatic.

—We're alone, she says.

I drink with them. I watch a bit of television, the computers bringing in the numbers. Then I walk down to the creek to blow a joint. The creek is now zigzagged by poles and sand, the construction of new highway. In a year or so there won't be a creek at all. The sun is dying.

I feel sad. The roofs of the houses are all black tile. Everyone under those roofs believes nothing of what I do. The cosiness of suburbia is a real thing, people want the comforts. But it bruises the soul sometimes.

I fucking hate it here. I throw the butt of the joint into the wind.

I am very aware, as the smoke gets me stoned, that I have no clarity, no vision or even a version of the future.

Only that I will have to live it through.

The Macinis are over when I come back. Dad's in the lounge, sinking piss with Tio Simon; Mum's cursing the earth and the heavens with Tia Cara. Pinnie's waiting for me. His real name is Pietro. But he's always been called Pinnie.

—What's up?

—The cunt has won the election.

—Right. Pinnie's not at all political. He voted on the basis of which candidate he'd most like to, fuck. Which, on this occasion, meant he voted Labor.

—What are you up to tonight?

I look over at him. He's stoned as well.

—Party.

—Where?

—Thornbury.

—What kind? Uni people?

—Some.

—I'm not going.

—Suit yourself.

We go into the kitchen and watch the television. I can't stand it and I ring a taxi. It takes almost twenty minutes to get through. The woman who answers is breathless.

—Sorry for the wait.

—That's all right. Busy night?

—I guess a lot of people are celebrating the election. Her voice is stiff.

—I won't be doing that.

She is so overjoyed, her voice turns sweet. I hear the lighting up of a cigarette and, amazingly, wonderfully, we talk for fifteen minutes. We talk of how stupid people are and we talk of how dirty the Liberals and the Nationals are. I realise she is drunk. Finally I give her an address. She promises the first available, tells me she'll put me on top priority. I find myself blowing her a kiss on the phone. I don't tell her I did not vote.

—Where are you going? Mum asks. Pinnie has left, bored by the waiting.

—To Soo-Ling's, then a party.

—You feel like partying, do you?

She is looking steel at me. I shuffle, I look down.

—Go. She softens, releases me. Get drunk tonight, curse tonight. She walks out of the room and returns with forty dollars, stuffs it in my jacket pocket.

—Take taxis tonight. And be careful. Lots of drunk idiots tonight.

I kiss them all goodbye. Getting into the taxi, I wave to Pinnie. He's sitting on the Mancinis' fence, smoking a cigarette.

—Sure you don't want to go to this party? I ask.

He shakes his head.

—Tomorrow, I promise.

—Tomorrow.

•

Soo-Ling is not pleased to see me. She's hitting the wine.

—What do you want?

I come in, scowling.

—Fuck you, I whinge, then immediately, Where's Betty?

—In bed. Did you vote?

I'm alarmed by her expression. She waits.

—No.

She slaps me. It hurts and I'm shocked. She slaps me again, soft.

—Want a wine?

She pours, hands me the glass, kisses me on my wounded cheek.

—You'll take anything from me, won't you?

I nod, furiously.

—I love you. I say it matter of fact and find a seat. We watch the television, saying nothing.

—Theo Louie.

Betty's at the door, tiny square blanket in her grip, the smooth silk corner in her mouth. I scoop her into my arms.

This child is so strikingly pretty, and I think she will grow to be a goddess. The beauty is Asian and Europe, every feature impossible to locate precisely. Even the eyes; yes, certainly Chinese yet also speaking a roundness. The beauty, then, is neither Asia nor Europe. Another country altogether. Betty gurgles and whispers in my ear.

—The bad people won.

—Yes. It's sad.

She comes and sits between us on the couch, Soo-Ling wraps her arm around her daughter; Betty's still sucking on her blanket.

I'm in love with Soo-Ling. I've got to be up front about that. In this silence, the meek disturbance of the television, I'm content. Betty keeps winking at me. I wink back.

The vanquished leader comes on stage to cheers from the Labor Party true believers. To the last he is confident and arrogant. I tune off. Soo-Ling has tears in her eyes.

He's just a politician.

—The best leader since Whitlam.

I wink at Betty. But she's only concerned for her mother.

—Why are you crying, Mummy?

—Because the bad people won, Soo-Ling sniffs. She hugs her daughter. Hugs her hard. You should go to bed.

—Can Uncle Louie put me to bed?

It's late so I'm firm. No reading. But she snuggles up to me and I smell the tanginess of the child, all soap and jam. She tickles my cheek.

—You're prickly.

—Sorry. I haven't shaved for a few days.

She looks up at the ceiling.

—Who are the bad people? The Liberals?

I nod.

—Why are they bad?

—They don't like us.

—Because we're not Australian?

—We're Australian, I answer angrily.

She laughs.

—Are they the bad word?

I smile.

—Shh. Don't let your mum hear.

—Are they?

—Yeah. What are they?

She hesitates, large olive eyes stare at me.

—They're . . . Pause. They're *fucked*, she whispers and collapses into giggles.

I collapse with her.

Soo-Ling looks up at me.

—She all right?

I nod and sit beside her. I take her hand.

—Should I stay? I want her to say yes. But she doesn't. If anything, I've exasperated her. She swigs the wine.

—No. I'm going to bed soon.

I fiddle with fluff on my jeans. There's a shaft of hurt in my heart. She stares at the television.

—You should go.

I know that I will never stop reminding her of Tommy, and

because of that I will never be whole to her. She wanted me to be a kid brother and now I'm a man who is trying to take the place of a father. I don't force anything on her, I obey. That's all I want to do. There is a tattoo under my heart. It's her name in Chinese characters. I showed her and she was furious.

—How dare you put me there.

She doesn't understand; anything she does to me, whatever hurt she thinks she can inflict, she will always be there, close to my heart. I promised her, I won't go. I won't disappear.

—How dare you.

I don't want to blow Mum's cash on fares so I hitch to the party, an easy ride down Whitehorse Road into town. The man who picks me up is a large quiet type. I ask about the election and he tells me he couldn't give a fuck. The shops, the lights, the world speeds by. I relax back in the seat. Bad commercial radio, but I don't care. The bittersweet songs fit my mood. I wonder how I can protect Betty and Soo-Ling from the world. Everyone else can disappear, they are really not important. That's brutal but that's the truth. Like this man driving me into the city. He's not close at all. Now I can smell him, tobacco and dry sweat. Tomorrow I won't be able to recall him at all. Maybe just the brand name of the cigarettes he smokes. I sit back, listen to pulp, relaxed. Soo-Ling spinning round my head.

It is, of course, the strangest of parties. In a matter of hours something has changed. There are people I glimpse from uni, from around the scenes. Yesterday they didn't care. Politics, we're over that. Tonight, the world is in shock. You can read it on everyone's faces. The queers and the hippies, the technoheads and the goth revivalists. Even the politicos, the spitting anarchists getting drunk, they too seem confused. Don't vote. It only encourages them.

I wish I'd voted.

I jump right into the party, slap Carin's hand, thrust into the dance. I close my eyes, wishing I was high. Dope is all around and I reach out for a roach. Electronic beats and African chants. I suck deeply on the joint.

The party is a dislocation, even the music does nothing for me tonight. I go from kitchen to backyard. A guy with a beard is singing The International. His voice is a wisp of thinness. He doesn't know all the words. I go from backyard to kitchen. A girl is splitting up with her boyfriend. She's giving him heaps, How could you, how could you? Stupid fucking cunt, she screams. He voted conservative.

—Just for a change.

He leaves the party. Before it all turns ugly. The mood swings from sadness to something more dangerous. There could be violence. I don't want to stay.

Only music can soften us. A big boy, big black T-shirt, stops the tape. The techno abruptly edits. He flicks through CDs, finds what he wants. 'Kids in America', not the original, the *Clueless* version. And it's a great idea. The crowd swirls into the lounge room and the music is jacked up high. No, we're not adults, we feel the relief. We're the kids in America, we're the kids in America. There's a new wave coming I tell you.

—They're all cunts they're all cunts in America, sings the big guy. There's loud cheers. The sweat is pouring off me. This is, finally, union.

Hoodoo Gurus, mining the past. The cackle of vinyl. 'What's My Scene'. Everyone is dancing now. I'm slipping back into the past, a boy, jumping around my bedroom. Tommy is there too. The night is banished, the world is safe again.

One line stops me. *Tell me am I crazy to believe in ideals*. I am still, jostled by the furious crowd. I escape, make my way outside.

A boy, golden hair, beautiful, is rolling a joint, alone on the porch. He smiles at me. I'm confronted by an immense desire simply to kiss him, to taste the salt of his lips. He speaks and the moment goes. I walk out, the street, black night, the fading bass of the music.

My family once lived around here, but before I was born. Dominic and Tommy spoke of it all the time. I think Dom, in particular, missed the city. This was the world he knew. I try to navigate myself down the dark streets, know the old house is just around the corner somewhere. But I get lost, find myself beneath the freeway that leads to the suburbs and to what I call, tentatively, home. A sweeping bridge offers a walk across the freeway. Above the city, watching the speeding cars below, I think that I can fly. I look down, wonder how long it would take to die from the fall. What would be the consciousness of pain before the extinction? A millisecond, hardly registrable to the mind? Quick and painless.

I can't off myself.

Across the concrete the fascists have scrawled in thick black paint, *Asians Out, National Action.* I have nothing on me, all I can do is spit on the words. Even as I do it I am aware of how ineffectual my protest is. I shiver, wondering who is lurking in the shadows. I tell myself off: there's nothing to be afraid of, the world cannot be as dangerous as the television says.

I start walking back to the party.

This is the New Age. This is the dawn of a New Millennium.

This is the New World Order. This is a New Dawn, in Australian politics.

I'm very lonely. I just need one person, one person who I trust, just one person to hold me.

2
Girls + boys

I know the crow is behind me, I've known it for a long time, but I'm not scared of it. This is not merely bravado. Tommy called it Satan once, when I was a kid, but I think that was just to scare me. I have no idea what Satan might mean. The crow was something we all heard of from very young, but being the youngest, and by such a loud passage of time, I was protected by my mother's scepticism. I'd be playing at her feet, lost in the trance of shapes and colour, and above me she'd laugh.

—The crow, the fucking crow. *That's* their excuse.

My mother believes firmly in God. She's not going to give up on that, otherwise her life is a waste. The evidence of God is there in her withered hands, her ruined back and her aged face. But she doesn't believe in heaven or in hell. That's just make-believe she tells me, this is it. The world and nothing beyond it.

Back from Greece I went to visit my great-grandmother's grave in Ballarat, a cold city. From what my father has said it is not the place for her. She hated this earth. The headstone—simple, just her name, Marta Kyriakos, a phrase in Greek—is vanishing with time. Crumbling. I just stood there looking down at the earth. Nothing leapt out at me, not even a crow around. The silence said nothing.

I'm in the toilet, masturbating. I've got the official Colling-wood Football Club yearbook open to pictures of Saverio Rocca and Nathan Buckley. I can hear Mum talking to Thea Yiota in the kitchen. I close my eyes, fantasise, and come quickly. I'm sure I'm blushing when I come out of the toilet.

Tonight I'm taking Soo-Ling out to dinner. I'm slightly ill at ease. Things are uptight between us, over Betty. And over God. Betty asked me about God, at Hungry Jack's, slowly nipping at her chips. It wasn't a question I was prepared for.

—Who's God, Louie?

A young couple were kissing in a corner.

—That's a hard question, Bet.

—Why?

—There's a lot of Gods.

She swirled her chip on the plastic tray, then gulped it down and reached for another.

—Mum says there is no God.

I don't answer.

—Who's Jesus?

—Some people say he was the son of God. I reckon he was just a good man.

—Mum says he's not real either. Mum says it's all bullshit.

—I think he was real.

The topic changes to *The Lion King*, the movie I'm taking her to. We finish the burgers and chips.

Soo-Ling rings up later. I can tell immediately that she's furious.

—What have you been saying to Betty?

—'Bout what?

—Religion.

—Nothing.

Religion is a sore topic with Soo-Ling. There was a lot of Jesus freak stuff around Tommy and the guy he killed. The journos whispered about sects.

—She keeps asking me about Jesus and God. I won't let her be fucked up by that.

—I didn't say a thing.

—Listen, she's my child.

That truth hurts because it cuts me right out.

—She's going to have to learn about it one day.

Soo-Ling says nothing, just the harsh beat of her breathing.

—I didn't say anything, I just told her what I think.

A cruel laugh.

—What do you know, Lou, what the fuck do you know? Religion just screws everything up. A stifled cry, then a stark ugly sarcasm. Just ask Tommy.

—This wasn't about Tommy.

—She's my child, okay, and I'll teach her my way.

You can't.

—Agreed. It is not a question, no room for negotiation.

—Agreed.

She hangs up.

Soo-Ling says that I have to learn how to make enemies, that without that skill I won't be able to go forward. She thinks it is as important as making friends, the ability to sift through people, find those that will deliberately hurt you. She dislikes my inability to ride through conflict. I just clam up, refuse the engagement, at my weakest pretend to agree just to avoid argument. She can't stand that.

—Some people will hurt you, believe me, through envy, through cruelty. You trust too easily.

My mother is totally in agreement. When I got my first tattoo she went hysterical, thought it was outrageous. But when I recently went for my third, she urged me to get an eye on my skin, to ward off evil.

—You need the eye, she ordered me, everyone is a saint to you. They'll do you great damage.

I got the eye, across my left shoulder, but I think they're both wrong. I want to be liked but what I give out is limited. It is easy for me to trust people because I don't let them move in deep, they only know my surfaces. The reality is that only Soo-Ling and my family can hurt me. Maybe Betty, but she's too young, I'm her favourite, she won't hurt me yet.

I don't believe anyone's a saint, I just don't believe anyone is the Devil.

The crow, I see it all the time. The old wog grandma and the old black crone, flying together. But maybe that too is bullshit.

I'm stopping myself loving but I'm falling in love all the time. I'm in love with Soo-Ling, in love with Sean, even in love with Saverio Rocca. That makes me a slut, I guess, but an emotional slut because I don't have lots of sex. I'm not very good at sex, it's all a pose. I clam up, don't talk, worry about my body. Sometimes I wish I was like the rootrats, those guys who can blow their load in anyone, enjoy it and not think about the moment afterwards. Except I've been with those type of guys and I know what it's like to be the receptacle. You feel fucking shithouse.

Let me make it clear. Don't assume that because I used the term receptacle I have ever let anyone fuck me up the arse. If that ever happens, it's going to have to be love, it's going to have to be with someone who makes it a pledge to be with me, it's going to have to be real and honest and good. That's not fashionable, that's too nineteenth century or something, but I don't give a shit. I'm doubting it will happen. Ever. I don't trust men. In my experience, men can't be trusted.

Take Sean. You'd think it would be easy for us to get together. He loves music, I make him laugh, he's tall and good looking and, though I hate my nose, dislike my feet and know I look wimpy, I'm not ugly. I try hard not to think of myself like that. I met Sean through friends at a party, and we danced to Sebodah together. It was an immediate crush. I was tired, my friends were leaving, the party was boring, but I stayed on. Sinking beers and meeting Sean's friends. I remember the excitement, of meeting someone and connecting. But the night had to end. The stereo was turned off and a bleating friend of Sean's was urging everyone to move on. I was invited, a poofter palace in Prahran, but I can't stand those places. Tacky music and too much aftershave. Instead, we exchanged numbers. He promised to give me a ring.

He didn't.

I waited five days, getting neurotic, boring my housemates, I was unable to work, to read, to study. I'd rush home every night, press the button on the answering machine. Soo-Ling cracked the shits by day five.

—Give the bastard a ring. I'm sick of hearing about him.

So I did. And you know what happened? Nada. He was stilted, standoffish. My confidence sunk to nil, beyond nil. He said he had to go, off to work. I put on my I-don't-feel-a-thing-just-rang-because-I-was-bored voice.

—See ya.

—See ya.

I hate poofters.

I really do.

Sean is six feet three inches, has the whisper of dimples and it is easy to forgive him everything when he smiles. All my friends love him. Except Soo-Ling. He's hurting me so she can't let herself like him. I think this must be something of what she means when she talks about the necessity of enemies.

If I could tear away the homosexuality from myself, I would gladly do it. If I believed aversion therapy would work, I would sign up. I wish for the bliss of being bisexual, because then I could appreciate the eroticism of men but also appreciate the eroticism of the gender I want to love. But I'm scared doing it with women. It's been a disaster, the soft drooping cock. The first girl said it didn't matter, but she told all her friends. The easy road to being a pariah in the schoolyard.

The second girl decided to suck me off. I closed my eyes and thought of football. I came in her mouth.

I went home, despising myself.

There are two men I have sex with. My friend Pinnie and an old man called Clive. Pinnie and I have been doing it for years, since our teens. I wish, often, that I could be like Pinnie. Pinnie's overweight, a dark Maltese boy, and he's shrill and he's tough. And he loves being fucked, adores it. He's a perpetual hole for any man who wants to put it up him and he's always been this way. He scares me sometimes, the way he moans, the explosive screams. He prefers I use spit, not lube. His hole is a big inviting space, protected by a veil of black tight curls. I don't always feel good after sex with him, and I don't know how he feels about it. We don't talk much, not about that. I go for weeks not touching him, not going near him, spending time with uni friends. And then I get that urge, the need to fuck, and I go over. He's usually at home, smoking bongs. I don't even have to say anything. We wordlessly strip, he blows me a little, and in I go. I come, I wipe myself with a hanky, I dress and we sit down to smoke and watch a video or television or play some Nintendo. What I do with Pinnie is somewhere between masturbation and making love. For him, I'm a chance to experience something he loves: the feel of semen shooting up his colon. He can't get that at the toiles and the sex clubs, he can't trust it. He trusts me because he knows I'm fucked up about sex and I don't get it enough. Sometimes I wonder if he's being straight with me, if he isn't letting himself get fucked without a condom in the toilet he uses.

—I swear, mate, it's all safe. Anyway, they're usually married men fucking too nervous of facing the wife to risk copping AIDS.

I've never been tested. That one I'm leaving to fate.

Clive is sixty-nine, has dentures and lives three blocks from Mum and Dad. I've been visiting him for two years, about once a month. I get fifty dollars but I don't think I'm doing it for the money. Pinnie put me onto Clive, though Pinnie can't be bothered with him any more. Clive sometimes has trouble getting an erection. I don't mind, I just go around to talk. I like him.

He was married, for forty years, to a woman called Sheila. He says he loved her and I believe him. Photos of Sheila are everywhere in the house, and photos of their two kids. Clive and I don't really do much. He may blow me, give me a hand-job. I lick him a bit and I try hard to kiss him because I know he likes it. But I have to close my eyes. He knows I'm doing it out of affection but I guess it still must hurt. The kisses are quick, friendly not passionate. He usually cooks me a meal.

Clive was in the army, served in Korea and Vietnam. He has tattoos, thick blue lines, all over his arms and chest. A mermaid hides underneath the sparse grey hairs.

—Have you always been into men?

He shook his head when I asked him, this the third time we had sex.

—No. Told you, I only had eyes for Sheila. And before marriage it was only whores, female, all of them.

—But did you know you were gay?

—I'm not gay.

—I mean, did you know you wanted to have sex with men?

Again, he shook his head no.

—Then why now?

This is what he told me. That five months after the funeral, alone, the kids all gone back to their homes, he looked up the escort services in the phone book and realised he had never seen, up close, what an uncircumcised cock looked like, how it functioned when erect. The thought just came to him and he was immediately excited. So he rang a service, specified he wanted an uncircumcised whore and a young blond man came over. They didn't do much. Clive just gave him a hand-job and the whore sucked him off. Twelve minutes and one hundred and ten dollars.

Clive takes out his dentures when he sucks me off. Clive occasionally hires a female whore, when he is feeling horny, when he's won at the pokies. But I'm cheaper and I think he genuinely likes me.

Soo-Ling knows about Clive. I pointed him out to her one day in Box Hill, shopping in the Plaza. He didn't know we were there.

—Oh yuck, that old geezer.

—He's all right. He's nice, he's got a good heart.

She blows a cool stretch of smoke, out of the side of her lips. She smiles at me.

—You're so weird. You could fuck anyone, why him?

I didn't tell her he pays. That would have only obscured the truth.

—I told you, he's nice.

—You reckon you've always been gay? she asks me abruptly.

—I'm not gay. I scowl.

—Bi then.

—I'm not bi.

—What the fuck are you then?

—Me.

She sighs. Then speaks slowly.

—All right, Mr Smarty-Pants. You reckon you've always been you?

—Yes.

She pounces.

—So it's biological?

—No.

—So it's society?

—No.

We look at each other. A pause. We break out laughing.

I think it's God.

Tommy never hurt me. Never. He put his cock in my mouth, when I was five, and that's it. Many people, maybe even most people, would trace a sexual history way back to that moment. But I think they'd be wrong. At three I remember vividly seeing Mum's pubes poking through her panties as she was getting undressed. The blackness shocked me. I saw Dad pissing when I was six. I can still masturbate to this. Tommy's dick in my mouth is just one more family snapshot.

Mum used to slap all of us when we were kids. And I saw Dad bash Tommy. No-one is a saint.

But Tommy never hurt me. I can't remember sucking him off, or yes, maybe I can, but it's all very blurry. Choppy. I remember getting excited when he showed me his cock, a little scared when he pushed me towards it. I think I remember it growing in my mouth and then all I remember is the wet, which I thought was fucking blood, and I must have panicked. Christ, I was only a kid. But Tommy didn't mean to hurt me, he was just a horny teenager, we were just playing.

I fucking loved Tommy. He was a good brother.

What hurt was seeing what they did to Tommy. And I blamed myself, for screaming, for getting scared. Tommy had zipped up, was crying by the time Dom smashed into the room, but I was still howling and semen was still a visible white trail across my face. Dad came in after Dom, and by then Dom was already knocking Tommy's head against the floor. Mum followed and when she saw me she went hysterical. She laid into Tommy, pushed Dom aside and she was fists and kicks. I had never seen this before and I never wish to see it again. The moment was a madness, a grand folly. Dad and Dom were holding Tommy down, by now the boy was silent, and Mum continued to beat him, to curse him, to destroy him. I was now only silent terror. I thought he was dead. And the voice, just yelling, I think it was Dom: You animal, you don't do that to your brother. Then, I see Tommy's face twitch, he's crying, and his nose is broken. He yelps like an animal and I start hoeing into Mum and Dad and Dom. This is what I remember most clearly, I want to kill them for what they are doing to Tommy. The fear is now just an instinct to punish.

My anger stopped the madness. Seeing what had happened to his child made my father repent. He scooped Tommy into his arms and asked forgiveness. Over and over and over. My mother was praying. This is all I remember.

No, I remember one more thing. The stretching touch of the semen as it dried on my cheek.

I don't know why Tommy did the things that he did. He didn't just cut his dick off, he scraped away at the insides, he scooped out from where he pisses, he tore his fucking urethra.

The balls were splattered flat on the floor. He had gutted himself. And nearly torn that poor fuck's head off.

Maybe, his getting me to suck him off fucked *him* up. Maybe, his being bashed so ruthlessly fucked him up. That's the risk of life which nothing, no religion, no belief, no promise will ever eradicate. I don't know why Tommy did the things he did. And because of that, everyone around me is now suspect, including myself.

Who killed my brother? Me. My mother. My father. My brother. His lover. The boy in the photograph. The media. The Church. The flap of a frigging butterfly's wing.

Tommy killed himself.

And I distrust everyone for letting it happen.

Except for Betty.

Soo-Ling picks me up for dinner on the corner of Rathdowne and Victoria Streets. I'm waiting at the edge of the Carlton Gardens, swinging my bag. The traffic is starting to bank up, the drizzle is gaining momentum, preparing for rain, and she laughs as I get into the car.

—What?

—You look so fucking young.

I fiddle with the radio stations, and because it's rush hour, all the commercial channels are synchronised to ads. I find something fluffy, some dance.

—No. Leave it on Radio National.

—It sucks. I fold my arms, frowning.

—You're to blame, you know.

—For what.

—That's why this bloody government can get away with cuts to public radio. She taps at my head. You should listen to more news.

—No way. I think about what she said. I want to listen to it, but they don't play any music.

The traffic has stalled, all the way to Punt Road. The announcer starts talking about the Racist.

—Switch it off, I order. I refuse to listen to that bitch.

—Heaps of people are listening to her. Soo-Ling's smile completely vanishes.

—Well, they're bloody idiots.

—There's a lot of them.

—Where?

—Lou, what do you mean? Look at the polls.

I sniff, look out to the orange bricks of a hospital. A little old woman, rugged up, is smoking on the steps. A thick branch of a tree provides shelter.

—Soo-Ling, most people are stupid. The polls are proof of that.

—But those people vote.

She wins on that.

We have dinner at a restaurant in Doncaster. It's Chinese, and good Chinese.

—You look happy.

I've been watching her study the menu and I am intrigued. When I first met Soo-Ling I was struck by her simple stylishness. She cared about clothes, and her clothes were European and exquisite. She told me that she spent half her time shopping in op shops and half her time in boutiques. No-one I knew dressed as beautifully as she did. The secret was wearing nothing gaudy. Now she dresses down a little. She no longer cares as passionately about the name on a label. But she is still breathtaking. Tonight she is giggly and soft, close to the first impression I had of her. Before we both got hard.

—I am happy.

—How come?

She pours another slosh of white wine.

—I'm going on a date Friday night.

I am up-front about resenting this piece of information.

—Why?

—What do you mean, why?

—I thought you were celibate.

She stops smiling.

—I am.

—You told him this?

Silence.

—So you haven't?

She explodes.

—Jesus, Lou, so fucking what? We've just talked bullshit so far. If I feel like telling him on Friday, I'll tell him.

—You want to have sex again, don't you?

I wait.

—Well?

I wait.

—Maybe.

I feel like grabbing the table and throwing it against a wall, I feel like being mean. Instead, I do something else. I stand up, say excuse me and walk to the toilet.

My behaviour, I know, is incredibly silly. I'm not going to pretend a justification. But Soo-Ling and Betty are all to me. I want them around me forever. I worship Soo-Ling and I only know, now anyway, how to be innocently happy, content, when I am around her. Without sex, because of her celibacy, because of my lust for cock, I can pretend we are somehow lovers. I am so jealous of this unseen unnamed man that I want to hurt her. This is a new sensation. This is shocking and this is why I have to hide in the toilet, why I have to cry.

When I piss, I feel a little better. My eyes are red and I splash cold water on my face. In the mirror, I see that I do look very young. Baby cheeks beneath the stubble.

—Are you all right? She takes my hand and I let her.

—Yeah. I decide to attempt a maturity. So who is it?

—His name is Patrick.

—So he's a man.

—Of course he's a man.

—Anglo?

She bites back on her lips.

—Kind of.

—Kind of?

—He's Irish.

—That's anglo.

—That is not!

I stare at her.

—Doesn't the Racist have some Irish blood?

—Shut the fuck up.

I can't seem to slow it down. I attempt to breathe in the jealousy. I can't eat the food.

—Celibacy hasn't been easy.

She is twirling the chopsticks around her finger. She drops them.

—Listen, Lou. I do love you but, and don't get upset about this, it's as a younger brother. You're a good friend but that's all we are.

I shake my head violently. She smiles at this and I lose it again.

—Don't treat me like a fucking child.

—Then don't act like one!

We sit in silence.

—What's he like?

She watches me cautiously.

—No, I mean it. I want to know.

She begins a spin, tells me about the way he looks and the way he sounds. She likes his voice. They met in class, he's worked with damaged kids. He sounds good, he sounds funny, he sounds handsome. Every single thing she tells me is a wound. The dinner is left not even half eaten on the table. Doncaster is the end of the universe, the coldest place on the planet.

She drives me home.

—How's the house hunting going?

—All right.

—You okay at your Mum and Dad's?

—Sure.

The drive is mercifully short. She keeps the lights on and the motor running. I dig into my jacket pocket. I hand her the tape.

—Present.

She takes it, and. as she takes it she holds tight, a moment, to my hand.

—Thank you.

I don't say anything, a peck on the cheek. I'm home, the house in darkness, a brutal brick negation. There is no sound in the neighbourhood.

Soo-Ling is the one who fills this nothing and makes life *something*. Only when Soo-Ling is around can the world be truly beautiful.

Mum wakes up as I come in and calls out to me. I answer back, softly, and she is again asleep. A light meal is on the table, covered in white paper napkins. The oil eats into the paper. I cover the plate with foil and put it in the fridge.

I go out on the back porch and call softly. The cat swiftly runs to my feet and I scoop it up, rub my face in the soft short hair.

—How are you, Man, how are you?

He is immediately purring.

I take him into my room and I put on the stereo. A world music show on 3PBS. I keep the music low and keep stroking the cat. Mum doesn't like him in the house but my rule-breaking is tolerated. Man is not yet two, he's sleek and mischievous, the perfect cat. Bass Guitar was like that, except Bass had no markings, just pure black. Man is black and white, Man is pretty sexy. Bass Guitar I had for years, she died at fourteen. She died not soon after Tommy. I cried more at the death of the cat. This doesn't mean anything except that the grief was simple. Bass Guitar loved me more than any other thing on the planet, a reciprocal love. That's a guarantee I have never achieved with an adult. I let Man sit on my chest and I am lost in some Arab rhythm.

When I think of Soo-Ling I think of my vast stupidity. This is a love that refuses the reality of my own body. I can't even love her in my imagination. This more than anything is the proof of my failed heterosexuality. I can love women but I consider it shameful to fuck them. I can fuck men but I consider it impossible to love them. I think of Soo-Ling with a man called Patrick, a dark shadow in my mind, and I am bereft of life. I sigh. I am immobile.

My treacherous libido resurrects me of course. I am patting the cat and my cock twitches. I try to think of a woman but it is only anatomy: fingers darting up a cunt, the silk taste of breast. Faces destroy the illusion.

I can't love those I fuck. Even Sean is impossible to wank to.

Instead I think of footballers and create a vision. I'm in a room, a motel, with a footballer. He is forcing me to his cock. On my chest the cat swirls, licks at my nose and then jumps off, angry. I unzip my fly and start tugging.

The image changes.

The footballer turns me over and enters me. Even as the fucking begins, I come. The cat jumps back on the bed. I clean my pants and shirt with my hanky. It stinks of decay. I pocket it.

I fall into sleep, Man on my shoulder, purring, my heart hurting, thinking of Soo-Ling. It takes a long time to leave consciousness behind.

3
Thesis: Taxi Driver

In 1968, as she was having a quick cigarette break outside her workplace, the Smithies & Sons Ladies Wear warehouse and factory, my mother was interviewed as part of a vox pop by the Channel Nine television program, *A Current Affair*. The reporter was asking people on Johnson Street for their views on conscription and the war in Vietnam. According to my mother's telling—for this story is now a family legend, and therefore there are numerous versions I have heard—she answered that she was opposed to conscription and, further, she was opposed to the war itself. She cited the United States' support for the military junta then in power in Greece as proof of America's selfish interference in other countries' affairs. She added that it was foolish for Australian young men to die for a cause they were ignorant about.

But then, Mum thinks that all of us Australians are ignorant about politics.

The journalist promised her that the segment would be televised that evening. Dominic says Mama was excited and proud. Everyone in the house, my brothers, my parents, Yiota and Spiro who were then living with my family, everyone was crowded around the television. The program comes on and the item is kept till the end. No-one can recall what the news story was that prompted the vox pop. Dom says it probably was more footage of soldiers dying in Vietnam but he can't really remember. But he remembers Mum.

For a few seconds she's squinting into the black and white

sun and she says, War is bad. That's it, that's all they had of her.

That incident changed my mother's attitude to the media forever. She was outraged. Growing up I remember a constant flow of invective hurtled towards the screen whenever the news or current affairs programs were on. Liars, fakers, charlatans, whores. Devils! She didn't mind the sitcoms or the nature documentaries, or the soaps and movies; they were fine because they did not conceal their fictions. She warned all of us against the deceits of the television but her three sons refused to listen; we found much solace there.

In the end, I think she was proved right.

The story of the interview just doesn't go away. I'm fascinated by it and angry about it, even though I was not yet born when all this occurred. They cut her up. I can see how it happened—her accent must have been much thicker then, and her emotive response a bit of an anomaly on Australian TV of the 1960s, which preferred to provide information with a Mother Country's stiff upper lip. When I see old black and white docos from the sixties, I mostly see frightened old ladies in Queen Mother hats or slightly pissed old guys. I never see anyone who reminds me of my mum. There's more hesitation, for me, about telling my mother's stories than there is about anyone else in our family. My mum's English is pretty good, it's excellent, but it's not her first language and I've seen her struggle with it, try and learn a vocabulary anew; to name things, to name herself. What she hated most was to be thought stupid. That's what hurt about the interview. War is bad. That's nothing, she still yells when telling the story, everyone *knows* war is bad. I said so much more and all they think fit to use is something that everybody already knows.

In 1997 an interview appeared in the English weekly, *New Musical Express*, an interview with the Anglo-Asian musicians Asian Dub Foundation. One member, speaking of the mythical aura surrounding the London of the 1960s, the swinging London of high fashion and high pop, sarcastically asks, What was so special about England in the sixties. Why don't you ask my mum about London in the sixties?

What would a Paki migrant woman in 1968 have told us about England? It wouldn't be a glamorous model's story, it wouldn't be Nicholas Roeg's *Performance*. But just because no-one sang the story, no-one wrote the book, no-one filmed it, that doesn't mean it didn't happen.

But as my mother would counter, even if someone had bothered to ask the wog Londoner a question, would it be the right question, would they have listened?

Mum has another great story, about a Yugoslav woman she worked with, Zita. Zita was an artist, had even trained in Belgrade, and she worked with Mum in the factories. She saved up and bought herself a black leather folio, quite expensive, gathered her drawings and her canvas and walked into a gallery in Toorak Road which specialised in modern and contemporary art. She had done her hair, she wore her new navy skirt and a white silk blouse she had bought in Myers. She walked into the gallery and the man behind the counter smiled, asked what she wanted. She started to speak and he stopped her and very slowly explained that the position was taken. What position? The cleaner, for the gallery. Oh, said Zita, and she turned around and walked through the door.

—What stopped her, Mum?

—History, she replies, history can be very wearing.

She was surrounded by men, my Mama. A husband and three sons. She always said of us that we were gullible, that our thinking betrayed a slackness which came from being born in the place we were born. All of us, I guess, were in awe of her strength. During the war, living in Athens, my mother had seen her youngest brother, still a toddler, die from starvation. Not that she talked much about her own suffering, not that she was any kind of martyr, but I think her three children grew up fearing that we could never live up to her strength. It hurt, a little, that she considered us gullible, merely Australian. It hurt that in small ways we were always reminded of being exiled from her.

No-one bothered to ask questions of my mother and the one time they did, they edited her out. Mum laughs at the crows, says they are a fairy tale. But, Mum, I'd argue as a kid, Dad believes in the crows.

—Lou, she'd tell me, just because you believe in something doesn't make it true.

•

There are maybe fourteen people in my Propaganda, Pornography and Dissidence tutorial. I say maybe because no-one, including myself, turns up regularly. There is a certain familiarity I have with these people, we acknowledge each other when we cross paths, but there are only three people in the tute I could confidently assess as personalities. The others all remain strangers. Sometimes, when I'm bored, looking out the window across the campus grounds, I start fantasising. There is a woman, Chloe, long red hair, quiet, private, who stuns me with her sweet beauty. There is Clinton, a simulation of an American; I wonder if his name is real. He is good-looking, blond, fit and healthy. What is he doing here, debating the intricacies of theory and culture? In my fantasies his soul leads a darker life. And there's Must, Mustapha, who is a bit of a joker, real sexy, and who likes an argument. The others, just faces.

The pressure is on. This is my final year. Sometimes, very occasionally, I think of going on, doing a Masters. But I resist. The pressure is economic. It will cost another two or three grand in fees to keep going. As it is I'll owe the taxation department twenty thousand when I graduate. There's no career path ahead of me. I contemplate journalism, I contemplate public relations, I contemplate film, I think about being a teacher, I contemplate being an office stiff. None of these options seems honest, from my core. I'm still fucking around, working out a direction, avoiding a white collar future.

—What are you going to do, asks my father, when you're finished?

—Don't know. Get a job somewhere.

The answer does not satisfy him but he is content to let me explore. My mother too, though she keeps her eyes on the unemployment figures.

—You should have done computers.

—I'd be hopeless.

—You're smart, you could have picked it up. She sips her coffee. If I was in your place, I would have done computer science.

That, of course, is not true. Maria Stefano, who loves her coffee and her wine, who adores argument and conversation, Maria Stefano, who still believes in struggle, would be in my tute if she ever had the chance. She would be arguing the world, class and politics, and getting straight As. But my mother never had the chance of any of this, never studied beyond the sixth grade. So I can't fail study, I couldn't betray her like that.

Maybe I should have done computers. This will be the last year for this seminar, the uni is going back to basics. Reading, writing and arithmetic. The humanities are dead.

Manoli, Mannie, is my boss. He's a bit of a wog, up himself and thinks he's God's gift. But he's fair. He doesn't pretend that we can or should be friends.

—Lou, next time you're even one fucking minute late, you're, out on your arse, right?

—Sorry, Mannie.

I don't go in late any more.

—I hear you're in the union.

—Who'd you hear it from?

—Forgot. So, are you?

—Yeah.

—Fine. Can you do a shift on Thursday?

—What time?

—From five-thirty.

—Sure.

That's how we talk to each other.

I work in a video shop in Nunawading. It has a section of Greek, Italian and Indian movies. Next, Mannie's bringing in some titles from Hong Kong. He can see the market for the product. Where I grew up prides itself as an anglo enclave but I can't ever remember that being true. It is not a wog area, we don't dominate, but we are there, in every street, in every classroom: Vietnamese, Chinese, Greeks, Indians and Italians. Mannie stocks the usual titles from the US, a tiny art-house section, and he gets the wog patronage as well. Times are tough.

—Mannie, I reckon you should expand into cult.

—We got some.

—Yeah?

—Yeah. *Blue Velvet.*

—That's not cult. That's like a classic.

—Yeah, that's right, a fucking cult classic.

The shop is clear of customers. He calls me intp the back and I stand in the doorway while he lights a cigarette in his office.

—That fucking cult shit costs. Those distributors are breaking my balls. All that poofter shit you like, all that Japanese sicko stuff, it costs heaps. Show me requests, a few of them, then I'll think about it. Not till then.

He winks at me.

—This is the fucking 'burbs, Lou, you got to take it slow.

There is a message book by the computer terminals. It's for the staff to leave notes to each other, keep informed about any harassing customers, any problems during the shift. After the discussion about unions, I leave this note:

Which one of you cunts informed on me about being a union member? When I find out, you're fucking mince.

Mannie has not said one word about it. Janet, who I can't stand, replied:

I find the word CUNT offensive.

Eva's favourite record is *Honey's Dead* by The Jesus and Mary

Chain and the song she loves most from it is 'Good For My Soul'. A friend, Sando, has a four track studio at home and he taught me some simple tricks with wires and buttons. I did a bit of a remix for Eva, taking the song and cutting it into the dub B-side of an old SOS Band song. I burnt it on a CD for her. It's simple, embarrassingly so, but Eva loved it. She hugged me and told me I was very talented. I blushed at this, I knew how naive it really was. But I was happy she was happy.

I'm working from their place, crashing a few weeks to complete my thesis. Ringwood, where they live, is on the train line, a quilt of red brick housing. It takes me half an hour to walk to the nearest convenience store. I don't mind. I like the walk.

Dom just smiled when Eva played him the song. He's made it listenable, is all he said, but he was proud of me. This is the generosity he was unable to offer Tommy.

•

They'll probably fail my thesis. It sure the fuck isn't classical, it sure the fuck isn't writing, reading or arithmetic. I'm not quite sure myself what I'm doing, but I'm trying hard to write something accessible and honest and which is worth spending a year of my life doing. I'm writing about a man who might be a rapist, Barry Bond, and I'm writing about Martin Scorsese's *Taxi Driver* and a film called *The Sum Of Us*. Two very different films, all very different stories. But I'm asking questions and making connections and hoping the connections spark more questions.

And I'm writing about Tommy.

I've cut down to two shifts a week at the video shop, just till I finish writing up the thesis. I should explain it, explain how it works, explain why it is. There is only one thing I know that I can do, and I don't even know if I can do it well. I can write. Somehow, I've got to trust it, somehow writing has to give me direction.

I have this theory that *Taxi Driver* vindicates the suburbs over the city. That might seem a fragile theory; after all, it's such a New York movie. But everything the protagonist Travis Bickle detests is a product and an effect of the urban. The fags, the whores, the niggers, the spooks. He wants to save the little whore-child, take her out of Manhattan, place her back into the womb of suburbia. Even though we, the audience, understand his mania, the coda of the film indicates that he has been made a hero. This is irony, quite thickly laid on irony, but I don't particularly wish to dwell on this. The ending is open to a variety of readings. I like that. I don't like anything being settled too comfortably.

Paul Schrader wrote the screenplay, and he's also a film director. Now, I've got another theory. I reckon Schrader is the brains. Scorsese is the more talented filmmaker but the script of *Taxi Driver* goes to places where Scorsese hasn't gone since. Reading the literature, the critical reception to his films, Schrader got his arse kicked in the US for being a reactionary, for being an intellectual. They're like Australians the Americans, suspicious of thinkers. That's why Scorsese gets the kudos and Schrader gets silence. This is a tangent, I can't explore it in my thesis, but I don't think Schrader is reactionary. A puritan, sure, but that allows him, in a film like *Hardcore*, to go places where the sexual liberationists can't go because they're protecting their turf. And in *Patty Hearst* Schrader deals the final blow to a politics of commitment Natasha Richardson, who plays Hearst, delivers a long final monologue to camera. Fuck them, fuck them all, she finishes. That's it. That's the politics of the post-Cold War, a fatigue with the right and with the left. And who better to know that than Patty Hearst herself? Growing up in the heartland of the right, grand-daughter of Randolph Hearst, Mr Citizen Kane himself, kidnapped and then a revolutionary member of the Symbionese Liberation Army (what the fuck is Symbionese?). What happens? Whatever role she assumes, she can't win because every act is open to criticism. So in the end, Fuck them, fuck them all.

But in *Taxi Driver* we still haven't got to that stage, there's still the game of morality and principles. If you were to remake *Taxi Driver* now, Travis Bickle wouldn't care a shit about some twelve year old hooker. Fuck, we all know twelve year old hookers, even if they're just the ones you pass on the streets. You don't need a reason for a massacre any more.

The thesis is really about the media, how it works. I feel that I can substantiate ideas with my own experience. Tommy's murder-suicide, the cameras and the papers were right on it. Great story. Tommy was:

Page 6 in the *Age*.

Page 3 in the *Herald*.

Page 7 in the *Australian*.

Three page spread in *Who Weekly*.

Interview with the man who owned the house in which it happened: *A Current Affair*.

Interview with Mum on Channel Ten news. She regrets it, they caught her, a camera in her face, asked the questions. She broke down. They played that again and again.

A photo of Tommy. We, the family, refused to give them anything. But someone contacted the place he worked. They found a file of photos from a Christmas bust-up party. Tommy, glass of beer raised, trying to hide his face from the lens, still smiling. This image was everywhere; blown up to half a page, full colour, in the *Who Weekly* spread.

I hate the media. They have made their image my last memory of my brother.

I don't use them, I avoid them. I don't read the papers, I don't watch the news. The most astounding thing I discovered in those first few hallucinatory months was how the story being communicated in the news is so removed from your everyday experience. I don't think I thought at all about the guy who was murdered. Just once, really, seeing footage of his family at the funeral.

He turned out to be an Aborigine. As much as I'd like it to be, that is no innocent fact.

An *Age* opinion piece about racist violence and anti-racist legislation law's referred to recent race hate crimes, mentioned the Tommy story.

The media created that story. That doesn't mean they might not have been right. No-one knows what happened in that house, on that night. Not the police, the investigating detectives, the victim's family, Tommy's family. No-one. That doesn't stop the media.

Was it a racist murder? I hate them, I hate them for leaving that question in my head.

It is the idea of Tommy suiciding that rocks me most. Me and Mum and Soo-Ling. Maybe not for Dad and Dom. I know Dom detests the idea of Tommy's murder. The one person I thought of most during that time was Mum, her spinning out of control. That's something that wasn't in the fucking media.

Mum came out of it, we all did, but we all got changed.

The media interest in my family had the effect of drawing us together. But now we're a family that doesn't trust easily, and that includes Soo-Ling. Fuck them, fuck them all.

My thesis may vindicate the family as well. Maybe. I won't know till it's done and I'm not one for stating firm conclusions. I'm here, at the university, and it's far away from my family. My thesis is also an argument about place. This is an argument that began last year, in another tutorial, between me and another man. He was arguing integrity. And I hated him for it.

—*The Sum Of Us* is bullshit. It's boring and it's conservative. All that crap about mateship.

He is a tall boy, an angry-boy, pierced mouth.

The rest of the class agrees. I'm thinking of my mother. Her tears at the end of the movie, how she cried when the old lesbian couple were split apart.

In Greek, she turns to me, A fantastic movie.

Here's the plot. Jeff (Russell Crowe) is a working class homosexual son, a plumber and amateur footballer, who lives with his accepting father (Jack Thompson). Jeff finds it hard to find a guy who will commit to a relationship and the father tries to assist him in his search. Father has stroke, Jeff looks after father and the film ends on the upbeat note that maybe the guy Jeff is interested in will reciprocate his love.

Also, an important subplot. Jeff's grandmother was a lesbian, lived for years with her girlfriend until the family decide to split them up and put them in separate nursing homes.

It's a film about family.

—I don't mind *The Sum Of Us*.

Everyone turns, eyes on me. The tall boy challenges me.

—Why?

—I like the characters.

He explodes.

—It's a fucking-fantasy, no-one, no-one lives like that. Certainly no working-class poofter. I come from that world.

—So do I.

—Then how can you like it?

There's the rub, there's the argument. There's the contradiction. We come from the same place, we end up different.

—I like the fag son, I like the father. I like the relationship.

—So being a poof is all right unless you happen to be a bit nancy, a bit effeminate. Don't you see, he is imploring me. The movie celebrates monogamy, traditional gender roles, can't you see how conservative it is?

My mother laughed a lot as well as cried watching *The Sum Of Us*. At the end of the movie, my mother switches off the television set, takes my hand. She begins in Greek. My child, if you decide to be with men, I'd like you to find a man like that boy in the movie. She finishes in English. Whoever you are, whoever you are with, I love you.

This is the first time that a non-heterosexual future has been discussed by my mother. I am shaking, scared, but also excited. We're both crying.

—I'll find a footballer, I joke with her, like the guy in the movie.

—Make it a soccer player, she says, deadpan. I don't want you to be with any Australian.

—I wouldn't mind finding someone like the Russell Crowe character, I argue back.

There are giggles in the classroom.

Let me put this straight. *Taxi Driver* is a great movie, an absolute masterpiece. *The Sum Of Us* is shoddy, a play unimaginatively transferred to screen. But I'm not interested, not in this thesis, in formal questions of aesthetics. I'm interested in what is being communicated. I want to understand two things. My mother's tears and pleasure in the movie, and the source of the giggles.

I've moved to Eva and Dom's because no matter how much she restrains herself, my mother can't stop interrupting, coming in, asking if I'm hungry, asking me questions. At Dom's I'm left alone, except for the children, and I don't mind the children. They watch *The Simpsons* on video, I am entertained by their laughter.

Eva and Dom aren't going well. I can sense it in the silences between them. The house is large, four bedrooms, and mercifully full of the gabbling of the kids. I'm reading them stories, rolling on the floor with them.

Lisa asks me, What are you doing? I'm at the kitchen table, punching the keys on the laptop Jay lent me.

—What's that?

—A computer.

She is disdainful.

—I know that. What are you doing on it?

—Writing my thesis.

—What's that?

—A story.

—Like a book?

—Kind of Shorter.

—What's it about?

—Me.

—What about you?

—It's about what I think. But it's also about a movie called *Taxi Driver*. Have you seen it?

She shakes her head.

—What's it rated?

—R.

She points a finger at me.

—Then I can't watch it. I'm not allowed to see any movies but G and PG.

I suppress a laugh. She's not yet ten, but she's so self-assured, a baby copper, ordering me around.

—It's all right, if there's any movies that you want to see, you can watch them with me. I'll explain anything you don't understand.

Lisa comes and sits next to me. She looks at the screen, squints to catch the notations.

—Am I in it?

I shake my head.

—You have to write your own story one day. I can't write it for you.

She bangs her feet against the kitchen chair.

—Can we watch *Aliens*?

—Sure.

She sniffs, and says, without looking at me, It's rated M.

—That's all right.

A big grin. She runs off to the garden.

Homosexuality is a sickness. This is what I'm writing. I need to write the truth or otherwise I only contribute to the din of evasions and lies. So, probably, is being hetero. Being black is a sickness, so too is being white: we're all living our templates. The first chapter of the thesis is set in the porno cinema where Travis Bickle takes Betsy, Cybill Shepherd, for a date. In the movie Betsy runs out, confused and appalled that Bickle would take her to a porno. The chapter begins just as she leaves. Unlike the actual film, my story stays in the cinema, following the shadows in the movie. I make up their stories. A young hustler, a stoned black straight couple, the lonely masturbation of an older Hispanic man. This is the most autobiographical part of the thesis, where I try to get to the reality of my own thoughts and emotions.

You see, every time I have had sex I have walked away perplexed and resentful. I've followed the rituals, got off, but got nowhere. Here's how it goes between fags.

—What do you like?

There is the menu.

Giving head.

Getting blown.

Top.

Bottom.

Leather.

—Can I come on you?

—Will you come on me?

There is no exchange of names.

Homosexuality is a sickness.

Travis Bickle always maintains a distance from the filth around him: we don't see him wank in the theatre, we don't see him fuck the hooker, we don't see his sleaze. We are only aware that it is all around him. This is why I have chosen to stay inside the theatre, to be honest about the attraction and the repulsion I feel about sex.

For five weeks, every Friday night, I had sex with a man in the back row of a porn theatre. He caught my eye; I was standing against the wall and I went and sat down next to him. The first time we hardly touched. I tried to masturbate him but he recoiled from my touch. At first I thought I had made a mistake, but he smiled at me and I placed my hand on his crotch. He crossed his legs and I moved away.

The second time we masturbated each other.

The third time we kissed, and the kiss was long and passionate, and I tasted his saliva, I tasted the cigarettes, I tasted the cheap coffee. He came on my jeans and wiped them clean with a handkerchief.

The fourth week, after a mutual wank, I asked him if he wanted to go for a coffee. He shook his head, stood up and walked out. As I left I saw him flicking through the magazines outside. He refused to look at me.

The final time we kissed again immediately. The same thing, the desire, the passion. I pleaded with him, I wanted to go outside, to talk, to discover his name. His agitation was violent. He pulled away. I went down on an old guy, flimsy wisps of white hair on his crotch. His come, when it came, was thin and runny. I spat it out.

When I say homosexuality is a sickness, I mean that I experience it truly alone. I am as alone as Travis is amid all the cum. I am ashamed to say that what I want is to love.

The second chapter of the thesis begins with a rewrite of another scene in *Taxi Driver*. The taxi drive picks up a customer, played by the director himself, who is going to murder his wife who's made a cuckold of him. I write that I identify with such jealousy, I can understand it. Then I write about *The Sum Of Us*. In one scene, early on, the homosexual protagonist is in bed with the man he wants, Greg, and they're beginning to fuck. Jeff's father, Harry, pokes his head in and asks how Greg wants his tea in the morning. Greg decides not to go through with the sex, he can't handle the domesticity between father and son. It's not sexy. I write an extra scene. After Greg walks out he goes to one of the twenty-four hour sex clubs in Sydney, stands next to a stranger, gets aroused, blows him, is fucked by him.

What's domesticity? Breakfast in bed? The cuckold going to shoot his wife? Does one inevitably lead to the other? I'm asking because there are no rules any more and I don't want to end up fucked up. I don't want to destroy anyone through my love. But I don't want to end up chasing intimacy from strangers either.

It strikes me that the love between Dominic and Eva has faded. They are both happy for my presence, they both fill their evenings together with the children and the television. Affection, however, seems to have gone. I don't see them kiss, they don't touch each other. We don't discuss any of this, and probably Dom would consider me too young arid too different to understand. Eva and I still have a closeness, a shared liking for each other, but she is also too aware of my kinship. The three of us are Australian but our emotions come from somewhere else.

—That's why you're not an Aussie. Aussie guys don't see further than a root.

I laugh when Eva says this to me, but I also withdraw and contemplate. What she says is what I'm learning.

They won't divorce. Not yet. Little Arthur is a new glue to hold them together. He has moved from the fragile whimpering of infanthood and is now a personality. He speaks in my ear, words made up, words learnt, words from the angels. He sits on my lap and tries to steal the laptop. He smells of shit and baby soap.

Friends, around me, on the carousel of sex, condemn the inertia of marriage. But though I don't know whether Eva and Dom love each other any more, I understand they can't easily forget the commitments made. I'm not at all sure I would be prepared to compromise the way they do, I don't know if I could face what Eva faces, after the kids are in bed, after Dom has fallen asleep on the couch. She roams the house then, quiet, smoking a joint, looking out of every window, checking on every door.

—What are you afraid of? I asked her.

—I'm not afraid of the outside, if that's what you mean, she replied. She goes stoned to bed.

Little Arthur, the only boy, is loved by them all. I adore his being a boy. He already plays at kick to kick with me, wanting me to send the football high above the trees. He wears the Collingwood colours, he makes guns from sticks. He stumbles forward differently to the girls, making noise and calling out his joy. Betty is so much more quiet, reserved. She sits quietly next to me, watching me write or watching me draw. Asks her questions. I adore the boy, the nephew, because I can see myself in him. With Betty I'm finding out, for the first time, how the world looks to the girl.

Last year, at uni, graffiti began to appear. *Barry Bond is a rapist.* It was painted on walls, scrawled on toilet doors. It was not because I knew him, though we had crossed paths at parties, that I was disturbed. Suddenly he was, for everyone to know, suddenly he was evil. The words were written by phantoms, I don't know who scribbled them across the walls. The blame was not one-sided. The feminist bitches, whoever they were, they too were condemned. Did he do it? To me that seemed to be the question that got lost in the heat of arguments. Who did he rape? No-one knew to tell me.

This has been the hardest part of my thesis, the one requiring the most work. I wanted to set my work within the university itself, to explore the age, the moment, the culture I am enmeshed in, rather than pretend that I can add anything else to the din of knowledge about the big wide world. I began by interviewing Barry Bond.

He is shy, he is thin and wears a uniform cobbled from last decade's hip-hop and the last generation's punk. He is attractive and his eyes are blue. He has his prejudices, those feminist bitches again, and though he says this is a response to the campaign against him, I think he was not too fond of feminists before. He pleads with me to believe: I have not raped.

—What happened?

—I told you, nothing.

—So why the graffiti?

—Donna wanted to get back at me.

The name of the woman.

—Who's Donna?

A bitch from fucking hell. He pauses. A girl, just a girl. I knew her, kind of, we had sex at a party. That's all.

—Did you rape her?

Fury. I can see that he hates the question.

—Fucking NO NO NO!

—Why does she day you did?

Silence. He looks at my tape recorder. He finally answers.

—This is killing me. Me, my friends, my family.

—Why does she say you raped her?

He begins to cry.

—I don't know.

The story he tells me is this. One Friday night at a party in Brunswick he flirts with a woman and they disappear into a bedroom with a half-bottle of vodka. He's taken half an E, a bad one, a weak one, and he does not know what she's on. They begin to kiss in the darkness. The sex is quick, he can't remember how he came. Inside her? Maybe. She leaves, buttoning her shirt. He rests a while on the pillows, sipping from the bottle. When he emerges she's dancing in the lounge room. She doesn't look at him. He walks home alone.

I try to interview the woman. She is scared of me, wants to know what for. I'm honest.

—For my thesis.

—What's your thesis?

—It's on *Taxi Driver*, the movie.

She giggles. Then is sad.

—Sorry, she answers. My life isn't yours to use.

I think of the graffiti.

—You're using Barry's life.

She storms off.

I approach the women's room. I knock on the door. A young smiling woman with gelatin black hair opens.

—Yeah?

I hand her a letter and walk away.

A woman called Nicole answers, leaves me a message at home.

—This is a message for Lou Stefano. I'm replying to the letter you wrote, regarding feminism and your thesis. Meet me at the union cafe, on the porch so we can smoke. Tomorrow, okay, three o'clock? My number is 9389 2424.

Nicole is Greek, or her origins are. She dresses in faux fur. I buy her a coffee.

—What are you doing this for?

It's a good question. She is asking something beyond my work.

—I want to know about the damage done, I finally get it out. I want to know if there's a way to argue for Barry without arguing against Donna. I hesitate. And maybe vice versa.

—You're presuming the guy didn't do it.

—No. I'm adamant on this and I won't lie. No, even if he did it, whatever it was he may have done, I want to know if public shaming is the best way to go. I stir my coffee and say, quietly, I don't think it is.

—You Italian?

—Half. Half Greek. Half Italian. Half Australian.

This makes her laugh. She stops and looks intently at me.

—Why this issue?

—Because it could happen to me.

—Good answer. She picks up another cigarette, lights it and drags hard on it.

—Some of the other women were pretty upset about your letter.

—Why?

—'Cause.

—What's that mean?

—'Cause you're a bloke. 'Cause Donna told them you upset her. 'Cause.

—Why did you answer?

—'Cause. 'Cause it was a good letter. It wasn't patronising, it was honest.

—So what should I do?

—Talk to me, ask away.

The story she tells me is this. There is a party in Brunswick.

Donna has been curious about this man Barry for a while. She thinks he's cute, they share a philosophy tute. Donna is quite stoned when Barry comes up for a chat. They talk nonsense, *Who Weekly* gossip, and he shows her a bottle of something, maybe whisky. They retreat to a bedroom. Donna wants to talk but Barry starts kissing her. She wants to talk and doesn't know if she wants sex. He has his hand up her cunt. She is beginning to cry because this woman Donna is far from as experienced as she would like to be. She is crying when he enters her; she's trying to kiss him. When he's finished, he falls asleep. She leaves the room, gets drunker and drunker, dances, walks home alone. She reaches home and finds, on entering the house, she can't stop screaming.

—Is that rape? Nicole asks me.

—I don't know. I think, screw up my face, try to find the right words. But then there's his story. Hers is different. I can't make a judgement. I just can't.

I want to take Nicole's hand.

—I don't know how the women, those who put up the graffiti, how did they come to their judgement?

I don't know if I've pissed her off. She's not looking at me, stirring her coffee. Her next question surprises me.

—Did you like Greece, have you been?

—Yes.

—Did you like it?

—No.

—I loved it. She's chain-smoking. I loved the women and the men, I loved it that they were free with their talk and their bodies. I loved it that they weren't ashamed of loving.

These final words really strike me because I think they are true. I think we, here, maybe elsewhere but definitely here, somehow we've fucked up, we've lost the way. If we're not scared of loving, we're certainly ashamed of it.

—No, I answer finally, I don't think it's rape. I look at her. Do you?

She actually laughs. It's a very big word, isn't it, she says, such a very big word for two such foolish kids.

Donna and Barry? Her and me? All of us?

•

—What are you doing?

Soo-Ling hates my thesis. Thinks it's a waste of time.

—Trying to make sense of something.

I can hear, over the phone, that she's annoyed with me.

—Can't you write about something more relevant?

—Like what?

She explodes.

—Luigi, you dickhead, I don't know what's wrong with you. With all the problems in the world, with all the things wrong in society, you are writing about some spoilt dickhead uni students. If you're going to write about uni life, can't you write about the cuts to education funding?

I have to laugh.

—That would bore me.

—Well, it shouldn't.

I try to explain.

—I care, Soo-Ling, you know I care, but I want to enjoy what I'm working on. If I'm going to spend a year of my life on this, I want it to be fun.

There is silence.

—So do you think he did it, did he rape her?

—I think if she thought he did, she should have given him a chance for a defence. I think she should have taken it to court.

Soo-Ling's laughter is harsh and sarcastic. It burns through me.

—You're a great believer in the system then, aren't you, little boy.

I am humiliated but I try to persist.

—Not *the* system, mate, but yes, *a* system. I think there's got to be *a* system.

•

There are three conclusions to my thesis. I consider them alternatives, a choice to be made. In the first, suburbia comes back into New York City. The brother of the pimp in *Taxi Driver*, the pimp played by Harvey Keitel, the guy Bickle murders, the guy the audience, the filmmakers have no sympathy for; the brother, comes to identify the body. The brother has been making a life for himself out in Wisconsin, away from the urban and the suburban. He is alone in my rewrite, in a room in a morgue, looking at the shattered bloody body of the brother who could not escape. He arranges the funeral, the headstone, the priest. He is alone in his grief. The rest of the world is with Travis. The pimp is evil.

In the second conclusion, a woman cleans her house. In *The Sum Of Us* Jeff dates a suburban boy, Greg, whose father chucks him out of home for being gay. Greg's mother is played by Sally Cahill. She is fantastic in the part; no more than five minutes of screen time, only whispers of dialogue, but she portrays a woman browbeaten by a husband and a life, a woman too scared to make a commitment to her son. Greg's mother is cleaning the house, locked into her misery. She receives a call from Greg, he tells her that he is travelling soon, off to America, LA, NY, San Francisco. He's split up with Jeff. Jeff is too concerned with Harry, his father, who has suffered a stroke. Greg can't put up with the work and Harry's dependence. He's not sure if he ever loved Jeff.

The woman puts down the phone. Goes back to cleaning the house.

Her son is also a man, and she can't answer back, can't say what she wants to say to him: I like Jeff, maybe you should stay with Jeff.

The last conclusion is an interview with my mother. Here are three fragments.

Q: Do you think what Travis Bickle did was right?
A: Yes. He wanted to save that poor young girl.

Q: So you think that killing is sometimes justified?

A: Yes. In war. When someone attacks you. When someone is evil.

Q: What is evil?

A: Being very bad. Hurting another.

Q: Wasn't the girl responsible, a little, for choosing to leave, to become a prostitute?

The interviewee's eyes flash. Her voice is angry.

A: She was just a little girl.

Q: She knew she wanted to get out. All Travis did was return her to a place she hated.

A: She's happier there.

Q: Why?

A: She's with her family.

Q: Maybe the pimp loved her more.

The interviewee laughs.

A: At her age, son, love isn't enough.

Q: Why do you like Jeff so much, in *The Sum Of Us*?

A: Because he is responsible, because he loves his father, because he is courageous, he is a pousti and happy about it, but he doesn't stop being a man.

Q: Would you have liked him if he was more feminine?

A: What do you mean?

Q: (In Greek) If he acted more like a woman.

A: I would have still liked him.

A pause.

A: I wouldn't have found him as attractive, but I would still have liked him. Don't you understand, I like him because he respects his father, his family. That's what's most important.

A pause.

A: (In Greek) The family in that film is like us, you and me, your dad, ordinary working people. They know what is real.

Q: What is real?

A pause. The interviewee taps the table.

A: This is real.

Second fragment.

Q: Why do you think *The Sum Of Us* is a good film?

A: Because I do.

Q: Why?

A: I like the actors, they're good people.

Q: But what makes it a good film?

The interviewee smiles.

A: Who am I to answer that?

Q: What do you mean?

A: What do I know about film?

Q: You watch them.

A: But who am I?

Q: Who are you?

A: My opinion doesn't matter.

Q: Yes it does.

The inteviewee is sad.

A: No it doesn't. No-one cares about my opinion.

—Are you Christian? asked Nicole.

—Why?

—There's something Christian about your letter. Very goody-goody.

—It's gone dusk.

—I'm not a Christian, I answer.

In the shadows of the trees, a crow is circling.

After I met Nicole I went home and tried to masturbate to her face. It wasn't easy, other people, mostly men, kept intruding. This masturbation I do, it's foolish. I'm trying to learn how to be straight, how to make my body respond to women. It's women who reach inside me, they don't reject my heart. Not all of them; some, like the guys, some laugh at me. But women don't make me feel small.

The house I'm working in is warm, Dominic and Eva have installed central heating. I stay in the kitchen, watching Eva

cook, laughing with the children. I have given the number to
no-one, except for Sean and Soo-Ling. I've been here three
weeks, I'm nearly finished. Soo-Ling rings twice a week, short
conversations in which I avoid asking about her life. Betty and I
talk, about school, about *The X Files*, about the possibility of
fairies. I have been here three weeks.

Sean hasn't rung.

It hurts but I haven't got the guts to ring him again. I'm
coping with the ramifications of rejection; it gets easier every
day, I promise myself. I know that when I see him I will die a
little death, but it will just be a passing collapse. Then I'll grin
and pretend to be strong. It's a good thing people can't see
straight into your heart. The world, as we know it, this world
would have to fall apart.

I'm trying to make my body love women. If I persist in
falling into men, continue feeling small, I'm scared that I will
completely disappear.

—*They weren't listening to Aretha Franklin in the seventies,
not in this country.*

That's a quote from my mother, it's the opening quote from
my thesis. It's a tangent but for me it says everything. I was
asking her about music, the conversation was freefalling and I
was asking her how authentic she thought *The Sum Of Us* was
about working class life. 'Cause that's the criticism, that a
working class father and a working class fag son could never find
reconciliation. And Mum said that working class lives were too
disparate, it depended on what kind of family you came from.

—They never listened to music, that's very Australian.

Her favourite music is Greek, by far, but her favourite song is
'You Make Me Feel Like A Natural Woman'.

Q: How did you get into Aretha Franklin? From the radio?
The interviewee laughs.

A: The radio (in Greek). No. They weren't listening to Aretha
Franklin in the seventies, not in this country. She's a nigger. You

know what they thought of niggers (in Greek). From my sons, I heard Aretha Franklin through my sons.

•

There is a question posed about *The Sum Of Us* which is not posed about *Taxi Driver*. Are Jeff and his father authentically working class, is Jeff authentically gay? But how about Travis? The psychotic murderer, how authentic is he? That's the paradox, isn't it? All of this is fiction, we know it's fiction, but it has to speak as truth. Then it gets fucked up, because the truth is in the fiction.

4

The last goodbye

The New Year stumbles to a close. The party is emptying, people around me are urging me on. Clubs, raves, the world awaits. This party is full of ghosts, all recognisable, faces from the borders of my world. Don't I know you from somewhere? I pretend to be friends.

In a corner of the room, next to a speaker blaring versions of 'Voodoo People', someone has connected the computer. Drunk, stoned, high, people take turns sending New Year's greetings across the world. I haven't had a shot yet, but my eyes keep getting attracted to the shimmering blue light of the screen.

A scream. Victory. A message from New York.

The music has been abandoned, it is so late in the evening. Hannah comes and sits next to me, takes my hand.

—You okay?

—Yep.

—What are you on?

—Some acid.

—Any good?

—It's okay. Not strong. Just buzzy.

We sit and watch the room, she smokes a cigarette. Her girlfriend is dancing with a woman I don't know. I follow Hannah's eyes. They are angry, jealous, she watches the women twirl around themselves. She lets go of my hand.

—You angry at Tina?

—Of course not. She's allowed to do what she likes, I'm not her wife.

I wish I could say what I thought should be said. Which is something like, No, you're not married and you don't want to be married. But you do love this girl and she's here, at a party, with a woman she's fucking and it's burning you up.

When Hannah left home, told her dad that she was a dyke, he beat her, pulped her, kicked her. I visited her in hospital, her face wrapped in bandages. Tina was there, holding her hand. Her mum, terrified, was in a corner, looking down on her daughter, fussing over her, endearments in Arabic which none of us understood. Her father eventually came to visit and all of us there, the urban us, the young us, the foreign us, we were asked to leave.

—Tina stays. In Arabic.

—If she must, replied the father. In English.

Hannah gets up, clasps my hand again.

—I'm going.

We hug.

—You want a lift?

—Nah, I'll find my way home.

—You still at home? With the folks?

—Sort of. I'm looking.

—You working?

—At the video shop.

—Happy 1997.

Hannah walks over to Tina, who kisses her, says something, turns back to the dancing girl. *Voodoo People Magic People*. On the Internet a message of cheer from a young guy, or he says he is a young guy, from Lyons in France.

Sean isn't here. He said he would be. In my pocket there's a tape, a collection I put together from Dom's old vinyl. Funk and disco from the golden era. I touch the pocket of my jeans, feel the hard surface of the cassette. It is four o'clock in the morning, I'm tired and it is time to go home.

•

—How was last night?

—All right. Just a party.

Soo-Ling pours me a coffee and Betty plays with her cereal.

—Eat up!

Betty and I exchange winks.

—How was your night?

—Good. You should have come along. Nadia and I just got drunk together, talked. Soo-Ling laughed. On second thoughts, you would have hated it. We're too old to keep pace with you.

—You're not old.

—I didn't say I was old. But I am older than you. By a few years, and don't I know it. She hesitates. Did he turn up?

I say nothing.

Soo-Ling explodes.

—Why the fuck do you persist with this stupid jerk?

—I'm not persisting with anything.

Betty looks scared at our shouting. I take her hand.

—I don't care. I reach inside my pocket, hand the tape to Soo-Ling. You can have this.

—What is it?

—Music. Music to dance to.

—Put it on, urges Betty.

I spend the first day of 1997 having breakfast with two people I adore, playing old James Brown and Betty Davis funk, feeling the summer's heat. The thick, inert sadness from last night vanishes.

•

The bus ride across the continent is stupendously long. The Nullarbor seduces the visitor with the unrelenting tease of its horizon. The plain is ferocious, the scale of the human world is reduced to a minuscule moment. The world does literally disappear within this landscape. When we stop at the border of two states, I don't go into the cafeteria, instead I walk as far as time will let me. This is not desert of sand and dune, it is all horizon and there is flowering everywhere. Stubby short grass, a carpet of dull yellow. But there are no trees, there is no height. This is the flat world, the edge of the universe. On the bitumen a silver truck is parked. Inside, the driver is sleeping. I simply turn and turn and turn, get dizzy in the vastness. The sky and the earth are one, announcing my insignificance. I am joyous and wish to remain here, in this circle, forever. Instead I hear an impatient honking. I walk back to the bus.

When we finally reach Perth and I emerge back into a city, I smell of sand and sweat. I am the stench of the prehistoric.

I am here to ask a question. That's all.

Perth is a small city, but from the first moment I am aware of its difference from the place I come from. The sand from the desert weaves itself in the wind, sticks to the modern plastic and metal. The city is all heat. Aboriginal people are obvious, refusing my white gaze.

My Aunt Sophia lives in Leederville, a ten minute train ride from the city. She is home when I knock on the door and at first she doesn't recognise me.

—Yes?

—Tia, it's me, Luigi.

She is shocked, then the politeness and, to be fair, also the warmth, kicks in. I enter the house and she hugs me.

The first three days are spent eating and drinking, catching up with a family I do not know. There are no questions about Tommy. The topic is carefully avoided, by them, by me. My cousins are now adults and we are shy of, each other. They have their Italian skins but their slouches, their long surfer hair, their casual clothes: distinctly Australian. In my black T-shirt and jeans, my coiled snake around my arm, I am distinctly from over east. From the other side of the desert, a vastness as intense as an ocean.

In Greece I could not be Greek. In Perth I cannot feel Australian. The racism slaps me immediately.

—What is happening to this country?

The boongs, the Asians, the homos, the trendies in the city. Everyone is to blame, except, of course, themselves. I cannot not remain in polite silence.

—I believe in Mabo, I say. I believe in Native Title. There's got to be compensation for what the Europeans did to the black man.

My Uncle Joseph, tough, a strong man, the elder brother, leans over. I smell the whisky, I want to fuck him.

—You don't even know any blackfellas, do ya?

I lie.

—A few.

—Nah, not real blackfellas. You probably know a few of those city types, bloody lawyers and that rot?

—They're real as well.

—Go ask the real black bastard, ask him what he thinks about Mabo. He'll tell you, he'll tell you it's just another white man's law.

My uncle reaches for his beer. The veins on his arm are thick with tension. The skin is noble in its weathered beauty.

—Put them in the bush, close it off, leave them there. That's all they want, they don't give a fuck about Mabo. My uncle points a finger towards me. I'll introduce you to my mate Johnny, he's a boong. He'll put you straight. Johnny doesn't give a fuck about land rights.

Again I don't say what I am thinking. That Johnny, then, is also wrong.

I wait till everyone has gone home. I pour a glass of wine for my Tia Sophia.

—I want to ask you some questions, Tia.

She has cleared the table of all the plates, the mountains of food. Soft candles perfume the room, dispel the lingering traces of meat and oil.

—What questions?

—Family questions.

She looks at me, hard. Her face is suspicion.

—I don't think I have much to tell you that you don't already know.

—Why did my father leave, why are relations so strained?

This was not a question I had even thought I wanted to ask.

—Your father left because our grandmother wished to leave. She took him early.

—Did you like her?

Sophia laughed. It was an explosion of heat. The candlelight danced.

—I couldn't stand the bitch. She hated me, hated all of us, all of us except Arto. Louie, Louie, the slaps I copped from that bitch, the ordering around. The hatred. My aunt leans over, there are tears in her eyes. She hated me, Louie, hated me. You don't know what that's like, to grow up, all of us in that small house in Freo, knowing that the old witch was going to be there, above you, staring you down. My aunt shivered, reclined back into her chair, into her wine. I'm glad she left, but all of us wished she had not taken Arto.

—Why him? Even in the night's liquid heat, I felt a shiver.

—She loved Arto.

—Why?

Sophia laughed again, but this time with softness.

—You're very young, my child, if you think that your question can have an answer. I don't know why I love the people I love. My aunt touches my knee. Do you know why you love the people you love?

I shake my head.

—My dad said that Nonna Marta's husband was a murderer.

Sophia is silent.

—Is that true?

Silence.

—Tia?

She is angry.

—Louie, your father had no right to say that. Our Nonno's first wife died, that's all I know. I didn't know the man. He probably was a bastard, they were tough times and it wasn't easy being a dago back then. She opens her hands to the world. Imagine it, a fucking wog married to a fucking boong. She died. I don't know how.

—But . . .?

The word shudders.

—But what?

—If he killed her, maybe that's why . . . I stop. I fall silent.

—What, Louie? My aunt grabs my hands. What? She is concerned, anxious, she scouts my face and I turn away.

—Maybe that's why Tommy died, I whisper. I think there was a curse.

The words are out. They are silly and they are frightening. Tia Sophia hugs me, close, kisses my face, my hands.

—No, she whispers. No, there is no curse, Louie. Or if there is, it is simply the curse of life. That's all. I push away. She won't let go of my hand.

—Luigi, listen. I don't know what my grandfather did. I never knew the man. Maybe he destroyed someone. That is no reason for that bitch to treat me the way she did, no reason for her to take your father away from us. There is no reason for these memories to keep singing in our blood.

—Look at me!

I follow her order.

—I'm not Italian. I'm an Australian woman. I have no time for these stories of curses and of revenge. I don't listen when the wogs tell me, I don't listen when the blacks go on about it. She finishes her wine. There are things that belong to the past, Louie. You don't need to understand them.

She is crying.

—Lou, my father and my mother were good people, please believe me. They worked hard, they looked after us, loved us. And she took their son away from them. I'm prepared to believe that Nonna suffered, I can believe that. It was a different world, a cruel world. But she also caused suffering.

I am crying.

—I don't know why Tommy died, I whispered.

I am howling.

•

I visit my grandparents' graves. They lie side by side, overgrown grass. Twice a year Aunt Sophia and Aunt Theresa clean the graves, chop away at the grass, light the incense and deposit the flowers. I am between visits. The earth is unkempt.

The headstones are scarred by weather, by rain and sun. The engravings are becoming illegible. The site is Catholic, but there are three Greek words on my grandmother's stone. They have faded to scratches, I can't make them out. I cross myself, twice, over both graves. Once I spiral my prayer to the east, and once to the west. The sun is oppressive and I cannot stay long in its weight. I light my two candles and place them across the graves. From nowhere a wind strikes up. My grandfather's candle shivers, whirls, extinguishes. I light it again and look up at the trees. The crows are watching me.

—Fuck you, I whisper. I am not on any side.

The wind is no more. The two candles burn.

When I get back to the house, Soo-Ling rings.

—How's it going?

—Fine.

—When are you coming back?

—Next week. How's Betty?

—Good. She misses you.

—Is she there?

—No. She's next-door.

—Give her my love.

—Sure. You all right?

—Yeah. I hesitate. I love you, Soo-Ling.

—I've got to go.

The line goes dead.

•

In the train a young Aboriginal girl is staring vacantly in my direction. She has a clear plastic bottle, a mineral water bottle, which she keeps bringing to her mouth and nose. She is not drinking from it, she's sniffing from it. When we arrive in the centre of the city she joins four other young girls who laugh and dance on the platform. She notices that I am looking at her.

—Fuck off.

I scout record shops, searching for music. I grab a drink, from a bar, I make myself tipsy. I walk around and around and around a block, taunting myself, hating myself. The entry to the porn shop is a narrow case of stairs. I look ahead, pass it one more time, then next time I enter.

I thumb magazines and video cases. Cunts and cocks. A man in a suit, a man in a tracksuit. The man at the counter, reading the newspaper, looks up and then, bored, looks down. I walk up to the counter.

—Can I go upstairs?

The man nods and takes my money. The man in the tracksuit follows me with his eyes. I walk to a white door and a buzzer rings. The man at the counter gives me a nod. I enter darkness.

These spaces are full of images of men without blemishes: the smoothest of chests, the most defined of muscles. These images make masculinity antiseptic. There is a flight of stairs through a narrow corridor. At the top there is a room, two couches and a television set that is playing a video. I sit on a couch, upright, wondering what I am doing here. The buzzer rings. I catch my breath and I wait. The man in the tracksuit enters and without looking at me sits on the other couch. His stare is fixed on the television screen.

—You want this big black cock up your arse?

The first actor is African-American, he is naked save for a policeman's cap on his head. A white man is sucking on his cock. The white man pulls away.

—Yeah, yeah, give it to me. I want to suck your black piece of meat.

The man in the tracksuit is about forty, he is tall and stocky. I want him to look at me. He doesn't.

—Fuck me with that black meat.

The white actor's face remains clear, for me, pale, his eyes are large and blue. The black man's face is a shadow, I cannot concentrate on him. This is a function of the editing. The white man is face, sucking; the black man is cock, thrusting.

—I want to taste your white ass.

The man across from me has his hand in his pants. The slight trembling motions of masturbation. I am aroused, by this stranger, by cock. I try to catch the stranger's eyes. He is keenly avoiding me.

—How are you?

My words shock him. He gets up quickly, moves out of the room. I sit, embarrassed. On the screen the black cock is about to enter the shaved white arsehole.

—Oh yeah, fuck! The white actor screams the last word as the cock enters his body. I get up and search for the stranger. A corridor of cubicles; a room with chains and graffiti. A corner leads to a shower and a toilet. The stranger is waiting. I approach him.

—Hi.

He looks at me. His eyes are cold, dismissive. He doesn't answer. I try to calm my voice.

—Do you want to go into one of the rooms?

He looks me up and down. I tighten my stomach.

—What are you into?

The voice is low, a growl.

—Whatever.

—You like getting fucked?

I shake my head no. He turns his face away, bored.

—I'll suck you.

I'm pleading, I'm angry. He looks me up and down again. Then he walks away.

These moments are a humiliation that strengthens my resolve to hate. This life, this homosexuality, is an ugliness that I would give anything to erase from my body.

I sit back on the couch. The stranger also returns. We do not look at each other. We watch the video.

—Come on my face, man. Come on my face, the white actor pleads. The black actor is pulling violently at his cock, there is a groan on the soundtrack. The white actor closes his eyes shut tight, closes his mouth. Semen falls on his cheeks, on his chest. He grabs the black man's cock, rubs it across his face, his eyes still shut, licks at the come. He pulls himself as he licks, his come falls on his stomach. The image fades. Another actor, white, a sailor cap and singlet, walks into a cubicle. Three glory holes. He sits on a stool and unzips his trousers, plays with his cock. He looks through the glory hole. Begs.

—Come on, come on, I want to suck your big black cock.

A long thin black cock comes through the hole. The white actor begins to suck it.

The stranger gets up from the couch, walks over to a coffee machine. He has an erection, straining at the polyester. I try to resist his rejection of me but the pain defeats me. I am ugly. I am weak. I have been made zero. The sound of a buzzer. We both turn our heads in the direction of the door. Footsteps. A good-looking blond man, a white shirt and wide deep blue tie. He checks both of us out, takes a seat next to me. I am vindicated.

On screen, three black cocks through three glory holes. The white actor sucks and pulls.

—I want to taste black meat.

The new man looks at me. I'm not sure if I even find him attractive. My aim is to conquer the other man, to make him feel rejection. I get up, walk down the corridor, enter a cubicle. I am in darkness.

The man in the tie follows. He comes in, turns on the light, closes the door behind him.

—Hello.

—Hi. I'm squeaking and I turn the sound into a cough.

—What do you like?

I am silent. The man smiles at me. He walks over, he touches my shoulder. I lean forward and begin to kiss him. His mouth tastes of the sourness of the day. I drink from him and he pulls at my T-shirt, unbuttons my jeans. My cock is lamely limp. He smiles and gets on his knees. He sucks and I'm thinking of the black cocks through glory holes, thinking of the hard-on in the trackpants. I'm hard.

He sucks me, unbuttons his shirt, flips his tie over his back. From his pants' pocket he pulls out a small brown vial and sniffs. He offers it to me and I shake my head. He caps it and his sucking is now ferocious, taking my cock in, his fingers explore my hole. I close my eyes and think of nothing except the urge to escape from this room.

I'm soft.

—Sorry.

I'm pulling up my jeans, put on my T-shirt.

—Sorry, I can't.

He plays with my dick.

—You sure?

I move away from him.

—Yeah, I'm sure.

He rests on the floor and winks. I open the door. The other man is there, hand in his pants, waiting. He again refuses to look at me. I turn away and he enters the cubicle. The door closes again.

The TV room is empty. A black cock comes on a white face.

Waiting for the train I notice a sticker on the bench I'm sitting on. It says *National Action*. A caricature of a Chinese man bringing suitcases of heroin and cocaine into Australia. A PO Box address.

A white businessman, reading the paper, looks over the top of it to where two Aboriginal kids are slouched on concrete steps.

The businessman looks over at the kids, then to me, raises his eyebrows; there is disgust on his face.

The train is on time.

•

Dad picks me up from the airport. He hugs me, clumsily. I hold onto him. We don't talk until we are out into the night air.

—How was it?

—Fine.

I put the radio on in the car. He laughs and turns down the volume.

—Hey, not so loud, right?

—Sure. I grin and look over at him. He is still handsome. Very grey, his skin coarse, speckled, but he still looks fit, healthy.

—Everyone says hello.

He doesn't answer. Jeff Buckley's 'Last Goodbye'. I turn it up. My father lets the song play loud.

—How's Mum?

—Anxious. She wanted to ring you every day.

I laugh.

—Just like Mum.

—She's got a big dinner for you.

—Good. I'm hungry.

—Didn't they feed you right?

—Of course. But not like Mum.

I relax back into the seat, enter the city of Melbourne, the flat snatches of dark, the low shimmering lights of the city.

—I went to Nonna and Nonno's graves.

—What for?

—Seemed right.

My father brakes as we leave the freeway. He turns to me, strokes my hair.

—You're looking good, tanned.

—I swam a lot.

I want to ask him many questions. I want to ask him how he

feels with all the death in his life. His grandmother, his son, his mother and his father. I want to ask him about love: is Mum the only person he has ever loved? I want to ask him if he feels as strange and confused and angry about my homosexuality as I do. But I also want to ask him something that is not dangerous, to begin an intimacy that is also a contentment. He does it for me.

—That's a good line.

—What?

—In that song. Dad whispers it. *Kiss me out of desire not consolation.*

—Have you felt like that?

—Sure. Haven't you?

I think of Sean, of Soo-Ling. Of some perfect stranger out there, waiting, burning down the cubicles, torching the porno cinemas.

—Yeah.

—I've felt it often with your mum.

I listen.

—I've been mad for her, mad for her for decades.

—You're lucky.

He touches my hair, like I'm his little boy again.

—Maybe you'll find it too.

—Maybe. Don't know. I look out the window. The parties of summer, drunk people in Royal Park.

—I love you, Dad.

He doesn't answer, he plays with my hair.

•

After dinner I have my visits to make.

—Where you going?

—Just around the corner.

Mum starts to curse in Greek.

—You've just got back.

—Give me a sec. I kiss her and leave, her insults fly after me.

I walk the quiet streets, everyone is in front of the television, safe in their closets. I grab flowers from the gardens. Two roses, a tulip, some snapdragons. I tear a thread from the bottom of my shirt, wrap it around the stems. I make a bouquet.

Clive laughs when I hand him the flowers.

—What's this for?

—For you.

He takes them and heads into the kitchen. The television is playing low and a half empty plate of vegetables lies on the table.

—Sorry, I interrupted.

—You interrupted nothing. He has put the flowers in a small purple vase. He places the vase next to a framed photo of himself and his wife. He sits down next to me.

—How was Perth?

—All right.

He laughs.

—You don't like talking much.

I blush. I tap my knee.

—What is it, mate?

I don't look at him as I speak.

—Clive, I can't do this any more. It's not you. I look at him, try to convince him. I don't want to do this casual sex thing any more.

There is silence except for the vapid muttering of the television.

—It's not you. I take his hand. He lets me.

—I understand.

He gets up, finds some whisky and pours two glasses. He stands above me and we clink.

On leaving, I grab him, bring him close and kiss him hard. At first he resists. Then he lets me touch him, hold him. Our mouths join, hold, there is no beginning and no end. We kiss for a long time. He pulls away.

—So long, kid.

—Can I come again? Please, just to visit.

He shakes his head. Then stops.

—Maybe.

The door closes, and I'm alone and I don't want to be alone, I want to be with someone I love.

I hitch a ride on Whitehorse Road and head to Ringwood. At Dom's I ring Mum.

—Where are you?

—Dominic's.

—You said around the corner.

—I'm staying here tonight.

She's pissed off, really pissed off.

—You just got back.

I make a promise. I'll take her to the cinema tomorrow.

Eva is bathing Arthur and Lisa is watching the television. Dom and I go out on the verandah, we smoke a joint. After my time in the west, the Melbourne night seems bitterly cold.

—How was it?

—All right. They're good people.

—Don't tell Mum that, she hates them.

—She doesn't know them.

I look over at my brother. He is so very definitely a man; his face has lines and age, it is a very handsome face. I wish I could ask him to sleep with me, and I don't mean sex, I mean a sleep in which he holds me with his strength. Instead, I just blow on the joint.

—Why did you go over?

—I wanted to ask stuff about our family?

—What kind of stuff?

I'm suddenly wary, everything's risky.

—About Tommy.

He is silent for a moment, and when he speaks it is of Eva.

—I'm worried about her.

—How come?

—She's not happy.

I know this.

—I'd like to take her on a holiday, maybe to Europe. She deserves a rest.

He loves her, he loves her very much.

—You going to do it?

When he answers it is with fury.

—How? He stands up. I'm going to watch some TV.

—Don't you want to know about my trip?

—No. He looks down at me, still angry. I don't want to know about your fucking trip. He grabs at me, pulls at my shirt. What the fuck are you looking for, arsehole? He's dead, gone, finito. That's it, that's all.

—He was our brother.

I'm scared.

—He killed a man.

And Dominic is shaking.

—He fucking killed a man, the bastard. Why'd he do that, eh, Louie, why that?

I'm crying his tears.

—Don't know, I say softly, sniffing. I don't care about that.

—You should. His voice is cold, he's straightened up. It's a debt. He goes inside.

Later I wander in, stoned, still shaky, wondering if I should head back home. Dominic is on the couch, the heating is on and he's wearing a singlet and boxer shorts, Eva is curled around his legs. They are watching the television. She smiles as I walk in.

—Come. She pats the space next to her. I sit down and we watch *The Footy Show*. Eva rests her head on my shoulder and Dominic is playing with my hair. On the television, Saverio Rocca is on the panel, shirt and tie, so very handsome. I sit up.

Eva punches me, softly.

—You like him, don't you?

I'm blushing.

—He's a good player, ain't he, Dom?

—He's a spunk is what you mean, giggles Eva.

Dominic says nothing, he's rubbing my shoulder.

In the morning I wake up with Lisa jumping on the bed. I kiss her warmly and she pulls me up, into the morning. Dominic is in his overalls, sipping a coffee. Eva is making breakfast. Arthur is in the lounge room watching cartoons. I look up at the clock. Seven-fifteen.

Dominic follows my stare. He puts down his coffee.

—Got to go.

—Where's the job?

—Fucking Mordialloc.

—Yow, I answer, that's a long way.

—It's all right. He kisses his wife, his daughter, his son and he comes around for me, grabs me, hugs me. Good to have you back, Luigi.

He's out.

Eva makes me bacon and eggs.

—He didn't sleep much last night, kept tossing and turning. Her eyes question me.

—What? I say defensively.

—Nothing. Did you talk about Tommy?

—Kind of. I look at her. He never really wants to talk about him.

—It's hard for Dom, he never understood Tommy. Everything's black and white for Dom.

I wonder if she's bitter. She touches my face.

—I don't think anything was simple for Tommy.

She starts clearing the breakfast table.

—Louie, maybe it's time to let go.

—Of what?

—Tommy. Let it rest.

I don't answer, play with the egg.

—That doesn't mean forget him, she whispers softly.

Eva prepares her daughter for school. I shower, I dress, I piss. And try to think of nothing, pure beautiful nothing.

5
Antipolitics

The night was bitter, cold. The wind's severity hurt. The crowd was fuelled by anger. There were songs, chanting, abuse and laughter. Betty was riding my shoulders and she was giggling.

—You cold up there?

—No. She hugs my neck.

—Where is she, Uncle Louie?

—Don't know.

The Racist had yet to appear. She was addressing a meeting. I wanted to go inside, now that I was here, mostly to check out the crowd. There were nervous men with mobile phones outside the entrance to the hall.

Nadia and Soo-Ling were hugging each other, challenging the cold. Young women and men weaved through the crowd, offering pamphlets and proclaiming meetings. They were dressed in black and in hippie. The church crowd, older, more sedate, eyed them suspiciously. But a camaraderie was being forged, through hatred directed against the Racist.

I felt nothing but my usual exclusion. The stale slogans, their misty humanism, annoyed me. Slowly, protected by the large frames of the police, people arrived to enter the meeting. They were greeted with insults, fire and brimstone. They cowered, the invective of the protesters, the flashing bulbs of the media. Betty's eyes were wide open. This was a circus.

I gripped tight to her hand. I was not going to let her go. The crowd's solidarity seemed tenuous. The anger that seethed through them, the angry insults to the police, was mounting to violence. And it was being returned with cold efficiency by the police. I tried to look at them, tried to catch the hazel eyes of a young blond cop. He refused to see me.

—Fuck off. This is a free country!

A burly bearded man, motorcycle jacket, was walking towards the hall.

—Racist! screamed back a young woman, socialist badges. The bearded man made as if to rush at her, but he was held back by one of the police. Instead he shook his head and walked grimly through the crowd. There was a chorus of abuse.

Soo-Ling laughed suddenly and pointed to the edge of the crowd. Three young Vietnamese boys, shivering in white T-shirts, had joined us.

—Check out their T-shirts.

One of the boys turned around. In bold black letters the T-shirt read: *White Trash And Proud Of It.*

I laughed with a deep enjoyment.

—Look, Betty, that's us.

She read the words and turned back, with curiosity, to the seething crowd.

I was here for her, more than for Soo-Ling, much more than for philosophy or belief. Yes, the Racist's venom against the non-European immigrant disgusted me. I detested her arrogant dismissal of the Aborigines. I thought her language and her petty hatreds abominable. But it was her refusal to see Betty, to acknowledge the mongrel child I loved, that I hated most. The Racist warned against a future where ethnicity was purged of purity. I was living only for that future.

The pamphlets tried to explain. But pamphlets were empty. The target, they claimed, was capitalism not immigration. There were no jobs. The solutions they spoke for belonged to a distant past, to something called rationality. And this protesting crowd contradicted the pamphlets. The working class were inside the hall. It was mostly the middle class doing the antiracist chanting. I don't believe in the logic of Apocalypse but I sensed that I was living through its history. One hundred metres down the road, as we were coming Up towards the rally, a young teenage girl was huddled behind a brick fence, shooting up.

—What's she doing? whispered Betty. At six she knew enough to whisper.

—She's taking drugs.

Soo-Ling glanced at me quickly, said nothing.

Betty kept looking back, over her shoulder.

A huge murmur was buzzing through the crowd. She's coming, she's coming. The numbers had swelled; the police formed a thick line along the corded barricade that separated us from the people arriving for the meeting. Spit was now being thrown along with the abuse. I dropped Betty from my shoulders and took her to the edge of the crowd. Soo-Ling and Nadia remained in the thick of it.

An elderly couple walked slowly towards the hall. He had his arm, tattooed arm, around the woman, protecting her, his head upright. She was frightened. They walked through and she shivered as the words fell on her.

—Racist bitch.

A young man aimed a powerful projectile of spit, caught the shoulder of her coat. There was laughter. The couple disappeared from my view.

The crowd was now feverish in its anticipation. I sat on a small park bench on the edge of the fury, Betty on my knees. The guests were now running into the hall and the whole street was ablaze with the flaming lights of the television crews. An elderly Chinese man, his hands in his pockets, stood silent, watching.

A young man arrived. He was blond and pissed. He walked, slowly towards the hall, laughed at the protesters. This accelerated their fury. He lifted his fingers towards them and his voice boomed.

—Kill all fucking boongs!

There was a silence, his words were a shock, and then a ferocious response. The crowd hurled itself against the barricade and the police scrambled to contain the force. There was pushing and screaming. A young woman was dragged away, thrown back into the crowd. The drunk man was still laughing. An object smashed against the back of his head. The juice of the tomato was as blood. The man stopped, wiped his neck and turned vicious onto the crowd. He tried to punch the protesters and two large policemen held him back.

This time it was the crowd laughing. He walked into the hall, cursing the boong and the gook, the poofter and the nigger. The crowd roared poison after him.

By now I could not feel the cold. A group of high-school kids had joined the protest and, rap style, were calling for the murder of all racists. Four news cameras were focused on them.

How about you? I thought to myself. Aren't we all racist? There was one black man, black African, the only one at this protest. I felt embarrassment, I just did, whenever I caught his eye.

The barricade was shifting. More guests arriving, more protest. Projectiles of fruit and spittle, of words, were thrown in the direction of the barricade. The air began to smell of vegetable. The police grabbed at protesters, but a young man broke through and smashed his weight against a large man who was trying to run into the hall. The man fell across the barricade and into the crowd and he was swept up. Police rushed towards the fall. There was screaming, I saw a flash of kicking. More protesters broke through and the police line fell. There was simply noise and the high pitched squeals of pain. A woman, young, short cropped hair, was dragged along the ground, swung violently into an awaiting police wagon. Betty screamed and pushed her face into my jacket. She started crying. I held her tight.

A man emerged, his face blood, bruises. I didn't know whether he was protester or guest. He collapsed. The sound of sirens.

Soo-Ling grabbed Betty from my arms. Beside her Nadia was shaking, trying unsuccessfully to light a cigarette. We were a moment of grace and around us there was chaos. The cameras, the protest, the police, the light, the shouting, the anger, all of it had formed a whirlpool around us.

—Let's go, Soo-Ling ordered. We followed, shifting our bodies around crying couples, furious cops. One of them, blue faced, pudgy, young, stopped in front of Soo-Ling. His eyes burnt towards her, hating her. She stood, stared, and he dropped his gaze. We walked past and he rushed back into the crowd. An ambulance screeched to a halt. It was followed by a van from National Nine News. We were flooded by the spotlight of a helicopter.

A few hundred metres from the hall the world again descended into suburban darkness. Only silence and the flickering of TV screens from inside the brick veneers. A Vietnamese man on a porch looked in the direction of the protest. He was clothed in a striped dressing gown, smoking. He looked at us, stubbed the cigarette, went inside.

We drove to Nadia's in silence. Betty's crying had stopped and she just wanted to be in my arms. We were together in the back. Nadia, driving, went to turn on the radio. Soo-Ling stopped her. We needed some silence.

Back home Nadia rushed to the television, flicked through a movie and an ad, found a news channel. The scene we had just been in but everything cut up and fractured. The rapping high school students, the flying fruit. Cops being pushed. The rushing guests. A helicopter view of the world below and the falsely anxious face of a journalist.

A man in hospital. A guest, not a protester. Nadia groaned. Nine arrests.

Nadia poured three vodkas.

—Betty, it's time for bed.

The girl shook her head.

—Bets, I pleaded, you know it's way past your bedtime.

She took hold of my fingers.

—Please. Just some quiet time. Her eyes were still a little red from the crying.

—How about some *Simpsons*?

Betty agreed gleefully.

—Just one episode, warned Soo-Ling.

The girl nodded.

Nadia went through her video tapes, put one on. Lisa Simpson hugging an older woman. She rewound. The episode made the four of us laugh. Homer finds his mother, who he thought was dead. She had left, had to go underground, because at the height of the sixties counterculture she had planned the destruction of a germ warfare laboratory built by Mr Burns. Lisa and her grandmother find a communion, a shared faith, a shared idealism. The episode ends with an old hippie driving the mother away in a beat-up Kombie.

—Why are you sad, Uncle Louie?

Tears must have been shivering in my eyes. Betty patted my cheek curiously.

—It's sad, don't you think, that she has to run away because of doing a good thing?

—I hate Mr Burns.

I put Betty to bed, kissed her forehead. She smelt of fruit and shit and piss and raspberry.

When I return to the lounge room—a second hand couch and posters for Circus Oz and *I Heard The Mermaids Singing*—Nadia has poured vodka for the three of us. Sinead O'Connor is on the stereo. The women are arguing about the protest, about the country, about division. Nadia believes the violence was a mistake. Soo-Ling hesitates, but she is also excited by the night's events.

—I don't care, you don't understand. I'm glad they hit back, that's something wonderful. You know how many times I've wanted to do that, kick some ugly redneck's head in? All my life.

—I'm a wog too, says Nadia quietly.

—Not like me, not the same kind of wog, flashes Soo-Ling.

And me? I have no contribution to make. All I felt from the night was fright. I felt fear, and I felt the desire to escape, with Betty, to remove us from the conflict. I wanted nothing more and possibly that means I am not prepared to fight for anything more than the right to safety. My weakness in the face of violence does not bother me. Quite the opposite. I want to exalt in it. Immune to the slasher video and the six o'clock news, I can't help but experience an immense relief at my abhorrence to real pain, to real blood and fury.

I am stretched, on your grave.

I turn up the volume.

—We're trying to talk. Soo-Ling is angry.

—Let him listen. He's done nothing wrong.

Soo-Ling stares at me, long. I turn away.

—What do you think?

—Of what? My happiness was gone. Evaporated. I'm sullen.

She is exasperated.

—Of tonight, of course. What do you think of what happened?

—It was stupid.

—Why?

—It proved nothing. It gave the racists more attention.

—Just lie down and take it, right? That's your fucking answer?

—I was there, remember? I was protesting.

—That's sometimes not enough.

The two women are looking at me, the man.

—I guess I'm not that angry.

My answer booms through the room. The music, the light, everything fades.

—Those people tonight, yeah sure, some were freaks, some were fascists. But mostly they were just ordinary folk, you know. I pause, struggle for articulation. The racists don't hate me. I look at Soo-Ling. I'm not Asian, I guess. I don't feel it the way you feel it.

—You are a fucking wog.

—No, I answer, sadly. Mum is, Dad even. But not me.

—You're pathetic. Soo-Ling drowns the vodka, she is trembling.

I'm not black, I'm white. I can't pretend a fury. I'm sad, depressed about it, confused about it. But I think of the pale white faces of the protesters tonight, faces twisted into ugliness, screaming abuse at other white faces entering the hall. Where does their anger come from? I'm disappointed, exasperated, frustrated and, above it all, I am an elitist. I think the whole mob of them fucking stupid. Most people, I'm discovering this, most people are ignorant: wilfully ignorant, wilfully stupid.

I look at Soo-Ling. I wish I could silence her fury.

I think of Betty. The racists also wish to hurt Betty.

—I do get angry, sure I do.

—Good. Soo-Ling turns away.

—But I get angry at everyone.

Nadia pours another drink.

—I don't like violence, I argue. Soo-Ling interrupts me.

—You're weak. Shoots for my heart.

Just like my brother, eh?

I don't, of course, say this.

We get shit-faced on vodka. Nadia asks Soo-Ling about Patrick. Her answers are hesitant. I know she is conscious that I'm in the room.

—So, come on. Are you two still together? Nadia pushes.

—No.

I can't pretend otherwise. I'm happy.

Soo-Ling on the way to the stereo, to change a CD, knocks over a box of videos. Naked black cases. Soo-Ling stoops and picks one up.

—What's this? The jacket features naked women, their legs apart.

Nadia laughs.

—Want to see one?

I'm titillated but I search Soo-Ling's face, wait for her approval. She simply smirks.

—Which one should we watch?

—Louie can choose.

All eyes on me. I look through the box.

—A gay one. Nadia is insistent.

—But you're a dyke, says Soo-Ling.

—I get off on the poofter ones, don't ask me why, I just do.

I'm surprised at how shocked I am at Nadia's words. I imagine her, alone, masturbating to the videos. I blush and glance through the covers. Most are LA, American custom bodies.

A cardboard box. A moustached dark haired man. A porno from the seventies.

—What's this like?

—Put it on.

We go quiet. The video is different to the pornography I'm used to. It's shot directly on film and so the colours are richer, the actors' skin by turn amber and gold, there is texture to the bodies, there is the absence of the dull flat yellow of video. And there are cuts, real edits. The sex scenes are fast, the men handsome, strong, but their beauty is not impossible. I am most aroused by the come shots, semen falling into mouths, over eyes, over cheeks and faces. I am hard. I can hear, above the instrumental funk, a soft breathing from Soo-Ling. We don't look at each other.

We watch for half an hour until we become bored; the women have descended to giggling. Nadia yawns, rises, wants to know if I want to spend the night, on the couch. I shake my head. I kiss Soo-Ling on the lips and she stays with me. She wets my top lip. It is cold, terribly cold, when I enter the night.

—You sure you don't want to stay? Soo-Ling asks me at the door. I can drop you off on my way back home tomorrow.

—I'm sure.

The anonymity of the dark, the suburb asleep, is intoxicating.

On Maroondah Highway I get a lift towards the city. I'm not ready to go home yet. The driver, a loudly polite Christian, drops me off in Richmond and I walk to a household I know in Abbotsford. Merryl and Slash are home, sucking on bongs. Merryl I used to share with. A boy, a stranger, is sitting with them. Our conversation is university, drugs, the new Palace Music CD. I'm thankful for the dope which takes me far away from where I am. I lie on the floor and concentrate on the music.

—We should have gone, says Merryl. They are talking about the demonstration.

Slash splutters into the bong.

—It was in fucking Dandenong. Long way, mate.

The boy takes the bong from her.

—It got exciting. Did you see the news?

—It's good they hospitalised that guy, answers Slash. I hate those fucking racists.

I keep numb, following the paths of the CD. I don't want to tell them where I have been tonight. I will close my eyes and think of the video I have just seen. The long cocks, the falling come.

I've never tasted come. Only Tommy's, so long ago.

—I went.

I speak to forget Tommy. Maybe I speak to forget the video.

—How was it?

—Stupid.

I should have kept my mouth shut.

—Why?

—It was, it just was. All of it was stupid. The rednecks, the protesters, me, everyone.

Slash doesn't like this.

—So what do you reckon they should have done instead?

It is a good question and the only answer I have is that there is nothing to be done; that it is not only the night, but the weeks and the months, the years and the century, that need to be undone. I know the embarrassment of being racist, the consciousness of another's skin, the oddity of manners to which I am unaccustomed. But I don't get the hatred; the hatred, its intensity, that's a sickness. It's psychotic.

In my final year at high school, at a party, I got it on with Melanie Jackson. She was hot, all the boys wanted to lay her. We were in some bedroom, drunk, and she was jerking me off, slowly. We were talking about school. I was hardly hard. We were talking about stuff, including racism. We were doing it in English.

—I'm not racist. But I can't stand the Asians.

And it was so weird, how cold my body became. I stopped touching her, zipped up my pants. She couldn't understand why I moved away. How could I explain it? Stupidity is unattractive. I can't explain it, how I got this way, how she got this way. But it separated us as firmly as any fortress, any barrier could. We stared at each other in mutual disbelief.

—I don't get the hatred, I tell the stoned group in the lounge room.

On this, we find agreement.

Merryl is in the kitchen, pouring tea. I try to explain to her what it was like, watching the porno with Soo-Ling, try to explain the tension which soured my pleasure in the erotic.

—I like porn, she answers defiantly.

This is not the point I am trying to make. I missed the solitaire of masturbation. There is a relief in masturbating to pornography, which comes right after orgasm. It is locking the video away, out of sight, washing the hands, a relief in knowing that for a while lust has been driven away.

—I felt a bit exposed.

Merryl tells me, nicely, with a pat on my shoulder, that she thinks I'm hung up about sex. The moon is only a sliver tonight and the light is distant, made brittle by the cold. I put my hands in the bomber's pockets and I keep walking, head erect, to the river. The water is loud, a rush, and the city disappears. I walk the boundaries of the children's farm and there are the sounds of goats and dogs. The world smells of rain. As I walk I begin to notice the graffiti, first the colourful tags, then the black calls for repeal of drug laws. I keep walking. On the path, graffiti in shaky red: *Every cop deserves a stiff cock up their arse every day*. I laugh into myself, I keep walking. In red, enormous letters, on a pillar to the bridge: *LSD*. On the path, thick black splashes: *Kill All Commies, Anarchists, Democrats and Nazis*. This time I laugh out loud.

I stop laughing. A flash, a memory of graffiti on a toilet door.

Old White Australia Wants War
Young White Australia wants Peace
Old Black Australia Wants Peace
Young Black Australia Wants War

I had told Soo-Ling of the scrawl. She had screwed up her face, gone thoughtful. I want war, she finally said. Does that make me old? No, I answered, it's just a slogan—it isn't necessarily so. But it is true for me. I don't want war.

Below the graffiti someone had written in black texta: *Into black meat—Negro, Indian, Koori—will suck any big black cock*. Then they had scrawled a mobile phone number.

I laugh again. At the end of the river I follow the path that leads underneath the freeway. The rushing of the water is drowned by the speeding noise of the traffic. I walk the steep climb and I am in the city. I make my way towards Hoddle Street and I realise I'm walking down the street into which I was born. I find the old house, one hundred and sixty-two. Lights are on and in the front yard there is a new fence being built. I don't know this street, I've only heard my family talk of it. I can't see the factories and the poverty of which they spoke. The houses are old but the street is new. The poverty has moved elsewhere.

Sean lives around here. I stop, try to recollect the address, cross Queens Parade and cross Edinburgh Gardens. I knock on the door and a woman who seems really out of it answers.

—Sean in?

—Yeah. That's all she says. I follow her down the empty hallway.

There are six of them in the room, Sean's sitting cross-legged, looking at the television. He smiles when he sees me, but he doesn't get up. Doesn't move.

He introduces me around. I immediately forget the names.

Their talk is slow, about nightclubs, about who is fucking who, about drugs and parties. Sean turns to me, looks away. I look at everyone's face and it hits me. Pinned, they're all pinned.

Got a hit?

The words are there, on the tip of my tongue, I'm close to asking for the heroin. And I don't. This isn't the connection I want to make. I get up quickly, tell them I have to go.

—I'll ring you, says Sean.

I want to smash his fucking face in.

There is no transport, it's too late. I walk into the city, even in the cold I begin to sweat and I buy a ticket to a porn show. I'm hungry for it, for sex, for bodies, for losing myself in it. A handful of men. On the screen a black woman fingers a blonde. I choose to stand, against the back wall. Three rows in front of me a young Vietnamese man has his hand in his crotch. He turns and glances at me. I walk and take the seat next to him. He turns away from me, takes his hand from between his thighs, crosses his legs. I'm not disappointed, I don't care.

I wank, not at the movie, but to the memories from the video I saw earlier in the night. I think of the back of Sean's neck. I come into my handkerchief and a little over the seat. As I get up to go to the bathroom, to wash my hands, I know that the young man is watching me. I return, sit in the back and promptly fall asleep.

When I awake it is five o'clock. In Flinders Street, as I hang outside the station, a frail old man offers me a pamphlet. I accept.

—God loves you.

—Thanks.

—You look like a good lad.

—I'm all right, I guess.

—You're a good lad, I can tell. Do you believe in God?

—Yes, I lie.

—Read it.

I promise that I will.

The pamphlet is titled, *An Exalted Saviour*. I begin to flick through it; I wake up, startled, as the train is leaving Box Hill Station. I get off at Laburnum and, too late, realise I've left the pamphlet behind, dropped, useless, under the seat. The train is moving away and I peer through the window to the empty carriage.

For some strange stupid reason I am angry at myself. The promise to the old man, of all promises I have made, it is one that I wish I could have kept.

SECTION FOUR

Epilogues

Too often the courage about dying is cowardice about living.

PULIKA

1

From the journal of Sean Sanders 1968–1997

1.

I went out with Monica and her new boyfriend Stuart. He's a strange guy, not sure that he's the kind of guy I wanted to spend New Year's Eve with. Monica was all talk, high on speed. I was pretty cruisy too, enjoying the high. We took it at his place, in Brunswick. Late in the morning, I ended up at the dance party with Marsh and Ben. I roamed the crowd, didn't pick up anyone. Didn't really want to, not anyone I wanted to pick up in front of Ben anyway. He's a bitch. There was an older guy in his forties, pretty beefy, who was tossing off in the urinal. It weirded me out even as it made me horny. The whole night weirded me out. It started at Stuart's.

He said he thought it was funny that I was a fag. He's a patronising bastard, said I'd make a bad drag queen. He kept calling me mate, but it was like he was sneering.

The speed was good and he shared it round. Got to give him that.

I think I'm being really stupid with drugs. But I'm scared I'll destroy myself faster without them. Even the thought of slowing down, let alone stopping, kills me. That's how I feel.

Stuart is on the Net. He showed us. Monica has been on, done the whole sex chat line bullshit. She came, she told me, having sex with another woman. Through the computer.

I laughed with her when she told me, teased her, but somehow the stories disturb my peace. No, it isn't that. I haven't got a peace to disturb. The stories make me feel embarrassed. I'm nearly thirty and I'm too old to be feeling all this. When am I going to work all this out?

Stuart collects all these images, on disk, porn stuff that he gets off the Net. He's quite methodical, the disks are all marked. Tits. Come Shots. Stars. Black. Asian. Gay. S/M. Pissing. He's got hundreds of them. He had a collection of disks marked TWS #1, #2, #3 and so on, in black texta. He told me they were for Totally Weird Shit. He and Mon were fooling around on the bed. He told me I should put one on.

I spent the whole time pretending that nothing was going through my mind as I flicked through his files. Stuart set me up, showed me how to surf it all, I guess. Monica squealed and got disgusted by some of the stuff on the screen, Stuart made crass jokes. There was a picture of this young Asian girl, some cheap motel, with a snake coming out of her cunt. I couldn't even look at it.

He had a series of photographs, bad black and white shots, they were of this boy, really thin, who these two dudes in leather had strung up and crucified. Real nails, one shot, a close-up, you could see that they had bunged the nails into his palm, heaps of blood. But not in his feet, they just had them tied up with rope onto the cross; and not through his torso—not an actual killing. It takes a while for each image to appear, you have to wait for the photo to download, section by section. At first I was just curious really, not shocked like I was with the pictures of bestiality or pictures with shit, but after a while something about the boy being so thin really got to me. And there was one shot where you could see his face and I know the look: he's drugged out to heaven, he's beyond pain. Getting so high, so numbed, anyone can do anything to you. It looks like they must have been popping amyl under his nose every second minute.

One shot—Stuart's got it marked as The Final Coming (ha

ha)—there's a close-up of the boy's face, covered in come, thick globules of it. He's wet, sweat and come. And there's all the blood. Close up, black and white, eyes rolled back, looking out away from the world. In that shot he does look like a Jesus.

Not that I know fuck about Jesus. Not that I know shit about religion. But I felt cold, scared, like something bad was in the room with us.

It hit Mon as well. She got upset about the pictures and Stuart got defensive. I pretended to remain cool about it all. Monica told Stuart she thought it was child pornography and he leapt off the bed, angry, told her that the guy wasn't a child, told us that he thought child pornography was evil, that people who traded in that filth should be shot. He shut down the system.

We went back to the lounge, snorted another line, drank some stubbies. We headed off to a party in Preston, a girl from Stuart's work. It was fine, the woman was a dyke and the crowd was friendly. But I couldn't stop thinking of those images. On the fridge at the party there was this postcard with the Virgin Mary on it. I really looked hard at this card, looked at her for the first time. She was almost African on this postcard, dark, very angular features. She looked a little stern.

I'm not as much freaked out by the boy in the photos as I am by wondering what the two men were doing there, why were they getting off this way. Or maybe they were just all models. Except that the young guy was so drug-fucked, except that the nails in the palms looked real. But it could have been make-up, like in the movies. What makes someone get off on this stuff? How much do they hate God? I'm glad I'm an atheist.

I'm getting tired, needing sleep. We've spent the night hopping from party to club, meeting up with Ben and Marsh, going off to a dance party.

I'm glad I wasn't tempted to have sex. It would have only disgusted me. The boy in the pictures, that girl with the shake. I wish I hadn't seen that shit.

I've just looked in the mirror. I'm not skin, I'm all lines.

Nineteen ninety fucking seven. Hooray! I don't want this, I don't think I want this. Even the Valium I've taken can't get me to sleep. It slows me down without cutting me off. I really need to sleep, I just need sleep.

2.

At the nursing home old Jossie is getting all excited about Pauline Hanson. That bitch, that's what she calls her, that racist ugly cunt. It cracks me up, though it's offending some of the more conservative ones. There are no Asians at the home, a few wogs. Old Jossie is in love with one of them, Mr Pericles. He's a funny old bugger, always so neat, so tidy. He agrees with Jossie about most things but he's more considered in what he says. I think he used to be a commie. He always asks me what I think about stuff and he's a pretty good listener. Jossie is fun but she's no listener. Mr Pericles remembers things, he's not lost any of his memory. He just stretches time. He doesn't talk about years or dates, but about long ago or when he was a child or when he was married. I don't know why he's here, I know he has children but they don't visit much. I was surprised about this when I started, I thought Greeks were into family, but that may just be another stereotype. He's not like Sandra, who is always crying, sniffling in Italian, moaning. She hates it here, feels abandoned, and there is nothing I can do that seems to make her happy. It's fucking horrible. This morning she refused to eat, just shook her head and repeated: I want to die, I want to die, I want to die, and I thought, Then just fucking die, will you?

Jossie believes in God. I asked her what that's like.

—Oh, He's definitely there. I know it now, for the first time I really know it. I can feel Him.

—What do you feel?

She said that now she can hear Him, and she laughed. I pray, she said, and in all the dreams He sends me I am dancing. I'm not always young again in these dreams but I am never tired. I just dance and dance.

Jossie is really in a prison here in the nursing home. Sometimes I feel like a warden. There's hot much they can do, it's a major effort getting permission to go outside the grounds.

I've wanted to tell Jossie for a long time that I'm a fag. She must know, she knows I don't have a girlfriend. She must know. I should just fucking tell her. But I don't know what to say. It sounds weak, so silly and finally so insignificant.

•

Marsh is tripping out, he's called again. He left a rambling message on the machine. He was fucked the other night, some taxi driver at Club 80, and the condom broke. He's freaking out but I can't be bothered. He can wait and get the test in a few weeks and work it out from there. I'll go over, I don't really want to but everyone else is out or away. It's all answering machines.

Jack's back but she's in a foul mood. She just had another fight with this new woman she's seeing. I heard her scream, Fuck off, as she played the machine and heard Marsh's hysterical voice.

I've still got a small deal from the cap of heroin Teddie got me. I'm going to take it, to handle Marsh being a drama queen.

3.

I wondered what it would be like to shoot myself. I've been thinking about it all day. Ben and I were at the footy and I couldn't face the thought of having to go to work. I just wanted a gun. I reckon it would be so easy, I'm not freaked out by it at all. One second, one split second, and it's all over. There would be a flash of pain, and then nothing. It would be over. Just nothing.

Ben thought I was hung over and he just concentrated on the game. We were pretty quiet.

St Kilda won.

4.

I got fucked up the arse last night. It hurt. I didn't let him do it for long. He seemed upset but I was scared about him coming, even with the condom. And I didn't like it, him over me like that. I haven't done it since being with Trent and I didn't like it then either. The guy last night wanted me to fuck him as well but I couldn't get hard.

He lived some place in the eastern suburbs. He was a snarly little prick when I got up to leave, came on all bitchy. I wouldn't give him my number. I can't figure out why I went home with him. He looked poonsy in bed. Last night I thought he was kind of hot, kind of tough.

Get real, Sean. Last night I was pissed out of my skull, I was tripping. I can't remember the sex much at all, apart from his trying to fuck me. I think I fell asleep during sex. I can't remember either of us coming.

I must have thought he was special, I must have. To even let him try fucking me.

5.

Postcard from Tara in Russia. From St Petersburg. A dog on the postcard, a dog in space. This is Laika, she wrote, the first living thing in space. Then she wrote about Russia and the crime and the poverty and how cheap everything was. She went to a rave, outside the city. That sounds cool.

I wonder what happened to the dog, up in space. I hope it came back, I hope it lived a long life. I hope they didn't let it die up there.

The dog's a fucking hero.

6.

Mum is hassling me to find a boyfriend. She thinks I'm lonely.

I saw Lou tonight. It was tough. He asked me these questions and I was slow to answer, kept stumbling, I was too fucked from the party last night. I pointed him out to Mon and she agreed he's sexy. I wish she didn't, she started flirting with him.

I made up a story for Mum, told her about a possibility of getting it together with Lou. I offered her my fantasy.

Jack found an old kitsch picture of Jesus on the Cross, found it in an op shop for fifty cents. She's placed it above the door to the kitchen. It's been freaking me out all night. I keep remembering those stupid porno files of Stuart's.

7.

An arsehole in a ute screamed out poofter at me this morning. He was just mouthing off, I jumped out in front of him, but I got really pissed off at what he said. I don't like it when they guess who I am. Sometimes I think fags know shit, know nothing, are the most selfish people on this planet.

Stephen's been on the phone, crying, telling me that he still loves me. I told him that I don't find him sexually attractive. I never have. I surprised myself. I felt shitty, a louse, but I did enjoy saying it.

I'm sick of that word love. I don't feel it. I don't even think I want it.

8.

I saw Lou at a party. He was with a group of people I don't know. We nodded to each other but we didn't talk at all. I left with Marsh and I patched *Pretty Woman* at Club 80 while he went off to have sex. I didn't look at anyone. I was pissed off with Lou, wanted to smash his face in. I think he likes me, that's about it. But I don't even think he's a fag. Marsh reckons he is, says he knows someone who knows someone who has fucked him. But that doesn't mean shit. That doesn't mean he's a fag. He comes on like a straight guy.

9.

Jossie's dead.

Jack scored some slow.

I wish I could cry.

10.

On Sunday I watched television till five p.m. and then fell asleep. I woke at nine in the evening and I took some speed and went to a night in Thornbury, with the ravers, to Taryaki. Someone had more speed. A girl told me I reminded her of a footballer but she didn't remember, which one. I was pleased. The guy who had the speed kept buying me beer.

It's seven a.m., back home, and I'm watching a video of *Rage*, taped a couple of years ago. I'm not listening to the video, I have the sound turned off and I'm listening to a compilation tape of Jack's. It's good, weird. Metallica has just segued into A Tribe Called Quest. Martika is on the screen, I barely remember her. She's some eighties bimbo, gorgeous. A bit woggy. George Michael's 'Freedom' is on the video and that's the only song I listen to. I don't want to see the images, I just lie back and listen, loud, to the song. But someone bangs on the wall, shouts at me to turn it down. I switch everything off, ready to go to bed.

I am writing all this down so I can pretend that I haven't

wasted all my time, all my money, that I haven't wasted another day.

I got really drunk tonight and I think someone went down on me in the men's toilet. What's worse, I don't think we were even in a cubicle. The thing I remember most clearly is that someone came in, a young Italian looking guy who stopped, then turned around and left. I think it was either the guy with the speed or the girl who thought I was a footballer who went down on me. They're the only people I remember spending time with.

I'm nothing but a fucking dirty poofter sleaze.

That guy, that guy who turned around and left, that guy was beautiful.

11.

I've spent the day wanking. That's it. The whole fucking day.

My cock feels like it is ready to drop off.

12.

I met Jossie's grand-daughter today, at the funeral. A woman called Becca. It's really Rebecca she said but in the east it's pronounced *Re-ve-kah*. In Australia they call her Becca.

She lives in Israel, in the capital (can't remember what it's called), and she tells me that no-one bothered telling her that her nan was in a nursing home. It turns out that old Jossie was Jewish. Becca tells me that Jossie was born in Greece, in Thessaloniki, to Spanish Jewish parents and they smuggled her to Turkey just before the war.

I told Becca that I once went to Salonika, when I was travelling, years ago, on the way to the islands.

Becca was furious that the funeral was Catholic. Our

grandmother was Jewish, she announced angrily to her uncles and aunts. They all seem to hate her.

Becca only seemed to want to talk to me. She noticed me at once. I was dressed down, I guess. I thought I was dressed up but not compared to everyone else. I was wearing jeans. Black but still jeans.

Becca took me to a pub after the funeral. I'd never been there, it was somewhere in South Yarra, near the Gardens, down an alley. She wanted to talk, insisted on buying me drinks.

I told her that she was the first Jewish person I had ever met. You knew my grandmother, she said.

She guessed I was a fag, asked me if I was gay. I wondered what it was that gave me away. I didn't ask but she answered the question anyway.

She said that I purposefully didn't look at men.

Jossie was born in Greece and it seems that there were a lot of Jews in Greece then, which is funny because none of the Greeks I know here told me that. Hitler killed them. Jossie was lucky, she was taken from Turkey to Lebanon, she got settled with a distant cousin. She grew up there and married an Italian. He wasn't a Jew. She married by choice, Becca tells me. She fell in love and they had to elope. They came here to Australia and at first things seemed to go well. Becca's mother was born and she was raised a Jew, but after a few years the husband began to change. He wanted to be respectable, fit in with the Italians. Becca's aunts and uncles, they all were baptised Catholic.

Becca's mum is dead and when I asked Becca if her mum remained a Jew, Becca didn't answer the question. I didn't push.

I think she must have, been about forty years old, Becca. Very very elegant. She wears her clothes, her sunglasses, like an ad from *Vogue*. She's like Paloma Picasso. She insisted on paying for every drink and I was high. I almost forgot that I had been to a funeral. When we said goodbye she kissed me twice, on both cheeks.

I walked home, it took ages, through the parks, across the

river, through Richmond and Abbotsford, trying always to follow the river. I realise Jossie kept a life from me, that's sad, but I guess she must have needed to. Maybe she told everything to Mr Pericles. He was at the funeral, crying. Sally took him back to work with her straight after. I wish I had invited him to the pub with us. He would have liked that.

I once asked Jossie, when we were speaking about the God stuff, what religion she was. She told me she was nothing, she didn't believe in religions, only in God.

I didn't tell Becca this. She seemed into being Jewish. Let her remember her grandmother any way she wants.

13.

I saw Lou yesterday, at Polyester, looking through CDs. We talked, or rather he talked, I mumbled. He'd been in the rain, his hair was wet and he smelt sweet, the sweetness of wood burning.

Back home last night I got some shit off Trev. He told me to take it easy, that it was strong, but I jacked it all up. I woke up, I don't know how long I was out, with vomit over my shirt, all over my trousers. The syringe was still sticking out of my arm.

It scares me, I don't like that all this is happening. I'm scared that my first thought on waking up was disappointment that I wasn't dead.

14.

A fucking shit of a day. Sally told me at work that they are thinking of reducing staff. I'm casual, that just may be in my favour, but who the fuck knows. I was also late for work, got up with a hangover, and Drummond screamed at me as soon as I walked through the door. I get home and everyone is there, not only Jack and Trev, but the fuckups they've picked up, all of them coming down from Es and speed. There's nothing left and I have to go to the pub and pick up beer. I get back, get drunk, share their joints and listen to their crap. It is all crap. Poofter gossip, dyke gossip, Fitzroy goss. Who the fuck cares? I try to watch telly and it's all the opening of the Casino. The girl with Jack says from now on she's dividing the world between those who have gone and those who haven't gone to the Casino. She's only going to talk to those who haven't gone.

How about those who have to work there? I wanted to ask her, but I didn't want to get into a shitfight and I know it's just words anyway. I hate the fucking Casino but we're all going to be in there at least once in our lives. It's half the size of Melbourne, for Christ's sake. The boy Trev has picked up is cute, dark and quiet. He kept looking at me. Trev didn't like that. I was pleased.

They're still going. I can hear them even with the bedroom door shut, even with the radio on.

Mr Pericles asked if I was going to the opening of the Casino. I said no, I wasn't interested. He winked at me, smiled. That was the only good thing that happened today.

15.

I visited Mum today. She gave me a card from Dad. It's a birthday card, not in time but, hey, it's the first contact in two years so I guess I should be happy. Mum got on my case, said I should write back, give him my address, my phone number. I don't want to. He'll just ring up pissed one night, telling me he needs money. His card reads:

Happy Birthday Sean. Sorry I haven't written but you probably know how it is. All work and girls. Come and visit soon, Townsville has changed, I think you'll like it. Work's all right but it's tough. Hope your work is going well. Happy Birthday again, son, Your Father.

The card is glossy, a photograph of a Porsche. I got drunk with Mum and she played Aretha Franklin. She asked about Lou and I fucked up because I'd forgotten I told her I was sort of going out with him. So now she thinks we've split up and she got sad and wanted to hug me so I decided to leave early without waiting for Claire to come home. I left her a note, on her bed, asked her to ring me.

The weirdest thing happens on the way back. I take the train from Lalor and get off at Collingwood Station, walk across the overpass to home. A Vietnamese woman is walking hand in hand with her daughter, walking towards me, on the overpass, and I get an urge to see them fall, to push them off. Of course I just pass them, I even smile, but I feel like the lowest scum on the planet. I mouth off about racists, say all the right things, but I'm no different. It makes me sick. I'm a fucking hypocrite.

The first thing I did on coming home, lying on the bed, was put a lighter under Dad's card. I torched the surface first, watched the paper form bubbles, then I streaked the flame across his words. Then I just started burning the corners. When it was a mangled sooty mess, when it was unreadable and indecipherable, I threw it in the bin. It was a stupid thing to do, I'm not even angry at him. I wasn't thinking when I did it.

The answering machine has just gone on. It's Mon, she says she's got some trips.

16.

Travis got drunk tonight, we were at the Tote and he asked if I could fuck him. I said no, wasn't interested. He lost it and started screaming at me. I got embarrassed and started to walk off. He tried to follow and I pushed him, hard, he fell on the floor. I walked out.

He's been crying, leaving messages, crying and apologising.

I'll ring him back tomorrow, when he isn't drunk, tell him it's okay, that I'm still his friend.

I'm really tired, I'm really fucking tired.

17.

I had a weird night at Stuart's tonight. I was supposed to meet Mon there but she didn't turn up. She was heading off to score. He had a bit of stuff and asked if I wanted some. I said sure. We hit up and Stuart wanted to play on the Internet. He hangs there all the time, it's giving Mon the shits. She says he's obsessed with sex, he knows all the porno sites, has accounts with heaps of them. I just want to get on and check out music and film, find some photos of Andy Garcia.

At some point while we're looking at a S/M site, Stuart starts stroking his crotch. He doesn't touch me. He unzips and his dick is huge. I go down on him for a while, I'm not quite into it, but his cock is the biggest I've seen. Amazing. It stretches my mouth and it hurts. I go back to surfing and he's wanking but he's too strung out from the slow to come. I ask him if he's still got the pictures of the boy on the cross but he tells me that he's got rid of them, to get Mon off his back. Instead he shows me pictures of people pissing on each other. This time I get a hard on-and he goes down on me. It hurts a bit and I lift his head, try to kiss him. He's not into that. Instead he pushes my mouth to his cock. He comes. I spit it out in my hand.

Mon turns up at midnight. She was at a piss up at work and didn't get round to the dealer's house until late. I know I won't tell her any of what happened. She'd hate me. She always says I'm the only guy she trusts, she wishes I was straight. She'd hate me if she knew.

We have another hit, it's good. I fall asleep during an infomercial.

After Stuart blew and his cock was lying across his thigh, still thick and long, I couldn't look at it. It almost made me sick. Just moments before all I wanted was to have it all, eat it all, his cock was the only thing that seemed real. But straight after—I mean, straight fucking after—I look at it and it's ugly. His cock is one of the most revolting things I have ever seen.

18.

Do I believe in evil? Mr Pericles asked me this question last night, or rather, he asked me early this morning. Do you believe in evil, Sean?

I was on the night shift. I was reading through the magazines, dozing a little, and I heard a noise from the television room. I went in to check and it was Mr Pericles, all alone, in his dressing gown, in the dark, watching television. It was about five in the morning, quite cold and I sat down with him. I'd never seen the show before, it was an infomercial but instead of selling exercise equipment or motivation tapes or that kind of shit, they were selling God. There was this funny looking American woman, with an old fashioned red beehive hairdo, and she was talking about the Ten Commandments.

Do you know the Commandments, Sean? That was the first thing Mr. Pericles said to me, looking up from the screen. I felt real ignorant. No, I said. Thou shalt not commit adultery, this woman was screaming on the television. And then there was a shot of all these people in the audience and they were cheering her, clapping their hands. Does it say in the Bible, this woman went on, that you can sleep with your boyfriend before marriage? The audience were shaking their heads. She raised a book in her hands. It doesn't say it in my Bible. There were more cheers. Mr Pericles was laughing, really loudly. I laughed with him. But inside I felt strange, like here were obviously thousands of Americans agreeing with her, you don't sleep with someone before marriage. And, I don't know why, I got scared. I thought:

Fuck, what would they think of me? They would hate me, they would loathe me. As for them, they were from another planet. There's all these people out there, must be, who think like that, live like that and we aren't on the same planet. We are not even in the same universe.

Then there was a switch to the same woman sitting on a chair in a living room, asking us to become a partner in her ministry. Which meant that she would pray for us and she would send us a book of Bible stuff and all it would cost would be a donation of twenty-seven dollars or more a month—whatever more you can afford, she said—to be a partner in Jesus. And Mr Pericles and I laughed together, really hard, and it was great. It was fantastic to laugh like that. Should we switch this rubbish off? he said, and I flicked the remote control.

And it was more Americans. But this time a program called *48 Hours* and there was this woman in prison and she was talking about how she was locked up, her husband too, for sexually abusing her children. But it turned out that what happened was that she and her husband caught their son, he was about fourteen, doing something to their youngest daughter, so they called in child protection, but what happened was that child protection took them in instead and said that they were the ones abusing their children and they got locked up for it. Then the oldest daughter—there were five kids and they all got fostered—when the daughter turned eighteen she was finally allowed to see her mum in prison because she was no longer in custody to welfare. So we see mum and daughter meet after two years and they are crying and hugging, and the mother is saying, I love you, and the daughter is saying, I love you, and fuck it I'm crying, and I feel so stupid I can't look at Mr Pericles. Then there's an ad break and I say, Do you want me to turn it off? and he says, No, I want to know what happens. So do I. So we watch. And it turns out that the daughter got into a car accident and got $100,000 in compensation—that's a shitload, we're talking US dollars—and so she can hire lawyers for her mum and dad. And it looks like the

appeal is going to be successful. But the report was filmed before
the couple are out of jail and it's mostly the mum talking, and she
talks of how she hasn't seen her kids for years, and how they are all
in different homes, and how the son who did things to his sister is
in an institution for underage sex offenders and I'm thinking what
the fuck would that be like, that would be like hell. And the
parents, the mum and the dad, both wearing these orange prison
uniforms, they just both looked really scared and really confused
and really hurt. And they both looked like good people, just weak
ordinary folk, just with those faces that say, What the fuck is
happening to me? And suddenly Mr Pericles says, and his voice is
really tired, Turn it off, Sean. Just turn the bloody thing off.

He looks really tired, really sad, and I ask him if he wants
anything, maybe he should go back to bed. He shakes his head.
We are still in the dark and there's silence and then he says, What
if she hadn't been in the car accident, Sean, what if she didn't get
that money to help her poor parents? They'd still be in jail. And
I guess he's right. That's when he asked me, Do you believe in
evil, Sean?

I don't know. Don't know what that would be. I guess I don't
because I don't believe in God, don't believe in anything. Then
he stood up, touched me on the shoulder and he pointed to the
television. What we just watched, all of it, especially the woman
selling God, that's evil, Sean, that's what it looks like. All of it, all
of it was evil. Then he tells me I'm a good boy and he tells me
that he feels sorry for me and he tells me he's glad his time is
coming to an end. Then he shuffles off, back to bed.

And I sat alone in the darkness for a long while. Then I
turned on the television again.

19.

Trev, pissed, back from work, has found this journal and has
been reading it. He's cracking up, tells me he's been laughing for

hours. You're a bad poofter, mate, he said to me, you're so fucking hung up about sex. Sex is nothing, he said, laughing, means absolutely nothing at all. Just enjoy it. It means shit, don't you get it, it's just zero. He said I'm too uptight.

I am too uptight.

I hate the cunt. I hate the cunt. I hate the cunt. I hate the cunt. I hate that fucking prick. I'd like to kill the prick. I'd love to kill the prick.

He's right. Sex, being a fag, being straight, all of it, it's nothing. It's nothing, it don't mean nothing.

2

Freedom '97

There's a new version of 'When Doves Cry', it's always on the radio, sung by a young boy, sung gospel. I'll always prefer the original but whatever version, it's a great song. I've loved the song since I was a kid in primary school. Such a long time ago.

Spring is around the corner, it's late August, but I can't get excited. Collingwood aren't in the finals, I haven't touched the thesis for weeks. And Sean, he's dead.

Tommy dead, Sean dead. I'm becoming a veteran of suicide.

Dad's retiring. Finally. He's still a strong man but the work is beginning to kill him. He and Mum, they've talked it over with Soo-Ling, they're going on a holiday to Europe, they'll take Betty with them. Some time next year. They want to go to Jerusalem as well. Since Tommy offed himself, Mum has got more and more religious. She wants to see the holy sites. Dad will go just to be with her. That's Dad.

I cried hard when I heard Sean was dead, that he cut his throat. I heard it from two queer students at uni, in the coffee lounge. They didn't know him either, they just knew him as that good-looking drug-taking cool guy. The guy that everyone wanted to fuck.

I didn't cry then, I cried later. I found out when Tommy died that my tears make sense only in private. Maybe, just maybe, that's where women are different from men: they know in their guts that boundaries are fluid. Mum, who is a cynic, who hates the Church, she can go back to God. Dad can't. He's put everything into work. I'm scared for him when he retires. He doesn't know stillness.

Dad drove me to the cemetery to find Sean's grave. He didn't ask questions, just asked if I wanted a lift. It's a real simple grave, there are flowers. It was an emptiness, and I couldn't feel. I didn't even know the guy. It's a little obscene that I'm crushed so much by someone who was only fantasy.

Fuck that! He was flesh and blood, he had a smell. He had a laugh.

On the way back, in the car, Dad asked me who he was.

—A friend.

—From uni?

—Nah. He wasn't at uni.

—Were you lovers?

The question stopped me. I shook my head. I can't remember what else was said.

Whatever he's done, Artie Stefano, my father, he will die knowing he was a good man. He has maintained a love, he's adored my mother for the length of a life. He's raised three kids, he's buried one; he never shut us out. There must have been temptations, there must have been a fiery urge to resist responsibility. I don't know who made the rules for my old man, maybe he made them for himself. I want, one day, what he has. His astounding faith in the soundness of living.

We also visited Tommy's grave. It is already ageing, there are deep cracks along the stone. I think both Dad and I were shocked at how quickly a death can turn to history.

Soo-Ling and Betty are at Apollo Bay, for a fortnight, staying with Nadia and her new girlfriend. Melbourne is silent. I watch film after film after film which I take from work, staying in my room, playing with the cat, not wishing to talk to anyone. All of clubland now simply makes me sick. I'm tired of young faces, especially beautiful faces.

I nearly took some smack the other day, it seems that it's

everywhere. I haven't touched it since high school. I didn't take up the offer. The time has passed.

I can still hate Tommy, and I may end up hating Sean for this as well, forcing me to live.

•

The hitch to Apollo Bay was spectacular. I took the train to Geelong and set off from there. A young Italian guy in a white Porsche picked me up at Anglesea. As the road followed the jagged cliffs, as we sped along, I felt as if we were flying. He played Natasha Atlas, Faith No More.

—You Italian too? he screamed over the music, across the ocean.

—Long way back.

—You still look it.

He was visiting his girlfriend, in Lorne.

—You got a girlfriend?

—No, I answered.

—A boyfriend? He laughed at my surprise. I'm just asking. I like gay people.

—I'm a poofter, I replied, but I can't stand gay people.

He laughed and turned down the radio.

—It's different for you. For me, it's just fun. You should hear the stuff I hear in the shop. I've got one guy working for me and all he seems to do is fuck. I mean, every night a different guy. And sometimes two or three. Fucking amazing. I reckon my dick would fall off if I fucked that often.

I looked at his hands, on the wheel. Smooth and dark, elegant, with rings. He began talking again.

—This one guy, Greek, pretty good looking, I didn't even realise he was a fag, I found him going down on one of the customers in the change room. And they weren't worried about being discreet. You could hear them going for it through the whole fucking shop. I got rid of him. Don't get me wrong, I wouldn't have minded what he did on his lunch break, but not on my fucking time.

He turned back to me.

—It's different for you, you might not want to end up like that. He smiled, widely, friendly. It's like being a wog, I reckon. You can be a wog but you don't have to act like a wog. You can be a poofter but you don't have to act like one.

I was smelling the new leather of the car. I took a chance.

—You act like a wog.

He turned up the music. He wasn't offended, he was laughing.

—Yeah, mate, he cried out, but you see, I don't mind being a wog. I like it.

We entered Lorne, the sun came through the clouds and it gilded the ocean. We entered Lorne singing 'Falling To Pieces'.

Soo-Ling and Betty picked me up from a cafe in the middle of town. Betty rushed to my arms and I lifted her, buried myself in her hair, hugged her so tight that she squirmed from under me. Soo-Ling gently kissed my cheek.

A strong wind, a savage wind, was blowing along the bay. I dug my hands deep into my pockets and we climbed a hill, moving away from the sea. Betty danced in front of us.

—It's good to see you.

—You too, replied Soo-Ling.

And we fell to silence.

I had come up for the weekend but decided, immediately, to stay the week. The house was new, roomy, it sat on the hill and from the verandah you could see the bay stretch to the gaping infinity of the south. The white noise of Melbourne had disappeared. I was not forgetting Sean but the world around him no longer seemed to matter, was no longer making me angry. Nadia's lover, Sally, was in her forties, red haired and red faced, plump and tough, and she welcomed me to the house. She chain smoked, drank wine all day, and she laughed at everything. She adored Betty. On our first night the conversation came around to children. Sally, drunk, was berating Nadia.

—Get yourself pregnant, love. I'd like a kid.

—Get pregnant yourself, retorted Nadia.

—Too late for me.

—Who's going to be the father?

Sally pointed to me.

—He'll do. He looks all right, got good genes.

Nadia winked at me and I winked back.

—He's too young to be a father. This from Soo-Ling.

—Oh fucking bullshit! roared Sally. My old man was eighteen when he got me mum pregnant.

—I'd like to be a father, I said.

Soo-Ling got up, excused herself, said it was time for bed.

Sometimes it hits me—it did at that moment, watching her leave without looking at me—I realise that it is not that Soo-Ling is angry at me, or that she doesn't care for me, but that I must remind her of Tommy. And no matter what her love for me is, he is dead and I'm alive and that is not what she wanted. I felt my youth profoundly at that moment. The sea was crashing below us, I regretted the journey I had taken.

On the third night we went to a local pub. We had a huge meal, we drank heaps, and we all noticed the young woman who was working behind the bar. She was pretty, her face shone and she moved with the quick sexy glide of a cat. She liked us and by the end of the evening, her boss drunk, she was with us, sharing a drink and Sally's smokes. Her name was Melissa, she was from Sydney and working the winter in Apollo Bay before heading back to a boyfriend in Melbourne. She entertained us with rapid-fire stories from her life. Next year she was going back to college.

—What do you study? I asked her, and she screwed up her face, said, Marketing, and then laughed.

—Boring, I know, but a girl needs a job, right? She raised her eyes and glanced around the pub. I don't want to do this the rest of my life. Not unless I can own it. She lowered her voice. These old drunks, they're all so boring. Most of them are unhappy and

I think that's sad. They talk more, to me than they do to their wives or their friends. Don't you reckon that's sad?

—That's life, answered Sally. That's why I never got married.

Melissa cocked an eyebrow.

—And because you're a dyke. She slammed hard down on the last word. And she quickly followed with, My mum's a dyke.

She butted out her cigarette and got up.

—Better get back to work. I like you all. Come again, please. I mean it. She touched my hand and she grinned. I can't wait to get back to the city.

On her way back to the bar she paused a moment to play with Betty's hair.

The week, as I remember it, was all the beach, the house and the pub. Every afternoon I'd take Betty for a long walk. She enjoyed the pier, watching the old men fish. On one of those days the wind came in so strong I held her hand tight, scared she would blow away. A soft rain began and we headed back, stopping to watch the fishermen lifting cages of fish from the hull of a boat. They were little sharks, petit rubbery carcasses, not at all threatening. It was cage after cage after cage, all the silver fish squirming. Betty covered her eyes. She stamped her feet.

—No. I don't want to see them die. Betty's not a screamer, not unless she is genuinely frightened, so I knew her agitation was real. I hoisted her on my shoulders, walked to the pub, and Melissa whispered that she'd organise her a free drink and chips.

—What's she drink?, she asked me.

—Coca-Cola, shot back Betty.

—You want one?

—Nah, I said, I don't really like Coke.

—You too, eh? She handed a glass to Betty. She turned back to me.

—It's funny, you know, whenever I drink a Coke I always think of the Antichrist. I think it's the colour or something, sulphur burning and shit.

—What's an Antichrish?, Betty stumbled.

—Antichrist, helped Melissa. Do you know who Jesus was?

Betty looked towards me for assistance. I shrugged my shoulders.

—Do you, Bets? I prodded.

Betty nodded slowly.

—People believe in him. He died, long ago.

—That's kind of it, laughed Melissa. Well, Jesus drank wine and the Antichrist drinks Coca-Cola.

Betty smiled, satisfied, and started eating her chips.

I chatted to Melissa. The pub was empty except for two drunk old men, sitting at the bar. They whispered to each other, occasionally glancing over at us. If by chance I caught their eye, they would dart their gaze away. Above us all a television played cable, Ricki Lake. She was interviewing welfare recipients, all single mothers, who were defending themselves from the vicious denunciations of the audience. One of the old men, coming back from the toilet, shook his head at the screen.

—Fucking black bastards. He called back to the bar. The nignongs are the same all over.

Most of the women interviewed for the show were black.

—Shut up, Geoff. Melissa mouthed, Sorry, at us.

—I'm right, aren't I, Joe? he pleaded with his friend, who turned around, looked at us, said, You're right, and went back to his drink.

For the first time the old man looked directly at me.

—Just like our boongs, fucking useless cunts. His eyes dared me. He turned and walked clumsily back to the bar, muttering loudly.

—We should have finished them off long ago. Useless bloody country, this one. Boongs controlling everything, fucking Vietnamese everywhere, and we're selling all of it to the slanty eye. This isn't Asia, he threatened.

These are, for me, and I suspect for most people, moments of fear. Inevitably. I'm the foreigner here and for whatever reason this old man distrusts me. But he's sick, a hopeless drunk, and I know he can't really hurt me. And there's Betty, who's looking at him curiously. If I let this moment go, I'd be ashamed, remembering it, for the rest of my life.

I got up. Melissa watched me carefully. I walked up to the old man.

—Excuse me, sir, but I just want to say one thing. I mean you no disrespect but my niece is half Chinese as well as being an Australian. As I said, I mean you no disrespect but all I want is to sit back with my niece and have a drink, and I don't want to hear talk of hate. Is that all right, sir, if I ask you not to do it in front of the both of us?

I think it had to do with two things, the way his face softened: the use of the word sir and the hint of anger in my voice. I ignored the other man who was younger.

—Son, replied the old man, I meant no harm.

Melissa, washing glasses, was looking over to us.

—They even say my nana was a black, the old man offered. Or half one.

I looked at his face. His skin was wretched, the veins protruded.

—See, I didn't mean everything I said, mate. He pointed at the television. It was that bloody thing that set me off. The old man signalled Melissa. Two pots, love. For me and the young man. He drank at his beer hungrily and I watched the screen.

—Why is this on? I ask Melissa. Why are we watching crap American television? Why can't we watch crap Australian TV?

—It's cable shit, man. She sneered. You got a complaint, tell the boss. Personally I'd prefer a jukebox.

I thanked the old man for the beer, he refused money, and I walked back to Betty. He continued talking to me, talking about a Chinaman friend, telling me he really liked the Greeks and the Italians.

—Wonderful people. He chuckled. Got to watch those Greek sheilas, eh? They're never satisfied. He smiled towards. Betty.

—How are you, little girl?

Betty stared at him.

—I'm fine, she said curtly. Then added, Thank you.

I turned my back to the old man and winked at the child.

—You don't like him, do you? I whispered.

—He was rude.

—Yes, but he said he was sorry.

She sucked on her straw.

—I'm going to Greece, she announced.

—I know. With your giagia and your nonno.

—But first I'll stay a little with Nana and Pop so they don't get jealous.

I smiled at her seriousness.

—What's the Chinese names for your nanna and nonno?

—We don't talk Chinese. They're like you and Mum, they talk Australian.

She slurped through the straw, scattering bubbles into her drink. When we left, the old man shouted his farewells.

•

The water is freezing. I'm up to my knees and shivering and all around me the hills form a cradle for the bay. Seagulls are feeding. Even bitterly cold I could stay here, by the water, for the rest of my life. I wouldn't be missing a thing.

•

Soo-Ling finally asked me about Sean, We were cooking pasta in the kitchen.

—How did he do it?

—He cut his throat.

She chopped furiously at the vegetables. I watched her hands.

—I'm so very sorry, Lou. You know that. She stopped her work and came over and kissed me. I wished to stay in the kiss but she pulled away.

—I wish you would let me kiss you. I had my face turned away from her as I spoke.

—You don't want to kiss me.

—I do.

She began to laugh.

—Seriously, Lou, you're ridiculous.

I took her hand and pulled her to me. I kissed her hard on the mouth and we were, both shocked. I was startled at the rush of a desire on experiencing the delicateness of her mouth. She pushed me away.

—Fuck off, you bastard.

She was shaking. I was stunned, still.

—Don't ever try that again.

—I love you, Soo-Ling.

Her voice was exhausted.

—You're a child, you don't know what love is.

I hate her. Her age, her experience, her refusal to believe my sincerity.

—I love you, I repeat.

She looks at me.

—I don't love you.

The sky is black with crows.

I left, ran into night, said nothing to anyone, not even glancing at Betty who cried after me. I got drunk in the pub.

—It's closing time. Melissa had her hand on my arm. You should go home.

—One more, I pleaded.

—You're out of money, remember. She poured me a shot of whisky, mindful of the boss who was snoozing by the fire.

—You should go home.

—I can't.

—Do you want to stay at my place?

I nodded. We walked clumsily the short distance to her flat.

How did we make love? By beginning in the dark, laughing, depending on touch. I stripped her slowly, rubbing my crotch gently against her leg. I touched as much of her as I could, entranced by the body of a woman. I kissed her mouth and her neck, her nipples and her shoulders. Her cunt, her thighs. She forced my head down and rubbed my face hard on her body. I worked at her cunt, with my tongue, my lips, my hair, the force of my chin. My face wet with her I grew excited; I chewed her tits, my rhythm against her became faster and she pulled down on my jeans. I was inside her.

That's all I wanted, to be inside her. I smelt of her. I closed my eyes and her moans were also the sounds of the sea. I came, shuddering, slamming my body hard into her. She kept me inside her, I opened my eyes and she was smiling at me. She kept me inside her till there was only softness and then she closed her eyes and began to masturbate. I remained raised above her, watching her approach climax, lowering my face, whispering to her, kissing her. She came, sweating, the mildest of moans.

After we fucked, I held her, we giggled together, her fingers played with mine.

In the morning I go to piss and am overwhelmed at the need to masturbate. I think of the first thing that will arouse me, think of pornography, a white man going down on a black man, I think of footballers in the showers, and I come quickly. Melissa is still asleep and I make us bacon and eggs. As I bring the plates to the bedroom the phone rings. It is her boyfriend, and as they talk she fondles my balls, I am stroking her hair. We hardly talk over breakfast, sit close to each other, and she puts on a tape, George Michael *Listen Without Prejudice*. She sings softly to 'Freedom'.

—You probably think this is daggy, right?

—Why should I?

I too start singing along.

—I used to have such a crush on George Michael. During primary school.

So did I.

—How old are you, Mel?

—Guess?

—Twenty.

—Close. I was born in 1975.

—What month?

—I was born the eleventh of November. Mum's contractions started when she heard Gough Whitlam got the sack. That's my middle name, Whitlam. She laughs, loudly. Don't tell many people that one.

I'm glad that I am one of them.

—Anyway, she continues, the important thing is I'm a Scorpio and that Scorpios are good in bed.

We both giggle, we both agree. She traces my tattoos, stops at the one beneath my heart.

—That Chinese?

—Yeah.

—What's it say?

—Love. I answer. Soo-Ling, Betty, Tommy, Sean. It says everything.

I leave after breakfast, after coffee. I leave without washing, still smelling of her, of her cigarettes.

The house is silent when I return. Sally and Nadia still asleep. I knock on Soo-Ling's door.

—Where the fuck have you been? She is smiling, she is not angry.

—I was safe.

She laughs.

—Good. You're lucky then, safe is hard.

—I know.

I sit on the bed, take her hand, trace my finger along her palm.

—Sorry about last night.

—Me too.

—I'm going back today. Back to Melbourne. Give you some peace.

She rubs her face into my chest.

—Will you be all right?

—Sure. I grin and get up.

There is a sadness between us, a sadness that won't go away. Betty's watching television in the lounge. My bedding sits neatly folded on the couch, reproaching me. She refuses to look at me, turns away from me, as I curl up beside her.

—I'm sorry, Bets.

Nothing.

—Aren't you going to forgive me?

—No.

—I love you, Bets.

—What?

I look at the cartoons, the crackle of TV noise.

—You pushed me away, as you were leaving.

—I'm sorry. I was an idiot.

—I was crying.

I nervously brush hair away from her cheek. She lets me. I reach over and hug her and she is immediately in my arms, in my lap, her short arms around my neck. I take her in: smell her, touch her, kiss her, love her.

We take a walk to the beach and we sit on the shore. It is cold and I envelop her in my jacket. She is watching the seagulls.

—They're noisy.

I make fists in the sand, feel the coarseness, the wetness. A crow flies low, and above us the seagulls scatter. Betty watches, the path of the black bird.

—I like those birds, she offers.

—I'm going to go home tonight, Bets.

—Why? She is petulant.

—I've got things to do in Melbourne. Work.

—Is it because you had a fight with Mummy?

—No. We made up.

—I don't like it when you two fight.

She bangs her fists in the sand, spraying yellow dust. She laughs, stops and looks at me.

—Mummy said you are sad, Uncle Louie, because your friend died.

—Yes, I am.

—Did you love him?

—Yes.

—Mummy says that when two men love each other then it's exactly the same as a man and a woman.

Oh, Betty, I want to say, if only it were that simple.

—Yes, Bets. That's right.

She leans closer into my jacket.

—How did he die?

—He killed himself.

We are silent, the seagulls are back, screeching.

—Like Daddy?

—Yeah, like Daddy.

She is tight around me.

—What was Daddy like?

This is the first time the question has been asked. The crow is still flying. I look at it as I answer.

—He was a real good man, handsome. I realise that Tommy is fading, that he is no longer clear before me. I am dependent on the clarity of photographs to describe him. He could be very sad.

—Why?

—I don't know.

She crawls out from the jacket, stands and points to the horizon.

—Look, a ship! She is excited, patient, as she stares into the ocean.

—I miss your dad, Bets.

She does not turn around.

—Mummy was crying about Daddy last night.

—How do you know?

She simply shrugs.

—'Cause.

—'Cause, eh? I grab her and we laugh and fall onto the sand. She squeals as I tickle her.

We walk past a church. Betty stops and peers through the gate. I walk up beside her.

—Do you want to light a candle for your daddy? For my friend Sean?

She looks up at me.

—Will they know?

I don't answer her. We walk in and the hall is empty and dark. I look for candles but I can't find any. I realise that this Protestant church is unfamiliar.

—Where are the candles?

—Sorry, Bets, they don't have any.

—I want to light a candle. She is scowling, she is insistent.

We buy two long red candles in town and we walk back towards the sea. I plant them in the ground, in the park, protected behind the solid girth of a fierce oak tree. Betty watches me.

—But this isn't a church.

—That doesn't matter.

I give her the matches and allow her to light the candles.

—This is for Tommy, I whisper, this is for Sean. And then I ask a God in whom I have no faith to look after, to protect, to make safe this little girl.

•

—I've seen Daddy.

We're climbing the hill towards home.

—Where?

—In the garden, at Nan's place in Ballarat. He was a little boy and he was playing with me. Then he just left. She is holding my hand.

—How did he leave?

—He just wasn't there. She carefully explains it to me again, with an exasperated patience. We were playing, he was there, and then he wasn't. She lets go of my hand and skips ahead of me. She turns, faces me.

—Uncle Louie, do you believe in God?

She is serious, intent on searching my face.

—No, I answer, I don't believe in God.

She starts skipping again, grabs my hand.

—I don't believe in God too, she says.

—Maybe you will one day.

She is silent.

—Do you believe in ghosts? She goes quiet.

—Yes, I answer, above me, around me, the crow. I believe in ghosts.

Again, she's skipping.

—Good, she says. So do I.

•

There is no traffic, no-one on the road. I walk along the edge of the water. I am confident that I will find a lift. Above me the clouds are dunes of greys and white in the sky; behind them the pale silhouette of the sun. The sea growls, the light shivers green and silver and blue. The sky is free, there are no seagulls, no machinery, no shadows from the crow. I walk out from the town, alone, with the wind a feeble pummelling against me. The gentle spray of the sea. I wish to keep moving, not to return to Melbourne, I'm requiring no destination. I simply wish for motion, the struggle against wind and sea, to keep moving and to never stop.